Satanstoe,

or The Littlepage Ma

A Tale of the Colony

The Writings of
James Fenimore Cooper

Satanstoe,

or The Littlepage Manuscripts

A Tale of the Colony

James Fenimore Cooper

Historical Introduction by

Kay Seymour House

Text Established, with Explanatory Notes

by Kay Seymour House and

Constance Ayers Denne

"The only amaranthine flower on earth

Is virtue; the only treasure, truth."

William Cowper, "The Task," iii, 268

State University of New York Press

The preparation of this volume was made possible (in part) by a grant from the Program for Editions of the National Endowment for the Humanities, an independent Federal agency.

```
┌─────────────────────────────┐
│      COMMITTEE ON           │
│    SCHOLARLY EDITIONS       │
│                             │
│   AN  APPROVED  EDITION     │
│                             │
│     MODERN LANGUAGE         │
│   ASSOCIATION OF AMERICA    │
└─────────────────────────────┘
```

The Center emblem means that one of a panel of textual experts serving the Center has reviewed the text and textual apparatus of the printer's copy by thorough and scrupulous sampling, and has approved them for sound and consistent editorial principles employed and maximum accuracy attained. The accuracy of the text has been guarded by careful and repeated proofreading according to standards set by the Center.

Published by
State University of New York Press, Albany

For information, address State University of New York
Press, State University Plaza, Albany, N.Y., 12246

Library of Congress Cataloging-in-Publication Data
Cooper, James Fenimore, 1789–1851.
    Satanstoe, or, The Littlepage manuscripts : a tale of the Colony /
  James Fenimore Cooper ; historical introduction by Kay Seymour House
  ; text established, with explanatory notes by Kay Seymour House and
  Constance Ayers Denne.
        p.   cm. — (The Writings of James Fenimore Cooper)
    Includes bibliographies.
    ISBN 0–88706–903–7.   ISBN 0–88706–904–5 (pbk.)
    1. New York (State)—History—Colonial period, ca. 1600–1775-
  -Fiction. I. House, Kay Seymour. II. Denne, Constance Ayers.
  III. Title. IV. Title: Satanstoe. V. Title: Littlepage
  manuscripts. VI. Series: Cooper, James Fenimore, 1789–1851. Works.
    1980.
PS1417.S3 1989   88–12196
813'.2—dc19   CIP
10 9 8 7 6 5 4 3 2 1

Contents

Acknowledgments

For institutional support in the preparation of this volume the editors wish to thank Martin Stevens, Dean of the School of Liberal Arts and Sciences, Baruch College, The City University of New York, and San Francisco State University. We are grateful to Herbert Cahoon, Robert H. Taylor Curator of Autograph Manuscripts at the Pierpont Morgan Library for making the manuscript of Chapters I–XV, available at the Pierpont Morgan Library; and to the late Dr. Paul Fenimore Cooper, Jr. for making the remainder of the manuscript—Chapters XVI–XXX and the Preface—available at the American Antiquarian Society. They are also grateful to the Fenimore Cooper family for its generous authorization to employ the manuscript as copy text for the present edition.

In preparing this book the editors also received invaluable help from Marcus McCorison, Director, and Barbara T. Simmons, Curator of Manuscripts at the American Antiquarian Society; from Elizabeth Orr, Barbara Quinn, Virginia Renner, Elsa Lee Sink, and Mary Wright of the Huntington Library; and from Inge Dupont and Stacy Berkheimer Glass at the Pierpont Morgan Library. The editors also wish to thank Professors James F. Beard. James P. Elliott, Donald A. Ringe, Thomas Philbrick, and Joel Meyerson for their encouragement and aid.

Additionally, Constance Denne would like to acknowledge the unfailing support of her husband, C. J. Denne, Jr., Associate Professor of English, College of New Rochelle. Kay House wishes to thank David Renaker, her colleague in San Francisco, and her friends Jeannette Carlson Stivers and Elizabeth Parker for identifying some difficult epigraphs in this volume.

For permission to reproduce the maps and the photograph of the Palisades from the T. Chalkley Matlack manuscript entitled "The Cooper Maps" (1911–1913), the editors wish to thank the Historical Society of Pennsylvania.

Illustrations

Historical Introduction

I

After *Satanstoe* had been published, Cooper asked his friend, Commodore Shubrick, "You see what anti-rentism is about? It is the great American question of the day."[1] *Satanstoe* is the foundation for a three-volume exposition of the principles and ideals at stake in the so-called "Anti-Rent War" in New York state following the death of Stephen Van Rensselaer (26 January 1839). Stephen's marriage to the daughter of General Philip Schuyler (the Philip Schuyler who appears in the novel) had united two powerful landowning families of Dutch descent. Known as the "Good Patroon," Stephen seems to have been a lenient landlord; his tenants owed him some $400,000 when he died. His will instructed his sons to collect these debts and settle the estate, but the tenants resisted so stoutly that Governor Seward had to call out the state militia in December to restore order. A commission the Governor appointed advised the heirs to forgive the past debts, but they refused and the Judiciary Committee of the New York State Assembly supported the landlords in an 1842 decision. The committee's action brought the Anti-Rent movement literally to the burning point since tenants seized and burned writs and warrants served against them, and the movement spread to other parts of the state. Often disguised as "Injins" in calico and warpaint, tenants and their sympathizers gathered to hear speakers denounce leases as "feudal" and "undemocratic," encourage the crowd to resistance against legal action, and even deny the validity of the landlords' titles to the land. Some law officers, including sheriffs, were tarred and feathered, and on 7 August 1845 an Undersheriff of Delaware County was murdered while attempting to make an arrest. The then governor of New York, Silas Wright, called out the militia and declared Delaware County to be in a state of insurrection.[2]

While Cooper was writing *Satanstoe*, tenants were organizing groups to finance the "Injins," to pay for their legal defense where necessary, and to support candidates (whether Whig or Democrat did not matter) who would back Anti-Rent measures. One of these groups, the National Reformers, adopted the slogan "Vote Yourself a Farm" and demanded the distribution of land from large estates. The struggle took on nationwide importance when newspapers like Horace Greeley's New York *Tribune* supported the Anti-Rent movement. Every candidate the Anti-Rent faction backed in the election of 1846 won, and a convention which met that same year to redraft the New York State Constitution declared certain provisions of existing leases illegal for the future.

Cooper was in no way personally involved in the kinds of complicated leases in question since his father had always insisted on selling outright to settlers (as the Mooseridge land will be sold in the novel). Yet Cooper saw as dangerous to the republic the demagogues' cloaking downright theft by inventing what they claimed were "republican principles." These included majority rule, curtailment of minority rights, invalidation of property deeds, denial of the power of civil law, and resistance to virtually any restraint of "the people." In spite of this agitation, however, no landlord's title was ever successfully challenged in the courts. Likewise, while certain provisions in the old leases were declared illegal for future contracts, the courts never found grounds for declaring an existing lease invalid. Yet, in spite of the decisions of the courts (and the efforts of Cooper), tenant violence combined with popular sentiment (influenced by demagogues inside and outside the press) and with political expediency to produce a situation in which the landowners were losers. Unable to collect their rents, they were forced to sell for whatever price they could get. Pressure groups had won in spite of the laws of the land. As Henry James would conclude sixty years later, "it was as if anything might be done there [in the U. S.] that any sufficient number of subscribers to any sufficient number of sufficiently noisy newspapers might want."[3]

Partly because of his personal acquaintance with the families involved and partly because of the threat it posed, the Anti-Rent movement had been on Cooper's mind since its beginning, and Thomas and Marianne Philbrick have rightly said of *Wyandotté*

(1843), "Insofar as Captain Willoughby's Hutted Knoll reflects the view of Hyde-Hall from Cooperstown, *Wyandotté* is less a novel of the Revolution than the first of Cooper's fictional treatments of the anti-rent controversy."[4] A year later, in the preface to Miles Wallingford, Cooper wrote:

> "The anti-rent combination," for instance, will prove . . . to be one of two things in this community—the commencement of a dire revolution, or the commencement of a return to the sounder notions and juster principles that prevailed among us thirty years since, than certainly prevail today.[5]

When the editor of the *Tomkins Democrat* of Ithaca, New York, wrote to Cooper 17 September 1844 to ask what he thought of the annexation of Texas and how it would affect "the perpetuity of our Republican Institutions," Cooper replied the next day:

> There is far more to apprehend to the Union and to the institutions from elements that are at work in our very vitals, than from slavery, Texas, and all ordinary political causes united. I allude to the wide spread and increasing demoralization of the people, themselves. Take the laws for the collection of debts, the impunity of the debtor, the whole history of the late bankrupt law, in its repeal as well as in its inception, and, as a climax, the anti-rent combination, as clues to what I mean.
>
> . . . This spirit must be put down, or we shall not only dissolve of our own weight, but we shall not have a shadow of liberty left among us. The worst description of tyranny— popular misrule—exists at this moment, in large portions of the counties of Rensselaer and Albany, and what is still more ominous, men defer to it, as a species of sublimated liberty.[6]

Once the entire trilogy was in print and the Hosmer girls wrote their admiration for the "irrefutable logic" of the three novels, Cooper answered:

> As to anti-rentism, in my judgment it is to be the test of the institutions. If men find that by making political combinations they can wipe out their indebtedness, adieu to every thing like liberty or government. The[re] will be but one alternative, and that will be the bayonet.[7]

To Thomas W. Field, a New Yorker who wrote to ask his advice about trying to recover a tract of land squatters had taken over, Cooper wrote, ". . . He who can look back for half a century, must see that a fearful progress has been made towards anarchy and its successor tyranny, in that period. Another such half a century will, in my judgment, bring the whole country under the bay-onet."[8] In the introduction to *The Towns of Manhattan*, left un-finished at his death, Cooper warned of the dangers of "loose-ness of law, legislation, and justice," and cited the conflict be-tween landlords and anti-renters in New York State as an exam-ple of what happened when "extra-legal pressures" took over.[9]

While the Anti-Rent wars were the immediate reason for Cooper's writing the trilogy of which *Satanstoe* is the first book, he had been accumulating the material he needed for years. His knowledge and memories of Albany, the setting for a third of the book (Chapters X through XIX), were vivid and, for the most part, pleasant. He had indicated as much in writing from Paris to the pastor of the Second Presbyterian Church at Albany 15 November 1831.

> To me Albany has always been a place of agreeable and friendly recollections—It was the only outlet we had, in my childhood, to the world, and many a merry week have I passed there with boys of my own age, while my father has waited for the opening of the river to go south. . . . A few years later, in 1801, I was sent to study under the direction and in the family of Mr. Ellison, the Rector of St. Peters. Of this gentleman I doubt not, you have often heard—We were five, and all in his family, for he took no others. There were two Rensselaers, of the Greenbush branch of the family, one of whom, Dr. Jeremiah Van Rensselaer of New York, is only living, a Livingston of the Upper Manor, who has died quite lately, William Jay, the youngest son of the Governor, and myself. . . . Still later, Albany was, to me, a town of excellent social feeling and friendly connexions. I could not visit my own County without passing it, and I always entered it with pleasure, and left it with regret. My father died in Albany, at the inn of Stewart Lewis, in 1809, and my eldest Brother Richard Fenimore Cooper, in his own house. So you see, dear Sir, that Albany is a name I love for a

multitude of associations that are connected with my earliest years.[10]

Mr. Ellison may well have been a model for the Reverend Mr. Worden of *Satanstoe*. Ellison was the last rector of old St. Peter's Church, which had the canopied pews and coats of arms described in Chapter XI.[11] Mention of the Rensselaers and Livingstons makes it clear that Cooper had long known the families of the great patroons, and his letters and journals show that he kept in touch with various members of these families all his life. The Pinkster celebration which Corny Littlepage describes as being "kept with more vivacity at Albany than in York" is nonetheless transferred to York in Chapter IV; yet Cooper was undoubtedly drawing on his memories of the Albany Pinkster (Pentecost or Whitsunday) which made an impression on him when he was in school there. The festivities had gone on for a week in Albany until 1811, and Cooper had mentioned the celebration in *The Spy*, which he wrote in 1820.

Later in his life, his friendship with William Dunlap, which began in 1823, further implicated him in studies of Dutch New York when he contributed to Dunlap's *History of the New Netherlands* (1838–1840). In the meantime, Dunlap had dedicated his *History of the American Theatre* to Cooper in 1832, and Cooper would use it as a reference for *Satanstoe's* theatrical scenes in the New York City section of the novel.

The neck of land sticking out into Long Island Sound that Cooper named "Satanstoe" belonged to his wife's family, the De Lanceys. Cooper's father-in-law, John Peter De Lancey, had inherited the property from his grandfather, Caleb Heathcote (Lord of the Manor of Scarsdale) through his mother, the former Ann Heathcote. The Coopers had lived there at Mamaroneck with the De Lanceys for a few months after their marriage in January of 1811, and had again been there from the time of the birth of their first child, Elizabeth, on 17 September, 1811, until after the birth of Susan Augusta, the second child, 17 April, 1813. The land was known as "East Neck" or "De Lancey's Neck" but Cooper's Corny Littlepage drew on Dutch folklore about the devil's retreat across Westchester and Long Island and christened it "Satanstoe."[12] The Mordaunt and Littlepage lands, handed down through five generations in the trilogy, are like the De

Lancey and Heathcote properties, and Cooper's daughter Susan had, as a nurse, a woman who had served five generations of Heathcotes and De Lanceys.[13]

Other connections between the novel and the Coopers' family history include the information that in the novel Captain Hugh Roger Littlepage, who knew Colonel Caleb Heathcote, had acquired Satanstoe about 1700. Colonel Caleb Heathcote had purchased Mamaroneck in 1697. Both estates enter the final families (Littlepage and De Lancey) through marriage, and the last Littlepage heir, Hugh Roger, inherits on his father's death in 1829, while De Lancey's Neck was conveyed to heirs on Cooper's father-in-law's death in 1828. Corny Littlepage's grandfather had been at the siege of Louisbourg in 1744, a battle that got Admiral Sir Peter Warren (who had married a De Lancey) a knighthood. Corny Littlepage's actions at Ticonderoga in 1758 resemble those of Captain James De Lancey, Cooper's wife's uncle, who had been aide-de-camp to Abercrombie during the same action. The De Lancey family history was also the source of Cooper's statement, as early as *Notions of the Americans* (1828), that the old Dutch stock had intermarried with the British to produce "a 'melange' of Dutch quietude and English aristocracy."[14] The De Lanceys had intermarried with people like the Van Cortlandts to produce the very "melange" we find in the Littlepage trilogy.

When the Coopers lived in New York City, from the fall of 1822 until they went to Europe in 1826, they grew familiar with the older portions of the city that had escaped the fire of 1778. Two of these, the Fly Market and Hanover Square, became settings for some of the early scenes of the book. Cooper had also been able to locate the sites in the city on which various De Lancey residences had stood—or still stood.

Yet another connection with the Coopers' family history is the fact that Cooper was still embroiled, while writing *Satanstoe* in 1845, in lawsuits stemming indirectly from a dispute over the public use of Three Mile Point. As executor of his father's will, Cooper was instructed to deliver a piece of ground known as Myrtle Grove or Three Mile Point to the youngest William Cooper existing among Judge Cooper's descendants in 1850. When he returned from Europe and resettled in Cooperstown, Cooper discovered that this area, which his family had let the villagers use for forty years, had been vandalized. Cooper placed a notice in the weekly paper reminding the public that Three Mile Point was private property that the public had been allowed to share because of the "liberality of the owners." Someone countered with a handbill, calling a meeting at a local inn in order

> to take means to meet, and defend against the arrogant pretensions of one James Fenimore Cooper, claiming title to the "Three Mile Point," and denying to the citizens, the right of using the same, as they have been accustomed to from time immemorial, without being indebted to the LIBERALITY of any one man, whether native or foreigner.
> JULY 22d 1837[15]

In asserting the public's right to unlimited use of private property, and in challenging the legality of the Coopers' title to the land the perpetrators of this handbill were dragging part of the Anti-Rent rationale to Cooper's own doorstep.

The handbill, however, did not truly represent local feeling, and Cooper would probably have overlooked the gall it took for a resident of Cooperstown to imply that Cooper was a foreigner, and the subsequent meeting that took place, had not an abusive editorial about the whole affair appeared in the *Chenango Telegraph* of Norwich and been reprinted in the *Otsego Republican* of Cooperstown and the *Albany Evening Journal*. When the editors refused to retract the errors in this editorial, Cooper sued for libel. He also embodied the story of this controversy and the principles he championed in a novel of social criticism, *Home as Found*, which stirred up a hornet's nest when it was published 15 November 1838. By 1845, when Cooper started to publish the Littlepage trilogy, his victories in court over various editors who had been found guilty of calumny gave them an excuse to sulk in silence.[16]

The close juxtaposition of Cooper's various concerns in 1845 is apparent to anyone going through that year's issues of the *Albany Argus* and Cooper's letters. On 2 March 1845, he wrote Mrs. Cooper, "I send, by mail, ... a copy of Weed's paper. The last is to be read by Paul, *and then kept for me*, as I wish to use it, in the new book [*Satanstoe*]. The Anti Rent speech is the matter I am in quest of."[17] On 11 May, the *Albany Argus* printed a letter from Cooper refuting a statement made by Thurlow Weed, one of the editors he was suing.[18] Sixteen days and seven pages later, the *Argus* ran this story:

> One of the most daring outrages that has taken place in this county since the breaking out of the Anti-Rent disturbances, took place in Taughkanic on Friday last, when an attempt was made by a party of disguised "Indians," to shoot down Deputy Sheriff Sedgwick and Constable Traver.
> The guns were loaded with buckshot, and on the first fire, Mr. Traver was hit on the side of his head; Mr. S. was next hit; he was staggered a little by this discharge, and had not fully recovered, before he received another charge in his thigh, where a number took effect. Mr. S. and those with him then left the road and got out of the range of the woods into the cleared fields; here the cowardly assassins dared not follow, and they met with no further opposition.[19]

Slightly more than two weeks later, the same publication reported, "A new tale by the author of the 'Spy' is announced simultaneously in London and New York, entitled 'Satanstoe.' "[20]

II

In thinking, and writing, of the trilogy as "The Family of Littlepage," Cooper was harking back to a line of thought that he had expressed in an article he wrote for *Brother Jonathan* in February, 1842:

> Now, it is expressly stated in Home as Found, that the Effinghams of that work are descended from the Oliver Effingham and Elizabeth Temple of the Pioneers. The motive for making the imaginary connection was simple enough. In the Pioneers I had attempted to pourtray a peculiar state of society in its commencement, and by preserving this connection, it saved much preliminary explanation, and enabled me to give a picture of the same again half a century later, and of obtaining some reflected interest for my scenes; a point of some moment in a country almost without a history.[21]

These same advantages should accrue to a triology which stretched beyond the half-century of the Effingham novels to a full century. Furthermore, Cooper wanted the expanse of four generations as a true and convincing gauge of the cost—in cash, energy, and lives—of establishing and maintaining a new settlement. Finally, in linking the past and present, he saw that he needed almost a century to depict realistically man's progress, or lack of it, from frontier life to civilization.[22]

Still embroiled with editors who ignored Eve Effingham as a spokeswoman and accused him of drawing his own portrait in the character of Edward Effingham, Cooper showed a good deal of caution in composing the trilogy. For one thing, he placed the narration in the hands of three members of the family, all of whom used first person narration. The self-deprecating revelations of Corny Littlepage, the first narrator, are quietly humorous and particularly disarming. As James Beard has remarked, when Cooper wrote from behind a mask (writing as A.B.C. for the New York *Evening Post* in the 1830s, for instance) he "could escape the too self-conscious and, at times, querulous tone that mars much of his controversial writing."[23] A relaxation of formality and increase in familiarity are notable in Cooper's first-person narratives—*Autobiography of a Pocket Handkerchief, Ned Myers*, and *Afloat and Ashore*—the books that immediately preceded the Littlepage triology. *Ned Myers* is important to the trilogy in still another way, as Cooper had assumed the function of editor, as well as recorder, of his old shipmate's memoirs. By continuing this role through the Littlepage trilogy, he gave himself the advantage of having two voices in one book.

Satanstoe also profits from Cooper's continuing a practice he had begun in *Afloat and Ashore* and its sequel, *Miles Wallingford*. For the first time in his career, he makes the narrator, who is a young gentleman, a central character, not peripheral (as the Effinghams were in the Leatherstocking Tales). The centrality of the man who will marry the heroine and establish a family underscores the importance of family in assuring continuity of culture as well as conservation of property. Since many Americans had never understood "breeding" to mean more than bloodlines, Cooper undertook to remedy the deficiency by spelling out the importance of gentlemen, who are "indispensable to civilization."[24] Corny Littlepage is responsible, a peacemaker, and a proper steward, getting the land surveyed so that it can be legally and peacefully transferred to posterity. He is flexible, acknowledging and accommodating differences in *mores* and manners between New York City and Albany, but his tolerance does not mean that truth is relative, nor that right and wrong can be determined by a show of hands. Corny has taste, manners, wellfounded opinions, and is generous and superior to any meanness. He is, in short, the gentleman who is not primarily a Christian, the gentleman Cooper described as having the "best qualities of a man unaided by God."[25] Yet it is important to notice that Corny cohabits comfortably with the Reverend Mr. Worden and clearly considers religion a normal part of the good life.

Besides being Corny's antagonist in the book, Jason Newcome functions as one way of defining a gentleman by negation. After discussing Jason's deficient education, Cooper crossed out "character" on line 20 of manuscript page 235 and substituted "feelings, tone, and tact" as the precise qualities Jason lacks. Cooper (like Faulkner later) knew what he was doing when he named Jason for the thief who stole the Golden Fleece with Medea's help and then deserted her. Jason has Mr. Worden and the Littlepages to thank for his opportunities, but he refuses to acknowledge the obligation and, like the classical Jason, will betray his benefactors.

Along with changing his narrative tactics to put the gentleman narrator in charge, Cooper increased the scope of the gentleman's family. Unlike the Effinghams, who are of English descent, the Littlepages are a mixture of Welsh, English, and Dutch, to begin with. Then they intermarry with such social inferiors as "Dus" Malbone, the Chainbearer's daughter of the second book. The family becomes increasingly democratic, but even in the first book Cooper was watching his language so as not to prejudice his case. Speaking of the lands they are about to locate and survey in *Satanstoe*, Cooper changed "an estate" and "estates" in the manuscript to "a property" and "tracts" in revision (at II.74.33 and II.74.35). Some of Cooper's old bugbears—squatters, usurers, demagogues, land speculators, attorneys, and Yankees—clearly underlie his attitude towards the Anti-Rent movement and such people end up aligned with the masked "Injins" of the third book. In opposition to them, Cooper places the real Indians (Susquesus and his tribe), the Dutch, and the other gentlemen—represented by the Littlepages. The contending forces predict

James's attribution of the "sordid ugliness and shabbiness" of rural America to "the suppression of the two great factors of the familiar English landscape, the squire and the parson."[26]

In establishing what is on the whole a favorable depiction of the Dutch, Cooper relied partly on a work he had earlier used for *The Pathfinder* and *Wyandotté*: Mrs. Grant's *Memoirs of an American Lady*. Ann MacVicar Grant, "commonly known as Mrs. Grant of Laggan to distinguish her from her friend Mrs. Grant of Carron,"[27] had first published her book in England in 1808, and it was reissued there in 1809 and again in 1817. Boston and New York both had editions in 1809, and it was again published in New York in 1836 and 1846 (the same year as the third volume of Cooper's trilogy). She mentioned the De Lancey family so frequently that it is very possible they would have had the book since it first appeared.

Beginning in 1758, when she was about three years old, Anne MacVicar had spent ten years with her mother and father, Captain MacVicar, in Oswego, Claverack, and other places in the colonies, and had resided for several years at or near Albany with Madame Schuyler, who is the American lady of the title. Having returned to Scotland with her parents in 1768, Anne MacVicar later married Grant, an army chaplain, and did not publish her account of her sojourn in America until she was fifty-three.[28] As Cooper frankly acknowledged in his footnotes in *Satanstoe* and in his 1851 note to Chapter X of *The Pathfinder*, Mrs. Grant's *Memoirs* were a valuable supplement to his own memories and to the records and memorabilia of the De Lancey family. Cooper may have been using her book as early as 1823 since certain beliefs about Indians—that they hold Negroes in contempt and that they never let an injury pass unrevenged—recorded in *The Pioneers* are also found in the *Memoirs*.[29]

Mrs. Grant tells about the Dutch custom of giving a child a slave of his or her own age and sex.[30] This custom explains Corny's Jaap and Anneke's Mari in the novel. Mrs. Grant's praise of the Albanian ways of having fun is generous: "The very idea of being ashamed of any thing that was neither vicious nor indecent never entered an Albanian head."[31] This attitude squares with Corny's and the Rev. Mr. Worden's indulgence of the antics of Guert and his friends, including the "frolick" in Chapter XII that expands on Mrs. Grant's statement that on such occasions the young men "never failed to steal either a roasting pig, or a fat turkey" for their supper.[32] Chapter X of Mrs. Grant's first volume takes up the "Winter Amusements of the Albanians" and not only describes their coasting down hills but suggests Anneke's attitude toward Corny's coasting. "In town all the *boys* were extravagantly fond of a diversion that to us would appear a very odd and childish one."[33] She and Anneke also have similar reactions to a performance of "the Beaux Stratagem; no favourable specimen of the delicacy or morality of the British theatre."[34] She stresses the fact that the river became the main highway for visits to friends at a distance, even at night, during the winter, and after describing the breaking up of the ice on the Hudson in the spring, she says, "I am absurdly attempting to paint a scene, under which the powers of language sink."[35] Cooper turned the breaking up of the Hudson ice, which he had seen for himself, into one of the most powerful scenes in the book.

Mrs. Grant was a great help in furnishing information about the military campaign of 1758. She described Lord Howe and the disaster of his early death,[36] and wrote of the battle of Ticonderoga: "They set out wrong however, by not having Indian guides, who are alone to be depended on in such a place. In a short time the columns fell in upon each other, and occasioned much confusion."[37] Cooper dramatizes the confusion and Corny says, "Want of guides was the great evil under which we labored; but it was an evil that it was now too late to remedy."[38] Of the disastrous attempt to take the fort itself, Mrs. Grant had written

> The fatal resolution was taken without consulting those who were best qualified to judge. An Indian or native American were here better skilled in the nature of the ground, and probabilities of success.[39]

Corny reports, "It was said that Abercrombie did not take counsel of any of the American officers with him, before he decided on the attack of the 8th of July."[40] Guert later remarks, " 'Had red-skin opinions been taken, Abercrombie might now have been a conqueror, instead of a miserable beaten man.' "[41]

For the description of the actual battle at Ticonderoga, Cooper drew both on Mrs. Grant and on William Dunlap's *History of the New Netherlands*.[42] Himself a painter, Dunlap had well described Abercrombie's army before and after the battle, an effective contrast that Cooper seized upon and incorporated into the novel by having Corny twice view the scene from above (as Cora views Fort William Henry before and after the massacre in *The Last of the Mohicans*). Corny's party's actions during the battle may have been suggested by Dunlap's report:

> This unexpected attack [of the French], and the fall of their commander [Howe], threw the British troops into confusion, already commenced by the labyrinth into which they had been led. . . . The provincials, who accompanied the party led by Lord Howe, more used to such scenes than Englishmen, rallied, pursued, and besides taking many prisoners, shot down many of the French before they could reach shelter.[43]

Yet another source, which Cooper mentions in a note on p. 331, was Abiel Holmes's *Annals of America* (1805). James H. Pickering has made an interesting table showing which details about the battle Cooper took from which of these three sources, and notes correctly that where they disagree, Cooper "remained loyal to Mrs. Grant."[44] Dunlap himself had used Mrs. Grant's *Memoirs* for some of the material in his own book.

Generally speaking, Mrs. Grant and Corny Littlepage have a lot in common. Both learn to like and trust Indians, and admire their sagacity. Both are suspicious of Yankees (New Englanders), detest their pushy ways and litigious tendencies, and shrink from their vulgarity and familiarity. To the extent that Yankeeisms underlie the whole trilogy, Cooper found a soul mate in Mrs. Grant, who described her family's reluctant decision to return to Scotland in terms that clearly connect with Cooper's theme. Prior to the revolution, her father's Yankee tenants had had a "revelation" that a line twenty miles inside New York—not the Connecticut River which had always been considered the dividing line—was the proper legal boundary, thus depriving her father at a stroke of half his property.

> Had not the revolution followed so soon, there was no doubt of this claim being rejected in Britain; but in the mean time it served as a pretext for daily encroachment and insolent bravadoes. . . . To give up every prospect of consequence and affluence, and return to Britain, leaving his

property afloat among these ungovernable people (to say no worse of them) was very hard. Yet to live among them, and by legal coercion force his due out of their hands, was no pleasing prospect."[45]

The same Green Mountain boys (and other Yankees) who drove Captain MacVicar from his land would prove to be equally hostile to Philip Schuyler, who appears in *Satanstoe* and expresses the Yankee-Yorker conflict in no uncertain terms. Not only did Mrs. Grant and Cooper agree in their admiration of the Schuylers, but Philip Schuyler's telling criticism of the Yankees (page 289) gives the Littlepages staunch support in the trilogy. Corny's statement, "Twenty years later in life, I had reason to remember this remark [that Yankees and Yorkers dislike each other], as well as to reflect on the character of the man who uttered it," alludes to the harassment Philip Schuyler would suffer during the revolution because of the Yankees. Meanwhile, in *Satanstoe* the Schuylers set the tone and standards of Albanian society and represent the kind of people who will be threatened, and possibly defeated, in the ensuing volumes of the trilogy.

III

There is no doubt that Cooper conceived of the Littlepage trilogy as a trilogy from the very first. Thus it differs from his other multi-volume tales. The Leatherstocking Tales were linked through the characters of Natty Bumppo, Chingachgook, and the Effingham family, but were separate works and did not appear in chronological order. *Homeward Bound* and *Home as Found* (1838), like *Afloat and Ashore* and *Miles Wallingford* (1844), however, were books that exceeded the author's original intentions and ran into continuations, as Cooper frankly admitted.[46]

Cooper may have had the trilogy in mind when he told Bentley, 29 August 1844, that he had "two plans in view" for the spring of 1845, and promised to "write you as soon as I have determined which to carry out."[47] In any event, he clearly had the entire trilogy laid out by 22 January, 1845, when he wrote Bentley about his "forth coming work, which I call 'The Family of Littlepage.'"

"The Family of Littlepage" will form three complete
Tales, each perfectly distinct from the other as regards
leading characters, love story &c, but, in this wise connected.
I divide the subjects into the "Colony," "Revolution" and
"Republic," carrying the same family, the same localities,
and same *things* generally through the three different
books, but exhibiting the changes produced by time &c. In
the Colony, for instance, the Littlepage of that day, first
visits an estate of wild land, during the operations of the
year 1758, the year that succeeded the scenes of the
Mohicans, and it is there that the most stirring events of the
book occur. In the "Revolution" this land is first settled, and
the principles are developed, on which this settlement takes
place, showing a book, in some respects resembling the
Pioneers, though varied by localities and incidents—In the
"Republic" we shall have the present aspect of things, with
an exhibition of the Anti-Rent commotion that now exists
among us, and which certainly threatens the destruction of
our system—You know I write what I think, in these
matters, and I shall not spare "The Republic" in all in which
it is faulty and weak, as faulty and weak it has been to a
grievous extent in these matters.

I think the Story of the Colony a very good one; the
others remain to be written. These books will be perfectly
distinct as Tales, and each will make an ordinary sized novel,
though I hope the interest of one will be reflected on the
others."[48]

Cooper added that the first book was "now far advanced, and will
go to press in a few days."

Bentley replied that the sequel to *Afloat* and *Ashore* had fallen
short, by more than a hundred copies, of the sale of the first
three-volume book, and that he could only credit Cooper with
£250 (not the customary £350) for the sequel, applying the other
£100 toward the purchase of *Satanstoe*. He added that the "taste"
for fiction had declined in England and that he was reducing the
size of printings.

With regard to your own Works on reviewing the sale of your
later productions, I find I must confine myself in future to

an impression of 750 copies. And this limit is the more
necessary when the subject is not at once completed—continuations never being so saleable as single works. This
number of copies will not enable me to offer you . . . more
than £250 for your next work in 3 volumes.[49]

Cooper answered, 24 April 1845, accepted the £350 for
Satanstoe, and said he would send the "remainder of Satanstoe,
by the steamer of the 16th May."[50] Yet he immediately wrote to
Robert Campbell, who frequently cashed his bills on Bentley,
that he was thinking of changing publishers.[51] Bentley wrote
Cooper, 18 June, that the second part of *Afloat and Ashore* had
sold only 570 copies, and complained that he would not have
paid £350 for the first part had he "known it was to be continued.
The same objection applies to Satanstoe."[52] Cooper answered
23 September, 1845, accepting payment of £250 for each book
of the trilogy, but protesting that the second book, "now nearly
stereotyped" was

> not a sequel, but a work in which the same scenes are used,
> as some of the old characters of Satanstoe are introduced,
> with new hero, heroine and love-story. The next book will
> be on the same plan, connecting one or two characters with
> the three books, as Leatherstocking appears in different
> tales.[53]

Bentley, who had published *Satanstoe* 10 June, 1845, accordingly
published *The Chainbearer* 19 November, 1845, and *The Redskins* 6
July, 1846.[54]

Small as the British sale of his books had come to be, they still
earned Cooper more money than he got from the editions he
published in the United States. Having become his own pub-
lisher when Lea and Blanchard refused to give him $1,500 for *A-
float and Ashore*, Cooper continued to have John Fagan sterotype
his books in Philadelphia and relied primarily on Burgess and
Stringer to distribute them.[55] Cooper wrote to Fagan from New
York City 4 March, 1845

> *By express* to-day, I send you a few chapters of new book.
> Begin *at once*, as I am in a great hurry, and wish to save time.
> I shall be at Heads on Tuesday or Wednesday night,

probably the last, and I hope to find a great bundle of proofs ready.

The running title must be, "Satanstoe."[56]

The following day he wrote Mrs. Cooper that he had "sold an edition entire of the New book, 3,500 copies, for $1050."[57] On Friday, 14 March, he wrote that he had just read the last proof of Volume I, which would "leave me nothing further to do with the new book, than to stereotype two thirds of a Volume, when I come down, next time."[58] On 2 May, he was in Philadelphia reading proof and in spite of taking four days out to attend the wedding of Shubrick's daughter he got corrected proofs to New York in time for the "sailing of the steamer of the 16th"[59] to England.

In the ensuing months, the optimism that characterizes Cooper's letters to his wife leads to some confusion about the book's success. On 3 October, 1845, he wrote to her from Philadelphia, "Chainbearer is a good book I think, and Satanstoe a good deal read. The edition of 3600 is nearly sold, and Burgess is negotiating for more."[60] Eleven days later, he wrote her, "You will be surprised to learn that Miles [the sequel to *Afloat and Ashore*] has not sold as well as Satanstoe."[61] Writing from Head's in Philadelphia in December of the same year, he told his wife, "Of Chainbearer, I can tell you nothing, though Griswold [editor and anthologist] does not think it as interesting as Satanstoe."[62] Yet he wrote to James Kirke Paulding the following spring, "I do not think the three last books will nett me much more than $500 a book. B. and S. say they have not sold the first editions of Satanstoe and Chainbearer."[63] Paulding had written to ask Cooper's advice about financial arrangements with publishers, and in his own lifetime the poor sales of the Littlepage trilogy supported another passage in his letter to Paulding:

> The cheap literature has destroyed the value of nearly all literary property, and after five and twenty years of hard work, I find myself comparatively a poor man. Had I employed the same time in trade, or in travelling as an agent for a manufacturer of pins, I do not doubt I should have been better off, and my children independent. The fact is, this country is not sufficiently advanced for any thing intellectual, and the man who expects to rise by any

such agency makes a capital mistake, unless he sell himself, soul and body, to a faction.

IV

The *U. S. Magazine and Democratic Review* announced the imminent publication of *Satanstoe* in April, 1845, but it did not appear until about the 4th of July, when Cooper wrote his wife, "No news of the Toe. I wait to hear from the publishers."[64] Few magazines in this country listed it in their "Books Received" column, suggesting that Burgess and Stringer were not sending many copies out for review. A second reason for the paucity of reviews is suggested by Cooper's report to Mrs. Cooper on the second book, 30 November, 1845, "I can hear nothing of Chainbearer. The papers are mum, as usual, but I know it sells pretty well. They cannot put me down entirely, though they do me infinite harm. A precious set of dishonest knaves are they!"[65] It may be that a story in the *New York Mirror* (a paper not involved in any Cooper lawsuits and one generally friendly to him) gives an accurate indication of the climate in which Cooper was publishing. Learning that Cooper himself was being sued for libel by a Rev. Mr. Tiffany, they wrote:

> We cannot exult, as many of our contemporaries do, at the prospect of bringing Cooper, the novelist, into a court of justice to be tried for libel. . . . It has been the misfortune of Mr. Cooper to have fallen under the displeasure of a large portion of the most distinguished conductors of the American press, not for what he has written, but for his nervousness and sensibility to their criticisms; but he mistook what they intended to be a fair view of his writings, for malicious slander . . . .
>
> We have often regretted that a man of Mr. Cooper's great and varied abilities, should have any infirmity of temper—should be impulsive or distrustful—or imagine that any injustice is intended toward him by his fellow-citizens of the press. How much he has to learn from the amiable deportment of Washington Irving, who, never distrustful, never impugning the motives of others, glides smoothly down the tide of time without an enemy. With a mind less vigorous, an

imagination less bold and vivid than Cooper's, he unites in
a sweetness of disposition, a mild and confiding temper, in
a graceful and beautiful style, as polished as Addison's—
with a wit keen, but never sarcastic—a fancy exuberant and
playful, yet full of judgement and sound principles. How
much Cooper would have gained by taking Irving for his
model thro' life.[66]

Similarly indicative of the *Zeitgeist* is a review in *The Harbinger*
which says "two reasons" make reviewing Cooper's books a
"serious matter." The first is his proclivity in suing for libel
"editors, whose manners had not the European perfection, for
which Mr. Cooper cherishes a profound and unwavering admiration," and the second is the fact that the "later productions of
our 'American Walter Scott,' are so unspeakably dull, that only
the most omnivorous and senseless appetite can succeed with
them."[67] The review accuses Cooper of offering "the stereotyped
characters and incidents which under various disguises appear
throughout Mr. Cooper's Romances."

The same hero and heroine, the same dangerous situations
and hair-breadth escapes, which in our earlier days we
learned by heart, out of Lionel Lincoln, the Pioneers, and
the Red Rover, are here with slight modifications served up
again. We entreat Mr. Cooper and ask his admirers—we
have faith that such rarae aves may exist,—to join in our
petition, to invent something new, and to allow the old
machinery to remain unused for a period. We should like to
see his talent for dramatic description, which is really good,
employed upon novel materials though we fear that we
shall never be so gratified.

Half of the review goes on to discuss the Anti-Rent movement,
and concludes:

The truth is, that *land* should be held not by *individuals* but
by *communities, in joint stock proprietorship*. By this means, and
by this only, the rights of individuals can be secured, and
the old conflict between the wealthy and those who are not
so entirely done away.

The review was written by Charles A. Dana, then twenty-five and a
member of the Brook Farm experiment until its collapse in 1846.

He wrote of the other two books with the same socialist single-mindedness and never discussed characters, themes, or actions—not even those that might be considered "dramatic description."

By contrast, the review in Hunt's *The Merchant's Magazine, and Commercial Review*, while giving the subtitle as the *Title-Page Manuscripts*, was favorable, praising the "curious and interesting points of information relative to the city, as it was" and the Indian characters. The "just and manly views" expressed in the preface found favor with the reviewer who professed to await the next two books of the series "with interest."[68] While publications at both ends of the economic spectrum were interested in *Satanstoe* as a political statement, only Hunt's suggested that it (and its successors) had any value as history or literature.

In England, *Satanstoe* was reviewed in the traditional manner, as a work of fiction, with long excerpts illustrating this or that quality. *The Critic* protested "With the memory of Cooper's former continuations, it will be no recommendation to this romance that it is intended to be the first of a series."[69] Yet the article repeated Cooper's promise that each volume would be independent. After describing various characters and the groups they represent, the critic wrote,

> Of such materials it would be difficult not to frame an interesting novel, and by help of a *few* striking incidents, such as an unexpected breaking up of the ice on the Hudson, and the perils thence encountered by the hero and heroine, and a vivid description of a journey into the interior to take possession of an estate, with divers warlike doings, that serve to re-introduce the Indians, and their skill, cunning, and magniloquence, make up a work that will sustain the reader's interest to the end.

By way of balancing the account, the critic complained that Cooper's "prosiness grows with age," that he produced "long, dull, wearisome dialogues," and "descriptions . . . elaborated with the tedious minuteness of a penny-a-liner . . . ." He declared that some of the characters were old friends in "new dress," but welcomed Jason Newcome as a "rich specimen of the genu*ine* New England . . . drawn not merely with the zest given by the hearty hatred of the species, but with an existing model before the author, from which he has caught the minutest shades, and worked them up into an admirable picture."

The London *Literary Gazette* announced the publication of *Satanstoe* on Saturday, 14 June, and gave it almost four columns of review the following week. Citing as notable the differences between "the New-Englanders and the New-Yorkites" and the "northern and midland states," the reviewer quoted liberally to illustrate "the American character" and the "prospects of that vast continent" and was amused by the account of Corny's education which was "whimsically described." While not giving away the story, the review assured the reader that the action does "move into the wide forest and Indian life and warfare, where the author is so much at home."[70] In subsequently reviewing the rest of the trilogy, the *Literary Gazette* declared that the "improvement or deterioration of the United States" was bound to affect the rest of the world, and that "it is of much interest to see the case probed by so intelligent a native operator as Mr. Cooper, whose observations may well be received as the sequel to Tocqueville and other foreign writers who have thrown most light on the *status quo* and prospects of the American people."[71]

In addition to the English-language editions listed in the stemma, *Satanstoe* was published in French by Baudry in Paris in 1845, and commencing 4 August 1845 it was also published as *feuilletons* by the *Bibiliotheque choisie* of the *Constitutionnel*.[72] A Defauconpret translation was published in Paris the following year by Charles Gosselin, and an edition in *Romans Populaires Illustres* was published by Barba in 1853 or 1854.[73] A German edition in six volumes was brought out by J. D. Sauerlander, Frankfurt-am-Main in 1845, and another edition appeared in 1845 and 1846 at Stuttgart, printed by Liesching; the same firm reprinted the novel in 1853.[74] Preston Barba also lists a German edition of 1848.[75]

At least Cooper was getting a hearing—or a reading—in England and Europe. George Sand, reading *Satanstoe* in *feuilleton* form as it came out in August, said she was delighted with it and praised Cooper's search for truth and his artistry. After complaining that other contemporary writers gave her a pain, she said she wanted "sentiment and imagination" in what she read.[76] A decade later, writing of Cooper's work in general, she pronounced *Satanstoe* one of his best novels and singled out for particular attention the sleigh ride on the river and the description of the sudden thaw as being

> all the more thrilling because, thanks to the confidence and clarity of the observations, it is among the most intelligible. These descriptions, in the form of straightforward and matter-of-fact report, are among Cooper's finest qualities. One senses there an observer who, from his own experience, has tried to give an account of everything, the effects and the causes, the details and the picture as a whole. Thus one's interest is held by the force of truth. The narrator has the calm objectivity of a mirror which reflects the great crises of nature, without adding any frills out of his own head, and, I repeat, this course flexibly taken, constitutes at times an important property which we perhaps underestimate a little.[77]

By contrast, Francis Parkman seems a fair sample of United States critics when he wrote, in *his* retrospective essay on Cooper in 1852, "... in speaking of Cooper's writings, we have reference only to those happier offspring of his genius which form the basis of his reputation; for, of that numerous progeny which of late years have swarmed from his pen, we have never read one...."[78]

NOTES

1. *The Letters and Journals of James Fenimore Cooper*; ed., James Franklin Beard (Cambridge, Mass.: Belknap Press of Harvard University Press, 1960–1968), V, 52 (hereafter cited as *Letters and Journals*).
2. Studies of the anti-rent movement in New York include Edward P. Cheyney, *The Anti-Rent Agitation in the State of New York, 1839–1846* (Philadelphia, 1887); Henry Christman, *Tin Horns and Calico* (New York, 1945), and David Maldwyn Ellis, *Landlords and Farmers in the Hudson-Mohawk Region, 1790–1850* (Ithaca, 1946). Typical terms of leases and the custom of basing them on three lives, the lives being those of persons the tenant chose, are described in Chapter XIII of Cooper's *The Chainbearer*.
3. *The American Scene* (New York: Horizon Press, 1967), p. 54. After

his tour of the United States in 1904–05 James first published *The American Scene* in 1906.

4. James Fenimore Cooper, *Wyandotté* (Albany: State University of New York Press, 1982), p. xviii.

5. James Fenimore Cooper, *Miles Wallingford* (New York: G. P. Putnam's Sons, "Pathfinder Edition," n.d.), p. iii.

6. *Letters and Journals*, IV, 477.

7. Ibid., V, 184.

8. Ibid., V, 388.

9. Ibid., VI, 205.

10. Ibid., II,155.

11. James H. Pickering, "James Fenimore Cooper and the History of New York," (Ph. D. dissertation, Northwestern University, 1964), p. 154.

12. Ibid., p. 302. Pickering cites Harold W. Thompson, *Body, Boots, & Britches, Folktales, Ballads and Speech from Country New York* (Philadelphia, 1940), p. 113 and Gabriel Furman, *Antiquities of Long Island*, ed. by Frank Moore (New York, 1874), pp. 56–57 as sources. Pickering has two additional articles useful for a study of *Satanstoe*: "Fenimore Cooper and Pinkster," *New York Folklore Quarterly*, XXII (March, 1966), pp. 15–19 and "*Satanstoe*: Cooper's Debt to William Dunlap," *American Literature*, XXXVIII (Jan., 1967), pp. 468–477.

13. James Fenimore Cooper, *Gleanings in Europe: England* (Albany: State University of New York Press, 1982), p. 77.

14. James Fenimore Cooper, *Notions of the Americans: Picked Up by a Travelling Bachelor* (Philadelphia, 1840), I, 90.

15. *Letters and Journals*, III, 272. On Tuesday, 25 January 1848, Cooper wrote in his journal: "Drove wife as far as Myrtle Grove, by the new road, which is a very pretty drive, and a great addition to our outlets. But the Grove is spoiled." *Letters and Journals*, V, 262.

16. *Letters and Journals*, IV, 370.

17. Ibid., V, 10.

18. *Albany Argus*, 11 May 1845, V, 171.

19. Ibid., 27 May 1845, V, 178.

20. Ibid., 13 June 1845, V, 201.

21. *Letters and Journals*, IV, 238.

22. Cooper agreed with Aristotle, Jefferson, John Adams and others that culture developed in stages culminating in what Aristotle called "the good life." See my chapter on the gentry in *Cooper's Americans* (Columbus, Ohio: Ohio State University Press, 1965) particularly pages 149–150, 176–77.

23. *Letters and Journals*, III, 64.

24. *The American Democrat* (New York: Vintage, 1956), p. 89. (First published in 1838).

25. James Fenimore Cooper, *The Chainbearer* (New York: G. P. Putnam's Sons, "Pathfinder Edition," n.d.), p. 161.

26. *The American Scene*, p. 23.

27. Anne Grant, *Memoirs of an American Lady*, ed. with memoir by James Grant Wilson (New York: Dodd Mead & Co., 1901), p. [xiii].

28. Ibid., p. xxiii. After Mr. Grant died in 1801, Mrs. Grant supported herself and her eight children partly by writing.

29. James Fenimore Cooper, *The Pioneers* (Albany: State University of New York Press, 1980), p. 294 and p. 140. Anne Grant, *Memoirs of an American Lady*, 2 vols. (Boston: W. Wells, Thomas B. Wait Co., 1809) I, 68 and I, 49. (This edition is hereafter referred to as *Memoirs*.)

30. *Memoirs*, Ibid., I, 33. Mrs. Grant said this occurred when the child was about three; Cooper said "six—, or eight." *Satanstoe*, p. 70.

31. *Memoirs*, Ibid., I, 53.

32. Ibid., I, 61.

33. Ibid., I, 58.

34. Ibid., II, 10.

35. Ibid., II, 154.

36. Ibid., II, 30–35.

37. Ibid., II, 35–36.

38 *Satanstoe*, p. 327.

39. *Memoirs*, II, 36.

40 *Satanstoe*, p. 331.

41. Ibid., p. 350.

42. *History of the New Netherlands, Province of New York, and State of New York* (New York, 1839), I, 391–393.

43. Ibid., I, 392.

44. Pickering, "Cooper and History," pp. 164–166.

45. *Memoirs*, II. 118–119. Pickering says on page 156 that "ill health" forced Mrs. Grant's father to "quit his promising estate," but she says her father's rheumatism was aggravated by his Connecticut persecutors, who "attacked him every where but in bed." II, 116.

46. In the preface to *Homeward Bound* (1860), Cooper said others who were reading as he wrote kept calling for "more ship" until the first book became all ship. He said of *Afloat and Ashore*, in a letter to Bentley, that he was halfway through the first book when he realized that he would need to divide the work into two parts. *Letters and Journals*, IV, 455.

47. *Letters and Journals*, IV, 472.

48. Ibid., V, 7.
49. Ibid., V, 8.
50. Ibid., V, 19.
51. Ibid., V, 21.
52. Ibid., V, 20.
53. Ibid., V, 55–56.
54. Robert E. Spiller & Philip C. Blackburn, *A Descriptive Bibliography of the Writings of James Fenimore Cooper* (New York: Burt Franklin, 1968), pp. 138, 141, 145.
55. *Letters and Journals*, IV, 436.
56. Ibid., V, 12.
57. Ibid., V, 13.
58. Ibid., V, 16.
59. Ibid., V, 24. The steamer is the one mentioned in his letter to Bentley; see note 50.
60. Ibid., V, 73.
61. Ibid., V, 84.
62. Ibid., V, 106–107.
63. Ibid., V, 131.
64. Ibid., V. 44.
65. Ibid., V, 101.
66. *New York Mirror*, Saturday, 27 September 1845, Vol. II, #XXV, p. 395.
67. *The Harbinger*, Saturday, 2 August 1845, Vol. I, #8, p. 122.
68. *The Merchants Magazine, and Commercial Review*, August, 1845, XIII, 206.
69. *The Critic*, Saturday, 28 June 1845, New Series Vol. II, #26, p. 175.
70. *The Literary Gazette*, Saturday, 21 June 1845, #1483, p. 392.
71. *The Literary Gazette*, Saturday, 1 August 1846, #1541, p. 681.
72. Spiller and Blackburn, *Bibliography*, p. 139 and George Sand, *Correspondance* (Paris: Editions Garnier Freres, 1970) VII, p. 60. The editor, George Lubin, bases the date of this letter #3218 on the beginning publication of *Satanstoe*.
73. Spiller and Blackburn, *Bibliography*, p. 140.
74. Ibid., pp. 140, 191, and 192.
75. "Cooper in Germany," *Indiana University Bulletin*, XII: 5 (15 May 1914), p. 85.
76. George Sand wrote to Pierre-Jules Hetzel about "le roman nouveau de Cooper" and said:
    ...j'en suis ravie. Planche hausserait les épaules, mais ne me dégoûterait [pas] de ce talent (de second ordre si l'on veut), mais simple, naïf, bon enfant, consciencieux, cherchant le vrai, enfin un artiste de la bonne école. Tous mes autres contemporains me

font une peine véritable . . . . Il me faut pourtant des émotions de sentiment et d'imagination. *Correspondance*, VII, 62.

77. George Sand, "Fenimore Cooper" in *Autour de la Table* (Paris, 1856), 261–72 and 281–2, translated by D. B. Wood and printed in George Dekker and John P. McWilliams, *Fenimore Cooper: The Critical Heritage* (London: Routledge & Kegan Paul, 1973), p. 265.

78. Francis Parkman, "The Works of James Fenimore Cooper," *North American Review*, LXXIV (January, 1852), 149.

SATANSTOE

Preface

EVERY chronicle of manners has a certain value. When customs are connected with principles, in their origin, development, or end, such records have a double importance, and it is because we think we see such a connection between the facts and incidents of the Littlepage Manuscripts and certain important theories of our own time, that we give the former to the world.

It is perhaps a fault of your professed historian, to refer too much to philosophical agencies, and too little to those that are humbler. The foundations of great events, are often remotely laid in very capricious and uncalculated passions, motives, or impulses. Chance has usually as much to do with the fortunes of states as with those of individuals; or, if there be calculations connected with them at all, they are the calculations of a power superior to any that exists in man.

We had been led to lay these manuscripts before the world, partly by considerations of the above nature, and partly on account of the manner in which the two works we have named "Satanstoe" and the "Chainbearer" relate directly to the great New York question of the day, ANTI-RENTISM, which question will be found to be pretty fully laid bare, in the third and last book of the series. These three works, which contain all the Littlepage manuscripts, do not form sequels to each other, in the sense of personal histories, or as narratives; while they do in that of principles. The reader will see that the early career, the attachment, the marriage, &c. of Mr. Cornelius Littlepage are completely related in the present book, for instance, while those of his son, Mr. Mordaunt Littlepage, will be just as fully given in the "Chainbearer," its successor. It is hoped that the connection, which certainly does exist between these three works, will have more tendency to increase the value of each, than to produce the ordinary effect of what are properly called sequels, which are known to lessen the interest a narrative might otherwise have with the reader. Each of these three books has its own hero, its own heroine, and its own picture of manners complete; though the latter may be, and is, more or less thrown into relief, by its *pendants*.

We conceive no apology is necessary for treating the subject of anti-rentism with the utmost frankness. Agreeably to our views of the matter, the existence of true liberty among us, the perpetuity of the institutions, and the safety of public morals are all dependent on putting down, wholly, absolutely, and unqualifiedly, the false and dishonest theories and statements that have been boldly advanced in connection with this subject. In our view, New York is, at this moment, much the most disgraced state in the Union, notwithstanding she has never failed to pay the interest on her public debt; and her disgrace arises from the fact that her laws are trampled under foot, without any efforts, at all commensurate with the object, being made to enforce them. If *words* and *professions* can save the character of a community, all may yet be well; but, if states, like individuals, are to be judged by their actions, and the "tree is to be known by its fruit," God help us!

For ourselves, we conceive that true patriotism consists in laying bare every thing like public vice, and in calling such things by their right names. The great enemy of the race has made a deep inroad upon us, within the last ten, or a dozen years, under cover of a spurious delicacy on the subject of exposing national ills, and it is time that they who have not been afraid to praise, when praise was merited, should not shrink from the office of censuring, when the want of timely warnings may be one cause of the most fatal evils. The great practical defect of institutions like ours is the circumstance that "what is every body's business, is nobody's business," a neglect that gives to the activity of the rogue a very dangerous ascendancy over the more dilatory correctives of the honest man.

Satanstoe,

or The Littlepage Manuscripts

Chapter I

"—Look you who comes here:
a young man, and an old, in solemn talk."
                    As You Like It, II. iv. 19–21.

I T is easy to foresee that this country is destined to undergo great and rapid changes. Those that more properly belong to history, history will doubtless attempt to record, and probably with the questionable veracity and prejudice that are apt to influence the labours of that particular muse, but there is little hope that any traces of American society, in its more familiar aspects, will be preserved among us, through any of the agencies usually employed for such purposes. Without a stage, in a national point of view at least, with scarcely such a thing as a book of memoirs that relates to a life passed within our own limits, and totally without light literature, to give us simulated pictures of our manners and the opinions of the day, I see scarcely a mode by which the next generation can preserve any memorials of the distinctive usages and thoughts of this. It is true, they will have traditions of certain leading features of the colonial society, but scarcely any records; and, should the next twenty years do as much as the last, towards substituting an entirely new race, for the descendants of our own immediate fathers, it is scarcely too much to predict that even these traditions will be lost in the whirl and excitement of a throng of strangers. Under all the circumstances, therefore, I have come to a determination to make an effort, however feeble it may prove, to preserve some vestiges of household life in New York, at least, while I have endeavoured to stimulate certain friends in New Jersey, and farther south, to undertake similar tasks in those sections of the country. What success will attend these last applications, is more than I can say, but, in order that the little I may do myself, shall not be lost for want of support, I have made a solemn request in my will, that those who come after me, will consent to continue this narrative, committing to paper their own experience as I have here committed mine, down as low at least as my grandson, if I ever have one. Perhaps, by the end of the latter's career, they will begin to publish books in America, and the fruits of our joint family labours may be thought sufficiently matured to be laid before the world.

It is possible that which I am now about to write, will be thought too homely, to relate to matters much too personal and private, to have sufficient interest for the public eye; but, it must be remembered that the loftiest interests of man are made up of a collection of those that are lowly, and, that he who makes a faithful picture of only a single important scene in the events of single life, is doing something towards painting the greatest historical piece of his day. As I have said before, the leading events of my time will find their way into the pages of far more pretending works than this of mine, in some form or other, with more or less of fidelity to the truth, and real events, and real motives, while the humbler matters it will be my office to record, will be entirely overlooked by writers who aspire to enrol their names among the Tacituses of former ages. It may be well to say here, however, I shall not attempt the historical mood at all, but content myself with giving the feelings, incidents and interests of what is purely private life, connecting them no farther with things that are of a more general nature, than is indispensable to render the narrative intelligible and accurate. With these explanations, which are made in order to prevent the person who may happen first to commence the perusal of this manuscript, from throwing it into the fire as a silly attempt to write a more silly fiction, I shall proceed at once to the commencement of my proper task.

I was born on the 3^d May 1737, on a neck of land, called Satanstoe, in the county of West-Chester, and in the colony of New York; a part of the widely extended empire that then owned the sway of His Sacred Majesty, George II^d King of Great Britain, Ireland, and France, Defender of the Faith; and I may add the shield and panoply of the Protestant Succession; God bless him! Before I say any thing of my parentage, I will first give the reader some idea of the *locus in quo,* and a more precise notion of the spot on which I happened first to see the light.

A "neck," in West-Chester and Long Island parlance, means something that might be better termed a "head and shoulders," if mere shape and dimensions are kept in view. Peninsula would be the true word, were we describing things on a geographical scale, but, as they are, I find it necessary to adhere to the local term, which is not altogether peculiar to our county, by the way. The "Neck" or peninsula of Satanstoe, contains just four hundred and sixty-three acres and a half of excellent West-Chester land, and, that when the stone is hauled and laid into wall, is saying as much in its favour, as need be said of any soil on earth. It has two miles of beach, and collects a proportionate quantity of sea-weed for manure, besides enjoying near a hundred acres of salt-meadow and sedges, that are not included in the solid ground of the neck proper. As my father, Major Evans Little-page, was to inherit this estate from his father, Capt. Hugh Little-page, it might even at the time of my birth be considered old fam-ily property, it having indeed been acquired by my grandfather, through his wife, about thirty years after the final cession of the colony to the English, by its original Dutch owners. Here we had lived, then, near half a century, when I was born, in the direct line, and considerably longer if we included maternal ancestors; here I now live, at the moment of writing these lines, and here I trust my only son is to live after me.

Before I enter into a more minute description of Satanstoe, it may be well perhaps to say a word concerning its somewhat peculiar name. The Neck lies in the vicinity of a well-known pass that is to be found in the narrow arm of the sea that separates the island of Manhattan from its neighbour, Long Island; and which is called Hell Gate. Now, there is a tradition, that I confess is somewhat confined to the blacks of the neighborhood, but which says that the Father of Lies, on a particular occasion, when he was violently expelled from certain roystering taverns in the New Netherlands, made his exit by this well-known dangerous pass, and drawing his foot somewhat hastily from among the lobster pots that abound in those waters, leaving behind him as a print of his passage by that route, the Hog's Back, the Pot, and all the whirlpools and rocks that render navigation so difficult in that celebrated strait, he placed it hurriedly upon the spot where there now spreads a large bay to the southward and eastward of the Neck, just touching the latter with the ball of his great toe, as he passed Down East; from which part of the country some of our people used to maintain he originally came. Some fancied re-semblance to an inverted toe (the devil being supposed to turn every thing with which he meddles, upside-down) has been im-agined to exist in the shape and swells of our paternal acres, a fact that has probably had its influence in perpetuating the name.

Satanstoe has the place been called, therefore, from time immemorial, as time is immemorial in a country in which civilized time commenced not a century and a half ago, and Satanstoe it is called to-day. I confess I am not fond of unnecessary changes, and I sincerely hope this neck of land will continue to go by its old appellation, as long as the House of Hanover shall sit on the throne of these realms, or as long as water shall run and grass shall grow. There has been an attempt made to persuade the neighborhood, quite lately, that the name is irreligious and unworthy of an enlightened people, like this of West-Chester, but it has met with no great success. It has come from a Connecticut man, whose father they say is a clergyman of the "*standing* order," so called I believe because they stand up at prayers, and who came among us himself in the character of a schoolmaster. This young man, I understand, has endeavoured to persuade the neighborhood, that Satanstoe is a corruption, introduced by the Dutch, from Devil's Town, which, in its turn, was a corruption from Dibbleston, the family from which my grandfather's father-in-law purchased having been, as he says, of the name of Dibblee. He has got half-a-dozen of the more sentimental part of our society to call the Neck, Dibbleton, but the attempt is not likely to succeed in the long run, as we are not a people much given to altering the language, any more than the customs of our ancestors. Besides, my Dutch ancestors did not purchase from any Dibblee, no such family ever owning the place, that being a bold assumption of the Yankee, to make out his case the more readily.

Satanstoe, as it is little more than a good farm in extent, so it is little more than a particularly good farm in cultivation and embellishment. All the buildings are of stone, even to the hog-sties and sheds, with well pointed joints, and field walls that would do credit to a fortified place. The house is generally esteemed one of the best in the Colony, with the exception of a few of the new school. It is of only a story and a half in elevation, I admit, but the rooms under the roof are as good as any of that description with which I am acquainted, and their finish is such as would do no discredit to the upper rooms of even a York dwelling. The building is in the shape of an L, or two sides of a parallelogram, one of which shows a front of seventy-five, and the other of fifty feet.

Twenty-six feet make the depth, from outside to outside of the walls. The best room had a carpet that covered two-thirds of the entire dimensions of the floor, even in my boyhood, and there were oil-cloths in most of the better passages. The buffet in the dining room, or smallest parlour, was particularly admired, and I question if there be, at this hour, a handsomer in the county. The rooms were well sized, and of fair dimensions, the larger parlors embracing the whole depth of the house, with proportionate widths, while the ceilings were higher than common, being eleven feet, if we except the places occupied by the larger beams of the chamber floors.

As there was money in the family, besides the Neck, and the Littlepages had held the King's commissions, my father having once been an ensign, and my grandfather a captain, in the regular army, each in the earlier portion of his life, we always ranked among the gentry of the county. We happened to be in a part of Westchester in which were none of the very large estates, and Satanstoe passed for a property of a certain degree of importance. It is true, the Morrises were at Morrisania, and the Felipes, or Philipses, as these Bohemian Counts were then called, had a manor on the Hudson, that extended within a dozen miles of us, and a younger branch of the de Lanceys had established itself even much nearer, while the Van Cortlandts, or a branch of them too, dwelt near Kingsbridge; but these were all people who were at the head of the Colony, and with whom none of the minor gentry attempted to vie. As it was, therefore, the Littlepages held a very respectable position between the higher class of the yeomanry and those, who, by their estates, education, connections, official rank and hereditary consideration, formed what might be justly called the aristocracy of the Colony. Both my father and grandfather had sat in the Assembly, in their time, and, as I have heard elderly people say, with credit, too. As for my father, on one occasion, he made a speech that occupied eleven minutes in the delivery, a proof that he had something to say, and which was a source of great, but I trust humble felicitation in the family, down to the day of his death, and even afterwards.

Then the military services of the family stood us in, for a great deal. In that day, it was something to be an ensign even in the militia, and a far greater thing to have the same rank in a regular regiment. It is true, neither of my predecessors served very long with the King's troops, my father in particular, selling out at the end of his second campaign, but the military experience, and I may add the military glory each acquired in youth, did them good service for all the rest of their days. Both were commissioned in the militia, and my father actually rose as high as Major, in that branch of the service, that being the rank he held, and the title he bore, for the last fifteen years of his life.

My mother was of Dutch extraction on both sides, her father having been a Blauvelt, and her mother a Van Busser. I have heard it said that there was even a relationship between the Stuyvesants and the Van Cortlandts, and the Van Bussers, but I am not able to point out the actual degree and precise nature of the affinity. I presume it was not very near, or my information would have been more minute. I have always understood that my mother brought my father thirteen hundred pounds for dowry (currency, not sterling) which, it must be confessed was a very genteel fortune for a young woman in 1733. Now, I very well know that six, eight and ten thousand pounds sometimes fall in, in this manner, and even much more in the high families, but no one need be ashamed, who looks back fifty years, and finds that his mother brought a thousand pounds to her husband.

I was neither an only child, nor the eldest born. There was a son who preceded me, and two daughters succeeded, but they all died in infancy leaving me in effect the only offspring for my parents to cherish and educate. My little brother monopolised the name of Evans, and living for some time after I was christened, I got the Dutch appellation of my maternal grandfather, for my share of the family nomenclature, which happened to be Cornelius. Corny was consequently the diminutive by which I was known to all the whites of my acquaintance, for the first sixteen or eighteen years of my life, and to my parents as long as they lived. Corny Littlepage is not a bad name, in itself, and I trust they who do me the favour to read this manuscript, will lay it down with the feeling that the name is none the worse for the use I have made of it.

I have said that both my father and grandfather, each in his day, sat in the assembly; my father twice, and my grandfather only once. Although we lived so near the borough of West-Chester, it was not for that place they sat, but for the county, the de Lanceys and the Morrises contending for the control of the borough, in a way that left little chance for the smaller fishes to swim in the troubled water they were so certain to create. Nevertheless, this political elevation, brought my father out, as it might be before the world, and was the means of giving him a personal consideration he might not have otherwise enjoyed. The benefits, and possibly some of the evils, of thus being drawn out from the more regular routine of our usually peaceable lives may be made to appear in the course of this narrative.

I have ever considered myself fortunate in not having been born in the earlier and infant days of the colony, when the interests at stake, and the events by which they were influenced, were not of a magnitude to give the mind and the hopes the excitement and enlargement that attend the periods of a more advanced civilization, and of more important incidents. In this respect, my own appearance in this world was most happily timed, as any one will see who will consider the state and importance of the Colony in the middle of the present century. New York could not have contained many less than seventy thousand souls, including both colours, at the time of my birth, for it is supposed to contain quite a hundred thousand, this day on which I am now writing. In such a community, a man has not only the room, but the materials on which to figure; whereas, as I have often heard him say, my father, when he was born, was one of less than half of the smallest number I have just named. I have been grateful for this advantage, and I trust it will appear, by evidence that will be here afforded, that I have not lived in a quarter of the world, or in an age, when and where, and to which great events have been altogether strangers.

My earliest recollections, as a matter of course, are of Satanstoe and the domestic fireside. In my childhood and youth, I heard a great deal said of the Protestant Succession, the House of Hanover, and King George II^{d}; all mixed up with such names as those of George Clinton, Gen. Monckton, Sir Charles Hardy, James de Lancey, and Sir Danvers Osborne, his official representatives in the colony. Every age has its *old* and its *last* wars, and I can well remember that which occurred between the French in the Canadas, and ourselves in 1744. I was then seven years old, and it was an event to make an impression on a child of that tender age. My honoured grandfather was then living, as he was long afterwards, and he took a strong interest in the military movements of the period, as was natural for an old soldier. New York had no connection with the celebrated expedition that captured Louisbourg, then the Gibraltar of America, in 1745, but this could not prevent an old soldier, like Capt. Littlepage from entering into the affair, with all his heart, though forbidden to use his hand. As the reader may not be aware of all the secret springs that set public events in motion, it may be well here to throw in a few words, in the way of explanation.

There was and is little sympathy, in the way of national feeling, between the Colonies of New England, and those which lie farther south. We are all loyal, those of the east, as well as those of the south-west and south, but there is, and ever has been, so wide a difference in our customs, origins, religious opinions, and histories, as to cause a broad moral line, in the way of feeling, to be drawn between the colony of New York, and those that lie east of the Byram River. I have heard it said, that most of the emigrants to the New England states came from the West of England, where many of their social peculiarities, and much of their language are still to be traced, while the colonies farther south have received their population from the more central counties, and those sections of the island that are supposed to be less provincial and peculiar. I do not affirm that such is literally the fact, though it is well known that we of New York, have long been accustomed to regard our neighbors of New England, as very different from ourselves, while, I dare say, our neighbors of New England have regarded us as different from themselves, and insomuch removed from perfection.

Let all this be as it may, it is certain New England is a portion of the empire that is set apart from the rest, for good or for evil. It got its name from the circumstance that the English possessions were met, on its western boundary, by those of the Dutch, and were thus separated from the other colonies of purely Anglo-Saxon origin, by a wide district that was much larger in surface than the mother country itself. I am afraid there is something in the character of these Anglo-Saxons that predisposes them to laugh, and turn up their noses, at other races, for I have remarked that the natives of the parent island itself, who come among us, show this disposition even as it respects us of New-York, and those of New England, while the people of the latter region manifest a feeling towards us, their neighbors, that

partakes of any thing but the humility that is thought to grace
that christian character to which they are particularly fond of
laying claim.

My grandfather was a native of the old country, however, and
he entered but little into the colonial jealousies. He had lived
from boyhood, and had married in New York, and was not apt to
betray any of the overweening notions of superiority that we
sometimes encountered in native-born Englishmen, though I
can remember instances in which he would point out the defects
in our civilization, and others in which he dwelt with pleasure on
the grandeur and power of his own island. I dare say this was all
right, for few among us have ever been disposed to dispute the
just supremacy of England, in all things that are desirable, and
which form the basis of human excellence.

I well remember a journey Capt. Hugh Littlepage made to
Boston, in 1745, in order to look at the preparations that were
making for the great expedition. Although his own colony had
no connection with this enterprise, in a military point of view, his
previous service rendered him an object of interest to the military men then assembled along the coast of New England. It has
been said the expedition against Louisbourg, then the strongest
place in America, was planned by a lawyer, led by a merchant,
and executed by husbandmen and mechanics; but this, though
true as a whole, was a rule that had its exceptions. There were
many old soldiers, who had seen the service of this continent in
the previous wars, and among them were several of my grandfather's former acquaintances. With these he passed many a
cheerful hour, previously to the day of sailing, and I have often
thought since, that my presence alone prevented him from making one in the fleet. The reader will think I was young, perhaps,
to be so far from home on such an occasion, but it happened in
this wise. My excellent mother thought I had come out of the
small pox with some symptoms that might be benefited by a journey, and she prevailed on her father-in-law to let me be of the
party, when he left home to visit Boston, in the winter of 1744–5.
At that early day, moving about was not always convenient in
these colonies, and my grandfather travelling in a sleigh that was
proceeding east with some private stores that had been collected
for the expedition, it presented a favourable opportunity to send
me along with my venerable progenitor, who very good na-

turedly consented to let me commence my travels under his own immediate auspices.

The things I saw on this occasion, have had a material influence on my future life. I got a love of adventure, and particularly of military parade and grandeur, that has since led me into more than one difficulty. Capt. Hugh Littlepage, my grandfather, was delighted with all he saw until after the expedition had sailed, when he began to grumble on the subject of the religious observances, that the piety of the Puritans blended with most of their other movements. On the score of religion, there was a marked difference; I may say there *is* still, a marked difference between New England and New-York. The people of New-England certainly did, and possibly may still, look upon us of New York, as little better than heathens, while we of New York, assuredly did, and for any thing I know to the contrary may yet, regard them as canters, and by necessary connection, hypocrites. I shall not take it on myself to say which party is right, though it has often occurred to my mind that it would be better had New England a little less self-righteousness, and New York a little more righteousness, without the self. Still, in the way of pounds, shillings and pence, we will not turn our backs upon them, any day, being on the whole rather the most trust-worthy of the two as respects money; more especially in all such cases in which our neighbor's goods can be appropriated without having recourse to absolutely direct means. Such, at any rate, is the New York opinion, let them think as they please about it, on the other side of Byram.

My grandfather met an old fellow campaigner, at Boston, of the name of Hight. Major Hight, as he was called, had come to see the preparations, too, and the old soldiers passed most of the time together. The Major was a Jersey man, and had been somewhat of a free-liver in his time, retaining some of the propensities of his youth, in old age, as is apt to be the case with those who cultivate a vice as if it were a hot-house plant. The Major was fond of his bottle, drinking heavily of Madeira, of which there was then a good stock in Boston, for he brought some on himself, and I can remember various scenes that occurred between him and my grandfather, after dinner, as they sat discoursing in the tavern on the progress of things, and the prospects for the future. Had these two old soldiers been of the troops of the Province in which they were, it would have been "Major" and "Captain" at every breath, for no part of the earth is fonder of titles than our eastern brethren,* whereas, I must think we had some claims to more true simplicity of character and habits, notwithstanding New York has ever been thought the most aristocratical of all the northern colonies. Having been intimate from early youth, my two old soldiers familiarly called each other Joey and Hodge, the latter being the abbreviation of one of my grandfather's names, Roger, when plain Hugh was not used, as sometimes happened between them. Hugh Roger Littlepage, I ought to have said was my grandfather's name.

"I should like these Yankees better, if they prayed less, my old friend," said the Major, one day, after they had been discussing the appearances of things, and speaking between the puffs of his pipe. "I can see no great use in losing so much time, by making these halts to pray, when the campaign is fairly opened."

"It was always their way, Joey," my grandfather answered, taking his time, as is customary with smokers. "I remember when we were out together, in the year '17, that the New England troops always had their parsons, who acted as a sort of second colonels. They tell me His Excellency has ordered a weekly fast, for public prayers, during the whole of this campaign."

"Ay, Master Hodge, praying and plundering; so they go on," returned the Major, knocking the ashes out of his pipe, preparatory to filling it anew, an employment that gave him an opportunity to give vent to his feelings, without pausing to puff—"Ay, Master Hodge, praying and plundering; so they go on. Now, do you remember old Watson, who was in the Massachusetts Levies, in the year '12? Old Tom Watson; he that was a sub under Barnwell, in our Tuscarora expedition?"

My grandfather nodded his head in assent, that being the only reply the avocation of smoking rendered convenient, just at that moment, unless a sort of affirmatory grunt could be construed into an auxiliary.

"Well, he has a son going in this affair, and old Tom, or Colonel Watson as he is now very particular to be called, is down here with his wife and two daughters, to see the ensign off. I went to pay the old fellow a visit, Hodge, and found him, and the mother and sis-

*It will be remembered Mr. Littlepage wrote more than seventy years ago, when this distinction might exclusively belong to the *East*; but the *West* has now some claim to it, also.

ters, all as busy as bees in getting young Tom's baggage ready for a march. There lay his whole equipment before my eyes, and I had a favorable occasion to examine it, at my leisure."

"Which you did, with all your might, or you're not the Joe Hight of the year '10," said my grandfather, taking his turn with the ashes and the tobacco box.

Old Hight was now puffing away, like a blacksmith, who is striving to obtain a white heat, and it was some time, before he could get out the proper reply, to this half-assertion, half-interrogatory sort of remark.

"You may be sure of that," he at length ejaculated; when, certain of his light, he proceeded to tell the whole story, stopping occasionally to puff, lest he should lose the "vantage ground" he had just obtained. "What d'ye think of half-a-dozen strings of red onions, for one item in a subaltern's stores?"

My grandfather grunted, again, in a way that might very well pass for a laugh.

"You're certain they were red, Joey?" he finally asked.

"As red as his regimentals. Then there was a jug, filled with molasses, that is as big as yonder demi john," glancing at the vessel which contained his own private stores. "But, I should have thought nothing of these, a large empty sack attracting much of my attention. I could not imagine what young Tom could want of such a sack, but, on broaching the subject to the Major, he very frankly gave me to understand that Louisbourg was thought to be a rich town, and there was no telling what luck, or Providence—Yes, by George!—he called it *Providence!*—might throw in his son Tommy's way. Now that the sack was empty, and had an easy time of it, the girls would put his bible and hymn book in it, as a place where the young man would be likely to look for them. I dare say, Hodge, you never had either bible, or hymn book, in any of your numerous campaigns?"

"No, nor a plunder-sack, nor a molasses jug, nor strings of red onions—" growled my grandfather in reply.

How well I remember that evening. A vast deal of colonial prejudice, and neighborly antipathy made themselves apparent in the conversation of the two veterans, who seemed to entertain a strange sort of contemptuous respect, for their fellow-subjects, of New England, who, in their turn, I make not the smallest doubt, paid them off in kind—with all the superciliousness and reproach, and with many grains less of the respect.

That night, Major Hight and Capt. Hugh Roger Littlepage, both got a little how-come-you-so, drinking bumpers to the success of what they called "the Yankee expedition," even at the moment they were indulging in constant side hits, at the failings and habits of the people. These marks of neighbourly infirmity, are not peculiar to the people of the adjacent provinces of New York and of New England. I have often remarked that the English think and talk very much of the French, as the Yankees speak of us, while the French, so far as I have been able to understand their somewhat unintelligible language—which seems never to have a beginning nor an end—treat the English as the Puritans of the Old World. As I have already intimated, we were not very remarkable for religion in New-York, in my younger days, while it would be just the word, were I to say that religion was *conspicuous* among our eastern neighbors. I remember to have heard my grandfather say he was once acquainted with a Col. Heathcote, an English man like himself by birth, and a brother of a certain Sir Gilbert Heathcote who was formerly a leading man in the Bank of England. This Col. Heathcote came among us young, and married here, leaving his posterity behind him, and was Lord of the Manors of Scarsdale and Mamaroneck, in our County of Westchester. Well, this Col. Heathcote told my grandfather, speaking on the subject of religion, that he had been much shocked, on arriving in this country, at discovering the neglected condition of religion in the Colony; more especially on Long Island, where the people lived in a sort of heathenish condition. Being a man of mark, and connected with the government, The Society for the Propagation of the Gospel in Foreign Parts, applied to him to aid it, in spreading the truths of the bible in the Colony. The Colonel was glad enough to comply, and I remember my grandfather said, his friend told him of the answer he returned to these good persons in England. "I was so struck with the heathenish condition of the people, on my arriving here," he wrote to them, "that, commanding the militia of the Colony, I ordered the captains of the different companies, to call their men together, each Sunday at sunrise, and to drill them until sunset, unless they would consent to repair to some convenient place, and listen to morning and evening prayer and to two wholesome sermons, read by some suitable person, in which case the men were to be excused from drill."* I do not think this would be found necessary in New England at least, where many of the people would be likely to prefer drilling to preaching.

But all this gossip about the moral condition of the adjacent colonies of New York and New England, is leading me from the narrative, and does not promise much for the connection and interest of the remainder of the manuscript.

*On the subject of this story, the editor can say he has seen a published letter from Col. Heathcote, who died more than a century since, at Mamaroneck, West-Chester Co., in which that gentleman gives the Society for the propagation of the gospel an account of his proceedings that agrees almost *verbatim*, with the account of the matter, that is here given by Mr. Cornelius Littlepage. The house in which Col. Heathcote dwelt, was destroyed by fire, a short time before the revolution, but the property on which it stood, and the present building, belong at this moment to his great-grandson, the Rt. Rev. Wm. *Heathcote* de Lancey, the Bishop of Western New-York.

On the subject of the *plunder*, the editor will remark, that a near connection, whose grandfather was a Major at the taking of Louisbourg, and who was subsequently one of the first Brigadiers appointed in 1775, has lately shown him a letter written to that officer, during the expedition, by *his* father, in which blended with a great deal of pious counsel, and some really excellent religious exhortation, is an earnest inquiry after the *plunder.*—EDITOR.

Chapter II

"I would there were no age between ten and three-and-twenty;
or that youth would sleep out the rest."

The Winters Tale, III. iii. 59–61.

I T is not necessary for me to say much of the first fourteen
years of my life. They passed like the childhood and youth of the
sons of most gentlemen in our Colony, at that day, with this distinction, however. There was a class among us, which educated its
boys at home. This was not a very numerous class certainly, nor
was it always the highest in point of fortune and rank. Many of
the large proprietors were of Dutch origin, as a matter of course,
and these seldom, if ever, sent their children to England to be
taught any thing, in my boyhood. I understand that a few are getting over their ancient prejudices, in this particular, and begin to
fancy Oxford, or Cambridge, may be quite as learned schools, as
that of Leyden; but, no Van, in my boyhood, could have been
made to believe this. Many of the Dutch proprietors gave their
children very little education, in any way or form, though most of
them imparted lessons of probity that were quite as useful as
learning, had the two things been really inseparable. For my part,
while I admit there is a great deal of knowledge going up and
down the land, that is just of the degree to trick a fellow creature
out of his rights, I shall never subscribe to the opinion, which is so
prevalent among the Dutch portion of our population, and
which holds the doctrine that the schools of the New-England
provinces are the reason the descendants of the Puritans do not
enjoy the best of reputations in this respect. I believe a boy may be
well taught, and made all the honester for it; though I admit
there may be, and is, such a thing as training a lad in false notions,
as well as training him in those that are true. But, we had a class,
principally of English extraction, that educated its sons well; usually sending them home, to the great English schools, and finishing at the Universities. These persons, however, lived principally
in town, or, having estates on the Hudson, passed their winters
there. To this class the Littlepages did not belong, neither their

habits, nor their fortunes, tempting them to so high a flight. For myself, I was taught enough Latin and Greek to enter college, by the Rev. Thomas Worden, an English divine who was rector of St. Jude's, the parish to which our family properly belonged. This gentleman was esteemed a good scholar, and was very popular among the gentry of the county; attending all the dinners, clubs, races, balls, and other diversions that were given by them, within ten miles of his residence. His sermons were pithy and short, and he always spoke of your half-hour preachers, as illiterate prosers, who did not understand how to condense their thoughts. Twenty minutes were his gauge, though I remember to have heard my father say, he had known him preach all of twenty-two. When he compressed down to fourteen, my grandfather invariably protested he was delightful.

I remained with Mr. Worden until I could translate the two first Æneids, and the whole of the Gospel of St. Matthew, pretty readily, and then my father and grandfather, the last in particular, for the old gentleman had a great idea of learning, began to turn over in their minds, the subject of the college to which I ought to be sent. We had the choice of two, in both of which the learned languages, and the sciences are taught, to a degree and in a perfection, that is surprising for a new Country. These Colleges are Yale, at New-Haven, in Connecticut, and Nassau Hall, which was then at Newark, New Jersey, after having been a short time at Elizabethtown, but which has since been established at Princeton. Mr. Worden laughed at both, said that neither had as much learning, as a second rate English grammar school, and that a lower form boy, at Eton, or Westminster, could take a Master's degree at either, and pass for a prodigy in the bargain. My father, who was born in the colonies, and had a good deal of the right colony feeling, was nettled at this, I remember, while my grandfather, being old country born, but colony educated, was at a loss how to view the matter. The captain had a great respect for his native land, and evidently considered it the paradise of this earth, though his recollections of it were not very distinct; but, at the same time he loved Old York, and Westchester in particular, where he had married, and established himself at Satan's Toe; or as he spelt it, and as we all have spelt it, now, this many a day, Satanstoe. I was present at the conversation which decided the question, as regarded my future education, and which took place in the common parlour, around a blazing fire, about a week before Christmas, the year I was fourteen. There were present, Capt. Hugh Roger, Major Evans, my mother, the Rev. Mr. Worden, and an old gentleman of Dutch designation and extraction, of the name of Abraham Van Valkenburgh, but who was familiarly called by his friends, 'Brom Follock, or Col. Follock, or Vollock, as the last happened to be more or less ceremonious, or more or less Dutch. Follock, I think however, was the favourite pronunciation. This Col. Van Valkenburgh, was an old brother soldier of my father's, and indeed a relation, a sort of a cousin through my great grandmother, besides being a man of much consideration and substance. He lived in Rockland, just across the Hudson, but never failed to pay a visit to Satanstoe, at that season of the year. On the present occasion, he was accompanied by his son Dirck, who was *my* friend, and just a year my junior.

"Vell, den—" the Colonel commenced the discourse by saying, as he tapped the ashes out of his pipe for the second time that evening, having first taken a draught of hot flip, a beverage much in vogue then, as well as now—"Vell, den, Evans, vat is your intention as to ter poy? Vill he pe college l'arnt, like as his grant-fat'er, or only school l'arnt, like as his own fat'er?" The allusion to the grandfather being a pleasantry of the Colonel's, who insisted that all the old-country born were "college-l'arnt" by instinct.

"To own the truth, 'Brom," my father answered, "this is a point that is not yet entirely settled, for there are different opinions as to the place to which he shall be sent, even admitting that he is to be sent, at all."

The Colonel fastened his full, projecting, blue eyes on my father, in a way that pretty plainly expressed surprise.

"Vat, den, is dere so many colleges, dat it is hart to choose?" he said.

"There are but two that can be of any use to us, for Cambridge is much too distant to think of sending the boy so far. Cambridge was in our thoughts at one time, but that is given up."

"Vhere, den, ist Camprige?" demanded the Dutchman, removing his pipe to ask so important a question, a ceremony he usually thought unnecessary.

"It is a New England college—near Boston; not half a day's journey distant, I fancy."

"Don't sent Cornelius dere," ejaculated the Colonel, contriving to get these words out, along side of the stem of the pipe.

"You think not, Col. Follock," put in the anxious mother—"May I ask the reason for that opinion?"

"Too much Suntay, Matam Littlepage—the poy wilt be sp'ilt by ter ministers. He will go away an honest lat, and come pack a rogue. He will l'arn how to bray and to cheat."

"Hoity toity! my noble Colonel!" exclaimed the Rev. Mr. Worden, affecting more resentment than he felt. "Then you fancy the clergy and too much Sunday, will be apt to convert an honest youth into a knave!"

The Colonel made no answer, continuing to smoke very philosophically, though he took occasion, while he drew the pipe out of his mouth, in one of its periodical removals, to make a significant gesture with it, towards the rising sun, which all present understood to mean "down east," as it is usual to say, when we mean to designate the colonies of New England. That he was understood by the Rev. Mr. Worden is highly probable; since that gentleman continued to turn the flip of one vessel into another, by way of more intimately blending the ingredients of the mixture, quite as coolly as if there had been no reflection on his trade.

"What do you think of Yale, friend 'Brom?" asked my father, who understood the dumb show as well as any of them.

"No tifference, Evans; dey all breaches and brays too much. *Goot* men have no neet of so much religion. Vhen a man is *really* goot, religion only does him harm:—I mean Yankee religion."

"I have another objection to Yale," observed Capt. Hugh Roger, "which is their English."

"Och!" exclaimed the Colonel—"Deir English is horriple! Wuss dan ast to us Tutch."

"Well, I was not aware of that," observed my father. "They are English, sir, as well as ourselves, and why should they not speak the language as well as we?"

"Why toes not a Yorkshireman, or a Cornishman speak as vell as a Lonnoner? I tell you what Evans, I'll pet the pest game cock on ter Neck, against the veriest tunghill the parson hast, ter Presitent of Yale calls peen, pen—ant—roof, ruff—and so on."

"My birds are all game," put in the divine; "I keep no other breed."

"Surely, Mr. Worden, *you* do not countenance cock-fights by your presence!" my mother said, using as much of reproach in her manner as comported with the holy office of the party she addressed, and with her own gentle nature. The Colonel winked at my father, and laughed *through his pipe*, an exploit he might have been said to perform almost hourly. My father smiled, in return; for, to own the truth, he *had* been present at such sports, on one or two occasions, when the parson's curiosity had tempted him to peep in also; but my grandfather looked grave and much in earnest. As for Mr. Worden himself, he met the imputation like a man. To do him justice, if he were not an ascetic, neither was he a whining hypocrite, as is the case with too many of those who aspire to be disciples and ministers of our blessed Lord.

"Why not, Madam Littlepage?" Mr. Worden stoutly demanded. "There are worse places than cock-pits, for, mark me, I never bet—no, not on a horse race, even; and *that* is an occasion on which any gentleman might venture a few guineas, in a liberal, frank, way. There are so few amusements for people of education in this country, Madam Littlepage, that one is not to be too particular. If there were hounds and hunting now, as there are at home, you should never hear of me at a cock-fight, I can assure you."

"I must say I do not approve of cock-fights," rejoined my mother meekly, "and I hope Corny will never be seen at one. No—never—never."

"Dere you're wrong, Matam Littlepage," the Colonel remarked, "for ter sight of ter spirit of ter cocks wilt give ter poy spirit himself. My Tirck, dere, goes to all in ter neighbourhoot, and he is a gamecock himself, let me tell you. Come, Tirck—come—cock-a-doodle-dooo!"

This was true all round, as I very well knew, young as I was. Dirck, who was as slow moving, as dull-seeming, and as anti-mercurial a boy to look at, as one could find in a thousand, was thorough game at the bottom, and he had been at many a main, as he had told me himself. How much of his spirit was derived from witnessing such scenes I will not take on me to affirm, for, in these later times, I have heard it questioned whether such exhibitions do really improve the spectator's courage, or not. But, Dirck had pluck, and plenty of it, and in that particular at least, his father was not mistaken. The Colonel's opinion always carried weight with my mother, both on account of his Dutch extraction, and on account of his well established probity; for, to own the truth, a text, or a sentiment from him, had far more weight with her, than the same from the clergyman. She was silenced on the subject of cock-fighting, for the moment therefore, which gave Capt. Hugh Roger further opportunity to pursue that of the English language. My grandfather, who was an inveterate lover of the sport, would have cut in to that branch of the discourse, but he had a great tenderness for my mother, whom everybody loved by the way, and he commanded himself, glad to find that so important an interest had fallen into hands as good as those of the Colonel. *He* would just as soon be absent from church, as be absent from a cock-fight, and he was a very good observer of religion.

"I should have sent Evans to Yale, had it not been for the miserable manner of speaking English they have in New England," resumed my grandfather, "and I had no wish to have a son who might pass for a Cornish man. We shall have to send this boy to Newark, in New Jersey. The distance is not so great, and we shall be certain he will not get any of your round-head notions of religion, too. Col. 'Brom, you Dutch are not altogether free from these dissenting follies."

"Debble a pit!" growled the Colonel, through his pipe, for no devotee of liberalism and latitudinarianism in religion, could be more averse to extra-piety than he. The Colonel, however, was not of the Dutch Reformed; he was an Episcopalian like ourselves, his mother having brought this branch of the Follocks into the church; and, consequently, he entered into all our feelings on the subject of religion, heart and hand. Perhaps, Mr. Worden was a greater favourite with no member of the four parishes over which he presided, than with Col. Abraham Van Valkenburgh.

"I should think less of sending Corny to Newark," added my mother, "was it not for crossing the water."

"Crossing the water!" repeated Mr. Worden—"The Newark we mean, Madam Littlepage, is not at home. The Jersey of which we speak, is the adjoining colony of that name."

"I am aware of that, Mr. Worden, but it is not possible to get to Newark, without making that terrible voyage between New-York and Powles Hook. No, sir, it is impossible, and every time the child comes home, that risk will have to be run. It would cause me many a sleepless night!"

"He can go by Tobb's Ferry, Matam Littlepage," quietly observed the Colonel.

"Dobb's Ferry can be very little better than that by Powles Hook," rejoined the tender mother. "A ferry is a ferry, and the Hudson will be the Hudson, from Albany to New York. So water is water."

As these were all self evident propositions, they produced a pause in the discourse, for men do not deal with new ideas as freely as they deal with the old.

"Dere is a way, Evans, as you and I know py experience," resumed the Colonel, winking again at my father, "to go rount the Hudson, altoget'er. To pe sure, it is a long way, and a pit in the woots, but petter to untertake dat, than to haf the poy lose his l'arnin'. Ter journey might be made in two mont's, and he none the wuss for ter exercise. Ter Major and I were never heartier dan when we were operating on the he't waters of the Hutson. I will tell Corny the roat."

My mother saw that her apprehensions were laughed at, and she had the good sense to be silent. The discussion did not the less proceed, until it was decided, after an hour more of weighing the *pros* and the *cons*, that I was to be sent to Nassau Hall, Newark, New Jersey, and was to move from that place with the college, whenever that event might happen.

"You will send Dirck there, too," my father added, as soon as the affair in my case, was finally determined. "It would be a pity to separate the boys, after they have been so long together, and have got to be so much used to each other. Their characters are so identical, too, that they are more like brothers than very distant relatives."

"Dey will like one anot'er all de petter for pein' a little tifferent, den," answered the Colonel, drily.

Dirck and I were no more alike, than a horse resembles a mule.

"Ay, but Dirck is a lad who will do honour to an education—he is solid and thoughtful, and learning will not be thrown away on such a youth. Was he in England, that sedate lad might get to be a bishop."

"I want no pishops, in my family, Major Evans, nor do I want any great l'arnin'. None of us ever saw a college, and we have got on fery vell. I am a Colonel and a memper; my fat'er was a Colonel and a memper, and my grandfat'er *woult* have peen a colonel and a memper, but dere vast no colonels and no mempers in his time, though Tirck, yonter, can be a colonel and a memper, wit'out crosting dat terriple ferry that frightens Matam Littlepage so much."

There was usually a little humour, in all Col. Follock said and did, though it must be owned it was humour after a very Dutch model; Dutch-built fun, as Mr. Worden used to call it. Nevertheless it was humour, and there was enough of Holland in all the junior generations of the Littlepages, to enjoy it. My father understood him, and my mother did not hear the last of the "terriple ferry," until not only I, but the college itself, had quitted Newark, for the institution made another remove to Princeton, the place where it is now to be found, some time before I got my degree.

"You have got on very well, without a college education, as all must admit, Colonel," answered Mr. Worden; "but, there is no telling how much *better* you would have got on, had you been an A. M. You might, in the last case, have been a general and a member of the King's Council."

"Dere ist no yeneral in ter colony, the Commander in Chief and His Majesty's representatif excepted," returned the Colonel. "We are no Yankees, to make yenerals of ploughmen."

Hereupon, the Colonel and my father knocked the ashes out of their pipes, at the same instant, and both laughed, a merriment in which the parson, my grandfather, my dear mother, and I myself joined. Even a negro boy, who was about my own age, and whose name was Jacob, or Jaap, but who was commonly called Yaap, grinned at the remark, for he too had a sovereign contempt for Yankee Land and all it contained; almost as sovereign a contempt as that which Yankee Land entertained for York itself, and its Dutch population. Dirck was the only person present who looked grave; but Dirck was habitually as grave and sedate, as if he had been born to become a burgomaster.

"Quite right, Brom," cried my father; "*Colonels* are good enough for us, and when we do make a man *that*, even, we are a little particular about his being respectable and fit for the office. Nevertheless, learning will not hurt Corny, and to college he shall go, let you do as you please with Dirck. So that matter is settled, and no more need be said about it."

And it was settled, and to college I *did* go, and that by the awful Powles Hook Ferry, in the bargain. Near as we lived to town, I paid my first visit to the island of Manhattan, the day my father and myself started for Newark. I had an aunt who lived in Queen Street, not a very great distance from the fort, and she had kindly invited me and my father to pass a day with her, on our way to New Jersey, which invitation had been accepted. In my youth, the world in general, was not as much addicted to gadding about, as it is now getting to be, and neither my grandfather, nor my father ordinarily went to town, their calls to the Legislature excepted, more than twice a year. My mother's visits were still less frequent, although Mrs. Legge, my aunt, was her own sister. Mr. Legge was a lawyer of a good deal of reputation, but he was inclined to be in the opposition, or espoused the popular side in politics, and there could be no great cordiality between one of that frame of mind, and our family. I remember we had not been in the house an hour, before a warm discussion took place between my uncle and my father, on the question of the right of the subject to canvass the acts of the government. We had left home, immediately after an early breakfast, in order to reach town before dark; but a long detention at the Harlem ferry compelled us to dine in that village, and it was quite night before we stopped in Queen Street. My aunt ordered supper early, in order that we might get early to bed, to recover from our fatigue, and be ready for sight-seeing next day. We sat down to supper, therefore, in less than an hour after our arrival, and it was while we were at table, that the discussion I have mentioned took place. It would seem that a party had been got up in town, among the disloyal, and I might almost say the disaffected, which claimed for the subject the right to know in what manner every shilling of the money raised by taxation was expended. This very obviously improper interference with matters that did not belong to them on the part of the ruled, was resisted by the rulers, and that with energy, inasmuch as such inquiries and investigations would naturally lead to results that might bring authority into discredit, make the governed presuming and prying in their dispositions, and cause much derangement and inconvenience to the regular and salutary action of government. My father took the negative of the proposition, while my uncle maintained its affirmative. I well remember that my poor aunt looked uneasy and tried to divert the discourse by exciting our curiosity on a new subject.

"Corny has been particularly lucky in having come to town just as he has, since we shall have a sort of gala-day, to-morrow, for the blacks and the children."

I was not in the least offended at being thus associated with the negroes, for they mingled in most of the amusements of us young people, but I did not quite so well like to be ranked with the children, now I was fourteen, and on my way to college. Notwithstanding this, I did not fail to betray an interest in what was to come next, by my countenance. As for my father, he did not hesitate about asking an explanation.

"The news came in this morning, by a fast sailing sloop that the Patroon of Albany is on his way to New York, in his coach and four, and with two out-riders, and that he may be expected to reach town in the course of to-morrow. Several of my acquaintances have consented to let their children go out a little way into the country to see him come in, and, as for the blacks, you know, it is just as well to give them *permission* to be of the party, as half of them would otherwise go without asking it."

"This will be a capital opportunity to let Corny see a little of the world," cried my father, "and I would not have him miss it, on any account. Besides, it is useful to teach young people early, the profitable lesson of honouring their superiors, and seniors."

"In that sense it may do," growled my uncle, who, though so much of a latitudinarian in his political opinions, never failed to inculcate all useful and necessary maxims for private life, "the Patroon of Albany being one of the most respectable and affluent of all our gentry. I have no objections to Corny's going to see that sight, and I hope, my dear, you will let both Pompey and Caesar be of the party. It won't hurt the fellows to see the manner in which the patroon has his carriage kept and horses groomed."

Pompey and Caesar were of the party, though the latter did not join us until Pompey had taken me all round the town, to see the principal sights; it being understood that the Patroon had slept at Kingsbridge, and would not be likely to reach town until near noon. New-York was certainly not the place in 1751, it is to-day; nevertheless it was a large and important town even when I went to college, containing not less than twelve thousand souls, blacks included. The Town Hall is a magnificent structure, standing at the head of Broad Street, and thither Pompey led me, even before my aunt had come down to breakfast. I could scarcely admire that fine edifice sufficiently, which for size, architecture, and position, has scarcely now an equal in all the Colonies. It is true that the town has much improved, within the last twenty years, but York was a noble place even in the middle of this century! After breakfast, Pompey and I proceeded up Broadway, commencing near the fort, at the Bowling Green, and walking some distance beyond the head of Wall Street, or quite a quarter of a mile. Nor did the town stop here, though its principal extent is, or was then, along the margin of the East River. Trinity Church I could hardly admire enough, either, for it appeared to me that it was large enough to contain all the church people in the colony.* It was a venerable structure, which had then felt the heats of summer and the snows of winter on its roofs and walls, near half a century, and it still stands a monument of pious zeal and cultivated taste. There were other churches, belonging to other denominations of course, that were well worthy of being seen; to say nothing of the markets. I thought I never should tire of gazing at the magnificence of the shops, particularly the silversmiths', some of which must have had a thousand dollars' worth of plate in their windows, or otherwise in sight. I might say

*The intelligent reader will, of course, properly appreciate the provincial admiration of Mr. Littlepage, who naturally fancied his own best, was other people's best. The Trinity of that day was burned in the great fire of 1776. The edifice that succeeded it, at the peace of 1783, has already given place to a successor, that has more claim to be placed on a level with modern, English, town church-architecture, than any other building in the Union. When another shall succeed this, which shall be as much larger and more elaborated than this is compared to its predecessor, and still another shall succeed, which shall bear the same relation to that, then the country will possess an edifice that is on a level with the first-rate Gothic cathedral-architecture of Europe. It would be idle to pretend that the new Trinity is without faults, some of which are probably the result of circumstances and necessity, but, if the respectable architect who has built it, had no other merit, he would deserve the gratitude of every man of taste in the country, by placing church towers of a proper comparative breadth, dignity and proportions before the eyes of its population. The diminutive meanness of American church towers, has been an eye-sore to every *intelligent* travelled American, since the country was settled.—EDITOR.

as much of the other shops, too, which attracted a just portion of my admiration.

About eleven, the number of children and blacks that were seen walking towards the Bowery Road, gave us notice that it was time to be moving in that direction. We were in the upper part of Broadway, at the time, and Pompey proceeded forthwith to fall into the current, making all the haste he could, as it was thought the traveller might pass down towards the East River, and get into Queen Street, before we could reach the point at which he would diverge. It is true, the old town residence of Stephen de Lancey, which stood at the head of Broadway, just above Trinity,* had been converted into a tavern, and we did not know but the Patroon might choose to alight there, as it was then the principal inn of the town; still, most people preferred Queen Street, and the new City Tavern was so much out of the way, that strangers in particular were not fond of frequenting it. Caesar came up, much out of breath, just as we got into the country.

Quitting Broadway, we went along the country road that then diverged to the east, but which is now getting to contain a sort of suburb, and passing the road that leads into Queen Street, we felt more certain of meeting the traveller, whose carriage we soon learned had not gone by. As there were and are several taverns for country people, in this quarter, most of us went quite into the country, proceeding as far as the villas of the Bayards, de Lanceys, and other persons of mark; of which there are several along the Bowery Road. Our party stopped under some cherry trees, that were not more than the mile from town, nearly opposite to Lt. Gov. de Lancey's country house† but many boys &c. went a long long way into the country, finishing the day by nutting and gathering apples in the grounds of Petersfield and Rosehill, the country residences of the Stuyvesant and Watt, or, as the last is now called, the Watts, families. I was desirous of going thus far myself, for I had heard much of both of those grand places, but Pompey told me it would be necessary to be back for dinner, by half-past one, his mistress having consented to postpone the hour a little, in order to indulge my natural desire to see all I could, while in town.

*The site of the present City Hotel.—ED.
†Now, de Lancey Street.—ED.

We were not altogether children and blacks, who were out on the Bowery Road, that day. Many tradesmen were among us, the leathern aprons making a goodly parade on the occasion. I saw one or two persons wearing swords, hovering round, in the lanes and in the woods, proof that even gentlemen had some desire to see so great a person as the Patroon of Albany pass. I shall not stop to say much of the *transit* of the Patroon. He came by, about noon, as was expected, and in his coach and four, with two out-riders, coachman, &c. in liveries, as is usual in the families of the gentry, and with a team of heavy, black, Dutch-looking horses, that I remember Caesar pronounced to be of the true Flemish breed. The patroon himself, was a sightly, well-dressed gentle-man, wearing a scarlet coat, flowing wig, and cocked hat; and I observed that the handle of his sword was of solid silver. But my father wore a sword with a solid silver handle, too, a present from my grandfather when the former first entered the army.* He bowed to the salutations he received in passing, and I thought all the spectators were pleased with the noble sight of seeing such an equipage pass into the town. Such a sight does not occur every day in the colonies, and I felt exceedingly happy that it had been my privilege to witness it.

A little incident occurred to myself, that rendered this day long memorable to me. Among the spectators assembled along the

*This patroon must have been Jeremiah Van Rensselaer who lived to be a bachelor of forty before he married. If there be no anachronism, this gentle-man married Miss Van Cortlandt, one of the seven daughters of Stephanus Van Cortlandt, who was proprietor of the great Manour of Cortlandt, West Chester county, and, who, in his day, was the principal personage of the Colony. The seven daughters of this Colonel Van Cortlandt, by marrying into the families of de Lancey, Bayard, Van Rensselaer, Beckman, M'Gregor-Skinner, &c. &c., brought together a connection, that was long felt in the political affairs of New York. The Schuylers were related through a previous marriage, and many of the Long Island and other families of weight, by other alliances. This connec-tion formed the court party, which was resisted by an opposition led by the Livingstons, Morris, and other names of *their* connection. This old bachelor, Jeremiah Van Rensselaer, believing he would never marry, alienated, in behalf of his next brother and anticipated heir, the Greenbush and Claverack estates, portions of those vast possessions which, in our day, and principally through the culpable apathy, or miserable demagogueism, of those who have been en-trusted with the care of the public weal, have been the pretext for violating some of the plainest laws of morality that God has communicated to man.— EDITOR.

road, on this occasion, were several groups of girls, who belonged to the better class, and who had been induced to come out into the country, either led by curiosity, or by the management of the different sable nurses who had them in charge. In one of these groups, was a girl of about ten, or possibly of eleven years of age, whose dress, air, and mien early attracted my attention. I thought her large, bright, full, blue eye, particularly winning, and boys of fourteen are not altogether insensible to beauty in the other sex, though they are possibly induced oftener to regard it in those who are older, than in those who are younger, than themselves. Pompey happened to be acquainted with Sylvy, the negress who had the care of my little beauty, to whom he bowed, and addressed as Miss Anneke (Anna Cornelia, abbreviated). Anneke I thought a very pretty name too, and some little advances were made towards an acquaintance, by means of an offering of some fruit that I had gathered by the way side. Things were making a considerable progress, and I had asked several questions, such as whether 'Miss Anneke had ever seen a patroon,' which 'was the greatest personage, a Patroon or a governor,' whether 'a nobleman who had lately been in the colony, as a military officer, or the Patroon would be likely to have the finest coach,' when a butcher's boy who was passing, rudely knocked an apple out of Anneke's hand, and caused her to shed a tear.

I took fire at this unprovoked outrage, and lent the fellow a dig in the ribs, that gave him to understand the young lady had a protector. My chap was about my own age and weight, and he surveyed me a minute, with a species of contempt, and then beckoned me to follow him into an orchard that was hard by, but a little out of sight. In spite of Anneke's entreaties I went, and Pompey and Caesar followed. We had both stripped before the negroes got up, for they were in a hot discussion whether I was to be permitted to fight, or not. Pompey maintained it would keep dinner waiting, but Caesar, who had the most bottom, as became his name, insisted as I had given a blow, I was bound to render satisfaction. Luckily, Mr. Worden was very skilful at boxing, and he had given both Dirck and myself many lessons, so that I soon found myself the best fellow. I gave the butcher's boy a bloody nose, and a black eye, when he gave in, and I came off victor; not, however, without a facer or two, that sent me to college with a reputation I hardly merited, or that of a regular pugilist.

When I returned to the Road, after this breathing, Anneke*
had disappeared, and I was so shy and silly, as not to ask her family name from Caesar the Great, or Pompey the Little.

* Pronounced On-na-*kay*, I believe.—EDITOR.

Chapter III

"Believe me, thou talkest of an admirable conceited fellow. Has he any unbraided wares?"
"Pr'ythee, bring him in; and let him approach singing."
The Winter's Tale, IV. iv. 202–3, 211–12.

I have no intention of taking the reader with me through college, where I remained the usual term of four years. These four years were not idled away, as sometimes happens, but were fairly improved. I read all of the New Testament, in Greek; several of Cicero's Orations; every line of Horace, Satires and Odes; four books of the Iliad; Tully de Oratore, throughout; besides paying proper attention to geography, mathematics, and other of the usual branches. Moral philosophy, in particular, was closely attended to, senior year, as well as Astronomy. We had a telescope that showed us all four of Jupiter's moons. In other respects Nassau might be called the seat of learning. One of our class purchased a second hand copy of Euripides, in town, and we had it in college all of six months, though it was never my good fortune to see it, as the young man who owned it, was not much disposed to let profane eyes view his treasure. Nevertheless, I am certain the copy of the work was in college, and we took good care to let the Yale men hear of it, more than once. I do not believe *they* ever saw even the outside of a Euripides. As for the telescope, I can testify of my own knowledge, having seen the moons of Jupiter, as often as ten times, with my own eyes, aided by its magnifiers. We had a tutor who was expert among the stars, and who, it was generally believed, would have been able to see the ring of Saturn, could he have found the planet, which, as it turned out, he was unable to do.

My four college years were very happy years. The vacations came often, and I went home invariably, passing a day or two with my aunt Legge, in going or coming. The acquisition of knowledge was always agreeable to me, and I may say it without vanity I trust at this time of life, I got the third honour of my class. We should have graduated four, but one of our class was compelled to quit us at the end of Junior year, on account of his health. He was an unusually hard student, and it was generally admitted that he would have taken the first honour had he remained. We were thought to acquit ourselves with credit, at the commencement; although I afterwards heard my grandfather tell Mr. Worden, that he was of opinion the addresses would have been more masculine and commendable, had less been said of the surprising growth, prosperity, and power of the Colonies. He had no objection to the encouragement of a sound, healthful, patriotic feeling, but to him it appeared that something more novel might have better pleased the audience. This may have been true, as all three of us had something to say on the subject, and it is a proof how much we thought alike, that our language was almost as closely assimilated as our ideas.

As for the Powles Hook Ferry, it was an unpleasant place I will allow, though by the time I was junior, I thought nothing of it. My mother, however, was glad when it was passed for the last time. I remember the very first words that escaped her, after she had kissed me on my final return from college, were—"Well, Heaven be praised, Corny! you will never again have any occasion to cross that frightful ferry, now college is completely done with!" My poor mother little knew how much greater dangers I was subsequently called on to encounter, in another direction. Nor was she minutely accurate in her anticipations, since I have crossed the ferry, in question, several times in later life, the distances not appearing to be as great of late years, as they certainly seemed to be in my youth.

It was a feather in a young man's cap to have gone through college, in 1755, which was the year I graduated. It is true, the University men, who had been home for their learning, were more or less numerous, but they were of a class that held itself aloof from the smaller gentry, and most of them were soon placed in office, adding the dignity of public trusts to their acquisitions, the former in a manner overshadowing the latter. But, I was nearer to the body of the community, and my position admitted more of comparative excellence, as it might be. No one thinks of certain habits, opinions, manners and tastes, in the circle where they are expected to be found, but, it is a different thing where all, or any of these peculiarities form the exception. I am afraid more was anticipated from my college education than has ever been realized, but I will say this for my *Alma Mater*, that I am not conscious my acquisitions at college, have ever been of any disadvantage to me, and I rather think they have, in some degree at least, contributed to the little success that has attended my humble career.

I kept up my intimacy with Dirck Follock, during the whole time I remained at college. He continued the classics with Mr. Worden, for two years after I left the school, but I could not discover that his progress amounted to any thing worth mentioning. The master used to tell the Colonel, that "Dirck's progress was slow and sure," and this did not fail to satisfy a man, who had a constitutional aversion to much of the head-over-heels rate of doing things, among the English population. Col. Follock, as we always called him, except when my father or grandfather asked him to drink a glass of wine, or drank to his health in the first glass after the cloth was removed, when he was invariably styled Col. Van Valkenburgh, at full length, but Col. Follock was quite content that his son and heir should know no more than he knew himself, after making proper allowances for the difference in years and experience. By the time I returned home, however, a material change had been made in the school. Mr. Worden fell heir to a moderate competency at home, and he gave up teaching, a business he had never liked, accordingly. It was even thought he was a shade less zealous in his parochial duties, after the acquisition of this fifty pounds sterling a year, than he had previously been, though I am far from insisting on the fact's being so. At any rate, it was not in the power of £50 per annum to render Mr. Worden apathetic on the subject of the church, for he continued a most zealous churchman down to the hour of his death; and this was something, even admitting that he was not quite so zealous as a Christian. The church being the repository of the faith, if not the faith itself, it follows that its friends are akin to religion, though not absolutely religious. I have always liked a man the better, for being what I call a sound, warm-hearted churchman though his habits may have been a little free.

It was necessary to supply the place left vacant by the resignation of Mr. Worden, or to abandon a school that had got to be the nucleus of knowledge in Westchester. There was a natural desire, at first, to obtain another scholar from home, but no such person offering, a Yale College graduate was accepted, though not without sundry rebellions, and plenty of distrust. The moment he appeared, Col. Follock, and Major Nicholas Oothout, another respectable Dutch neighbor, withdrew their sons, and from that hour Dirck never went to school again. It is true, Westchester was not properly a Dutch county, like Rockland, and Albany, and Orange, and several others along the river, but it had many respectable families in it, of that extraction, without alluding to such heavy people as the Van Cortlands, Philipses, Beekmans, and two or three others of that stamp. Most of our important county families had a different origin, as in the case of the Morrises, of Morrisania, and of the Manor of Fordham, the Pells, of Pelham, the Heathcotes, of Mamaroneck, the branch of the de Lanceys, at West Farms, the Jays, of Rye, &c. &c. All these came of the English, or the Huguenot stock. Among these last, more, or less, Dutch blood was to be found, however, though Dutch prejudices were a good deal weakened. Although few of these persons sent their boys to this school, they were consulted in the selection of a master, and I have always supposed that their indifference was the cause that the county finally obtained the services of a Yankee, from Yale.

The name of the new pedagogue was Jason Newcome, or, as he pronounced the latter appellation himself, Noocome. As he affected a pedantic way of pronouncing the last syllable long, or as it was spelt, he rather called himself Noo-comb—instead of New-cum, as is the English mode, whence he soon got the nick-name of Jason Old Comb, among the boys; the lank, orderly arrangement of his jet-black, and somewhat greasy-looking locks, contributing their share towards procuring for him the *sobriquet*, as I believe the French call it. As this Mr. Newcome will have a material part to play in the succeeding portions of this narrative, it may be well to be a little more minute in his description.

I found Jason fully established in the school, on my return from college. I remember we met very much like two strange birds, that see each other for the first time, on the same dunghill; or two quadrupeds in their original interview in a common herd. It was New Haven against Newark, though the institution, after making as many migrations as the House of Loretto, finally settled down at Princeton, a short time before I took my degree. I was consequently entitled to call myself a graduate of Newark,— a sort of scholar that is quite as great a curiosity in the country, as a Queen Anne's farthing, or a book printed in the fifteenth century. I remember the first evening we two spent in company, as well as if the meeting occurred only last night. It was at Satanstoe, and Mr. Worden was present. Jason had a liberal supply of puritanical notions, which were bred in-and-in in his moral, and I had almost said in his physical, system; nevertheless he could unbend, and I did not fail to observe that very evening a gleam of covert enjoyment on his sombre countenance, as the hot-stuff, the cards, and the pipes were produced, an hour or two before supper,—a meal we always had hot and comfortable. This covert satisfaction, however, was not exhibited without certain misgiving looks, as if the neophyte in these innocent enjoyments distrusted his right to possess his share. I remember in particular, when my mother laid two or three new, clean packs of cards on the table, that Jason cast a stealthy glance over his shoulder, as if to make certain that the act was not noted by the minister, or the "neighbours." The neighbours!—what a contemptible being a man becomes, who lives in constant dread of the comments and judgments of these social supervisors! and what a wretch the habit of deferring to no principle better than their decision, has made many a being, who has had originally the materials of something better in him, than has been developed by the *surveillance* of ignorance, envy, vulgarity, gossiping and lying! In those cases in which education, social position, opportunities and experience have made any material difference between the parties, the man who yields to such a government, exhibits the picture of a giant held in bondage by a pigmy. I have always remarked too, that they who are best qualified to sit in this neighborhood-tribunal, generally keep most aloof from it, as repugnant to their tastes and habits, thus leaving its decisions to the portion of the community least qualified to make such as are either just, or enlightened.

I felt a disposition to laugh outright, at the manner in which Jason betrayed a sneaking consciousness of crime, as he saw my meek, innocent, simple-minded, just and warm-hearted mother, lay the cards on the table, that evening. His sense of guilt was purely conventional, while my mother's sense of innocence existed in the absence of false instruction, and in the purity of her intentions. One had been taught no exaggerated and false notion of sin—nay, a notion that is impious, as it is clearly impious

in man to torture acts that are perfectly innocent, *per se*, into formal transgressions of the law of God—while the other had been
educated under the narrow and exaggerated notions of a provincial sect, and had obtained a species of conscience that was purely
dependent on his miserable schooling. I heard my grandfather
say that Jason actually showed the white of his eyes, the first time
he saw Mr. Worden begin to deal, and he still looked, the whole
time we were at whist, as if he expected some one might enter,
and tell of his delinquency. I soon discovered that Jason had a
much greater dread of being told of, than of doing such things as
taking a hand at whist, or drinking a glass of punch, from which
I inferred his true conscience drew perceptible distinctions between the acts, and the penalties he had been accustomed to see
inflicted on them. He was much disposed to a certain sort of
frailty, but it was a sneaking disposition to the last.

But, the amusing part of the exhibition that first evening of
our acquaintance, was Mr. Worden's showing off his successor's
familiarity with the classics. Jason had not the smallest notion of
quantity, and he pronounced the Latin very much as one would
read Mohawk, from a vocabulary made out by a hunter, or a sav-
ant of the French Academy. As I had received the benefit of Mr.
Worden's own instruction, I could do better, and generally my
knowledge of the classics went beyond that of Jason's. The latter's
English, too, was long a source of amusement with us all, though
my grandfather often expressed strong disgust at it. Even Col.
Follock did not scruple to laugh at Newcome's English, which, as
he frequently took occasion to say, "hat a ferry remarkaple sount
to it." As this peculiarity of Jason's extended a good way into the
Anglo-Saxon race in the part of the country, in which he was
born, it may be well to explain what I mean, a little more at large.

Jason was the son of an ordinary Connecticut farmer, of the
usual associations, and with no other pretension to education,
than such as was obtained in a common school, or any reading
which did not include the scriptures, some half-dozen volumes
of sermons, and polemical works, all the latter of which were vig-
orously as well as narrowly one-sided, and a few books that had
been expressly written to praise New England, and to under-
value all the rest of the earth. As the family knew nothing of the
world, beyond the limits of its own township, and an occasional
visit to Hartford on what is called "election-day," Jason's early life

was necessarily of the most contracted experience. His English, as a matter of course, was just that of his neighbourhood and class of life, which was far from being either very elegant, or very Doric. But, on this rustic, provincial, or rather hamlet foundation, Jason had reared a superstructure of New Haven finish and proportions. As he kept school before he went to college, while he was in college, and after he left college, the whole energies of his nature became strangely directed to just such reforms of language, as would be apt to strike the imagination of a pedagogue of his calibre. In the first place, he had brought from home with him a great number of sounds that were decidedly vulgar and vicious, and with these in full existence in himself, he had commenced his system of reform on other people. As is common with all tyros, he fancied a very little knowledge sufficient authority for very great theories. His first step was to improve the language, by adapting sound to spelling, and he insisted on calling Angel, *An*-gel, because a-n spelt an; chamber, *cham*-ber for the same reason, and so on, through a long catalogue of similarly constructed words. "English," he did not pronounce as "*Ing*lish," but as "*Eng*lish," for instance, and "nothing" (anglice *nuth*ing) as *noth*-ing, or perhaps it were better to say "*naw*thin'." While Jason showed himself so much of a purist with these and many other words, he was guilty of some of the grossest possible mistakes, that were directly in opposition to his own theory. Thus, while he affectedly pronounced "none," (nun,) as "known" he did not scruple to call "stone," "stun," and "home," "hum." The idea of pronouncing "clerk" as it should be, or "clark," greatly shocked him, as it did to call "hearth," "h'arth;" though he did not hesitate to call this good earth of ours, the "'arth." "Been," he pronounced "ben," of course, and "roof," he called "ruff," in spite of all his purism.

From the foregoing specimens, half a dozen among a thousand, the reader will get an accurate notion of this weakness in Jason's character. It was heightened by the fact that the young man commenced his education, such as it was, late in life, and it is rare indeed that either knowledge or tastes thus acquired, are entirely free from exaggeration. Though Jason was several years my senior, like myself, he was a recent graduate, and it will be easy enough to imagine the numberless discussions that took place between us, on the subject of our respective acquisitions. I say 'respective,' instead of mutual acquisitions, because there was nothing mutual about it, or *them*. Neither our classics, our philosophy, nor our mathematics would seem to have been the same, but each man apparently had a science, or a language of his own, and which had been derived from the institution where he had been taught. In the classics I was much the strongest, particularly in the quantities, but Jason had the best of it, in mathematics. In spite of his conceit, his vulgarity, his English, his provincialism, and the awkwardness with which he wore his tardily acquired information, this man had strong points about him, and a native shrewdness that would have told much more in his favour had it not been accompanied by a certain evasive manner, that caused one constantly to suspect his sincerity, and which often induced those who were unaccustomed to him, to imagine he had a sneaking propensity that rendered him habitually hypocritical. Jason held New York in great contempt, a feeling he was not always disposed to conceal, and of necessity his comparisons were usually made with the state of things in Connecticut, and much to the advantage of the latter. To one thing, however, he was much disposed to defer, and that was money. Connecticut had not then, nor has it now, a single individual who would be termed rich in New York, and Jason, spite of his provincial conceit, spite of his overweening notions of moral and intellectual superiority, could no more prevent this profound deference for wealth, than he could substitute for a childhood of vulgarity and neglect, the grace, refinement and knowledge, which the boys of the more fortunate classes in life, obtain as it might be without knowing it. Yes, Jason bowed down to the golden calf, in spite of his puritanism, his love of liberty, his pretension to equality and the general strut of his disposition and manner.

Such is an outline of the character and qualifications of the man whom I found, on my return from college, at the head of Mr. Worden's school. We soon became acquainted, and I do not know which got the most ideas from the other, in course of the first fortnight. Our conversation and arguments were free, almost to rudeness, and little mercy was shown to our respective prejudices. Jason was ultra leveling in his notions of social intercourse, while I had the opinions of my own colony, in which the distinctions of classes, are far more strongly marked than is usual in New England, out of Boston, and its immediate association.

Still Jason deferred to names, as well as money, though it was in a way very different from my own. New England was, and is, loyal to the crown, but having the right to name many of its own governors, and possessing many other political privileges through the charters that were granted to her people, in order to induce them to settle that portion of the continent, they do not always manifest the feeling in a way to be agreeable to those who have a proper reverence for the crown. Among other points, growing out of this difference in training, Jason and I had sundry arguments on the subject of professions, trades and callings. It was evident he fancied the occupation of a schoolmaster next in honour, to that of a clergyman. The clergy formed a species of aristocracy, according to his notions, but no man could commence life under more favourable auspices than by taking a school. The following dialogue occurred between us, on this subject, and I was so much struck with the novelty of my companion's notions as to make a note of it, as soon as we parted.

"I wonder your folks don't think of giving you suthin' to do, Corny," commenced Jason, one day, after our acquaintance had ripened into a sort of belligerent intimacy. "You're near nineteen, now, and ought to begin to think of bringing suthin' in, to pay for all the outgoin's."

By "your folks," Jason meant the family of Littlepage, and the blood of that family quickened a little within me, at the idea of being profitably employed, in the manner intimated, because I had reached the mature and profitable age of nineteen.

"I do not understand you exactly, Mr. Newcome, by your bringing something in," answered I, with dignity enough to put a man of ordinary delicacy on his guard.

"Bringing suthin' in is good English I hope, Mr. Littlepage. I mean that your edication has cost your folks enough to warrant them in calling on you for a little interest. How much do you suppose, now, has been spent on your edication, beginning at the time you first went to Mr. Worden, and leaving off the day you quitted Newark?"

"Really, I have not the smallest notion; the subject has never crossed my mind."

"Did the old folks never say any thing to you about it?—Never foot up the total?"

"I am sure it is not easy to see how this could be done, for I could not help them in the least."

"But your father's books would tell that, as doubtless it all stands charged against you."

"Stands charged against me!—How, sir; do you imagine my father makes a charge in a book against me, whenever he pays a few pounds for my education?"

"Certainly; how else could he tell how much you have had:— Though on reflection, as you are an only child it does not make so much difference. You probably will get all, in the end."

"And had I a brother, or a sister, do you imagine, Mr. New-come, each shilling we spent would be set down in a book, as charges against us?"

"How else, in natur', could it be known which had had the most, or any sort of justice be done between you?"

"Justice would be done, by our common father's giving to each just as much of his own money, as he might see fit. What is it to me, if he chose to give my brother a few hundred pounds more than he chose to give to me? The money is his, and he may do with it as he choose."

"An hundred pounds is an awful sight of money!" exclaimed Jason, betraying by his countenance how deeply he felt the truth of this. "If you have had money in such large sums, so much the more reason why you should set about doing suthin' to repay the old gentleman. Why not set up a school?"

"Sir!"

"Why not set up a school, I say. You might have had this of mine had you been a little older, but once in, fast in, with me. Still, schools are wanted, and you might get a tolerable good recom-mend. I dare say your tutor would furnish a certificate."

This word "recommend" was used by Jason for "recommenda-tion;" the habit of putting verbs in the places of substantives, and *vice versa*, being much in vogue with him.

"And do you really think that one who is destined to inherit Satanstoe, would act advisedly to set up a school! Recollect, Mr. Newcome, that my father and grandfather have both borne the King's commission, and that the last bears it, at this very moment through his representative, the governor."

"What of all that? What better business is there than keeping a good school? If you are high in your notions, get to be made a tutor in that New Jersey college. Recollect that a tutor in a college is somebody. I did hope for such a place, but having a governor's son against me, as a candidate, there was no chance."

"A governor's son a candidate for a tutorship in a college! You are pleased to trifle with me, Mr. Newcome."

"It's true as the Gospel. You thought some smaller fish put me down, but he was the son of the governor. But, why do you give that vulgar name to your father's farm—Satanstoe is not decent; yet, Corny, I've heard you use it before your own mother!"

"That you may hear every day, and my mother use it, too, before her own son. What fault do you find with the name of Satanstoe?"

"Fault!—In the first place it is irreligious and profane; then it is ungenteel and vulgar, and only fit to be used in low company. Moreover, it is opposed to history and revelation, the Evil One having a huff if you will, but no toes. Such a name couldn't stand a fortnight before public opinion, in New England."

"Yes, that may be very true, but we do not care enough for His Satanic Majesty, in the colony of New York, to treat him with so much deference. As for the 'huffs,' as you call them—"

"Why, what do *you* call 'em, Mr. Littlepage?"

"Hoofs, Mr. Newcome; that is the New York pronunciation of the word."

"I care nothing for York pronunc'ation, which everybody knows is Dutch and full of corruptions. You'll never do any thing, worth speaking of in this colony, Corny, until you pay more attention to your schools."

"I do not know what you call attention, Mr. Jason, unless we have paid it already. Here, I have the caption, or rather preamble of a law, on that very subject, that I copied out of the statute-book on purpose to show you, and which I will now read in order to prove to you how things really stand in the colony."

"Read away—" rejoined Jason with an air of sufficient disdain.

Read I did, and in the following sententious and comprehensive language, viz:—"Whereas the youth of this colony are found, by manifold experience, to be not inferior in their natural geniuses to the youth of any other country in the world, therefore, be it enacted &c."*

*This quotation would seem to be accurate, and it is somewhat curious to

"There, sir," I said in exultation, "you have chapter and verse for the true character of the rising generation in the colony of New-York."

"And what does that preamble lead to?" demanded Jason, a little staggered at finding the equality of our New York intellects established so clearly, by legislative enactment.

"It is the preamble to an act establishing the free schools of New York, in which the learned languages have now been taught these twenty years, and you will please to remember that another law has not long been passed establishing a college in town."

"Well, curious laws sometimes do get into the statute books, and a body must take them as he finds them. I dare say Connecticut might have a word to say on the same subject, if you would give her a chance. Have you heard the wonderful news from Philadelphia, Corny, that has just come among us?"

"I have heard nothing of late, for you know I have been over in Rockland, with Dirck Follock, for the last two weeks, and news never reaches that family, or indeed that county."

"No, that is true enough," answered Jason drily—"News and a Dutchman have no affinity, or attraction, as we would say in philosophy; though there is gravitation enough on one side, ha! boy?"

Here Jason laughed outright, for he was always delighted whenever he could get a side hit at the children of Holland, whom he appeared to regard as a race occupying a position

---

trace the reason why a preamble so singular, should have been prefixed to the law. Was it not owing to the oft-repeated and bold assertions of Europeans, that man deteriorated in this hemisphere? Any American who has been a near observer of European opinion, even in our day, must have been frequently amused at the expressions of surprise and doubt, that so often escape the residents of the Old World, when they discover any thing that particularly denotes talent, coming from the New. I make little question that this extraordinary preamble is a sort of indirect answer to an imputation that was known to be as general, in that age, as it was felt to be unjust. My own experience would lead me to think native capacity more abundant in America, than in the midland countries of Europe, and quite as frequently met with as in Italy itself; and I have often heard teachers, both English and French, admit that their American and West-Indian scholars, were generally the readiest and cleverest in their schools. The great evil under which this country labors, in this respect, is the sway of numbers, which is constantly elevating mediocrity and spurious talent to high places. In America, we have a *higher average* of intelligence, while we have far less of the *higher class*; and I attribute the latter fact to the control of those who have never enjoyed the means of appreciating excellence.—EDITOR.

between the human family and the highest class of the unintellectual animals. But it is unnecessary to dwell longer on this dialogue, my object being merely to show the general character of Jason's train of thought, in order to be better understood when I come to connect his opinions with his acts.

Dirck and myself were much together, after my return from college. I passed weeks at a time, with him, and he returned my visits with the utmost freedom and good will. Each of us had now got his growth, and it would have done the heart of Frederick of Prussia good, to have seen my young friend, after he had ended his nineteenth year. In stature, he measured exactly six feet three, and he gave every promise of filling up in proportion. Dirck was none of your roundly turned, Apollo-built fellows, but he had shoulders that his little, short, solid, but dumpy looking mother, who was of the true stock, could scarcely span, when she pulled his head down to give him a kiss; which she did regularly, as Dirck told me himself, twice each year, that is to say Christmas and New-Year. His complexion was fair, his limbs large and well proportioned, his hair light, his eyes blue, and his face would have been thought handsome by most persons. I will not deny, however, that there was a certain ponderosity, both of mind and body, about my friend, that did not very well accord with the general notion of grace and animation. Nevertheless, Dirck was a sterling fellow, as true as steel, as brave as a game-cock, and as honest as noon-day light.

Jason was a very different sort of person, in many essentials. In figure, he was also tall, but he was angular, loose-jointed and swinging—slouching would be the better word, perhaps. Still he was not without strength, having worked on a farm until he was near twenty, and he was as active as a cat; a result that took the stranger a little by surprise, when he regarded only his loose, quavering sort of build. In the way of thought, Jason would think two feet to Dirck's one, but I am far from certain that it was always in so correct a direction. Give the Dutchman time, he was very apt to come out right; whereas Jason, I soon discovered, was quite liable to come to wrong conclusions, and particularly so in all matters that were a little adverse and which affected his own apparent interests. Dirck, moreover, was one of the best natured fellows that breathed, it being almost impossible to excite him to anger; when it did come, however, the earthquake was scarcely

more terrific. I have seen him enraged, and would as soon encounter a wild-boar in an open field, as run against his course,
while in the fit.

Modesty will hardly permit me to say much of myself. I was
well grown, active, strong for my years, and, I am inclined to
think, reasonably well-looking, though I would prefer that this
much should be said by any one but myself. Dirck and I often
tried our manhood, together, when youngsters, and I was the
better chap until my friend reached his eighteenth year, when
the heavy metal of the young Dutch giant told in our struggles.
After that period was past, I found Dirck too much for me in a
close gripe, though my extraordinary activity rendered the in-
equality less apparent than it might otherwise have proved. I
ought not to apply the term of "extraordinary" to any thing
about myself, but the word escaped me unconsciously, and I shall
let it stand. One thing I will say, notwithstanding, let the reader
think of it, as he may. I was good-natured and well disposed to my
fellow creatures, and had no greater love of money than was
necessary to render me reasonably discreet.

Such is an outline of the characters and persons of three of the
principal actors in the scenes I am about to relate; scenes that will
possess some interest for those who love to read accounts of adventures in a new country, however much they may fail in interesting others, when I speak of the condition and events of the
more civilized condition of society, that was enjoyed even in my
youth, in such old counties as West-chester, and such towns as
York.

Chapter IV

"Let us, then, be up and doing,
With a heart for any fate;
Still achieving, still pursuing,
Learn to labour and to wait."
  Longfellow, "A Psalm of Life," ll. 33–36.

THE spring of the year I was twenty, Dirck and myself paid our first visit to town, in the characters of young men. Although Satanstoe was not more than five-and-twenty miles from New-York, by the way of Kingsbridge, the road we always travelled in order to avoid the ferry, it was by no means as common to visit the capital, as it has since got to be. I know gentlemen who pass in and out, from our neighbourhood, now, as often as once a fortnight, or even once a week, but thirty years since this was a thing very seldom done. My dear mother always went to town twice a year; in the spring to pass Easter week and in the autumn to make her winter purchases. My father usually went down four times, in the course of the twelve months, but he had the reputation of a gadabout, and was thought by many people to leave home quite as much as he ought to do. As for my grandfather, old age coming on, he seldom left home now, unless it were to pay stated visits to certain old brother campaigners, who lived within moderate distances, and with whom he invariably passed weeks, each summer.

The visit I have mentioned occurred some time after Easter, a season of the year that many of our country families were in the habit of passing in town, to have the benefit of the daily services of Old Trinity, as the Hebrews resorted to Jerusalem, to keep the feast of the passover. My mother did not go to town this year, on account of my father's gout, and I was sent to supply her place with my aunt Legge, who had been so long accustomed to have one of the family with her at that season, that I was substituted. Dirck had relatives of his own, with whom he staid, and thus every thing was rendered smooth. In order to make a fair start, my friend crossed the Hudson the week before, and, after taking breath at Satanstoe, for three days, we left the Neck for the capital, mounted on a pair of as good roadsters as were to be found in the county: and that is saying a good deal; for the Morrises, and de Lanceys and Van Cortlandts, all kept racers, and sometimes gave us good sport, in the autumns, over the county course. Westchester, to say no more than she deserved, was a county with a spirited gentry, and one of which no colony need be ashamed.

My mother was a tender-hearted parent, and full of anxiety in behalf of an only child. She knew that travelling always has more or less of hazard, and was desirous we should be off betimes, in order to make certain of our reaching town before the night set in. Highway robbers, Heaven be praised! were then, and are still, unknown to the Colonies; but there were other dangers that gave my excellent parent much concern. All the bridges were not considered safe; the roads were, and are yet, very circuitous, and it was possible to lose one's way; while it was said persons had been known to pass the night on Harlem Common, an uninhabited waste that lies some seven or eight miles on our side of the city. My mother's first care, therefore, was to get Dirck and myself off, early in the morning; in order to do which she rose with the light, gave us our breakfasts immediately afterwards, and thus enabled us to quit Satanstoe just as the sun had burnished the eastern sky with its tints of flame-colour.

Dirck was in high good humour, that morning, and, to own the truth, Corny did not feel the depression of spirits which, according to the laws of propriety, possibly ought to have attended the first really free departure of so youthful an adventurer from beneath the shadows of the paternal roof. We went our way laughing, and chatting like two girls, just broke loose from boarding school. I had never known Dirck more communicative, and I got certain new insights into his feelings, expectations and prospects, as we rode along the Colony's Highway, that morning, that afterwards proved to be matters of much interest with us both. We had not got a mile from the chimney tops of Satanstoe, ere my friend broke forth as follows—

"I suppose you have heard, Corny, what the two old gentlemen have been at, lately?"

"Your father and mine? I have not heard a syllable of any thing new."

"They have been suing out, before the Governor and Council,

a joint claim to that tract of land they bought of the Mohawks, the last time they were out together on service, in the Colony Militia."

I ought to mention, here, that though my predecessors had made but few campaigns in the regular army, each had made several in the more humble capacity of a militia officer.

"This is news to me, Dirck," I answered. "Why should the old gentlemen have been so sly about such a thing?"

"I cannot tell you, lest they thought silence the best way to keep off the yankees. You know, my father has a great dread of a yankee's getting a finger into any of his bargains. He says the yankees are the locusts of the west."

"But, how came you to know any thing about it, Dirck?"

"I am no yankee, Corny."

"And your father told *you*, on the strength of this recommendation?"

"He told me, as he tells me most things that he thinks it best I should know. We smoke together, and then we talk together."

"I would learn to smoke too, if I thought I should get any useful information by so doing."

"Dere is much to be l'arnt from ter pipe!" said Dirck, dropping into a slightly Dutch accent, as frequently happened with him, when his mind took a secret direction towards Holland, though in general he spoke English quite as well as I did myself, and vastly better than that miracle of taste, and learning, and virtue, and piety, Mr. Jason Newcome, A. B., of Yale, and prospective president of that, or some other institution.

"So it would seem, if your father is telling you secrets all the time you are smoking together. But where is this land, Dirck?"

"It is in the Mohawk country—or, rather it is in the country near the Hampshire Grants, and at no great distance from the Mohawk country."

"And how much may there be of it?"

"Forty thousand acres; and some of it of good, rich flats, they say; such as a Dutchman loves."

"And your father and mine have purchased all this land in company, you say—share and share alike, as the lawyers call it."

"Just so."

"Pray how much did they pay for so large a tract of land?"

Dirck took time to answer this question. He first drew from his breast, a pocket book, which he opened as well as he could under the motion of his roadster, for neither of us abated his speed, it being indispensable to reach town before dark. My friend succeeded at length, in putting his hand on the paper he wanted, which he gave to me.

"There;" he said; "that is a list of the articles paid to the Indians, which I have copied, and then there have been several hundred pounds of fees paid to the governor and his officers."

I read from the list, as follows; the words coming out by jerks as the trotting of my horse permitted. "Fifty blankets, each with yellow strings and yellow trimmings; ten iron pots, four gallons each; forty pounds of gunpowder; seven muskets; twelve pounds of small beads; ten strings of wampum; fifty gallons of rum, pure Jamaica, and of high proof; a score of jews-harps, and three dozen first quality English-made tomahawks."

"Well, Dirck," I cried, as soon as through reading, "this is no great matter to give for forty thousand acres of land, in the colony of New York. I dare say a hundred pounds currency ($250) would buy every thing here, even to the rum and the first quality of English-made tomahawks."

"Ninety-six pounds, t'irteen shillings, seven pence 't'ree fart'in's, was the footing of the whole bill," answered Dirck deliberately, preparing to light his pipe; for he could smoke very conveniently while trotting no faster than at the rate of six miles the hour.

"I do not find that dear for forty thousand acres; I suppose the muskets, and rum, and other things were manufactured expressly for the Indian trade."

"Not they, Corny: you know how it is with the old gentlemen; they are as honest as the day."

"So much the better for them, and so much the better for us. But what is to be done with this land, now they own it?"

Dirck did not answer, until we had trotted twenty rods, for by this time the pipe was at work, and the moment the smoke was seen, he kept his eye on it, until he saw a bright light in front of his nose.

"The first thing will be to find it, Corny. When a patent is signed and delivered, then you must send forth some proper person to find the land it covers. I have heard of a gentleman who got a grant of ten thousand acres, five years since, and though he has had a hunt for it every summer since, he has not been able to find it yet. To be sure ten thousand acres is a small object to look for, in the woods."

"And our fathers intend to find their land, as soon as the season opens?"

"Not so fast, Corny; not so fast! That was the scheme of your father's Welsh blood, but mine takes matters more deliberately. 'Let us wait until next year,' he said, 'and then we can send the boys. By that time, too, the war will take some sort of a shape, and we shall know better how to care for the children.' The subject has been fairly talked over between the two patentees, and we are to go early *next* spring; not this."

The idea of land-hunting was not in the least disagreeable to me; nor was it unpleasant to think that I stood in reversion, or as heir, to twenty thousand acres of land, in addition to those of Satanstoe. Dirck and I talked the matter over, as we trotted on, until both of us began to regret that the expedition was so far in perspective.

The war to which Dirck alluded had broken out a few months before our visit to town, a Mr. Washington, of Virginia—the same who has since become so celebrated as the Col. Washington of Braddock's defeat and other events at the south—having been captured, with a party of his men, in a small work thrown up in the neighborhood of the French somewhere on the tributaries of the Ohio; a river that is known to run into the Mississippi, a vast distance to the west. I knew very little then, nor do I know much now of these remote regions, beyond the fact that there are such places, and that they are sometimes visited by detachments, war-parties, hunters and other adventurers from the Colonies. To me, it seems scarce worth fighting about such distant and wild territory; for ages and ages must elapse before it can be of any service for the purposes of civilization. Both Dirck and myself regretted that the summer would be likely to go by without our seeing the enemy, for we came of families that were commonly employed on such occasions. We thought both our fathers might be out, though even that was a point that still remained under discussion.

We dined and baited at Kingsbridge, intending to sup in town. While the dinner was cooking, Dirck and I walked out on the heights, that overlook the Hudson, for I knew less of this noble river than I wished to know of it. We conversed as we walked, and my companion, who knew the river much better than myself, having many occasions to pass up and down it between the village of Haverstraw and town, in his frequent visits to his relatives below, gave me some useful information.

"Look here, Corny," said Dirck, after betraying a good deal of desire to obtain a view of some object in the distance, along the river side, "Look here, Corny; do you see yonder house, in the little bay below us, with the lawn that extends down to the water, and that noble orchard behind it?"

I saw the object to which Dirck alluded. It was a house, that stood near the river, but, sheltered, and secluded, with the lawn and orchard as described, though at the distance of some two or three miles, all the beauties of the spot could not be discovered, and many of them had to be received on the faith of my companion's admiration. Still I saw very plainly, all the principal objects named, and, among others the house, the orchard and the lawn. The building was of stone—as is common with most of the better sort of houses in the country—was long, irregular, and had that air of solid comfort about it, which it is usual to see in buildings of that description. The walls were not whitewashed, according to the lively tastes of our Dutch fellow colonists, who appear to expend all their vivacity in the pipe and the brush, but were left in their native gray, a circumstance that rendered the form and dimensions of the structure, a little less distinct, at a first glance, than they might otherwise have proved. As I gazed at the spot, however, I began to fancy it a charm to find the picture thus sobered down, and found a pleasure in drawing the different angles, and walls, and chimneys, and roofs from this background, by means of the organ of sight. On the whole, I thought the little sequestered bay, the wooded and rocky shores, the small but well distributed lawn, the orchard, with all the other similar accessories, formed together one of the prettiest places of the sort I had ever seen. Thinking so, I was not slow in saying as much to my companion. I was thought to have some taste in these matters, and had been consulted on the subject of laying out grounds by one or two neighbours, in the county.

"Whose house is it Dirck," I enquired; "and how came you to know any thing about it?"

"That is Lilacsbush," answered my friend; "and it belongs to my mother's cousin, Herman Mordaunt."

I had heard of Herman, or, as it is pronounced, Harman Mordaunt. He was a man of considerable note in the colony, having been the son of a Major Mordaunt, of the British Army, who had married the heiress of a wealthy Dutch merchant, whence the name of Herman; which had descended to the son along with the money. The Dutch were so fond of their own blood, that they never failed to give this Mr. Mordaunt his Christian name, and he was usually known in the colony as Herman Mordaunt. Further than this, I knew little of the gentleman, unless it might be that he was reputed rich, and was admitted to be in the best society, though not actually belonging to the territorial, or political aristocracy of the colony.

"As Herman Mordaunt is your mother's cousin, I suppose, Dirck," I resumed, "that you have been at Lilacsbush, and ascertained whether the inside of the house is as pleasant and respectable, as the outside."

"Often, Corny; while Madam Mordaunt lived my mother and I used to go there every summer. The poor lady is now dead, but I go there still."

"Why did you not ride on, as far as Lilacsbush, and levy a dinner on your relations? I should think Herman Mordaunt would feel hurt, were he to learn that an acquaintance, or a relation, had put up at an inn, within a couple of miles of his own house. I dare say he knows both Major and Capt. Littlepage, and I protest I shall feel it necessary to send him a note of apology, for not calling. These things ought not to be done, Dirck, among persons of a certain stamp, and who are supposed to know what is proper."

"This would be all right enough, Corny, had Herman Mordaunt, or his daughter, been at Lilacsbush; but they live in Crown Street, in town, in the winter, and never come out here, until after the Pinkster holidays, let *them* come when they may."

"Oh! he is as great a man as that, is he?—A town and country house; after all, I do not know whether it would do to be quite so free with one of his standing, as to go to dine with him without sending notice."

"Nonsense, Corny. Who hesitates about stopping at a gentleman's door, when he is travelling? Herman Mordaunt would have given us a hearty welcome, and I should have gone on to Lilacsbush, did I not know that the family is certain to be in town, at this season. Easter came early this year, and to- morrow will be the first day of the Pinkster Holidays. As soon as they are over, Herman Mordaunt and Anneke, will be out here to enjoy their lilacs and roses."

"Oh! ho—There is an Anneke, as well as the old gentleman— Pray how old may Miss Anneke be, Master Dirck?"

As this question was asked, I turned to look my friend in the face, and I found that his handsome, smooth, fair Dutch linea- ments were covered with a glow of red that it was not usual to see extended so far from his ruddy cheeks. Dirck was too much of a man, however, to turn away, or to try to hide blushes so ingenu- ous, but he answered stoutly—

"My cousin, Anneke Mordaunt, is just turned of seventeen; and, I'll tell you what, Corny—"

"Well—I am listening with both ears, to hear your *what?* Out with it, man; both ears are open."

"Why, Anneke (On-na-*kay*) is one of the very prettiest girls in the Colony!—What is more, she is as sweet and goot—" Dirck grew Dutch, as he grew animated—"as she is pretty."

I was quite astounded at the energy and feeling with which this was said. Dirck was such a matter-of-fact fellow, that I had never dreamed he could be sensible to the passion of love, nor had I ever paused to analyze the nature of our own friendship. We liked each other, in the first place, most probably, from habit; then, we were of characters so essentially different, that our attachment was in- fluenced by that species of excitement which is the child of opposi- tion. As we grew older, Dirck's good qualities began to command my respect, and reason entered more into my affection for him. I was well convinced that my companion could, and would, prove to be a warm friend, but the possibility of his ever becoming a lover had not before crossed my mind. Even then the impression made was not very deep, or lasting, though I well remember the sort of admiration and wonder with which I gazed at his flushed cheek, animated eye, and improved mien. For the moment, Dirck really had a commanding and animated air.

"Why, Anneke is one of the prettiest girls in the colony!" my friend had exclaimed.

"And your cousin?"

"My second cousin—her mother's father and my mother's mother, were brother and sister."

"In that case I shall hope to have the honour of being introduced one of these days, to Miss Anneke Mordaunt, who is just turned of seventeen, and is one of the prettiest girls in the colony, and is as good, as she is pretty."

"I wish you to see her, Corny, and that before we go home," Dirck replied, all his philosophy, or phlegm, which ever the philosophy of other people may term it, returning; "come; let us go back to the inn; our dinner will be getting cold."

I mused on my friend's unusual manner, as we walked back towards the inn, but it was soon forgotten in the satisfaction produced, by eating a good substantial meal of broiled ham, with hot potatoes, boiled eggs, a beef steak done to a turn, with the accessories of pickles, cold-slaw, apple pie and cider. This is a common New York tavern dinner for the way-farer, and I must say I have got to like it. Often have I enjoyed such a repast, after a sharp forenoon's ride; ay, and enjoyed it more than I have relished entertainments at which have figured turkies, oysters, hams, hashes, and other dishes that have higher reputations. Even turtle soup, for which we are somewhat famous in New York, has failed to give me the same delight.

Dirck, to do him justice, ate heartily, for it is not an easy matter to take away his appetite. As usual, I did most of the talking, and that was with our landlady, who, hearing I was a son of her much esteemed and constant customer, Major Littlepage, presented herself with the dessert and cheese, and did me the honour to commence a discourse. Her name was Light, and light was she certain to cast on every thing she discussed, that is to say, innkeeper's light, which partakes somewhat of the darkness that is so apt to overshadow no small portion of the minds of her many customers.

"Pray, Mrs. Light," I asked, when there was an opening, which was not until the good woman had exhausted her breath in honour of the Littlepages, "do you happen to know any thing of a family, hereabouts, of the name of Mordaunt?"

"Do I *happen* to know, sir!—Why, Mr. Littlepage, you might almost as well have asked me, if I had ever heard of a Van Cortlandt, or a Philipse, or a Morris, or any other of the gentry hereabouts. Mr. Mordaunt has a country place, and a very pretty one it is, within two miles and a half of us, and he and Madam Mordaunt, never passed our door, when they went into the country to see Madam Van Cortlandt, without stopping to say a word, and leave a shilling. The poor lady is dead, but there is a young image of her virtues that is coming a'ter her, that will be likely to do some damage in the colony. She is modesty itself, sir, so I thought it could do her no harm, the last time she was here, just to tell her, she ought to be locked up for the thefts she was likely to commit, if not for them she had committed already. She blushed, sir, and looked for all the world like the shell of the most delicate boiled lobster, you ever laid eyes on. She is truly a charming young lady!"

"Thefts of hearts, you mean of course, my good Mrs. Light?"

"Of nothing else, sir; young ladies are apt to steal hearts, you know. My word for it, Miss Anneke will turn out a great robber, after her own fashion, you know, sir."

"And whose hearts is she likely to run away with, pray? I should be pleased to hear the names of some of the sufferers?"

"Lord, sir!—she is too young, to have done much *yet*; but, wait a twelvemonth, and I'll answer the question."

I could see, all this time, that Dirck was uneasy, and had some amusement in watching the workings of his countenance. My malicious intentions, however, were suddenly interrupted. As if to prevent further discourse, and, at the same time, further *espionage* my young friend rose from table, ordering the horses and the bill.

During the ride to town no more was said of Lilacsbush, Herman Mordaunt, or his daughter, Anneke. Dirck was silent, but this was his habit after dinner, and I was kept a good deal on the alert, in order to find the road which crossed the common, it being our desire to go in that direction. It is true, we might have gone into town, by the way of Bloomingdale, Greenwich, the meadows and the Collect, and so down past the common, upon the head of Broadway, but my mother had particularly desired we would fall into the Bowery Lane, passing the seats that are to be found in that quarter, and getting into Queen Street as soon as possible. By taking this course, she thought we should be less likely to miss our way within the town itself, which is certainly full of narrow and intricate passages. My uncle Legge had removed into Duke Street, in the vicinity of Hanover Square, and, Queen Street, I well knew, would lead us directly to his door. Queen Street, indeed, is the great artery of New York, through which most of its blood circulates.

It was drawing towards night, when we trotted up to the stable, where we left our horses, and, obtaining a black to shoulder our portmanteaus, we began to thread the mazes of the capital on foot. New-York was certainly, even in 1757, a wonderful place for commerce! Vessels began to be seen some distance east of Fly Market, and there could not have been fewer than twenty ships, brigs and schooners lying in the East River, as we walked down Queen Street. Of course I include all descriptions of vessels that go to sea, in this estimate. At the present moment, it is probable twice that number would be seen. There Dirck and I stopped more than once, involuntarily, to gaze at the exhibitions of wealth and trade, that offered themselves as we went deeper into the town. My mother had particularly cautioned me against falling into this evidence of country habits, and I felt much ashamed at each occurrence of the weakness; but I found it irresistible. At length my friend and I parted; he to go to the residence of his aunt while I proceeded to that of mine. Before separating, however, we agreed to meet next morning, in the fields at the head of Broadway, on the Common, which as it was understood, was to be the scene of the Pinkster sports.

My reception in Duke Street was cordial, both on the part of my uncle, and on the part of my aunt; the first being a good hearted person, though a little too apt to run into extravagance on the subject of the rights of the rabble. I was pleased with the welcome I received, enjoyed an excellent hot supper, to which we sat down at half-past eight, my aunt being fond of town hours, both dining and supping a little later than my mother, as being more fashionable and genteel.* As I was compelled to confess fatigue, after so long a ride, as soon as we quitted the table, I retired to my own room.

*The dinner of the last half century, is, in one sense, but a substitute for the *petits soupers*, of the century, or two, that preceded. It is so entirely rational and natural, that the cultivated and refined should meet for the purposes of social enjoyment, after the business of the day has terminated, that the supper has only given place to the same meal under another name, and at hours little varying from those of the past. The Parisian dines at half-past six, remaining at table until eight; the Englishman, later in all his hours, and more ponderous in all his habits, sits down to table about the time the Frenchman gets up; quitting it between nine and ten. The Italian pays a tribute to his climate, and has his early dinner and light supper, both usually alone, the habits of the country carrying him to the opera and the *conversazione* for social communion. But what is

The next day was the first of the three that are devoted to Pinkster, the great Saturnalia of the New York blacks. Although this festival is always kept with more vivacity at Albany, than in York, it is far from being neglected, even now, in the latter place. I had told my aunt before I left her, I should not wait for breakfast, but should be up with the sun, and off in quest of Dirck, in order that we might enjoy a stroll along the wharves before it was time to repair to the Common where the fun was to be seen. Accordingly, I got out of the house betimes, though it was an hour later than I had intended, for I heard the rattling of cups in the little parlour, the sign that the table was undergoing the usual process of arrangement for breakfast. It then occurred to me that most, if not all of the servants, seven in number, would be permitted to enjoy the holiday, and that it might be well if I took all my meals, that day, in the fields. Running back to the room, I communicated this intention to Juno, the girl I found doing Pompey's work, and left the house on a jump. There was no great occasion for starving I thought, in a town as large and as full of eatables as New York, and the result fully justified this reasonable opinion.

Just as I got into Hanover Square, I saw a gray headed negro, who was for turning a penny before he engaged in the amusements of the day, carrying two pails that were scoured to the neatness of Dutch fastidiousness, and which were suspended from the yoke he had across his neck and shoulders. He cried "White wine—white wine!" in a clear sonorous voice, and I was at his side in a moment. White wine was, and is still my delight of a morning, and I bought a delicious draught of the purest and best of a Communipaw vintage, eating a cake at the same time. Thus refreshed, I proceeded into the square, the beauty of which had

---

the American? A jumble of the same senseless contradictions in his social habits, as he is fast getting to be in his political creeds and political practices; a being that is *in transitu*, pressed by circumstances on the one side, and by the habit of imitation on the other; unwilling, almost unable, to think and act for himself. The only American who is temporarily independent in such things, is the unfledged provincial, fresh from his village conceit and village practices, who, until corrected by communion with the world, fancies the south-east corner, of the north-west parish, in the town of Hebron, in the county of Jericho, and the State of Connecticut, to be the only portion of this globe that is perfection. If he should happen to keep a school, or conduct a newspaper, the community becomes, in a small degree, the participant of his rare advantages and vast experience!—EDITOR.

struck my fancy, as I walked through it, the previous evening. To my surprise, whom should I find in the very centre of Queen Street, gaping about him, with a most, indomitable Connecticut air, but Jason Newcome! A brief explanation let me into the secret of his presence. His boys had all gone home to enjoy the Pinkster holiday, with the black servants of their respective families, and Jason had seized the opportunity to pay his first visit to the great capital of the colony. He was on his travels, like myself.

"And what has brought you down here?" I demanded, the pedagogue having already informed me that he had put up at a tavern in the suburbs, where horsekeeping and lodgings were "reasonable." "The Pinkster fields are up near the head of Broadway; on the common."

"So I hear," answered Jason; "but I want to see a ship, and all the sights this way, in the first place. It will be time enough for Pinkster, two or three hours hence, if a Christian ought even to look at such vanities. Can you tell me where I am to find Hanover Square, Corny?"

"You are in it, now, Mr. Newcome; and to my fancy, a very noble area it is!"

"*This* Hanover Square!" repeated Jason. "Why, its shape is not that of a square at all; it is nearer a *triangle*."

"What of that, Sir? By a square in a town, one does not necessarily understand an area with four equal sides and as many right angles, but an open space that is left for air and beauty. There are air and beauty enough to satisfy any reasonable man. A square may be a parallelogram, or a triangle, or any other shape one pleases."

"This, then, is Hanover Square!—A New York Square, or a Nassau Hall Square, Corny, but not a Yale College Square, take my word for it. It is so small, moreover!"

"Small!—the width of the street at the widest end, must be near a hundred feet; I grant you it is not half that at the other end, but that is owing to the proximity of the houses."

"Ay, it is all owing to the proximity of the houses, as you call it. Now, according to my notion, Hanover Square, of which a body hears so much talk in the country, ought to have had fifty or sixty acres in it, and statues of the whole House of Brunswick, besides. Why is that nest of houses, left in the middle of your square?"

"It is not, sir. The square ceases when it reaches *them*. They are too valuable to be torn down, although there has been some talk of it. My uncle Legge told me, last evening, that those houses have been valued as high as twelve thousand dollars, and some persons put them as high as six thousand pounds."

This reconciled Jason to the houses, for he never failed to defer to money, come in what shape it would. It was the only source of human distinction that he could clearly comprehend, though he had some faint impressions touching the dignity of the crown, and the respect due to its representatives.

"Corny," said Jason, in an under-tone, and taking me by the arm to lead me aside, though no one was near, like a man who has a great secret to ask, or to communicate—"What was that I saw you taking for your bitters, a little while ago?"

"Bitters! I do not understand you, Jason. Nothing bitter have I tasted to-day; nor can I say I have any great wish to put any thing bitter into my mouth."

"Why, the draught you got from the nigger who is now coming back across the square, as you call it, and which you seemed to enj'y, particularly. I am dry, myself, and should wonderfully like a drink."

"Oh! that fellow sells 'white wine,' and you will find it delicious. If you want your 'bitters,' as you call them, you cannot do better than stop him, and give him a penny."

"Will he let it go so desperate cheap as that?" demanded Jason, his eyes twinkling with a sort of "bitters" expectation.

"That is the stated price. Stop him boldly; there is no occasion for all this Connecticut modesty—Here, uncle, this gentleman wishes a cup of your white wine."

Jason turned away in alarm, to see who was looking on; and, when the cup was put into his hands, he shut his eyes determined to gulp its contents at a swallow, in the most approved "bitters" style. About half the liquor went down his throat; the rest being squirted back in a small white stream.

"Buttermilk, by Jingo!" exclaimed the disappointed pedagogue, who expected some delicious combination of spices with rum. St. Jingo was the only saint, as "darnation" or "darn you" were the only oaths, his puritan education ever permitted him to use.

Chapter V

"Here's your fine clams!
As white as snow!
On Rockaway, these clams do grow."

New York Cries.

I T was some time before Jason's offended dignity and disappointment would permit him to smile at the mistake, and we had walked some distance towards Old Slip, where I was to meet Dirck, before the pedagogue even opened his lips. Then, the only allusion he made to the white wine, was to call it "a plaguy Dutch cheat," for Jason had implicitly relied on having that peculiar beverage of his caste, known as "bitters." What he meant by a *Dutch* cheat, I do not know, unless he thought the butter-milk was particularly Dutch, and *this* butter-milk an imposition.

Dirck was waiting for me at the Old Slip, and, on enquiry, I found he had enjoyed his draught of white wine as well as myself, and was ready for immediate service. We proceeded along the wharves in a body, admiring the different vessels that lined them. About nine o'clock, all three of us passed up Wall-Street, on the stoops of which no small portion of its tenants were already seated, enjoying the sight of the negroes, as, with happy, "shining," faces they left the different dwellings, to hasten to the Pinkster field. Our passage through the street attracted a good deal of attention, for, being all three strangers it was not to be supposed we could be thus seen in a body, without exciting a remark. Such a thing could hardly have been expected in London itself.

After showing Jason the City Hall, Trinity Church, and the City Tavern, we went out of town, taking the direction of a large common that the King's officers had long used for a parade ground, and which has since been called the Park, though it would be difficult to say why, since it is barely a paddock in size, and certainly has never been used to keep any animals wilder than the boys of the town. A park I suppose it will one day become, though it has little at present that comports with my ideas of such a thing. On this common there was the Pinkster ground, which was now quite full of people, as well as of animation.

There was nothing new in a Pinkster frolic either to Dirck, or to myself, though Jason gazed at the whole procedure with wonder. He was born within seventy miles of that very spot, but had not the smallest notion, before, of such a holiday as Pinkster. There are few blacks in Connecticut, I believe, and those that are there, are so ground down in the Puritan mill, that they are neither fish, flesh, nor red herring, as we say of a non-descript. No man ever heard of a festival in New-England that had not some immediate connection with the saints, or with politics.

Jason was at first confounded with the noises, dances, music, and games that were going on. By this time, nine-tenths of the blacks of the city, and of the whole country within thirty, or forty miles, indeed, were collected in thousands in those fields, beating banjoes, singing African songs, drinking, and most of all laughing, in a way that seemed to set their very hearts rattling within their ribs. Every thing wore the aspect of good humour, though it was good humour in its broadest and coarsest forms. Every sort of common game was in requisition while drinking was far from being neglected. Still, not a soul was drunk. A drunken negro, indeed, is by no means a common thing. The features that distinguish a Pinkster frolic from the usual scenes at fairs, and other merry makings, however, were of African origin. It is true, there are not now, nor were there then, many blacks among us of African birth; but the traditions and usages of their original country were so far preserved as to produce a marked difference between this festival, and one of European origin. Among other things, some were making music, by beating on skins drawn over the ends of hollow logs, while others were dancing to it, in a manner to show that they felt infinite delight. This, in particular, was said to be a usage of their African progenitors.

Hundreds of whites were walking through the fields, amused spectators. Among these last, were a great many children of the better class, who had come to look at the enjoyment of those who attended them in their own ordinary amusements. Many a sable nurse did I see that day, chaperoning her young master, or young mistress, or both together, through the various groups, demanding of all, and receiving from all the respect that one of these classes was accustomed to pay to the other.

A great many young ladies between the ages of fifteen and twenty were also in the fields, either escorted by male companions, or, what was equally as certain of producing deference, under the care of old female nurses, who belonged to the race that kept the festival. We had been in the field ourselves two hours, and even Jason was beginning to condescend to be amused, when, unconsciously, I got separated from my companions, and was wandering through the groups by myself, as I came on a party of young girls, who were under the care of two or three wrinkled and gray headed negresses, so respectably attired, as to show at once they were confidential servants in some of the better families. As for the young ladies themselves, most were still of the age of school girls; though there were some of that equivocal age, when the bud is just breaking into the opening flower, and one or two, that were even a little older; young women in forms and deportment, though scarcely so in years. One of a party of two, of the last, appeared to me to possess all the grace of young womanhood, rendered radiant by the ingenuous laugh, the light-hearted playfulness, and the virgin innocence of sweet seventeen. She was simply, but very prettily dressed, and every thing about her attire, air, carriage and manner, denoted a young lady of the better class, who was just old enough to feel all the proprieties of her situation, while she was still sufficiently youthful to enjoy all the fun. As she came near me, it seemed as if I knew her, but, it was not until I heard her sweet, mirthful voice, that I recollected the pretty little thing in whose behalf I had taken a round with the butcher's boy, on the Bowery Road near six years before. As her party came quite near the spot where I stood, what was only conjecture at first, was reduced to a certainty.

In the surprise of the moment, happening to catch the eye of the young creature, I was emboldened to make her a low bow. At first she smiled, like one who fancies she recognizes an acquaintance, then her face became scarlet, and she returned my bow, with a very lady-like, but, at the same time, a very distant curtsey; upon which, bending her blue eyes to the ground, she turned away seemingly to speak to her companion. After this, I could not advance to speak, though I was strongly in hopes the old black nurse who was with her, would recognise me, for she had manifested much concern about me, on the occasion of the quarrel with the young butcher. This did not occur, and old Katrinke, as I heard the negress called, jabbered away, explaining the meaning of the different ceremonies of her race, to a cluster of very interested listeners, without paying any attention to me. The tongues of the pretty little things went, as girls' tongues will go, though my unknown fair one maintained all the reserve and quiet of manner that comported with her young womanhood, and apparent condition in life.

"Dere, Miss Anneke!" exclaimed Katrinke, suddenly, "dere come a genttleum dat will bring a pleasure, I know."

"*Anneke*," I repeated mentally, and "gentleman that will cause pleasure by his appearance." "Can it be Dirck?" I thought. Sure enough, Dirck it proved to be, who advanced rapidly to the group, making a general salute, and finishing by shaking my beautiful young stranger's hand and addressing her by the name of "cousin Anneke." This, then, was Annie Mordaunt, as the young lady was commonly called in the English circles, the only child and heiress of Herman Mordaunt, of Crown Street, and of Lilacsbush. Well, Dirck has more taste than I had ever given him credit for. Just as this thought glanced through my mind, my figure caught my friend's eye, and with a look of pride and exultation he signed to me to draw nearer, though I had managed to get pretty near as it was, already.

"Cousin Anneke," said Dirck, who never used circumlocution, when direct means were at all available, "this is Corny Littlepage, of whom you have heard me speak so often, and for whom I ask one of your best curtsies, and sweetest smiles."

Miss Mordaunt was kind enough to comply literally, both curtsying and smiling precisely as she had been desired to do, though I could see, she was also slightly disposed to laugh. I was still making my bow, and mumbling some unintelligible compliment, when Katrinke gave a little exclamation, and using the freedom of an old and confidential servant, she eagerly pulled the sleeve of her young mistress, and hurriedly whispered something in her ear. Anneke coloured, turned quickly towards me, bent her eyes more boldly and steadily on my face—and then it was that I fancied the sweetest smile which mortal had ever received, or that with which I had just before been received, was much surpassed.

"Mr. Littlepage, I believe, is not a total stranger, Cousin Dirck," she said. "Katrinke remembers him, as a young gentleman who once did me an important service, and now I think I can trace the resemblance myself. I allude to the boy who insulted me on the Bowery Road, Mr. Littlepage, and your handsome interference, in my behalf."

"Had there been twenty boys, Miss Mordaunt, an insult to *you* would have been resented by any man of ordinary spirit."

I do not know that any youth, who was suddenly put to his wits to be polite, or sentimental, or feeling, could have done a great deal better than *that*! So Anneke thought too, I fancy, for her colour increased, rendering her ravishingly lovely, and she looked surprisingly pleased.

"Yes," put in Dirck, with energy—"let twenty, or a hundred try it, if they please, Anneke, men or boys, and they'll find those that will protect you."

"You, for one, of course, cousin Dirck," rejoined the charming girl, holding out her hand towards my friend, with a frankness I could have dispensed with in her; "but, you will remember, Mr. Littlepage, or *Master* Littlepage, as he then was, was a stranger, and I had no such claim on *him*, as I certainly have on you."

"Well, Corny, it is odd you never said a word of this to me! when I was showing him Lilacsbush, and talking of you, and of your father, not a word did he say on the subject!"

"I did not then know it was Miss Mordaunt I had been so fortunate as to serve. But, here is Mr. Newcome at your elbow, Follock, and dying to be introduced, as he sees I have been."

Anneke turned to smile and curtsey again to Jason, who made his bow in a very school-master sort of a fashion, while I could see that the circumstance I had not boasted of my exploit gave it new importance in the sweet creature's eyes. As for Jason, he had no sooner got along with the introduction, the first, I fancy, he had ever gone regularly through, than, profiting by some questions Miss Mordaunt was asking Dirck about his mother and the rest of the family, he came round to me, drew me aside by a jerk of the sleeve, and gave me to understand he had something for my private ear.

"I did not know before, that you had ever kept school, Corny," he half whispered earnestly.

"Nor do you know it, now, Mr. Newcome, since the thing never happened."

"How comes it then, that this young woman called you *Master* Littlepage?"

"Bah! Jason, wait a year, or two, and you will begin to get truer notions of us New Yorkers."

"But, I heard her with my own ears—*Master* Littlepage; as plain as words were ever uttered."

"Well, then, Miss Mordaunt must be right, and I have forgotten the affair. I must, once, have kept a woman's school, somewhere, in my younger days, but forgotten it."

"Now, this is nothing (nawthin', as expressed) but your desperate York pride, Corny, but I think all the better of you for it. Why, as it could not have taken place after you went to college, you must have got the start of even me! But, the Rev. Mr. Worden is enough to start a youth with a large capital, if he be so minded. I admit he does understand the dead languages. It is a pity he is so very dead in religious matters."

"Well—well—I will tell you all about it, another time; you perceive, now, that Miss Mordaunt wishes to move on, and does not like to quit us too abruptly. Let us follow."

Jason complied, and for an hour, or two we had the pleasure of accompanying the young ladies, as they strolled among the booths and different groups of that singular assembly. As has been said, most of the blacks had been born in the colony, but there were some native Africans among them. New York never had slaves on the system of the southern planters, or in gangs of hundreds, to labour in the fields under overseers, and who lived apart in cabins of their own; but, our system of slavery was strictly domestic, the negro almost invariably living under the same roof with the master, or, if his habitation was detached, as certainly sometimes happened, it was still near at hand, leaving both races as parts of a common family. In the country, the negro men toiled in the fields, but it was as ordinary husbandmen; and, in the cases of those who laboured on their own property, or as tenants of some extensive landlord, the black did his work at his master's side. Then all, or nearly all, our household servants were, and still are, blacks, leaving that department of domestic economy almost exclusively in their hands, with the exception of those cases in which the white females busied themselves also in such occupations, united to the usual supervision of the mistresses. Among the Dutch, in particular, the treatment of the negro was of the kindest character, a trusty field slave often having quite as much to say on the subject of the tillage and the crops, as the man who owned both the land he worked, and himself.

A party of native Africans kept us for half an hour. The scene seemed to have revived their early associations, and they were carried away with their own representation of semi-savage sports. The American-born blacks gazed at this group with intense interest also, regarding them as so many ambassadors from the land of their ancestors, to enlighten them in usages, and superstitious lore, that were more peculiarly suited to their race. The last even endeavoured to imitate the acts of the first, and, though the attempt was often ludicrous, it never failed on the score of intention and gravity. Nothing was done in the way of caricature, but much in the way of respect and affection.

Lest the habits of this generation should pass away and be forgotten, of which I see some evidence, I will mention a usage that was quite common among the Dutch, and which has passed in some measure, into the English families that have formed connections with the children of Holland. Two of these intermarriages had so far brought the Littlepages within the pale, that the usage to which I allude, was practised in my own case. The custom was this: when a child of the family reached the age of six, or eight, a young slave of the same age and sex, was given to him, or her, with some little formality, and from that moment the fortunes of the two were considered to be, within the limits of their respective pursuits and positions, as those of man and wife. It is true, divorces do occur, but it is only in cases of gross misconduct, and quite as often the misconduct is on the side of the master, as on that of the slave. A drunkard may get in debt, and be compelled to part with his blacks; this one among the rest; but this particular negro remains with him as long as any thing remains. Slaves that seriously misbehave, are usually sent to the islands, where the toil on the sugar plantations proves a very sufficient punishment.

The day I was six, a boy was given to me, in the manner I have mentioned, and he remains not only my property, but my factotum to this moment. It was Yaap, or Jacob, the negro to whom I have already had occasion to allude. Anneke Mordaunt, whose grandmother was of a Dutch family, it will be remembered, had with her, there in the Pinkster field, a negress of just her own age, who was called Ma*ri*; not Mary, or Maria, but the last as it would be pronounced without the final a. This Ma*ri* was a buxom, glistening, smooth faced, laughing, red-lipped, pearl-toothed, black eyed hussy, that seemed born for fun, and who was often kept in order by her more sedate and well mannered young mistress with a good deal of difficulty. My fellow was on the ground somewhere, too, for I had given him permission to come to town to keep Pinkster, and he was to leave Satanstoe in a sloop, within an hour after I left it myself. The wind had been fair, and I made no question of his having arrived, though as yet I had not seen him.

I could have accompanied Anneke, and her party, all day, through that scene of unsophisticated mirth, and felt no want of interest. Her presence immediately produced an impression, even the native Africans moderating their manner, and lowering their yells, as it might be the better to suit her more refined tastes. No one in our set was too dignified to laugh, but Jason. The pedagogue, it is true, often expressed his disgust, at the amusements and antics of the negroes, declaring they were unbecoming human beings, and otherwise manifesting that disposition to hyper-criticism which is apt to distinguish one who is only a tyro in his own case.

Such was the state of things when Ma*ri* came rushing up to her young mistress, with distended eyes, and uplifted hands, exclaiming on a key that necessarily made us all sharers in the communication—

"Oh! Miss Anneke!—What you t'ink, Miss Anneke! Could you ever s'pose sich a t'ing, Miss Anneke!—"

"Tell me at once, Mari, what it is you have seen, or heard, and leave off these silly exclamations;" said the gentle mistress with a colour that proved she was unused to her own girl's manner.

"Who *could* t'ink it, Miss Anneke! Dese, here, werry niggers have sent all 'e way to deir own country, and have had a lion cotched for Pinkster!"

This was news, indeed, if true. Not one of us all had ever seen a lion; wild animals then being exceedingly scarce in the colonies, with the exception of those that were taken in our own woods. I had seen several of the small brown bears, and many a wolf, and one stuffed panther, in my time, but never supposed it within the range of possibilities that I could be brought so near a living lion. Inquiry showed, nevertheless, that Mari was right, with the exception of the animal's having been expressly caught for the occasion. It was the beast of a showman, who was also the proprietor of a very active and amusing monkey. The price of admission was a quarter of a dollar, for adult whites, children and negroes going in for half price. These preliminaries understood, it was at once settled that all who could muster enough of money and courage should go in a body, and gaze on the King of Beasts. I say of courage, for it required a good deal for a female novice to go near a living lion.

The lion was kept in a cage, of course, which was placed in a temporary building of boards, that had been erected for the Pinkster field. As we drew near the door, I saw that the cheeks of several of the pretty young creatures who belonged to the party of Anneke, began to turn pale, a sign of weakness that, singular as it may appear, very sensibly extended itself to most of their attendant negresses. Mari did not flinch, however, and when it came to the trial, of that sex, she and her mistress were the only two who held out in the original resolution of entering. Some time was thrown away, in endeavouring to persuade two or three of her older companions to go in with her, but finding it useless, with a faint smile Miss Mordaunt calmly said—

"Well, gentlemen, Mari and myself must compose the female portion of the party. I have never seen a lion and would not, by any means, miss this opportunity. We shall find my friends waiting for such portions of us as shall not be eaten, on our return."

We were now near the door, where stood the man who received the money, and gave the tickets. It happened that Dirck had been stopped by a gentleman of his acquaintance, who had just left the building, and who was laughingly relating some incident that had occurred within. I stood on one side of Anneke, Jason on the other, while Mari was close in the rear.

"A quarter for each gentleman and the lady," said the door keeper, "and a shilling for the wench."

On this hint, Jason, to my great surprise, for usually he was very backward on such occasions, drew out a purse, and emptying some silver into his hand, he said with a flourish—

"Permit me, Miss, it is an honour I covet; a quarter for yourself, and a shilling for Mari."

I saw Anneke colour, and her eye turn hastily towards Dirck.

Before I had time to say any thing, or to do any thing in fact, she answered steadily—

"Give yourself no trouble, Mr. Newcome. Mr. Littlepage will do me the favour to obtain tickets for me."

Jason had the money in his fingers, and I passed him and bought the tickets, while he was protesting—

"It gave him pleasure—he was proud of the occasion—another time her brother could do the same for his sisters, and he had six," and other matters of the sort.

I simply placed the tickets in Anneke's hand, who received them with an expression of thanks and we all passed; Dirck enquiring of his cousin as he came up, if he should get her tickets. I mention this little incident as showing the tact of woman, and will relate all that pertains to it, before I proceed to other things. Anneke said nothing on the subject of her tickets until we had left the booth, when she approached me, and with that grace and simplicity which a well bred woman knows how to use on such an occasion, she quietly observed—

"I am under obligations to you, Mr. Littlepage, for having paid for my tickets. They cost three shillings, I believe?"

I bowed, and had the pleasure of almost touching Miss Mordaunt's beautiful little hand, as she gave me the money. At this instant, a jerk at my elbow came near causing me to drop the silver. It was Jason, who had taken this liberty, and who now led me aside with an earnestness of manner, it was not usual for him to exhibit. I saw by the portentous look of the pedagogue's countenance, and his swelling manner, that something extraordinary was on his mind, and waited with some little curiosity to learn what it might be.

"Why, what in human natur', Corny, do you mean?" he cried, almost angrily. "Did ever mortal man hear of a gentleman's making a lady pay for a treat! Do you know you have made Miss Anneke pay for a treat?"

"A treat, Mr. Newcome!"

"Yes, a treat, Mr. Corny Littlepage! How often do you think young ladies will accompany you to shows, and balls, and other sights, if you make them *pay*!"

Then a laugh of derision added emphasis to Jason's words.

"Pay;—could I presume to think Miss Mordaunt would suffer me to pay money for her, or for her servant?"

"You almost make me think you a nat'ral! Young men *always* pay for young women, and no questions asked. Did you not remark how smartly I offered to pay for this Miss, and how well she took it, until you stepped forward and cut me out. I bore it, for it saved me three nine-pences."

"I observed how Miss Mordaunt shrunk from the familiarity of being called Miss, and how unwilling she was to let you buy the tickets, and that I suspect was solely because she saw you had some notion of what you call a treat."

I cannot enter into the philosophy of the thing, but certainly nothing is more vulgar in English, to address a young lady as Miss, without affixing a name, whereas I know it is the height of breeding to say Mademoiselle in French, and am told the Spaniards, Italians and Germans use its synonyme in the same manner. I had been indignant at Jason's familiarity when he called Anneke—the pretty Anneke!—Miss; and felt glad of an occasion to let him understand how I felt on the subject.

"What a child you be, a'ter all, Corny!" exclaimed the pedagogue, who was much too good natured to take offence at a trifle. "You a bachelor of arts! But this matter *must* be set right, if it be only for the honour of my school. Folks"—Jason never blundered on the words 'one' or 'people' in this sense—"Folks may think that you have been in the school since it has been under my care, and I wouldn't for the world, have it get abroad that a youth from my school had neglected to treat a lady under such circumstances."

Conceiving it useless to remonstrate with *me* any farther, Jason proceeded forthwith to Anneke, with whom he begged permission to say a word in private. So eager was my companion to wipe out the stain, and so surprised was the young lady, who gently declined moving more than a step, that the conference took place immediately under my observation, neither of the parties being aware that I necessarily heard or saw all that passed.

"You must excuse Corny, Miss," Jason commenced, producing his purse again, and beginning to hunt anew for a quarter and a shilling—"he is quite young, and knows nawthin' worth speaking of, of the ways of mankind. Ah! here is just the money;—three nine-pennies, or three York shillings. Here, Miss, excuse Corny, and overlook it all; when he is older, he will not make such blunders."

"I am not certain that I understand you, sir!" exclaimed Anneke, who had shrunk back a little at the 'Miss,' and who now saw Jason hold out the silver, with a surprise she took no pains to conceal.

"This is the price of the tickets—yes, that's all. Nawthin' else, on honour. Corny, you remember, was so awful dumb as to let you pay, just as if you had been a gentleman."

Anneke now smiled, and glancing at me at the same instant, a bright blush suffused her face, though the meaning of my eye, as I could easily see, strongly tempted her to laugh.

"It is very well as it is, Mr. Newcome, though I feel much indebted to your liberal intentions," she said, turning to rejoin her friends; "it is customary in New York, for ladies to pay themselves for every thing of this nature. When I go to Connecticut, I shall feel infinitely indebted to you for another such offer."

Jason did not know what to make of it! He long after insisted that the young lady was 'huffed,' as he called it, and that she had refused to take the money, merely because she was thus offended.

"There is a manner, you know, Corny," he said, "of doing even a genteel thing, and that is to do it genteelly. I much doubt if a genteel thing *can* be done ungenteelly. One thing I'm thankful for, and that is that she don't know that you ever were at the 'Seminarian Institute' in your life;" such being the appellation Jason had given to that which Mr. Worden had simply called a "Boys' School." To return to the booth.

The lion had many visitors, and we had some difficulty in finding places. As a matter of course, Anneke was put in front, most of the men who were in the booth, giving way to her, with respectful attention. Unfortunately, the young lady wore an exceedingly pretty shawl, in which scarlet was a predominant colour, and that which occurred has been attributed to this circumstance, though I am far from affirming such to have been literally the case. Anneke, from the first, manifested no fear, but, the circle pressing on her from without, she got so near the cage, that the beast thrust a paw through, and actually caught hold of the shawl, drawing the alarmed girl quite up to the bars. I was at Anneke's side, and, with a presence of mind that now surprises me, I succeeded in throwing the shawl from the precious creature's shoulders, and of fairly lifting her from the ground and setting her down again, at a safe distance from the beast. All this passed so soon, that half the persons present were unconscious of what had occurred, until it was all over; and what astonishes me most is, that I do not retain the least recollection of the pleasure I ought to have felt while my arm encircled Anneke Mordaunt's slender waist, and, while she was altogether supported by me. The keeper interposed immediately, and the lion relinquished the shawl, looking like a disappointed beast, when he found it did not contain its beautiful owner.

Anneke was rescued, before she had time fully to comprehend the danger she had been in. Even Dirck could not advance to her aid, though he saw and comprehended the imminent risk run by the being he loved best in the world; but Dirck was always so slow! I must do Jason the credit to say that he behaved well, though so situated as to be of no real use. He rushed forward to assist Anneke, and remained to draw away the shawl, as soon as the keeper had succeeded in making the lion relinquish his hold. But, all this passed so rapidly, as to give little opportunity for noting incidents.

Anneke was certainly well frightened, by this adventure with the lion, as was apparent by her changing colour, and a few tears that succeeded. Still, a glass of water, and a minute or two, seated in a chair, were sufficient to restore her self composure, and she remained with us, for half an hour, examining and admiring her terrible assailant.

And, here, let me add, for the benefit of those who have never had an opportunity of seeing the King of Beasts, that he is a sight well worthy to behold! I have never viewed an elephant, which travelled gentlemen tell me, is a still more extraordinary animal, though I find it difficult to imagine any thing finer, in its way, than the lion which came so near injuring "sweet Anne Mordaunt." I question if any of us were aware of the full extent of the danger she ran, until we began to reflect on it coolly, after time and leisure were afforded. As soon as the commotion naturally produced at first, had subsided, the incident seemed forgotten, and we left the booth, after a long visit, expatiating on the animal, and its character, apparently in forgetfulness of that which, by one blow of his powerful paw, the lion might have rendered fatal to one of the very sweetest and happiest innocents of the whole province, but for the timely and merciful interposition of a kind providence.

After the little affair of the tickets, I walked on with Anneke, who declared her intention of quitting the field, her escape beginning to affect her spirits, and she was afraid that some particularly kind friend might carry an exaggerated account of what had happened to her father. Dirck offered to accompany her home, for Mr. Mordaunt kept no carriage; or, at least nothing that was habitually used as a town equipage. We had all gone as far as the verge of the Common, with Anneke, when the sweet girl stopped, looked at me earnestly, and, while her colour changed and tears rose to her eyes, she said—

"Mr. Littlepage, I am just getting to be fully conscious of what I owe to you. The thing passed so suddenly, and I was so much alarmed, that I did not know how to express myself at the time, nor am I certain that I do now. Believe me, notwithstanding, that I never can forget this morning, and I beg of you, if you have a sister, to carry to her the proffered friendship of Anneke Mordaunt, and tell her that her own prayers in behalf of her brother will not be more sincere than mine."

Before I could recollect myself, so as to make a suitable answer, Anneke had curtsied and walked away, with her handkerchief to her eyes.

Chapter VI

"Nay, be brief:
I see into thy end, and am almost
A man already."
> *Cymbeline*, III. iv. 165–167.

As Dirck accompanied Miss Mordaunt to her father's house, in Crown Street,* I took an occasion to give Jason the slip, being in no humour to listen to his lectures on the proprieties of life, and left the Pinkster field, as fast as I could. Notwithstanding the size and importance of New York, a holiday like this could not fail to draw great crowds of persons to witness the sports. In 1757, James de Lancey was at the head of the government of the province, as indeed he had been, in effect, for much of his life, and I remember to have met his chariot carrying the younger children of the family to the field, on my way into the town. As the day advanced, carriages of one sort and another, made their appearance in Broadway, principally conveying the children of their different owners. All these belonged to people of the first mark, and I saw the Ship, that denotes the arms of Livingston, the Lance, of the de Lanceys, the Burning Castle of the Morrises, and other armorial bearings that were well known in the province. Carriages, certainly, were not as common in 1757, as they have since become, but most of our distinguished people rode in their coaches, chariots, or phaetons, or conveyances of some sort or other, when there was occasion to go so far out of town, as the Common, which is the site of the present "Park". The roads on the island of Manhattan, were very pretty and picturesque, winding among rocks and through valleys, being lined with groves and copses in a way to render all the drives rural and retired. Here and there, one came to a country-house, the residence of some person of importance, which, by its comfort and snugness, gave all the indications of wealth and of a prudent taste. Mr. Speaker Nicoll† had occupied a dwelling of this sort for

*Now, Liberty Street.
†The person meant here, was William Nicoll Esquire, Patentee of Islip, a

a long series of years, that was about a league from town, and which is still standing, as I pass it constantly in travelling between Satanstoe and York. I never saw the Patentee myself, as he died long before my birth, but his house near town, still stands, as I have said, a memorial of past ages!

The whole town seemed alive, and everybody had a desire to get a glance at the sports of the Pinkster field, though the more dignified and cultivated had self-denial enough to keep aloof, since it would hardly have comported with their years and stations to be seen in such a place. The war had brought many regiments into the Province, however, and, I met at least twenty young officers strolling out to the scene of amusement, as I walked into town. I will confess I gazed at these youths with admiration, and not entirely without envy, as they passed me in pairs, laughing and diverting themselves with the grotesque groups of blacks, that were occasionally met, coming in from their sports. These young men, I knew, had enjoyed the advantages of being educated at home, some of them quite likely in the Universities, and all of them amid the high civilization and taste of England. I say all of them, too hastily, as there were young men

---

large estate on Long Island, that is still in the family, under a Patent granted in 1683. This gentleman was a son of Mr. Secretary Nicoll, who is supposed to have been a relative of Col. Nicoll, the first English Governor. Mr. Speaker Nicoll, as the son was called in consequence of having filled that office for nearly a generation, was the direct ancestor of the Nicolls of Islip and Shelter Island, as well as of a branch long settled at Stratford, Connecticut. The house alluded to by Mr. Littlepage, as a relic of antiquity in *his* day,—American antiquity, be it remembered,—was standing a few years since, if it be not still standing, at the point of junction between the Old Boston Road, and the New Road, and nearly opposite to the termination of the long avenue that led to Rosehill, originally a seat of the Watts'. The house stood a short distance above the present Union Square, and not far from that of the present Gramercy. It was, or is, a brick-house of one story, with a small courtyard in front; the House of Refuge being at a little distance on its right. If still standing, it must now be one of the oldest buildings of any sort, in a town of 400,000 souls! As Mr. Speaker Nicoll resigned the chair in 1718, this house must be at least a hundred and thirty or forty years old, and it may be questioned if a dozen as old, public or private, can be found on the whole island.

As the regular family residences of the Nicolls were in Suffolk or on their estates, it is probable that the abode mentioned was, in a measure, owing to an intermarriage with the Watts, as much as to the necessity of the Speaker's passing so much time at the seat of government.—EDITOR.

of the Colonies among them, who probably had not enjoyed these advantages. The easy air, self-possession, and quiet, what shall I call it?—insolence would be too strong a word, and a term that I, the son and grandson of old King's officers would not like to apply, and yet it comes nearest to what I mean as applicable to the covert manner of these young men—but, whatever it was, that peculiar air of metropolitan superiority over provincial ignorance and provincial dependence, which certainly distinguished all the younger men of this class, had an effect on me, I find it difficult to describe. I was a loyal subject, loved the King, most particularly since he was so identified with the Protestant succession, loved all of the blood royal, and wished for nothing more than the honour and lustre of the English Crown. One thus disposed could not but feel amicably towards the King's officers, yet, I will confess there were moments when this air of ill-concealed superiority, this manner that so much resembled that of the master towards the servant, the superior to the dependant, the patron to the client, gave me deep offence, and feelings so bitter that I was obliged to struggle hard to suppress them. But, this is anticipating, and is interrupting the course of my narrative. I am inclined to think there must always be a good deal of this feeling, where the relation of principal and dependant exists, as between distinct territories.

I was a good deal excited, and a little fatigued with the walk and the incidents of the morning, and determined to proceed at once to Duke Street, and share the cold dinner of my aunt, for few private families in York, that depended on regular cooks for their food, had any thing served warm on their tables, for that and the two succeeding days. Here and there, a white substitute was found, it is true, and we had the benefit of such an assistant, at half-past one. It was the English servant of a Col. Mosely, an officer of the army, who was intimate at my uncle's, and who had had the civility to offer a man for this occasion. I afterwards ascertained, that many officers manifested the same kind spirit, towards various other families in which they visited on terms of friendship.

Marriages between young English officers, and our pretty, delicate, York belles, were of frequent occurrence, and I had felt a twinge or two, on the subject of Anneke, that morning, as I passed the youths of the 55th, 60th, or Loyal Americans, 17th, and other regiments that were then in the province.

My aunt was descending from the drawing-room, in dinner dress, for that no lady ever neglects even though she dines on a cold dumpling, as I opened the street-door. Mrs. Legge was not coming down alone to take her seat at table, but, having some extra duty to perform in consequence of the absence of most of her household, she was engaged in that service. Seeing me, however, she stopped on the landing of the stairs, and beckoned me to approach.

"Corny," she said, "what have you been doing, my child, to have drawn this honour upon you?"

"Honour!—I am ignorant of having even received any. What can you mean, my dear aunt?"

"Here is Herman Mordaunt waiting to see you, in the drawing room. He asked particularly for *you*;—wishes to *see* you—expresses his regrets that *you* are not in, and talks only of *you!*"

"In which case, I ought to hasten up stairs in order to receive him, as soon as possible. I will tell you all about it at dinner, aunt; excuse me, now."

Away I went, with a beating heart, to receive a visit from Anneke's father. I can scarcely give a reason why this gentleman was usually called, when he was spoken of, and sometimes when he was spoken to, *Herman* Mordaunt; unless, indeed, it were that being in part of Dutch extraction, the name which denoted the circumstance (Hermanus—pronounced by the Hollanders, Her-*maa*nus) was used by a portion of the population in token of the fact, and adopted by others in pure compliance. But *Herman* Mordaunt was he usually styled, and this, too, in the way of respect, and not as coarse-minded persons affect to speak of their superiors, or in a way to boast of their own familiarity. I should have thought it an honour, at my time of life, to receive a visit from Herman Mordaunt, but my heart fairly beat, as I have said, as I went hastily up stairs, to meet Anneke's father.

My uncle was not in, and I found my visiter waiting for me, alone, in the drawing room. Aware of the state of the family, and of all families, indeed, during Pinkster, he had insisted on my aunt's quitting him, while he looked over some new books, that had recently been received from home; among which was a new and very handsome edition of the Spectator, a work that enjoys a just celebrity throughout the colonies.

Mr. Mordaunt advanced to receive me with studied politeness, yet a warmth that could not well be counterfeited, the instant I approached. Nevertheless, his manner was easy and natural, and to me he appeared to be the highest-bred man I had ever seen.

"I am thankful that the debt of gratitude I owe you, my young friend," he said, at once, and without preface of any sort, unless that of manner be so received, "is due to the son of a gentleman I so much esteem, as Evans Littlepage. A loyal subject, an honest man, and a well connected and well descended gentleman, like him, may well be the parent of a brave youth, who does not hesitate to face even lions, in defence of the weaker sex."

"I cannot affect to misunderstand you, sir," I answered, "and I sincerely congratulate you that matters are no worse, though you greatly overrate the danger. I doubt if even a lion would have the heart to hurt Miss Mordaunt, were she in his power."

I think this was a very pretty speech, for a youth of twenty, and I confess I look back upon it, even now, with complacency. If I occasionally betray weakness of this character, I beg the reader to recollect that I am acting in the part of an honest historian, and that it is my aim to conceal nothing that ought to be known.

Herman Mordaunt did not resume his seat, on account of the lateness of the hour, (half-past one) but he made me professions of friendship, and named Friday, the first moment when he could command the services of his domestics, when I should dine with him. The army had introduced later hours than was usual, and this invitation was given for three o'clock, it being said, at the time, as I well remember, that persons of fashion, in London, sat down to table even later than this. After remaining with me five minutes, Herman Mordaunt took his leave. Of course, I accompanied him to the door, where we parted with many bows.

At dinner I told my uncle and aunt all that had occurred, and was glad to hear them both speak so favorably of my new acquaintances.

"Herman Mordaunt might be a much more considerable man than he is," observed my uncle, "were he disposed to enter into public life. He has talents, a good education, a very handsome estate, and is well connected in the Colony, certainly; some say at home, also."

"And Anneke is a sweet young thing," added my aunt, "and, since Corny was to assist any young lady, I am heartily glad it was Anneke. She is an excellent creature, and her mother was one of my most intimate friends; as she was of my sister Littlepage, too. You must go and enquire after her health, this evening, Corny. Such an attention is due, after what has passed all round."

Did I wish to comply with this advice? Out of all question; and yet I was too young, and too little at my ease, to undertake this ceremony, without many misgivings. Luckily, Dirck came in, in the evening, and, my aunt repeating her opinion before my friend, he at once declared it was altogether proper, and that he thought Anneke would have a right to expect it. As he offered to be my companion, we were soon on our way to Crown Street, in which Mr. Mordaunt owned, and inhabited, a very excellent house. We were admitted by Mr. Mordaunt himself, not one of his blacks having yet returned from the Pinkster field.

Dirck appeared to be on the best terms, not only with Herman Mordaunt, but with his charming daughter. I had observed that the latter always called him "*cousin* Dirck," and I hardly knew whether to interpret this as a sign of particular, or of family regard. That Dirck was fonder of Anneke Mordaunt than of any other human being, I could easily see, and I confess that the discovery already began to cause uneasiness. I loved Dirck, and wished he loved any one else but the very being I feared he did.

Herman Mordaunt showed me the way, up the noble wide, mahogany garnished staircase of his dwelling, and ushered us into a very handsome, though not very large, but well lighted drawing room. There sat Anneke, his daughter, in the loveliness of her maiden charms, a little more dressed than usual perhaps, for she had three or four young and lovely girls with her, and five or six young men, among whom were no less than three scarlet coats.

I shall not attempt to conceal my weakness. Only twenty, inexperienced, and unaccustomed to town society, I felt awkward and unpleasantly, the instant I entered the room; nor did the feeling subside during the first half-hour. Anneke came forward, one or two steps, to meet me, and I could see she was almost as much confused, as I was myself. She blushed, as she thanked me for the service I had rendered, and expressed her satisfaction that her father had been fortunate enough to find me at home, and had had an opportunity of saying a little of what he felt, on the occasion. She then invited me to be seated, naming me to the company, and telling me who two or three of the young ladies were. From these last I received sundry approving smiles, which I took as so many thanks for serving their friend, while I could not help seeing that I was an object of examination to most of the men present. The three officers, in particular, looked at me the most intently, and the longest.

"I trust your little accident, which could have been of no great moment in itself, since you escaped so well, did not have the effect to prevent you from enjoying the rare fun of this Pinkster affair?" said one of the scarlet coats, as soon as the movement caused by my reception had subsided.

"You call it a 'little accident,' Mr. Bulstrode," returned Anneke, with a reproachful shake of her pretty head, "but, I can assure you, it is not a trifle to a young lady to find herself in the paws of a lion."

"*Serious* accident, then, since I see you are resolved to consider yourself a victim," rejoined the other—"but, not serious enough, I trust, to deprive you of the fun?"

"Pinkster fields, and Pinkster frolicks are no novelties to us, sir, as they occur every year, and I am just old enough not to have missed one of them all, for the last twelve years."

"We heard you had been 'out'," put another red-coat, whom I had heard called Billings, "accompanied by a little army of what Bulstrode called the Light Infantry."

Here three or four of the other young ladies joined in the discourse, at once, protesting against Mr. Bulstrode's placing their younger sisters in the army, in so cavalier a manner, an accusation that Mr. Bulstrode endeavoured to parry, by declaring his hopes of having them all not only in the army, but in his own regiment, one day or other. At this, there was a certain amount of mirth, and various protestations of an unwillingness to enlist, in which I was glad to see that neither Anneke, nor her most intimate friend, Mary Wallace, saw fit to join. I liked their reserve of manner, far better than the girlish trifling of their companions, and I could see that all the men respected them the more for it. There was a good deal of general and disjointed conversation that succeeded, which I shall not pretend to follow or relate, but confine myself to such observations as had a bearing on matters that were connected with myself.

As none of the young soldiers were addressed by their military titles, such things never occurring in the better circles, as I now discovered, and least of all in those connected with the army, I was not able at the time to ascertain the rank of the three red-coats, though I afterwards ascertained that the youngest was an ensign of the name of Harris, a mere boy and the younger son of a member of parliament; the next oldest, Billings, was a captain and was said to be a natural son of a nobleman; while Bulstrode was actually the oldest son of a Baronet, of three or four thousand a year, and had already bought his way up as high as a Majority, though only four-and-twenty. This last was a handsome fellow, too, nor had I been an hour in his company, before I saw plainly enough that he was a strong admirer of Anneke Mordaunt. The other two, evidently admired themselves too much, to have any very lively feeling on the subject of other persons. As for Dirck, younger than myself, and diffident as well as slow by nature, he kept himself altogether in the background, conversing most of the time with Herman Mordaunt on the subject of farming.

We had been together an hour, and I had acquired sufficient ease to change my seat, and to look at a picture or two, which adorned the walls, and which were said to be originals from the old world; for to own the truth, the art of painting has not made much progress in the Colonies. We *have* painters, it is true, and one or two are said to be men of rare merit, the ladies being very fond of sitting to them for their portraits, but these are exceptions. At a future day, when critics shall have immortalized the names of a Smybert, and a Watson, and a Blackburn, the people of these provinces will become aware of the talents they once possessed among them, and the grandchildren of those who neglected these men of genius in their day—ay, their descendants to the latest generations—will revenge the wrongs of merit and talent, to the end of civilized time. It is a failing of colonies to be diffident of their own opinions, but I have heard gentlemen who were educated at home, and who possessed cultivated and refined tastes, affirm that the painters of Europe, when visiting this hemisphere, have retained all their excellence, and have painted as freely and as well under an American, as under a European sun. As for a sister art, the Thespian Muse had actually made her appearance among us, five years before the time of my visit to town in 1757, or in 1752, a theatre having actually been built and opened in Nassau Street in 1753, with a company under the care of the celebrated Hallam, and his family. This theatre I had been dying to visit while it stood for as yet I had never witnessed a theatrical performance; but my mother's injunctions prevented me from entering it while at college. "When you are old enough, Corny," she used to say, "you shall have my permission to go as often as is proper, but you are now of an age when Shakspeare and Rowe, might unsettle your Latin and Greek." My task of obedience had not been very difficult, inasmuch as the building in Nassau Street, the second regular theatre ever erected in British America was taken down, and a church erected in its place.* The comedians went to the islands, and had not re-appeared on the continent down to the period of which I am now writing; nor did their return occur until the following year. That they were expected, however, and that a new house had been built for them, in another part of the town, I was aware, though month after month passed away, and the much expected company did not appear. I had understood, however, that the large military force collecting in the Colony, would be likely to bring them back soon, and the conversation soon took a turn that proved how much interest the young, the gay and the fair, felt in the result. I was still looking at a picture, when Mr. Bulstrode approached me, and entered into conversation. It will be remembered that this gentleman was four years my senior, that he had been at one of the universities, was the heir to a baronetcy, knew the world, had risen to a Majority in the army, and was by nature, as well as training, agreeable when he had a mind to be, and genteel. These circumstances, I could not but feel, gave him a vast advantage over me, and I heartily wished that we stood any where but in the presence of Anneke Mordaunt, as he thus saw fit to single me out for invidious comparison, by a sort of *tête-a-tête*, or aside. Still I could not complain of his manner, which was both polite and respectful, though I could scarce divest myself of the idea that he was covertly amusing himself, the whole time.

"You are a fortunate man, Mr. Littlepage," he commenced, "in having had it in your power to do so important a service to Miss

*The church is now (1845) being converted into a Post Office.—EDITOR.

Mordaunt. We all envy you your luck, while we admire your spirit, and I feel certain the men of our regiment will take some proper notice of it. Miss Anneke is in possession of half our hearts, and we should be still more heartless to overlook such a service."

I muttered some half intelligible answer to this compliment, and my new acquaintance proceeded.

"I am almost surprised, Mr. Littlepage," he added, "that a man of your spirit does not come among us, in times as stirring as these. They tell me both your father and grandfather served, and that you are quite at your ease. You will find a great many men of merit and fashion among us, and I make no doubt they would contribute to make your time pass agreeably enough. Large reinforcements are expected, and if you are inclined for a pair of colours, I think I know a battalion in which there are a vacancy or two, and which will certainly serve in the colonies. It would afford me great pleasure to help to further your views, should you be disposed to turn them towards the army."

Now, all this was said with an air of great apparent frankness and sincerity, which I fancied was only the more visible from the circumstance that Anneke was so seated, as unavoidably to hear every word of what was said. I observed that she even turned her eyes on me, as I made my answer, though I did not dare so far to observe her in turn, as to note their expression.

"I am very sensible, Mr. Bulstrode, of the liberality and kindness of your intentions," I answered steadily enough, for pride came to my assistance, "though I fear it will not be in my power to profit by it, at once, if ever. My grandfather is still living, and he has much influence over me and my fortune, and I know it is his wish that I should remain at Satanstoe."

"Where?" demanded Bulstrode, with more quickness and curiosity than strictly comported with good breeding perhaps.

"Satanstoe; I do not wonder you smile, for it has an odd sound, but it is the name my grandfather has given the family place in West-Chester. Given I have said, though translated would be better, as I understand the present appellation is pretty literally rendered into English from the Dutch."

"I like the name exceedingly, Mr. Littlepage, and I feel certain I should like your good, old, honest Anglo-Saxon grandfather. But pardon me—it is his wish you should remain at Satansfoot?"

"Satans*toe*, sir; we do not aspire to the whole foot. It is my grandfather's wish that I remain at home until of age, which will not be, now, for some months."

"By way of keeping you out of Satan's footsteps, I suppose—Well, these old gentlemen are often right. Should you alter your views, however, my dear Littlepage, do not forget me, but remember you can count on one who has some little influence, and who will ever be ready to exert it, in the behalf of one who has proved so serviceable to Miss Mordaunt. Sir Harry is a martyr to the gout, and talks of letting me stand in his place at the dissolution. In that case my wishes will naturally carry more weight. I like that name of Satanstoe, amazingly!"

"I am infinitely obliged to you, Mr. Bulstrode, though I will confess I have never looked forward to rising in the world by taxing my friends. One may own that he has had some hopes founded on merit and honesty—"

"Poh! poh!—my dear Littlepage, honesty is a very pretty thing to talk about, but I suppose you remember what Juvenal says on that interesting subject—*"probitas laudatur et alget."* I dare say, you are fresh enough from college to remember that comprehensive sentiment."

"I have never read Juvenal, Mr. Bulstrode, and never wish to, if such be the tendency of what he teaches—"

"Juvenal was a satirist, you know," interrupted Bulstrode a little hastily, for, by this time, he too had ascertained that Anneke was listening, and he betrayed some eagerness to get rid of so flagitious a sentiment, "and satirists speak of things as they are, rather than as they ought to be. I dare say Rome deserved all she got, for the moralists give a very sad account of her condition. Of all the large capitals of which we have any account, London is the only town of even tolerable manners."

What young Bulstrode would have ventured to say next, it is out of my power to guess, for a certain Miss Warren who was of the company, and who particularly affected the youth, luckily called out, at this critical instant—

"Your attention one moment, if you please, Mr. Bulstrode; is it true that the gentlemen of the army have been getting the new theatre in preparation, and that they intend to favour us with some representations? A secret something like this has just leaked out, from Mr. Harris, who even goes so far as to add that you can tell us all about it."

"Mr. Harris must be put under an arrest for this, though I hear the Colonel let the cat out of the bag, at the Lt. Governor's table, as early as last week."

"I can assure you, Mr. Bulstrode," Anneke observed calmly, "that I have heard rumours to this effect, for quite a fortnight. You must not blame Mr. Harris solely, for your whole regiment has been hinting to the same purpose, far and near."

"Then the delinquent will escape, this time. I confess the charge; we have hired the new theatre, and do intend to solicit the honour of the ladies coming to hear me murder Cato, and Scrub; a pretty climax of characters, you will admit, Miss Mordaunt?"

"I know nothing of Scrub, though I have read Mr. Addison's play, and think you have no need of being ashamed of the character of Cato. When is the theatre to open?"

"We follow the sable gentry. As soon as St. Pinkster has received his proper share of attention, we shall introduce Dom-Cato, and Mr. Scrub to your acquaintance."

All the young ladies, but Anneke, and her friend Mary Wallace, laughed, two or three repeating the words 'St. Pinkster,' as if they contained something much cleverer than it was usual to hear. A general burst of exclamations, expressions of pleasure, and of questions and answers followed, in which two or three voices were heard at the same moment, during which time, Anneke turned to me, who was standing near her, at the spot occupied by Bulstrode a minute before, and seemed anxious to say something.

"Do you seriously think of the army, Mr. Littlepage?" she asked, changing colour at the freedom of her own question.

"In a war like this, no one can say when he may be called on to go out," I answered. "But, only as a defender of the soil, if at all."

I thought Anneke Mordaunt seemed pleased with this answer. After a short pause she resumed the dialogue.

"Of course you understand Latin, Mr. Littlepage, although you have not been at the universities?"

"As it is taught in our own colleges, Miss Mordaunt."

"And that is sufficient to tell me what Mr. Bulstrode's quotation means, if it be proper for me to hear."

"He would hardly presume to use even a Latin saying, in your presence, that is unfit for your ear. The maxim which Mr. Bulstrode attributes to Juvenal simply means 'that honesty is praised and starves.' "

I thought that something like displeasure settled on the fair, polished, brow of Miss Mordaunt, who, I could now see, possessed much character and high principles for one of her tender years. She said nothing, however, though she exchanged a very meaning glance with her friend Mary Wallace. Her lips were moved, and I fancied I could trace the formation of the sounds "honesty is praised and starves!"

"And *you* are to be Cato I hear, Mr. Bulstrode," cried one of the young ladies, who thought more of a scarlet coat, I fancy, than was for her own good. "How very charming! Will you play the character in regimentals or in mohair—in a modern, or in an ancient dress?"

"In my *robe de chambre*, a little altered for the occasion, unless St. Pinkster and his sports should suggest some more appropriate costume," answered the young man, lightly.

"Are you quite aware what feast Pinkster is?" asked Anneke, a little gravely.

Bulstrode actually changed colour, for it had never crossed his mind to enquire into the character of the holiday; and, to own the truth, the manner in which it is kept by the negroes of New York never would enlighten him much on the subject.

"That is information, for which I perceive I am now about to be indebted to Miss Mordaunt."

"Then you shall not be disappointed, Mr. Bulstrode; Pinkster is neither more nor less than the Festival of Whitsunday, or the Feast of Pentecost. I suppose we shall now hear no more of your saint."

Bulstrode took this little punishment, which was very sweetly but quite steadily uttered, with perfect good humour, and with a manner so rebuked, as to prove that Anneke possessed great control over him. He bowed, in submission, and she smiled so kindly, that I wished the occasion for the little pantomime had not occurred.

"*Our* ancestors, Miss Mordaunt, never heard of any Pinkster, you will remember, and that must explain my ignorance," he said meekly.

"But some of *mine* have long understood it, and observed the festival," answered Anneke.

"Ay, on the side of Holland—but, when I presume to speak of *our* ancestors, I mean those which I can claim the honour of boasting as belonging to me in common with yourself."

"Are you and Mr. Bulstrode, then, related?" I asked, as it might be involuntarily, and almost too abruptly.

Anneke replied, however, in a way to show that she thought the question natural for the circumstances, and not in the least out of place.

"My grandfather's mother, and Mr. Bulstrode's grandfather were brother and sister," was the quiet answer. "This makes us a sort of cousins, according to those Dutch notions which he so much despises, though I fancy it would not count for much at home."

Bulstrode protested to the contrary, stating that he knew his father valued his relationship to Mr. Mordaunt, by the earnest manner in which he had commanded him to cultivate the acquaintance of the family, the instant he reached New York. I saw by this, the footing on which the formidable Major was placed in the family, everybody seeming to be related to Anneke Mordaunt but myself. I took an occasion, that very evening, to question the dear girl on the subject of her Dutch connections, giving her a clue to mine, but with all our industry, and some assistance from Herman Mordaunt, who took an interest in such a subject, as it might be *ex officio*, we could make out no affinity worth mentioning.

Chapter VII

"Sir Valentine, I care not for her, I;
I hold him but a fool, that will endanger
His body for a girl that loves him not:
I claim her not, and therefore she is thine."
Two Gentlemen of Verona, V. iv. 132–135.

I saw Anne Mordaunt several times, either in the street, or in her own house, between that evening and the day I was to dine with her father. The morning of the last named day Mr. Bulstrode favoured me with a call, and announced that he was to be of the party in Crown Street, and that the whole company was to repair to the theatre, to see his own Cato and Scrub, in the evening.

"By giving yourself the trouble to call at the Crown and Bible, kept hard by, here, in Hanover Square, or Queen Street, by honest Hugh Gaine, you will find a package of tickets for yourself, Mr. and Mrs. Legge, and your relative Mr. Dirck Follock, as I believe the gentleman is called. These Dutch have extraordinary patronymics, you must admit, Littlepage."

"It may appear so to an Englishman, though our names are quite as odd to strangers. But Dirck Van Valkenburgh is not a kinsman of mine, though he is related to the Mordaunts, *your* relatives."

"Well, it's all the same! I knew he was related to somebody that I know, and I fancied it was to yourself. I am sure I never see him but I wish he was in our grenadier company."

"Dirck would do honour to any corps, but you know how it is with the Dutch families, Mr. Bulstrode. They still retain much of their attachment to Holland, and do not as often take service in the army, or navy, as we of English descent."

"I should have thought a century might have cooled them off, a little, from their veneration of the meadows of Holland. It is the opinion at home, that New York is a particularly well affected colony."

"So it is, as I hear from all sides. As respects the Dutch, among ourselves, I have heard my grandfather say that the reign of King William had a powerful influence in reconciling them to the new government, but, since his day, that they are less loyal than formerly. The Van Valkenburghs, notwithstanding, pass for as good subjects as any that the House of Hanover possesses. On no account would I injure them in your opinion."

"Good, or bad, we shall hope to see your friend, who is a connection, in some way, as you believe, of the Mordaunts. You will get but a faint idea of what one of the Royal Theatres is, Littlepage, by this representation of ours, though it may serve to kill time. But, I must go to rehearsal; we shall meet at three."

Here my gay and gallant major made his bow, and took his leave. I proceeded on to the sign of the Crown and the Bible, where I found a large collection of people, coming in quest of tickets. As the *élite* of the town, would not of themselves, form an audience sufficiently large to meet the towering ambition of the players, more than half the tickets were sold, the money being appropriated to the sick families of soldiers; those who were not entitled to receive aid from government. It was deemed a high compliment to receive tickets gratis, though all who did, made it a point to leave a donation to the fund, with Mr. Gaine. Receiving my package, I quitted the shop, and it being the hour for the morning promenade, I went up Wall Street to the Mall, as Trinity Church Walk was even then called. Here, I expected to meet Dirck, and hoped to see Anneke, for the place was much frequented by the young and gay, both in the mornings and in the evenings. The bands of different regiments were stationed in the church yard, and the company was often treated to much, fine, martial, music. Some few of the more scrupulous, objected to this desecration of the church yard, but the army had every thing pretty much in its own way. As they were supposed to do nothing but what was approved of at home, the dissenters were little heeded, nor do I think the army would have greatly cared, had they been more numerous.

I dare say there were fifty young ladies promenading the Church Walk when I reached it, and nearly as many young men, in attendance on them; no small portion of the last being scarlet-coats, though the mohairs had their representatives there, too. A few blue jackets were among us, also, there being two or three King's cruisers in port. As no one presumed to promenade the

Mall, who was not of a certain stamp of respectability, the company was all gaily dressed, and I will confess that I was much struck with the air of the place, the first time I showed myself among the gay idlers. The impression made on me that morning, was so vivid, that I will endeavour to describe the scene, as it now presents itself to my mind.

In the first place there was the noble street, quite eighty feet in width in its narrowest part, and gradually expanding as you looked towards the bay, until it opened into an area of more than twice that width, at the place called the Bowling Green.* Then came the Fort, crowning a sharp eminence, and overlooking every thing in that quarter of the town. In the rear of the Fort, or in its front, taking a water view, lay the batteries that had been built on the rocks which form the south-western termination of the island. Over these rocks, which were black and picturesque, and over the batteries they supported, was obtained a view of the noble Bay, dotted, here and there, with some speck of a sail, or possibly with some vessel anchored on its placid bosom. Of the two rows of elegant houses, most of them of brick, and with very few exceptions principally of two stories in height, it is scarcely necessary to speak, as there are few who have not heard of, and formed some notion of Broadway; a street that all agree is one day to be the pride of the western world.

In the other direction, I will admit that the view was not so remarkable, the houses being principally of wood, and of a somewhat ignoble appearance. Nevertheless, the army was said to frequent those habitations quite as much as they did any other in the place. After reaching the Common, or present Park, where the great Boston Road, led off into the country, the view was just the reverse of that which was seen in the opposite quarter. Here, all was inland, and rural. It is true, the New Bridewell had been erected in that quarter, and there was also a new gaol, both facing the Common, and the King's troops had barracks in their rear, but high, abrupt, conical hills, with low marshy land, orchards and meadows, gave to all that portion of the island a peculiarly

*Mr. Cornelius Littlepage betrays not a little of provincial admiration, as the reader will see. I have not thought it necessary to prune these passages, their causes being too familiar to leave any danger of their insertion's being misunderstood. Admiration of Broadway, certainly not more than a third-class street, as streets go in the old world, is so very common among us, as to need no apology.—EDITOR.

novel, and somewhat picturesque character. Many of the hills, in that quarter, and indeed all over the widest part of the island, are now surmounted by country houses, as some were then, including Petersfield, the ancient abode of the Stuyvesants, or that farm which, by being called after the old Dutch Governor's retreat, has given the name of Bowery, or Bouerie, to the road that led to it; as well as the Bowery House, as it was called, the country abode of the then Lieutenant Governor, James de Lancey; Mount Bayard, a place belonging to that respectable family; Mount Pitt, another that was the property of Mrs. Jones, the wife of Mr. Justice Jones, a daughter of James de Lancey, and various other Mounts, Houses, Hills, and Places, that are familiar to the gentry and people of New York.

But, the reader can imagine for himself the effect produced by such a street as Broadway, reaching very nearly half a mile in length, terminating at one end, in an elevated, commanding fort, with its back-ground of batteries, rocks and bay, and, at the other, with the Common, on which troops were now constantly parading, the Bridewell and gaol, and the novel scene I have just mentioned. Nor is Trinity itself, to be forgotten. This edifice, one of the noblest, if not the most noble of its kind, in all the colonies, with its gothic architecture, statues in carved stone, and flanking walls, was a close accessory of the view, giving to the whole grandeur, and a moral.*

As has been said, I found the Mall crowded with young persons of fashion and respectability. This Mall was near a hundred yards in length, and it follows that there must have been a goodly show of youth and beauty. The fine weather had commenced, spring had fairly opened, Pinkster Blossoms (the wild Honeysuckle) had been seen in abundance throughout the week, and every thing and person, appeared gay and happy.

I could discover that my person in this crowd, attracted attention as a stranger. I say as a stranger, for I am unwilling to betray so much vanity as to ascribe the manner in which many eyes followed me, to any vain notion that I was known, or admired. Still,

---

*The provincial admiration of Mr. Cornelius Littlepage was not quite as much in fault, as respects the church, as the superciliousness of our more modern tastes and opinions may lead us to suspect. The church that was burned in 1776, was a larger edifice, than that just pulled down, and, in many respects, was its superior.—EDITOR.

I will not so far disparage the gifts of a bountiful providence as to leave the impression that my face, person, or air was particularly disagreeable. This would not be the fact, and I have now reached a time of life when something like the truth may be told, without the imputation of conceit. My mother often boasted to her intimates that "Corny was one of the best made, handsomest, most active, and genteelest youths in the Colony." This I know, for such things will leak out, but mothers are known to have a remarkable weakness on the subject of their children. As I was the sole surviving offspring of my dear mother, who was one of the best hearted women that ever breathed, it is highly probable that the notions she entertained of her son partook largely of the love she bore me. It is true, my aunt Legge, on more than one occasion has been heard to express a very similar opinion, though nothing can be more natural than that sisters should think alike, on a family matter of this particular nature, more especially as my aunt Legge never had a child of her own to love and praise.

Let all this be as it may, well stared at was I, as I mingled among the idlers on Trinity Church Walk, on the occasion named. As for myself, my own eyes were bent anxiously on the face of every pretty, delicate young creature that passed, in the hope of seeing Anneke. I both wished and dreaded to meet her, for, to own the truth, my mind was dwelling on her beauty, her conversation, her sentiments, her grace, her gentleness and withal her spirit, a good deal more than half the time. I had some qualms on the subject of Dirck, I will confess; but Dirck was so young that his feelings could not be much interested, after all, and then Anneke was a second cousin, and that was clearly too near to marry. My grandfather had always put his foot down firmly, against any connection between relations that were nearer than *third* cousins, and I now saw how proper were his reasons. If they were even farther removed, so much the better he said; and so much the better it was.

If the reader should ask me why I *dreaded* to meet Anne Mordaunt, under such circumstances, I might be at a loss to give him a very intelligible answer. I feared even, to see the sweet face I sought—and oh! how soft, serene, and angel-like it was, at that budding age of seventeen!—but, though I almost feared to see it, when at last I saw her I had so anxiously sought, approaching me, arm and arm with Mary Wallace, having Bulstrode next herself, and Harris next her friend, my eyes were instantly averted, as if they had unexpectedly lighted on something disagreeable. I should have passed without even the compliment of a bow, had not my friends been more at their ease, and more accustomed to the free ways of town life than I happened to be myself.

"How's this, Cornelius, *Coeur de Lion!*" exclaimed Bulstrode, stopping, thus causing the whole party to stop with him, or to appear to wish to avoid me; "will you not recognise us, though it is not an hour since you and I parted? I hope you found the tickets, and when you have answered, 'yes,' I hope you will turn and do me the honour to bow to these ladies."

I apologized, I am afraid I blushed, for I detected Anneke looking at me, as I thought, with some little concern, as if she pitied my awkward, country embarrassment. As for Bulstrode, I did not understand him at that time, it exceeding my observation to be certain whether he considered me of sufficient importance, or not, to feel any concern on my account, in his very obvious suit with Anneke. Nevertheless, as he treated me with cordiality and respect, while he dealt with me so frankly, there was not room to take offence. Of course, I turned and walked back with the party, after I had properly saluted the ladies and Mr. Harris.

"*Coeur de Lion* is a better name for a soldier, than for a civilian," said Anneke, as we moved forward, "and, however much Mr. Littlepage may *deserve* the title, I am not certain, Mr. Bulstrode, he would not prefer leaving it among you gentlemen who serve the king."

"I am glad of this occasion, Mr. Littlepage, to enlist you on my side, in a warfare I am compelled to wage with Miss Anne Mordaunt," said the Major, gaily. "It is on the subject of the great merit of us poor fellows who have crossed the wide Atlantic, in order to protect the Colonies, New York among the number, and their people, Miss Mordaunt and Miss Wallace, inclusively, from the grasp of their wicked enemies, the French. The former young lady has a way of reasoning on the matter, to which I cannot assent, and I am willing to choose you as arbitrator between us."

"Before Mr. Littlepage accepts the office, it is proper he should know its duties and responsibilities," said Anneke, smiling. "In the first place, he will find Mr. Bulstrode, with loud professions of attachment to the colonies, much disposed to think them provinces that owe their very existence to England, while I maintain it is English*men*, and that it is not England, that have done so much in America. As for New York, Mr. Littlepage, and especially as for you and me, we can also say a word in favour of Holland. I am very proud of my Dutch connections and Dutch descent."

I was much gratified with the "as for you and me," though I believe I cared less for Holland than she did herself. I made an answer much in the vein of the moment, but the conversation soon changed to the subject of the military theatre that was about to open.

"I shall dread you as a critic, cousin Annie," so Bulstrode often termed Anneke, as I soon discovered; "I find you are not too well disposed to us of the cockade, and I think you have a particular spite to our regiment. I know that Billings and Harris, too, hold you in the greatest possible dread."

"They then feel apprehensive of a very ignorant critic, for I never was present at a theatrical entertainment in my life," Anneke answered with perfect simplicity. "So far as I can learn, there never has been but one season of any regular company, in this colony, and that was when I was a very little and a very young girl, as I am now neither very large, nor very old as a young woman."

"You see, Littlepage, with how much address, my cousin avoids adding 'and very uninteresting, and very ugly, and very disagreeable, and very much unsought,' and fifty other things she *might* add with such perfect truth and modesty! But is it true, that the theatre was open only one season, here?"

"So my father tells me, though I know very little of the facts themselves. To-night will be my first appearance in *front* of any stage, Mr. Bulstrode, as I understand it will be your first appearance *on* it."

"In one sense, the last will be true, though not altogether in another. As a school boy, I have often played, school-boy fashion, but this is quite a new thing with us, to be *amateur* players."

"It may seem ungrateful, when you are making so many efforts, principally to amuse us young ladies I feel convinced, to enquire if it be quite as wise, as it is novel. I must ask this, as a cousin you know, Henry Bulstrode, to escape entirely from the imputation of impertinence."

"Really, Anneke Mordaunt; I am not absolutely certain that it is. Our manners are beginning to change in this respect, however, and I can assure you that various noblemen have permitted sports of this sort at their seats. The custom is French, as you probably know, and whatever is French has much vogue with us, during times of peace. Sir Harry does not altogether approve of it, and, as for my lady mother, she has actually dropped more than one discouraging hint, on the subject in her letters."

"The certain proof that you are a most dutiful son. Perhaps, when Sir Harry and Lady Bulstrode learn your great success, however, they will overlook the field on which your laurels have been won. But, our hour has come, Mary; we have barely time to thank these gentlemen for their politeness, and to return in season to dress. I am to enact a part myself, at dinner, as I hope you will all remember."

Saying this, Anneke made her curtsies in a way to preclude any offer of seeing her home, and went her way with her silent, but sensible-looking and pretty friend. Bulstrode took my arm, with an air of easy superiority, and led the way towards his own lodgings, which happened to be in Duke Street. Harris joined another party, making it a point to be always late at dinner.

"That is not only one of the handsomest, but she is one of the most charming girls in the Colonies, Littlepage!" my companion exclaimed, as soon as we had separated, speaking at the same time with an earnestness and feeling I was far from expecting. "Were she in England, she would make one of the first women in it, by the aid of a little fashion and training. And very little would do, too; for there is a charm in her *naïveté* that is worth the art of fifty women of fashion."

"Fashion is a thing that any one may want, who does not happen to be in vogue," I answered, notwithstanding the great degree of surprise I felt. "As for training, I can see nothing but perfection in Miss Mordaunt as she is, and should deprecate the lessons that produced any change."

I believe it was now Bulstrode's turn to feel surprise, for I was conscious of his casting a keen look into my face, though I did not like to return it. My companion was silent, for a minute; then, without again adverting to Anneke he began to converse very sensibly on the subject of theaters and plays. I was both amused and instructed; for Mr. Bulstrode was an educated and a clever man, and a strange feeling came over the spirit of my dream, even then as I listened to his conversation. "This man," I thought, "admires Anne Mordaunt, and he will probably carry her with him to England, and obtain for her that fashion and training, of which he has just spoken. With his advantages of birth, air, fortune, education and military rank, he can scarcely fail in his suit, should he seriously attempt one, and it will be no more than prudent to command my own feelings, lest I become the hopeless victim of a serious passion." Young as I was, all this I saw, and thus I reasoned, and when I parted from my companion I fancied myself a much wiser man than when we had met. We separated in Duke Street, with a promise on my part, to call at the Major's lodgings half an hour later, after dressing, and walk with him to Herman Mordaunt's door.

"It is fortunate that it is the fashion of New York to walk to a dinner party," said Bulstrode, as he again took my arm, on our way to Crown Street, "for these narrow streets must be excessively inconvenient for chariots, though I occasionally see one of them. As for sedan chairs I detest them as things unfit for a man to ride in."

"Many of our leading families keep carriages, and *they* seem to get along well enough," I answered. "Neverthess it is quite in fashion, even for ladies to walk. I understand that many, perhaps most of your auditors will walk to the play-house door, this evening."

"They tell me as much," said Bulstrode, curling his lip a little, in a way I did not exactly like. "Notwithstanding, there will be many charming creatures among them, and they shall be welcome. Well, Littlepage, I do not despair of having you among us, for, to be candid without wishing to boast, I think you will find the ———th, as liberal a set of young men as there is in the service. There is a wish to have the mohairs among us, instead of shutting ourselves up altogether in scarlet. Then your father and grandfather have both served, and that will be a famous introduction."

I protested my unfitness for such an amusement, never having seen such an exhibition in my life; but, to this, my companion would not listen, and we picked our way, as well as we could, through William Street, up Wall, and then by Nassau into Crown, Herman Mordaunt owning a new house that stood not far from Broadway, in the latter street. This was rather in a remote part of the town, but the situation had the advantage of good air, and as a place extends, it is necessary some persons should live on its skirts.

"I wish my good cousin did not live quite so much in the suburbs," said Bulstrode, as he knocked in a very patrician manner; "it is not altogether convenient to go quite so much out of one's ordinary haunts in order to pay visits. I wonder Mr. Mordaunt came so far out of the world, to build."

"Yet the distances of London must be much greater, though *there* you have coaches."

"True; but not a word more on *this* subject; I would not have Anneke fancy I ever find it far to visit *her*."

We were the last but one; the tardy Mr. Harris making it a point always to be the last. We found Anneke Mordaunt supported by two or three ladies of her connection, and a party of quite a dozen assembled. As most of those present saw each other every day, and frequently two or three times a day, the salutations and compliments were soon over, and Herman Mordaunt began to look about him, to see who was wanting.

"I believe everybody is here, but Mr. Harris," the father observed to his daughter, interrupting some of Bulstrode's conversation to let this fact be known. "Shall we wait for him, my dear; he is usually so uncertain and late?"

"Yet, a very important man," put in Bulstrode, "as being entitled to lead the lady of the house to the table in virtue of his birthright. So much for being the fourth son of an Irish baron! Do you know Harris's father has just been ennobled?"

This was news to the company, and it evidently much increased the doubts of the propriety of sitting down without the young man in question.

"Failing of this son of a new Irish baron, I suppose you fancy I shall be obliged to give my hand to the eldest son of an English Baronet," said Anneke, smiling so as to take off the edge of a little irony that I fancied just glimmered in her manner.

"I wish to Heaven you *would*, Anne Mordaunt," whispered Bulstrode, loud enough for me to hear him, "so that the heart were its companion!"

I thought this both bold and decided, and I looked anxiously at Anneke to note the effect, but she evidently received it as trifling, certainly betraying no emotion at a speech I thought so pointed. I wished she had manifested a little resentment. Then she was so very young to be thus importuned!

"Dinner had better be served, sir," she calmly observed to her father. "Mr. Harris is apt to think himself ill-treated, if he do not find everybody at table. It would be a sign his watch was wrong, and that he had come half an hour too soon."

Herman Mordaunt nodded assent, and left his daughter's side to give the necessary order.

"I fancy Harris will regret this," said Bulstrode. "I wish I dared repeat what he had the temerity to say to me on this very subject, no later than yesterday."

"Of the propriety of so doing, Mr. Bulstrode must judge for himself, though *repetitions* of this nature, are usually best avoided."

"No, the fellow deserves it, so I will just tell you and Mr. Little-page in confidence. You must know, as his senior in years, and his senior officer, in the bargain, I was hinting to Harris the inexpediency of always being so late at dinner, and here is my gentleman's answer—'You know,' said he, 'that excepting my lord Loudon, the commander in chief, the Governor and a few public officers, I shall now take precedence of almost every man here, and I find, if I go early to dinner, I shall have to hand in all the elderly ladies, and to take my place at *their* sides, whereas, if I go a little late, I can steal in alongside of their daughters.' Now, on the present occasion, he will be altogether a loser, the lady of the house not yet being quite fifty."

"I had not given Mr. Harris credit for so much ingenuity," said Anneke, quietly. "But here he is to claim his rights."

"Ay, the fellow has remembered *your* age, and quite likely your *attractions!*"

Dinner was announced, at that instant, and all eyes were turned on Harris, in expectation that he would advance to lead Anneke down stairs. The young man, even more youthful than myself, had a good deal of *mauvaise honte*, for though the son of an Irish peer, of two months' creation, the family was not strictly Irish, and he had very little ambition to figure in this manner. From what I saw of him subsequently, I do believe that nothing but a sense of duty to his order, made him respect these privileges of rank at all, and that he would really just as soon go to a dinner table last, as first. In the present case, however, he was soon relieved by Herman Mordaunt, who had been educated at home, and understood the usages of the world very well.

"Gentlemen," he said, "I must ask you to waive the privileges of rank in favour of Mr. Cornelius Littlepage, to-day. This good company has met to do honour especially to his courage and devotion to his fellow creatures, and he will do me the favour to hand Miss Mordaunt down stairs."

Herman Mordaunt then pointed out to the Hon. Mr. Harris, the next lady of importance, and to Mr. Bulstrode a third; after which all the rest took care of themselves. As for myself, I felt my face in a glow, at this unexpected order, and scarcely dared to look at Anneke as we led the way to the dining room door. So much abashed was I, that I scarce touched the tips of her slender little fingers, and a tremor was in the limb that performed this office, the whole time it was thus employed. Of course, my seat was next to that of the young and lovely mistress of the house, at this banquet.

What shall I say of the dinner? It was the very first entertainment of the sort, at which I had ever been present, though I had acquired some of the notions of town habits, on such occasions, at my aunt Legge's table. To my surprise, there was soup, a dish that I never saw at Satanstoe, except in the most familiar way, while here it was taken by every one, seemingly as a matter of course. Every thing was elegant, and admirably cooked. Abundance, however, was the great feature of the feast, as I have heard it said is apt to be the case with most New York entertainments. Nevertheless, I have always understood that, in the way of eating and drinking, the American colonies have little reason to be ashamed.

"Could I have foreseen this dinner, Miss Mordaunt," I said, when everybody was employed, and I thought there was an opening to say something to my beautiful neighbor; "it would have made my father very happy to have sent a sheep's head to town, for the occasion."

Anneke thanked me, and then we began to converse about the game. Westchester was, and is still, famous for partridges, snipe, quails, ducks and meadow-larks, and I understood expatiating on such a subject, as well as the best of them. All the Littlepages were shots, and I have known my father bag ten brace of woodcock, among the wet thickets of Satanstoe, of a morning; and this with merely a second class dog, and only one. Both Bulstrode and Harris listened to what I said on this subject, with great attention, and it would soon have been the engrossing discourse, had not Anneke pleasantly said—

"All very well, gentlemen; but you will remember that neither Miss Wallace, nor I, shoot."

"Except with the arrows of Cupid," answered Bulstrode, gaily; "with these you do so much execution, *between you*," emphasizing the words, so as to make me look foolish, for I sat between them, "that you ought to be condemned to hear nothing but fowling conversation, for the next year."

This produced a laugh, a little at my expense I believe, though I could see that Anneke blushed, while Mary Wallace smiled indifferently, but as the healths now began, there was a truce to trifling. And a serious thing it is, to drink to everybody by name, at a large table; serious I mean to a new beginner. Yet, Herman Mordaunt went through it with a grace and dignity, that I think would have been remarked at a royal banquet. The ladies acquitted themselves admirably, omitting no one, and even Harris felt the necessity of being particular with this indispensable part of good breeding. So well done was this part of the ceremony, that I declare I believe everybody had drunk to everybody within five minutes after Herman Mordaunt commenced, and it was very apparent that there was more ease and true gaiety *after* all had got through, than there had previously been.

But the happy period of every dinner party, is after the cloth is removed. With the dark polished mahogany for a background, the sparkling decanters making their rounds, the fruit and cake-baskets, the very scene seems to inspire one with a wish for gaiety. Herman Mordaunt called for toasts, as soon as the cloth disappeared, with a view I believe of putting everybody at ease, and to render the conversation more general. He was desired to set the example, and immediately gave, "Miss Markham," who, as I was told, was a single lady of forty, with whom he had carried on a little flirtation. Anneke's turn came next, and she chose to give a sentiment, notwithstanding all Bulstrode's remonstrances, who insisted on a gentleman. He did not succeed, however; Anneke very steadily gave "The Thespian corps of the ———th; may it prove as successful in the arts of peace, as, in its military character, it has often proved itself to be, in the art of war." Much applause followed this toast, and Harris was persuaded by Bulstrode to stand up, and say a few words, for the credit of the regiment. Such a speech!—It reminded me of the horse that was advertised as a show, in London, about this time, and which was said 'to have its tail where its head ought to be.' But, Bulstrode clapped his hands, and cried 'hear,' at every other word, protesting that the regiment was honoured as much in the thanks, as in the sentiment. Harris did not seem displeased with his own effort, and, presuming on his rank, he drank without being called on, "to the fair of New York; eminent alike for beauty, and wit, may they only become as merciful as they are victorious!"

"Bravo!" again cried Bulstrode—"Harris is fairly inspired, and is growing better and better. Had he said imminent, instead of eminent, it would be more accurate, as their frowns are as threatening, as their smiles are bewitching."

"Is that to pass for *your* sentiment, Mr. Bulstrode, and are we to drink it?" demanded Herman Mordaunt.

"By no means sir; I have the honor to give Lady Dolly Merton."

Who Lady Dolly was, nobody knew, I believe, though we of the colonies always drank a titled person, who was known to be at home, with a great deal of respectful attention, not to say veneration. Other toasts followed, and then the ladies were asked to sing. Anneke complied, with very little urging, as became her position, and never did I hear sweeter strains than those she poured forth! The air was simple, but melody itself, and the sentiment had just enough of the engrossing feeling of woman in it, to render it interesting, without in the slightest degree impairing its fitness for the virgin lips from which it issued. Bulstrode, I could see, was actually entranced; and I heard him murmur "an angel, by Heavens!" He sang, himself, a love song, full of delicacy and feeling, and in a way to show that he had paid much attention to the art of music. Harris sang, too, as did Mary Wallace; the former, much as he spoke; the last plaintively, and decidedly well. Even Herman Mordaunt gave us a strain, and my turn followed. Singing was somewhat of a *forte* with me, and I have reason to think I made out quite as well as the best of them. I know that Anneke seemed pleased, and I saw tears in her eyes, as I concluded a song that was intended to produce just such an effect.

At length, the youthful mistress of the house arose, reminding her father that he had at table the principal performer of the evening, by way of a caution, when three or four of us handed the ladies to the drawing room door. Instead of returning to the table, I entered the room, and Bulstrode did the same, under the plea of its being necessary for him to drink no more, on account of the work before him.

Chapter VIII

"God's bodkin, man, much better: use
every man after his desert, and who shall 'scape
whipping? Use them after your own honour
and dignity: the less they deserve, the more
merit is in your bounty."

Hamlet, II. ii. 529–532.

"HARRIS will be *hors de combat*," Bulstrode soon observed, "unless I can manage to get him from the table. You know he is to play Marcia this evening; and, though a *little* wine will give him fire and spirit for the part, too much will impair its feminine beauties. Addison never intended that 'the virtuous Marcia,' in towering above her sex, was to be picked out of a kennel, or from under a table. Harris is a true Irish peer, when claret is concerned."

All the ladies held up their hands, and protested against Mr. Harris' being permitted to act a travestie on their sex. As yet, no one had known how the characters were to be cast beyond the fact that Bulstrode himself was to play Cato, for great care had been taken to keep the bills of the night from being seen, in order that the audience might have the satisfaction of finding out, who was who, for themselves. At the close of each piece a bill was to be sent round, among the favoured few, telling the truth. As Anneke declared that her father never locked in his guests, and had faithfully promised to bring up everybody for coffee, in the course of half an hour, it was determined to let things take their own way.

Sure enough, at the end of the time mentioned, Herman Mordaunt appeared, with all the men, from the table. Harris was not tipsy, as I found was very apt to be the case with him, after dinner, but neither was he sober. According to Bulstrode's notion, he may have had just fire enough to play the 'virtuous Marcia.' In a few minutes, he hurried the ensign off, declaring that, like Hamlet's ghost, their hour had come. At seven, the whole party left the house in a body, to walk to the theatre. Herman Mordaunt did not keep a proper town equipage, and, if he had, it would not have contained a fourth of our company. In this, however, we were not singular, as nine in ten of the audience that night, I mean nine in ten of the gentle sex, went to the theatre on foot.

Instead of going directly down Crown Street, into Maiden Lane, which would have been the nearest way to the theatre, we went out into Broadway, and round by Wall Street, the walking being better, and the gutters farther from the ladies; the centre of the street being at no great distance from the houses, in the narrower passages of the town. We found a great many well dressed people moving in the same direction with ourselves. Herman Mordaunt remarked that he had never before seen so many hoops, cardinals, cocked hats and swords in the streets at once, as he saw that evening. All the carriages in town rolled past us, as we went down Wall Street, and by the time we reached William Street, the pavements resembled a procession, more than any thing else. As every one was in full dress, the effect was pleasing, and the evening being fine, most of the gentlemen carried their hats in their hands, in order not to disturb their curls, thus giving to the whole the air of a sort of vast drawing room. I never saw a more lovely creature, than Anneke Mordaunt appeared, as she led our party, on this occasion. The powder had got a little out of her fine auburn hair, and on the part of the head that was not concealed by a cap that shaded half her beautiful face, it seemed as if the rich covering bestowed by nature was about to break out of all restraint, and shade her bust with its exuberance. Her negligée was a rich satin, flounced in front, while the lace that dropped from her elbows seemed as if woven by fairies, expressly for a fairy to wear. She had paste buckles in her shoes, and I thought I had never beheld such a foot, as was occasionally seen peeping from beneath her dress, while she walked daintily, yet, with the grace of a queen at my side. I do not thus describe Anneke, with a view of inducing the reader to fancy her stately and repulsive; on the contrary, winning ease and natural grace were just as striking in her manner, as were beauty, and sentiment, and feeling in her countenance. More than once, as we walked side by side, did I become painfully conscious how unworthy I was to fill the place I occupied. I believe this humility is one of the surest signs of sincere love.

At length we reached the theatre, and were permitted to enter.

All the front seats were occupied by blacks, principally in New York liveries; that is to say, with cuffs, collars and pocket flaps of a cloth different from the coat, though a few were in lace. These last belonged to the topping families, several of which gave colours and ornaments, almost as rich as those that I understand are constantly given at home. I well remember that two entire boxes were retained by servants, in shoulder knots, and much richer dresses than common, one of whom belonged to the Lt. Governor, and the other to my Lord Loudon, who was then commander in chief. As the company entered, these domestics disappeared, as is usual, and we all took our seats on the benches thus retained for us. Bulstrode's care was apparent in the manner in which he had provided for Anneke, and her party, which, I will take it on myself to say, was one of the most striking for youth and good looks, that entered the house that evening.

Great was the curiosity, and deep the feeling that prevailed among the younger portion of the audience in particular, as party after party was seated, that important evening. The house was ornamented as a theatre, and I thought it vast in extent, though Herman Mordaunt assured me it was no great thing, in that point of view, as compared with most of the playhouses at home. But the ornaments, and the lights, and the curtain, the pit, the boxes, the gallery, were all so many objects of intense interest. Few of us said any thing, but our eyes wandered over all with a species of delight that I am certain can be felt in a theatre only once. Anneke's sweet face was a picture of youthful expectation; an expectation, however, in which intelligence and discretion had their full share. The orchestra was said to have an undue portion of wind instruments in it, though I perceived ladies all over the house, including those in our own box, returning the bows of many of the musicians, who I was told were *amateurs* from the army, and the drawing rooms of the town.

At length the Commander in Chief and the Lt. Governor entered together, occupying the same box, though two had been provided, their attendants having recourse to the second. The commotion produced by these arrivals had hardly subsided, when the curtain arose, and a new world was presented to our view! Of the playing, I shall not venture to say much, though to me it seemed perfection. Bulstrode gained great applause that night, and I understand that divers gentlemen, who had either been educated at home, or who had passed much time there, declared that his Cato would have done credit to either of the Royal Theatres. His dress appeared to me to be every thing it should be, though I can not describe it. I remember that Syphax wore the uniform of a Colonel of Dragoons, and Juba that of a General Officer, and that there was a good deal of criticism expended, and some offence taken, because the gentlemen who played these parts, came out in wool and with their faces blacked. It was said in answer to these feelings, that the characters were Africans, and that any one might see, by casting his eyes at the gallery, that Africans are usually black and that they have woolly hair; a sort of proof that I imagine only aggravated the offence.* Apart from this little mistake, every thing went off well, even to Harris's Marcia. It is true, that some evil inclined persons whispered that the "virtuous Marcia" was a little how-came-you-so, but Bulstrode afterwards assured me that his condition helped him along amazingly, and that it added a liquid lustre to his eyes, that might otherwise have been wanting. The high-heeled shoes appeared to trouble him; but some persons fancied it gave him a pretty tottering in his walk, that added very much to the deception. On the whole, the piece went off surprisingly, as I could see by Lord Loudon and the Lt. Governor both of whom seemed infinitely diverted. Herman Mordaunt smiled, once or twice, when he ought to have looked grave, but this I ascribed to a want of practice, of late years, in scenic representations. He certainly was a man of judgment, and must have known the proper moments to exhibit particular emotions.

During the interval between the play and the farce, the actors came among us, to receive the homage they merited, and loud were the plaudits that were bestowed on them. Anneke's bright eyes sparkled with pleasure as she admitted, without reserve, to Bulstrode the pleasure she had received, and confessed she had formed no idea, hitherto, of the beauty and power of a theatrical representation, aided as was this, by the auxiliaries of lights, dress and scenery. It is true, the women had been a little absurd, and the "virtuous Marcia" particularly so, but the fine sentiments

*In England, Othello is usually played as a black, while in America he is played as a nondescript; or of no colour that is ordinarily seen. It is not clear that England is nearer right than America, however, the Moor not being a negro, any more than he is of the colour of a dried herring.—EDITOR.

of Addison, which, though as Herman Mordaunt observed, they had all the accuracy and all the stiffness of a pedantic age, were sufficiently beautiful and just, to cover the delinquencies of the Hon. Mr. Harris. She hoped the after piece would be of the same general character, that they might all enjoy it, as much as they had the play, itself.

The other young ladies were equally decided in their praise, though it struck me that Anneke *felt* the most, on the occasion. That the Major had obtained a great advantage by his efforts, I could not but see, and the folly of my having any pretensions with one who was courted by such a rival, began to impress itself on my imagination with a force I found painful. But the bell soon summoned away the gallant actors, in order to dress for the farce.

The long interval that occurred between the two pieces, gave ample opportunity for visiting one's acquaintances, and to compare opinions. I went to my aunt's box, and found her well satisfied, though less animated than the younger ladies, in the expression of her pleasure. My uncle was altogether himself; good natured, but not disposed to award any indiscreet amount of praise.

"Pretty well for boys, Corny," he said, "though the youngster who acted Marcia had better been at school. I do not know his name, but he completely took all the virtue out of Marcia. He must have studied her character from some of the ladies who follow the camp."

"My dear uncle, how differently you think from all in our box! That gentleman is the Hon. Mr. Harris, who is only eighteen, and has a pair of colours in the ——th, and is a son of Lord Ballybannon, or Bally something else, and is said to have the softest voice in the army!"

"Ay, and the softest head, too, I'll answer for it. I tell you, Corny, the Hon. Mr. Ballybilly, who is only eighteen, and has a pair of colours in the ——th, and the softest voice in the army, had better been at school, instead of undermining the virtue of the 'virtuous Marcia,' as he has so obviously done. Bulstrode did well enough; capitally well, for an amateur, and must be a first-rate fellow. By the way, Jane"—that was my aunt's name—"they tell me, he is likely to marry that exceedingly pretty daughter of Herman Mordaunt's, and make her Lady Bulstrode one of these days."

"Why not, Mr. Legge?—Anne Mordaunt is as sweet a girl as there is in the colony, and is very respectably connected. They even say the Mordaunts are of a high family at home. Mary Wallace told me that Herman Mordaunt and Sir Henry Bulstrode are themselves related, and you know, my dear, how intimate the Mordaunts and the Wallaces are?"

"Not I; I know nothing of their intimacies, though I dare say it may be all true. Mordaunt's father was an English gentleman of some family, I have always heard, though he was as poor as a church mouse, when he married one of our Dutch heiresses; and as for Herman Mordaunt himself, he proved he had not lost the instinct by marrying another, though she did not happen to be Dutch. Here comes Anneke to inherit it all, and I'll answer for it that care is had that she shall marry an heir."

"Well, Mr. Bulstrode is an heir, and the eldest son of a baronet. I am always pleased when one of our girls makes a good connection at home, for it does the colony credit. It is an excellent thing, Corny, to have our interest well sustained at home—especially before the Privy Council, they tell me."

"Well, I am not," answered my uncle. "I think it more to the credit of the colony for its young women to take up with its young men, and its young men with its young women. I wish Anne Mordaunt had been substituted for the Hon. Ballyshannon to-night. She would have made a thousand times better 'virtuous Marcia.'"

"You surely would not have had a young lady, of respectability, appear in public, in this way, Mr. Legge."

My uncle said something to this, for he seldom let "Jane" get the better of it for want of an answer, but as I left the box, I did not hear his reply. It seemed then to be settled, in the minds of most persons, that Bulstrode was to marry Anneke! I cannot describe the new shock this opinion gave me, but it served to make me more fully sensible of the depth of the impression that had been made on myself, in the intercourse of a single week. The effect was such that I did not return to the party I had left, but sought a seat in a distant part of the theatre, though one in which I could distinctly see those I had abandoned.

The Beaux Stratagem soon commenced, and Bulstrode was again seen in the character of Scrub. Those who were most familiar with the stage, pronounced his playing to be excellent;—far better in the footman, than in the Roman Senator. The play, it-self, struck me as being as broad and coarse as could be tolerated, but, as it had a reputation at home, where it had a great name, our matrons did not dare to object to it. I was glad to see the smiles soon disappear from Anneke's face, however, and to dis-cover that *she* found no pleasure in scenes so unsuited to her sex and years. The short, quick glances that were exchanged between Anneke and Mary Wallace, did not escape me, and the manner in which they both rose, as soon as the curtain dropped, told quite plainly the haste they were in to quit the theatre. I reached their box door, in time to assist them through the crowd.

Not a word was said by any of us, until we reached the street, where two or three of Miss Mordaunt's female friends became loud in the expression of their satisfaction. Neither Anneke, nor Mary Wallace said any thing, and so well did I understand the na-ture of their feelings, that I made no allusion whatever to the farce. As for the others, they did but chime in with what ap-peared to be the common opinion, and were to be pitied rather than condemned. It was perhaps the more excusable in them to imagine such a play right, inasmuch as they must have known it was much extolled at home, a fact that gave any custom a certain privilege in the Colonies. A mother country, has much of the same responsibility as a natural mother, herself, since its opin-ions and example are apt to be quoted in the one case by the de-pendant, in justification of its own opinions and conduct, as it is by the natural offspring in the other. I fancy, notwithstanding, this sort of responsibility gives the ministers or people of Eng-land very little trouble, since I never could discover any sensitive-ness to their duties on this score.

We all went in at Herman Mordaunt's, after walking to the house as we had walked from it, and were made to take a light supper, including some delicious chocolate. Just as we sat down to table, Bulstrode joined us, to receive the praises he had earned, and to enjoy his triumph. He got a seat directly opposite to mine, on Anneke's left hand, and soon began to converse.

"In the first place," he cried, "you must all admit that Tom Har-ris did wonders to-night as Miss Marcia Cato. I had my own trou-ble with the rogue, for there is no precedent for a tipsy Marcia, but we managed to keep him straight, and that was the nicest part of my management, let me assure you."

"Yes," observed Herman Mordaunt, drily; "I should think keeping Tom Harris straight after dinner, an exploit of no little difficulty, but a task that would demand a very judicious management, indeed."

"You were pleased to express your satisfaction with the performance of Cato, Miss Mordaunt," said Bulstrode, in a very deferential and solicitous manner, "but I question if the entertainment gave you as much pleasure?"

"It certainly did not. Had the representation ended with the first piece, I am afraid I should too much regret that we are without a regular stage; but, the farce will take off much of the keenness of such regrets."

"I fear I understand you, cousin Anne, and greatly regret that we did not make another choice," returned Bulstrode, with a humility that was not usual in his manner, even when addressing Anneke Mordaunt; "but, I can assure you the play has great vogue at home, and the character of Scrub in particular, has usually been a prodigious favourite. I see by your look, however, that enough has been said, but after having done so much to amuse this good company, to-night, I shall feel authorised to call on every lady present, at least for a song, as soon as the proper moment arrives. Perhaps I have a right to add a sentiment, and a toast."

And songs and toasts, and sentiments, we had as usual, the moment we had done eating. It was, and indeed *is*, rather more usual to indulge in this innocent gaiety after supper, than after dinner with us, and that night everybody entered into the feeling of the moment, with spirit. Herman Mordaunt gave "Miss Markham," as he had done at dinner, and this with an air so determined, as to prove no one else would ever be got out of *him*.

"There is a compact between Miss Markham and myself, to toast each other, for the remainder of our lives," cried the master of the house, laughing, "and we are each too honest ever to violate it."

"But, Miss Mordaunt is under no such engagement," put in a certain Mr. Benson, who had manifested much interest in the beautiful young mistress of the house throughout the day, "and I trust we shall not be put off by any such excuse from her."

"It is not in rule to ask two of the same race for toasts in succession," answered Herman Mordaunt. "There is Mr. Bulstrode dying to give us another English belle."

"With all my heart," said Bulstrode, gaily. "This time it shall be Lady Betty Boddington."

"Married, or single, Bulstrode?" enquired Billings, as I thought with some little point.

"No matter which; so long as she be a beauty and a toast. I believe it is now my privilege to call on a lady, and I beg a gentleman from Miss Wallace."

There had been an expression of pained surprise, at the trifling between Billings and Bulstrode, in Anneke's sweet countenance, for, in the simplicity of our provincial habits, we of the colonies did not think it exactly in rule for the single to toast the married, or *vice versa*; but the instant her friend was thus called on, it changed for a look of gentle concern. Mary Wallace manifested no concern, however, but gave "Mr. Francis Fordham."

"Ay, Frank Fordham, with all my heart," cried Herman Mordaunt; "I hope he will return to his native country as straight-forward, honest, and good as he left it."

"Mr. Fordham is then abroad?" inquired Bulstrode—"I thought the name new to me."

"If being at home, can be called being abroad. He is reading law at the Temple."

This was the answer of Mary Wallace, who looked as if she felt a friendly interest in the young Templar, but no more. She now called on Dirck for his lady. Throughout the whole of that day, Dirck's voice had hardly been heard; a reserve that comported well enough with his youth and established diffidence. This appeal, however, seemed suddenly to arouse all that there was of manhood in him, and that was not a little, I can tell the reader, when there was occasion to use it. Dirck's nature was honesty itself, and he felt that the appeal was too direct, and the occasion too serious, to admit of duplicity. He loved but one, esteemed but one, felt for one only; and it was not in his nature to cover his preference by any attempt at deception. After colouring to the ears, appearing distressed, he made an effort, and pronounced the name of—"Anneke Mordaunt."

A common laugh rewarded this blunder; common with all but the fair creature, who had extorted this involuntary tribute, and myself, who knew Dirck's character too well not to understand how very much he must be in earnest thus to lay bare the most cherished secret of his heart. The mirth continued some time,

Herman Mordaunt appearing to be particularly pleased, and applauding his kinsman's directness, with several 'bravos' very distinctly uttered. As for Anneke, I saw she looked touched, while she looked concerned, and as if she would be glad to have the thing undone.

"After all, Dirck, much as I admire your spirit and plain dealing, boy," cried Herman Mordaunt, "Miss Wallace can never let such a toast pass. She will insist on having another."

"I!—I protest I am well pleased with it, and ask for no other—" exclaimed the lady in question. "No toast can be more agreeable to me than Anneke Mordaunt, and I particularly like the quarter from which this comes."

"If friends can be trusted in a matter of this nature," put in Bulstrode, with a little pique, "Mr. Follock has every reason to be contented. Had I known, however, that the customs of New York allowed a lady who is present to be toasted, that gentleman would not have had the merit of being the first to make this discovery."

"Nor is it;" said Herman Mordaunt, "and Dirck must hunt up another, to supply my daughter's place."

But no other was forth-coming from the stores of Dirck Follock's mind. Had he a dozen names in reserve, not one of them would he have produced under circumstances that might seem like denying his allegiance to the girl already given, but he *could* not name any other female. So, after some trifling, the company attributing Dirck's hesitation to his youth and ignorance of the world, abandoned the attempt, desiring him to call on Anneke, herself, for a toast in turn.

"*Cousin* Dirck Van Valkenburgh," said Anneke, with the greater self-possession and ease of her sex, though actually my friend's junior by more than two years; laying some emphasis, at the same time, on the word *cousin*.

"There!" exclaimed Dirck, looking exultingly at Bulstrode; "you see, gentlemen and ladies, that *it* is permitted to toast a person present, if you happen to respect and esteem that person!"

"By which, sir, we are to understand how much Miss Mordaunt respects and esteems Mr. Dirck Van Valkenburgh," answered Bulstrode, gravely. "I am afraid there is only too much justice in an opinion that might, at the first blush, seem to savour of self-love."

"An imputation I am far from denying," returned Anneke,

with a steadiness that showed wonderful self-command, did she really return any of Dirck's attachment. "My kinsman gives me as his toast, and I give him as mine. Is there any thing unnatural in that?"

Here, there was an outbreak of raillery, at Anneke's expense, which the young lady bore with a calmness and composure that at first astonished me. But, when I came to reflect that she had been virtually at the head of her father's house, for several years, and that she had always associated with persons older than herself, it appeared more natural; for, it is certain we can either advance or retard the character, by throwing a person into intimate association with those who, by their own conversation, manners, or acquirements are most adapted for doing either. In a few minutes, the interruption was forgotten by those who had no interest in the subject, and the singing commenced. I had obtained so much credit by my attempt at dinner, that I had the extreme gratification of being asked to sing another song, by Anneke, herself. Of course I complied, and I thought the company seemed pleased. As for my young hostess, I knew she looked more gratified with my song, than with the after piece, and that I felt to be something. Dirck had an occasion to recover a little of the ground lost by the toast, for he sang a capital comic song, in Low Dutch. It is true, not half the party understood him, but the other half laughed until the tears rolled down their cheeks, and there was something so droll in my friend's manner, that everybody was delighted. The clocks struck twelve before we broke up.

I staid in town, but a day or two longer, meeting my new acquaintances every day, and sometimes twice a day, however, on Trinity Church Walk. I paid visits of leave-taking, with a heavy heart, and most of all to Anneke and her father.

"I understood from Follock," said Herman Mordaunt, when I explained the object of my call, "that you are to leave town tomorrow. Miss Mordaunt, and her friend Miss Wallace, go to Lilacsbush, this afternoon; for it is high time to look after the garden and the flowers, many of which are now in full bloom. I shall join them in the evening, and I propose that you young men take a late breakfast with us, on your way to Westchester. A cup of coffee before you start, and getting into your saddle at six, will bring all right. I promise you, that you shall be on the road again by one, which will give you plenty of time to reach Satanstoe before dark."

I looked at Anneke, and fancied that the expression of her countenance was favourable. Dirck left every thing to me, and I accepted the invitation. This arrangement shortened my visit in Crown Street, and I left the house with a lighter heart than that with which I had entered it. It is always so agreeable to get an unpleasant duty deferred!

Next day, Dirck and I were in the saddle at six precisely, and we rode through the streets just as the blacks were washing down their stoops and side walks, though there were but very few of the last, in my youth. This is a commodious improvement, and one that it is not easy to see how the ladies could dispense with, and which is now getting to be pretty common, all the new streets, I see, being provided with the convenience.

It was a fine May morning, and the air was full of the sweet fragrance of the lilacs, in particular, as we rode into the country. Just as we got into the Bowery Lane, a horseman was seen walking out of one of the by streets, and coming our way. He no sooner caught sight of two travellers going in his own direction, than he spurred forward to join us, being alone, and probably wishing company. As it would have been churlish to refuse to travel in company with one thus situated we pulled up, walking our horses until the stranger joined us, when to our surprise it turned out to be Jason Newcome. The pedagogue was as much astonished when he recognised us, as we were in recognising him, and I believe he was a little disappointed; for, Jason was so fond of making acquaintances, that it was always a pleasure to him to be thus employed. It appeared that he had been down on the island, to visit a relative, who had married and settled in that quarter, and this was the reason we had not met since the morning of the affair of the lion. Of course we trotted on together, neither glad nor sorry, at having this particular companion.

I never could explain the process by means of which Jason wormed his way into everybody's secrets. It is true, he had no scruples about asking questions, putting those which most persons would think forbidden by the usages of society, with as little hesitation as those which are universally permitted. The people of New England have a reputation this way, and I remember to have heard Mr. Worden account for the practice in the following way. Every thing, and everybody was brought under rigid church government among the puritans, and, when a whole community gets the notion that it is to sit in judgment on every act of one of its members, it is quite natural that it should extend that right to an enquiry into all his affairs. One thing is certain; our neighbours of Connecticut do assume a control over the acts and opinions of individuals, that is not dreamed of in New York, and I think it very likely that the practice of pushing inquiry into private things, has grown up under this custom.

As one might suppose, Jason, whenever baffled in an attempt to obtain knowledge by means of inquiries, more or less direct, sought to advance his ends through conjectures; taking those that were the most plausible, if any such could be found, but putting up with those that had not even this questionable recommendation, if nothing better offered. He was, consequently, for ever falling into the grossest errors, for, necessarily making his conclusions on premises drawn from his own ignorance and inexperience, he was liable to fall into serious mistakes at the very outset. Nor was this the worst; the tendency of human nature not being very directly to charity, the harshest constructions were sometimes blended with the most absurd blunders, in his mind, and I have known him to be often guilty of assertions, that had no better foundation than these conjectures, which might have subjected him to severe legal penalties.

On the present occasion, Jason was not long in ascertaining where we were bound. This was done in a manner so characteristic and ingenious, that I will attempt to relate it.

"Why you're out early, this morning, gentlemen!" exclaimed Jason, affecting surprise. "What in natur' has started you off before breakfast?"

"So as to be certain not to lose our suppers at Satanstoe, this evening," I answered.

"Suppers? why you will almost reach home (Jason *would* call this word *hum*) by dinner time; that is your York dinner time. Perhaps you mean to call by the way?"

"Perhaps we do, Mr. Newcome; there are many pleasant families between this and Satanstoe."

"I know there be. There's the great Mr. Van Cortlandt's at Yonker's; perhaps you mean to stop there."

"No sir, we have no such intention."

"Then, there's the rich Count Philipse's, on the river; that would be no great matter out of the way?"

"It's farther than we intend to turn."

"Oh! so you *do* intend to turn a bit aside! Well, there's that Mr. Mordaunt, whose daughter you pulled out of the lion's paws;—he has a house near Kingsbridge, called Lilacsbush."

"And, how did you ascertain that, Jason?"

"By asking. Do you think I would let such a thing happen, and not enquire a little about the young lady? Nothing is ever lost by putting a few questions, and inquiring round, and I did not forget the rule in her case."

"And you ascertained that the young lady's father has a place called Lilacsbush, in this neighbourhood?"

"I did; and a queer York fashion it is to give a house a name, just as you would a Christian being; that must be a Roman Catholic custom, and some way connected with idolatry."

"Out of all doubt. It is far better to say, for instance, that we are going to breakfast at Mr. Mordaunt's-es-es—than to say we intend to stop at Lilacsbush."

"Oh! you be, be you? Well, I thought it would turn out that some such place must have started you off so early. It will be a desperate late breakfast, Corny!"

"It will be at ten o'clock, Jason, and that is rather later than common; but our appetites will be so much the better."

To this Jason assented, and then commenced a series of manoeuvres to be included in the party. This we did not dare to do, however, and all Jason's hints were disregarded; until, growing desperate by our evasions, he plumply proposed to go along, and we as plumply told him we would take no such liberty with a man of Herman Mordaunt's years, position and character. I do not know that we should have hesitated so much had we considered Jason a gentleman, but this was impossible. The custom of the Colony admitted of great freedom in this respect, being very different from what it is at home, by all accounts, in these particulars, but there was always an understanding that the persons one brought with him should be of a certain stamp and class in life; recommendations to which Jason Newcome certainly had no claim.

The case was getting to be a little embarrassing, when the appearance of Herman Mordaunt himself, fortunately removed the difficulty. Jason was not a man to be thrown off, very easily, but here was one who had the power, and who showed the disposition to set things right. Herman Mordaunt had ridden down the road a mile or two to meet us, intending to lead us by a private and shorter way to his residence, than that which was already known to us. He no sooner saw that Jason was of our company, than he asked that as a favor, which our companion would very gladly have accepted as a boon.

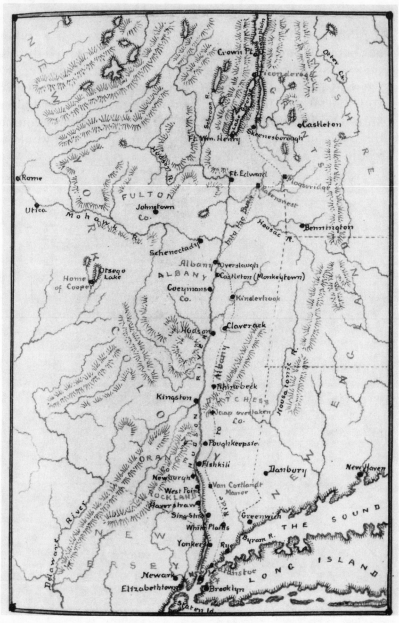

I. T. Chalkley Matlack's map of the Hudson River Valley showing real and imaginary routes and places associated with the action of *Satanstoe*.

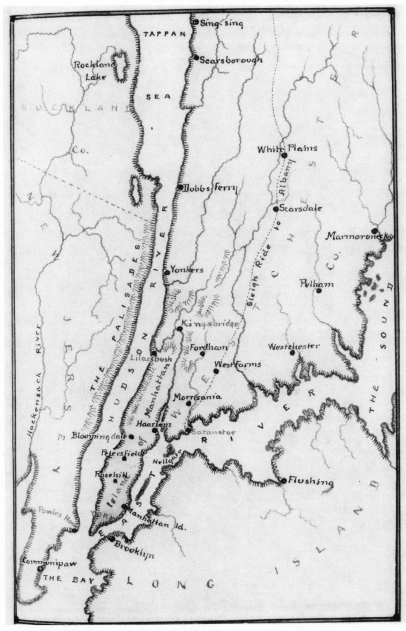

II. Matlack's map of Westchester county and the setting for the early chapters.

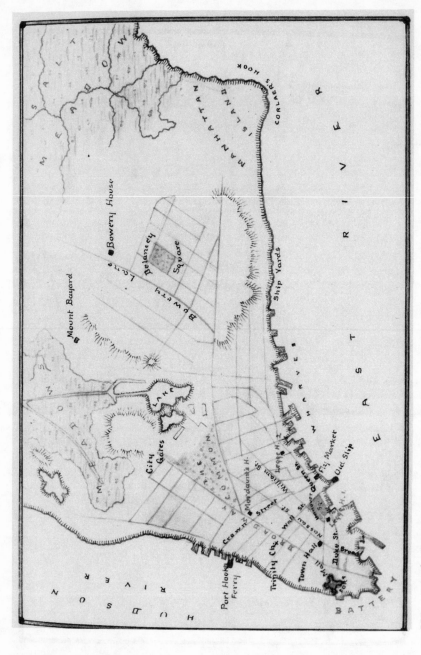

III. Matlack's map of old New York, setting for much of the first nine chapters.

IV.   A view of the Palisades from a photograph in the Matlack manuscript.

Chapter IX

"I question'd love, whose early ray
So heavenly bright appears;
And love, in answer, seem'd to say,
His light was dimm'd by tears."
                    Reginald Heber, "Happiness," ll. 17–20.

I T was not long after the explanation occurred as respects Jason, and the invitation was given to include him in our party, before Herman Mordaunt opened a gate, and led the way into the fields. A very tolerable road conducted us, through some woods, to the heights, and we soon found ourselves on an eminence, that overlooked a long reach of the Hudson, extending from Haverstraw to the north, as far as Staten Island to the south; a distance of near forty miles. On the opposite shore, rose the wall-like barrier of the Palisadoes, lifting the table land on their summits to an elevation of several hundred feet. The noble river, itself, fully three-quarters of a mile in width, was unruffled by a breath of air, lying in one single, extended, placid sheet, under the rays of a bright sun, resembling molten silver. I scarce remember a lovelier morning, every thing appearing to harmonize with the glorious but tranquil grandeur of the view, and the rich promises of a bountiful nature. The trees were mostly covered with a beautiful clothing of a young verdure, the birds had mated, and were building in nearly every tree, the wild flowers started up beneath the hoofs of our horses, and every object, far and near, seemed to my young eyes to be attuned to harmony and love.

"This is a favorite ride of mine, in which Anneke often accompanies me," said Herman Mordaunt, as we gained the commanding eminence I have mentioned. "My daughter is a spirited horse-woman, and is often my companion in these morning rides. She and Mary Wallace should be somewhere on the hills, at this moment, for they promised to follow me, as soon as they could dress for the saddle."

A cry of something like wild delight burst out of Dirck, and, the next moment he was galloping away for an adjoining ridge, on the top of which the beautiful forms of the two girls were just then visible, embellished by neatly fitting habits, and beavers with drooping feathers. I pointed out these charming objects to Herman Mordaunt, and followed my friend, at half-speed. In a minute or two, the parties had joined.

Never had I seen Anneke Mordaunt so perfectly lovely, as she appeared that morning. The exercise and air had deepened a bloom that was always rich, and her eyes received new lustre from the glow on her cheeks. Though expected, I thought she received us as particularly acceptable guests, while Mary Wallace manifested more than an usual degree of animation, in her reception. Jason was not forgotten, but was acknowledged as an old acquaintance, and was properly introduced to the friend.

"You frequently take these rides, Mr. Mordaunt tells me," I said, reining my horse to the side of that of Anneke's, as the whole party moved on; "and I regret that Satanstoe is so distant, as to prevent our oftener meeting of a morning. We have many noted horse women in Westchester, who would be proud of such an acquisition."

"I know several ladies on your side of Harlem River," Anneke answered, "and frequently ride in their company, but none so distant as any in your immediate neighbourhood. My father tells me he used often to shoot over the fields of Satanstoe, when a youth, and still speaks of your birds with great affection."

"I believe our fathers were once brother sportsmen. Mr. Bulstrode has promised to come and imitate their good example. Now, you have had time to reflect on the plays you have seen, do you still feel the same interest in such representations as at first?"

"I only wish there was not so much to condemn. I think Mr. Bulstrode might have reached eminence as a player, had not fortune put it, in one sense, beyond his reach, as an elder son and a man of family."

"Mr. Bulstrode they tell me is not only the heir of an old baronetcy, but of a large fortune?"

"Such are the facts, I believe. Do you not think it creditable to him, Mr. Littlepage, that one so situated, should come so far to serve his king and country, in a rude war like this of our colonies?"

I was obliged to assent, though I heartily wished that Anneke's manner had been less animated and sincere, as she put the question. Still, I hardly knew what to think of her feelings towards that gentleman, for, otherwise, she always heard him named with a calmness and self-possession that I had observed was not shared by all her young companions, when there was occasion to allude to the gay and insinuating soldier. I need scarcely say it was no disadvantage to Mr. Bulstrode to be the heir of a baronetcy, in an English Colony. Somehow or other, we are a little apt to magnify such accidental superiority, at a distance from home, and I *have* heard Englishmen, themselves, acknowledge that a baronet was a greater man in New York, than a duke was in London. These were things, that passed through my mind, as I rode along at Anneke's side, though I had the discretion not to give utterance to my thoughts.

Herman Mordaunt rode in advance, with Jason, and he led the party, by pretty bridle-paths, along the heights, for nearly two miles, occasionally opening a gate, without dismounting, until he reached a point that overlooked Lilacsbush, which was soon seen, distant from us less than half a mile.

"Here we are, on my own domain," he said, as he pulled up to let us join him; "that last gate separating me from my nearest neighbor south. These hills are of no great use, except as early pastures, though they afford many beautiful views."

"I have heard it predicted," I remarked, "that the time would come, some day, when the banks of the Hudson would contain many such seats as that of the Philipses, at Yonkers, and one or two more like it, that I am told are now standing above the Highlands."

"Quite possibly; it is not easy to foretell what may come to pass in such a country. I dare say, that in time, both towns and seats will be seen on the banks of the Hudson, and a powerful and numerous nobility to occupy the last. By the way, Mr. Littlepage, your father and my friend Col. Follock have been making a valuable acquisition in lands, I hear; having obtained a patent for an extensive estate somewhere in the neighbourhood of Albany?"

"It is not so very extensive, sir, there being only some forty thousand acres of it, altogether; nor is it very near Albany, by what I can learn; since it must lie at a distance of some forty miles, or more, from that town. Next winter, however, Dirck and myself are to go in search of the land, when we shall learn all about it."

"Then we may meet in that quarter of the country. I have affairs of importance at Albany, which have been too long neglected, and it has been my intention to pass some months, at the north, next season, and early in the season, too. We may possibly meet in the woods."

"You have been at Albany, I suppose, Mr. Mordaunt?"

"Quite often, sir; the distance is so great that one has not much inducement to go there, unless carried by affairs; however, as has been my case. I was at Albany before my marriage, and have had various occasions to visit it since."

"My father was there, when a soldier, and he tells me it is a part of the province well worth seeing. At all events, I shall encounter the risk and fatigue next season, for it is useful to young persons to see the world. Dirck and myself may make the campaign, should there be one in that direction."

I fancied Anneke manifested some interest in this conversation, but we rode on, and soon alighted at the door of Lilacsbush. Bulstrode was not in the way, and I had the supreme pleasure of helping Miss Mordaunt to alight, when we paused a moment before entering the house, to examine the view. I have given the reader some idea of the general appearance of the place, but it was necessary to approach it, in order to form a just conception of its beauties. As its name indicated, the lawn, house, and out-buildings were all garnished, or buried in lilacs, the whole of which were then in full blossom. The flowers filled the air with a species of purple light, that cast a warm and soft radiance even on the glowing face of Anneke, as she pointed out to me the magical effect. I know no flower that does so much to embellish a place as the lilac, on a large scale, common as it is, and familiar as we have become with its hues and its fragrance.

"We enjoy the month our lilacs are out, beyond any month in the year," Anneke said, smiling at my surprise and delight, "and we make it a point to pass most of it, here. You will at least own, Mr. Littlepage, that Lilacsbush is properly named."

"The effect is more like enchantment than any thing else!" I cried. "I did not know that the simple, modest lilac could render any thing so very beautiful."

"Simplicity and modesty are such charms in themselves, sir, as to be potent allies," observed the sensible, but taciturn Mary Wallace.

To this I assented of course, and we all followed Mr. Mordaunt into the house. I was as much delighted with the appearance of things in the interior of Lilacsbush, as I had been with the exterior. Everywhere, it seemed to me, I met with the signs of Anneke's taste and skill. I do not wish the reader to suppose that the residence itself was of the very first character and class, for this it could not lay claim to be. Still it was one of those staid, story and a half dwellings, in which most of our first families were, and are content to dwell, in the country; very much resembling the good old habitation at Satanstoe, in these particulars. The furniture, however, was of a higher town-finish than we found it necessary to use, and the little parlour in which we breakfasted was a model for an eating room. The buffets in the corners were so well polished that one might see his face in them, the cellarets were ornamented with plated hinges, locks &c., and the table itself shone like a mirror. I know not how it was, but the china appeared to me richer and neater than common under Anneke's pretty little hand, while the massive and highly-finished plate of the breakfast service, was such as could be wrought only in England. In a word, while every thing appeared rich and respectable, there was a certain indescribable air of comfort, gentility and neatness about the whole, that impressed me in an unusual manner.

"Mr. Littlepage tells me, Anneke," observed Herman Mordaunt, while we were at breakfast, "that he intends to make a journey to the north, next winter, and it may be our good fortune to meet him there. The ——th expects to be ordered up as high as Albany, this summer, and we may all renew our songs and jests, with Bulstrode and his gay companions, among the Dutchmen."

I was charmed with this prospect of meeting Anneke Mordaunt at the north, and took occasion to say as much, though I was afraid it was in an awkward and confused manner.

"I heard as much as this, sir, while we were riding," answered the daughter. "I hope cousin Dirck is to be of the party?"

Cousin Dirck assured her he was, and we discussed, in anticipation, the pleasure it must give to old acquaintances to meet so far from home. Not one of us, Herman Mordaunt excepted, had ever been one hundred miles from his, or her birth place, as was ascertained on comparing notes. I was the greatest traveller, Princeton lying between eighty and ninety miles from Satanstoe, as the road goes.

"Perhaps I come nearer to it, than any of you," put in Jason, "for my late journey on the island must have carried me nearly that far from Danbury. But, ladies, I can assure you, a traveller has many opportunities for learning useful things, as I know by the difference there is between York and Connecticut."

"And which do you prefer, Mr. Newcome?" asked Anneke, with a somewhat comical expression about her laughing eyes.

"That is hardly a fair question, Miss—"no reproof could break Jason of this vulgarism—"since it might make enemies for a body to speak *all* of his mind in such matters. There are comparisons that should never be made, on account of circumstances that overrule all common efforts. Now, York is a great colony—a very great colony, Miss—but it was once Dutch, as everybody knows, begging Mr. Follock's pardon, and it must be confessed Connecticut has, from the first, enjoyed almost unheard of advantages, in the moral and religious character of her people, the excellence of her laws, and the purity—" Jason called this word "poority," but that did not alter the sentiment—though I must say, once for all, it is out of my power to spell every word as this man saw fit to pronounce it—"of her people and church."

Herman Mordaunt looked up with surprise, at this speech, but Dirck and I had heard so many like it, that we saw nothing out of the way on this particular occasion. As for the ladies, they were too well bred to glance at each other as girls sometimes will, but I could see that each thought the speaker a very singular person.

"You find, then, a difference in customs, between the two colonies, sir?" said Herman Mordaunt.

"A vast difference truly, sir. Now there was a little thing happened about your daughter, 'Squire Mordaunt, the very first time I saw her"—the present was the *second* interview—"that could no more have happened in Connecticut, than the whole of the province could be put into that tea cup."

"To my daughter, Mr. Newcome!"

"Yes, sir, to your own daughter; Miss, that sits there looking as innocent as if it had never come to pass."

"This is so extraordinary, sir, that I must beg an explanation."

"You may well call it extr'ornary, for extr'ornary it would be called all over Connecticut, and I'll never give up, that York, if this be a York usage, is or can be right in such a matter, at least."

"I entreat you to be more explicit, Mr. Newcome."

"Why, sir, you must know, Corny, here, and I, and Dirck there, went in to see the lion, about which no doubt you've heard so much, and Corny paid for Miss's ticket. Well, *that* was all right enough, but—"

"Surely, Anneke, you have not forgotten to return to Mr. Littlepage the money!"

"Listen patiently, my dear sir, and you will get the whole story; my delinquencies and debts included, if any there are."

"That's just what she did, 'Squire Mordaunt, and I maintain there is not the man in all Connecticut that would have taken it. If ladies can't be treated to sights, and other amusements, I should like to know who is to be so."

Herman Mordaunt, at first, looked gravely at the speaker, but catching the expression of our eyes, he answered with the tact of a perfectly well bred man, as he certainly was, on all occasions that put him to the proof—

"You must overlook Miss Mordaunt's adhering to her own customs, Mr. Newcome, on account of her youth, and her little knowledge of any world but that immediately around her. When she has enjoyed an opportunity of visiting Danbury, no doubt she will improve by the occasion."

"But, Corny, sir—think of Corny's falling into such a mistake!"

"As for Mr. Littlepage, I must suppose he labours under somewhat of the same disadvantage. We are less gallant, here, than you happen to be in Connecticut; hence our inferiority. At some future day, perhaps, when society shall have made a greater progress among us, our youths will come to see the impropriety of permitting the fair sex to pay for any thing, even their own ribands. I have long known, sir, that you of New England, claim to treat your women better than they are treated in any other portion of the inhabited world, and it must be owing to that circumstance, that they enjoy the advantage of being 'treated' for nothing."

With this concession, Jason was apparently content. How much of this provincial feeling, arising from provincial ignorance, have I seen since that time! It is certain that our fellow subjects of the eastern provinces, are not addicted to hiding their lights under bushels, but make the most of all their advantages. That they are superior to us of York, in some respects, I am willing enough to allow, but there are certainly points on which this

superiority is far less apparent. As for Jason, he was entirely satisfied with the answer of Herman Mordaunt, and often alluded to
the subject afterwards, to my prejudice, and with great self-com-
placency. To be sure, it is a hard lesson to beat into the head of the
self-sufficient colonist, that his own little corner of the earth does
not contain all that is right, and just, and good, and refined.

I left Lilacsbush, that day, deeply in love. I hold it to be unmanly to attempt to conceal it. Anneke had made a lively impression on me, from the very first, but that impression had now gone
deeper than the imagination, and had very sensibly touched the
heart. Perhaps it was necessary to see her in the retirement of the
purely domestic circle, to give all her charms their just ascendancy. While in town, I had usually met her in crowds, surrounded by admirers, or other young persons of her own sex,
and there was less opportunity for viewing the influence of nature and the affections, on her manner. With Mary Wallace, at
her side, however, there was always one on whom she could
exhibit just enough of these feelings to bring out the loveliness of
her nature, without effort or affectation. Anne Mordaunt never
spoke to her friend, without a change appearing in her manner.
Affection thrilled in the tones of her voice, confidence beamed in
her eye, and esteem and respect were to be gathered from the expectation and deference that shone in her countenance. Mary
Wallace was two years the oldest, and these years taken in connection with her character, entitled her to receive this tribute from
her nearest associate, but all these feelings flowed spontaneously
from the heart, for never was an intercourse between two of the
sex more thoroughly free from acting.

It was a proof that passion was getting the mastery over me,
that I now forgot Dirck, his obvious attachment, older claims,
and possible success. I know not how it was, or why it was, but it
was certain that Herman Mordaunt had a great regard for Dirck
Van Valkenburgh. The affinity may have counted for something,
and it was possible that the father was already weighing the advantages that might accrue from such a connection. Col. Follock
had the reputation of being rich, as riches were then counted
among us, and the young fellow himself, in addition to a fine
manly figure, that was fast developing itself into the frame of a
youthful Hercules, had an excellent temper, and a good reputation. Still, this idea never troubled me. Of Dirck I had no fears,

while Bulstrode gave me great uneasiness, from the first. I saw all his advantages; may have even magnified them; while those of my near and immediate friend, gave me no trouble whatever. It is possible, had Dirck presented himself oftener, or more distinctly to my mind, a feeling of magnanimity might have induced me to withdraw in time, and leave him a field to which he had the earliest claim. But, after the morning at Lilacsbush it was too late for any such sacrifice on my part, and I rode away from the house, at the side of my friend, as forgetful of his interest in Anneke, as if he had never felt any. Magnanimity and I had no further connection in relation to my pretensions to Anneke Mordaunt.

"Well," commenced Jason, as soon as we were fairly in the saddle, "these Mordaunts are even a notch above your folks, Corny! There was more silver vessels in that room where we ate, than there is at this moment, in all Danbury! The extravagance amounts to waste. The old gentleman must be desperate rich, Dirck?"

"Herman Mordaunt has a good estate, and very little of it has gone for plate, Jason; that which you saw is old, and came either from Holland, or England; one home, or the other."

"Oh! Holland is no home for me, boy. Depend on it, all that plate is not put there for nothing. If the truth could be come at, this Herman Mordaunt, as you call him, though I do not see why you cannot call him 'Squire Mordaunt, like other folks, but this Mr. Mordaunt has some notion, I conclude, to get his daughter off on one of these rich English officers, of whom there happen to be so many in the province, just at this time. I never saw the gentleman, but there was one Bulstrode named pretty often, this forenoon—" Jason's morning always terminated at his usual breakfast hour—"and I rather conclude he will turn out to be the chap, in the long run. Such is my calculation, and *they* don't often fail."

I saw a quick, surprised start in Dirck, but I felt such a twinge myself, that there was little opportunity to inquire into the state of my friend's feelings, at this coarse, but unexpected remark.

"Have you any particular reason, Mr. Newcome, for venturing such an opinion?" I asked, a little sternly.

"Come, don't let us, out here in the highway, begin to mister one another. You are Corny, Dirck is Dirck, and I am Jason. The shortest way is commonly the best way, and I like given names among friends. Have I any particular reason?—Yes; plenty on 'em, and them that's good. In the first place, no man has a daughter,"—darter à la Jason—"that he does not begin to think of setting her out in the world, accordin' to his abilities; then, as I said before, these folks from home" (hum) "are awful rich, and rich husbands are always satisfactory to parents, whatever they may be to children. Besides, some of these officers will fall heirs to titles, and that is a desperate temptation to a woman, all over the world. I hardly think there is a young woman in Danbury that could hold out agin' a real title."

It has always struck me as singular, that the people of Jason's part of the provinces, should entertain so much profound respect for titles. No protion of hte world is of simpler habits, nor is it easier to find any civilized people among whom there is greater equality of actual condition, which one would think, must necessarily induce equality of feeling, than in Connecticut, at this very moment. Notwithstanding these facts, the love of titles is so great, that even that of serjeant is often prefixed to the name of a man on his tombstone, or in the announcement of his death, or marriage; and as for the militia ensigns and lieutenants, there is no end to them. Deacon is an important title, which is rarely omitted, and woe betide the man who should forget to call a magistrate, "Esquire." No such usages prevail among us; or, if they do, it is among that portion of the people of this colony, which is derived from New England, and still retains some of its customs. Then, in no part of the colonies, is English rank more deferred to, than in New England, generally, notwithstanding most of those colonies possess the right to elect nearly every officer they have among them. I allow that we of New York defer greatly to men of birth and rank from home, and it is right we should so do; but I do not think our difference is as great, or by any means as general, as it is in New England. It is possible the influence of the Dutch may have left an impression on our state of society, though I have been told that the colonies farther south exhibit very much the same characteristics as we do, ourselves, on this head.*

*As respects the love of titles that are derived from the people, there is nothing opposed to strict republican, or if the reader will democratic, principles, since it is deferring to the power that appoints, and manifests a respect for that which the community chooses to elevate. But, the deference to *English* rank, mentioned by Mr. Littlepage, is undeniably greater among the mass in New Eng-

We reached Satanstoe a little late, in consequence of the delay at Lilacsbush, and were welcomed with affection and warmth. My excellent mother was delighted to see me at home again, after so long an absence, and one which she did not think altogether without peril, when it was remembered that I had passed a whole fortnight amid the temptations and fascinations of the capital. I saw the tears in her eyes as she kissed me, again and again, and felt the gentle, warm, embrace as she pressed me to her bosom, in maternal thanksgiving.

Of course, I had to render an account of all I had seen and done, including Pinkster, the theatre, and the lion. I said nothing, however, of the Mordaunts, until questioned about them by my mother, quite a fortnight after Dirck had gone across to Rockland. One morning as I sat, endeavouring to write a sonnet in my own room, that excellent parent entered and took a seat near my table, with the familiarity the relation she bore me justified. She was knitting at the time, for never was she idle, except when asleep. I saw by the placid smile on her face, which, Heaven bless her! was still smooth and handsome, that something was on her mind, that was far from disagreeable, and I waited with some curiosity for the opening. That excellent mother! How completely did she live out of herself, in all that had the most remote bearing on my future hopes and happiness!

"Finish your writing, my son," commenced my mother, for I

---

land, than it is anywhere else, in this country, at this very moment. One leading New York paper, edited by New England men, during the last controversy about the indemnity to be paid by France, actually styled the Duc de Broglie "his grace," like a Grub Street Cockney, a mode of address that would astonish that respectable statesman, quite as much as it must have amused every man of the world who saw it. I have been much puzzled to account for this peculiarity, unquestionably one that exists in the country, but have supposed it must be owing to the diffusion of information, which carries intelligence sufficiently far to acquaint the mass with leading social features, without going far enough to compensate for a provincial position and provincial habits. Perhaps the exclusively English origin of the people may have an influence. The writer has passed portions of two seasons in Switzerland, and, excluding the small Forest Cantons, he has no hesitation in saying that the habits and general notions of Connecticut are more inherently democratical than those of any part of that country. Notwithstanding, he thinks a nobleman, particularly an English nobleman, is a far greater man in New England, than he is among the real middle-state families of New-York.—EDITOR.

had instinctively striven to conceal the sonnet, "finish your writing; until you have done, I will be silent."

"I have done, now, mother; 't was only a copy of verses I was endeavouring to write out—you know—that is—write out, you know."

"I did not know you were a poet, Corny," returned my mother, smiling still more complacently; for it *is* something to be the parent of a poet.

"I!—I a poet, mother!—I'd sooner turn school master than turn poet. Yes, I'd sooner be Jason Newcome, himself, than even suspect it possible I *could* be a poet."

"Well, never mind; people never turn poets, I fancy, with their eyes open. But, what is this I hear of your having saved a beautiful young lady from the jaws of a lion, while you were in town; and why was I left to learn all the particulars from Mr. Newcome?"

I believe my face was of the colour of scarlet, for it felt as if it were on fire, and my mother smiled still more decidedly than ever. Speak! I could not have spoken to be thus smiled on by Anneke.

"There is nothing to be ashamed of, Corny, in rescuing a young lady from a lion, or in going to her father's to receive the thanks of the family. The Mordaunts are a family any one can visit with pleasure. Was the battle between you and the beast, a very desperate conflict, my child?"

"Poh! Mother:—Jason is a regular dealer in marvels, and he makes mountains of mole hills. In the first place, for 'jaws,' you must substitute 'paws,' and for a 'young lady,' 'her shawl.' "

"Yes, I understand it was the shawl, but it was on her shoulders, and could not have been disengaged time enough to save her, had you not shown so much presence of mind, and courage. As for the 'jaws' I believe that was my mistake, for Mr. Newcome certainly said 'claws.' "

"Well, mother, have it your own way. I was of a little service to a very charming young woman, and she and her father were civil to me, as a matter of course. Herman Mordaunt is a name we all know, and, as you say, his is a family that any man may be proud of visiting; ay, and pleased too."

"How odd it is, Corny," added my mother, in a sort of musing, soliloquizing way—"You are an only child, and Anneke Mordaunt is also an only child, as Dirck Follock has often told me."

"Then, Dirck has spoken to you frequently of Anneke, before this, Mother?"

"Time and again; they are relations, you must have heard; as, indeed, you are yourself, if you did but know it."

"I!—I related to Anneke Mordaunt, without being too *near!*"

My dear mother smiled again, while I felt sadly ashamed of myself, at the next instant. I believe that a suspicion of the truth, as respects my infant passion, existed in that dear parent's mind from that moment.

"Certainly related, Corny, and I will tell you how. My great-great-grandmother, Alida van der Heyden, was a first cousin of Herman Mordaunt's great-great-grandmother, by his mother's side, who was a Van Kleeck. So you see, you and Anneke are actually related."

"Just near enough, mother, to put one at ease in their house, and not so near as to make relationship troublesome."

"They tell me, my child, that Anneke is a sweet creature!"

"If beauty, and modesty, and grace, and gentleness, and spirit, and sense, and delicacy, and virtue and piety, can make any young woman of seventeen, a sweet creature, mother, then Anneke is sweet."

My dear mother seemed surprised at my warmth, but she smiled still more complacently than ever. Instead of pursuing the subject, however, she saw fit to change it, by speaking of the prospects of the season, and the many reasons we all had for thankfulness to God. I presume, with a woman's instinct, she had learned enough to satisfy her mind, for the present.

The summer soon succeeded to the May that proved so momentous to me, and I sought occupation in the fields. Occupation, however, would not do. Anneke was with me, go where I would, and glad was I when, Dirck, about midsummer, in one of his periodical visits to Satanstoe, proposed that we should ride over, and make another visit to Lilacsbush. He had written a note, to say we should be glad to ask a dinner and beds, if it were convenient, for a day a short distance ahead, and he waited the answer at the Neck. This answer arrived duly by mail, and was every thing we could wish. Herman Mordaunt offered us a hearty welcome, and sent the grateful intelligence that his daughter and Mary Wallace would both be present to receive us. I envied Dirck the manly feeling which had induced him to take this plain and respectable course to his object.

We went across the county, accordingly, and reached Lilacsbush, several hours before dinner. Anneke received us with a bright suffusion of the face, and kind smiles, though I could not detect the slightest difference in her manner to either. To both was she gracious, gentle, attentive, and lady-like. No allusion was made to the past, except a few remarks that were given on the subject of the theatre. The officers had continued to play until the ———th had been ordered up river, when Bulstrode, Billings, Harris, virtuous Marcia and all, had proceeded to Albany in company. Anneke thought there was about as much to be displeased with, as there was to please in these representations, though her removal to the country had prevented her seeing more than three of them all. It was admitted all round, however, that Bulstrode played admirably, and it was even regretted by certain persons, that he should not have been devoted to the stage.

We passed the night at Lilacsbush, and remained an hour or two after breakfast, next morning; I had carried a warm invitation from both my parents to Herman Mordaunt, to ride over, with the young ladies, and taste the fish of the Sound, and the visit was returned in the course of the month of September. My mother received Anneke as a relation, though I believe that both Herman Mordaunt and his daughter were surprised to learn that they came within even the wide embrace of Dutch kindred. They did not seem displeased, however, for the family name of my mother was good, and no one need have been ashamed of affinity to *her*, on her own account. Our guests did not remain the night, but they left us in a sort of a chaise that Herman Mordaunt kept, for country use, about an hour before sunset. I mounted my horse, and rode five miles with the party, on its way back, and then took my leave of Anneke, as it turned out, for many many, weary months.

The year 1757 was memorable in the colonies, by the progress of the war, and as much so in New York as in any other province. Montcalm had advanced to the head of Lake George, had taken Fort William Henry, and a fearful massacre of the garrison had succeeded. This bold operation left the enemy in possession of Champlain, and the strong post of Ticonderoga was adequately

garrisoned by a formidable force. A general gloom was cast over
the political affairs of the colony, and it was understood that a great
effort was to be made, the succeeding campaign, to repair the
loss. Rumour spoke of large reinforcements from home, and of
greater levies in the colonies themselves, than had been hitherto
attempted. Lord Loudon was to return home, and a veteran, of
the name of Abercrombie was to succeed him in the command of
all the forces of the king. Regiments began to arrive from the
West-Indies, and, in the course of the winter of 1757–8, we heard
at Satanstoe of the gaieties that these new comers had introduced
into the town. Among other things a regular corps of Thespians
had arrived from the West-Indies.

Chapter X

"Dear Hasty Pudding, what unpromised joy
Expands my heart to meet thee in Savoy!
Doom'd o'er the world through devious paths to roam,
Each clime my country, and each house my home,
My soul is sooth'd, my cares have found an end:
I greet my long-lost, unforgotten friend."

Joel Barlow, "The Hasty Pudding,"
Canto I. 57–62.

THE winter was soon drawing to a close, and my twenty-first birth-day was past. My father, and Col. Follock, who came over to smoke more than usual that winter with my father, began to talk of the journey Dirck and I were to take, in quest of the Patent. Maps were produced, calculations were made, and different modes of proceeding were proposed, by the various members of the family. I will acknowledge that the sight of the large, coarse, parchment map, of the Mooseridge Patent, as the new acquisition was called, from the circumstance of the surveyors having shot a moose on a particular ridge of land in its centre, excited certain feelings of avarice within my mind. There were streams meandering among hills and valleys, little lakes, or ponds, as they were erroneously called in the language of the country, dotted the surface, and there were all the artistical proofs of a valuable estate, that a good map-maker could devise, to render the whole pleasing and promising.* If it were a good thing to be the heir of Satanstoe, it was far better to be the tenant in common, with my friend Dirck, of all these ample plains, rich bottoms, flowing streams and picturesque lakes. In a word, for the first time, in the history of the Colonies, the Littlepages had become the owners

---

*Forty years ago, a gentleman in New York purchased a considerable body of wild land, on the faith of the map. When he came to examine his new property, it was found to be particularly wanting in water-courses. The surveyor was sought, and rebuked for his deception, the map having numerous streams &c. "Why, did you lay down all these streams here, where none are to be found?" demanded the irritated purchaser, pointing to the document. "Why?—Why, who the d—l ever saw a map without rivers?" was the answer.—EDITOR.

of what might be termed an estate. According to our New York parlance, six or eight hundred acres are not an estate; nor two or three thousand, scarcely; but ten, or twenty, and much more, forty thousand acres of land might be dignified with the name of an estate!

The first knotty point discussed, was to settle the manner in which Dirck and myself, should reach Mooseridge. Two modes of going as far as Albany offered, and on one of these it was our first concern to decide. We might wait until the river opened, and go as far as Albany in a sloop, of which one or two left town each week, when business was active, as it was certain to be in the spring of the year. It was thought, however, that the army would require most of the means of transportation of this nature, that offered, and it might put us to both inconvenience and delay, to wait on the tardy movements of quarter-masters and contractors. My grandfather shook his head, when the thing was named, and advised us to remain as independent as possible.

"Have as little, as possible, to do with such people, Corny," put in my grandfather, now a grey-headed, venerable-looking old gentleman, who did not wear his wig, half the time, but was content to appear in a pointed night-cap, and gown, at all hours, until just before dinner was announced, when he invariably came forth dressed as a gentleman—"Have as little as possible to do with these gentry, Corny. Money, and not honour, is their game, and you will be treated like a barrel of beef, or a bag of potatoes, if you fall into their hands. If you move with the army at all, keep among the real soldiers, my boy, and above all things, avoid the contractors."

It was consequently determined that there was too much uncertainty and delay in waiting for a passage to Albany by water, for, it was known that the voyage itself often lasted ten days, or a fortnight, and it would be so late before we could sail, as to render this delay very inconvenient. The other mode of journeying was to go before the snow had melted from the roads, by the aid of which, it was quite possible to make the distance between Satanstoe and Albany, in three days.

Certain considerations of economy next offered, and we settled down on the following plan, which, as it strikes me, is even now, worthy of being mentioned, on account of its prudence and judgment. It was well known that there would be a great demand for horses for the army, as well as for stores, provisions &c. of various sorts. Now, we had on the Neck several stout horses, that were falling into years, though still serviceable and good for a campaign. Col. Follock had others, of the same description, and, when the cavalry of the two farms were all assembled at Satanstoe, there were found to be no fewer than fourteen of the venerable animals. These made just three four-horse teams, besides leaving a pair for a lighter load. Old, stout lumber sleighs were bought, or found, and repaired, and Yaap, having two other blacks with him, was sent off at the head of what my father called a brigade of lumber sleighs, all of which were loaded with the spare pork and flour of the two families. The war had rendered these articles quite high, but the hogs that were slaughtered at Christmas had not yet been sold, and it was decided that Dirck and myself could not commence our careers, as men who had to buy and sell from the respective farms, in any manner more likely to be useful to us, and to our parents, than this. As Yaap's movements were necessarily slow, he was permitted to precede Dirck and myself by two entire days, giving him time to clear the Highlands before we left Satanstoe. The negroes carried the provender, for their horses, and no small portion of the food, and all of the cider that was necessary for their own consumption. No one was ashamed of economising with his slaves, in this manner, the law of slavery itself, existing principally as a money-making institution. I mention these little matters, that posterity may understand the conventional feeling of the colony, on such points.

When every thing was ready, we had to listen to much good advice, from our friends, previously to launching ourselves into the world. What Col. Follock said to Dirck, the latter never told me; but the following was pretty much the form and substance of that which I received from my own father; the interview taking place in a little room he called his "office," or "study," as Jason used to term it.

"Here, Corny, are all the bills, or invoices, properly made out," my father commenced, handing me a small sheaf of papers; "and you will do well to consult them, before you make any sales. Here are letters of introduction to several gentlemen in the army whose acquaintance I could wish you to cultivate. This, in particular, is to my old captain, Charles Merrewether, who is now a Lt. Col. and commands a battalion in the Royal Americans. You will find him of great service to you, while you remain with the army, I make no doubt. Pork, they tell me, if of the quality of that you will have, ought to bring three half joes, the barrel, and you might ask that much. Should accident procure you an invitation to the table of the Commander in Chief, as may happen through Col. Merrewether's friendship, I trust you will do full credit to the loyalty of the Littlepages. Ah! There's the flour, too; it ought to be worth two half joes the barrel, in times like these. I have thrown in, a letter or two to some of the Schuylers, with whom I served when of your age. They are first rate people, remember, and rank among the highest families of the colonies; full of good old Van Cortlandt blood, and well crossed with the Rensselaers. Should any of them ask you about the barrel of tongues, that you will find marked T—"

"Any of whom, sir; the Schuylers, the Cortlandts, or the Rensselaers?"

"Poh! Any of the sutlers, or contractors, I mean of course. You can tell them that they were cured at home, and that you dare recommend them as fit for the Commander in Chief's own table."

Such was the character of my father's parting instructions. My mother held a different discourse.

"Corny, my beloved child," she said; "this will be an all important journey to you. Not only are you going far from home, but you are going to a part of the country where much will be to be seen. I hope you will remember what was promised for you, by your sponsors in baptism, and also what is owing to your own good name, and that of your family. The letters you take with you, will probably introduce you to good company, and that is a great beginning to a youth. I wish you to cultivate the society of reputable females, Corny. My sex has great influence on the conduct of yours, at your time of life, and both your manners and principles will be aided by being as much with women of character as possible—"

"But, mother, if we are to go any distance with the army, as both my father and Col. Follock wish, it will not be in our power to be much in ladies' society."

"I speak of the time you will pass in, and near Albany. I do not expect you will find accomplished women at Mooseridge, nor, should you really go any distance with the troops, though I see no occasion for your going with them a single foot, since you are not a soldier, do I suppose you will find many reputable women in the camp; but, avail yourself of every favourable opportunity to go into good company. I have procured a letter for you, from a lady of one of the great families of this county, to Madam Schuyler, who is above all other women, they tell me, in and around Albany. Her, you must see, and I charge you, on your duty, to deliver this letter. It is possible, too, that Herman Mordaunt—"

"What of Herman Mordaunt, and Anneke, Mother?"

"I spoke only of Herman Mordaunt, himself, and did not mention Anneke, boy," answered my mother smiling, "though I doubt not that the daughter is with the father. They left town, for Albany, two months since, my sister Legge writes me, and intend to pass the summer north. I will not deceive you, Corny, so you shall hear all that your aunt has written on the subject. In the first place, she says Herman Mordaunt has gone on public service, having an especial appointment for some particular duty of importance, that is private, but which it is known will detain him near Albany, and among the northern posts, until the close of the season though he gives out to the world, he is absent on account of some land he has in Albany county. His daughter and Mary Wallace are with him, with several servants, and they have taken up with them a sleigh-load of conveniences; that looks like remaining. Now, you ought to hear the rest, my child, though I feel no apprehension when such a youth as yourself is put in competition with any other man in the colony—Yes, though your own mother, I think I may say *that!*"

"What is it, mother?—Never mind me; I shall do well enough, depend on it—that is—but what is it, dear mother?"

"Why, your aunt says, it is whispered among a few in town, a very few only, but whispered, that Herman Mordaunt got the appointment named, merely that he might have a pretence for taking Anneke near the ———th, in which regiment it seems there is a baronet's son, who is a sort of relative of his, and whom he wishes to marry to Anneke."

"I am sorry, then, that my aunt Legge listens to any such unworthy gossip!" I indignantly cried. "My life on it, Anneke Mordaunt never contemplated so indelicate a thing."

"No one supposes Anneke does, or did. But fathers are not daughters, Corny; no, nor mothers neither, as I can freely say, seeing you are my only child. Herman Mordaunt may imagine all this in *his* heart, and Anneke be every thing that is innocent and delicate."

"And how can my aunt Legge's informants know what is in Herman Mordaunt's heart?"

"How?—I suppose they judge by what they find in their own, my son; a common means of coming at a neighbour's failings, though I believe virtues are rarely detected by the same process."

"Ay, and judge of others, by themselves. The means may be common, mother, but they are not infallible."

"Certainly not, Corny, and that will be a ground of hope to you. Remember, my child, you can bring me no daughter I shall love half as well as I feel I can love Anneke Mordaunt. We are related too, her father's great-great-grandmother—"

"Never mind the great-great-grandmother, my dear, good, excellent, parent. After this, I shall not attempt to have any secret from you. Unless Anneke Mordaunt consent to be your daughter, you will never have one."

"Do not say that, Corny, I beseech you," cried my mother, a good deal frightened. "Remember there is no accounting for tastes; the army is a formidable rival, and, after all, this Mr. Bulstrode, I think you call him, may prove as acceptable to Anneke as to her father. Do not say so cruel a thing, I entreat of you, dearest, dearest, Corny."

"It is not a minute, mother, since you said how little you apprehended for me, when opposed by any other man in the province!"

"Yes, child; but that is a very different thing from seeing you pass all your days as a heartless, comfortless old bachelor. There are fifty young women in this very county, I could wish to see you united to, in preference to witnessing such a calamity."

"Well, mother, we will say no more about it. But, is it true that Mr. Worden actually intends to be of our party ?"

"Both Mr. Worden and Mr. Newcome, I believe. We shall scarcely know how to spare the first, but he conceives he has a call to accompany the army, in which there are so few chaplains, and souls are called to their last dread account so suddenly in war, that one does not know how to refuse to let him go."

My poor, confiding mother! When I look back at the past, and remember the manner in which the Rev. Mr. Worden discharged the duties of his sacred office, during the campaign that succeeded, I cannot but smile at the manner in which confidence manifests itself in woman. The sex has a natural disposition to place their trust in priests, by a very simple process of transferring their own dispositions to the bosoms of those they believe set apart for purely holy objects. Well, we live and learn. I dare say that many are what they profess to be, but I have lived long enough, now, to know *all* are not. As for Mr. Worden, he had one good point about him, at any rate. His friends and his enemies saw the worst of him. He was no hypocrite, but his associates saw the man very much as he was. Still, I am far from wishing to hold up this imported minister as a model of christian graces, for my descendants to admire. No one can be more convinced than myself, how much sectarians are prone to substitute their own narrow notions of right and wrong, for the Law of God, confounding acts that are perfectly innocent in themselves with sin; but, at the same time, I am quite aware too, that appearances are ever to be consulted in cases of morals, and that it is a minor virtue to be decent in matters of manners. The Rev. Mr. Worden, whatever might have been his position as to substantials, certainly carried the external of liberality to the verge of indiscretion.

A day, or two, after the conversation I have related, our party left Satanstoe, with some *éclat*. The team belonged equally to the Follocks, and the Littlepages, one horse being the property of my father, while the other belonged to Col. Follock. The sleigh, an old one new painted for the occasion, was the sole property of the latter gentleman, and was consigned, in mercantile phrase, to Dirck, in order to be disposed of, as soon as we should reach the end of our journey. On its exterior it was painted a bright sky-blue, while its interior was of vermilion, a colour that was and is much in vogue for this species of vehicle, inasmuch as it carries with it the idea of warmth, so, at least, the old people say, though I will confess I never found my toes any less cold in a sleigh thus painted, than in one painted blue, which is usually thought a particularly cold colour to the feet.

We had three buffalo skins, or, rather, two buffalo (bison) skins, and one bear skin. The last being trimmed with scarlet cloth had a particularly warm and comfortable appearance. The largest skin was placed on the hind-seat, and thrown over the back of the sleigh, as a matter of course; and, though this back was high enough to break off the wind from our heads and necks, the skin not only covered it, but it hung two or three feet down behind, as is becoming in a gentleman's sleigh. The other buffalo was spread in the bottom of the sleigh, as a carpet for all four, leaving an apron to come in front upon Dirck's, and my lap, as a protection against the cold, in that quarter. The bear skin, formed a cushion for us in front, and an apron for Mr. Worden and Jason, who sat behind. Our trunks had gone on the lumber sleighs, that is mine and Dirck's had thus been sent, while our two companions found room for theirs in the conveyance in which we went ourselves.

It was March 1st 1758, the morning we left Satanstoe, on this memorable excursion. The winter had proved as was common in our latitude, though there had been more snow along the coast, than was usual. Salt air and snow do not agree well together, but I had driven in a sleigh over the Neck, most of the month of February, though there were symptoms of a thaw, and of a southerly wind, the day we left home. My father observed this, and he advised me to take the road through the centre of the county, and get among the hills, as soon as possible. Not only was there always more snow in that part of the country, but it resisted the influence of a thaw much longer, than that which had fallen near the sea, or Sound. I got my mother's last kiss, my father's last shake of the hand, my grandfather's blessing, stepped into the sleigh, took the reins from Dirck, and drove off.

A party in a sleigh, must be composed of a very sombre sort of persons, if it be not a merry one. In our case, everybody was disposed to good humour, though Jason could not pass along the highway, in York Colony, without giving vent to his provincial, Connecticut, hypercriticism. Every thing was Dutch, according to his view of matters, and when it failed of being Dutch, why, it was York-Colony. The doors were not in the right places; the windows were too large, when they were not too small; things had a cabbage-look; the people smelt of tobacco; and hasty-pudding was called "suppaan." But these were trifles; and being used to them, nobody paid much attention to what our puritanical neighbor saw fit to pour out, in the humility and meekness of his soul. Mr. Worden chuckled, and urged Jason on, in the hope of irritating Dirck; but Dirck smoked through it all, with an indifference that proved how much he really despised the critic. I was the only one who resented this supercilious ignorance, but even I was often more disposed to laugh, than to be angry.

The signs of a thaw increased, as we got a few miles from home, and by the time we reached White Plains, the "south wind" did not blow "softly," but freshly, and the snow in the road became sloppy, and rills of water were seen running down the hillsides, in a way that menaced destruction to the sleighing. On we drove, however, and deeper and deeper we got among the hills, until we found not only more snow, but fewer symptoms of immediately losing it. Our first day's work carried us well into the Manor of the Van Cortlandts, where we passed the night. Next morning the south wind was still blowing, sweeping over the fields of snow charged with the salt air, of the ocean, and bare spots began to show themselves on all the acclivities and hillsides, an admonition for us to be stirring. We breakfasted in the Highlands, and in a wild and retired part of them, though in a part where snow and beaten roads were still to be found. We had escaped from the thaw, and no longer felt any uneasiness on the subject of reaching the end of our journey on runners.

The second day brought us fairly through the mountains, out on the plains of Dutchess, permitting us to sleep at Fishkill. This was a thriving settlement, the people appearing to me to live in abundance, as certainly they did in peace and quiet. They knew little of the war, and asked us many questions concerning the army, its commanders, its force and its objects. They were a simple, and judging from appearances, an honest people, who troubled themselves very little with what was going on in the world.

After quitting Fishkill we found a great change, not only in the country, but in the weather. The first was level, as a whole, and was much better settled than I could have believed possible, so far in the interior. As for the weather, it was quite a different climate from that we had left below the highlands. Not only was the morning cold, cold as it had been a month earlier with us, but the snow still lay two or three feet in depth, on a level, and the sleighing was as good as heart could wish.

That afternoon, we overtook Yaap and the brigade of lumber-sleighs. Every thing had gone right, and, after giving the fellow some fresh instructions I passed him, proceeding on our route. This parting did not take place, however, until the following had been uttered between us:

"Well, Yaap," I inquired, as a sort of close to the previous discourse, "how do you like the upper counties?"

A loud negro laugh succeeded, and a repetition of the question was necessary to extort an answer.

"Lor', Masser Corny, how you t'ink I know, when dere not'in but snow to be seen!"

"There was plenty of snow in West-Chester; yet, I dare say you could give some opinion of our own county!"

"'Cause I know him, sah; inside and out; and all over, Masser Corny."

"Well, but you can see the houses, and orchards, and barns, and fences, and other things of that sort."

"'Em pretty much like our'n, Masser Corny; why you bother nigger with sich question?"

Here another burst of loud, hearty "yah—yah—yahs" succeeded, and Yaap had his laugh out before another word could be got out of him, when I put the question a third time.

"Well, den, Masser Corny, sin' you *will* know, dis is my mind. Dis country is oncomparable wid our ole county, sah. De houses seem mean, de barns look empty, de fences be low, and de niggers, ebbery one of 'em, look cold, sah—yes, sah—'ey look berry cold!"

As a "cold negro" was a most pitiable object in negro eyes, I saw by this summary that Yaap had commenced his travels in much of the same temper of superciliousness, as Jason Newcome. It struck me as odd at the time, but, since that day, I have ascertained that this feeling is a very general travelling companion for those who set out on their first journey.

We passed our third night at a small hamlet called Rhinebeck, in a settlement in which many German names were to be found. Here we were travelling through the vast estates of the Livingstons, a name well known in our colonial history. We breakfasted at Claverack, and passed through a place called Kinderhook, a village of Low Dutch origin, and of some antiquity. That night we succeeded in coming near Albany, by making a very hard day's drive of it. There was no village at the place where we slept, but the house was a comfortable, and exceedingly neat Dutch tavern. After quitting Fishkill we had seen more or less of the river, until we passed Claverack, where we took our leave of it. It was covered with ice, and sleighs were moving about it, with great apparent security; but we did not like to try it. Our whole party preferred a solid highway, in which there was no danger of the bottom's dropping out.

As we were now about to enter Albany, the second largest town in the Colony, and one of the largest inland towns of the whole country, if such a word can properly be given to a place that lies on a navigable river, it was thought necessary to make some few arrangements, in order to do it decently. Instead of quitting the tavern at day-light, therefore, as had been our practice previously, we remained until after breakfast, having recourse to our trunks in the mean time. Dirck, Jason and myself, had provided ourselves with fur caps for the journey, with ear-laps and other contrivances for keeping oneself warm. The cap of Dirck, and my own, were of very fine marten's skin, and as they were round and high, and each was surmounted with a handsome tail, that fell down behind, they had both a smart and military air. I thought I had never seen Dirck look so nobly and well, as he did in his cap, and I got a few compliments on my own air in mine; though they were only from my mother, who, I do think, would feel disposed to praise me, even if I looked wretchedly. The cap of Jason was better suited to his purse, being lower and of fox skins, though it had a tail also. Mr. Worden had declined travelling in a cap, as unsuited to his holy office. Accordingly he wore his clerical beaver, which differed a little from the ordinary cocked hats, that we all wore as a matter of course, though not so much so as to be very striking.

All of us had over-coats well trimmed with furs, mine and Dirck's being really handsome, with trimmings of marten, while those of our companions were less showy and expensive. On a consultation, Dirck and I decided that it was better taste to enter the town in travellers' dress, than to enter it in any other, and we merely smartened up a little, in order to appear as gentlemen. The case was very different with Jason. According to his idea a man should wear his best clothes on a journey, and I was surprised to see him appear at breakfast, in black breeches, striped woollen stockings, large plated buckles in his shoes, and a coat that I well knew he religiously reserved for high-days and holidays. This coat was of a light pea-green colour, and but little adapted to the season, but Jason had not much notion of the fitness of things, in general, in matters of taste. Dirck and myself wore our ordinary snuff-coloured coats, under our furs, but Jason threw aside all the overcoats, when we came near Albany, in order to enter the place in his best. Fortunately for him, the day was mild, and there was a bright sun to send its warm rays through the pea-green covering, to keep his blood from chilling. As for Mr. Worden, he wore a cloak of black cloth, laying aside all the furs, but a tippet and muff, both of which he used habitually in cold weather.

In this guise then we left the tavern, about nine in the morning, expecting to reach the banks of the river about ten. Nor were we disappointed; the roads being excellent, a light fall of snow having occurred in the night, to freshen the track. It was an interesting moment to us all, when the spires and roofs of that ancient town, Albany, first appeared in view! We had journeyed from near the southern boundary of the Colony, to a place that stood at no great distance from its frontier settlements on the north. The town itself, formed a pleasing object, as we approached it, on the opposite side of the Hudson. There it lay, stretching along the low land on the margin of the stream, and on its western bank, sheltered by high hills, up the side of which, the principal street extended, for the distance of fully a quarter of a mile. Near the head of this street, stood the fort, and we saw a brigade paraded in the open ground near it, wheeling and marching about. The spires of two churches were visible, one, the oldest, being seated on the low land, in the heart of the place, and the other on the height at no great distance from the fort; or, about half way up the acclivity, which forms the barrier to the inner country, on that side of the river. Both these buildings were of stone, of course, shingle tenements being of very rare occurrence in the Colony of New York, though common enough further east.*

*In nothing was the difference of character between the people of New England, and those of the Middle Colonies, more apparent than in the nature of the dwellings. In New York, for instance, men worth thousands dwelt in humble low, (usually one story) dwellings of stone, having window-shutters, frequently within as well as without, and the other appliances of comfort; whereas the farmer farther east, was seldom satisfied, though his means were limited, unless he lived in a house as good as his neighbour's; and the strife dotted the whole of their colonies with wooden buildings, of great pretension for the age, that rarely had even exterior shutters, and which frequently stood for generations unfinished. The difference was not of Dutch origin, for it was just as

I will own that not one of our party liked the idea of crossing the Hudson, in a loaded sleigh, on the ice, and that in the month of March. There were no streams about us, to be crossed in this mode, nor was the cold usually sufficient to render such a transit safe, and we felt as the inexperienced would be apt to feel, in circumstances so unpleasant. I must do Jason the credit to admit that he showed more plain, practical, good sense than any of us, determining our course in the end, by his view of the matter. As for Mr. Worden, however, nothing could induce him to venture on the ice in a sleigh, or *near* a sleigh, though Jason remonstrated in the following terms—

"Now, look here, Rev. Mr. Worden," Jason seldom omitted anybody's *title*, "you've only to turn your eyes on the river to see it is dotted with sleighs, far and near. There are highways north and south, and if that be the place, where the crossing is at the town, it is more like a thoroughfare, than a spot that is risky. In my judgment, these people, who live hereabouts ought to know whether there is any danger, or not."

Obvious as was this truth, 'Rev. Mr. Worden' made us stop on terra firma, and permit him to quit the sleigh, that he might cross the river on foot. Jason ventured a hint, or two, about faith, and its virtues, as he stripped himself to the pea-green, in order to enter the town in proper guise, throwing aside every thing that concealed his finery. As for Dirck and myself, we kept our seats manfully, and trotted on the river, at the point where we saw sleighs and foot-passengers, going and coming, in some numbers. The Rev. Mr. Worden, however, was not content to take the beaten path, for he knew there was no more security in being out on the ice, *near* a sleigh, than there was in being *in* it; so he diverged from the road, which crossed at the ferry, striking diagonally athwart the river, towards the wharves of the place.

It seemed to me to be sort of a holiday, among the young and idle, one sleigh passing us after another, filled with young men and maidens, all sparkling with the excitement of the moment, and gay with youth and spirits. We passed no less than four of

---

apparent in New Jersey or Pennsylvania, as in New York, and I think it may be attributed to a very obvious consequence of a general equality of condition in a state of society in which no one is content to wear even the semblance of poverty but those who cannot by any means, prevent it; but, in which all strive to get as high as possible, in appearances at least.—EDITOR.

these sleighs on the river, the jingling of the bells, the quick movement, the laughter and gaiety, and the animation of the whole
scene, far exceeding any thing of the sort, I had ever before witnessed. We were nearly across the river, when a sleigh more handsomely equipped than any we had yet seen, dashed down the
bank, and came whirling past us like a comet. It was full of ladies,
with the exception of one gentleman, who stood erect in front,
driving. I recognised Bulstrode, in furs like all of us, capped and
tailed, if not plumed, while among the half-dozen pairs of brilliant eyes, that were turned with their owner's smiling faces on
us, I saw one which never could be forgotten by me, that belonged to Anneke Mordaunt. I question if we were recognised,
for the passage was like that of a meteor, but I could not avoid
turning to gaze after the gay party. This change of position, enabled me to be a witness of a very amusing consequence of Mr.
Worden's experiment. A sleigh was coming in our direction, and
the party in it seeing one who was known for a clergyman *walking*
on the ice, turned aside, and approached him on a gallop, in
order to offer the courtesy of a seat to a man of his sacred profession. Our divine heard the bells, and fearful of having a sleigh so
near him, he commenced a downright flight, pursued by the
people in the sleigh, as fast as their horses could follow. Everybody on the ice, pulled up to gaze in wonder, at this strange spectacle, until the whole party reached the shore, the Rev. Mr. Worden pretty well blown, as the reader may suppose.

Chapter XI

"But bid physician talk our veins to temper,
And with an argument new-set a pulse;
Then think, my lord, of reasoning into love."
                    Edward Young, *The Revenge*, I. i. 86–88.

As the road from the ferry into the town, ran along the bank of the river, we reached the point where the Rev. Mr. Worden had landed, precisely at the same instant with his pursuers, who had been obliged to make a little circuit, in order to get off the ice. I do not know which party regarded the other in the greatest astonishment; the hunted, or the hunters. The sleigh had in it, two fine looking young fellows, that spoke English with a slight Dutch accent, and three young women, whose bright, coal-black eyes betokened surprise a little mitigated by a desire to laugh. Seeing that we were all strangers, I suppose, and that we claimed the runaway as belonging to our party, one of the young men raised his cap very respectfully, and opened the discourse by asking in a very civil tone—

"What ails the reverent gentleman, to make him run so fast?"

"Run!" exclaimed Mr. Worden, whose lungs had been playing like a blacksmith's bellows—"Run! and who would not run to save himself from being drowned?"

"Drowned!" repeated the young Dutchman, looking round at the river, as if to ascertain whether the ice were actually moving—"Why does the Dominie suppose there was any danger of *that*?"

As Mr. Worden's bellows were still hard at work, I explained to the young Albanians that we were strangers just arrived from the vicinity of New-York; that we were unaccustomed to frozen rivers, and had never crossed one on the ice before; that our reverend companion had chosen to walk at a distance from the road, in order to be in less danger should any team break in, and that he had naturally run to avoid their sleigh, when he saw it approaching. The Albanians heard this account in respectful silence, though I could see the two young men casting sly glances at each other, and that even the ladies had some little difficulty in altogether suppressing their smiles. When it was through, the oldest of the Dutch men, a fine, dare-devil, roystering looking fellow of four or five-and-twenty, whose dress and mien however denoted a person of the upper class, begged a thousand pardons for his mistake, quitting his sleigh and insisting on having the honour of shaking hands with the whole of us. His name was 'Ten Eyck' he said; 'Guert Ten Eyck,' and he asked permission, as we were strangers, of doing the honours of Albany to us. Everybody in the place knew him, which, as we afterwards ascertained was true enough, for he had just as much reputation for fun and frolick, as at all comported with respectability; keeping along, as it were, on the very verge of the pale of reputable people, without being thrown entirely out of it. The young females with him, were a shade below his own natural position in society, tolerating his frolicks on account of this circumstance, aided as it was by a singularly manly face and person, a hearty and ready laugh, a full purse, and possibly by the secret hope of being the happy individual who was designed by Providence to convert 'a reformed rake into the best of husbands.' In a word, he was always welcome with them, when those a little above them felt more disposed to frown.

Of course, all this was unknown to us, at the time, and we accepted Guert Ten Eyck's proffers of civility in the spirit in which they were offered. He inquired at what tavern we intended to stop, and promised an early call. Then, shaking us all round by the hand again, with great cordiality, he took his leave. His companion doffed a very dashing, high, wolf-skin cap to us, and the black-eyed trio, on the hind seat, smiled graciously, and away they drove, at a furious rate, startling all the echoes of Albany, with their bells. By this time, Mr. Worden was seated, and we followed more moderately, our team having none of the Dutch courage of a pair of horses fresh from the stable. Such were the circumstances under which we made our entrance into the ancient city of Albany. We were all in hopes, the little affair of the chase would soon be forgotten, for no one likes to be associated with a ridiculous circumstance, but we counted without our host. Guert Ten Eyck was not of a temperament to let such an affair sleep, but, as I afterwards ascertained, he told it with the laughing embellishments that belonged to his reckless character, until in time, the Rev. Mr. Worden came to be known, throughout all that region, by the nickname of the "Loping Dominie."

The reader may be assured our eyes were about us, as we drove through the streets of the second town in the Colony. We were not unaccustomed to houses constructed in the Dutch style, in New York, though the English mode of building had been most in vogue there, for half a century. It was not so with Albany, which remained, essentially, a Dutch town, in 1758. We heard little beside Dutch, as we passed along. The women scolded their children in Low Dutch, a use, by the way for which the language appears singularly well adapted; the negroes sang Dutch songs; the men called to each other in Dutch, and Dutch rang in our ears, as we walked our horses through the streets, towards the tavern. There were many soldiers about, and other proofs of the presence of a considerable military force were not wanting; still, the place struck me as very provincial and peculiar, after New York. Nearly all the houses were built with their gables to the streets, and each had heavy wooden Dutch stoops, with seats, at its door. A few had small court-yards in front, and, here and there, was a building of somewhat more pretension than usual. I do not think, however, there were fifty houses in the place, that were built with their gables off the line of the street.*

We were no sooner housed than Dirck and I sallied forth, to look at the place. Here we were, in one of the oldest towns of America; a place that could boast of much more than a century's existence, and it was natural to feel curious to look about one. Our inn was in the principal street, that which led up the hill towards the fort. This street was a wide avenue, that quite put Broadway out of countenance, so far as mere width was concerned. The streets that led out of it, however, were principally little better than lanes, as if the space that had been given to two or three of the main streets, had been taken off of the remainder.

*The population of Albany could not have reached 4000, in 1758. Its Dutch character remained down to the close of this century, with gradual changes. The writer can remember when quite as much Dutch, as English, was heard in the streets of Albany, though it has now nearly disappeared. The present population must be near 40,000.

Mr. Littlepage's description was doubtless correct at the time he wrote, but Albany would now be considered a first-class country town, in Europe. It has much better claims to compare with the towns of the old world, in this character, than New York has to compare with their capitals.—EDITOR.

The High Street, as we English would call it, was occupied by sleds filled with wood for sale; sleds loaded with geese, turkeys, tame and wild, and poultry of all sorts; sleds with venison, still in the skin, piled up in heaps, &c., all these eatables being collected, in unusual quantities as we were told, to meet the extraordinary demand created by the different military messes. Deer were no strangers to us, for Long Island was full of all sorts of game, as were the upper counties of New Jersey. Even Westchester, old and well settled as it had become, was not yet altogether clear of deer, and nothing was easier than to knock over a buck in the Highlands. Nevertheless, I had never seen venison, wild turkeys and sturgeons in such quantities, as they were to be seen that day in the principal street of Albany.

The crowd collected in this street, the sleighs that were whirling past, filled with young men and maidens, the incessant jingling of bells, the spluttering and jawing in Low Dutch, the hearty English oaths, of serjeants and sutler's men, and cooks of messes, the loud laughs of the blacks, and the beauty of the cold clear day, altogether produced some such effect on me, as I had experienced when I went to the theatre. Not the least striking picture of the scene, was Jason, in the middle of the street, gaping about him, in the cocked hat, the pea-green coat, and the striped woollen stockings.

Dirck and myself naturally examined the churches. These were two, as has been said already; one for the Dutch, and the other for the English. The first was the oldest. It stood at the point where the two principal streets crossed each other, and in the centre of the street, leaving sufficient passages all round it. The building was square, with a high pointed roof, having a belfry and weathercock on its apex, windows with diamond panes and painted glass, and a porch that was well suited, both to the climate, and to appearances.*

We were examining this structure, when Guert Ten Eyck accosted us, in his frank, off-hand way—

"Your servant, Mr. Littlepage; your servant, Mr. Follock," he

---

*There were two churches, of this character, built on this spot. The second, much larger than the first, but of the same form, was built *around* the other, in which service was held to the last, when it was literally thrown out of the windows of its successor. The last edifice disappeared about forty years since.— EDITOR.

cried, again shaking each cordially by the hand. "I was on the way to the tavern to look you up, when I accidentally saw you, here. A few gentlemen of my acquaintance, who are in the habit of supping together, in the winter time, meet for the last jollification of the season to-night, and they have all express't a wish to have the pleasure of your company. I hope you will allow me to say you will come? We meet at nine, sup at ten, and break up at twelve, quite regularly, in a very sedate and prutent manner."

There was something so frank and cordial, so simple and straight forward in this invitation, that we did not know how to decline it. We both knew that the name of Ten Eyck was respectable in the colony, our new acquaintance was well dressed, he seemed to be in good company when we first met him, his sleigh and horses had been actually of a more dashing stamp than usual, and his own attire had all the peculiarities of a gentleman's, with the addition of something even more decided and knowing than was common. It is true, the style of these peculiarities was not exactly such as I had seen in the air, manners and personal decorations of those of Billings and Harris, but they were none the less striking, and none the less attractive; the two Englishmen being "macaronis" from London, and Ten Eyck, being a "buck" of Albany.

"I thank you very heartily, Mr. Ten Eyck," I answered, "both for myself and for my friend"—

"And will let me come for you at half-past eight, to show you the way?"

"Why, yes, sir; I was about to say as much, if it be not giving you too much trouble."

"Do not speak of tr-r-ouple—" This last word will give a very good notion of Guert's accent, which I cannot stop to imitate at all times, in writing, "and do not say your *fre'nt*, but your *fre'ntz*."

"As to the two that are not here, I cannot positively answer—yonder, however, is one that can speak for himself."

"I see him, Mr. Littlepage, and will answer for *him*, on my own account. Depent on it, *he* will come. But the Dominie—he has a hearty look, and can help eat a turkey, and swallow a glass of goot Madeira, I think I can rely on. A man cannot take all that active exercise without food."

"Mr. Worden is a very companionable man, and is excellent

company at a supper table. I will communicate your invitation, and hope to be able to prevail on him to be of the party."

"T'at is enough, sir," returned Ten Eyck, or Guert, as I shall henceforth call him, in general, "vere dere ist a vill, dere ist a vay." Guert frequently broke out in such specimens of broken English, while at other times he would speak almost as well as any of us. "So Got pless you, my dear Mr. Littlepage, and make us lasting friends. I like your countenance, and my eye never deceives me in these matters."

Here, Guert shook us both by the hand again, most cordially, and left us. Dirck and I next strolled up the hill, going as high as the English church, which stood also in the centre of the principal street, an imposing and massive edifice in stone. With the exception of Mother Trinity in New York, this was the largest and altogether the most important edifice devoted to the worship of my own church I had ever seen. In Westchester, there were several of Queen Anne's churches, but none on a scale to compare with this. Our small edifices, were usually without galleries, steeples, towers, or bells, while St. Peter's, Albany, if not actually St. Peter's, Rome, was a building of which a man might be proud. A little to our surprise, we found the Rev. Mr. Worden and Mr. Jason Newcome had met at the door of this edifice, having sent a boy to the sexton in quest of the key. In a minute, or two, the urchin returned, bringing not only the key of the church, but the excuses of the sexton for not coming himself. The door was opened, and we went in.

I have always admired the decorous and spiritual manner in which the Rev. Mr. Worden entered a building that had been consecrated to the service of the Deity. I know not how to describe it, but it proved how completely he had been drilled in the decencies of his profession. Off came his hat, of course, and his manner, however facetious and easy it may have been, the moment before, changed on the instant to gravity and decorum. Not so with Jason. He entered St. Peter's, Albany, with exactly the same indifferent and cynical air with which he had seemed to regard every thing but money, since he entered "York Colony." Usually, he wore his cocked hat, on the back of his head, thereby lending himself a lolloping, negligent, and, at the same time, defying air; but I observed that, as we all uncovered, he brought his own beaver up over his eye-brows, in a species of military bravado. To uncover to a church, in his view of the matter, was a sort of idolatry; there might be images about, for any thing he knew, "and a man could never be enough on his guard ag'in being carried away by such evil deceptions," as he had once before answered to a remonstrance of mine, for wearing his hat in our own parish church.

I found the interior of St. Peter's quite as imposing as its exterior. Three of the pews were canopied, having coats of arms on their canopies. These, the boy told us belonged to the Van Rensselaer and Schuyler families. All these were covered with black cloth, in mourning for some death in those ancient families, which were closely allied. I was very much struck with the dignified air, that these patrician seats gave the house of God.* There were also several hatchments suspended against the walls, some being placed there in commemoration of officers of rank, from home, who had died in the king's service in the colony; and others to mark the deaths of some of the more distinguished of our own people.

Mr. Worden expressed himself well pleased with appearances of things, in and about this building, though Jason regarded all with ill-concealed disgust.

"What is the meaning of them pews, with tops to them, Corny?" the pedagogue whispered me, afraid to encounter the parson's remarks, by his own criticism.

"They are the pews of families of distinction, in this place, Mr. Newcome, and the canopies, or tops, as you call them, are honourable signs of their owners' conditions."

*I cannot recollect one of these canopied pews that is now standing, in this part of the Union. The last, of my knowledge, were in St. Mark's, New York, and, I believe, belonged to the Stuyvesants; the patron family of that church. They were taken down when that building was repaired, a few years since. This is one of the most innocent of all our innovations of this character. Distinctions in the House of God are opposed to the very spirit of the Christian religion, and it were far more fitting that pews should be altogether done away with, the true mode of assembling under the sacred roof, than that men should be classed even at the foot of the altar.

It may be questioned if a hatchment is now hung up, either on the dwelling, or in a church, in any part of America. They were to be seen, however, in the early part of the present century. Whenever any such traces of ancient usages are met with among us, by the traveller from the old world, he is apt to mistake them for the shadows "that coming events cast before," instead of those of the past.—EDITOR.

"Do you think their owners will set under such coverings, in paradise, Corny?" continued Jason, with a sneer.

"It is impossible for me to say, sir; it is probable, however, the just will not require any such mark to distinguish them from the unjust."

"Let me see," said Jason, looking round and affecting to count—"there are just three—Bishop, Priest, and Deacon, I suppose. Waal, there's a seat for each, and they can be comfortable *here*, whatever may turn up, *herea'ter*."

I turned away unwilling to dispute the point, for I knew it was as hopeless to expect that a Danbury man would feel like a New Yorker, on such a subject, as it was to expect that a New Yorker could be made to adopt Danbury sentiments. As for the *argument*, however, I have heard others of pretty much the same calibre often urged against the three orders of the ministry.

On quitting St. Peter's, I communicated the invitation of Guert Ten Eyck to Mr. Worden, and urged him to be of the party. I could see that the notion of a pleasant supper, was any thing but unpleasant to the missionary. Still he had his scruples, inasmuch as he had not yet seen his reverend brother who had the charge of St. Peter's, did not know exactly the temper of his mind, and was particularly desirous of officiating for him, in the presence of the principal personages of the place, on the approaching Sunday. He had written a note to the chaplain, for the person who had the cure of the Episcopalians held that rank in the army, St. Peter's being as much of an official chapel, as a parish church, and he must have an interview with that individual before he could decide. Fortunately, as we descended the street, towards our inn, we saw the very person in question. The marks of the common office, that these two divines bore about their persons in their dress, sufficed to make them known to each other, at a glance. In five minutes, they had shaken hands, heard each man's account of himself, had given and accepted the invitation to preach, and were otherwise on free and easy terms. Mr. Worden was to dine in the fort, with the chaplain. We then walked forward towards the tavern.

"By the way, Mr.———," said Mr. Worden, in a parenthesis of the discourse, "the family of Ten Eyck is quite respectable, here in Albany?"

"Very much so, sir—a family that is held in much esteem. I shall count on your assisting me morning and evening, my dear Mr. Worden."

It is surprising how the clergy do depend on each other for "assistance!"

"Make your arrangements accordingly, my good brother—I am quite fresh, and have brought a good stock of sermons, not knowing how much might remain to be done in the army. Corny," in a half whisper, "you can let our new friends know that I will sup with them; and, harkee—just drop a hint to them, that I am none of your puritans."

Here, then, we found every thing in a very fair way, to bring us all out in society, within the first two hours of our arrival. Mr. Worden was engaged to preach the next day but one, and he was engaged to supper that same day. All looked promising, and I hurried on in order to ascertain if Guert Ten Eyck had made his promised call. As before, he was met in the street, and the acceptance of the Dominie was duly communicated. Guert seemed highly pleased at this success, and he left me promising to be punctual to his hour. In the mean time, we had to dine.

The dinner proved a good one, and, as Mr. Worden remarked, it was quite lucky that the principal dish was venison, a meat that was so easy of digestion, as to promise no great obstacle to the accommodation of the supper. He should dine on venison, therefore, and he advised all three of us to follow his example. But, certain Dutch dishes attracted the eye and taste of Dirck, while Jason had alighted on a hash of some sort or other, that he did not quit until he had effectually disposed of it. As for myself, I confess the venison was so much to my taste that I stuck by the parson. We had our wine, too, and left the table early, in order not to interfere with the business of the night.

After dinner it was proposed to walk out in a body, to make a further examination of the place, and to see if we could not fall in with an army contractor, who might be disposed to relieve Dirck and myself of some portion of our charge. Luck again threw us in the way of Guert Ten Eyck, who seemed to live in the public street. In the course of a brief conversation that took place, as a passing compliment, I happened to mention a wish to ascertain where one might dispose of a few horses, and of two or three sleigh-loads of flour, pork &c. &c.

"My dear Mr. Littlepage," said Guert, with a frank smile and a friendly shake of the hand, "I am delighted that you have mentioned these matters to me; I can take you to the very man you wish to see; a heavy army-contractor, who is buying up every thing of the sort he can lay his hands on."

Of course, I was as much delighted as Guert could very well be, and left my party to proceed at once to the contractor's office, with the greatest alacrity, Dirck accompanying me. As we went along, our new friend advised us not to be very backward in the way of price, since the king paid in the long run.

"Rich dealers ought to pay well," he added, "and I can tell you, as a useful thing to know, that orders came on no later than yesterday to buy up every thing of the sort that offered. Put sleigh and harness, at once, all in a heap, on the King's servants."

I thought the idea not a bad one, and promised to profit by it. Guert was as good as his word, and I was properly introduced to the contractor. My business was no sooner mentioned, than I was desired to send a messenger round to the stables, in order that my conveyance, team &c., might make their appearance. As for the articles that were still on the road, I had very little trouble. The contractor knew my father, and he no sooner heard that Mr. Littlepage, of Satanstoe, was the owner of the provisions, than he purchased the whole, on the guaranty of his name. For the pork, I was to receive two half-joes the barrel, and for the flour, one. This was a good sale. The horses would be taken, if serviceable, as the contractor did not question, as would the lumber-sleighs, though the prices could not be set, until the different animals and objects were seen and examined.

It is amazing what war will do for commerce, as well as what it does against it! The demand for every thing that the judgment of my father had anticipated, was so great, that the contractor told me very frankly, the sleighs would not be unloaded in Albany at all, but would be sent on North, on the line of the expected route of the army, so as to anticipate the disappearance of the snow, and the breaking up of the roads.

"You shall be paid liberally for your teams, harness and sleighs," he continued, "though no sum can be named until I see them. These are not times, when operations are to be retarded on account of a few joes, more or less, for the King's service must go on. I very well know that Major Littlepage and Col. Follock both understand what they are about, and have sent us the right sort of things. The horses are very likely a little old, but are good for one campaign; better than if younger, perhaps, and were they colts we could get no more than that out of them. These movements in the woods destroy man and beast, and cost mints of money. Ah! There comes your team."

Sure enough, the sleigh drove round from the tavern, and we all went out to look at the horses &c. Guert now became an important person. On the subject of horses, he was accounted an oracle, and he talked, moved, and acted like one, in all respects. The first thing he did, was to step up to the animal's head, and to look into the mouth of each, in succession. The knowing way in which this was done, the coolness of the interference, and the fine, manly form of the intruder, would have given him, at once, a certain importance, and a connection with what was going on, had not his character for judgment in horse-flesh, been well established, far and near, in that quarter of the country.

"Upon my word, wonderfully good mouths!" exclaimed Guert, when through. "You must have your grain ground, Mr. Littlepage, or the teeth never could have stood it so well!"

"What age do you call the animals, Guert?" demanded the contractor.

"That is not so easily told, sir. I admit that they are aged horses; but they may be eight, or nine, or even ten, as for what can be told by their teeth. By the looks of their limbs, I should think they might be nine, coming grass."

"The near horse is eleven," I said, "and the off horse is supposed to be—"

"Poh! poh! Littlepage," interrupted Guert, making signs to me to be quiet—"you may *think* the off horse ten, but I should place him at about nine. His teeth are excellent, and there is not even a wind-gall on his legs. There is a cross of the Flemish in that beast."

"Well, and what do you say the pair is worth, Master Guert," demanded the contractor, who seemed to have a certain confidence in his friend's judgment, notwithstanding the recklessness and freedom of his manner. "Twelve half-joes for them both?"

"That will never do, Mr. Contractor," answered Guert, shaking his head. "In times like these, such stout animals, and beasts too in such heart and condition, ought to bring fifteen."

"Fifteen let it be then, if Mr. Littlepage assents. Now for the

sleigh, and harness, and skins. I suppose Mr. Littlepage will part
with the skins, too, as he can have no use for them without the
sleigh?"

"Have *you*, Mr. Contractor?" asked Guert, a little abruptly.
"That bear skin fills my eye beautifully, and, if Mr. Littlepage will
take a guinea for it, here is his money."

As this was a fair price, it was accepted, though I pressed the
skin on Guert as a gift, in remembrance of our accidental acquaintance. This offer, however, he respectfully but firmly resisted. And, here I will take occasion to say, lest the reader be mis-
led by what is met with in works of fiction, and other light and
vain productions, that in all my dealings and future connection
with Guert, I found him strictly honorable in money matters. It is
true, I would not have purchased a horse on his recommendation, if he owned the beast, but we all know how the best men
yield in their morals, when they come to deal in horses. I should
scarcely have expected Mr. Worden to be orthodox, in making
such bargains. But, on all other subjects connected with money,
Guert Ten Eyck was one of the honestest fellows I ever dealt with.

The contractor took the sleigh, harness and skins at seven
more half-joes, making twenty-three for the whole outfit. This
was certainly receiving two half-joes more than my father had expected, and I owed the gain of sixteen dollars to Guert's friendly
and bold interference. As soon as the prices were settled, the
money was paid me in good Spanish gold, and I handed over to
Dirck the portion that properly fell to his father's share. As it was
understood that the remaining horses, sleighs, harness, provisions &c. were to be taken at an appraisal, the instant they arrived, this hour's work relieved my friend and myself from any
further trouble, on the subject of the property entrusted to our
care. And a relief it was to be so well rid of a responsibility that was
as new, as it was heavy, to each of us.

The reader will get some idea of the pressure of affairs, and
how necessary it was felt to be on the alert in the month of
March—a time of the year when twenty-four hours might bring
about a change in the season—by the circumstance that the contractor sent his new purchase to be loaded up, from the door of
his office, with orders to proceed on north, with supplies for a
depot that he was making as near to Lake George as was deemed
prudent; the French being in force at Ticonderoga and Crown

Point, two posts at the head of Champlain; a distance considerably less than a hundred miles from Albany. Whatever was forwarded as far as Lake George, while the snow lasted, could then be sent on with the army, in the contemplated operations of the approaching summer, by means of the two lakes, and their northern outlets.

"Well, Mr. Littlepage," cried Guert, heartily; "*that* affair is well disposed of. You got goot prices, and I hope the King has got goot horses. They are a little venerable, perhaps, but what of that? The army would knock up the best and youngest beast in the colony, in one campaign in the woots, and it can do no more with the oldest and worst. Shall we walk rount into the main street, gentlemen? This is about the hour when the young ladies are apt to start for their afternoon sleighing."

"I suppose the ladies of Albany are remarkable for their beauty, Mr. Ten Eyck," I rejoined, wishing to say something agreeable, to a man who seemed so desirous of serving me. "The specimens I saw in crossing the river, this morning, would induce a stranger to think so."

"Sir," replied Guert, walking towards the great avenue of the town, "we are content with our ladies, in general, for they are charming, warm-hearted and amiable; but there has been an arrival among us this winter, from your part of the Colony, that has almost melted the ice on the Hudson!"

My heart beat quicker, for I could only think of one being of her sex, as likely to produce such a sensation. Still, I could not abstain from making a direct inquiry on the subject.

"From *our* part of the colony, Mr. Ten Eyck? You mean from New-York, probably?"

"Yes, sir, as a matter of course. There are several beautiful English women, who have come up with the army, but no Colonel, Major, or Captain, has brought such paragons with him as Herman Mordaunt; a gentleman who may be known to you by name?"

"Personally too, sir—Herman Mordaunt is even a kinsman of Dirck Follock, my friend, here."

"Then is Mr. Follock to be envied, since he can call cousin with so charming a young lady, as Anneke Mordaunt—"

"True, sir, most true!" I interrupted, eagerly; "Anne Mordaunt passes for the sweetest girl in York!"

"I do not know that I should go quite as far as that, Mr. Little-page," returned Guert, moderating his warmth, in a manner that a little surprised me, though his handsome face still glowed with honest, natural admiration; "since there is a Miss Mary Wallace in her company, that is quite as much thought of, here in Albany, as her friend, Miss Mordaunt."

Mary Wallace! The idea of comparing the silent, thoughtful, excellent though she were—Mary Wallace, with Anneke could never have crossed my mind. Still, Mary Wallace certainly *was* a very charming girl. She was even handsome; had a placid, saint-like character of countenance that had often struck me, singular beauty and development of form, and, in any other company than that of Anneke's, might well have attracted the first attention of the most fastidious beholder.

And Guert Ten Eyck admired, perhaps, loved Mary Wallace! Here, then, was fresh evidence how much we are all inclined to love our opposites; to form close friendships with those who resemble us least, principles excepted, for virtue can never cling to vice, and how much more interest, novelty possesses in the human breast, than the repetition of things to which we are accustomed. No two beings could be less alike than Mary Wallace and Guert Ten Eyck, yet the last admired the first.

"Miss Wallace is a very charming young lady, Mr. Ten Eyck," I rejoined, as soon as wonder would allow me to answer, "and I am not surprised you speak of her in terms of so much admiration."

Guert stopped short in the street, looked me full in the face with an expression of truth that could not well be feigned, squeezed my hand fervently and rejoined with a strange frankness, that I could not have imitated, to be master of all I saw—

"Admiration, Mr. Littlepage, is not a wort strong enough for what I feel for Mary! I would marry her in the next hour, and love and cherish her for all the rest of my life. I worship *her*, and love the earth she treads on."

"And you have told her this, Mr. Ten Eyck?"

"Fifty times, sir. She has now been two months in Albany, and my love was secured within the first week. I offered myself too soon, I fear; for Mary is a prutent, sensible young woman, and girls of that character, are apt to distrust the youth who is too quick in his advances. They like to be served sir, for seven years and seven years, as Joseph served for Potiphar."

"You mean, most likely, Mr. Ten Eyck, as Jacob served for Rachel."

"Well, sir, it may be as you say, dough I t'ink that in our Dutch Bibles, it stands as Joseph served for Potiphar—but you know what I mean, Mr. Littlepage. If you wish to see the ladies, and will come with me, I will go to a place where Herman Mordaunt's sleigh invariaply passes at this hour, for the ladies almost live in the air. I never miss the occasion of seeing them."

I had now a clue to Guert's being so much in the street. He was as good as his word, however, for he took a stand near the Dutch church, where I soon had the happiness of seeing Anneke and her friend driving past, on their evening's excursion. How blooming and lovely the former looked! Mary Wallace's eyes turned, I fancied understandingly, to the corner where Guert had placed himself, and her colour deepened as she returned his bow. But, the start of surprise, the smile, and the lightening eye of Anneke, as she unexpectedly saw me, filled my soul with delight, almost too great to be borne.

Chapter XII

"Then the wine it gets into their heads,
And turns the wit out of its station;
Nonsense gets in, in its stead,
And their puns are now all botheration."

The Punning Society.

GUERT Ten Eyck looked at me expressively, as the sleigh whirled round an angle of the building and disappeared. He then proposed that we should proceed. On ascending the main street, I was not a little surprised at discovering the sort of amusement that was going on, and in which it seemed to me all the youths of the place, were engaged. By youths, I do not mean lads of twelve and fourteen, but young men of eighteen and twenty, the amusement being that of sliding down hill, or "coasting," as I am told it is called in Boston. The acclivity was quite sharp, and of sufficient length, to give an impetus to the sled that was set in motion at a short distance above the English Church; an impetus that would carry it past the Dutch Church—a distance that was somewhat more than a quarter of a mile. The hand-sleds employed, were of a size and construction suited to the dimensions of those that used them, and, as a matter of course, there was no New Yorker that had not learned how to govern the motion of one of these vehicles, even when gliding down the steepest descent, with the nicest delicacy, and greatest ease. As children, or boys as late in life, as fourteen even, every male in the colony, and not a few of the females, had acquired this art, but this was the first place in which I had ever known adults to engage in the sport. The accidental circumstance of a hill's belonging to the principal street, joined to the severity of the winters, had rendered an amusement suited to grown people, that, elsewhere, was monopolized by the children.

By the time we had ascended as high as the English church, a party of young officers came down from the fort, gay with the glass and the song of the regimental mess. No sooner did they reach the starting point, than three or four of the more youthful, got possession of as many sleds, and off they went, like the shot starting from its gun. Nobody seemed to think it strange, but, on the contrary, I observed that the elderly people looked on, with a complacent gravity, that seemed to say how vividly the sight recalled the days of their own youth. I cannot say, however, that the strangers succeeded very well in managing their sleds, generally meeting with some stoppage before they reached the bottom of the hill.

"Will you take a slide, Mr. Littlepage?" Guert demanded, with a courteous gravity that showed how serious a business he fancied the sport. "Here is a large and strong sled, that will carry double, and you might trust yourself with me, though a regiment of horse were paraded down below."

"But, are we not a little too *old* for such an amusement, in the streets of a large town, Mr. Ten Eyck?" I answered, doubtingly, looking round me in an uncertain manner, as one who did not like to adventure, even while he hesitated to refuse. "Those King's officers are privileged people, you know."

"No man has a higher privilege to use the streets of Albany, than Mr. Cornelius Littlepage, sir, I can assure you. The young ladies often honour me with their company, and no accident has ever happened."

"Do the young ladies venture to ride down *this* street, Mr. Ten Eyck?"

"Not often, sir, I grant you; though that *has* been done too, of a moonlight night. There is a more retired spot, at no great distance from this street, however, to which the ladies are rather more partial. Look, Mr Littlepage!—There goes the Hon. Capt. Monson, of the ———th, and he will be down the hill and up again, before we are off, unless you hurry. Take your seat, lady-fashion, and leave me to manage the sled."

What could I do?—Guert had been so very civil, was so much in earnest, everybody seemed to expect it of me, and the Hon. Capt. Monson was already a hundred yards on his way to the bottom, shooting ahead with the velocity of an arrow. I took my seat, accordingly, placing my feet together on the front round, "*lady-fashion*," as directed. In an instant Guert's manly frame was behind me, with a leg extended on each side of the sled, the government of which, as every American who has been born north of the Potomac well knows, is effected by delicate touches of the heels. Guert called out to the boys, for a shove, and away we went, like the ship that is bound for her "destined element," as the poets say. We got a good start, and left the spot as the arrow leaves its bow.

Shall I own the truth, and confess I had a momentary pleasure, in the excitement produced by the rapidity of the motion, by the race we were running with another sled, and by the skill and ease with which Guert, almost without touching the ground, carried us unharmed through sundry narrow passages, and along the line of wood and venison-loaded sleighs, barely clearing the noses of their horses. I forgot that I was making this strange exhibition of myself, in a strange place, and almost in strange company. So rapid was our motion, however, that the danger of being recognized, was not very great, and there were so many to divide attention, that the act of folly would have been over-looked, but for a most untimely and unexpected accident. We had gone the entire length between the two churches with great success, several steady, grave, and respectable-looking old burgh-ers calling out, on a high key, "Vell done, Guert!"—for Guert ap-peared to be a general favourite, in the sense of fun and frolic at least,—when, turning an angle of the Old Dutch Temple, in the ambitious wish of shooting past it, in order to run still lower and shoot off the wharf upon the river, we found ourselves in immi-nent danger of running under the fore-legs of two foaming horses, that were whirling a sleigh around the same corner of the church. Nothing saved us but Guert's readiness and physical power. By digging a heel into the snow, he caused the sled to fly round, at a right angle to its former course, and us to fly off it, heels over head, without much regard to the proprieties, so far as postures, or grace was concerned. The negro who drove the sleigh pulled up, at the same instant, with so much force, as to throw his horses on their haunches. The result of these combined movements was to cause Guert and myself to roll over in such a way, as to regain our feet directly along side of the sleigh. In ris-ing to my feet, indeed, I laid a hand on the side of the vehicle, in order to assist me in the effort.

What a sight met my eyes! In the front, stood the negro, grin-ning from ear to ear; for *he* deemed every disaster that occurred on runners, a fit subject for merriment. Who ever did any thing but laugh at seeing a sleigh upset? And it was consequently quite in rule to do so on seeing two overgrown boys roll over from a hand-sled. I could have knocked the rascal down, with a good will, but it would not have done to resent mirth that proceeded from so legitimate a cause. Had I been disposed to act differently, however, the strength and courage necessary to effect such a purpose, would have been annihilated in me, by finding myself standing within three feet, and directly in front of Anneke Mordaunt and Mary Wallace! The shame at being thus detected in the disastrous termination of so boyish a flight, at first nearly overcame me. How Guert felt I do not know, but, for a single instant, I wished him in the middle of the Hudson, and all Albany, its Dutch Church, sleds, hill, and smoking burghers included, on top of him.

"Mr. Littlepage!" burst out of the rosy lips of Anneke, in a tone of voice that was not to be misunderstood.

"Mr. Guert Ten Eyck!" exclaimed Mary Wallace, in an accent and manner that bespoke chagrin.

"At your service, Miss Mary," answered Guert, who looked a little sheepish at the result of his exploit, though for a reason I did not at first comprehend, brushing some snow from his cap at the same time—"At your service, now and ever, Miss Mary. But, do not suppose it was awkwardness that produced this accident, I entreat of you. It was altogether the fault of the boy who is stationed to give warning of sleighs below the church, who must have left his post. Whenever, either of you young ladies will do me the honour to take a seat with me, I will pledge my character as an Albanian, to carry her to the foot of the highest and steepest hill in town, without disturbing a riband!"

Mary Wallace made no answer, and I fancied she looked a little sad. It is possible Anneke saw and understood this feeling, for she answered with a spirit that I had never seen her manifest before.

"No—no—Mr. Ten Eyck," she said; "when Miss Wallace, or I wish to ride down hill, and become little girls, again, we will trust ourselves with boys, whose constant practice will be likely to render them more expert than men can be, who have had time to forget the habits of their childhood. Pompey, we will return home."

The cold inclination of the head that succeeded, while it was sufficiently gracious to preserve appearances, proved too plainly that neither Guert, nor myself had risen in the estimation of his mistress by this boyish exhibition of his skill with the hand-sled. Had either of these young ladies been Albanians, it is probable they would have laughed at our mishap, but no high hill running directly into New-York, the custom that prevailed at Albany, did not prevail in the capital. Small boys alone used the hand-sled in that part of the colony, while the taste continued longer among the more stable and constant Dutch. Of course, we had nothing to do, but to make profound bows, and suffer the negro to move on.

"There it is, Littlepage," exclaimed Guert, with a species of sigh. "I shall have nothing but iced looks for the next week, and all for riding down hill four or five years later than is the rule. Everybody, hereabouts, uses the hand-sled until eighteen, or so, and I am only five-and-twenty. Pray what may be your age, my dear fellow?"

"Twenty-one, only about a month since—I wish with all my heart, it were ten!"

"Turned the corner!—well, that's unlucky, but we must make the best of it. My taste is for *fun*, and so I have admitted to Miss Wallace, twenty times, but she tells me that, after a certain period, men should look to graver things, and think of their country. She has lectured me already once, on the subject of slid-ing—though she allows that skating is a manly exercise."

"When a lady takes the trouble to lecture, it is a sure sign she feels some interest in the subject."

"By St. Nicholas! I never thought of that, Littlepage!" cried Guert, who, notwithstanding the great advantages he possessed in the way of face and figure, turned out to have less personal vanity about him, than almost any man I ever met with. "*Lecture* me she has and that more than once, too!"

"The lady who lectures *me*, sir, will not get rid of me, at the end of the discourse."

"That's manly! I like it, Littlepage; and I like *you*. I foresee we shall be great friends, and we'll talk more of this matter another time. Now, Mary has spoken to me of the war, and hinted that a single man like myself, with the world before him, might do something to make his name known in it. I did not like that; for a girl who loved a fellow would not wish to have him shot."

"A girl who took no interest in her suitor, Mr. Ten Eyck, would not care whether he did any thing or not. But, I must now quit you, being under an engagement to meet Mr. Worden at the inn, at six."

Guert and I shook hands, for the tenth or twelfth time that day, parting with an understanding that he was to call for us, to accompany our party to the supper at the previously appointed hour. As I walked towards the inn, I pondered on what had just occurred, in a most mortified temper. That Anneke was displeased was only too apparent, and I felt fearful that her displeasure was not entirely free from contempt. As for Guert's case, it did not strike me as being half as desperate as my own, for there was nothing unnatural, but something quite the reverse, in women of sense and stability, when they admire any youths of opposite temperament, and I remembered to have heard my grandfather say that such was apt to be the case, wishing to elevate their suitors in their pursuits and characters. Had Anneke taken the pains to remonstrate with me about the folly of what I had done, I should have been encouraged, but the cold indifference of her manner, not to call it contempt, cut me to the quick. It is true, Anneke seemed to feel most on her friend's account; but, I could not mistake the look of surprise with which she saw me, Cornelius Littlepage, rise from under her sleigh, and stand brushing the snow from my clothes, like a great oaf as I was! No man can bear to be rendered ridiculous in the presence of the woman he loves.

Near the inn I met Dirck, his whole face illuminated with a look of pleasure.

"I have just met Anneke and Mary Wallace!" he cried, "and they stopped their sleigh to speak to me. Herman Mordaunt has been here half the winter, and he means to remain most of the summer. There will be no Lilacsbush this season, the girls told me, but Herman Mordaunt has got a house, where he lives with his own servants, and boils his own pot, as he calls it. We shall be at home there, of course, for you are such a favourite, Corny, ever since that affair of the lion! As for Anneke, I never saw her looking so beautiful!"

"Did Miss Mordaunt say she would be happy to see us, on the old footing, Dirck?"

"Did she?—I suppose so. She said I shall be glad to see you, cousin Dirck, whenever you can come, and I hope you will bring with you, sometimes the clergyman of whom you have spoken."

"But nothing of Jason Newcome, or Corny Littlepage? Tell the truth at once, Dirck; my name was not mentioned?"

"Indeet it was, t'ough. *I* mentioned it several times, and told them how long we had been on the roat, and how you trove, and how you had sold the sleigh and horses already, and a dozen other t'ings. Oh! we talket a great deal of you, Corny; that is, I dit, and the girls listened."

"Was my name mentioned by either of the young ladies, Dirck, in direct terms?"

"To be sure. Anneke had something to say about you, though it was so much out of the way, I can hardly tell you what it was, now. Oh! I remember;—she said 'I have seen Mr. Littlepage, and think he has grown since we last met; he promises to make a *man*, one of these days.' What could t'at mean, Corny?"

"That I am a fool, a great overgrown boy, and wish I had never seen Albany; that's what it means. Come; let us go in; Mr. Worden will be expecting us—ha! Who the devil's that, Dirck?"

A loud Dutch shout from Dirck broke out of him, regardless of the street, and his whole face lighted up into a broad sympathetic smile. I had caught a glimpse of a sled coming down the acclivity we were slowly ascending, which sled glided past us, just as I got the words out of my mouth. It was occupied by Jason, alone, who seemed just as much charmed with the sport, as any other grown up boy, on the hill. There he went, the cocked-hat uppermost, the pea green coat beneath, and the striped woollens and heavy plated buckles stuck out, one on each side, governing the movement of the sled with the readiness of a lad accustomed to the business.

"That must be capital fun, Corny!" my companion said, scarce able to contain himself for the pleasure he felt. "I have a great mind to borrow a sled and take a turn myself."

"Not if you intend to visit Miss Mordaunt, Dirck. Take my word for it, she does not like to see men following the pleasures of boys."

Dirck stared at me, but, being taciturn by nature, he said nothing, and we entered the house. There we found Mr. Worden reading over an old sermon, in readiness for his next Sunday's business; and, sitting down, we began to compare notes on the subject of the town, and its advantages. The divine was in raptures. As for the Dutch he cared little for them, and had seen but little of them; overlooking them in a very natural, metropolitan sort of way; but he had found so many English officers, had heard so much from home, and had received so many invitations, that *his* campaign promised nothing but agreeables. We sat chatting over these matters, until the tea was served, and for an hour or two afterwards. My bargains were applauded, my promptitude—the promptitude of Guert would have been more just—was commended, and I was told that my parents should hear the whole truth in the matter. In a word, our Mentor being in good humour with himself, was disposed to be in good humour with every one else.

At the appointed hour, Guert came to escort us to the place of meeting. He was courteous, attentive, and as frank as the air he breathed, in manner. Mr. Worden took to him excessively, and it was soon apparent that he and young Ten Eyck were likely to become warm friends.

"You must know, gentlemen, that the party to which I have had the honour of inviting you, will be composed of some of the heartiest young men in Albany, if not in the colony. We meet once a month, in the house of an old bachelor, who belongs to us, and who will be delighted to converse with you, Mr. Worden, on the subject of religion. Mr. Van Brunt is very expert in religion, and we make him the umpire of all our disputes and bets, on *that* subject."

This sounded a little ominous I thought, but Mr. Worden was not a man to be frightened from a good hot supper, by half a dozen inadvertent words. He could tolerate even a religious discussion, with such an object in view. He walked on, side by side with Guert, and we were soon at the door of the house of Mr. Van Brunt, the Bachelor in Divinity, as I nick-named him. Guert entered without knocking, and ushered us into the presence of our *quasi* host.

We found in the room a company of just twelve, Guert included; that being the entire number of the club. It struck me, at the first glance, that the whole set had a sort of slide-down-hill aspect, and that we were likely to make a night of it. My acquaintance with Dirck, and indeed my connection with the old race, had not left me ignorant of a certain peculiarity in the Dutch character. Sober, sedate, nay phlegmatic, as they usually appeared to be, their roystering was on a pretty high key, when it once fairly commenced. We thought one lad of the old race, down in Westchester, fully a match for two of the Anglo-Saxon breed, when it came to a hard set-to; no ordinary fun appeasing the longings of an excited Dutchman. Tradition had let me into a good many secrets connected with their excesses, and I had heard the young Albanians often mentioned as being at the head of their profession, in these particulars.

Nothing could be more decorous, or considerate, however, than our introduction and reception. The young men seemed particularly gratified at having a clergyman of their party, and I make no doubt it was intended that the evening should be one of unusual sobriety and moderation. I heard the word "Dominie" whispered from mouth to mouth, and it was easy to see the effect it produced. Most eyes were fastened on Van Brunt, a red faced, square-built, somewhat dissolute-looking man of forty-five, who seemed to find his apology for associating with persons so much his juniors, in his habits, and possibly in the necessity of the case; as men of his own years might not like his company.

"And, gentlemen, it is dry business standing here looking at each other," observed Mr. Van Brunt, "and we will take a little punch, to moisten our hearts, as well as our throats. Guert, yon is the pitcher."

Guert made good use of the pitcher, and each man had his glass of punch, a beverage, then as now, much used in the colony. I must acknowledge that the mixture was very knowingly put together, though I had no sooner swallowed my glass, than I discovered it was confounded strong. Not so with Guert. Not only did he swallow *one* glass, but he swallowed *two*, in quick succession, like a man who was thirsty; standing at the time in a fine, manly, erect attitude, as one who trifled with something, that did not half tax his powers. The pitcher, though quite large, was emptied at that one assault, in proof of which it was turned bottom upwards, by Guert himself.

Conversation followed, most of it being in English, out of compliment to the Dominie, who was not supposed to understand Dutch. This was an error, however, Mr. Worden making out tolerably well in that language, when he tried. I was felicitated on the bargains I had made with the contractor, and many kind and hospitable attempts were made to welcome me in a frank, hearty manner among strangers. I confess I was touched by these hon-

est and sincere endeavours to put me at my ease, and when a second pitcher of punch was brought round, I took another glass
with right good will, while Guert, as usual took two; though the
liquor *he* drank, I had many occasions to ascertain subsequently,
produced no more visible effect on him, in the way of physical
consequences, than if he had not swallowed it. Guert was no
drunkard; far from it; he could only drink all near him, under
the table, and remain firm in his chair himself. Such men usually
escape the imputation of being sots, though they are very apt to
pay the penalty of their successes, at the close of their careers.
These are the men who break down at sixty, if not earlier, becoming subject to paralysis, indigestion and other similar evils.

Such was the state of things, the company gradually getting
into a very pleasant humour, when Guert was called out of the
room, by one of the blacks, who bore a most ominous physiog-
nomy while making his request. He was gone but a moment,
when he returned with a certain sort of consternation painted in
his own handsome face. Mr. Van Brunt was called into a corner,
where two or three more of the principal persons present, soon
collected, in an earnest, half-whispered discourse. I was seated so
near this group, as occasionally to overhear a few expressions,
though to get no clear clue to its meaning. The words I overheard
were "old Cuyler"—"capital supper"—"venison and ducks"—
"partridges and quails"—"old Doortje"—"knows us all"—"never
do"—"Dominie the man"—"strangers"—"how to do it?" and several other similar expressions, which left a vague impression on
my mind that our supper was in great peril, from some cause or
other, but what that cause was, I could not learn. Guert was evidently the principal person in this consultation, everybody appearing to listen to his suggestions with respect and attention. At
length, our friend came out of the circle, and in a courteous, self-
possessed manner communicated the difficulty, in the following
words:

"You must know, Rev. Mr. Worden, and Mr. Littlepage, and
Mr. Follock, and Mr. Newcome, that we have certain customs of
our own, among us youths of Albany, that perhaps are not familiar to you gentlemen, nearer the capital. The trut' is that we are
not always as wise, and as sober, as our parents, and grand-
parents in particular, could wish us to be. It is t'ought a good
thing, among us sometimes, to rummage the hen-roosts and

poultry yards of the burghers, and to sup on the fruits of such a forage. I do not know how it is with you, gentlemen, but I will own that to me, ducks and geese got in this innocent game-like way, taste sweeter than when they are bought in the market-hall: our own supper for to-night was a *bought* supper, but it has become the victim of a little enlargement of the practice I have mentioned—"

"How!—How's that, friend Ten Eyck!" exclaimed Mr. Worden, in no affected consternation. "The *supper* a victim, do you say?"

"Yes, sir; to be frank at once, it is gone; gone to a pullet, a steak, and a potatoe. They have not left us a dish!"

"They!" echoed the parson—"And who can *they* be?"

"That is a point yet to be ascertained, for the operation has been carried on in so delicate and refined a way, that none of our blacks know any thing of the matter. It seems there was a cry of fire just now, and it took every one of the negroes into the street, during which time all our game has been put up, and has flown."

"Bless me! Bless me! What a calamity!— What a rascally theft! Did you not mark it down?"

"No sir, I am sorry to say we have not; nor do we apply such hard names to a frolic, even when we lose our supper by it. It is the act of some of our associates and friends, who hope to feast at our expense to-night, and who will, gentlemen, unless you will consent to aid us in recovering our lost dishes."

"Aid you, my dear sir—I will do any thing you can wish—what will you have me attempt? Shall I go to the fort, and ask for succour from the army?"

"No, sir; our object can be effected short of t'at. I am quite certain we can find what we want, only two or three doors from this, if you will consent to lend us a little—a very little of your assistance."

"Name it—Name it, at once, for Heaven's sake, Mr. Guert— The dishes must be getting cold all this time," cried Mr. Worden, jumping up with alacrity, and looking about him, for his hat and cloak.

"The service we ask of you, gentlemen, is just this," rejoined Guert, with a coolness that, when I came to reflect on the events of that night, has always struck me as singularly astonishing. "Our supper, and an excellent one it is, is close at hand, as I have said. Nothing will be easier than to get it on our own table, in the next room, could we only manage to call old Doortje off duty, and detain her for five minutes at the area gate of her house. She knows every one of *us*, and would smell a rat in a minute, did *we* show ourselves; but Mr. Worden and Mr. Littlepage, here, might amuse her for the necessary time, without any trouble. She is remarkably fond of Dominies, and would not be able to trace *you*, back to this house, leaving us to eat the supper in peace. After t'at, no one cares for the rest."

"I'll do it!—I'll do it!" cried Mr. Worden, hurrying into the passage, in quest of his hat and cloak. "It is no more than just that you should have your own, and the supper will be either eaten, or overdone, should we go for constables."

"No fear of constables, Mr. Worden; we never employ them in our poultry wars. All we, who will get the supper back again, can expect, will be merely a little hot water, or a skirmish with our friends."

The details of the movement were now intelligibly and clearly settled. Guert, was to head a party, provided with large clothes-baskets, who were to enter the kitchen, during Doortje's absence, and abstract the dishes, which could not yet be served, as all in Albany, of a certain class, sat down to supper, at nine precisely. As for Doortje, a negro who was in the house, in waiting on one of the guests, his master, would manage to get her out to the area gate, the house having a cellar kitchen, where it would depend on Mr. Worden to detain her, three or four minutes. To my surprise, the parson entered on the execution of this wild scheme, with boyish eagerness, affirming that he could keep the woman half an hour if it were necessary, by delivering her a lecture on the importance of observing the eighth commandment. As soon as the preliminaries were thus arranged, the two parties proceeded on their respective duties, the hour admonishing us of the necessity of losing no time unnecessarily.

I did not like this affair from the first, the experiment of sliding down-hill, having somewhat weakened my confidence in Guert Ten Eyck's judgment. Nevertheless, it would not do for *me* to hold back, when Mr. Worden led, and, after all, there was no great harm in recovering a supper that had been abstracted from our own house. Guert did not proceed, like ourselves, by the street, but he went with his party, out of a back gate into an alley, and was to enter the yard of the house he assailed, by means of a similar gate in its rear. Once in that yard, the access to the kitchen, and the retreat were very easy, provided the cook could be drawn away from her charge at so important a moment. Every thing, therefore, depended on the address of the young negro who was in the house, and ourselves.

On reaching the gate of the area, we stopped while our negro descended to invite Doortje forth. This gave us a moment to examine the building. The house was large, much larger than most of those round it, and what struck me as unusual, there was a lighted lamp over the door. This looked as if it might be a sort of a tavern, or eating house, and rendered the whole thing more intelligible to me. Our roystering plunderers, doubtless intended to sup on their spoils at that tavern.

The negro was gone but a minute, when he came out with a young black of his own sex, a servant whom he was leading off his post, on some pretence of his own, and was immediately followed by the cook. Doortje made many curtsies, as soon as she saw the cocked hat and black cloak, of the Dominie, begging his pardon, and asking his pleasure. Mr. Worden now began a grave and serious lecture on the sin of stealing, holding the confounded Doortje in discourse, quite three minutes. In vain the cook protested she had taken nothing; that her master's property was sacred in her eyes, and ever had been; that she never gave away even cold meats without an order, and that she could not imagine why *she* was to be talked to in this way. To give him his due, Mr. Worden performed his part to admiration, though it is true, he had only an ignorant wench, who was awed by his profession, to manage. At length we heard a shrill whistle, from the alley, the signal of success, when Mr. Worden wished Doortje a solemn good night, and walked away with all the dignity of a priest. In a minute or two, we were in the house, again, and were met by Guert, with cordial shakes of the hand, thanks for our acceptable service, and a summons to supper. It appears that Doortje had actually dished up every thing, all the articles standing before a hot fire, waiting only for the clock to strike nine to be served. In this state, then, the only change the supper had to undergo, was to bring it a short distance through the alley, and to place it on our table, instead of that for which it was so lately intended.

Notwithstanding the rapidity with which the change had been made, it would not have been very easy for a stranger to detect

any striking irregularity in our feast. It is true, there were two sets
of dishes on the table, or, rather dishes of two different sets, but
the ducks, game &c., were not only properly cooked, but were
warm and good. To work everybody went, therefore, with an appetite, and, for five minutes little was heard beyond the clatter of
knives and forks. Then came the drinking of healths, and finally
the toasts and the songs, and the stories.

Guert sang capitally, in a fine, clear, sweet, manly voice, and he
gave us several airs, with words both in English and in Dutch. He
had just finished one of these songs, and the clapping of hands
was still loud and warm, when the young man called on Mr. Worden for a lady, or a sentiment.

"Come, Dominie," he called out, for by this time the feast had
produced its familiarity—"Come, Dominie, you have acquitted
yourself so well as a lecturer, that we are all dying to hear you
preach."

"A lady do you say, sir?" asked the parson, who was as merry as
any of us.

"A laty—a laty—" shouted six, or seven at once—"The Tominie's laty—the Tominie's laty."

"Well, gentlemen, since you will have it so, you shall have one.
You must not complain if she prove a little venerable, but I give
you 'Mother Church.'"

This produced a senseless laugh, as such things usually do, and
then followed my turn. Mr. Van Brunt very formally called on me
for a lady. After pausing a moment I said, as I flatter myself, with
spirit—

"Gentlemen, I will give you another almost as heavenly—Miss
Anneke Mordaunt!"

"Miss Anneke Mordaunt!" was echoed round the table, and I
soon discovered that Anneke was a general favourite, and a very
common toast already at Albany.

"I shall now ask Mr. Guert Ten Eyck for his lady," I said, as soon
as silence was restored, there being very little pause between the
cups that night.

This appeal changed the whole character of the expression of
Guert's face. It became grave in an instant, as if the recollection of
her whose name he was about to utter, produced a pause in his almost fierce mirth. He coloured, then raised his eyes and looked
sternly round, as if to challenge denial, and gave—

"Miss Mary Wallace."

"Ay, Guert, we are used to that name, now," said Van Brunt, a little drily—. "This is the tenth time I have heard it from you, within two months."

"You will be likely to hear it twenty more, sir, for I shall give Mary Wallace, and nobody but Mary Wallace, while the lady remains Mary Wallace—How, now, Mr. Constable! What may be the reason we have the honour of a visit from you, at this time of night?"*

* In this whole affair of the supper, the reader will find incidents that bear a striking resemblance to certain local characteristics pourtrayed, by Mrs. Grant, of Laggan, in her Memoirs of an American Lady; thus corroborating the fidelity of the pictures of our ancient manners, as given by that respectable writer, by the unquestioned authority of Mr. Cornelius Littlepage.—EDITOR.

Chapter XIII

"Masters, it is proved already
That you are little better than false knaves;
And it will go near to be thought so shortly."
                    Much Ado About Nothing, IV. ii. 20–22.

THE sudden appearance of the City Constable, a functionary whose person was not unknown to most of the company, brought every man at table to his feet, the Rev. Mr. Worden, Dirck and myself, included. For my own part I saw no particular reason for alarm, though, it at once struck me that this visit might have some connection with the demolished supper, since the law does not, in all cases, suffer a man to reclaim even his own, by trick or violence. As for the constable himself, a short, compact, snub nosed, Dutch built person, who spoke English as if it disagreed with his bile, he was the coolest of the whole party.

"Vell, Mr. Guert," he said, with a sort of good-natured growl of authority, "here I moost coome, ag'in! Mr. Mayor woult be happy to see you, and ter Tominie, dat ist of your party; and ter gentleman dat acted as clerk, ven he lectured old Doortje, Mr. Mayor's cook."

Mr. Mayor's cook! Here, then, a secret was out, with a vengeance! Guert had not reclaimed his own lost supper, which, having passed into the hands of the Philistines was hopelessly gone, but he had actually stolen and eaten the supper prepared for the Mayor of Albany; Peter Cuyler, a man of note, and standing, in all respects; a functionary who had held his office, from time immemorial. The lamp was the symbol of authority, and not the sign of an inn, or an eating house. The supper, moreover, was never prepared for one man, or one family, but had certainly been got up for the honorable treatment of a goodly company. Fifteen stout men, had mainly appeased their appetites on it, and the fragments were that moment under discussion among half-a-dozen large-mouthed, shining negro-faces, in the kitchen! Under circumstances like these, I looked inquiringly, at the Rev. Mr. Worden, and the Rev. Mr. Worden looked inquiringly at me.

There was no apparent remedy, however; but, after a brief consultation with Guert, we, the summoned parties, took our hats
and followed Dogberry to the residence of Mr. Mayor.

"You are not to be uneasy, gentlemen, at this little interruption
of our amusements," said Guert, dropping in between Mr. Worden and myself, as we proceeded on our way, "these things happening very often among us. You are innocent, you know, under
all circumstances, since you supposed that the supper was our
own, brought back by direct means, instead of having recourse to
the shabby delays of the law."

"And whose supper may this have been, sir, that we have just
eaten?" demanded Mr. Worden.

"Why, there can be no harm, now, in telling you the trut',
Dominie, and I will own, therefore, it belonged in law to Mr.
Mayor Cuyler. There is no great danger, however, as you will see,
when I come to explain matters. You must know that the Mayor's
wife was a Schuyler, and my mother has some of that blood in her
veins, and we count cousins as far as we can see, in Albany. It is
just supping with one's relatives, a little out of the common way,
as you will perceive, gentlemen."

"Have you dealt fairly with Mr. Littlepage and myself, sir, in
this affair?" Mr. Worden asked, a little sternly. "I might, with
great propriety, lecture to a cook on the eighth commandment,
when that cook was a party to robbing you of your supper, but
how shall I answer to His Honour, Mr. Mayor, on the charge
which will now be brought against me? It is not for myself, Mr.
Guert, that I feel so much concern, as for the credit and reputation of my sacred office, and that, too, among your disciples of
the schools of Leyden!"

"Leave it all to me, my dear Dominie—leave it all to me,"
answered Guert, well disposed to sacrifice himself, rather than
permit a friend to suffer. "I am used to these little matters, and
will take care of you."

"I vill answer for t'at," put in the constable, looking over his
shoulder. "No young fly-away, in All*ponny* hast more knowletge
in t'ese matters t'an Mr. Guert, here. If any potty can draw his
heat out of the yoke, Mr. Guert can. Yaas—yaas—he know all
apout t'ese little matters, sure enough."

This was encouraging of a certainty! Our associate was so well
known for his tricks and frolicks, that even the constable who

took him, calculated largely on his address in getting out of scrapes! I did not apprehend that any of us were about to be tried and convicted of a downright robbery, for I knew how far the Dutch carried their jokes of this nature, and how tolerant the seniors were to their juniors, and especially how much all men are disposed to regard any exploit of the sort of that in which we had been engaged, when it has been managed adroitly, and in a way to excite a laugh. Still it was no joke to rob a Mayor of his supper, these functionaries usually passing to their offices through the probationary grade of Alderman.* Guert was not free from uneasiness, as was apparent by a question he put to the officer, on the steps of Mr. Cuyler's house, and under the very light of the official lamp.

"How is the old gentleman, this evening, Hans?" the principal asked, with some little concern in his manner. "I hope he and his company have supped?"

"Vell, t'at is more t'an I can telt you, Mr. Guert. He look't more as like himself, when he hat the horse t'ieves from New Englant taken up, t'an he hast for many a tay. 'Twas most too pat, Mr. Guert, to run away wit' the Mayor's *own* supper! I coult have tolt you who hast your own tucks and venison."

"I wish you had, Hans, with all my heart; but we were hard pushed, and had a strange Dominie to feed—You know a body must provide *well* for company."

"Yaas—yaas—I understants it, and knows how you moost have peen nonplush't to do sich a t'ing; put it was *mo-o-st* too pat. Vell, we are all young, afore we live to pe olt—t'at effery potty knows."

By this time the door was open, and we entered. Mr. Mayor had issued orders we should all be shown into the parlour, where I rather think, from what subsequently passed, he intended to cut Guert up a little more than common, by exposing him before the eyes of a particular person. At all events, the reader can judge

*The American Mayor is usually a different person, from the English mayor. Until within the last five-and-twenty, or thirty years, the Mayor of New-York was invariably a man of social and political importance, belonging strictly to the higher class of society. The same was true of the Mayor of Albany. At the present time, the rule has been so far enlarged, as to admit a selection from all of the more reputable classes, without any rigid adherence to the highest. The elective principle has produced the change. During the writer's boyhood, Philip Van Rensselaer, the brother of the late Patroon, was so long Mayor of Albany, as to be universally known by the *sobriquet* of "*The* Mayor."—EDITOR.

of my horror at finding that the party whose supper I had just helped to demolish, consisted, in addition to three or four sons and daughters of the house, of Herman Mordaunt, Mary Wallace and Anneke! Of course everybody knew *what* had been done; but, until we entered the room, Mr. Mayor alone knew *who* had done it. Of Mr. Worden and myself, even he knew no more than he had learned from Doortje's account of the matter, and the cook, quite naturally, had represented us as rogues feigning our divinity.

Guert was a thoroughly manly fellow, and he did us the justice to enter the parlour first. Poor fellow! I can feel for him, even at this distance of time, when his eye first fell on Mary Wallace's pallid and distressed countenance. It could scarcely be less than I felt myself, when I first beheld Anneke's flushed features, and the look of offended propriety that I fancied to be sparkling in her estranged eye.

Mr. Mayor evidently regarded Mr. Worden with surprise, as indeed he did me, for, instead of strangers he probably expected to meet two of those delinquents whose faces were familiar to him, by divers similar jocular depredations, committed within the limits of his jurisdiction. Then the circumstance that Mr. Worden was a real Dominie, could not be questioned by those who saw him standing, as he did, face to face, with all the usual signs of his sacred office in his dress and air.

"I believe there must be some mistake here, constable!" exclaimed Mr. Mayor. "Why have you brought these two strange gentlemen, along with Guert Ten Eyck?"

"My orters, Mr. Mayor, wast to pring 'Doortje's rapscallion Tominie,' and his 'rapscallion frient,' and t'at is one, and t'is ist t'ot'er."

"This gentleman has the appearance of being a *real* clergyman, and that too, of the church of England."

"Yaas, Mr. Mayor—t'at is yoost so. He wilt preach fifteen minutes, wit'out stopping, if you wilt give him a plack gownt, and pray an hour, in a white shirt."*

---

*This opinion of the constable's must refer to the notion common amongst the non-Episcopal sects, that the value of spiritual provender, was to be measured by the quantity. Preaching, however, *might* be overdone in the Dutch Reformed Churches; for, quite within my recollection, a half-hour glass stood on the pulpit of the Dutch edifice named in the text, to regulate the dominie's wind. It was

"Will you do me the favour, Guert Ten Eyck, to let me know the names of the strangers I have the pleasure to receive," said the Mayor, a little authoritatively.

"Certainly, Mr. Mayor; certainly, and with very great pleasure. I should have done this at once, had we been ushered into your house, by any one but the city constable. Whenever I accompany that gentleman anywhere, I always wait to ascertain my welcome."

Guert laughed with some heart, at this allusion to his own known delinquencies, while Mr. Cuyler only smiled. I could see, notwithstanding the severe measures to which he had resorted in this particular case, that the last was not unfriendly to the first, and that our friend Guert had not fallen literally among robbers, in being brought to the place where we were.

"This reverend dominie," continued Guert, as soon as he had had his laugh, and had ventured to cast a short, inquiring glance at Mary Wallace, "is a gentleman from England, Mr. Mayor, who is to preach in St. Peter's the day after to-morrow, by special invitation from the chaplain, when, I make no doubt, we shall all be much edified; Miss Mary Wallace, among the rest, if she will do him the honour to attend the service, good, and angelic, and *forgiving*, as I know she is by nature."

This speech caused all eyes to turn on the young lady, whose face crimsoned, though she made no reply. I now felt satisfied that Guert's manly, frank avowed and sincere admiration had touched the heart of Mary Wallace, while her reason condemned that which her natural tenderness encouraged, and the struggle in her mind was then, and long after, a subject of curious study with me. As for Anneke, I thought she resented this somewhat indiscreet, not to say indelicate though indirect avowal of his feelings towards his mistress, and that she looked on Guert with even more coldness than she had previously done. Neither of the ladies, however, said any thing. During this dumb show, Mr. Cuyler had leisure to recover from the surprise of discovering that one of his prisoners was really a clergyman, and to enquire who the other might be.

"That gentleman, then, is in fact a clergyman!" he answered. "You have forgotten to name the other, Guert."

said it might be turned *once* with impunity; but woe betide him who should so far trespass on his people's patience, as to presume to turn it *twice*.—EDITOR.

"This is Mr. Corny Littlepage, Mr. Mayor; the only son of Major Littlepage, of Satanstoe, Westchester."

The Mayor looked a little puzzled, and I believe felt somewhat embarrassed as to the manner in which he ought to proceed. The incursion of Guert upon his premises, much exceeded in boldness, any thing of the kind that had ever before occurred in Albany. It was common enough for young men of his stamp, to carry off poultry, pigs &c., and feast on the spoils; and cases had occurred, as I afterwards learned, in which rival parties of these depredators preyed on each other, the same materials for a supper having been known to change hands two, or three times before they were consumed; but no one had ever presumed, previously to this evening, to make an inroad even on Mr. Mayor's hencoop, much less to molest the domains of his cook. In the first impulse of his anger, Mr. Cuyler had sent for the constable, and Guert's club, with its place of meeting being well known, that functionary having had many occasions to visit it, the latter proceeded thither, forthwith. It is probable, however, a little reflection satisfied the mayor that a frolick could not well be treated as a larceny, and that Guert had some of his own wife's blood in his veins. When he came to find that two respectable strangers were implicated in the affair, one of whom was actually a clergyman, this charitable feeling was strengthened and he changed his course of proceeding.

"You can return home, Hans," said Mr. Mayor, very sensibly mollified in his manner. "Should there be occasion for your further services, I will send for you. Now, gentlemen," as soon as the door closed on the constable, "I will satisfy you that old Peter Cuyler can cover a table, and feed his friends, even though Guert Ten Eyck be so near a neighbour. Miss Wallace, will you allow me the honour to lead you to the table? Mr. Worden will see Mrs. Cuyler in safety to the same place."

On this hint, the missionary stepped forward with alacrity, and led Mrs. Mayoress after Mary Wallace, with the utmost courtesy. Guert did the same to one of the young ladies of the house, Anneke was led in by one of the young men, and I took the remaining young lady, who I presumed was also one of the family. It was very apparent we were respited, and all of us thought it wisest to appear as much at our ease as possible, in order not to balk the humour of the principal magistrate of the ancient town of Albany.

To do Mr. Mayor justice, the lost time had been so well improved by Doortje, that, on looking around the table, I thought the supper to which we were thus strangely invited, was of the two, the best I had seen that evening. Luckily game was plenty, and by means of quails, partridges, oysters, venison patties and other dishes of that sort, the cook had managed to send up quite as good a supper at ten o'clock as she had previously prepared for nine.

I will not pretend that I felt quite at my ease, as I took my seat at the table, for the second time that night. All the younger members of the party looked exceedingly grave, as if they could very well dispense with our company, the old people alone appearing to enter into the scene with any spirit. Anneke did not even look at me, after the first astounded look given on my entrance, nor did Mary Wallace once cast her eyes towards Guert, when we reached the supper room. Mr. Mayor, notwithstanding, had determined to laugh off the affair, and he and Mr. Worden soon became excellent friends, and began to converse freely and naturally.

"Come, cousin Guert," cried Mr. Mayor, after two or three glasses of Madeira had still further warmed his heart, "fill, and pledge me—unless you prefer to give a lady. If the last, everybody will drink to her, with hearty good will. You eat nothing, and must drink the more."

"Ah! Mr. Mayor, I have toasted one lady to-night, and cannot toast another."

"Not present company excepted, my boy?"

"No, sir, not even with that license. I pledge you with all my heart, and thank you with all my heart for this generous treatment, after my own foolish frolic—but, you know how it is, Mr. Mayor, with us Albany youths, when our pride is up, and a supper must be had—"

"Not I, Guert; I know nothing about it, but should very well like to learn. How came you, in the first place, to take such a fancy to my cook's supper?—Did you imagine it better than Van Brunt's cook could give you?"

"The supper of Arent Van Brunt's cook, has disappeared—

gone on the hill, I fancy, among the red coats; and, to own the truth, Mr. Mayor, it was yours, or nothing. I had invited these gentlemen, to pass the evening with us. One of our blacks happened to mention what was going on here, and hospitality led us all astray. It was nothing more, I do assure you, Mr. Mayor."

"And so your hospitable feelings made your guests work for their supper, by sending them to preach to old Doortje, while you were dishing up my ducks and game?"

"Your pardon, Mr. Mayor; Doortje had dished up before she went to lecture. Your cook is too well trained to neglect her duty even to hear a sermon by the Rev. Mr. Worden! But, these gentlemen were quite as much deceived as the old woman, for they supposed we were after our own lost goods, and did not know that you dwelt here, and were as much my dupes, as old Doortje herself. Truth obliges me to own this much, in their justification."

There was a general clearing up of countenances at this frank avowal, and I saw that Anneke, herself, turned her looks inquiringly upon the speaker, and suffered a smile to relieve the extreme gravity of her sweet countenance. From that moment, a very sensible change came over the feelings and deportment of the younger part of the company, and the conversation became easier and more natural. It was certainly much in our favour to have it known we had not officiously and boyishly joined in a gratuitous attempt to rob and insult this particular and unoffending family, but that Mr. Worden and I supposed we were simply aiding in getting back those things which properly belonged to our hosts, and getting them back, too, in a manner of which the party we supposed we were acting against, would certainly have no right to complain, inasmuch as they had set the example. Guert was encouraged to go on further with his explanations, which he did in his own honest, candid manner, exculpating us, in effect, from every thing but being a little too much disposed to waggery, for a minister of the church, and his pupil who had just commenced his travels.

Anneke's face brightened up, more and more, as the explanations proceeded, and soon after they were ended, she turned to me, in a very gracious manner, and inquired after my mother. As I sat directly opposite to her, and the table was narrow, we could converse, without attracting much attention to ourselves, Mr. Mayor and his other guests keeping up a round of reasonably noisy jokes, on the events of the evening, nearer the foot of the table.

"You find some customs in Albany, Mr. Littlepage, that are not known to us, in New York;" Anneke observed, after a few preliminary remarks had opened the way to further communication.

"I scarce know, Miss Anneke, whether you allude to what has occurred this evening, or to what occurred this afternoon?"

"To both, I believe;" answered Anneke, smiling, though she coloured, as I thought, with a species of feminine vexation, "for, certainly, one is no more a custom with us, than the other."

"I have been most unfortunate, Miss Mordaunt, in the exhibitions I have made of myself, in the course of the few hours I have passed in this, to me, strange place. I am afraid you regard me as little more than an overgrown boy, who has been permitted by his parents, to leave home sooner than he ought."

"This is your construction, and not mine, Mr. Littlepage. I suppose you know—but, we will talk of this in the other room, or at some other time."

I took the hint, and said no more on the subject while at table. Mr. Mayor, I suppose in consideration of our having gone through the exactions of one feast already, that evening, permitted us to leave the supper room much earlier than common, and the hour being late, the whole party broke up immediately afterwards. Before we separated, however, Herman Mordaunt approached me, in a friendly, free way, and invited me to come to his house at eight the next morning to breakfast, requesting the pleasure of Dirck's company, at the same time; the invitation to the latter going through me. It is scarcely necessary to say how gladly I accepted, and how much I was relieved by this termination of an adventure that, at one moment, menaced me with deep disgrace. Had Mr. Mayor seen fit to pursue the affair of the abstraction of his first supper, in a serious vein, although the legal consequences could not probably have amounted to any thing very grave, they might prove very ridiculous; and I have no doubt they would have brought about a very abrupt termination of my visit to the north. As it was, my mind was vastly relieved, as I believe was the case also with that of the Rev. Mr. Worden.

"Corny," said that gentleman, after we had wished Guert good night, and were well on our way to the inn, again, "this second supper has helped surprisingly to digest the first. I doubt if our new acquaintance, here, will be likely to turn out very profitable to us."

"Yet, sir, you appeared to take to him exceedingly, and I had thought you excellent friends."

"I like the fellow well enough, too, for he is hearty, and frank, and good natured; but there was some little policy, in keeping on good terms with him. I'm afraid, Corny, I did not altogether consult the dignity of my holy office, this morning, on the ice! It is exceedingly unbecoming in a clergyman, to be seen running in a public place, like a school boy, or a youngster contending in a match. I thought, moreover, I overheard one of those young Dutchmen call me the 'Loping Dominie,' and, so, taking altogether, it struck me it would be wisest to keep on good terms with this Guert Ten Eyck."

"I see your policy, sir, and it does not become me to deny it. As for myself, I confess I like Guert, surprisingly, and shall not give him up, easily, though he has already got me into two serious scrapes, in the short time we have been acquainted. He is a hearty, good natured, thoughtless young fellow, who, Dutchman like, when he does make an attempt to enjoy life, does it with all his heart."

I then related the affair of the hand-sled to Mr. Worden, who gave me some of that sort of consolation of which a man receives a great deal, as he elbows his way through this busy, selfish, world.

"Well, Corny," said my old master, "I am not certain you did not look more like a fool, as you rolled over from that sled, than I looked while 'loping' from our friends in the sleigh!"

We both laughed as we entered the tavern; I, to conceal the vexation I really felt, and Mr. Worden, as I presume, because he was flattered with the belief that I must have appeared quite as ridiculous as himself.

Next morning I proceeded to Herman Mordaunt's residence, at the earliest hour, the rules of society would allow. I found the family established in one of those Dutch edifices, of which Albany was mainly composed, and which stood a little removed from the street, having a tiny yard in front, with the *stoop* in the gable, and that gable towards the yard. The battlement walls of this house, diminished towards the high apex of a very steep roof, by steps, as we are all so much accustomed to see, and the whole was surmounted by an iron weathercock, that was perched on a rod of some elevation. It was always a matter of importance with the Dutch, to know which way the wind blew, nor did it comport with their habits of minute accuracy, to trust to the usual indications of the feeling on the skin, the bending of branches, the flying of clouds, or the driving of smoke, but they must and would have the certainty of a machine that was constructed expressly to let them know the fact. Smoke might err, but a weathercock would not!

No one was in the little parlor into which I was shown, by the servant who admitted me to the house, and, in whom I recognised Herman Mordaunt's principal male attendant, of the household in New York. How pleasantly did that little room appear to me, in the minute, or two, that I was left in it alone. There lay the very shawl, that Anneke had on, the day I met her in the Pinkster Field, and a pair of gloves that it seemed to me no other hands but hers were small enough to wear, had been thrown on the shawl, carelessly, as one casts aside a thing of that sort, in a hurry. A dozen other articles, were put here and there, that denoted the habits and presence of females of refinement. But the gloves most attracted my attention, and I must needs rise, and examine them. It is true, these gloves might belong to Mary Wallace, for she, too, had a pretty little hand, but I fancied they belonged to Anneke. Under this impression, I raised them to my lips, and was actually pressing them there, with a good deal of romantic feeling, when a light footstep in the room, told me I was not alone. Dropping the gloves, I turned and beheld Anneke, herself. She was regarding me with an expression of countenance I did not then know how to interpret, and which I now hardly know how to describe. In the first place, her charming countenance was suffused with blushes, while her eyes were filled with an expression of softened interest, that caused my heart to beat so violently, that I did not know but it would escape by the channel of the throat. How near I was to declaring all I felt, at that moment; of throwing myself at the feet of the dear, dear, creature, and of avowing how much and engrossingly she had filled both my waking and sleeping thoughts during the last year, and of beseeching her to bless the remainder of my days, by becoming my wife! Nothing prevented this sally, but the remark which Anneke made, the instant she had gracefully curtsied, in return to my confused and awkward bow, and which happened to be this—

"What do you find so much to admire in Miss Wallace's gloves?" asked the wilful girl, biting her lip as I fancied, to suppress a smile, though her cheeks were still suffused and her eyes continued to give forth that indescribable expression of bewitching softness. "It is a pair my father presented to her, and she wore them last evening in compliment to him."

"I beg pardon, Miss Mordaunt—Miss Anneke—that is—I beg pardon. Is there not a very delightful odour about those gloves—that is, I was thinking so, and was endeavoring to ascertain what it might be, by the scent."

"It must be the lavender with which we young ladies are so coquettish as to sprinkle our gloves and handkerchiefs—or, it may be musk. Mary is rather fond of musk, though I prefer lavender. But, what an evening we had, Mr. Littlepage!—And what an introduction you have had to Albany, and, most of all, what a master of ceremonies!"

"Do you then dislike Guert Ten Eyck, as an acquaintance, Miss Anneke?"

"Far from it:—it is quite impossible to *dislike* Guert; he is so manly; so ready to admit his own weaknesses; so sincere in all he does and says; so good natured, and, in short, so much that, were one his sister, she might wish him to be, and yet so much that a sister must regret."

"I thought, last evening, that all the ladies felt an interest in him, notwithstanding the numberless wild and ill-judged things he does. Is he not a favourite with Miss Wallace?"

The quick, sensitive glance that Anneke gave me, said plainly enough that my question was indiscreet, and it was no sooner put, than it was regretted. A shadow passed athwart the sweet face of my companion, and a moment of deep, and, as I fancied, of painful thought succeeded. Then a light broke over all, a smile illumined her features, after which a light girlish laugh came to show how active were the agents within, and how strong was the native tendency to happiness and humour.

"After all, Corny Littlepage," said Anneke, turning her face towards me with an indescribable character of fun and feeling so blended in it, as fairly to puzzle me—"you must admit that your exploit in the hand-sled was sufficiently ridiculous to last a young man for some time!"

"I confess it all, Anneke, and shall have a care, how I turn boy again, in a strange place. I am rejoiced to find, however, that you look upon the foolish affair of the slide, as more grave than that of the supper, which I was fearful might involve me in serious disgrace."

"Neither is very serious, Mr. Littlepage, though the last might have proved awkward, had not the Mayor known the ways of the young men of the town; they say, however, that nothing so bold has ever before been attempted in that way, in Albany, great as are the liberties that are often taken with the neighbors' hencoops."

Anneke laughed, and this time it was naturally, and without the least restraint.

"I hope you will not think it shabby in me, if I seem to wish to throw all the blame on this harum scarum Guert Ten Eyck. He drew me into both affairs, and into the last, in a great measure, innocently and ignorantly."

"So it is understood, and so it would be understood the moment Guert Ten Eyck was found to be connected with the affair at all."

"I may hope, then, to be forgiven, Anneke?" I said, holding out a hand, to invite her to accept it as a pledge of pardon.

Anneke did not prudishly decline putting her own little hand in mine, though I got only the ends of two or three slender delicate fingers, and her colour increased as she bestowed this grace.

"You must ask forgiveness, Corny," she answered—I believe she now used this familiar name, simply to show how completely she had forgotten the little spleen she had certainly felt at my untoward exhibition in the street. "You must ask forgiveness of those who possess the right to pardon. If Corny Littlepage chooses to slide down hill, like a boy, what right has Anneke Mordaunt to say him nay?"

"Every right in the world—the right of friendship—the right of a superior mind, of superior manners—the right that my—"

"Hush—that is Mr. Bulstrode's footstep in the passage, and he will not understand this discussion on the subject of my manifold rights. It takes him some time, however, to throw aside his overcoats and furs, and sword, and I will just tell you that Guert Ten Eyck is a dangerous master of ceremonies for Corny Littlepage."

"Yet, he has sense enough, feeling enough, *heart* enough to admire and love Mary Wallace."

"Has he told you this, so soon! But, I need not ask, as he tells his love to every one who will listen."

"And to Miss Wallace herself, I trust, among the number. The man who loves, and loves truly should not long permit its object to remain in any doubt of his feelings and intentions. It has ever appeared to me, Miss Mordaunt, as a most base and dastardly feeling in a man to wish to be certain of a woman's returning his love, before he has the manliness to let his mistress understand his wishes. How is a sensitive female to know when she is safe in yielding her affections, without this frankness on the part of her suitor? I'll answer for it that Guert Ten Eyck has dealt thus honestly and frankly with Mary Wallace."

"That is a merit which cannot be denied him," answered Anneke, in a low, thoughtful tone of voice. "Mary has heard this from his own mouth, again and again. Even my presence, has been no obstacle to his declarations, for three times have I heard him beg Mary to consider him as a suitor for her hand, and entreat her not to decide on his offer, until he has had a longer opportunity to win her esteem."

"And this you will admit, Miss Mordaunt, is to his credit; is manly, and like himself?"

"It is certainly frank and honourable, Mr. Littlepage, since it enables Miss Wallace to understand the object of his attentions, and leaves nothing to doubt, or uncertainty."

"I am glad you approve of such fair and frank proceedings; though but a moment remains to say what I wish, it will suffice to add that the course Guert Ten Eyck has taken towards Mary Wallace, Cornelius Littlepage would wish to pursue towards Anneke Mordaunt."

Anneke started, turned pale; then showed cheeks that were suffused with blushes, and looked at me with timid surprise. She made no answer; though that earnest, yet timid gaze, long remained, and, for that matter still remains, vividly impressed upon my recollection. It seemed to express astonishment, startled sensiblity, feminine bashfulness, and maiden coyness, but it did not appear to me that it expressed displeasure. There was no time, however, to ask for explanations, since the voices of Herman Mordaunt and Bulstrode were now heard at the very door, and, at the next instant, both entered the room.

Chapter XIV

"My beautiful! my beautiful! that standest meekly by,
With thy proudly arch'd and glossy neck, and dark
   and fiery eye—
Thus, thus, I leap upon thy back, and scour the distant plains,
Away! who overtakes me now, shall claim thee for his pains."
      Caroline Norton, "The Arab to His Favorite Steed,"
        ll. 1–2, 47–48.

BULSTRODE seemed happy to meet me, complaining that I had quite forgotten the satisfaction with which all New York, agreeably to his account of the matter, had received me, the past spring. Of course, I thanked him for his civility, and we soon became as good friends as formerly. In a minute or two, Mary Wallace joined us, and we all repaired to the breakfast table, where we were soon joined by Dirck who had been detained by some affairs of his own.

Herman Mordaunt and Bulstrode had the conversation principally to themselves, for the first few minutes. Mary Wallace was habitually silent, but Anneke, without being loquacious, was sufficiently disposed to converse. This morning, however, she said little beyond what the civilities of the table required from the mistress of the house, and that little in as few words as possible. Once, or twice, I could not help remarking that her hand remained on the handle of a richly chased tea-pot, after that hand had performed its office; and that her sweet, deep blue eye was fixed on vacancy, or on some object before her with a vacant regard in the manner of one that thought intensely. Each time as she recovered from these little *reveries*, a slight flush appeared on her face, and she seemed anxious to conceal the involuntary abstraction. This absence of mind continued until Bulstrode, who had been talking with our host, on the subject of the movements of the army, suddenly directed his discourse to me.

"I hope we owe this visit to Albany," he said, "to an intention on your part, Mr. Littlepage, to make one among us, in the next campaign. I hear of many gentlemen of the colonies, who intend to accompany us in our march to Quebec."

"That is somewhat farther than I had thought of going, Mr. Bulstrode," was my answer, "inasmuch as I have never supposed the King's forces contemplated quite so distant a march. It is the intention of Mr. Follock and myself, to get permission to attach ourselves to some regiment, and to go forward as far as Ticonderoga at least; for we do not like the idea of the French holding a post like that, so far within the limits of our own province."

"Bravely said, sir, and I trust I shall be permitted to be of some assistance when the time comes to settle details. Our mess would always be happy to see you, and you know that I am at its head, since the Lt. Colonel has left us."

I returned my thanks, and the discourse took another direction.

"I met Harris, as I was walking hither, this morning," Bulstrode continued, "and he gave me, in his confused Irish way, for I insist he is Irish although he was born in London, but he gave me a somewhat queer account of a supper he was at, last night, which he said had been borne off by a foraging party of young Albanians, and brought into the barracks, as a treat to some of our gentlemen. This was bad enough, though they tell me a Dutchman always pardons such a frolick, but Harris makes the matter much worse, by adding that the supperless party indemnified itself by making an attack on the kitchen of Mr. Mayor, and carrying off his ducks and partridges, in a way to leave him without even a potatoe!"

I felt that my face was as red as scarlet, and I fancied everybody was looking at me, while Herman Mordaunt took on himself the office of making a reply.

"The story does not lose in travelling, as a matter of course," answered our host, "though it is true, in the main. We all supped with Mr. Cuyler, last evening, and know that he had much more than a potatoe on the table."

"All!—What the ladies?"

"Even to the ladies—and Mr. Littlepage in the bargain," returned Herman Mordaunt, casting a glance at me, and smiling. "Each and all of us will testify he not only had a plenty of supper, but that which was good."

"I see by the general smile," cried Bulstrode, "that there is a *sous entendu*, here, and shall insist on being admitted to the secret."

Herman Mordaunt now told the whole story, not being particularly careful to conceal the more ludicrous parts, dwelling with some emphasis on the lecture Mr. Worden had delivered to Doortje, and appealing to me to know whether I did not think it excellent. Bulstrode laughed of course, though I fancied both the young ladies wished nothing had been said on the subject. Anneke even attempted, once or twice, to divert her father from certain comments that he made, in which he spoke rather lightly of such sort of amusements, in general.

"That Guert Ten Eyck is a character!" exclaimed Bulstrode, "and one I am sometimes at a loss to comprehend. A more manly looking, fine, bold young fellow, I do not know, and he is often as manly and imposing in his opinions and judgments, as he is to the eye; while, at times, he is almost childish in his tastes and propensities. How do you account for this, Miss Anneke?"

"Simply that nature intended Guert Ten Eyck for better things than accident and education, or the want of education, have enabled him to become. Had Guert Ten Eyck been educated at Oxford, he would have been a very different man from what he is. If a man has only the instruction of a boy, he will long remain a boy."

I was surprised at the boldness and decision of this opinion, for it was not Anneke's practice to be so open in delivering her sentiments of others; but, it was not long ere I discovered that she did not spare Guert, in the presence of her friend, from a deep conviction he was not worthy of the hold he was sensibly gaining on the feelings of Mary Wallace. Herman Mordaunt, as I fancied, favoured his daughter's views, in this behalf, and there was soon occasion to observe that poor Guert had no other ally, in that family, than the one his handsome, manly, person, open disposition, and uncommon frankness had created in his mistress's own bosom. There was certainly a charm in Guert's habitual manner of underrating himself, that inclined all who heard him to his side, and, for myself, I will confess I early became his friend in all that matters, and so continued to the last.

Bulstrode and I left the house together, walking arm and arm, to his quarters, leaving Dirck with the ladies.

"This is a charming family," said my companion, as we left the door, "and I feel proud of being able to claim some affinity to it, though it is not so near as I trust it may one day become."

I started, almost twitching my arm away from that of the Major's, turning half round, at the same instant, to look him in the face. Bulstrode smiled, but preserved his own self-possession in the stoical manner common to men of fashion and easy manners, pursuing the discourse.

"I see that my frankness has occasioned you some little surprise," he added, "but, the truth is the truth, and I hold it to be unmanly for a gentleman who has made up his mind to become the suitor of a lady, to make any secret of his intentions—is not that your own way of thinking, Mr. Littlepage?"

"Certainly, as respects the lady; and possibly as respects her family; but not as respects all the world."

"I take your distinction, which may be a good one, in ordinary cases; though, in the instance of Anneke Mordaunt, it may be merciful to let wandering young men, like yourself, Corny, comprehend the real state of the case. I very well understand your own particular relation to the family of the Mordaunts, but others may approach it with different and more interested views."

"Am I to understand, Mr. Bulstrode, that Miss Mordaunt is your betrothed?"

"Oh! by no means, for she has not yet made up her mind to accept me. You are to understand, however, that I have proposed to Herman Mordaunt, with my father's knowledge and approbation, and that the affair is *in petto*. You can judge for yourself of the probable termination, being a better judge, as a looker on, than I, as a party interested, of Anneke's manner of viewing my suit."

"You will remember I have not seen you together these ten months, until this morning, and I presume you do not wish me to suppose you have been waiting all that time, for an answer."

"As I consider you an *ami de famille*, Corny, there is no reason why there should not be a fair statement of things laid before you, for that affair of the lion will ever render you half a Mordaunt, yourself. I had proposed to Anneke, when you first saw me, and got the usual lady-like answers that the dear creature was too young to think of contracting herself, which was certainly truer then than now; that I had friends at home, who ought to be consulted, that time must be given, or the answer would necessarily be 'no,' and all the usual substance of such replies, in the preliminary state of a negotiation."

"And there the matter has stood ever since?"

"By no means, my dear fellow; as far from that as possible. I heard Herman Mordaunt, for he did most of the talking on that side, with the patience of a saint, observed how proper it all was, and stated my intention to lay every thing before my father, and then advance to the assault anew, reinforced by his consent, and authority to offer settlements."

"All of which you got, by return of vessel, on writing home," I added, unable to imagine how any man could hesitate about receiving Anneke Mordaunt for a daughter-in-law.

"Why, not exactly by return of vessel, though Sir Harry is much too well bred to neglect answering a letter. I never knew him to do such a thing in his life; no, not when I have pushed him a little closely on the subject of my allowance, having been out, before the quarter was up, as will sometimes happen at college, you know, Corny. To tell you the truth, my dear boy, Sir Harry's consent did *not* come by return of vessel, though an answer did. It is a confounded distance across the Atlantic, and it takes time to argue a question, when the parties are 'a thousand leagues asunder.'"

"Argue!—What argument could be required to convince Sir Harry Bulstrode of the propriety of your getting Anneke Mordaunt for a wife, *if you could?*"

"Quite plain and sincere, upon my honour!—But, I love you for the simplicity of your character, Corny, and so shall view all favourably. If I *could*! Well, we shall know at the end of the approaching campaign, when you and I come back from our trip to Quebec."

"You have not answered my question, in the mean time, concerning Sir Harry Bulstrode."

"I beg Sir Harry's and your pardon. What argument could be required to convince my father?—Why, you have never been at home, Littlepage, and cannot easily understand, therefore, what the feeling is precisely, in relation to the colonies—much depends on that, you know."

"I trust the mother loves her children, as I am certain the children love their mother."

"Yes, you are all loyal;—I will say that for you, though Albany is not exactly Bath, or New York, Westminster. I suppose you know, Littlepage, that the church upon the hill, yonder, which is called St. Peter's, though a very good church, and a very respectable church, with a very reputable congregation, is not exactly Westminster Abbey, or even St. James's?"

"I believe I understand you, sir; and so Sir Harry proved obstinate?"

"As the devil!—It took no less than three letters, the last of which was pretty bold, to get him round, which I did at last, and his consent, in due form, has been handed in to Herman Mordaunt. I contended, with some advantages in the affair, or I never should have prevailed. But, you will see how it was. Sir Harry is gouty and asthmatic both, and no great things of a life, at the best, and every acre he has on earth, is entailed, just making the whole thing a question of time."

"All of which you communicated, of course, to Anneke and Herman Mordaunt?"

"If I did, I'll be hanged! No, no; Master Corny, I am not so green as that would imply. You provincials are as thin-skinned as *raisins de Fontainebleau*, and are not to be touched so rudely. I do not believe Anneke would marry the Duke of Norfolk, himself, if the family raised the least scruple about receiving her."

"And would not Anneke be right, in acting under so respectable a feeling?"

"Why, you know she would only marry the duke, and not his mother, and aunts, and uncles. I cannot see the necessity of a young woman's making herself uncomfortable on that account. But, we have not come to that yet, for I would wish you to understand, Littlepage, that I am not accepted. No—no—justice to Anneke demands that I should say this much. She knows of Sir Harry's consent, however, and that is a good deal in my favour, you must allow. I suppose her great objection will be to quitting her father, who has no other child, and on him it *will* bear a little hard; and, then, it is likely she will say something about a change of country, for you Americans are all great sticklers for living in your own region."

"I do not see how you can justly accuse us of that, since it is universally admitted among us that every thing is better at home, than it is in the Colonies."

"I really think, Corny," rejoined Bulstrode, smiling good naturedly, "were you to pay the old island a visit, now, you yourself would confess that some things *are!*"

"I to visit!—I am at a loss to imagine why I am named as one disposed to deny it. Had it been Guert Ten Eyck, now, or even Dirck Follock, one might imagine such a thing; but, I, who come from English blood, and who have an English born grandfather, at this moment, alive and well, at Satanstoe, am not to be included among the disaffected to England."

Bulstrode pressed my arm, and his conversation took a more confidential air, as it proceeded. "I believe you are right, Corny," he said; "the colony is loyal enough, Heaven knows, yet I find these Dutch look on us red coats more coldly than the people of English blood, below. Should it be ascribed to the phlegm of their manners, or to some ancient grudge connected with the conquest of their colony?"

"Hardly the last, I should think, since the colony was traded away, under the final arrangement, in exchange for a possession the Dutch now hold in South America. There is nothing strange, however, in the descendants of the people of Holland preferring the Dutch to the English."

"I assure you, Littlepage, the coldness with which we are regarded by the Albanians has been spoken of among us; though most of the leading families treat us well, and aid us all they can. They should remember that we are here to fight their battles, and to prevent the French from overrunning them."

"To that they would probably answer that the French would not molest them, but for their quarrel with England. Here, we must part, Mr. Bulstrode, as I have business to attend to. I will add one word, however, before we separate, and that is, that King George II^d, has not more loyal subjects in his dominions, than those who dwell in his American provinces."

Bulstrode smiled, nodded in assent, waved his hand, and we parted.

I had plenty of occupation, for the remainder of that day. Yaap arrived with his 'brigade of sleighs' about noon, and I went in search of Guert, in whose company, I repaired once more to the office of the contractor. Horses, harness, sleighs, provisions and all, were taken at high prices, and I was paid for the whole in Spanish gold; joes and half-joes being quite as much in use among us, in that day, as the coin of the realm. Spanish silver has always formed our smaller currency, such a thing as an English shilling, or a sixpence, being quite a stranger among us. Pieces of eight, or dollars, are our commonest coin, it is true, but we make good use of the half-joe, in all heavy transactions. I have seen two or three, Bank of England notes in my day, but they are of very rare occurrence in the colonies. There have been colony bills among us, but they are not favourites, most of our transactions being carried on by means of the Spanish gold and Spanish silver, that find their way up from the islands and the Spanish main. The war of which I am now writing, however, brought a great many guineas among us, most of the troops being paid in that species of coin; but the contractors, in general, found it easier to command the half-joe than the guinea. Of the former, when all our sales were made, Dirck and myself had, between us, no less than one hundred and eleven, or eight hundred and eighty-eight dollars, in value.

I found Guert just as ready, and just as friendly on this occasion, as he had been on the previous day. Not only were all our effects disposed of, but all our negroes were hired to the army, for the campaign, Yaap excepted. The boys went off with their teams, towards the north, that same afternoon, in high spirits, as ready for a frolick, as any white youths in the Colony. I permitted Yaap to go on with his sleigh, to be absent for a few days, but he was to return and join us before we proceeded in quest of the 'Patent,' after the breaking up of the winter.

It was late in the afternoon, before every thing was settled, when Guert invited me to take a turn with him on the river in his own sleigh. By this time, I had ascertained that my new friend was a young man of very handsome property, without father or mother, and that he lived in as good style, as was common for the simple habits of those around him. Our principal families in New York, were somewhat remarkable for the abundance of their plate, table linen, and other household effects of the latter character, while, here and there, one was to be found that possessed some good pictures. The latter, I have reason to think, however, were rare, though occasionally the work of a master did find its way to America, particularly from Holland and Flanders. Guert kept bachelor's hall, in a respectable house, that had its gable to the street, as usual, and which was of no great size; but every thing about it proved that his old black housekeeper had been trained under a *régime* of thorough neatness; for that matter, every thing around Albany, wore the appearance of being periodically scoured. The streets themselves could not undergo that process with snow on the ground, but once beneath a roof, and every thing that had the character of dirt was banished. In this particular, Guert's bachelor residence was as faultless, as if it had a mistress at its head, and that mistress were Mary Wallace.

"If she ever consent to have me," said Guert, actually sighing as he spoke, and glancing his eyes round the very pretty little parlour I had just been praising, on the occasion of the visit I first made to his residence that afternoon; "If she ever consent to have me, Corny, I shall have to build a new house. This is now a hundred years old, and though it was thought a great affair in its day, it is not half good enough for Mary Wallace. My dear fellow, how I envy you that invitation to breakfast this morning; what a favourite you must be with Herman Mordaunt!"

"We are very good friends, Guert—" for with the freedom of our Colony manners, we had already dropped into the familiarity of calling each other 'Corny' and 'Guert'—"We are very good friends, Guert," I answered, "and I have some reason to think Herman Mordaunt does not dislike me. It was in my power to be of a trifling service to Miss Anneke, last spring, and the whole family is disposed to remember it."

"So I can see, at a glance; even Anneke remembers it. I have heard the whole story from Mary Wallace; it was about a lion. I would give half of what I am worth to see Mary Wallace in the paws of a lion, or any other wild beast, just to let her see that Guert Ten Eyck has a heart, as well as Corny Littlepage. But, Corny my boy, there is one thing you must do; you are in such favour that it will be easy for you to effect it, though I might try in vain, forever."

"I will do any thing that is proper, to oblige you, Guert; for you have a claim on me for services rendered by yourself."

"Pshaw!—Say nothing of such matters; I am never happier than when buying or selling a horse; and in helping you to get off your old cattle, why, I did the King no harm, and you some good. But, it was about horses I was thinking. You must know, Littlepage, there is not a young man, or an old man, within twenty miles of Albany, that drives such a pair of beasts as myself."

"You surely do not wish me to sell these horses, to Mary Wallace, Guert!" I rejoined, laughing.

"Ay, my lad, and this house, and the old farm, and two or three stores along the river, and all I have, provided you can sell me with them. As the ladies have no present use for horses, however, Herman Mordaunt having brought up with him a very good pair that came near running over you and me, Corny; so, there is no need of any sale; but I *should* like to drive Mary and Anneke, a turn of a few miles, with that team of mine, and in my own sleigh!"

"That cannot prove such a difficult affair, young ladies ordinarily consenting readily enough to be diverted with a sleigh ride."

"The off one carries himself more like a colonel at the head of his regiment, than like an ignorant horse!"

"I will propose the matter to Herman Mordaunt, or to Anneke herself, if you desire it."

"And the near one has the movement of a lady in a minuet, when you rein him in a little. I drove those cattle, Corny, across the pine plains to Schenectady, in one hour and twenty-six minutes; sixteen miles as the crow flies, and nearer sixty if you follow all the turnings of the fifty roads."

"Well, what am I to do? tell this to the ladies, or beg them to name a day?"

"Name a day!—I wish it had come to that, Corny, with my whole soul. They are two beauties!"

"Yes, I think everybody will admit *that*"—I answered innocently—"Yet, very different in their charms."

"Oh! Not a bit more alike than is just necessary for a good match. I call one Jack and the other Moses. I never knew an animal that was named 'Jack,' who would not do his work. I would give a great deal, Corny, that Mary Wallace could see that horse move!"

I promised Guert that I would use all my influence with the ladies to induce them to trust themselves with his team, and, in order that I might speak with authority, the sleigh was ordered round to the door forthwith, with a view first to take a turn with me. The winter equipage of Guert Ten Eyck, was really a tasteful and knowing thing. I had often seen handsomer sleighs, in the way of paint, varnish, tops, and mouldings, for to these he appeared to pay very little attention. The points on which its owner most valued his sleigh, was the admirable manner in which it rested on its runners, pressing lightly both behind and before. Then the traces were nearer on a level with the horses, than was common, though not so high as to affect the draft. The colour without, was a sky blue, a favourite Dutch tint, while within it was fiery red. The skins were very ample, all coming from the grey wolf. As these skins were lined with scarlet cloth, the effect of the whole was sufficiently cheering and warm. I ought not to forget the bells. In addition to the four sets buckled to the harness, the usual accompaniment of every sort of sleigh-harness, Guert had provided two enormous strings (always leathern straps) that passed from the saddles quite down under the bodies of Jack and Moses, and another string around each horse's neck thus increasing the jingling music of his march, at least fourfold beyond the usual quantity.*

In this style, then, we dashed from the door of the old Ten Eyck house, all the blacks in the street gazing at us in delight, and shaking their sides with laughter; a negro always expressing his admiration of any thing, even to a sermon, in that mode. I remember to have heard a traveller who had been as far as Niagara,

---

*As it is possible this book may pass into the hands of others than Americans, it may be well to say that a sleigh-bell, is a small hollow ball made of bell-metal, having a hole in it, that passes round half of its circumference, and containing a small *solid* ball, of a size not to escape. These bells are fastened to leathern straps, which commonly pass round the necks of the horses. In the time of Guert Ten Eyck, most of the bells were attached to small plates, that were buckled to various parts of the harness; but, as this caused a motion annoying to the animals, Mr. Littlepage evidently wishes his readers to understand that his friend Ten Eyck, was too knowing to have recourse to the practice. Even the straps are coming into disuse, the opinion beginning to obtain that sleigh bells are a nuisance, instead of an advantage. Twenty years since, the laws of most large towns rendered them necessary, under the pretense of preventing accidents by apprising the footman of the approach of a sleigh, but more horses are now driven, in the state of New York without than with bells, in winter.

"Sleigh," as spelt, is purely an American word. It is derived from "slee," in Dutch; which is pronounced like "sleigh." Some persons contend that the Americans ought to use the old English words "sled," or "sledge." But these words do not precisely express the thing we possess. There is as much reason for calling a pleasure-conveyance by a name different from "sled," as there is for saying "coach" instead of "wagon." "Sleigh" *will* become English, ere long, as it is now American. Twenty millions of people not only can make a word, but they can make a language, if it be needed.—EDITOR.

declare that his black did nothing but roar with laughter, the first half-hour he stood confronted with that mighty cataract.

Nor did the blacks alone stop to admire Guert Ten Eyck, his sleigh and his horses. All the young men in the place paid Guert this homage, for he was unanimously admitted to be the best whip, and the best judge of horse-flesh, in Albany; that is, the best judge for his years. Several young women who were out in sleighs, looked behind them, as we passed, proving that the admiration extended even to the other sex. All this Guert felt and saw, and its effect was very visible in his manner as he stood guiding his spirited pair, amid the wood-sleds that still crowded the main street.

Our route lay towards the large flats, that extend for miles, along the west shore of the Hudson, to the north of Albany. This was the road usually taken by the young people of the place, in their evening sleigh-rides, not a few of the better class, stopping to pay their respects to Madam Schuyler, a widow, born of the same family, as that into which she had married, and who, from her character, connections and fortune, filled a high place in the social circle of the vicinity. Guert knew this lady, and proposed that I should call and pay my respects to her, a tribute she was accustomed to receive from most strangers of respectability. Thither, then, we drove as fast as my companion's blacks could carry us. The distance was only a few miles, and we were soon dashing through the open gate, into what must have been a very pretty, though an inartificial, lawn, in the summer.

"By Jove, we are in luck!" cried Guert, the moment his eyes got a view of the stables. "Yonder is Herman Mordaunt's sleigh, and we shall find the ladies here!"

All this turned out as Guert had announced. Anneke and Mary Wallace had dined with Madam Schuyler, and their coats and shawls had just been brought to them, preparatory to returning home as we entered. I had heard so much of Madam Schuyler as not to approach this respectable person without awe, and I had no eyes at first for her companions. I was well received by the mistress of the house, a woman of so large a size as to rise from her chair with great difficulty, but whose countenance expressed equally intelligence, principles, refinement and benevolence. She no sooner heard the name of Littlepage, than she threw a meaning glance towards her young female friends, mine following and perceiving Anneke colouring highly, and looking a little distressed. As for Mary Wallace, she appeared to me then, as I fancied was usually the case whenever Guert Ten Eyck approached her, to be struggling with a species of melancholy pleasure.

"It is unnecessary for me to hear your mother's name, Mr. Littlepage," said Madam Schuyler, extending a hand, "since I knew her, as a young woman. In *her* name you are welcome; as indeed, you would be in your own, after the all-important service I hear you have rendered my sweet young friend, here."

I could only bow, and express my thanks, but it is unnecessary to say how grateful to me was praise of this sort, coming as I knew it must from Anneke, in the first instance. Still, I could hardly refrain from laughing at Guert, who shrugged his shoulders, and turned towards me with a look that repeated his ludicrous regrets he could not see Mary Wallace in a lion's paws! The conversation then took the usual turn, and I got an opportunity of speaking to the young ladies.

After the character I had heard of Madam Schuyler, I was a good deal surprised to find that Guert was somewhat of a favourite. But, even the most intellectual and refined women, I have since had occasion to learn, feel a disposition to judge handsome, manly, frank, flighty fellows like my new acquaintance, somewhat leniently. With all his levity, and his disposition to run into the excesses of animal spirits, there was that about Guert, which rendered it difficult to despise him. The courage of a lion was in his eye, and his front and bearing were precisely those that are particularly attractive to women. To these advantages were added a seeming unconsciousness of his superiority to most around him, in the way of looks, and a humility of spirit that caused him often to deplore his deficiencies in those accomplishments which characterize the man of study and of intellectual activity. It was only among the hardy, active, and reckless, that Guert manifested the least ambition to be a leader.

"Do you still drive those spirited blacks, Guert," demanded Madam Schuyler, in a gentle, affable way that inclined her to adapt her discourse to the tastes of those she might happen to be with; "those, I mean, which you purchased in the autumn?"

"You may be certain of that, aunt," every one who could claim the most distant relationship to this amiable woman, and whose years did not render the appellation disrespectful, called her "aunt"—"You may be certain of that, aunt, for their equals are not to be found in *this* colony. The gentlemen of the army pretend that no horse can be good that has not what they call *blood*; but Jack and Moses are both of the Dutch breed, and the Schuylers and the Ten Eycks will never own there is no "blood" in such a stock. I have given each of these animals my own name, and call them Jack Ten Eyck and Moses Ten Eyck."

"I hope you will not exclude the Littlepages and the Mordaunts from your list of dissenters, Mr. Ten Eyck," observed Anneke, laughing, "since both have Dutch blood in their veins, too."

"Very true, Miss Anneke, Miss Wallace being the only true, thorough, English woman here. But, as Aunt Schuyler has spoken of my team, I wish I could persuade you and Miss Mary, to let me drive you back to Albany, with it, this very evening. Your own sleigh can follow, and, your father's horses being English, we shall have an opportunity of comparing the two breeds. The Anglo-Saxons will have no load, while the Flemings will; still I will wager animal against animal, that the last do the work the most neatly, and in the shortest time."

To this proposition, however, Anneke would not consent; her instinctive delicacy, I make no doubt, at once presenting to her mind the impropriety of quitting her own sleigh, to take an evening's drive, in that of a young man of Guert's established reputation for recklessness and fun, and who was not always fortunate enough to persuade young women of the first class to be his companions. The turn the conversation had taken, nevertheless, had the effect to produce so many urgent appeals, that were seconded by myself, to give the horses a trial, that Mary Wallace promised to submit the matter to Herman Mordaunt, and, should he approve, to accompany Guert, Anneke and myself, in an excursion, the succeeding week.

This concession was received by poor Guert with profound gratitude, and he assured me, as we drove back to town, that he had not felt so happy for the last two months.

"It is in the power of such a young woman—young angel I might better say," added Guert, "to make any thing she may please of me! I know I am an idler, and too fond of our Dutch amusements, and think I have not paid the attention I ought to have paid to books; but let that precious creature only take me by the hand, and I should turn out an altered man in a month. Young women can do any thing they please with us, Mr. Little-page, when they set their minds about it, in earnest. I wish I were a horse, to have the pleasure of dragging Mary Wallace in this excursion!"

Chapter XV

"When lo! the voice of loud alarm
His inmost soul appalls;
'What ho! Lord William, rise in haste!
The water saps thy walls!'"
                Robert Southey, "Lord Wiliam," ll. 73–76.

T HE visit to Madam Schuyler, occurred of a Saturday evening, and the matter of our adventure in company with Jack and Moses, was to be decided on the following Monday. When I rose and looked out of my window on the Sunday morning, however, there appeared but very little prospect of its being effected that spring, inasmuch, as it rained heavily, and there was a fresh south wind. We had reached the 21st of March, a period of the year, when a decided thaw was not only ominous to the sleighing, but when it actually predicted a permanent breaking up of the winter. The season had been late, and it was thought the change could not be distant.

The rain and south wind continued all that day, and torrents of water came rushing down the short, steep streets, effectually washing away every thing like snow. Mr. Worden preached, notwithstanding, and to a very respectable congregation. Dirck and myself attended, but Jason preferred sitting out a double half-hour-glass sermon in the Dutch church, delivered in a language of which he understood very little, to lending his countenance to the rites of the English service. Both Anneke and Mary Wallace found their way up the hill, going in a carriage, though I observed that Herman Mordaunt was absent. Guert was in the gallery, in which we also sat, but I could not avoid remarking that neither of the young ladies raised her eyes once, during the whole service, as high as our pews. Guert whispered something about this, as he hastened down stairs to hand them to their carriage, when the congregation was dismissed, begging me, at the same time, to be punctual to the appointment for the next day. What he meant by this last remembrancer I did not understand, for the hills were beginning to exhibit their bare breasts, and it was somewhat surprising with what rapidity a rather unusual amount of snow, had disappeared. I had no opportunity to ask an explanation, as Guert was too busy in placing the ladies in the carriage, and the weather was not such as to admit of my remaining a moment longer in the street than was indispensably necessary.

A change occurred in the weather during the night, the rain having ceased, though the atmosphere continued mild and the wind was still from the south. It was the commencement of the spring, and, as I walked round to Guert Ten Eyck's house, to meet him at breakfast, I observed that several vehicles with wheels were already in motion in the streets, and that divers persons appeared to be putting away their sleighs and sleds, as things of no further use, until the next winter. Our springs do not certainly come upon us as suddenly as some of which I have read, in the old world, but when the snow and winter endure as far into March, as had been the case with that, of the year 1758, the change is often nearly magical.

"Here, then, is the spring opening," I said to Dirck, as we walked along the well washed streets "and, in a few weeks, we must be off to the bush. Our business on the Patent must be got along with, before the troops are put in motion, or we may lose the opportunity of seeing a campaign."

With such expectations and feelings I entered Guert's bachelor abode, and the first words I uttered, were to sympathize in his supposed disappointment.

"It is a great pity you did not propose the drive to the ladies for Saturday," I began, "for that was not only a mild day, but the sleighing was excellent. As it is, you will have to postpone your triumph until next winter."

"I do not understand you!" cried Guert. "Jack and Moses never were in better heart, or in better condition. I think they are equal to going to Kinderhook, in two hours!"

"But who will furnish the roads with snow? By looking out of the window, you will see that the streets are nearly bare."

"Streets and roads! Who cares for either, while we have the river. We often use the river, here, weeks at a time, when the snow has left us. The ice has been remarkably even the whole of this winter, and now the snow is off it, there will be no danger from the air-holes."

I confess I did not much like the notion of travelling twenty miles on the ice, but was far too much of a man to offer any objections.

We breakfasted, and proceeded in a body to the residence of Herman Mordaunt. When the ladies first heard that we had come to claim the redemption of the half-promise given at Madam Schuyler's, their surprise was not less than mine had been, half an hour before, while their uneasiness was probably greater.

"Surely, Jack and Moses cannot exhibit all their noble qualities without snow!" exclaimed Anneke, laughing; "Ten Eycks though they be!"

"We Albanians have the advantage of travelling on the ice when the snow fails us," answered Guert. "Here is the river, near by, and never was the sleighing on it, better than at this moment."

"But, it has been many times safer, I should think. This looks very much like the breaking up of winter!"

"That is probable enough, and so much greater the reason why we should not delay, if you and Miss Mary ever intend to learn what the blacks can do. It is for the honour of Holland that I desire it, else would I not presume so far. I feel every condescension of this sort, that I receive from you two ladies, in a way I can not express, for no one knows, better than myself, how unworthy I am of your smallest notice."

This brought the signs of yielding, at once, into the mild countenance of Mary Wallace. Guert's self-humiliation never failed to do this. There was so much obvious truth in his admission, so sincere a disposition to place himself where nature and education, or a *want* of education had placed him, and most of all so profound a deference for the mental superiority of Mary herself, that the female heart found it impossible to resist. To my surprise, Guert's mistress, contrary to her habit in such things, was the first to join him, and to second his proposal. Herman Mordaunt entering the room at this instant, the whole thing was referred to him, as in reason it ought to have been.

"I remember to have travelled on the Hudson, a few years since," returned Herman Mordaunt, "the entire distance between Albany and Sing-Sing. And a very good time we had of it; much better than had we gone by land, for there was little or no snow."

"Just our case now, Miss Anneke!" cried Guert. "Good sleighing on the river, but none on the land."

"Was that near the end of March, dear Papa?" asked Anneke, a little inquiringly.

"No, certainly not, for it was early in February. But the ice, at this moment, must be near eighteen inches thick, and strong enough to bear a load of hay."

"Yes, Masser Herman," observed Cato, a gray headed black, who never called his master by any other name, having known him from an infant. "Yes, Masser Herman, a load do come over, dis minute."

It appeared unreasonable to distrust the strength of the ice, after this proof to the contrary, and Anneke submitted. The party was arranged forthwith, and in the following manner. The two ladies, Guert and myself, were to be drawn by the blacks, while Herman Mordaunt, Dirck, and any one else they could enlist, were to follow in the New York sleigh. It was hoped that an elderly female connection, Mrs. Bogart, who resided at Albany, would consent to be of the party, as the plan was to visit and dine with another and a mutual connection of the Mordaunts, at Kinderhook. While the sleighs were getting ready, Herman Mordaunt walked round to the house of Mrs. Bogart, made his request, and was successful.

The clock in the tower of the English church struck ten, as both sleighs drove from Herman Mordaunt's door. There was literally no snow in the middle of the streets, but enough of it, mingled with ice, was still to be found nearer the houses, to enable us to get down to the ferry, the point where sleighs usually went upon the river. Here Herman Mordaunt, who was in advance, checked his horses, and turned to speak to Guert on the propriety of proceeding. The ice near the shore had evidently been moved, the river having risen a foot or two, in consequence of the rains and the thaw, and there was a sort of icy wave cast up near the land, over which it was indispensable to pass, in order to get fairly on the river. As the top of this ridge, or wave, was broken, it exposed a fissure that enabled us to see the thickness of the ice, and this Guert pointed out in proof of its strength. There was nothing unusual in a small movement of the covering of the river, which the current often produced; but, unless the vast fields below got in motion, it was impossible for those above materially to change their positions. Sleighs were passing, too, still bringing to town, hay from the flats on the eastern bank, and there was no longer any hesitation. Herman Mordaunt's sleigh passed slowly over the ridge, having a care to the legs of the horses, and ours followed in the same cautious manner, though the blacks jumped across the fissure in spite of their master's exertions.

Once on the river, however, Guert gave his blacks the whip and rein, and away we went like the wind. The smooth, icy surface of the Hudson was our road, the thaw having left very few traces of any track. The water had all passed beneath the ice, through cracks and fissures of one sort and another, leaving us an even, dry, surface to trot on. The wind was still southerly, though scarcely warm, while a bright sun contributed to render our excursion as gay to the eye, as it certainly was to our feelings. In a few minutes every trace of uneasiness had vanished. Away we went, the blacks doing full credit to their owner's boasts, seeming scarcely to touch the ice, from which their feet appeared to rebound with a sort of elastic force. Herman Mordaunt's bays followed on our heels, and the sleighs had passed over the well known shoal of the Overslaugh, within the first twenty minutes after they touched the river.

Every northern American is familiar with the effect that the motion of a sleigh produces on the spirits, under favourable circumstances. Had our party been altogether composed of Albanians, there would probably have been no drawback on the enjoyment, for use would have prevented apprehension; but it required the few minutes I have mentioned to give Anneke and Mary Wallace full confidence in the ice. By the time we reached the Overslaugh, however, their fears had vanished, and Guert confirmed their sense of security, by telling them to listen to the sounds produced by his horses' hoofs, which certainly conveyed the impression of moving on a solid foundation.

Mary Wallace had never before been so gay in my presence, as she appeared to be that morning. Once, or twice, I fancied her eyes almost as bright as those of Anneke, and certainly her laugh was as sweet and musical. Both the girls were full of spirits, and some little things occurred that gave me hopes Bulstrode had no reason to fancy himself as secure, as he sometimes seemed to be. A casual remark of Guert's had the effect to bring out some of Anneke's private sentiments on the subject; or, at least, so they appeared to be to me.

"I am surprised that Mr. Mordaunt forgot to invite Mr. Bulstrode to be one of our party, to-day," cried Guert, when we were below the Overslaugh. "The Major loves sleighing, and he would have filled the fourth seat, in the other sleigh, very agreeably. As for coming into this, that would be refused him, were he even a general!"

"Mr. Bulstrode is English," answered Anneke, with spirit, "and fancies American amusements beneath the tastes of one who has been presented at the Court of St. James."

"Well, Miss Anneke, I cannot say that I agree with you at all, in this opinion of Mr. Bulstrode," Guert returned, innocently. "It is true, he is English; that he fancies an advantage, as does Corny Littlepage, here, but we must make proper allowances for home-love and foreign-dislike."

" 'Corny Littlepage, here,' is only *half* English, and that half is Colony born and Colony bred," answered the laughing girl, "and he has loved a sleigh from the time when he first slid down hill—"

"Ah! Miss Anneke—let me entreat—"

"Oh! No allusion is intended to the Dutch church and its neighbourhood; but, the sports of childhood are always dear to us, as are sometimes the discomforts. Habit and prejudice are sister hand-maidens, and I never saw one of these gentlemen from home, taking extraordinary interest in any of our peculiarly Colony usages, but I distrusted an extra amount of complaisance, or a sort of enjoyment in which we do not strictly share."

"Is this altogether liberal to Bulstrode, Miss Anneke," I ventured to put in— "he seems to like us, and I am sure he has good reason so to do. That he likes *some* of us, is too apparent to be concealed or denied."

"Mr. Bulstrode is a skilful actor, as all who saw his Cato must be aware," retorted the charming girl, compressing her pouting lips in a way that seemed to me to be inexpressibly pleasing, "and those who saw his Scrub must be equally convinced of the versatility of his talents. No—no—Major Bulstrode is better where he is, or will be to-day, at four o'clock; at the head of the mess of the ————th, instead of dining in a snug Dutch parlour, with my cousin, worthy Mrs. Van der Heyden, at a dinner got up with Colony hospitality and Colony good will, and Colony plainness. The entertainment we shall receive to-day, sweetened, as it will be, by the welcome which will come from the heart, can have no competitor in countries where a messenger must be sent two days before the visit, to ask permission to come, in order to escape cold looks and artificial surprise. I would prefer surprising my friends from the heart, instead of from the head."

Guert expressed his astonishment that any one should not always be glad and willing to receive his friends, and insisted on it, that no such inhospitable customs *could* exist. I knew, however, that society could not exist on the same terms, in old and in new countries, among a people that was pressed upon by numbers, and a people that had not yet felt the evils of a superabundant population. Americans are like dwellers in the country, who are always glad to see their friends, and I ventured to say something of the causes of these differences in habits.

Nothing occurred worthy of being dwelt on, in our ride to Kinderhook. Mrs. Van der Heyden resided at a short distance from the river, and the blacks and the bays had some difficulty in dragging us through the mud to her door. Once there, however, our welcome fully verified the theory of the Colony habits which had been talked over in our drive down. Anneke's worthy connection was not only glad to see her, as anybody might have been, but she would have been glad to receive as many as her house would hold. Few excuses were necessary, for we were all welcome. The visit would retard her dinner an hour, as was frankly admitted; but that was nothing, and cakes and wine were set before us, in the interval, did we feel hungry, in consequence of a two hours' ride. Guert was desired to make free, and go to the stables to give his own orders. In a word, our reception was just that which every colonist has experienced, when he has gone unexpectedly to visit a friend, or a friend's friend. Our dinner was excellent, though not accompanied by much form. The wine was good, Mrs. Van der Heyden's deceased husband having been a judge of what was desirable in that respect. Everybody was in good-humour, and our hostess insisted on giving us coffee before we took our departure.

"There will be a moon, cousin Herman," she said, "and the night will be both light and pleasant. Guert knows the road, which cannot well be missed, as it is the river; and if you quit me at eight, you will reach home in good season to go to rest. It is so seldom I see you, that I have a right to claim every minute you can spare. There remains much to be told concerning our old friends and mutual relatives."

When such words are accompanied by looks and acts that prove their sincerity, it is not easy to tear ourselves away from a pleasant house. We chatted on, laughed, listened to stories and Colony anecdotes that carried us back to the last war, and heard a great many eulogiums on beaux and belles, that we young people had, all our lives, considered as respectable, elderly, commonplace sort of persons.

At length the hour arrived, when even Mrs. Van der Heyden, herself, admitted we ought to part. Anneke and Mary, were kissed, enveloped in their furs and kissed again, and then we took our leave. As we left the house, I remarked that a clock in the passage struck eight. In a few minutes every one was placed, and the runners were striking fire from the flints of the bare ground. We had less difficulty in descending, than in ascending the bank of the river, though there was no snow. It did not absolutely freeze, nor had it actually frozen since the commencement of the thaw, but the earth had stiffened, since the disappearance of the sun. I was much rejoiced when the blacks sprang upon the ice, and whirled us away, on our return road, at a rate even exceeding the speed with which they had come down it, in the morning. I thought it high time we should be in motion on our return, and in motion we were, if flying at the rate of eleven miles in the hour could thus be termed.

The light of the moon was not clear and bright, for there was a haze in the atmosphere, as is apt to occur in the mild weather of March; but there was enough to enable Guert to dash ahead with as great a velocity as was at all desirable. We were all in high spirits; us two young men, so much the more, because each of us fancied he had seen that day, evidence of a tender interest existing in the heart of his mistress towards himself. Mary Wallace had managed, with a woman's tact, to make her suitor appear even respectable in female society, and had brought out in him, many sentiments that denoted a generous disposition and a manly heart, if not a cultivated intellect, and Guert was getting confidence, and with it the means of giving his capacity fairer play. As for Anneke, she now knew my aim, and I had some right to construe several little symptoms of feeling, that escaped her in the course of the day, favourably. I fancied that, gentle as it always was, her voice grew softer, and her smile sweeter and more winning, as she addressed herself to, or smiled on me, and she did just enough of both not to appear distant, and just little enough to appear conscious. At least such were the conjectures of one who I do not think could be properly accused of too much confidence, and whose natural diffidence was much increased by the self-distrust of the purest love.

Away we went, Guert's complicated chimes of bells jingling their merry notes, in a manner to be heard half a mile, the horses bearing hard on the bits, for they knew that their own stables lay at the end of their journey, and Herman Mordaunt's bays keeping so near us, that, notwithstanding the noise we made with our own bells, the sounds of his were constantly in our ears. An hour went swiftly by, and we had already passed Coejeman's, and had a hamlet that stretched along the strand, and which lay quite beneath the high bank of the river, in dim, distant view. This place has since been known by the name of Monkey Town, and is a little remarkable as being the first cluster of houses, on the shores of the Hudson, after quitting Albany. I dare say it has another name in law, but Guert gave it the appellation I have mentioned.

I have said that the night had a sombre, misty, light, the moon wading across the heavens through a deep, but thin curtain of vapour. We saw the shores plainly enough, and we saw the houses and trees, but it was difficult to distinguish smaller objects at any distance. In the course of the day, twenty sleighs had been met, or passed, but at that hour everybody but ourselves appeared to have deserted the river. It was getting late for the simple habits of those who dwelt on its shores. When about half way between the islands opposite to Coejeman's and the hamlet just named, Guert, who stood erect to drive, told us that some one who was out late, like ourselves, was coming down. The horses of the strangers were in a very fast trot, and the sleigh was evidently inclining towards the west shore, as if those it held intended to land at no great distance. As it passed, quite swiftly, a man's voice called out something on a high key, but our bells made so much noise that it was not easy to understand him. He spoke in Dutch, too, and none of our ears, those of Guert excepted, were sufficiently expert in that language to be particularly quick in comprehending what he said. The call passed unheeded, then, such things being quite frequent among the Dutch, who seldom passed each other on the highway, without a greeting of some sort, or other. I was thinking of this practice, and of the points that distinguished our own habits from those of the people of this part of the Colony, when sleigh bells sounded quite near me, and turning my head, I saw Herman Mordaunt's bays galloping close to us, as if wishing to get alongside. At the next moment the object was effected, and Guert pulled up.

"Did you understand the man who passed down, Guert?" demanded Herman Mordaunt, as soon as all noises ceased. "He called out to us, at the top of his voice, and would hardly do that without an object."

"These men seldom go home, after a visit to Albany, without filling their jugs," answered Guert drily; "what could he have to say, more than to wish us good night?"

"I cannot tell, but Mrs. Bogart thought she understood something about 'Albany,' and 'the river.' "

"The ladies always fancy Albany is to sink into the river after a great thaw," answered Guert, good-humouredly; "but I can show either of them that the ice is sixteen inches thick, here where we stand."

Guert then gave me the reins, stepped out of the sleigh, went a short distance to a large crack that he had seen while speaking, and returned with a thumb placed on the handle of the whip, as a measure to show that his statement was true. The ice, at that spot, was certainly nearer eighteen than sixteen inches thick. Herman Mordaunt showed the measure to Mrs. Bogart, whose alarm was pacified by this positive proof. Neither Anneke, nor Mary exhibited any fear; but, on the contrary as the sleighs separated again, each had something pleasant, but feminine, to say at the expense of poor Mrs. Bogart's imagination.

I believe I was the only person in our own sleigh, who felt any alarm, after the occurrence of this little incident. Why uneasiness beset *me*, I cannot precisely say. It must have been altogether on Anneke's account, and not in the least on my own. Such accidents as sleighs breaking through, on our New York lakes and rivers, happened almost every winter, and horses were often drowned; though it was seldom the consequences proved so serious to their owners. I recalled to mind the fragile nature of ice, the necessary effects of the great thaw and the heavy rains, remembering that frozen water might still retain most of its apparent thickness, after its consistency was greatly impaired. But, I could do nothing! If we landed, the roads were impassable for runners, almost for wheels, and another hour might carry the ladies, by means of the river, to their comfortable homes. That day, however, which down to the moment of meeting the unknown sleigh, had been the very happiest of my life, was entirely changed in its aspect, and I no longer regarded it with any satisfaction. Had Anneke been at home, I could gladly have entered into a contract to pass a week on the river myself, as the condition of her safety. I thought but little of the others, to my shame be it said, though I cannot do myself the injustice to imagine, had Anneke been away, that I would have deserted, even a horse, while there was a hope of saving him.

Away we went! Guert drove rapidly, but he drove with judgment, and it seemed as if his blacks knew what was expected of them. It was not long, before we were trotting past the hamlet I have mentioned. It would seem that the bells of the two sleighs attracted the attention of the people on the shore, all of whom had not yet gone to bed; for the door of a house opened, and two men issued out of it, gazing at us, as we trotted past at a pace that defied pursuit. These men also hallooed to us, in Dutch, and again Herman Mordaunt galloped up alongside, to speak to us.

"Did you understand these men?" he called out, for this time Guert did not see fit to stop his horses; "they, too, had something to tell us."

"These people always have something to tell an Albany sleigh, Mr. Mordaunt," answered Guert; "though it is not often that which it would do any good to hear."

"But Mrs. Bogart thinks they, also, had something to say about 'Albany' and the 'river.'"

"I understand Dutch, as well as excellent Mrs. Bogart—" said Guert, a little drily, "and I heard nothing; while I fancy I understand the river better. This ice would bear a dozen loads of hay, in a close line."

This again satisfied Herman Mordaunt, and the ladies, but it did not satisfy me. Our own bells made four times the noise of those of Herman Mordaunt; and it was very possible that one, who understood Dutch perfectly, might comprehend a call in that language, while seated in his own sleigh, when the same call could not be comprehended by the same person, while seated in Guert's. There was no pause, however; on we trotted, and another mile was passed, before any new occurrence attracted attention.

The laugh was again heard among us, for Mary Wallace consented to sing an air, that was rendered somewhat ludicrous by the accompaniment of the bells. This song, or verse or two, for the singer got no further on account of the interruption, had drawn Guert's and my attention behind us, or away from the horses, when a whirling sound was heard, followed immediately by a loud shout. A sleigh passed within ten yards of us, going down, and the whirling sound was caused by its runners, while the shout came from a solitary man who stood erect, waving his whip and calling to us in a loud voice, as long as he could be heard. This was but for a moment, however, as his horses were on the run, and the last we could see of the man, through the misty moon-light, he had turned his whip on his team, to urge it ahead still faster. In an instant, Herman Mordaunt was at our side, for the third time that night, and he called out to us somewhat authoritatively to stop.

"What can all this mean, Guert?" he asked. "Three times have we had warnings about 'Albany' and the 'river.' I heard this man myself utter those two words, and cannot be mistaken."

"I dare say, sir, that you may have heard something of the sort," answered the still incredulous Guert, "for these chaps have generally some impertinence to utter, when they pass a team that is better than their own. These blacks of mine, Herman Mordaunt, awaken a good deal of envy, when ever I go out with them, and a Dutchman will forgive you any other superiority sooner, than he will overlook your having the best team. That last man had a spur in his head, moreover, and is driving his cattle, at this moment, more like a spook than like a humane and rational being. I dare say he asked if we owned Albany and the river."

Guert's allusion to his horses, occasioned a general laugh, and laughter is little favourable to cool reflection. We all looked out on the solemn and silent night, cast our eyes along the wide, and long reach of the river, in which we happened to be, and saw nothing but the calm of nature, rendered imposing by solitude and the stillness of the hour. Guert smilingly renewed his assurances that all was right and moved on. Away we went! Guert evidently pressed his horses, as if desirous of being placed beyond this anxiety as soon as possible. The blacks flew, rather than trotted, and we were all beginning to submit to the exhilaration of so rapid and easy a motion, when a sound which resembled that which one might suppose the simultaneous explosion of a thousand rifles would produce, was heard, and caused both drivers to pull up; the sleighs stopping quite near each other, and at the same instant! A slight exclamation escaped old Mrs. Bogart, but Anneke and Mary remained still as death.

"What means that sound, Guert?" enquired Herman Mordaunt, the concern he felt being betrayed by the very tone of his voice. "Something seems wrong!"

"Something *is* wrong," answered Guert coolly, but very decidedly; "and it is something that must be seen to."

As this was said, Guert stepped out on the ice, which he struck a hard blow with the heel of his boot, as if to make certain of its solidity. A second report was heard, and it evidently came from *behind* us. Guert gazed intently down the river; then he laid his head close to the surface of the ice, and looked again. At the same time, three or four more of these startling reports followed each other in quick succession. Guert instantly rose to his feet.

"I understand it, now," he said, "and find I have been rather too confident. The ice, however, is safe and strong, and we have nothing to fear from its weakness. Perhaps it would be better to quit the river, notwithstanding, though I am far from certain the better course will not be to push on."

"Let us know the danger at once, Mr. Ten Eyck," said Herman Mordaunt, "that we may decide for the best."

"Why, sir, I am afraid that the rains and the thaw, together, have thrown so much water into the river, all at once, as it might be, as to have raised the ice, and broken it loose, in spots, from the shores. When this happens, *above*, before the ice has disappeared below, it sometimes causes dams to form, which heap up such a weight, as to break the whole plain of ice, far below it, and thus throw cakes over cakes, until walls twenty, or thirty feet high are formed. This has not happened *yet*, therefore there is no immediate danger; but by bending your heads low, you can see that such a break *has* taken place about half a mile below us."

We did as Guert directed, and saw that a mound had arisen

across the river, nearer than the distance, named by our companion, completely cutting off retreat by the way we had come. The bank on the west side of the Hudson, was high, at the point where we were, and looking intently at it, I saw by the manner in which the trees disappeared, the more distant behind those that were nearer, that we were actually in motion! An involuntary exclamation, caused the whole party to comprehend this startling fact, at the same instant. We were certainly in motion, though very slowly, on the ice of that swollen river, in the quiet and solitude of a night, in which the moon rather aided in making danger apparent, than in assisting us to avoid it! What was to be done? It was necessary to decide, and that promptly and intelligently.

We waited for Herman Mordaunt to advise us, but he referred the matter at once to Guert's greater experience.

"We cannot land, here," answered the young man, "so long as the ice is in motion, and I think it better to push on. Every foot will bring us so much nearer to Albany, and we shall get among the islands, a mile or two higher, where the chances of landing will be greatly increased. Besides, I have often crossed the river on a cake, for they frequently stop; and I have known even loaded sleighs profit by them, to get over the river. As yet, there is nothing very alarming; let us push on, and get nearer to the islands."

This, then, was done, though there was no longer heard the laugh, or the song among us. I could see that Herman Mordaunt was uneasy about Anneke, though he could not bring her into his own sleigh, leaving Mary Wallace alone; neither could he abandon his respectable connection, Mrs. Bogart. Before we re-entered the sleighs, I took an occasion to assure him that Anneke should be my especial care.

"God bless you, Corny, my dear boy," Herman Mordaunt answered, squeezing my hand, with fervour. "God bless you, and enable you to protect her. I was about to ask you to change seats with me, but, on the whole, I think my child will be safer with you, than she could be with me. We will await God's pleasure as accident has placed us."

"I will desert her only with life, Mr. Mordaunt. Be at ease, on that subject."

"I know you will not—I am *sure* you will not, Littlepage; that affair of the lion is a pledge that you will not. Had Bulstrode come, we should have been strong enough to—but, Guert is impatient to be off. God bless you, boy,—God bless you. Do not neglect my child."

Guert *was* impatient, and no sooner was I in the sleigh than we were once more in rapid motion. I said a few words to encourage the girls, and then no sound of a human voice, mingled with the gloomy scene.

Chapter XVI

"He started up, each limb convulsed
With agonizing fear,
He only heard the storm of night—
'Twas music to his ear."
                    Robert Southey, "Lord William," ll.69–72.

AWAY we went! Guert's aim was the islands, which carried him nearer home, while it offered a place of retreat, in the event of the danger's becoming more serious. The fierce rapidity with which we now moved prevented all conversation, or even much reflection. The reports of the rending ice, however, became more and more frequent, first coming from above, and then from below. More than once it seemed as if the immense mass of weight that had evidently collected somewhere near the town of Albany, was about to pour down upon us in a flood—when the river would have been swept for miles, by a resistless torrent. Nevertheless, Guert held on his way; firstly, because he knew it would be impossible to get on either of the main shores, any-where near the point where we happened to be, and secondly be-cause, having often seen similar dammings of the waters, he fan-cied we were still safe. That the distant reader may understand the precise character of the danger we ran, it may be well to give him some notion of the localities.

The banks of the Hudson are generally high and precipitous, and, in some places they are mountainous. No flats worthy of being mentioned occur, until Albany is approached, nor are those which lie south of that town, of any great extent, compared with the size of the stream. In this particular, the Mohawk is a very different river, having extensive flats that, I have been told, resemble those of the Rhine, in miniature. As for the Hudson, it is generally esteemed in the colony, as a very pleasing river, and I remember to have heard intelligent people from home, admit, that even the majestic Thames, itself, is scarcely more worthy to be visited, or that it better rewards the trouble and curiosity of the enlightened traveller.*

*This remark of Mr. Cornelius Littlepage's, may induce a smile in the reader. But,

While there are flats on the shores of the Hudson, and of some extent, in the vicinity of Albany, the general formation of the adjacent country is preserved, being high, bold, and in some quarters, more particularly to the northward and eastward, mountainous. Among these hills the stream meanders for sixty or eighty miles north of the town, receiving tributaries as it comes rushing down towards the sea. The character of the river changes entirely, a short distance above Albany, the tides flowing to that point, rendering it navigable, and easy of ascent in summer, all the way from the sea. Of the tributaries, the principal is the Mohawk, which runs a long distance towards the west—they tell me, for I have never visited those remote parts of the colony— among fertile plains, that are bounded, north and south, by precipitous highlands. Now, in the spring, when the vast quantities of snow, that frequently lie four feet deep in the forests, and among the mountains and valleys of the interior, are suddenly melted by the south winds and rains, freshets necessarily succeed, which have been known to do great injury. The flats of the Mohawk, they tell me, are annually overflown, and a moderate freshet is deemed a blessing; but, occasionally, a union of the causes I have mentioned, produces a species of deluge that has a very opposite character. Thus it is, that houses are swept away, and bridges from the smaller mountain streams, have been known to come floating past the wharves of Albany, holding their way towards the ocean. At such times, the tides produce no counter current, for it is a usual thing in the early months of the spring, to have the stream pour downwards for weeks, the whole length of the river, and to find the water fresh even as low as New York.

Such was the general nature of the calamity we had been so

---

few persons of fifty can be found, who cannot recall the time, when it was a rare thing to imagine *any thing* American, as good as its English counterpart. The American who could write a book—a real, live, book—forty years since, was a sort of prodigy. It was the same with him, who could paint any picture, beyond a common portrait. The very fruits and natural productions of the country were esteemed, doubtingly, and he was a bold man who dared to extol even canvass-back ducks, in the year 1800! At the present day, the feeling is fast undergoing an organic change. It is now the fashion to extol every thing American, and from submitting, to a degree that was almost abject, to the feeling of colonial dependency, the country is filled to-day with the most profound, provincial, self-admiration. It is to be hoped that the next change will bring us to something like the truth.—EDITOR.

unexpectedly made to encounter. The winter had been severe, and the snows unusually deep, and, as we drove furiously onward, I remembered to have heard my grandfather predict extraordinary freshets in the spring, from the character of the winter, as we had found it, even previously to my quitting home. The great thaw and the heavy rains of the late storm had produced the usual effect, and the waters thus let loose, among the distant, as well as the nearer, hills, were now pouring down upon us in their collected might. In such cases, the first effect is to loosen the ice from the shores, and, local causes forcing it to give way, at particular points, a breaking up of its surface occurs, and dams are formed that set the stream back in floods upon all the adjacent low land, such as the flats in the vicinity of Albany.

We did not then know it, but, at the very moment Guert was thus urging his blacks to supernatural efforts—actually running them as if on a race-course—there was a long reach of the Hudson, opposite to, for a short distance below, and for a considerable distance above, the town, which was quite clear of stationary ice. Vast cakes continued to come down, it is true, passing on to increase the dam that had formed below, near and on the overslaugh, where it was buttressed by the islands, and rested on the bottom; but the whole of that firm field, on which we had first driven forth that morning, had disappeared! This we did not know at the time, or it might have changed the direction of Guert's movements, but I learned it afterwards, when placed in a situation to enquire into the causes of what had occurred.

Herman Mordaunt's bells, and the rumbling sound of his runners, were heard close behind us, as our own sleigh flew along the river, at a rate that I firmly believe could not have been much less than that of twenty miles in the hour. As we were whirled northward, the reports made by the rending of the ice, increased in frequency and force. They really became appalling! Still, the girls continued silent, maintaining their self-command, in a most admirable manner; though I doubt not that they felt, in the fullest extent, the true character of the awful circumstances in which we were placed. Such was the state of things, as Guert's blacks began sensibly to relax in their speed, for want of wind. They still galloped on, but it was no longer with the swiftness of the wind, and their master became sensible of the folly of hoping to reach the town, ere the catastrophe should arrive. He reined in his panting horses, therefore, and was just falling into a trot, as a violent report was heard directly in our front. At the next instant, the ice rose, positively beneath our horses' hoofs, to the height of several feet, taking the form of the roof of a house. It was too late to retreat, and Guert shouting out "Jack"—"Moses," applied the whip, and the spirited animals actually went over the mound, leaping a crack three feet in width, and reaching the level ice beyond. All this was done, as it might be, in the twinkling of an eye. While the sleigh flew over this ridge, it was with difficulty I held the girls in their seats, though Guert stood nobly erect, like the pine that is too firmly rooted to yield to the tempest. No sooner was the danger passed, however, than he pulled up, and came to a dead halt.

We heard the bells of Herman Mordaunt's sleigh, on the other side of the barrier, but could see nothing. The broken cakes, pressed upon by millions of tons' weight above, had risen fully ten feet, into an inclination that was nearly perpendicular, rendering crossing it next to impossible even to one afoot. Then came Herman Mordaunt's voice, filled with paternal agony, and human grief, to increase the awe of that dreadful moment!

"Shore!—Shore!—" he shouted, or rather yelled—"In the name of a righteous providence, to the shore, Guert!"

The bells passed off towards the western bank, and the rumbling of the runners accompanied their sound. That was a breathless moment to us four. We heard the rending and grinding of the ice, on all sides of us, saw the broken barriers behind and in front, heard the jingling of Herman Mordaunt's bells, as it became more and more distant, and finally ceased, and felt as if we were cut off from the rest of our species. I do not think either of us felt any apprehension of breaking through, for use had accustomed us to the field of the river, while the more appalling grounds of alarm were so evident, that no one thought of such a source of danger. Nor was there much, in truth, to apprehend from that cause. The thaw had not lasted long enough materially to diminish either the thickness, or tenacity, of the common river ice, though it was found unequal to resisting the enormous pressure that bore upon it, from above. It is probable that a cake of an acre's size, would have upheld not only ourselves, but our sleigh and horses, and carried us, like a raft, down the stream, had there been such a cake, free from stationary impediments.

Even the girls now comprehended the danger, which was in a manner suspended over us,—as the impending wreath of snow menaces the fall of the *avalanche*. But, it was no moment for indecision, or inaction.

Cut off as we were, by an impassable barrier of ice, from the route taken by Herman Mordaunt, it was necessary to come to some resolution on our own course. We had the choice of endeavoring to pass to the western shore, on the upper side of the barrier, or of proceeding towards the nearest, of several low islands which lay in the opposite direction. Guert determined on the last, walking his horses to the point of land, there being no apparent necessity for haste, while the animals greatly needed breath. As we went along, he explained to us that the fissure below cut us off from the only point, where landing on the western shore could be practicable. At the same time, he put in practice a pious fraud, which had an excellent effect on the feelings and conduct of both the girls, throughout the remainder of the trying scenes of that fearful night; more especially on those of Anneke. He dwelt on the good fortune of Herman Mordaunt, in being on the right side of the barrier that separated the sleighs, in a way to induce those, who did not penetrate his motive, to fancy the rest of the party was in a place of security, as the consequence of this accident. Thus did Anneke believe her father safe, and thus was she relieved from much agonizing doubt.

As soon as the sleigh came near the point of the island, Guert gave me the reins, and went ahead to examine whether it were possible to land. He was absent fifteen minutes, returning to us only after he had made a thorough search into the condition of the island, as well as of that of the ice in its eastern channel. These were fifteen fearful minutes, the rending of the masses above and the grinding of cake on cake, sounding like the roar of the ocean in a tempest. Notwithstanding all the awful accessories of this dreadful night, I could not but admire Guert's coolness of manner and his admirable conduct. He was more than resolute, for he was cool, collected, and retained the use of all his faculties in perfection. As plausible as it might seem, to one less observant and clear-headed, to attempt escaping to the western shore, Guert had decided right in moving towards the island. The grinding of the ice, in another quarter, had apprised him that the water was forcing its way through, near the main land, and that escape would be nearly hopeless on that side of the river. When he rejoined us, he called me to the heads of the horses, for a conference, first solemnly assuring our precious companions that there were no grounds for immediate apprehension. Mary Wallace anxiously asked him to repeat this to *her*, on the faith due from man to woman, and he did it; when I was permitted to join him without further opposition.

"Corny," said Guert, in a low tone, "Providence has punished me for my wicked wish of seeing Mary Wallace in the claws of lions, for all the savage beasts of the old world, could hardly make our case more desperate than it now is. We must be cool, however, and preserve the girls, or die like men."

"Our fates are, and must be, the same. Do you devote yourself to Mary, and leave Anneke to me. But, why this language; surely our case is by no means so desperate."

"It might not be so difficult for two active, vigorous, young men to get ashore, but it would be different with females. The ice is in motion all around us, and the cakes are piling and grinding on each other, in a most fearful manner. Were it light enough to see, we should do much better; but, as it is, I dare not trust Mary Wallace any distance from this island, at present. We may be compelled to pass the night here, and must make provision accordingly. You hear the ice grinding on the shore; a sign that every thing is going down stream.—God send that the waters break through ere long; though they may sweep all before them when they do come. I fear me, Corny, that Herman Mordaunt and his party are lost!"

"Merciful Providence!—Can it be as bad as that!—I rather hope they have reached the land."

"*That* is impossible, on the course they took. Even a man would be bewildered and swept away, in the torrent that is driving down under the west shore. It is that vent to the water, which saves us. But, no more words.—You now understand the extent of the danger, and will know what you are about. We must get our precious charge on the island, if possible, without further delay. Half an hour—nay, half a minute, may bring down the torrent."

Guert took the direction of every thing. Even while we had been talking the ice had moved materially, and we found ourselves fifty feet further from the island, than we had been. By causing the horses to advance, this distance was soon recovered, but it was found impossible to lead, or drive them over the broken cakes with which the shore of the island now began to be lined. After one or two spirited and determined efforts, Guert gave the matter up, and asked me to help the ladies from the sleigh. Never did women behave better than did these delicate and lovely girls, on an occasion so awfully trying. Without remonstrances, tears, exclamations, or questions, both did as desired, and I cannot express the feeling of security I felt, when I had helped each over the broken and grinding border of white ice, that separated us from the shore. The night was far from cold, but the ground was now frozen sufficiently to prevent any unpleasant consequences from walking on what would otherwise have been a slimy, muddy, alluvion, for the island was so very low, as often to be under water when the river was particularly high. This, indeed, formed our danger, after we had reached it.

When I returned to Guert, I found him already drifted down some little distance, and this time we moved the sleigh so much above the point, as to be in less danger of getting out of sight of our precious wards. To my surprise, Guert was busy in stripping the harness from the horses, and Jack already stood only in his blinkers. Moses was soon reduced to the same state. I was wondering what was to be done next, when Guert drew each bridle from its animal, and gave a smart crack of his whip. The liberated horses started back with affright—snorted, reared, and, turning, away, they went down the river, free as air, and almost as swift; the incessant and loud snapping of their master's whip, in no degree tending to diminish their speed. I asked the meaning of this.

"It would be cruel not to let the poor beasts make use of the strength and sagacity nature has given them to save their lives," answered Guert, straining his eyes after Moses, the horse that was behind, so long as his dark form could be distinguished, and leaning forward to listen to the blows of their hoofs, while the noises around us permitted them to be heard. "To us, they would only be an encumbrance, since they never could be forced over the cracks and caked ice in harness; nor would it be at all safe to follow them, if they could. The sleigh is light and we are strong enough to shove it to land, when there is an opportunity; or, it may be left on the island."

Nothing could have served more effectually to convince me of the manner in which Guert regarded our situation, than to see him turn loose beasts which I knew he so highly prized. I mentioned this, and he answered me with a melancholy seriousness that made the impression so much the stronger—

"It is possible they may get ashore, for Nature has given a horse a keen instinct. They can swim, too, where you and I would drown. At all events, they are not fettered with harness, but have every chance it is in my power to give them. Should they land, any farmer would put them in his stable, and I should soon hear where they were to be found—if, indeed, I am living in the morning to make the inquiry."

"What is next to be done, Guert?" I asked, understanding at once, both his feelings and his manner of reasoning.

"We must now run the sleigh on the island; after which, it will be time to look about us, and to examine if it be possible to get the ladies on the main land."

Accordingly, Guert and I applied ourselves to the task, and had no great difficulty in dragging the sleigh over the cakes, grinding and in motion as they were. We pulled it as far as the tree beneath which Anneke and Mary stood, when the ladies got into it, and took their seats, enveloped in the skins. The night was not cold for the season, and our companions were thickly clad, having tippets and muffs; still, the wolves' skins of Guert, contributed to render them more comfortable. All apprehension of immediate danger now ceased, for a short time, nor do I think either of the females fancied they could run any more risk, beyond that of exposure to the night air, so long as they remained on *terra firma.* Such was not the case, however, as a very simple explanation will render apparent to the reader.

All the islands in this part of the Hudson are low, being rich, alluvial meadows, bordered by trees and bushes; most of the first being willows, sycamores, or nuts. The fertility of the soil had given to these trees rapid growths, and they were generally of some stature, though not one among them had that giant size which ought to mark the body and branches of a venerable tenant of the forest. This fact of itself proved that no one tree of them all, was *very* old, a circumstance that was certainly owing to the ravages of the annual freshets. I say annual, for, though the freshet which now encompassed us, was far more serious than usual, each year brought something of the sort; and the islands were constantly increasing, or diminishing, under their action.

To prevent the last, a thicket of trees was left at the head of each is-land, to form a sort of barricade against the inroads of the ice in the spring. So low was the face of the land, or meadow, however, that a rise of a very few feet in the river, would be certain to bring it entirely under water. All this will be made more apparent, by our own proceedings, after we had placed the ladies in the sleigh, and more especially by the passing remarks of Guert, while employed in his subsequent efforts.

No sooner did Guert Ten Eyck believe the ladies to be tem-porarily safe, than he proposed to me that we should take a closer look at the state of the river, in order to ascertain the most fea-sible means of getting on the main land. This was said aloud, and in a cheerful way, as if he no longer felt any apprehension, and, evidently to me, to encourage our companions. Anneke desired us to go, declaring that now she knew herself to be on dry land, all her own fears had vanished. We went accordingly, taking our first direction towards the head of the island.

A very few minutes sufficed to reach the limits of our narrow domain, and, as we approached them, Guert pointed out to me the mound of ice, that was piling up behind it, as a most fearful symptom.

"*There* is our danger," he said, with emphasis; "and we must not trust to these trees. This freshet goes beyond any I ever saw on the river, and not a spring passes that we have not more, or less, of them. Do you not see, Corny, what saves us now?"

"We are on an island, and cannot be in much danger from the river, while we stay here."

"Not so, my dear friend, not at all so. But, come with me and look for yourself."

I followed Guert, and did look for myself. We sprang upon the cakes of ice, which were piled quite thirty feet in height, on the head of the island, extending right and left as far as our eyes could see, by that misty light. It was by no means difficult moving about on this massive pile, the movement in the cakes being slow and frequently interrupted, but there was no concealing the true character of the danger. Had not the island and the adjacent main interposed their obstacles, the ice would have continued to move bodily down the stream, cake shoving over cake, until the whole found vent in the wider space below, and floated off to-wards the ocean. Not only was our island there, however, but

other islands lay near us, straitening the different channels, or
passages, in such a way as to compel the formation of an icy dam;
and, on the strength of this dam rested all our security. Were it to
be ruptured anywhere near us, we should inevitably be swept off,
in a body. Guert thought, however, as has been said already, that
the waters had found narrow issues, under the main land, both
east and west of us; and should this prove to be true, there was a
hope that the great calamity might be averted. In other words, if
those floodgates sufficed, we *might* escape; otherwise, the catastrophe was certain.

"I cannot excuse it to myself to remain here, without endeavouring to see what is the state of things, nearer to the shore,"
said Guert, after we had viewed the fast accumulating mass of
broken ice above us, as well as the light permitted, and we had
talked over together the chances of safety, and the character of
the danger. "Do you return to the ladies, Corny, and endeavour
to keep up their spirits, while I cross this channel on our right, to
the next island, and see what offers in that direction."

"I do not like the idea of your running all the risk alone; besides, something may occur to require the strength of two, instead of that of one, to overcome it."

"You can go with me as far as the next island, if you will, where
we shall be able to ascertain, at once, whether it be ice, or water,
that separates us from the eastern shore. If the first, you can return as fast as possible, for the ladies, while I look for a place to
cross. I do not like the appearance of this dam, to be honest with
you, and have great fears for those who are now in the sleigh."

We were in the very act of moving away, when a loud, cracking,
noise, that arose within a few yards alarmed us both, and running to the spot whence it proceeded, we saw that a large willow
had snapped in two, like a pipe stem, and that the whole barrier
of ice was marching slowly, but grandly, over the stump, crushing
the fallen trunk and branches beneath its weight, as the slow-
moving wheel of the loaded cart, crushes the twig. Guert grasped
my arm, and his fingers nearly entered the flesh, under his iron
pressure.

"We must quit this spot—" he said firmly, "and at once. Let us
go back to the sleigh."

I did not know Guert's intentions; but I saw it was time to act
with decision. We moved swiftly down to the spot where we had

left the sleigh, and the reader will judge of our horror, when we
found it gone! The whole of the low point of the island where we
had left it, was already covered with cakes of ice that were in motion, and which had doubtless swept off the sleigh during the few
minutes that we had been absent! Looking around us, however,
we saw an object on the river, a little distance below, that I fancied
was the sleigh, and was about to rush after it, when a voice, filled
with alarm, took us in another direction. Mary Wallace came out
from behind a tree, to which she had fled for safety, and seizing
Guert's arm, implored him not to quit her, again.

"Whither has Anneke gone?" I demanded, in an agony, I cannot describe. "I see nothing of Anneke!"

"She would not quit the sleigh—" answered Mary Wallace, almost panting for breath—"I implored—entreated her to follow
me—said you *must* soon return, but she refused to quit the sleigh.
Anneke is in the sleigh, if that can now be found."

I heard no more, but springing on the still moving cakes of ice,
went leaping from cake to cake, until my sight showed me that,
sure enough, the sleigh was on the bed of the river, over which it
was in slow motion, forced downward before the new coating of
ice that was fast covering the original surface. At first, I could see
no one in the sleigh; but, on reaching it, I found Anneke buried
in the skins. She was on her knees: the precious creature was asking succour from God!

I had a wild but sweet consolation in thus finding myself, as it
might be, cut off from all the rest of my kind, in the midst of that
scene of gloom and desolation, alone with Anneke Mordaunt.
The moment I could make her conscious of my presence, she enquired after Mary Wallace, and was much relieved on learning
that she was with Guert, and would not be left by him, for a single
instant, again that night. Indeed, I saw their figures dimly, as
they moved swiftly across the channel that divided the two islands, and disappear in that direction, among the bushes that
lined the place to which they had gone.

"Let us follow," I said, eagerly. "The crossing is yet easy, and
we, too, may escape to the shore."

"Go you!" said Anneke, over whom a momentary physical tor-
por appeared to have passed. "Go you, Corny," she said—"A man
may easily save himself, and you are an only child—the sole hope
of your parents."

"Dearest, beloved Anneke!—Why this indifference, this apathy on your own behalf? Are *you* not an only child, the sole hope of a widowed father?—do you forget *him?*"

"No, no, no!" exclaimed the dear girl, hurriedly. "Help me out of the sleigh, Corny; there, I will go with you anywhere—any-how—to the end of the world to save my father from such anguish!"

From that moment the temporary imbecility of Anneke vanished, and I found her for the remainder of the time we remained in jeopardy, quick to apprehend, and ready to second all my efforts. It was this passing submission to an imaginary doom, on the one hand, and the headlong effect of sudden fright on the other, which had separated the two girls, and which had been the means of dividing the whole party, as described.

I scarcely know how to describe what followed. So intense was my apprehension in behalf of Anneke, that I can safely say, I did not think of my own fate, in the slightest degree, as disconnected from hers. The self-devoted reliance with which the dear girl seemed to place all her dependence on me, would of itself have produced this effect, had she not possessed my whole heart, as I was now so fully aware. Moments like those, make one alive to all the affections, and strip off every covering that habit, or the dissembling of our manners, is so apt to throw over the feelings. I believe I both spoke and acted towards Anneke, as one would cling to, or address the being dearest to him in the world, for the next few minutes, but, I can suppose the reader will naturally prefer learning what we did, under such circumstances, rather than what we said, or how we felt.

I repeat, it is not easy for me to describe what followed. I know we first rather ran, than walked, across the channel on which I had last seen the dim forms of Guert and Mary, and even crossed the island to its eastern side, in the hope of being able to reach the shore in that quarter. The attempt was useless, for we found the water running down over the ice, like a race-way. Nothing could be seen of our late companions, and my loud and repeated calls to them, were unanswered.

"Our case is hopeless, Cornelius," said Anneke, speaking with a forced calmness when she found retreat impossible, in that direction. "Let us return to the sleigh, and submit to the will of God!"

"Beloved Anneke!—Think of your father, and summon your whole strength. The bed of the river is yet firm; we will cross it, and try the opposite shore."

Cross it we did, my delicate companion being as much sustained by my supporting arm, as by her own resolution; but, we found the same obstacle to retreat interposing there, also. The island above had turned the waters aside, until they found an outlet under each bank—shooting along their willowy shores, with the velocity of arrows. By this time, owing to our hurried movement, I found Anneke so far exhausted, that it was absolutely necessary to pause a minute, to take breath. This pause was also necessary, in order to look about us, and to decide understandingly, as to the course it was necessary now to pursue. This pause, brief as it was, moreover, contributed largely to the apparent horrors of our situation.

The grating, or grinding of the ice above us, cake upon cake, now sounded like the rushing of heavy winds, or the incessant roaring of a surf upon the sea shore. The piles were becoming visible, by their height and their proximity, as the ragged barrier set slowly, but steadily down upon us, and the whole river seemed to me to be in motion, downwards. At this awful instant, when I began to think it was the will of Providence that Anneke and I were to perish together, a strange sound interrupted the fearful, natural accessories of that frightful scene. I certainly heard the bells of a sleigh. At first they seemed distant, and broken; then nearer and incessant, attended by the rumbling of runners on the ice. I took off my cap, and pressed my head, for I feared my brain was unsettled. There it came, however, more and more distinctly, until the trampling of horses' hoofs mingled in the noise.

"Can there be others as unhappy as ourselves!" exclaimed Anneke, forgetting her own fears, in generous sympathy. "See, Littlepage!—see, *dear* Cornelius—yonder, surely, comes another sleigh!"

Come it did, like the tempest, or the whirlwind; passing within fifty feet of us. I knew it at a glance. It was the sleigh of Herman Mordaunt, empty, with the horses, maddened by terror, running wherever their fears impelled. As the sleigh passed, it was thrown on one side; then, it was whirled up again, and it went out of sight, with the rumbling sound of the runners, once more mingling with the jingling of bells and the tramp of hoofs.

At this instant, a loud, distant cry, from a human voice, was certainly heard. It seemed to me as if some one called my name, and Anneke said she so understood it, too. The call, if call it was, came from the south, and from under the western shore. At the next moment, awful reports proceeded from the barrier above, and, passing an arm around the slender waist of my lovely companion to support her, I began a rapid movement in the direction of that call. While attempting to reach the western shore, I had observed a high mound of broken ice, that was floating down, or rather was pressed down on the smooth surface of the frozen river, in advance of the smaller cakes that came by in the current. It was increasing in size, by accessions from these floating cakes, and threatened to form a new dam, at some narrow pass below, as soon as of sufficient size. It occurred to me we should be temporarily safe, could we reach that mound, for it rose so high as to be above danger from the water. Thither then I ran, almost carrying Anneke on my arm, our speed increased by the terrific sounds from the dam above us.

We reached the mound, and found the cakes so piled, as to be able to acsend them, though not without an effort. After getting up a layer or two, the broken mass became so irregular and ragged, as to render it necessary for me to mount first, and then to drag Anneke up after me. This I did, until exhausted, and we both seated ourselves on the edge of a cake, in order to recover our breath. While there, it struck me, that new sounds arose from the river, and bending forward to examine, I saw that the water had forced its way through the dam above, and was coming down upon us in a torrent.

V.   Corny and Anneke crossing the ice, engraving from a drawing by F. O. C. Darley.

VI.   Corny and Guert consult the fortune teller, engraving
from a drawing by William A. McCullough.

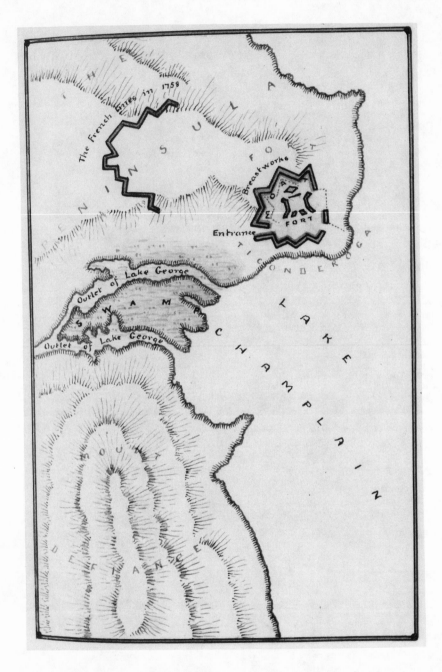

Within the map:
The French Lines in 1758
The Peninsula
Fort
Breastworks
Entrance
Fort
Ticonderoga
Outlet of Lake George
Swamp
Outlet of Lake George
Lake Champlain
Mount Defiance

VII. Matlack's map of Fort Ticonderoga and the surrounding area (Chapters XXII–XXIV).

VIII.   Engraving from a drawing by F. O. C. Darley
of Corny and Susquesus in the forest (Chapter XXV).

Chapter XVII

"My heart leaps up when I behold
  A rainbow in the sky;
So was it when my life began;
So is it now I am a man;
So be it when I shall grow old,
  Or let me die!
The Child is father of the Man;
  And I could wish my days to be
  Bound each to each by natural piety."
Wordsworth

FIVE minutes longer on the ice of the main channel, and we should have been swept away. Even as we still sat, looking at the frightful force of the swift current, as well as the dim light of that clouded night would permit, I saw Guert Ten Eyck's sleigh whirl past us; and, only a minute later, Herman Mordaunt's followed, the poor exhausted beasts struggling in the harness for freedom, that they might swim for their lives. Anneke heard the snorting of those wretched horses, but her unpracticed eyes did not detect them, immersed as they were in the current, nor had she recognised the sleigh that whirled past us as her father's. A little later, a fearful shriek came from one of the fettered beasts, such a heart-piercing cry as it is known the horse often gives. I said nothing on the subject, knowing that love for her father was one of the great incentives which had aroused my companion to exertion, and being unwilling to excite fears that were now latent.

Two, or three, minutes of rest were all that circumstances permitted. I could see that every thing visible on the river was in motion downwards; the piles of ice on which we were placed, as well as the cakes that glanced by us, in their quicker descent. Our own motion was slow on account of the mass, which doubtless pressed on the shoals of the west side of the river, as well as on account of the friction against the lateral fields of ice and occasionally against the shore. Still we were in motion, and I felt the necessity, on every account, of getting as soon as possible on the western verge of our floating island, in order to profit by any favourable occurrence that might offer.

Dear Anneke!—How admirably did she behave that fearful night! From the moment she regained her entire consciousness, after I found her praying in the bottom of the sleigh, down to that instant, she had been as little of an encumbrance to my own efforts, as was at all possible. Reasonable, resolute, compliant and totally without any ill-timed exhibition of womanly apprehension, she had done all she was desired to do unhesitatingly, and with intelligence. In ascending that pile of ice, by no means an easy task under any circumstances, we had acted in perfect concert, every effort of mine being aided by one of her own, directed by my advice and greater experience.

"God has not deserted us, dearest Anneke," I said, now that my companion's strength appeared to have returned, "and we may yet hope to escape. I can anticipate the joy we shall bring to your father's heart, when he again takes you to his arms, safe and uninjured."

"Dear, *dear* Father! What agony he must, now, be suffering on my account.—Come, Corny; let us go to him, at once, if it be possible."

As this was said, the precious girl arose, and adjusted her tippet, in a way that should cause her no incumbrance, like one ready to set about the execution of a serious task with all her energies. The muff had been dropped on the river, for neither of us had any sensibility to cold. The night, however, was quite mild for the season, and we probably should not have suffered, had our exertions been less violent. Anneke declared herself ready to proceed, and I commenced the difficult and delicate task of aiding her across an island composed of icy fragments, in order to reach its western margin. We were quite thirty feet in the air, and a fall into any of the numerous caverns, among which we had to proceed, might have been fatal; certainly would have crippled the sufferer. Then the surface of the ice was so smooth as to render walking on it an exceedingly delicate operation, more especially as the cakes lay at all manner of inclinations to the plane of the horizon. Fortunately I wore buckskin moccasins, over my boots, and their rough leather aided me greatly in maintaining my footing. Anneke, too, had socks of cloth, without which I do not think she could have possibly moved. By these aids, however, and by proceeding with the utmost caution, we had actually succeeded in attaining our object, when the floating mass shot into an eddy, and turning slowly round under this new influence, placed us, on the outer side of the island again! Not a murmur escaped Anneke at this disappointment, but with a sweetness of temper that spoke volumes in favour of her natural disposition, and a resignation that told her training, she professed a readiness to renew her efforts. To this I would not consent, however; for I saw that the eddy was still whirling us about, and I thought it best to escape from its influence altogether, before we threw away our strength fruitlessly. Instead of re-crossing the pile therefore, I told my fair companion that we would descend to a cake that lay level on the water, and which projected from the mass to such a distance, as to be close to the shore, should we again get near it. This descent was made, after some trouble, though I was compelled to receive Anneke entirely into my arms, in order to effect it. Effect it I did, placing the sweet girl safely at my side, on the outermost and lowest of all the cakes in our confused pile.

In some respects this change was for the better, while it did not improve our situation in others. It placed both Anneke and myself behind a shelter, as respected the wind; which, though neither very strong nor very cold, had enough of March about it, to render the change acceptable. It took my companion, too, from a position where motion was difficult, and often dangerous, leaving her on a level, even spot, where she could walk with ease and security, and keep the blood in motion, by exercise. Then it put us both, in the best possible situation to profit by any contact with that shore, along and near which our island was now slowly moving.

There could no longer be any doubt of the state of the river in general. It had broken up; spring had come, like a thief in the night, and the ice below having given way, while the mass above had acquired too much power to be resisted, every thing was set in motion, and like the death of the strong man, the disruption of fields in themselves so thick and adhesive, had produced an agony surpassing the usual struggle of the seasons. Nevertheless, the downward motion had begun in earnest, and the centre of the river was running like a sluice, carrying away in its current, those masses which had just before formed so menacing an obstacle above.

Luckily our own pile was a little aside from the great downward rush. I have since thought that it touched the bottom, which caused it to turn, as well as retarded its movement. Be this as it might, we still remained in a little bay, slowly turning in a circle; and glad was I to see our low cake coming round again, in sight of the western shore. The moment now demanded decision, and I prepared Anneke to meet it. A large, low, level cake had driven up on the shore, and extended out so far as to promise that our own cake would touch it, in our evolutions. I knew that the ice, in general, had not broken, in consequence of any weakness of its own, but purely under the weight of the enormous pressure from above, and the mighty force of the current, and that we ran little, or no, risk in trusting our persons on the uttermost limits of any considerable fragment. A station was taken, accordingly, near a projection of the cake we were on, when we waited for the expected contact. At such moments, the slightest disappointment carries with it the force of the gravest circumstance. Several times did it appear to us that our island was on the point of touching the fastened cake, and as often did it incline aside, at no time coming nearer than within six, or eight feet. This distance it would have been easy enough for *me* to leap across; but to Anneke, it was a barrier as impassable as the illimitable void. The sweet girl saw this, and she acted like herself, under the circumstances. She took my hand, pressed it, and said earnestly and with patient sweetness—

"You see how it is, Corny; I am not permitted to escape; but you can easily reach the shore. Go, then, and leave me in the hands of Providence. Go; I never can forget what you have already done; but it is useless to perish together!"

I have never doubted that Anneke was perfectly sincere in her wish that I should, at least, save my own life. The feeling with which she spoke, the despair that was coming over her, and the movement of our island, which, at that moment gave signs of shooting away from the shore altogether, roused me to a sudden, and certainly to a very bold attempt. I tremble, even at this distance of time, as I write the particulars. A small cake of ice, was floating in between us and that which lay firmly fastened to the shore. Its size was such as to allow it to pass between the two, though not without coming nearly, if not absolutely in contact with one, if not with both. I observed all this, and saying one word of encouragement to Anneke, I passed an arm around her waist, waited the proper moment, and sprang forward. It was necessary to make a short leap, with my precious burthen on my arm, in order to gain this floating bridge; but it was done and successfully. Scarcely permitting Anneke's foot to touch this frail support, which was already sinking under our joint weight, I crossed it at two or three steps, and threw all my power into a last and desperate effort. I succeeded, here also, and fell upon the firmer cake, with a heart filled with gratitude to God. The touch told me that we were safe, and, in the next instant, we reached the solid ground. Under such circumstances, one usually looks back to examine the danger he has just gone through. I did so, and saw that the floating cake of ice, had already passed down, and was out of reach, while the mass that had been the means of saving us, was slowly following, under some new impulse, received from the furious currents of the river. But we were saved, and most devoutly did I thank my God, who had mercifully aided our escape from perils so imminent.

I was compelled to wait for Anneke, who fell upon her knees, and remained there quite a minute, before I could aid her in ascending the steep acclivity which formed the western bank of the Hudson, at this particular point. We reached the top, however, after a little delay, and pausing, once or twice, to take breath, when we first became really sensible of the true character of the scene from which we had been delivered. Dim as was the light, there was enough to enable us to overlook a considerable reach of the river, from that elevated stand. The Hudson resembled chaos rushing headlong between the banks. As for the cakes of ice,— some darting past singly, and others piled as high as houses—of course the stream was filled with such; but, a large dark object was seen coming through that very channel, over which Anneke and I had stood, less than an hour before, sailing down the current, with fearful rapidity. It was a house, of no great size it is true, but large enough to present a singular object on the river. A bridge of some size followed, and a sloop, that had been borne away from the wharves of Albany, soon appeared in the strange assemblage that was thus suddenly collected on this great artery of the colony.

But the hour was late; Anneke was yet to care for; it was necessary to seek a shelter. Still supporting my lovely companion, who now began to express her uneasiness on account of her father, and her other friends, I held the way inland, knowing that there was a high road parallel to the river, and at no great distance from it. We reached the highway, in the course of ten minutes, and turned our faces northward, as the direction which led towards Albany. We had not advanced far before I heard the voices of men, who were coming towards us, and glad was I to recognize that of Dirck Follock among the number. I called aloud, and was answered by a shout of exultation, which, as I afterwards discovered, spontaneously broke out of his mouth, when he recognised the form of Anneke. Dirck was powerfully agitated when we joined him; I had never previously seen any thing like such a burst of feeling from him, and it was some time before I could address him.

"Of course your whole party is safe?" I asked a little doubtingly, for I had actually given up all who had been in Herman Mordaunt's sleigh for lost.

"Yes, thank God, all but the sleigh and horses. But where are Guert Ten Eyck and Miss Wallace?"

"Gone ashore on the other side of the river; we parted, and they took that direction, while we came hither." I said this to quiet Anneke's fears, but I had misgivings about their having got off the river at all. "But let me know the manner of your own escape."

Dirck then gave us a history of what had passed, the whole party turning back to accompany us, as soon as I told them that their errand—a search for the horses—was useless. The substance of what we heard, was as follows:—In the first effort to reach the western shore, Herman Mordaunt had been met by the very obstacle which Guert had foreseen, and he turned south, hoping to find some spot at which to land, by going farther from the dam that had formed above. After repeated efforts, and having nearly lost his sleigh, and the whole party, a point was reached at which Herman Mordaunt determined to get his female companion on shore, at every hazard. This was to be done only by crossing floating cakes of ice, in a current that was already running at the rate of four or five miles in the hour. Dirck was left in charge of the horses, while the experiment was made, but seeing the adventurers in great danger, he flew to their assistance— when the whole party were immersed, though not in deep water.

Left to themselves, and alarmed with the floundering in the river, and the grinding of the cakes, Herman Mordaunt's bays went off in the confusion. Mrs. Bogart was assisted to the land, and was helped to reach the nearest dwelling—a comfortable farm-house, about a quarter of a mile beyond the point where we had met the party. There Mrs. Bogart had been placed in a warm bed, and the gentlemen were supplied with such dry clothes, as the rustic wardrobes of these simple people could furnish. The change made, Dirck was on his way to ascertain what had become of the sleigh and horses, as has been mentioned.

On inquiry, I found that the spot where Anneke and myself had landed was quite three miles below the island on which Guert and I had drawn the sleigh. Nearly the whole of this distance had we floated with the pile of broken ice, in the short time we were on it; a proof of the furious rate at which the current was setting downward. No one had heard any thing of Guert and Mary, but I encouraged my companion to believe that they were necessarily safe on the other shore. I certainly deemed this to be very questionable, but there was no use in anticipating evil.

On reaching the farm house, Herman Mordaunt's delight and gratitude may more easily be imagined than described. He folded Anneke to his heart, and she wept like an infant on his bosom. Nor was I forgotten in this touching scene, but came in for a full share of notice.

"I want no details, noble young man—" I am professing to write the truth, and must be excused from relating such things as these, but—"I want no details, noble young man," said Herman Mordaunt, squeezing my hand, "to feel certain that, under God, I owe my child's life, for the second time, to you. I wish to Heaven!—but, no matter—it is now too late—some other way may and *must* offer. I scarce know what I say, Littlepage, but what I *mean*, is to express faintly some small portion of the gratitude I feel, and to let you know how sensibly and deeply your services are felt and appreciated."

The reader may think it odd, that this incoherent, but pregnant speech, made little impression on me at the time, beyond the grateful conviction of having really rendered the greatest of all services to Anneke and her father, though I had bitter occasion to remember it afterwards.

It is unnecessary to dwell more particularly on the occurrences at the farm-house. The worthy people did what they could to make us comfortable, and we were all warm in bed, in the course of the next half-hour.

On the following morning, a wagon was harnessed and we left these simple countrymen and women—who refused every thing like compensation as a matter of course—and proceeded homeward. I have heard it said that we Americans are mercenary; it may be so, but not a man probably exists in the colonies who would accept money for such assistance. We were two hours in reaching Albany, on wheels, and entered the place about ten, in a very different style from that in which we had quitted it the day before. As we drove along, the highway frequently led us to points that commanded views of the river, and we had so many opportunities of noting the effects of the freshet. Of ice, very little remained. Here and there, a cake or a pile, was seen still adhering to the shore, and occasionally fragments floated downwards; but, as a rule, the torrent had swept all before it. I particularly took notice of the island on which we had sought refuge. It was entirely under water, but its outlines were to be traced by the bushes which lined its low banks. Most of the trees, on its upper end, were cut down, and all that grew on it would unquestionably have gone, had not the dam given way as early as it did. A great number of trees had been broken down, on all the islands, and large tops and heavy trunks, were still floating in the current, that were lately tenants of the forests, and had been violently torn from their places.

We found all the lower part of Albany too, under water. Boats were actually moving through the streets, a considerable portion of its inhabitants having no other means of communicating with their neighbors. A sloop of some size lay up in one of the lowest spots, and, as the water was already subsiding, it was said she would remain there, until removed by the shipwrights. Nobody was drowned, in the place, for it is not usual for the people of these colonies to remain in their beds, at such times, to await the appearance of the enemy in at their windows. We often read of such accidents destroying hundreds in the old world; but, in the new, human life is of too much account to be unnecessarily thrown away, and so we make some efforts to preserve it.

As we drove into the street in which Herman Mordaunt lived, we heard a shout, and, turning our heads, we saw Guert Ten

Eyck, waving his cap to us, with joy delineated in every feature of his handsome face. At the next moment, he was at our side.

"Mr. Herman Mordaunt," he cried, shaking that gentleman most cordially by the hand, "I look upon you, as on one raised from the dead; you and my excellent neighbour, Mrs. Bogart, and Mr. Follock, here! How you got off the river is a mystery to me, for I well know that the water commonly breaks through first, under the west shore. Corny and Miss Anneke—God bless you, both! Mary Wallace is in terror lest ill news come from some of you; but I will run ahead and let her know the glad tidings. It is but five minutes, since I left her, starting at every sound, lest it prove the foot of some ill-omened messenger."

Guert stopped to say no more. In a minute he was inside of Herman Mordaunt's house—in another Anneke and Mary Wallace were locked in each other's arms. After exchanging salutes, Mrs. Bogart was conveyed to her own residence, and there was a termination to that memorable expedition.

Guert had less to communicate in the way of dangers and marvels, than I had anticipated. It seemed that, when he and Miss Wallace reached the inner margin of the last island, a large cake of ice had entered the strait, and got jammed; or, rather, that it went through, forced by the tremendous pressure above, though not without losing large masses, as it came in contact with the shores, and grinding much of its material into powder, by the attrition. Guert's presence of mind and decision did him excellent service here. Without delaying an instant, the moment it was in his power, he led Mary on that cake, and crossed the narrow branch of the river, which alone separated him from the main land, on it, dry shod. The water was beginning to find its way, over this cake, as it usually did on all those that lay low, and which were stopped in their progress; but this did not offer any serious obstacles to persons who were so prompt. Safe themselves, our friends remained to see if we could not be induced to join them, and the call we heard, was from Guert, who had actually recrossed to the island, in the hope of meeting us, and directing us to a place of safety. Guert never said any thing to me on the subject, himself, but I subsequently gathered from Mary Wallace's accounts, that the young man did not rejoin her without a good deal of hazard and difficulty, and after a long and fruitless search for his companions. Finding it useless to remain any longer on the river side, Guert and his companion, held their way towards Albany. About midnight they reached the ferry, opposite to the town, having walked quite six miles, filled with uneasiness on account of those who had been left behind. Guert was a man of decision, and he wisely determined it would be better to proceed, than to attempt waking up the inmates of any of the houses he passed. The river was now substantially free from ice, though running with great velocity. But, Guert was an expert oarsman, and finding a skiff, he persuaded Mary Wallace to enter it, actually succeeding, by means of the eddies, in landing her within ten feet of the very spot where the hand sled had deposited him and myself, only a few days before. From this point, there was no difficulty in walking home, and Miss Wallace actually slept in her own bed, that eventful night; if, indeed, she *could* sleep.

Such was the termination of this adventure; one that I have rightly termed memorable. In the end, Jack and Moses came in, safe and sound, having probably swum ashore. They were found in the public road, only a short distance from the town, and were brought in to their master the same day. Every one who took any interest in horses,—and what Dutchman does not?—knew Jack and Moses; and there was no difficulty in ascertaining to whom they belonged. What is singular, however, both sleighs were recovered; though at long intervals of time, and under very different circumstances. That of Guert, wolves' skins and all, actually went down the whole length of the river on the ice, passing out to sea through the Narrows. It must have gone by New York in the night, or doubtless it would have been picked up, while the difficulty of reaching it was its protector on the descent, *above* the town. Once outside of the Narrows, it was thrown by the tide and winds upon the shore of Staten Island, where it was hauled to land, housed, and, being properly advertised in one New York paper, Guert actually got tidings of it, in time to receive it, skins and all, by one of the first sloops that ascended the Hudson that year; which was within a fortnight after the river had opened. The year 1758 was one of great activity, on account of the movements of the army, and no time was then unnecessarily lost.

The history of Herman Mordaunt's sleigh was very different. The poor bays must have drowned soon after we saw them floating past us in the torrent. Of course, life had no sooner left them, than they sank to the bottom of the river, carrying with them the sleigh to which they were still attached. In a few days, the animals rose to the surface—as is usual with all swollen bodies—bringing up the sleigh again. In this condition the wreck was overtaken by a downward bound sloop, the men of which saved the sleigh, harness, skins, foot-stoves, and such other articles as would not float away.

Our adventure made a good deal of noise, in the circle of Albany, and I have reason to think that my own conduct was approved, by those who heard of it. Bulstrode paid me an especial visit of thanks, the very day of my return, when the following conversation took place between us.

"You seem fated, my dear Corny," the Major observed, after he had paid the usual compliments, "to be always serving me in the most material way, and I scarcely know how to express all I feel on the occasion. First the lion, and now this affair of the river—but, that Guert will drown, or make away with the whole family, before the summer is over, unless Mr. Mordaunt puts a stop to *his* interference."

"This accident was one that might have overtaken the oldest and most prudent man in Albany. The river seemed as solid as the street, when we went on it, and another hour, even as it was, would have brought us all home, in entire safety."

"Ay, but that hour came near bringing death and desolation into the most charming family in the colony, and you have been the means of averting the heaviest part of the blow. I wish to Heaven, Littlepage, that you would consent to come into the army! Join us as a volunteer, the moment we move, and I will write to Sir Harry to obtain a pair of colours for you. As soon as he hears that we are indebted to your coolness and courage for the life of Miss Mordaunt, he will move heaven and earth, to manifest his gratitude. The instant this good parent made up his mind to accept Miss Mordaunt as a daughter, he began to consider her as a child of his own."

"And, Anneke—Miss Mordaunt herself, Mr. Bulstrode—does she regard Sir Harry as a father?"

"Why, that must be coming, by slow degrees, as a matter of course, you know. Women are slower than us men to admit such totally novel impressions, and I dare say Anneke fancies one father enough for her, just at this moment:—though she sends very pleasant messages to Sir Harry, I can assure you, when in the humour! But, what makes you so grave, my good Corny?"

"Mr. Bulstrode, I conceive it no more than fair to be as honest as yourself, in this matter. You have told me that you are a suitor for Miss Mordaunt's hand; I will now own to you that I am your rival."

My companion heard this declaration with a quiet smile, and the most perfect good nature.

"So you actually wish to become the husband of Anneke Mordaunt, yourself, my dear Corny, do you?" he said so coolly that I was at a loss to know of what sort of materials the man could be made.

"I do, Major Bulstrode—it is the first and last wish of my heart."

"Since you seem disposed to reciprocate my confidence, you will not take offence, if I ask you a question, or two?"

"Certainly not, sir; your own frankness shall be a rule for my government."

"Have you ever let Miss Mordaunt know that such are your wishes?"

"I have, sir; and that in the plainest terms—such as cannot well be misunderstood."

"What! Last night?—On that infernal ice?—While she thought her life was in your hands!"

"Nothing was said on the subject, last night, for we had other thoughts to occupy our minds."

"It would have been a most ungenerous thing to take advantage of a lady's fears—"

"Major Bulstrode! I cannot submit—"

"Hush, my dear Corny," interrupted the other, holding out a hand in a most quiet and friendly manner; "there must be no misunderstanding between you and me. Men are never greater simpletons than when they let the secret consciousness of their love of life, push them into swaggering about their honour, when their honour has, in fact, nothing to do with the matter in hand. I shall not quarrel with you, and must beg you, in advance, to receive my apologies for any little indecorum into which I may be betrayed by surprise; as for great pieces of indecorum, I shall endeavour to avoid *them*."

"Enough has been said, Mr. Bulstrode; I am no wrangler to

quarrel with a shadow, and I trust not in the least, that most contemptible of all human beings, a social bully, to be on all occasions, menacing the sword, or the pistol. Such men usually *do* nothing, when matters come to a crisis. Even when they fight, they fight bunglingly and innocently."

"You are right, Littlepage, and I honour your sentiments. I have remarked that the most expert swordsman with his tongue, and the deadest shot at a shingle, are commonly as innocent as lambs of the shedding of blood on the ground. They can sometimes screw themselves up to *meet* an adversary, but it exceeds their powers to use their weapons properly, when it comes to serious work. The swaggerer is ever a coward at heart, however well he may wear a mask for a time. But enough of this— we understand each other, and are to remain friends, under all circumstances. May I question, further?"

"*Ask* what you please, Bulstrode—I shall answer, or not, at my own discretion."

"Then permit me to inquire if Major Littlepage has authorized you to offer proper settlements?"

"I am authorized to offer nothing—nor is it usual for the husband to make settlements on his wife, in these colonies, further than what the law does for her, in favour of her own. The father sometimes has a care for the third generation. I should expect Herman Mordaunt to settle *his* estate on his daughter and her rightful heirs, let her marry whom she may."

"Ay, that is a very American notion, and one on which Herman Mordaunt, who remembers his extraction, will be little likely to act. Well, Corny, we are rivals, as it would seem; but that is no reason we should not remain friends. We understand each other—though, perhaps I ought to tell you all."

"I should be glad to know *all*, Mr. Bulstrode, and can meet my fate, I hope, like a man. Whatever it may cost me, if Anneke prefer another, her happiness will be dearer to me than my own."

"Yes, my dear fellow, we all say and think so at one-and-twenty; which is about your age I believe. At *two*-and-twenty, we begin to see that our own happiness has an equal claim on us, and at *three*-and-twenty, we even give it the preference. However, I will be just, if I am selfish. I have no reason to believe Anne Mordaunt does prefer me, though my *perhaps* is not altogether without a meaning either."

"In which case I may possibly be permitted to know to what it refers?"

"It refers to the father; and I can tell you, my fine fellow, that fathers are of some account in the arrangement of marriages between parties of any standing. Had not Sir Harry authorized my own proposals, where should I have been? Not a farthing of settlement could I have offered while he remained Sir Harry, notwithstanding I had the prodigious advantage of the entail. I can tell you what it is, Corny; the existing power is always an important power, since we all think more of the present time, than of the future. That is the reason so few of us get to Heaven. As for Herman Mordaunt, I deem it no more than fair to tell you he is on my side, heart and hand. He likes my offers of settlement; he likes my family; he likes my rank, civil and military; and I am not altogether without the hope, that he likes *me*."

I made no direct answer, and the conversation soon changed. Bulstrode's declaration, however, caused me to remember both the speech and manner of Herman Mordaunt when he thanked me for saving his daughter's life. I now began to reflect on it, and reflected on it much during the next few months. In the end, the reader will learn the effect it had on my happiness.

Chapter XVIII

"Good Sir, why do you start; and seem to fear
Things that do sound so fair? I' the name of truth,
Are ye fantastical, or that indeed
Which outwardly ye show?"

Macbeth, I.iii.51–54.

As I have said already, the adventure on the river made a good deal of noise, in that simple community, and it had the effect to render Guert and myself a sort of heroes, in a small way; bringing me much more into notice than would otherwise have been the case. I thought that Guert, in particular, would be likely to reap its benefit, for various elderly persons who were in the habit of frowning whenever his name was mentioned, I was given to understand, could now smile; and two or three of the most severe among the Albany moralists, were heard to say that, "after all, there was some good about that Guert Ten Eyck." The reader will not require to be told, that a high-school moralist, in a place as retired and insulated as Albany, must necessarily be a being that became subject to a very severe code. Morality, as I understand the matter, has a good deal of convention about it. There is town-morality and country-morality, all over the world, as they tell me. But, in America, our morals were and long have been, separated into three great and very distinct classes; viz.—New England, or puritan-morals; Middle Colonies', or liberal morals; and Southern Colonies', or latitudinarian morals. I shall not pretend to point out all the shades of difference in these several schools, though that in which I had myself been taught, was necessarily the most in conformity with my own tastes. There were minor shades to be found in the same school, Guert and myself belonging to different classes. His morals were of the Dutch class, while mine more properly belonged to the English. The great characteristic of the Dutch school was the tendency to excess that prevailed, when indulgencies were sought. With them, it did not rain often; but when it did rain, it was pretty certain to pour. Old Col. Follock was a case in point, on this score, nor was his son Dirck,

young and diffident as he was, altogether an exception to the
rule. There was not a more respectable man in the colony, in the
main, than Col. Van Valkenburgh. He was well connected, had a
handsome unincumbered estate and money at interest, was a
principal prop in the church of his neighbourhood, was esteemed as a good husband, a good father, a true friend, a kind
neighbour, an excellent and loyal subject, and a thoroughly honest man. Nevertheless, Col. Van Valkenburgh had his weak times
and seasons. He *would* have a frolic, and the Dominie was obliged
to wink at this propensity. Mr. Worden often nick-named him Col.
Frolick. His frolicks might be divided into two classes; viz. the
moderate, and the immoderate. Of the first, he had two or three
turns a year, and these were the occasions on which he commonly
visited Satanstoe, or had my father with him at Rockrockarock,
as his own place in Rockland was called. On these visits, whether
to or from, there was a large consumption of tobacco, beer, cider,
wine, rum, lemons, sugar, and the other ingredients of punch,
toddy and flip, but no outrageously durable excesses. There
was much laughing, a great deal of good feeling, many stories, and
regular repetitions of old adventures in the way of traditional
narrations, but nothing that could be called decided excesses. It
is true, that my grandfather, and my father, and the Rev. Mr.
Worden, and Col. Follock were much in the habit of retiring to their
beds a little confused in their brains; the consequence of so much
tobacco smoke as Mr. Worden always maintained; but, every thing
was decent, and in order. The parson, for instance, invariably
pulled up on a Friday, and did not take his place in the circle, until
Monday evening, again, which gave him fully twenty-four hours to
cool off in, before he ascended the pulpit. I will say this for Mr.
Worden, that he was very systematic and methodical in the obser-
vance of all his duties and I have known him, when he happened
to be late at dinner, on discovering that my father had omitted to
say grace, insist on everybody's laying down their knives and
forks, while he asked a blessing, even though it were after the fish
was actually eaten. No, no; Mr. Worden was a particular person
about all such things, and it was generally admitted that he had
been the means of causing grace to be introduced into several
families in Westchester, in which it had never been the practice to
have it, before his example and precepts were known to them.

I had not been acquainted with Guert Ten Eyck a fortnight, before I saw he had a tendency to the same sort of excesses as those to which Col. Van Valkenburgh was addicted. There was an old French Huguenot living near Satanstoe—or rather, the son of one, who still spoke his father's language—and who used to call Col. Follock's frolicks his "*grands couchers*," and his "*petit couchers*,"* inasmuch as he usually got to bed at the last, without assistance; while at the first, it was indispensable that some aid should be proffered. It was these "grands couchers" at which my father never assisted. On these occasions, the Colonel invariably had his orgies, over in Rockland, in the society of men of purely Dutch extraction; there being something exclusive in the enjoyment. I have heard it said that these last frolicks sometimes lasted a week, on really important occasions; during the whole of which time, the Colonel and all near him, were as happy as lords. These "*grands couchers*," however, occurred but rarely—coming round, as it might be, like leap years, just to regulate the calendar, and adjust the time.

As for my new friend, Guert, he made no manifestation towards a "*grand coucher*" during the time I remained at Albany— this his attachment to Mary Wallace forbade—but, I discovered by means of hints and allusions, that he *had* been engaged in one, or two, such affairs, and that there was still a longing for them in his bones. It was owing to her consciousness of the existence of such weaknesses, and her own strong aversion to any thing of the sort, that, I am persuaded, Mary Wallace was alone induced to hesitate about accepting Guert's weekly offer of his hand. The tenderness she evidently felt for him, now shone too obviously in her eyes, to leave any doubt in my mind of Guert's final success,

---

*In plain English, the "great go-to-bed," and the "little go-to-bed." There may be a portion of our readers who are not aware that the word "levee," meaning a morning reception by a great man, is derived from the French "lever," which means "to rise," or "to get up." The Kings of France were in the habit of receiving homage at their morning toilets, a strange custom that doubtless had its origin in the *empressement* of the courtier to enquire how his master had slept, which receptions were divided into two classes, the "*grand lever*" and the "*petit lever*"—the "great getting-up" or the "little getting-up." The first was an occasion of more state, than the last. Even down to the time of Charles X., the court papers seldom went a week without announcing that the King had signed the contract of marriage—a customary compliment in France among friends, of this or that personage—at the "grand lever," or at the "petit lever," the first, I believe, but am not certain, being the greater honour of the two.—EDITOR.

for what woman ever refused long to surrender, when the image of the besieger had taken its place in the citadel of her heart! Even Anneke received Guert with more favour, after his excellent behaviour on the river, and I fancied that every thing was going on most flatteringly for my friend, while it seemed to me that I made no advance in my own suit. Such, at least, were my notions on the subject, at the very moment when my new friend, as it appeared, was nearly driven to desperation.

It was near the end of April, or about a month after our perilous adventure on the ice, that Guert came to seek me, one fine spring morning, with something very like despair depicted in his fine, manly face. During the whole of that month, it ought to be premised, I had not dared to speak of love to Anneke. My attentions and visits were incessant and pointed; but my tongue had been silent. The diffidence of real admiration had held me tongue-tied, and I foolishly fancied there would be something like presuming on the service I had so lately rendered, in urging my suit so soon after the occurrence of the events I have described. I had even the romance to think it might be taking an undue advantage of Bulstrode, to wish to press my claims at a moment when the common object of our suit might be supposed to feel the influence of a lively gratitude. These were the notions and sentiments of a very young man, it must be confessed, but I do not know that I ought to feel ashamed of them. At all events, they existed; and they had produced the effect I have mentioned, leaving me to fall, each day, more desperately in love, while I made no sensible advances in preferring my suit. Guert was very much in the same situation, with this difference, however; he made it a point to offer himself, distinctly each Monday morning, invariably receiving for an answer "no," if the lady were to be pressed for a definite reply; but leaving some glimmering of hope, should time be given for her to make up her mind. The visit of Guert's, to which I have just alluded, was after one of the customary offers, and usual replies; the offer direct, and the "no" tempered by the doubting and thoughtful brow, the affectionate smile, and the tearful eye.

"Corny," said my friend, throwing down his hat with a most rueful aspect, for, winter having departed, and spring come, we had all laid aside our fur-caps—"Corny, I have just been refused again! That word 'no,' has got to be so common with Mary Wallace, that I am afraid her tongue will never know how to utter a 'yes.' Do you know, Corny, I have a great mind to consult Mother Doortje!"

"Mother who?—You do not mean Mr. Mayor's cook, surely?"

"No; *Mother* Doortje. She is said to be the best fortune-teller that has ever lived in Albany. But, perhaps you do not believe in fortune-tellers; some people I know do not?"

"I cannot say that I have much belief, or unbelief, on the subject, never having seen any thing of that sort."

"Have they, then, no fortune-teller, no person who has the dark art, in New York?"

"I have heard of such people, but have never had an opportunity of seeing, or hearing, for myself. If you *do* go to see this Mother Dorrichy, or whatever you call her, I should like amazingly to be of the party."*

Guert was delighted to hear this, and he caught eagerly at the offer. If I would stand his friend, he would go at once, but he confessed he did not like to trust himself all alone in the old woman's company.

"I am, perhaps, the only man of my time of life, in Albany, who has not, sooner or later, consulted Mother Doortje," he added. "I do not know how it is, but, *somehow*, I have never liked to tempt fortune, by going to question her! One never can tell what such a being may say, and should it be evil, why it might make a man very miserable. I am sure I want no more trouble, as it is, than to find Mary Wallace so undetermined about having me!"

"Then you do not mean to go, after all? I am not only ready, but anxious, to accompany you."

"You mistake me, Corny. Go I will, now, though she tell me that which will cause me to cut my throat—but, we must not go as we are; we must disguise ourselves, in order that she may not know us. Every body goes disguised, and, then, they have an opportunity of learning if she is in a good vein, or not, by seeing if she can tell any thing about their business, or habits, in the first place. If she fail in that, I should not care a straw for any of the rest. So, go to work, Corny, and dress yourself for the occasion—borrow

*Doortje—pronounced Doort-yay—means Dorothea. Mr. Littlepage uses a sort of corruption of the pronunciation. I well remember a fortune-teller of that name, in Albany, though it could not have been the Doortje of 1758.— EDITOR.

some clothes of the people in the house here, and come round to me, as soon as you please; I shall be ready, for I often go disguised to frolicks— yes, unlucky devil that I am, and come back disguised too!"

Every thing was done, as desired. By means of a servant in the tavern, I was soon equipped in a way that satisfied me was very successful, inasmuch as I passed Dirck, in quitting the house, and my old, confidential friend did not recognize me. Guert was in as good luck, as I actually asked himself, for himself, when he opened the door for my admission. The laugh, and the handsome face, however, soon let me into the secret, and we sallied forth, in high spirits, almost forgetting our misgivings concerning the future, in the fun of passing our acquaintances in the streets, without being known.

Guert was much more artistically and knowingly disguised, than I was myself. We both had put on the clothes of labourers, Guert wearing a smock-frock that he happened to own for his fishing occupations in summer, but I had my usual linen, in view, and wore all the ordinary minor articles of my daily attire. My friend pointed out some of these defects, as we went along, and an attempt was made to remedy them. Mr. Worden coming in view, I determined to stop him, and speak to him in a disguised voice, in order to ascertain if it were possible to deceive him.

"Your servant, Tominie," I said, making an awkward bow, as soon as we got near enough to the parson to address him; "be you ter Tominie that marries folk on a pinch?"

"Ay, or on a handful, liking the last best—Why, Corny, thou rogue, what does all this mean?"

It was necessary to let Mr. Worden into the secret, and he no sooner learned the business we were on, than he expressed a wish to be of the party. As there was no declining, we now went to the inn, and gave him time to assume a suitable disguise. As the divine was a rigid observer of the costume of his profession, and was most strictly a man of his *cloth*, it was a very easy matter for him to make such a change in his exterior, as completely to render him *incognito*. When all was ready, we went finally forth, on our errand.

"I go with you, Corny, on this foolish business," said the Rev. Mr. Worden, as soon as we were fairly on our way, "to comply with a promise made your excellent mother, not to let you stray into any questionable company, without keeping a fatherly eye over you. Now, I regard a fortune-teller's as a doubtful sort of society; therefore, I feel it to be a duty, to make one of this party."

I do not know whether the Rev. Mr. Worden succeeded in deceiving himself, but, I very well know he did not succeed in deceiving me. The fact was, he loved a frolic, and nothing made him happier than to have an opportunity of joining in just such an adventure, as that we were on. Judging from the position of her house, and the appearance of things in and around it, the business of Mother Doortje, was not of the most lucrative sort. Dirt and poverty were two things not easily encountered in Albany, and I do not say that we found very positive evidence of either, here; but there was less neatness than was usual in that ultra-tidy community, and, as for any great display of abundance, it was certainly not to be met with.

We were admitted by a young woman, who gave us to understand that Mother Doortje had a couple of customers, already, but she invited us to sit down in an outer room, promising that our turn should be the next. We did so, accordingly, listening, through a door that was a little ajar, with no small degree of curiosity, to what was passing within. I accidentally took a seat in a place that enabled me to see the legs of one of the fortune-teller's customers, and I thought, immediately, that the striped stockings were familiar to me; when the nasal and very peculiar intonation of Jason put the matter out of all doubt. He spoke in an earnest manner, which rendered him a little incautious, while the woman's tones were low and mumbled. Notwithstanding, we all overheard the following discourse.

"Well, now, Mother Dorrichay," said Jason, in a very confiding sort of way, "I've paid you well, for this here business, and I want to know if there is any chance for a poor man in this colony, who doesn't want for friends, or, for that matter, merit?"

"That's *yourself*," mumbled the female voice—in the way one announces a discovery—"yes, I see by the cards, that your question applies to yourself. You are a *young* man that wants not for friends, and you have *merit*! You have friends that you deserve; the cards tell me *that*!"

"Well, I'll not deny the truth of what you assert, and I must say, Dirck, it *is* a little strange, this woman, who never saw me before, should know me so well—my very natur', as it might be. But, do you think I shall do well to follow up the affair I am now on, or that I had best give it up?"

"Give up nothing," answered the oracle, in a very oracular manner, shuffling the cards as she spoke. "No, give up nothing, but keep all you can. That is the way to thrive in this world."

"By the Hokey, Dirck, she gives good advice, and I think I shall follow it! But, how about the land and the mill seat—or, rather, how about the particular things, I'm thinking about?"

"You are thinking of purchasing—yes—the cards say, purchasing, or is it disposing—"

"Why, as I've got none to sell, it can't very well be disposing, Mother."

"Yes, I'm right—this Jack of Clubs settles the matter—you are thinking of buying some land—Ah! there's water running down hill, and here I see a pond—why, you are thinking of buying a mill seat."

"By the Hokey!—Who would have thought this, Dirck!"

"Not a *mill*; no, there is *no* mill built; but a mill *seat*. Six, king, three and an ace; yes, I see how it is—and you wish to get this mill seat at much less than its real value. *Much* less; not less, but *much* less."

"Well, this is wonderful! I'll never gainsay fortin-tellin' ag'in!" exclaimed Jason. "Dirck, you are to say nothin' of this, or *think* nothin' of this, as it's all in confidence, you know. Now, jist put in a last word, about the end of life, Mother, and I'll be satisfied. What you have told me about my fortin, and earnin's must be true, I think, for my whole heart is in them, but I should like to know, after enjoying so much wealth and happiness as you've foretold, what sort of an end I am to make of it?"

"An excellent end—full of grace, and hope, and christian faith. I see here, something that looks like a clergyman's gown—white sleeves—book under the arm—"

"That can't be *me*, Mother, as I'm no lover of forms, but belong to the platform."

"Oh! I see how it is, now; you dislike Church of England people, and could throw dirt at them. Yes, yes—here *you* are, a presbyterian deacon, and one that can lead in a private meeting, on an occasion."

"Come, Dirck, I'm satisfied. Let us go; we have kept Mother Doorichaise long enough, and I heard some visitors come in, just now. Thank you, mother—thank you, with all my heart—I think there *must* be some truth in this fortin-tellin' after all!"

Jason now rose, and walked out of the house, without even deigning to look at us, and consequently without our being recognized. But, Dirck lingered a minute, not yet satisfied with what had been already told him.

"Do you really think I shall never be married, Mother?" he asked, in a tone that sufficiently betrayed the importance he attached to the answer. "I wish to know that particularly, before I go away!"

"Young man," answered the Fortune-Teller in an oracular manner; "what has been said, has been said! I cannot *make* fortunes, but only reveal them. You have heard that Dutch blood is in your veins; but you live in an English colony. *Your* king, is *her* king; while *she* is your *queen*, and you are not her master. If you can find a woman of English blood, that has a Dutch heart, and has no English suitors, go forward and you will succeed; but, if you do not, remain as you are, until time shall end. These are my words, and these are my thoughts. I can say no more."

I heard Dirck sigh—poor fellow! he was thinking of Anneke—and he passed through the outer room, without once raising his eyes from the floor. He left Mother Doortje, as much depressed in spirits, as Jason had left her elated; the one looking forward to the future, with a selfish and niggardly hope, while the other regarded it with a feeling as forlorn as the destruction of all his youthful fancies could render any view of his after-life. The reader may feel disposed to smile at the idea of Dirck Van Valkenburgh's possessing youthful fancies, regarding the young man in the quiet, unassuming manner in which he has hitherto been portrayed by me, but it would be doing great injustice to his heart and feelings, to figure him to the mind, as a being without deep sensibilities. I have always supposed that this interview with Mother Doortje had a lasting influence on the fortunes of poor Dirck, nor am I at all certain its effects did not long linger in the temperaments of some others that might be named.

As our turns had now come, we were summoned to the presence of this female soothsayer. It is unnecessary to describe the apartment in which we found Mother Doortje. It had nothing unusual in it, with the exception of a raven, that was hopping about the floor, and which appeared to be on the most familiar terms with its mistress. Doortje, herself, was a woman of quite sixty, wrinkled, lean, and hag-like; and, I thought, some care had been taken, in her dress, to increase the effect of this, certainly her natural, appearance. Her cap was entirely of black muslin, though her dress itself was grey. The eye of this woman was of the colour of her gown, and it was penetrating, restless, and deep-seated. Altogether, she looked the character well.

On our entrance, after saluting the Fortune-Teller, each of us laid a French crown on the table, at which she was seated. This coin had become quite current among us, since the French troops had penetrated into our colony, and it was even said they purchased supplies with it, from certain of our own people. As we had paid the highest price ever given for these glimpses into futurity, we thought ourselves entitled to have the pages of the sealed book freely opened to us.

"Do you wish to see me together, or shall I communicate with one at a time?" demanded Doortje, in her husky, sepulchral voice, which, it struck me, obtained its peculiar tones partly from nature, and partly from art.

It was settled that she should commence with Mr. Worden, but that all might remain in the room the whole time. While we were talking over this point, Doortje's eyes were by no means fixed, but I remarked that they wandered from person to person, like those of one who was gathering information. Many persons do not believe, at all, in the art of the Fortune Teller; but insist that there is nothing more in it than trick and management, pretending that this very woman kept the blacks of the town, in pay, to bring her information, and that she never told any thing of the past which was true, that had not been previously communicated to herself. I shall not pretend to affirm that the art goes as far as many imagine, but it strikes me that it is very presuming to deny that there is some truth in these matters. I do not wish to appear credulous, though, at the same time, I hold it to be wrong to deny our testimony to facts that we are convinced are true.*

*It is quite evident that Mr. Cornelius Littlepage was, to a degree at least, a believer in the Fortune-Teller's art. This was, however, no more than was common a century since. Quite within my recollection, the Albanians had a celebrated dealer in the Black Art, who was regularly consulted on the subject of all lost spoons, and the pilfering of servants, by the good housewives of the town, as recently as my school-boy days. The Dutch, like the Germans, appear to have been prone to this species of superstition, from which even the English of education

Doortje commenced by shuffling an exceedingly dirty pack of cards, which had probably been used five hundred times, on similar duty. She next caused Mr. Worden to cut these cards, when a close and musing examination succeeded. All this time not a syllable was said; though we were startled by a low whistle, from the woman, which brought the raven upon her shoulder.

"Well, Mother," cried Mr. Worden with a little impatience at what he fancied mummery, "I am dying to hear what *has* happened, that I may put the more faith in what *is* to happen. Tell me something of the crop of wheat I put into the ground last autumn; how many bushels I sowed, and on how many acres; whether on new land, or on old?"

"Ay, ay, you have sowed!—and you have sowed!" answered the woman on a high key, for her; "but your seed fell among tares, and on the flinty ground, and you'll never reap a soul among 'em all! Broadcast may you sow, but narrow will be your harvest."

The Rev. Mr. Worden gave a loud hem, placed his arms akimbo, and seemed determined to brazen it out, though, I could easily perceive, that he felt excessively awkward.

"How is it with my cattle, and shall I send much mutton to market, this season?"

"A wolf, in sheep's clothing!" muttered Doortje. "No—no—you like hot suppers and ducks, and lectures to cooks, more than gathering in the harvest of the Lord!"

"Come, this is folly, woman!" exclaimed the parson, angrily. "Give me some common sense for my good French crown. What do you see in that Knave of Diamonds, that you study its face so closely?"

"A loping Dominie!—a loping Dominie!" screamed the hag several times, rather than exclaiming aloud. "See!—he runs for life, but Beelzebub will overtake him!"

There was a sudden, and dead pause; for the Rev. Mr. Worden had caught up his hat, and darted from the room, quitting the house as if already busily engaged in the race alluded to. Guert shook his head, and looked serious; but, perceiving that the woman was already tranquil, and was actually shuffling the cards anew, in his behalf, he advanced to learn his fate. I saw the eyes

---

were far from being free, a century since. Mademoiselle Normand existed in the present century, even in the sceptical capital of France. But, the somnambulist is taking the place of the ancient soothsayer, in our own times.—EDITOR.

of Doortje fastened keenly on him, as he took his stand near the table, and the corners of her mouth curled in a significant smile. What that meant exactly, I have never been able to ascertain.

"I suppose you wish to know something of the past, like all the rest of them," mumbled the woman, "so that you may have faith in what you hear about the future?"

"Why, Mother," answered Guert, passing his hand through his own fine head of natural curls, and speaking a little hastily, "I do not know that it is any great matter about the past. What is done, is done, and there is an end of it. A young man may not wish to hear of such things, at the moment, perhaps, when he is earnestly bent on doing better. We are all young, once in our lives, and we can grow old only after having been so."

"Yes—yes—I see how it is!"—muttered Doortje. "So—so—turkeys—turkeys; ducks—ducks—quaack—quaack— quaack—gobble, gobble, gobble—" Here, the old hag set up such an imitation of ducks, geese, turkeys, game-cocks, and other birds, that one who was in an outer room, might well have imagined he heard the cries of a regular poultry-yard. I was startled myself, for the imitation was very admirable, but Guert was obliged to wipe the perspiration from his face.

"That will do—that will do, Mother!" the young man exclaimed. "I see you know all about it, and there is no use in attempting disguises with you. Now, tell me if I am ever to be a married man, or not. My errand, here, is to learn that fact, and I may as well own it, at once."

"The world has many women in it, and fair faces are plenty in Albany," once more mumbled the woman, examining her cards with great attention. "A youth like you might marry twice, even."

"No, *that* is impossible; if I do not marry a particular lady, I shall never marry at all."

"Yes—yes—I see how it is!—You are in love, young man."

"D'ye hear that, Corny! Isn't it wonderful how these creatures can tell? I admit the truth of what you say, but, describe to me the lady that I love."

Guert had forgotten altogether, that the use of the word *lady*, completely betrayed the fact of his disguise, since no man truly of his dress and air would think of applying such a word to his sweetheart.* I could not prevent these little betrayals of himself,

*This might have been true, in 1758, but is not true for 1845.—EDITOR.

however, for, by this time my companion was too much excited to hear reason.

"The lady that you love," answered the Fortune Teller, deliberately, and with a manner of one that proceeded with great confidence—"is *very* handsome, in the first place."

"True as the sun in the heavens, Mother!"

"Then she is virtuous, and amiable, and wise, and witty, and good."

"The Gospel is not more certain! Corny, this surpasses belief!"

"Then she is *young*. Yes, she is young, and fair, and good; three things that make her much sought after."

"Why is she so long reflecting on my offers, Mother; tell me that, I beg of you; or will she ever consent to have me?"

"I see—I see—it is all here, on the cards. The lady cannot make up her mind."

"Listen to that, now, Corny, and do not tell me there is nothing in this art. *Why* does she not make up her mind? For Heaven's sake, let me know *that*? A man may tire of offering to marry an angel, and getting no answer. I wish to know the reason of her doubts."

"A woman's mind is not easily read. Some are in haste, while some are not. I am of opinion you wish to get an answer, before the lady is ready to give it. Men must learn to wait."

"She really seems to know all about it, Corny! Much as I have heard of this woman, she exceeds it all! Good Mother, can you tell me how I can gain the consent of the woman I love?"

"That is only to be had by asking. Ask once, ask twice, ask thrice."

"By St. Nicholas! I have asked, already, twenty times! If asking would do it, she would have been my wife a month since. What do you think, Corny—no, I'll not do it—it is not manly to get the secrets of a woman's heart, by means like these—I'll not ask her!"

"The crown is paid, and the truth must be said. The lady you love, loves you, and she doesn't love you; she will have you, and she won't have you; she thinks *yes*, and she says *no*."

Guert now trembled all over, like an aspen-leaf.

"I do not believe there is any harm, Corny, in asking whether I gained or lost by the affair of the river? I *will* ask her that much, of a certainty. Tell me, Mother, am I better, or worse, for a certain thing that happened about a month ago—about the time that the ice went, and that we had great freshet?"

"Guert Ten Eyck, why do you try me thus?" demanded the fortune teller solemnly. "I knew your father, and I knew your mother; I knew your ancestors in Holland, and their children in America. Generations on generations have I known your people, and you are the first that I have seen so ill clad! Do you suppose, boy, that old Doortje's eyes are getting dim, and that she cannot tell her own nation? I saw you on the river—ha! ha! 'T was a pleasant sight—Jack and Moses too, how they snorted, and how they galloped! Crack—crack—that's the ice—there comes the water— See, that bridge may hit you on the head! Do *you* take care of this bird, and do *you* take care of *that*, and all will come round with the seasons. Answer me one thing, Guert Ten Eyck, and answer me truly. Know you ever a young man who goes quickly into the bush?"

"I do, Mother; this young man, my friend intends to go in a few days, or as soon as the weather is settled."

"Good! go you with him—absence makes a young woman know her own mind, when asking will gain nothing. Go you with him I say; and if you hear muskets fired, go near them; *fear* will sometimes make a young woman speak. You have your answer and I will tell no more. Come hither, young owner of many half-joes, and touch that card."

I did as ordered, when the woman began to mumble to herself, and to run over the pack as rapidly as she could. Kings, aces, and knaves were examined, one after another, until she had got the Queen of Hearts in her hand, which she held up to me in triumph.

"That is *your* lady. She is queen of too many hearts! The Hudson did that for you, that it has done for many a poor man before you. Yes, yes; the river did you good. But water will drown, as well as make tears. Do *you* beware of Knights Barrownights!"*

*In the colony of New York there lived but one titled man, for a considerable period. It was the celebrated Sir William Johnson, Bart, of Johnson Hall, Johnstown, Albany, now, Fulton County. The son of Sir William Johnson was knighted during his father's life-time, and was Sir John while Sir William was living. At the death of his father he was Sir John Johnson, Kt. & Bart. and it was usual for the common class of people to style him a Knights-Barrow*night*.— EDITOR.

Here Mother Doortje came to a dead stand in her communications, and not another syllable, of any sort, could either of us get from her; though between us as many as twenty questions were asked. Signs were made for us to depart, and when the woman found our reluctance, she laid a crown for each of us, on the table, with a dignified air, and went into a corner, seated herself, and began to rock her body like one impatient of our presence. After so unequivocal a sign that she considered her work as done, we could not well do less than return, leaving the money behind us as a matter of course.

Chapter XIX

"Virtue, how frail it is!
   Friendship, too rare!
   Love, how it sells poor bliss
For proud despair!
But we, though soon they fall,
Survive their joy, and all
Which ours we call."
                    Shelley, "Mutability," ll. 8–14.

GUERT Ten Eyck was profoundly impressed with what he had heard, in his visit to the fortune-teller. It affected his spirits, and, as will be seen, it influenced all his subsequent conduct. As for myself, I will not say that I totally disregarded what had passed, though the effect was greatly less on me, than it was on my friend. The Rev. Mr. Worden, however, treated the matter with great disdain. He declared that he had never before been so insulted in his life. The old hag, no doubt, had seen us all before, and recognised him. Profiting by a knowledge of this sort—that was very easily obtained in a place of the size of Albany—she had taken the occasion to make the most of the low gossip that had been circulated at his expense. "Loping Dominie, indeed," he added, "as if any man would not run to save his life! You saw how it was with the river, Corny, when it once began to break up, and know that my escape was marvellous. I deserve as much credit for that retreat, boy, as Xenophon did for his retreat with the Ten Thousand. It is true, I had not thirty-four thousand six hundred and fifty stadia to retreat over, but acts are to be estimated more by quality, than by quantity. The best things are always of an impromptu character; and, generally, they are on a small scale. Then, as for all you tell me about Guert, why the hussy knew him—*must* have known him in a town like Albany, where the fellow has a character that identifies him with all sorts of fun and roguery. Jack and Moses, too! Do you think the inspiration of even an evil spirit, or, of forty thousand devils would lead a fortune teller to name any horse Moses? Jack might do, perhaps;

but *Moses* would never enter the head of even an imp! Remember, lad, Moses was the great law-giver of the Jews; and such a creature would be as apt to suppose a horse was named Confucius, as to suppose he was named Moses!"

"I suppose the inspiration, as you call it, sir, would lead a clever fortune teller to give things as they are, and to call the horses by their real names, let them be what they might."

"Ay, such inspiration as this miserable, old, wrinkled, impudent she-devil enjoys! Don't tell me, Corny; there is no such thing as fortune telling; at least nothing that can be depended on, in all cases, and this is one of downright imposition. 'Loping Dominie' forsooth!"

Such were the Rev. Mr. Worden's sentiments on the subject of Mother Doortje's revelations. He exacted a pledge from us all, to say nothing about the matter, nor were we much disposed to be communicative on the subject. As for Guert, Dirck, Jason and myself, we did not hesitate to converse on the circumstances of our visits, among ourselves, however; and each and all of us, viewed the matter somewhat differently from our Mentor. I ascertained that Jason had been highly gratified with what had been predicted on his own behalf, for what was wealth in his eyes had been foretold as his future lot; and a man rarely quarrels with good fortune, whether in prospective, or in possession. Dirck, though barely twenty, began to talk of living a single life from this time, and no laughter of mine could induce the poor lad to change his views, or to entertain livelier hopes. Guert was deeply impressed, as has been said, and feeling no restraint in the matter of his own case, he took occasion to speak of his visit to the woman, one morning that Herman Mordaunt, the two ladies, Bulstrode and myself, were sitting together, chatting in the freedom of what had now become a very constant intercourse.

"Are such things as fortune tellers known in England, Mr. Bulstrode?" Guert abruptly commenced, fastening his eyes on Mary Wallace, as he asked the question; for on her were his thoughts running at the time.

"All sorts of silly things are to be found in Old England, Mr. Ten Eyck, as well as some that are wise. I believe London has one, or two, soothsayers, and I think I have heard elderly people say that the fashion of consulting them has somewhat increased, since the court has been so German."

"Yes," Guert innocently replied; "I find it easy to believe that, for it is a common saying among our people that the German and Low Dutch fortune tellers are the best known. They have had or pretend to have had witches in New England, but no one, hereabouts, puts any faith in the pretence. It is like all the bragging of these boastful Yankees!"

I observed that Mary Wallace's colour deepened, and, that in biting off a thread, she profited by the occasion to avert her face in such a manner, that Bulstrode, in particular, could not see it.

"The meaning of all this," put in Major Bulstrode "is, that our friend Guert has been to pay a visit to Mother Doortje, a woman of some note, who lives on the hill, and who has a reputation in that way, among these good Albanians! Several of our mess have been to see the old woman."

"It is, Mr. Bulstrode," Guert answered, in his manly way, and with a gravity which proved how much he was in earnest. "I have been to see Mother Doortje, for the first time in my life, and Corny Littlepage, here, was my companion. Long as I have known the woman by reputation, I have never had any curiosity to pay her a visit, until this spring. We have been, however, and I must say I have been greatly surprised at the extent of the knowledge of this very extraordinary person."

"Did she tell you to look into the sweet-meat pot for the lost spoon, Mr. Ten Eyck?" Anneke inquired, with an archness of eye and voice that sent the blood to my own face, in confusion. "They say these fortune tellers send all prudent, yet careless housewives to the sweet-meat pots to look for the lost spoons! Many have been found, I hear, by this wonderful prescience."

"Well, Miss Anneke, I see you have no faith," answered Guert, fidgeting, "and people who have no faith never believe. Notwithstanding, *I* put so much confidence in what Doortje has told me, that I intend to follow her advice, let matters turn out as they may."

Here Mary Wallace raised her thoughtful, full, blue eyes to the face of the young man, and they expressed an intense interest, rather than any light curiosity, that even her woman's instinct and woman's sensitiveness could not so far prevail, as to enable her to conceal. Still, Mary Wallace did not speak, leaving the others present to maintain the discourse.

"Of course you mean to tell us all about it, Ten Eyck," cried the Major—"There is nothing more likely to succeed with an audience than a good history of witchcraft, or something so very marvellous as to do violence to common sense, before we give it our faith."

"Excuse me, Mr. Bulstrode; these are things I cannot well mention, though Corny Littlepage will testify that they are very wonderful. At any rate, I shall go into the bush, this spring, and Littlepage and Follock being excellent companions, I propose to join their company. It will be late before the army will be ready to move, and, by that time all three of us propose to join you before Ticonderoga; if, indeed, you succeed in getting so far."

"Say, rather, in front of Montreal, for I trust this new Commander in Chief will find something more for us to do, than the last one did. Shall I have a sentinel placed at Doortje's door in your absence, Guert?"

The smile this question produced was general, Guert himself joining in it, for his good nature was of proof. When I say the smile was general, however, I ought to except Mary Wallace, who smiled little that morning.

"We shall be neighbours, then," Herman Mordaunt quietly observed; "that is to say, if you mean by accompanying Corny and Dirck to the bush, you intend to go with them to the Patent lately obtained by Messrs. Littlepage and Van Valkenburgh. I have an estate in that quarter, which is now ten years old, and these ladies have consented to accompany me thither, as soon as the weather is a little more settled, and I can be assured that our army will be of sufficient force to protect us from the French and Indians."

It is unnecessary for me to say with what delight Guert and I heard this announcement! On Bulstrode, however, it produced an exactly contrary effect. He did not appear to me to be surprised at a declaration that was so new to us, but several expressions fell from him that showed he had no idea the two estates, that of Herman Mordaunt, and that which belonged to us, lay so near together. It was by means of *his* questions indeed that I learned the real facts of the case. It appeared that Herman Mordaunt's business in Albany, was to make some provisions in behalf of this property, on which he had caused mills to be erected, and some of the other improvements of a new settlement to be made, two or three years before; and which, by the progress and events of the war, was getting to be in closer proximity to the enemy than was desirable. Even when the French lay at Ticonderoga, his mills, in particular, might be thought in some danger, though forty, or more, miles distant; for parties of savages, led on by white men, frequently marched that distance through the forests, in order to break up a settlement and to commit depredations. But the enemy had crossed Lake George, the previous summer, and had actually taken Fort William Henry, at its southern extremity, by siege. It is true, this was the extent of their inroad, and it was now known that they had abandoned this bold conquest, and had fallen back upon Ty and Crown Point, two of the strongest military positions in the British Colonies. Still, Ravensnest, as Herman Mordaunt's property was called, was far from being beyond the limits of sorties, and the residence at Albany was solely to watch the progress of events in that quarter, and to be near the scene. If he had any public employment, it remained a profound mystery. A new source of embarrassment had arisen, however, and this it was that decided the proprietor to visit his lands in person. The fifteen, or twenty, families he had succeeded in establishing on the estate, at much cost and trouble, had taken the alarm at the prospect of a campaign in their vicinity, and had announced an intention of abandoning their huts and clearings, as the course most expedient for the times. Two or three had already gone off towards the Hampshire Grants, whence they had originally come, profiting by the last of the snow, and it was feared that others might imitate their caution.

Herman Mordaunt saw no necessity for this abandonment of advantages over the wilderness that had been obtained at so much cost and trouble. The labour of a removal and a return, was sufficient of itself to give a new direction to the movements of his settlers, and as their first entrance into the country had been effected through his agency, and aided by his means, he naturally wished to keep the people he had got to his estate with so much difficulty, and at so much cost, at their several positions as long, at least, as he conceived it to be prudent. In these circumstances, therefore, he had determined to visit Ravensnest in person, and to pass a part, if not most of the summer among his people. This would give them confidence, and would enable him to infuse

new life into their operations. It would seem that Anneke and
Mary Wallace had refused to let Mr. Mordaunt go alone, and, believing, himself, there was no danger in the course he was about
to take, the father and guardian, for Mary Wallace was Herman
Mordaunt's ward, had yielded to the importunities of the two
girls, and it had been formally decided that they were all to proceed together, as soon as the season should get to be a little more
advanced. Intelligence of this intention had been sent to the
settlers, and its effect was to induce them to remain at their posts,
by pacifying their fears.

I might as well add here, what I learned subsequently, in the
due course of events. Bulstrode had been made acquainted with
Herman Mordaunt's plans, they being sworn friends, and the latter warmly in the interest of the former's suit, and he had known
how to profit by the information. It was now time to put the
troops in motion, and several parties had already marched towards the north, taking post at different points that it was
thought desirable to occupy, previously to the commencement of
the campaign. Among other corps under orders of this nature,
was that commanded by Bulstrode, and he had sufficient interest
at head-quarters to get it sent to the point nearest to Ravensnest,
where it gave him the double advantage of having it in his power
to visit the ladies, on occasion, while, at the same time, he must
appear to them somewhat in the character of a protector. The object of Dirck and myself, in visiting the north, was no secret, and,
it was generally understood that we were to go to Mooseridge,
but we did not know ourselves that Herman Mordaunt had an
estate so near us. This intelligence, as has been said, I now ascertained was as new to Bulstrode as it was to myself.

The knowledge of many little things I have just mentioned,
was obtained by me only at intervals, and by means of observation and discourse. Nevertheless, the main points were determined the morning on which Guert referred to his visit to the fortune-teller, and in the manner named. The conversation lasted
an hour, nor did it cease until all present got a general idea of the
course intended to be pursued by the different parties present,
during the succeeding summer.

It happened that morning, that Bulstrode, Dirck and Guert
withdrew together, the two last to look at a horse the former
had just purchased, leaving me alone with the young ladies. No

sooner was the door closed on the retiring members of our party, than I saw a smile struggling about the handsome mouth of Anneke; Mary Wallace continuing the whole time, thoughtful if not sad.

"And *you* were of the party at the fortune-teller's, too, it seems, Mr. Littlepage," Anneke remarked, after appearing to be debating with herself on the propriety of proceeding any farther in the subject. "I knew there was such a person in Albany, and that thrifty housekeepers *did* sometimes consult her, but I was ignorant that men, and *educated* men, paid her that honour."

"I believe there is no exception, in the way of sex or learning, to her influence or her authority. They tell me that most of the younger officers of the army, visit her, while they remain here."

"I would much like to know if Mr. Bulstrode has been of the number! He is young enough in years, though so high in rank. A major may have as much curiosity as an ensign; or, as it may appear, dear Mary, of a woman who has lost her grandmother's favourite dessert spoon."

Mary Wallace gave a gentle sigh, and she even raised her eyes from her work; still she made no answer.

"You are severe on us, Anneke," for, since the affair on the river, the whole family treated me with the familiarity of a son or a brother—"I fancy we have done no more, than Mr. Mordaunt has done in his day."

"This may be very true, Corny, and not make the consultation the wisest thing in nature. I hope, however, you do not keep your fortune a secret, but let your friends share in your knowledge."

"To me the woman was far from being communicative, though she treated Guert Ten Eyck better. Certainly she told him many extraordinary things, of the past even; unless, indeed, she knew who he was."

"Is it probable, Mr. Littlepage," said Mary Wallace, "that any person in Albany should not know Guert Ten Eyck, and a good deal of his past history? Poor Guert makes himself known wherever he is."

"And, often, much to his advantage," I added, a remark that cost me nothing, but which caused Mary Wallace's face to brighten, and even brought a faint smile to her lips. "All that is true; yet there *was* something wild and unnatural in the woman's manner, as she told these things!"

"All of which you seem determined to keep to yourself?" observed Anneke, as one asks a question.

"It would hardly do to betray a friend's secrets. Let Guert answer for himself; he is as frank as broad day, and will not hesitate about letting you know all."

"I wish Corny Littlepage were only as frank as twilight!"

"I have nothing to conceal, and least of all from you, Anneke. The fortune teller told me that the queen of my heart was the queen of *too many* hearts; that the river had done me no harm; and, that I must particularly beware of what she called Knights-Barrow*nights*."

I watched Anneke closely, as I repeated this warning of Mother Doortje's, but could not read the expression of her sweet and thoughtful contenance. She neither smiled, nor frowned; but she certainly blushed. Of course, she did not look at me; for that would have been to challenge observation. Mary Wallace, however, *did* smile, and she *did* look at me.

"You believe all the wizzard told you, Corny?" said Anneke, after a short pause.

"I believed that the queen of my heart was the queen of many hearts; that the river had done me no harm, though I could not say, or see, that it had done me much good; and that I had much to fear from Knights-Barrow*nights*. I believed all this, however, before I ever saw the fortune teller."

The next remark that was made came from Anneke, and it referred to the weather. The season was opening finely and fast, and it could not be long, before the great movements of the year must commence. Several regiments had arrived in the colonies, and various officers of note and rank had accompanied them. Among others who had thus crossed the Atlantic for the first time, was my Lord Howe, a young soldier of whom fame spoke favourably, and from whom much was expected in the course of the anticipated service of the year. While we were talking over these things, Herman Mordaunt re-entered the room, after a short absence, and he took me with him, to examine his preparations for transporting the ladies to Ravensnest. As we went along, the discourse was maintained, and I learned many things from my older and intelligent companion, that were new to me.

"New lords, new laws, they say, Corny," continued Herman Mordaunt, "and this Mr. Pitt, the great Commoner, as some persons call him, is bent on making the British empire feel the truth of the axiom. Every thing is alive in the colonies, and the sluggish period of Lord Loudon's command is passed. Gen. Abercrombie, an officer from whom much is expected, is now at the head of the King's troops, and there is every prospect of an active and most important campaign. The disgraces of the few last years *must* be wiped out, and the English name be made once more to be dreaded on this continent. The Lord Howe of whom Anneke spoke, is said to be a young man of merit, and to possess the blood of our Hanoverian monarchs; his mother being a half-sister, in the natural way, of His present Majesty."

Herman Mordaunt then spoke more fully of his own plans for the summer, expressed his happiness at knowing that Dirck and myself were to be what he called his neighbors, though, on a more exact computation it was ascertained, that the nearest boundaries of the two patents, that of Ravensnest, and that of Mooseridge, lay quite fourteen miles apart, with a dense and virgin forest between them. Nevertheless, this would be making us neighbors, in a certain sense as gentlemen always call men of their own class neighbors, when they live within visiting distance, or near enough to be seen once or twice in a year. And such men *are* neighbors, in the sense that is most essential to the term. They know each other better, understand each other better, sympathize more freely, have more of the intercourse that makes us judges of motives, principles and character, twenty-fold, than he who lives at the gate, and merely sees the owner of the grounds pass in and out, on his daily avocations. There is, and can be no greater absurdity than to imagine that the sheer neighborhood or proximity of position, makes men acquainted. That was one of Jason Newcome's Connecticut notions. Having been educated in a state of society in which all associated on a certain footing of intimacy, and in which half the difficulties that occurred were "told to the church," he was for ever fancying he knew all the gentry of Westchester, because he had lived a year or two in the county, when in fact he had never spoken to one in a dozen of them. I never could drive this notion out of his head, however, for *looking* often at a man, or occasionally exchanging a bow with him on the highway, he would insist was knowing him; or what he called being "well acquainted," a very favourite expression of the Danbury man's, though their sympathies, habits, opinions, and feelings created so vast a void between the parties, they hardly understood each other's terms and ordinary language, when they did begin to converse, as sometimes happened. Notwithstanding all this, Jason insisted to the last, that he *knew* every gentleman in the county, whom he had been accustomed to hear alluded to in discourse, and when he had seen them once or twice, though it were only at church. But Jason had a very flattering notion, generally, of his own acquisitions on all subjects.

Herman Mordaunt had made careful provision for the contemplated journey, having caused a covered vehicle to be constructed that could transport not only himself and the ladies, but many articles of furniture that would be required during their residence in the forest. Another conveyance, strong, spacious, and covered, was also prepared for the blacks, and another portion of the effects. He pointed out all these arrangements to me, with great satisfaction, dwelling on the affection and spirit of the girls, with a pleasure he did not affect to conceal. For my own part, I have always been of opinion, that Anneke was solely influenced by pure, natural, regard, in forming her indiscreet resolution, while her father was governed by the secret expectation that the movement would leave open the means of receiving visits and communications from Bulstrode, during most of the summer. I commended the arrangements, made one or two suggestions of my own in behalf of Anneke and Mary, and we returned to our several homes.

A day, or two, after this visit to the work-shops, and the conversation related, the ———th took up its line of march, for the north. The troops defiled through the narrow streets in the neighborhood of the barracks, half an hour after the appearance of the sun, preceded and followed by long trains of baggage wagons. They marched without tents, however, it being well understood that they were going into a region where the axe could at any time, cover thousands of men, in about the time that a camp could be laid out, and the canvass spread. Hutting was the usual mode of placing an army under cover, in the forest, and a dozen marches would take the battalion to the point where it was intended it should remain, as a support to two or three other corps still further in advance, and to keep open the communications.

Bulstrode, however, did not quit Albany in company with his

regiment. I had been invited, with Guert and Dirck, to breakfast at Herman Mordaunt's that morning, and as we approached the door, I saw the Major's groom, walking his own, and his master's horse, in the street, near by. This was a sign we were to have the pleasure of Bulstrode's company at breakfast. Accordingly, on entering the room, we found him present, in the uniform of an officer of his rank, about to commence a march, in the forests of America. I thought him melancholy, as if sad at parting; but my most jealous observation could detect no sign of similar feeling on the part of Anneke. She was not quite as gay as usual, but she was far from being sad.

"I leave you, ladies, with the deepest regret," said Bulstrode, while at table, "for you have made this country more than a home to me—you have rendered it *dear.*"

This was said with feeling; more than I had ever seen Bulstrode manifest before, and more than I had given him credit for possessing. Anneke coloured a little, but there was no tremor in the beautiful hand that held a highly wrought little tea-pot suspended over a cup, at that very moment.

"We shall soon meet again, Harry," Herman Mordaunt remarked, in a tone of strong affection; "for our party will not be a week behind you. Remember, we are to be *good* neighbours, as well as neighbours; and, if the mountain will not come to Mahomet, Mahomet must go to the mountain."

"Which means, Mr. Bulstrode," said Mary Wallace, with one of her sweet smiles, and one that was as open and natural as childhood itself, "that you are Mahomet and we are the mountain. Ladies can neither travel with comfort in a wilderness, nor visit a camp, with propriety, if they would."

"They tell me I shall not be in a camp at all—" answered the soldier; "but in good, comfortable, log barracks, that have been built for us, by the battalion we relieve. I am not without hopes, they will be such as even ladies will not disdain to use, on an emergency. There ought to be no Mahomet and no mountain, between such old and intimate friends."

The conversation then turned on the plans and expectations of the respective parties, and the usual promises were made of being sociable and good neighbours, as had just been suggested. Herman Mordaunt evidently wished to consider Bulstrode as one of his family, a feeling that might excuse itself to the world, on the score of consanguinity; but which, it was easy enough for me to see, had its origin in a very different cause. When Bulstrode rose to take his leave, I wished myself away, on account of the exhibition of concern it produced, while the desire to watch the effect on Anneke, would have kept me rooted to the floor, even had it been proper that I should retire.

Bulstrode was more affected than I could have thought possible. He took one of Herman Mordaunt's hands into his own, and pressed it warmly for some little time, before he could speak at all.

"God only knows what this summer is to see, and whether we are ever to meet again, or not," he then said. "But, come what may, the past, the *happy past* is so much gained from the commonplace. If you never hear of me again, my dear kinsman, my letters to England will give you a better account of my gratitude, than any thing I can say in words. They have been written as your kindnesses have been bestowed, and they faithfully portray the feelings to which your hospitality and friendship have given rise. In a possible event, I have requested that every one of them may be sent to America for your special perusal—"

"My dear Harry, this is foreboding the very worst—" interrupted Herman Mordaunt, dashing a tear from his eye, "and is making a very short separation, a more serious matter than one ought—"

"Nay, sir, a soldier, who is about to be posted within striking distance of his enemy, can never speak with confidence of separations that are to be short. This campaign will be decisive for me," glancing towards Anneke—"I must return a conqueror, in one sense, or I do not wish to return at all. But, God bless you, Herman Mordaunt, as your own countrymen call you; a thousand years could not efface from my heart the remembrance of all your kindness."

This was handsomely expressed, and the manner in which it was uttered, was as good as the language. Bulstrode hesitated a moment, looked at the two girls in doubt, and first approached Mary Wallace.

"Adieu, excellent Mary Wallace," he said, taking her offered hand, and kissing it with a freedom from emotion, that denoted it was only friendship and respect which induced the act—"I believe you are a severe critic on Catos and Scrubs, but I forgive all your particular backbitings, on account of your general indulgence and probity. You may meet with a thousand mere acquaintances, before you find another who shall have the same profound respect for your many virtues, as myself."

This was handsomely said, too, and it caused Mary Wallace to remove the handkerchief from her eyes, and to utter her adieus cordially and with some emotion. Strangers say that our women want feeling, passion; or, if they have it, that it is veiled behind a mask of coldness that takes away from its loveliness and warmth; that they are girlish and familiar where they might better be reserved, and distant, and unnatural, where feeling and nature ought to assert their sway. That they have less *manner*, in all respects, in that of self-control and perhaps of self-respect in their ordinary intercourse, and in that of *acting* where it may seem necessary so to do, I believe to be true; but, he who denies an American girl a heart, knows nothing about her. She is *all* heart, and the apparent coldness is oftener the consequence of not daring to trust her feelings, and her general dislike to every thing artificial, than to any want of affections. Two girls, educated however as had been Anneke and Mary Wallace, could not but acquit themselves better in such a scene, than those who had been less accustomed to the usages of polite life, which are always, more or less, the usages of convention.

On the present occasion, Mary Wallace was strongly affected; it would not have been possible for one of her gentle nature and warm affections to be otherwise, when an agreeable companion, one she had now known intimately near two years, was about to take his leave of her, on an errand that he himself, either thought, or affected so well to seem to think, might lead to the most melancholy issue. She shook hands with Bulstrode warmly, wished him good fortune, and various other pleasant things, thanked him for his good opinion, and expressed her hope as well as her belief that they should all meet again before the summer was over, and again be happy in each other's society.

Anneke's turn came next. Her handkerchief was at her eyes, and when it was removed, the face was pale, and the cheeks were covered with tears. The smile that followed was sweetness itself, and I will own it caused me a most severe pang. To my surprise, Bulstrode said nothing. He took Anneke's hand, pressed it to his heart, kissed it, left a note in it, bowed, and moved away. I felt ashamed to watch the countenance of Miss Mordaunt, under such circumstances, and turned aside that the observation might not increase the distress and embarrassment she evidently felt. I saw enough, notwithstanding, to render me more uncertain than ever, as to the success of my own suit. Anneke's colour had come and gone, as Bulstrode stood near her, acting his dumb-show of leave-taking, and, to me, she seemed far more affected than Mary Wallace had been. Nevertheless, her feelings were always keener and more active than those of her friend, and that which my sensitiveness took for the emotion of tenderness might be nothing more than ordinary womanly feeling and friendship. Besides Bulstrode was actually her relative.

We men all attended Bulstrode to his horse. He shook us cordially by the hand, and, after he had got into the saddle he said—"This summer will be warmer than is usual, even in your warmy-cold climate. My letters from home give me reason to think that there is, at last, a man of talents at the head of affairs, and the British empire is likely to feel the impulse he will give it, at its most remote extremities. I shall expect you three young men to join the ———th, as volunteers, as soon as you hear of our moving in advance. I wish I had a thousand like you; for that affair of the river tells where a man will be found when the time comes. God bless you, Corny," leaning forward in his saddle to give me another shake of the hand; "we *must* remain friends, *coute qui coute*."

There was no withstanding this frankness and so much good temper. We shook hands most cordially, Bulstrode raised his hat and bowed, after which he rode away, as I fancied, at a slow, thoughtful, reluctant pace. Notwithstanding the kindness of this parting, I had more cause than ever to regret Bulstrode had appeared among us, and the scenes of that morning only confirmed me in a resolution previously adopted, not to urge Anneke to any decision in my case, at a moment when I felt there might be so much danger it would be adverse.

Chapter XX

"Come, let a proper text be read,
An' touch it aff wi' vigour,
How graceless Ham leugh at his dad,
Which made Canaan a nigger."
                    Burns, "The Ordination," IV. 28–31.

TEN days after the departure of the ———th, Herman Mordaunt and his family, with our own party, left Albany, on the summer's business. In that interval, however, great changes had taken place in the military aspect of things. Several regiments of King's troops ascended the Hudson, most of the sloops on the river, of which there could not have been fewer than thirty or forty, having been employed in transporting them, and their stores. Two or three corps came across the country, from the eastern colonies, while several provincial regiments appeared, every thing tending to a concentration at this point, the head of navigation on the Hudson. Among other men of mark who accompanied the troops, was Lord Viscount Howe, the nobleman of whom Herman Mordaunt had spoken. He bore the local rank of Brigadier,* and seemed to be the very soul of the army. It was not his personal consideration alone that placed him so high in the estimation of the public and of the troops, but his professional reputation, and professional services. There were many young men of rank in the army present, and, as for younger sons of peers, there were enough to make honourables almost as plenty at Albany, as they were at Boston. Most of the colonial families of mark had sons in the service, too, those of the Middle and Southern colonies, bearing commissions in regular regiments, while the provincial troops from the eastern were led, as was very usual

*The ordinary American reader may not know that the rank of Brigadier, in the British army, is not a step in the regular line of promotion, as with us. In England, the regular military gradations are from Colonel to Major General, Lieut. General, General, and Field Marshal. The rank of Brigadier is barely recognised, like that of Commodore in the navy, to be used on emergencies, usually as brevet, *local*, rank, to enable the government to employ clever colonels at need.

in that quarter of the country, by men of the class of yeomen, in a great degree; the habits of equality that prevailed in those provinces making few distinctions on the score of birth, or fortune.

Yet it was said, I remember, that obedience was as marked among the provincials from Massachusetts and Connecticut, as among those that came from farther south; the men deferring to authority, as the agent of the laws. They were fine troops, too; better than our own colony regiments, I must acknowledge; seeming to belong to a higher class of labourers; while it must be admitted that most of their officers were no very brilliant representatives of manners, acquirements, or habits that would be likely to qualify them for command. It must have been that the officers and men suited each other, for it was said all round, that they stood well, and fought very bravely, whenever they were particularly well led, as did not always happen to be the case. As a body of mere physical men, they were universally allowed to be the finest corps in the army, regulars and all included.

I saw Lord Howe, two or three times, particularly at the residence of Madam Schuyler, the lady I have already had occasion to mention, and to whom I had given the letter of introduction, procured by my mother, the Mordaunts visiting her with great assiduity, and frequently taking me with them. As for Lord Howe himself, he almost lived under the roof of excellent Madam Schuyler, where, indeed, all the good company assembled at Albany, was at times to be seen.

Our party was a large one, and it might have passed for a small corps of the army itself, moving on in advance, as was the case with corps, or parts of corps, now, almost daily. Herman Mordaunt had delayed our departure, indeed, expressly with a view to render the country safe, by letting it fill with detachments from the army, and our progress, when we were once in motion, was literally from post to post; encampment to encampment. It may be well to enumerate our force, and to relate the order of our march, that the reader may better comprehend the sort of business we were on.

Herman Mordaunt took with him, in addition to the ladies, a black cook, and a black serving girl, a negro man to take care of his horses, and another as his house servant. He had three white labourers in addition, men employed about the teams, and as axe-men to clear the roads, bridge the streams, and to do other work of that nature, as it might be required. On our side, there were us three gentlemen, Yaap, my own faithful negro, Mr. Traverse, the surveyor, two chain bearers, and two axe-men. Guert Ten Eyck carried with him also, a negro man, who was called Pete, it being contrary to *bonos mores* to style him Peter, or Petrus; the latter being his true appellation. This made us ten men strong, of whom eight were white, and two black. Herman Mordaunt mustered, in all, just the same number, of which however, four were females. Thus by uniting our forces, we made a party of twenty souls, altogether. Of this number, all the males, black and white, were well armed, each man owning a good rifle, and each of the gentlemen a brace of pistols in addition. We carried the latter belted to our bodies, with the weapons, which were small and fitted to the service, turned behind, in such a way as to be concealed by our outer garments. The belts were also hid by the flaps of our nether garments. By this arrangement, we were well armed without seeming to be so; a precaution that is sometimes useful in the woods.

It is hardly necessary to say that we did not plunge into the forest, in the attire in which we had been accustomed to appear in the streets of New York and Albany. Cocked hats were laid aside, altogether, forest caps resembling in form those we had worn in the winter, with the exception that the fur had been removed, being substituted. The ladies wore light beavers, suited to their sex, there being little occasion for any shade for the face, under the dense canopies of the forest. Veils of green, however, were added as the customary American protection for the sex. Anneke and Mary travelled in habits, made of light woman's cloth, and in a manner to fit their exquisite forms like gloves. The skirts were short, to enable them to walk with ease, in the event of being compelled to go afoot. A feather or two, in each hat, had not been forgotten, the offering of the natural propensity of their sex to please the eyes of man.

As for us men, buckskin formed the principal material of our garments. We all wore buckskin breeches, and gaiters, and moccasins. The latter, however, had the white man's soles, though Guert took a pair, or two, with him that were of the pure Indian manufacture. Each of us had a coatee, made of common cloth, but we all carried hunting-shirts, to be worn as soon as we entered the woods. These hunting-shirts, green in colour, fringed, and ornamented garments, of the form of shirts to be worn over all, were exceedingly smart in appearance, and were admirably suited to the woods. It was thought that the fringes, form, and colour blended them so completely with the foliage, as to render them in a manner invisible to one at a distance; or, at least, undistinguished. They were much in favour with all the forest corps of America, and formed the usual uniform of the riflemen of the woods, whether acting against man, or only against the wild beasts.

Neither Mr. Worden, nor Jason, moved with the main party, and it was precisely on account of these distinctions of dress. As for the divine, he was so great a stickler for appearances, he would have worn the gown and surplice, even on a mission to the Indians, which, by the way, was ostensibly his present business; and, at the several occasions, on which I saw him at cock-fights, he kept on the clerical coat and shovel hat. In a word, Mr. Worden never neglected externals, so far as dress was concerned, and I much question if he would have consented to read prayers without the surplice, or to preach without the gown, let the desire for spiritual provender be as great as it might. I very well remember to have heard my father say, that, on one occasion, the parson had refused to officiate of a Sunday, when travelling, rather than bring discredit on the church, by appearing in the discharge of his holy office, without the appliances that belonged to the clerical character.

"More harm than good is done to religion, Mr. Littlepage," said the Rev. Mr. Worden, on that occasion, "by thus lessening its rites in vulgar eyes. The first thing is to teach men to respect holy things, my dear sir, and a clergyman in his gown and surplice, commands threefold the respect of one without them. I consider it, therefore, a sacred duty to uphold the dignity of my office, on all occasions."

It was in consequence of these opinions, that the divine travelled in his clerical hat, clerical coat, black breeches, and band, even when in pursuit of the souls of red men, among the wilds of North America! I will not take it upon myself to say, these observances had not their use; but I am very certain they put the reverend gentleman to a great deal of inconvenience.

As for Jason, he gave a Danbury reason for travelling in his best. Every body did so, in his quarter of the country, and, for his part, he thought it disrespectful to strangers, to appear among them in old clothes! There was, however, another and truer reason, and that was economy; for the troops had so far raised the price of every thing, that Jason did not hesitate to pronounce Albany the dearest place he had ever been in. There was some truth in this allegation, and the distance from New York, being no less than one hundred and sixty miles—so reported—the reader will at once see, it was the business of quite a month, or even more, to refurnish the shelves of the shop that had been emptied. The Dutch not only moved slow, but they were methodical, and the shopkeeper whose stores were exhausted in April, would not be apt to think of replenishing them, until the regular time and season returned.

As a consequence of these views and motives, the Rev. Mr. Worden and Mr. Jason Newcome left Albany twenty-four hours in advance of the rest of our party, with the understanding they were to join us, at a point where the road led into the woods, and where it was thought the cocked hat and the skin cap might travel in company harmoniously. There was, however, a reason for the separation I have not yet named, in the fact that all of my own set travelled on foot, three or four pack-horses carrying our necessaries. Now Mr. Worden had been offered a seat in a government conveyance, and Jason managed to worm himself into the party, in some way that to me was ever inexplicable. It is, however, due to Mr. Newcome to confess that his faculty of obtaining favours of all sorts, was of a most extraordinary character, and he certainly never lost any chance of preferment for want of asking. In this respect, Jason was always a moral enigma to me, there being an absolute absence, in his mind, of every thing like a perception of the fitness of things, so far as the claims and rights of persons were connected with rank, education, birth, and experience. Rank, in the official sense, once possessed, he understood and respected; but of the claims to entitle one to its enjoyment, he seemed to have no sort of notion. For property, he had a profound deference, so far as that deference extended to its importance and influence; but it would have caused him not the slightest qualm, either in the way of conscience, or feeling, to find himself suddenly installed in the mansion of the patroons, for instance, and placed in possession of their estates, provided only he fancied he could maintain his position. The circumstance that he was dwelling under the roof that was erected by another man's ancestors, for instance, and that others were living who had a better moral right to it, would give him no sort of trouble, so long as any quirk of the law would sustain him in possession. In a word, all that was allied to sentiment, in matters of this nature, was totally lost on Jason Newcome, who lived and acted from the hour he first came among us, as if the game of life were merely a game of puss in the corner, in which he who inadvertently left his own post unprotected, would be certain to find another filling his place as speedily as possible. I have mentioned this propensity of Jason's, at some little length, as I feel certain, should this history be carried down by my own posterity, as I hope and design, it will be seen that this disposition to regard the whole human family, as so many tenants in common of the estate left by Adam, will lead in the end to something extraordinary. But, leaving the Rev. Mr. Worden and Mr. Jason Newcome to journey in their public conveyance, I must return to our own party.

All of us men, with the exception of those who drove the two wagons of Herman Mordaunt, marched afoot. Each of us carried a knapsack, in addition to his rifle and ammunition, and it will be imagined that our day's work was not a very long one. The first day, we halted at Madam Schuyler's, by invitation, where we all dined; including the surveyor. Lord Howe was among the guests that day, and he appeared to admire the spirit of Anneke and Mary Wallace greatly, in attempting such an expedition, at such a time.

"You need have no fears, however, ladies, as we shall keep up strong detachments between you and the French," he said, more gravely, after some pleasant trifling on the subject. "Last summer's work, and the disgraceful manner in which poor Munro was abandoned to his fate, has rendered us all keenly alive to the importance of compelling the enemy to remain at the north end of Lake George, too many battles having already been fought on this side it, for the credit of the British arms. We pledge ourselves to your safety."

Anneke thanked him for this pledge, and the conversation changed. There was a young man present, who bore the name of Schuyler, and who was nearly related to Madam, with whose air, manner and appearance I was much struck. His aunt called him

'Philip,' and being about my own age, during this visit I got into conversation with him. He told me he was attached to the commissariat under Gen. Bradstreet, and that he should move on with the army, as soon as the preparations for its marching were completed. He then entered into a clear, simple explanation of the supposed plan of the approaching campaign.

"We shall see you, and your friends among us then, I hope," he added, as we were walking on the lawn together, previously to the summons to dinner, "for, to own to you the truth, Mr. Littlepage, I do not half like the necessity of our having so many eastern troops among us, to clear this colony of its enemies. It is true, a nation must fight its foes wherever they may happen to be found, but there is so little in common between us and the Yankees, that I could wish we were strong enough to beat back the French alone."

"We have the same sovereign and the same allegiance," I answered, "if you can call that something in common."

"That is true; yet, I think you must have enough Dutch blood about you, to understand me. My duty calls me much among the different regiments, and I will own that I find more trouble with one New England regiment, than with a whole brigade of the other troops. They have generals, and colonels, and majors enough, for the army of the Duke of Marlborough!"

"It is certain there is no want of military rank among them, and they are particularly fond of referring to it."

"Quite true," answered young Schuyler smiling. "You will hear the word 'general' or 'colonel,' oftener used in one of their cantonments in a day, than you shall hear it at Head Quarters in a month. They have capital points about them, too; yet, somehow or other, we do not like each other."

Twenty years later in life, I had reason to remember this remark, as well as to reflect on the character of the man who had uttered it. I, or my successors, will probably have occasion to advert to matters connected with this feeling, in the later passages of this record.

I had also a little conversation with Lord Howe, who complimented me on what had passed on the river. He had evidently received an account of that affair from some one who was much my friend, and saw fit to allude to the subject in a way that was very agreeable to myself. This short conversation was not worth repeating, but it opened the way to an acquaintance that subsequently was connected with some events of interest.

About an hour after dinner, our party took its leave of Madam Schuyler and moved on. The day's march was intended to be short, though, by this time the roads were settled, and tolerably good. Of roads, however, we were not long to enjoy the advantages, for they extended only some thirty miles to the north of Albany, in our direction. With the exception of the military route which led direct to the head-waters of Lake Champlain, this was about the extent of all the avenues that penetrated the interior, in that quarter of the country. Our direction was to the northward and eastward, both Ravensnest and Mooseridge lying slightly in the direction of the Hampshire Grants.

As soon as we reached the point on the great northern road, or that which led towards Skeenesborough, Herman Mordaunt was obliged to quit his wagons, and to put all the females on horseback. The most necessary of the stores were placed on pack horses, and after a delay of half a day, time lost in making these arrangements, we proceeded. The wagons were to follow, but at a slow pace, the ladies being compelled to abandon them on account of the ruggedness of the ways, which would have rendered their motion not easy to be borne. Our cavalcade and train of footmen made a respectable display along the uneven road, which soon became very little more than a line cut through the forest, with an occasional wheel track, but without the least attempt to level the surface of the ground by any artificial means. This was the place where we were to overtake Mr. Worden and Jason, and where we did find their effects; the owners themselves having gone on in advance, leaving word that we should fall in with them somewhere on the route.

Guert and I marched in front, our youth and vigour enabling us to do this with great ease to ourselves. Knowing that the ladies were well cared for, on horseback, we pushed on, in order to make provision for their reception, at a house a few miles distant, where we were to pass the night. This building was of logs, of course, and stood quite alone in the wilderness, having, however, some twenty or thirty acres of cleared land around it, and it would not do to pass it, at that hour of the day. The distance from this solitary dwelling, to the first habitation on Herman Mordaunt's property, was eighteen miles; and that was a length of road that would require the whole of a long May day to over-come, under our circumstances.

Guert and myself might have been about a mile in advance of the rest of the party, when we saw a sort of semi-clearing before us, that we mistook at first for our resting place. A few acres had been chopped over, letting in the light of day upon the gloom of the forest, but the second growth was already shooting up, cover-ing the area with high bushes. As we drew nearer we saw it was a small, abandoned, clearing. Entering it, voices were heard at no great distance, and we stopped; for the human voice is not heard, in such a place, without causing the traveller to pause, and look to his arms. This we did; after which we listened with some curiosity and caution.

"High!" exclaimed some one, very distinctly in English.

"Jack!" said another voice, in a sort of answering second, that could not well be mistaken.

"There's three for low;—is that good?" put in the first speaker.

"It will do, sir; but here are a ten and an ace. Ten and three, and four and two make nineteen—I'm game."

"High, low, Jack and game!" whispered Guert; "here are fel-lows playing at cards, near us; let us go on and beat up their quar-ters."

We did so, and pushing aside some bushes, broke quite unex-pectedly to all parties on the Rev. Mr. Worden and Jason New-come, playing the game of 'All Fours on a stump;' or, if not liter-ally in the classic position of using 'the stump,' substituting the trunk of a fallen tree for their table. As we broke suddenly in upon the card players, Jason gave unequivocal signs of a disposi-tion to conceal his hand, by thrusting the cards he held into his bosom, while he rapidly put the remainder of the pack, under his thigh, pressing it down in a way completely to conceal it. This sudden movement was merely the effect of a puritanical educa-tion, which, having taught him to consider that as a sin which was not necessarily a sin at all, exacted from him that hypocrisy which 'is the tribute that vice pays to virtue'. Very different was the con-duct of the Rev. Mr. Worden. Taught to discriminate better, and unaccustomed to set up arbitrary rules of his own as the law of God, this loose observer of his professional obligations in other matters, made a very proper distinction in this. Instead of giving the least manifestation of confusion, or alarm, the log on which he was seated, was not more unmoved than he remained at our sudden appearance at his side.

"I hope, Corny, my dear boy," Mr. Worden cried, "that you did not forget to purchase a few packs of cards, which, I plainly see, will be a great resource for us, in this woody region. These cards of Jason's are so thumbed and handled, that they are not fit to be touched by a gentleman, as I will show you.—Why, what has become of the pack, Master Newcome?—It was on the log, but a minute ago!"

Jason actually blushed! Yes, for a wonder, shame induced Jason Newcome to change colour! The cards were reluctantly produced from beneath his leg, and there the schoolmaster sat, as it might be in presence of his school, actually convicted of being engaged in the damning sin of handling certain spotted pieces of paper, invented for, and used in the combinations of a game played for amusement.

"Had it been push-pin, now," Guert whispered, "it would give Mr. Newcome no trouble at all, but he does not admire the idea of being caught at 'All Fours, on a stump.' We must say a word to relieve the poor sinner's distress. I have cards, Mr. Worden, and they shall be much at your service, as soon as we can come at our effects. There is one pack in my knapsack, but it is a little soiled by use, though somewhat cleaner than that. If you wish it I will hand it to you. I never travel without carrying one or two clean packs with me."

"Not just now, sir, I thank you. I love a game of Whist, or Picquet, but cannot say I am an admirer of All Fours. As Mr. Newcome knows no other, we were merely killing half an hour, at that game, but I have enough of it, to last me for the summer. I am glad that cards have not been forgotten, however, for, I dare say, we can make up a very respectable party at Whist, when we all meet."

"That we can, sir, and a party that shall have its good players. Miss Mary Wallace plays as good a hand at Whist, as a woman should, Mr. Worden, and a very pretty accomplishment it is, for a lady to possess; useful, sir, as well as entertaining, for any thing is preferable to dummy. I do not think a woman should play quite as well as a man, our sex having a natural claim to lead in all such things, but it is very convenient sometimes to find a lady who can hold her hand with coolness and skill."

"I would not marry a woman who did not understand Picquet," exclaimed the Rev. Mr. Worden, "to say nothing of Whist, and one or two other games. But, let us be moving, since the hour is getting late."

Move on we did, and in due time we all reached the place at which we were to halt for the night. This looked like plunging into the wilderness, indeed, for the house had but two rooms, one of which was appropriated to the use of the females, while most of us men took up our lodgings in the barn. Anneke and Mary Wallace, however, showed the most perfect good humour, and our dinner, or supper might better be the name, was composed of deliciously fat and tender broiled pigeons. It was the pigeon season, the woods being full of the birds, and we were told we might expect to feast on the young, to satiety.

About noon the next day, we reached the first clearing on the estate of Ravensnest. The country through which we were traveling was rolling rather than bold, but it possessed a feature of grandeur in its boundless forests. Our route that day, lay under lofty arches of young leaves, the buds just breaking into the first green of the foliage, tall, straight, columns, sixty, eighty, and sometimes a hundred feet of the trunks of the trees, rising almost without a branch. The pines, in particular, were really majestic, most of them being a hundred and fifty feet in height, and a few, as I should think, nearly if not quite two hundred. As every thing grows towards the upper light, in the forest, this ought not to surprise those who are accustomed to see vegetation expand its powers in wide-spreading tops, and low, knarled branches that almost touch the ground, as is the case in the open fields, and on the lawns of the older regions. As is usual in the American virgin forest, there was very little under-brush, and we could see frequently, a considerable distance, through these long vistas of trees; or, indeed, until the number of the stems intercepted the sight.

The clearings of Ravensnest were neither very large, nor very inviting. In that day, the settlement of new lands was a slow and painful operation, and was generally made at a great outlay to the proprietor. Various expedients were adopted to free the earth from its load of trees,* for, at that time, the commerce of the colonies did not reward the toil of the settler, in the same liberal manner, as has since occurred. Herman Mordaunt, as we moved along, related to me the cost and trouble he had been at already, in getting the ten or fifteen families who were on his property, in the first place, to the spot itself; and in the second place to induce them to remain there. Not only was he obliged to grant leases for three lives, or, in some cases, for thirty or forty years, at rents that were merely nominal, but, as a rule, the first six, or eight years, the tenants were to pay no rent at all. On the contrary, he was obliged to extend to them many favours, in various ways, that cost no inconsiderable sum in the course of the year. Among other things, his agent kept a small shop, that contained the most ordinary supplies used by families of the class of the settlers, and these he sold at little more than cost, for their accommodation, receiving his pay in such articles as they could raise from their half-tilled fields, or their sugar-bushes, and turning those again into money, only after they were transported to Albany, at the end of a considerable period. In a word, the commencement of such a settlement, was an arduous undertaking, and the experiment was not very likely to succeed, unless the landlord had both capital and patience.

The political economist can have no difficulty in discovering the causes of the circumstances just mentioned. They were to be found in the fact that people were scarce, while land was superabundant. In such a condition of society, the tenant had the choice of his farm, instead of the landlord's having a selection of

*The late, venerable Hendrick Frey was a man well know to all who dwelt in the valley of the Mohawk. He had been a friend, contemporary, and it is believed an executor of the celebrated Sir William Johnson, Bart. Thirty years since, he related to the writer the following anecdote.—Young Johnson first appeared in the valley, as the agent of a property belonging to his kinsman, Admiral Sir Peter Warren, K.B.; who, having married in the colony, had acquired several estates in it. Among other tracts was one called Warrensbush, on the Mohawk, on which young Johnson first resided. Finding it difficult to get rid of the trees, around his dwelling, Johnson sent down to the Admiral at New York, to provide some purchases with which to haul the trees down to the earth, after grubbing and cutting the roots on one side. An acre was lowered in this manner, each tree necessarily lying at a larger angle to the earth than the next beneath it. An easterly wind came, one night, and to Johnson's surprise, he found half his trees erect again, on rising in the morning! The mode of clearing lands by 'purchases' was then abandoned.—EDITOR.

his tenants, and the latter were to be bought only on such conditions, as suited themselves.

"You see," continued Herman Mordaunt, as we walked together, conversing on this subject, "that my twenty thousand acres are not likely to be of much use to myself, even should they prove to be of any to my daughter. A century hence, indeed, my descendants may benefit from all this outlay of money, and trouble; but, it is not probable that either I, or Anneke will ever see the principal and interest of the sums that will be expended in the way of roads, bridges, mills, and other things of that sort. Years must go by, before the light rents which will only begin to be paid a year or two hence, and then only by a very few tenants, can amount to a sufficient sum to meet the expenses of keeping up the settlement, to say nothing of the quit-rents to be paid to the crown."

"This is not very encouraging to a new beginner in the occupation of a landlord," I answered, "and, when I look into the facts, I confess I am surprised that so many gentlemen in the colony are willing to invest the sums they annually do, in wild lands."

"Every man who is at his ease, in his moneyed affairs, Corny, feels a disposition to make some provision for his posterity. This estate, if kept together, and in single hands, may make some descendant of mine a man of fortune. Half a century will produce a great change in this colony, and, at the end of that period, a child of Anneke's may be thankful that his mother had a father who was willing to throw away a few thousands of his own, the surplus of a fortune that was sufficient for his wants without them, in order that his grandson may see them converted into tens, or possibly into hundreds of thousands."

"Posterity will, at least, owe us a debt of gratitude, Mr. Mordaunt, for I now see that Mooseridge is not likely to make either Dirck, or myself, very affluent patroons."

"On that you may rely. Satanstoe will produce you more than the large tracts you possess in this quarter."

"Do you no longer fear, sir, that the war and apprehension of Indian ravages may drive your people off?"

"Not much, at present, though the danger was great at one time. The war *may* do me good, as well as harm. The armies consume every thing they can get—soldiers resembling locusts in this respect. My tenants have had the commissaries among them, and I am told every blade of grass they can spare, all their surplus grain, potatoes, butter, cheese, and, in a word, every thing that can be eaten, and with which they are willing to part, has been contracted for, at the top of the market. The King pays in gold, and the sight of the precious metals will keep even a Yankee from moving.

About the time this was said, we came in sight of the spot Herman Mordaunt had christened Ravensnest, a name that had since been applied to the whole property. It was a log building, that stood on the verge of a low cliff of rocks, at a point where a bird of that appellation had originally a nest on the uppermost branches of a dead hemlock. The building had been placed, and erected, with a view to defence, having served for some time as a sort of rallying point to the families of the tenantry, in the event of an Indian alarm. At the commencement of the present war, taking into view the exposed position of his possessions on that frontier,—frontier as to settlement, if not as to territorial limits— Herman Mordaunt had caused some attention to be paid to his fortifications; which, though they might not have satisfied Mons. Vauban, were not altogether without merit, considered in reference to their use in case of a surprise.

The house formed three sides of a parallelogram, the open portion of the court in the centre, facing the cliff. A strong picket served to make a defence against bullets on that side, while the dead walls of solid logs were quite impregnable against any assault known in forest warfare, but that of fire. All the windows opened on the court, while the single outer door was picketed, and otherwise protected by coverings of plank. I was glad to see by the extent of this rude structure, which was a hundred feet long by fifty in depth, that Anneke and Mary Wallace would not be likely to be straitened for room. Such proved to be the fact, Herman Mordaunt's agent, having prepared four or five apartments for the family that rendered them as comfortable as people could well expect to be in such a situation. Every thing was plain, and many things were rude; but shelter, warmth and security had not been neglected.

Chapter XXI

"And long shall timorous fancy see
　The painted chief and pointed spear;
And Reason's self shall bow the knee
　To shadows and delusions here."
　　　　　　　Freneau, "The Indian Burying Ground," ll. 37–40.

IT is not necessary to dwell on the manner in which Herman Mordaunt, and his companions became established at Ravensnest. Two or three days, sufficed to render them as comfortable as circumstances would permit; then Dirck and I bethought us of proceeding in quest of the lands of Mooseridge. Mr. Worden and Jason both declined going any further, the mill seat of which the last was in quest, being, as I now learned, on the estate of Herman Mordaunt, and having been for some time the subject of a negotiation between the pedagogue and its owner. As for the divine, he declared that he saw a suitable 'field' for his missionary labour where he was, while, it was easy to see, that he questioned if there were fields of any sort, where we were going.

Our party, on quitting Ravensnest, consisted of Dirck and myself, Guert, Mr. Traverse, the surveyor, three chain-bearers, Jaap, or Yaap, Guert's man Pete, and one woodsman, or hunter. This would have given us ten vigorous and well-armed men, for our whole force. It was thought best, however, to add two Indians to our number, in the double character of hunters, and runners; or messengers. One of these red-skins was called Jumper, in the language of the settlement where we found them, and the other Trackless; the latter *sobriquet* having been given him on account of a faculty he possessed of leaving little, or no trail, in his journeys and marches. This Indian was about six and twenty years of age, and was called a Mohawk, living with the people of that tribe, though, I subsequently ascertained that he was, in fact, an Onondago* by birth. His true name was Susquesus, or Crooked

---

*Pronounced On-on-daw-ger, the latter syllable hard; or like ga, as it is sometimes spelled. This is the name of one of the midland counties of New York. The tribe from which it is derived, in these later times has ever borne a better name

Turns; an appellation that might, or might not speak well of his character, as the 'turns' were regarded in a moral, or in a physical sense.

"Take that man, Mr. Littlepage, by all means," said Herman Mordaunt's agent, when the matter was under discussion. "You will find him as useful in the woods, as your pocket compass, besides being a reasonably good hunter. He left here, as a runner, during the heaviest of the snows, last winter, and a trial was made to find his trail, within half an hour after he had quitted the clearing, but without success. He had not gone a mile in the woods, before all traces of him were lost, as completely as if he had made the journey in the air."

As Susquesus had a reputation for sobriety, as was apt to be the case with the Onondagos, the man was engaged, though one Indian would have been sufficient for our purpose. But Jumper had been previously hired, and it would have been dangerous, under our circumstances to offend a red man, by putting him aside for another, even after compensating him fully for the disappointment. By Mr. Traverse's advice, therefore, we took both. The Indian, or Mohawk name of Jumper, was Quissquiss, a term that, I fancied, signified nothing very honourable, or illustrious.

The girls betrayed deep interest in us, on our taking leave; more, I thought, than either had ever before manifested. Guert had told me privately, of an intention on his part, to make another offer to Mary Wallace, and I saw the traces of it, in the tearful eyes, and flushed cheeks of his mistress. But, at such a moment, one does not stop to think much of such things, there being tears in Anneke's eyes, as well as in those of her friend. We had a thousand good wishes to exchange, and we promised to keep open the communication between the two parties, by means of our runners, semi-weekly. The distance, which would vary from fifteen to thirty miles, would readily admit of this, since either of the Indians would pass over it, with the greatest ease to himself, in a day, at that season of the year.

After all, the separation was to be short, for we had promised to come over and dine with Herman Mordaunt on his fiftieth birth-day, which would occur within three weeks. This arrange-

for morals, than its neighbours, the Oneidas, the Mohawks &c. &c. The Onondagoes belonged to the Six Nations.—EDITOR.

ment made the parting tolerable to us young men, and our constitutional gaiety did the rest. Half an hour after the last breakfast at Ravensnest, saw us all on our road, cheerful if not absolutely happy. Herman Mordaunt accompanied us three miles, which led him to the end of his own settlements, and to the edge of the virgin forest. There he took his leave, and we pursued our way, with the utmost diligence for hours, with the compass for our guide, until we reached the banks of a small river that was supposed to lie some three or four miles from the southern boundaries of the Patent we sought. I say 'supposed to lie,' for there existed then, and I believe there still exists, much uncertainty concerning the landmarks of different estates in the woods. On the banks of this stream, which was deep but not broad, the surveyor called a halt, and we made our dispositions for dinner. Men who had walked as far, and as fast as we had done, made but little ceremony, and for twenty minutes every one was busy in appeasing his hunger. This was no sooner accomplished, however, than Mr. Traverse summoned the Indians to the side of the fallen tree on which we had taken our seats, when the first occasion occurred, for putting the comparative intelligence of the two runners to the proof. At the same time, the principal chainbearer, a man whose life had been passed in his present occupation, was brought into the consultation, as follows.

"We are now on the banks of this stream, and about this bend in it," commenced the surveyor, pointing to the precise curvature of the river, on a map he had spread before him, at which he supposed we were actually situated; "and the next thing is to find that ridge, on which the moose was killed, and across which the line of the patent we seek, is known to run. This abstract of the title tells us to look for a corner somewhere off here, about a mile, or a mile and a half from this bend in the river; a black oak with its top broken off by the wind, and standing in the centre of a triangle made by three chestnuts. I think you told me, David, that you had never borne a chain on any of these ridges?"

"No, sir, never," answered David, the old chain-bearer already mentioned, "my business never having brought me out so far east. A black oak, with corner blazes on it, and its top broken down by the wind, and standing atween three chestnuts, howsomedever, can be nothing so very hard to find, for a person that's the least acquainted. These Injins will be the likeliest bodies to know that tree, if they've any nat'ral knowledge of the country."

Know a tree! There we were, and had been for many hours, in the bosom of the forest, with trees in thousands ranged around us; trees had risen on our march, as horizon extends beyond horizon on the ocean, and this chain-bearer fancied it might be in the power of one who often passed through these dark and untenanted mazes, to recognise any single member of those countless oaks, and beeches, and pines! Nevertheless, Mr. Traverse did not seem to regard David's suggestion as so very extravagant, for he turned towards the Indians and addressed himself to them.

"How's this?" he asked. "Jumper, do you know any thing of the sort of tree I have described?"

"No—" was the short, sententious, answer.

"Then I fear there is little hope that Trackless is any wiser, as you are Mohawk born, and *he*, they tell me, is at bottom an Onondago. What say you, Trackless; can you help us to find the tree?"

My eyes were fastened on Susquesus, as soon as the Indians were mentioned. There he stood, straight as the trunk of a pine, light and agile in person, with nothing but his breech-cloth, moccasins, and a blue calico shirt belted to his loins with a scarlet band, through which was thrust the handle of his tomahawk, and to which were attached his shot-pouch and horn, while his rifle rested against his body, butt downward. Trackless was a singularly handsome Indian, the unpleasant peculiarities of his people being but faintly portrayed in his face and form; while their nobler and finer qualities came out in strong relief. His nose was almost aquiline, his eye, dark as night, was restless and piercing, his limbs Apollo-like, and his front and bearing had all the fearless dignity of a warrior, blended with the grace of nature. The only obvious defects were in his walk, which was Indian, or in-toed and bending at the knee; but, to counterbalance these, his movements were light, springy and swift. I fancied him, in figure, the very *beau-ideal* of a runner.

During the time the surveyor was speaking, the eye of Susquesus was seemingly fastened on vacancy, and I would have defied the nicest observer to detect any consciousness of what was in hand, in the countenance of this forest stoic. It was not his business to speak, while an older runner and an older warrior was present—for Jumper was both—and he waited for others, who might know more, to reveal their knowledge ere he produced his own. Thus directly addressed, however, all reserve vanished, and he advanced two or three steps, cast a curious glance at the map, even put a finger on the river, the devious course of which it followed across the map, much as a child would trace any similar object that attracted his attention. Susquesus knew but little of maps, it was clear enough, but the result showed that he knew a great deal about the woods, his native field of action.

"Well, what do you make of my map, Trackless," repeated the surveyor. "Is it not drawn to suit your fancy?"

"Good—" returned the Onondago, with emphasis. "Now, show Susquesus, *your* oak tree."

"Here it is, Trackless. You see it is a tree drawn in ink, with a broken top, and here are the three chestnuts, in a sort of triangle, around it."

The Indian examined the tree with some interest, and a slight smile illumined his handsome though dark countenance. He was evidently pleased at this proof of accuracy in the Colony surveyors, and no doubt thought the better of them for the fidelity of their work.

"Good," he repeated, in his low, guttural, almost feminine voice, so soft and mild were its tones. "*Very* good. The pale-faces know every thing! Now, let my brother find the tree."

"That is easier said than done, Susquesus," answered Traverse, laughing. "It is one thing to sketch a tree on a map, and another to go to its root, as it stands in the forest, surrounded by thousands of other trees."

"Pale-face must first see him, or how paint him? Where painter?"

"Ay, the surveyor saw the tree once, and marked it once, but that is not finding it again. Can you tell me where the oak stands? Mr. Littlepage will give the man who finds that corner a French crown. Put me anywhere on the line of the old survey, and I will ask favours of no one."

"Painted tree, *there*," said Susquesus, pointing a little scornfully at the map, as it seemed to me. "Pale-face can't find him in wood. Live tree out yonder; Injin know."

Trackless pointed, with quiet dignity, towards the northeast, standing motionless as a statue the while, as if inviting the closest possible scrutiny into the correctness of his assertion.

"Can you lead us to the tree?" demanded Traverse, eagerly. "Do it, and the money is yours."

Susquesus made a significant gesture of assent; then he set about collecting the scanty remains of his dinner, a precaution in which we imitated him, as a supper would be equally agreeable as the meal just taken, a few hours later. When every thing was put away, and the packs were on our shoulders—not on those of the Indians, for *they* seldom condescended to carry burthens, which was an occupation for women—Trackless led the way, in the direction he had already pointed out.

Well did the Onondago deserve his name, as it seemed to me, while he threaded his way through that gloomy forest, without path, mark, or sign of any sort, that was intelligible to others. His pace was between a walk and a gentle trot, and it required all our muscles to keep near him. He looked to neither the right nor the left, but appeared to pursue his course guided by an instinct, or as the keen-scented hound follows the viewless traces of his game. This lasted for ten minutes, when Traverse called another halt, and we clustered together in council.

"How much further do you think it may be to the tree, Onondago?" demanded the surveyor, as soon as the whole party was collected in a circle. "I have a reason for asking."

"So many minutes," answered the Indian holding up five fingers, or the four fingers and thumb of his right hand. "Oak with broken top, and pale-face marks, *there*."

The precision and confidence with which the Trackless pointed, not a little surprised me, for I could not imagine how any human being could pretend to be minutely certain of such a fact, under the circumstances in which we were placed. So it was, however, and so it proved in the end. In the mean time, Traverse proceeded to carry out his own plans.

"As we are so near the tree," he said, for the surveyor had no doubt of the red-man's accuracy, "we must also be near the line. The last runs north and south, on this part of the patent, and we shall shortly cross it. Spread yourselves, therefore, chain-bearers, and look for blazed trees; for, put me anywhere on the boundaries, and I'll answer for finding any oak, beech, or maple that is mentioned in the corners."

As soon as this order was received, all the surveyor's men obeyed, opening the order of their march, and spreading themselves in a way to extend their means of observing materially. When all was ready, a sign was made to the Indian to proceed. Susquesus obeyed, and we were all soon in quick motion, again.

Guert's activity enabled him to keep nearest to the Onondago, and a shout from his clear, full throat, first announced the complete success of the search. In a moment, the rest of us pressed forward, and were soon at the end of our journey. There was Susquesus, quietly leaning against the trunk of the broken oak, without the smallest expression of triumph in either his manner, or his countenance. That which he had done, he had done naturally, and without any apparent effort, or hesitation. To him the forest had its signs, and metes and marks, as the inhabitant of the vast capital has his means of threading its mazes, with the readiness of familiarity and habit. As for Traverse, he first examined the top of the tree, where he found the indicated fracture, then he looked round for the three chestnuts, each of which was in its place; after which he drew near to look into the more particular signs of his craft. There they were, three of the inner sides of the oak being blazed, the proof it was a corner, while that which had no scar on its surface looked outward, or from the Patent of Mooseridge. Just as all these agreeable facts were ascertained, shouts from the chain-bearers south of us, announced that they had discovered the line, men of their stamp being quite as quick-sighted in ascertaining their own peculiar traces, as the native of the forest is in finding his way to any object in it which he has once seen, and may desire to revisit. By following the line, these men soon joined us, when they gave us the additional information that they had also actually found the skeleton of the moose that had given its name to the estate.

Thus far, all was well, our success much exceeding our hopes. The hunters were sent to look for a spring, and one being found at no great distance, we all repaired to the spot, and hutted for the night. Nothing could be more simple than our encampment, which consisted of coverings made of the branches of trees, with leaves and skins for our beds. Next day, however, Traverse finding the position favorable for his work, he determined to select the spot as head quarters, and we all set about the erection of a log-house, in which we might seek a shelter in the event of a storm, and where we might deposit our implements, spare ammunition, and such stores as we had brought with us, on our backs. As everybody worked with good-will at the erection of this rude building, and the laborers were very expert with the axe, we had it nearly complete, by the setting of the next day's sun. Traverse chose the place because the water was abundant and good, and because a small knoll was near the spring, that was covered with young pines that were about forteen or fifteen inches in diameter, while they grew to the height of near a hundred feet, with few branches and straight as the Onondago. These trees were felled, cut into lengths of twenty and thirty feet, notched at the ends, and rolled alternately on each other, so as to enclose an area that was one-third longer than it was wide. The notches were deep, and brought the logs within two or three inches of each other, and the interstices were filled with pieces of riven chestnut, a wood that splits easily and in straight lines, which pieces were driven hard into their beds, so as to exclude the winds and the rains. As the weather was warm, and the building somewhat airy at the best, we cut no windows, though we had a narrow door, in the centre of one of the longer sides. For a roof, we used the bark of the hemlock, which, at that season, came off in large pieces, and which was laid on sticks, raised to the desired elevation by means of a ridge-pole.

All this was making no more than one of the common log-houses of the new settlements, though in a more hurried and less artificial manner than was usual. We had no chimney, for our cooking could be done in the open air, and less attention was paid to the general finish of the work than might have been the case had we expected to pass the winter there. The floor was somewhat rude, but it had the effect of raising us from the ground, and giving us perfectly dry lodgings; an advantage not always obtained in the woods. It was composed of logs roughly squared on three sides, and placed on sleepers. To my surprise, Traverse directed a door to be made of riven logs, that were pinned together, with cross-pieces, and which was hung on the usual wooden hinges. When I spoke of this as unnecessary labour, occupying two men an entire day to complete, he reminded me that we were much in advance from the settlements, that an active war was being waged around us, and that the agents of the French had been very busy among our own tribes, while those in Canada often pushed their war parties far within our borders. He had always found a great satisfaction, as well as security, in having a sort of citadel to retreat to, when on these exposed surveys; and he never neglected the necessary precaution, when he fancied himself in the least danger.

We were quite a week in completing our house, though, after the first day, neither the surveyor nor his chain-bearers troubled themselves with the labour, any further than to make an occasional suggestion. Traverse and his men went to work in their own pursuit, running lines to divide the patent into its great lots, each of which was made to contain a thousand acres. It should be mentioned that all the surveys, in that day, were made on the most liberal scale, our forty thousand acres turning out, in the end, to amount to quite three thousand more. So it was with the subdivisions of the Patent, each of which was found to be of more than the nominal dimensions. Blazed trees, and records cut into the bark, served to indicate the lines, while a map went on *pari passu* with the labour, the field-book containing a description of each lot, in order that the proprietor of the estate might have some notions of the nature of its soil and surface, as well as of the quality and sizes of the trees it bore.

The original surveyors, those on whose labours the patent of the King was granted, had a comparatively trifling duty to perform. So long as they gave a reasonably accurate outline of an area that would contain forty thousand acres of land, more or less, and did not trespass on any prior grant, no material harm could be done, there being no scarcity of surface in the colony; but, Mr. Traverse had to descend to a little more particularity. It is true, he ran out his hundreds of acres daily, duly marking his corners and blazing his line trees, but something very like a summer's work lay before him. This he understood, and his proceedings were as methodical and deliberate as the nature of his situation required.

In a very few days, things had gotten fairly in train, and every body was employed in some manner that was found to be useful. The surveying party was making a very satisfactory progress, running out their great lots between sun and sun, while Dirck and myself made the notes concerning their quality, under the dictation of Mr. Traverse. Guert did little besides shoot and fish, keeping our larder well supplied with trout, pigeons, squirrels, and such other game as the season would allow, occasionally knocking over something in the shape of poor venison. The hunters brought us their share of eatables also, and we did well enough in this particular, more especially as trout proved to be very abundant. Yaap, or Jaap, as I shall call him in future, and Pete performed domestic duty, acting as scullions and cooks, though the first was much better fitted to perform the service of a forester. The two Indians did little else, for the first fortnight, but come and go between Ravensnest and Mooseridge, carrying missives and acting as guides to the hunters who went through, once or twice, within that period, to bring out supplies of flour, groceries and other similar necessaries, no inducement being able to prevail on the Indians to carry any thing that approached a burthen, either in weight or appearance.

The surveying party did not always return to the hut at night, but it 'camped out,' as they called it, whenever the work led them to a distance, on the other side of the tract. Mr. Traverse had chosen his position for head quarters more in reference to its proximity to the settlement at Ravensnest, than in reference to its position on the patent. It was sufficiently central to the latter, as regarded a north and south line, but was altogether on the western side of the property. As his surveys extended east, therefore, he was often carried too far from the building to return to it each night, though his absences never extended beyond the evening of the third day. In consequence of this arrangement, his people were enabled to carry the food they required without inconvenience, for the periods they were away, coming back for fresh supplies, as the lines brought them west again. Sundays were strictly observed by us all, as days of rest, a respect to the day that is not always observed in the forest; he who is in the solitude of the woods, like him who roams athwart the wastes of the ocean, often forgetting that the spirit of the Creator is abroad equally on the ocean and on the land, ready to receive that homage of his creatures, which is a tribute due to beneficence without bounds, a holiness that is spotless, and a truth that is inherent.

As Jumper, or the Trackless returned from the constantly recurring visits to our neighbours, we young men waited with impatience for the letter that the messenger was certain to bear. This letter was sometimes written by Herman Mordaunt himself, but oftener by Anneke, or Mary Wallace. It was addressed to no one by name, but uniformly bore the superscription of 'To the Hermits of Mooseridge,' nor was there any thing in the language to betray any particular attention to either of the party. We might have liked it better, perhaps, could we have received epistles that were a little more pointed in this particular, but those we actually got, were much too precious to leave any serious grounds of complaint. One from Herman Mordaunt, reached us on the evening of the second Saturday, when our whole party was at home, and assembled at supper. It was brought in by the Trackless, and, among other matters, contained this paragraph:—

"We learn that things hourly assume a more serious aspect, with the armies. Our troops are pushing north, in large bodies, and the French are said to be reinforcing. Living as we do, out of the direct line of march, and fully thirty miles in the rear of the old battle grounds, I should feel no apprehension were it not for a report, I hear, that the woods are full of Indians. I very well know that such a report invariably accompanies the near approach of hostilities in the frontier settlements, and is to be received with many grains of allowance, but it seems so probable the French should push their savages on this flank of our army, to annoy it on the advance, that I confess the rumour has some influence on my feelings. We have been fortifying still more, and I would advise you not to neglect such a precaution, altogether. The Canadian Indians are said to be more subtle than our own, nor is government altogether without the apprehension that our own have been tampered with. It was said at Albany, that much French silver had been seen in the hands of the people of the Six Nations, and that even French blankets, knives and tomahawks were more plentiful among them, than might be accounted for, by the ordinary plunder of their warfare. One of your runners, the man who is called the Trackless, is said to live out of his own tribe, and such Indians are always to be suspected. Their absence is sometimes owing to reasons that are creditable, but far oftener to those that are not. It may be well to have an eye on the conduct of this man. After all, we are in the hands of a beneficent and gracious God, and we know how often his mercy has saved us, on occasions more trying than this."

This letter was read several times, among ourselves, including Mr. Traverse. As the *oi polloi* of our party were eating out of ear-shot, and the Indians had left us, it naturally induced a conversation that turned on the risks we ran, and on the probability of Susquesus's being false.

"As for the rumour that the woods are full of Indians," the surveyor quietly observed, "it is very much as Herman Mordaunt says—there is never a blanket seen, but fame magnifies it into a whole bale. There is danger to be apprehended from savages, I will allow, but not one-half that the settlers ordinarily imagine. As for the French, they are likely to need all their savages at Ty, for they tell me, Gen. Abercrombie will go against them with three men to their one."

"With that superiority, at least," I answered; "but, after all, would not a sagacious officer be likely to annoy his flank, in the manner here mentioned?"

"We are every mile of forty to the eastward of the line of march, and why should parties keep so distant from their enemies?"

"Even such a supposition would place our foes between us and our friends; no very comfortable consideration of itself. But, what think you of this hint concerning the Onondago?"

"There may be truth in *that*—more than in the report that the woods are full of savages. It is usually a bad sign when an Indian quits his tribe, and this runner of ours is certainly an Onondago; *that* I know, for the fellow has twice refused rum. Bread he will take, as often as offered; but rum has not wet his lips since I have seen him, offered in fair weather, or foul."

"T'at *is* a bad sign—" put in Guert, a little dogmatically for him. "T'e man t'at refuses his glass, in good company, has commonly something wrong in his morals. I always keep clear of such chaps."

Poor Guert!—How true that was, and what an influence the opinion had on his character and habits. As for the Indian, I could not judge him so harshly. There was something in his countenance that disposed me to put confidence in him, at the very moment his cold, abstracted manner—cold and abstracted even for a red-skin in pale-face company—created doubts and distrust.

"Certainly, nothing is easier than for a man in his situation to sell us," I answered, after a short pause, "if he be so disposed. But, what could the French gain by cutting off a party as peaceably employed as this? It can be of no moment to them whether Mooseridge be surveyed into lots, this year, or the next."

"Quite true, and I am of opinion that Mons. Montcalm is very indifferent whether it be ever surveyed at all," returned Traverse, who was an intelligent and tolerably educated man. "You forget, however, Mr. Littlepage, that both parties offer such things as premiums on scalps. A Huron may not care about our lines, corners, and marked trees; but he *does* care a great deal whether he is to go home with an empty string, or with half-a-dozen human scalps at his girdle."

I observed that Dirck thrust his fingers through his bushy hair, and that his usually placid countenance assumed an indignant and semi-ferocious appearance. A little amused at this, I walked towards the log on which Susquesus was seated, having ended his meal, in silent thought.

"What news do you bring us, from the red-coats, Trackless?" I asked, with as much of an air of indifference as I could assume. "Are they out in sufficient numbers to eat the French?"

"Look at leaves; count 'em;" answered the Indian.

"Yes, I know they are in force; but, what are the red-skins about? Is the hatchet buried among the Six Nations, that you are satisfied with being a runner when scalps may be had near Ticonderoga?"

"Susquesus *Onondago*—" the red man replied, laying a strong emphasis on the name of his tribe. "No Mohawk blood run in him. *His* people no dig up hatchet, this summer."

"Why not, Trackless? You are allies of the Yengeese, and ought to give us your aid, when it is wanted."

"Count leaves—count Yengeese. Too much for one army. No want Onondago."

"That may be true, possibly, for we are certainly very strong. But, how is it with the woods—are they altogether clear of redskins, in times as troublesome as these?"

Susquesus looked grave, but he made no answer. Still, he did not endeavour to avoid the keen look I fastened on his face, but sat composed, rigid and gazing before him. Knowing the uselessness of attempting to get anything out of an Indian, when he was indisposed to be communicative, I thought it wisest to change the discourse. This I did by making a few general enquiries as to the state of the streams, all of which were answered, when I walked away.

Chapter XXII

"Fear not, till Birnam Wood
Shall come to Dunsinane."
Macbeth, V. v. 43–44.

I cannot say I was quite satisfied with the manner of Susquesus, nor, on the other hand, was I absolutely uneasy. All
might be well; and, if it were not, the power of this man to injure
us could not be very great. A new occurrence, however, raised
very unpleasant doubts of his honesty. Jumper being out on a
hunt, the Onondago was sent across to Ravensnest the next trip,
out of his turn; but, instead of returning, as had been the practice of both, the next day, we saw no more of him for near a
fortnight. As we talked over this sudden and unexpected disappearance, we came to the conclusion, that, perceiving he was distrusted, the fellow had deserted, and would be seen no more.
During his absence, we paid a visit to Ravensnest, ourselves,
spending two or three happy days with the girls, whom we found
delighted with the wildness of their abode, and as happy as innocence, health, and ceaseless interest in the forest, and its habits,
could make them. Herman Mordaunt, having fortified his house
sufficiently, as he fancied, to remove all danger of an assault, returned with us to Mooseridge, and passed two or three days in
walking over, and examining the quality of the land, together
with the advantages offered by the water-courses. As for Mr. Worden and Jason, the former had gone to join the army, craving the
flesh-pots of a regimental mess, in preference to the simple fare
of the woods, while Jason had driven a hard bargain with Herman Mordaunt for the possession of the mill seat, which had
been the subject of frequent discussions between the parties, and
about which the pedagogue had deemed it prudent to draw on
the wisdom of Mother Doortje. As the reader may have some
curiosity to know how such things were conducted in the Colony,
in the year 1758, I will recapitulate the terms of the bargain that
was finally agreed on; signed and sealed.

Herman Mordaunt expected no emolument to himself, from

Ravensnest, but looked forward solely to a provision for posterity. In consequence of these views, he refused to sell, but gave leases on such conditions as would induce tenants to come into his terms, in a country in which land was far plentier than men. For some reason, that never was very clear to me, he was particularly anxious to secure Jason Newcome, and no tolerable terms seemed extravagant to effect his purpose. It is not surprising, therefore, that our miller in perspective, got much the best of the bargain, as its conditions will show.

The lease was for three lives, and twenty-one years afterwards. This would have been thought equal to a lease for forty-two years, in that day, in Europe, but experience is showing that it is, in truth, for a much longer period in America.* The first ten years, no rent at all was to be paid. For the next ten, the land, five hundred acres, was to pay six-pence currency an acre, the tenant having the right to cut timber at pleasure. This was a great concession, as the mill-lot contained much pine. For the remainder of the lease, be it longer or shorter, a shilling an acre, or about six-pence sterling, was to be paid for the land, and forty pounds currency, or one hundred dollars a year, for the mill-seat. The mills to be taken by the landlord at an appraisal 'made by men', at the expiration of the lease, the tenant to pay the taxes. The tenant had the privilege of using all the materials for his dams, buildings, &c., he could find on the land.

The policy of the owners of Mooseridge was different. We intended to sell, at low prices at first, reserving for leases hereafter, such farms as could not be immediately disposed of, or for which the purchaser failed to pay. In this manner it was thought we should sooner get returns for our outlays, and sooner 'build up a settlement' as the phrase goes. In America, the reader should know, every thing is 'built.' The priest 'builds up' a flock; the speculator, a fortune; the lawyer a reputation and the landlord a settlement; sometimes, with sufficient accuracy in language, he even builds a town.

Jason was a very happy man, the moment he got his lease, signed and sealed, in his own possession. It made him a sort of a land-holder on the spot, and one who had nothing to pay for ten years to come. God forgive me if I do the man injustice, but,

*It has been found that a three lives' lease, in the State of New York, is equal to a term of more than thirty years.—EDITOR.

from the first, I had a suspicion that Jason trusted to fortune, to prevent any pay-day from ever coming at all. As for Herman Mordaunt, he seemed satisfied, for he fancied that he had got a man of some education on his property, who might answer a good purpose in civilizing, and in otherwise advancing the interests of his estate.

Just as the rays of the rising sun streamed through the crevices of our log tenement, and ere one of us three idlers had risen from his pallet, I heard a moccasined foot moving near me, in the nearly noiseless tread of an Indian. Springing to my feet, I found myself face to face with the missing Onondago!

"You here, Susquesus!" I exclaimed; "we supposed you had abandoned us. What has brought you back?"

"Time to go, now—" answered the Indian, quietly. "Yengeese and Canada warrior soon fight."

"Is this true!—And do you, *can* you know it to be true! Where have you been this fortnight past?"

"Been see—have see—know him just so. Come—call young men; go on war-path."

Here, then, was an explanation of the mystery of the Onondago's absence! He had heard us speak of an intention of moving with the troops, at the last moment, and he had gone to reconnoitre, in order that we might have seasonable notice when it would be necessary to quit the 'Ridge,' as we familiarly termed the Patent. I saw nothing treasonable in this, but rather deemed it a sign of friendly interest in our concerns, though it was certainly 'running' much farther than the Indian had been directed to proceed, and 'running' a little off the track. One might overlook such an irregularity in a savage, however, more especially as I began to weary of the monotony of our present manner of living, and was not sorry to discover a plausible apology for a change.

The reader may be certain, it was not long before I had communicated the intelligence brought by the Trackless, to my companions, who received it as young men would be apt to listen to tidings so stirring. The Onondago was summoned to our council, and he renewed his protestation that it was time for us to be moving.

"No stop—" he answered, when questioned again on the sub-

ject. "Time go. Canoe ready—gun loaded—warrior counted—
chief woke up—council fire gone out. Time, go."

"Well then, Corny," said Guert, rising and stretching his fine
frame like a lion roused from his lair, "here's off. We can go to
Ravensnest to sleep, to-day; and, to-morrow we will work our way
out into the highway, and fall into the line of march of the army.
I shall have another opportunity of seeing Mary Wallace, and of
telling her how much I love her. That will be so much gained, at
all events."

"No see squaw—no go to Nest!" said the Indian, with energy.
"War path *this* way," pointing in a direction that might have varied a quarter of a circle from that to Herman Mordaunt's settlement. "Bad for warrior to see squaw when he dig up hatchet—
only make woman of him. No; go this way—path there—no
here—scalp there—squaw here."

As the gestures of the Onondago were quite as significant as
his language, we had no difficulty in understanding him. Guert
continued his questions, however, while dressing, and we all soon
became convinced by the words of the Indian, broken and
abrupt as they were, that Abercrombie was on the point of embarking with his army on Lake George, and that we must needs
be active, if we intended to be present at the contemplated operations in front of Ticonderoga.

Our decision was soon reached, and our preparations made.
By packing and shouldering his knapsack and arming himself
each man would be ready, though a short delay grew out of the
absence of Traverse and his chain-bearers. We wrote a letter, however, explaining the reason of our intended absence, promising
to return as soon as the operations in front of Ty should be terminated. This letter we left with Pete, who was to remain as cook,
though Jaap bestirred himself, loaded his broad shoulders with
certain indispensables for our march, took his rifle, pouch and
horn, and was ready to move as soon as any of us. All this the fellow did, moreover, without orders; deeming it a part of his duty
to follow his young master, even if he followed him to evil. No
dog, indeed, could be truer in this particular than Jaap, or Jacob,
Satanstoe, for he had adopted the name of the Neck as his pat-
ronymic; much as the nobles of other regions style themselves
after *their* lands.

When all was ready, and we were on the point of quitting the hut, the question arose seriously whether we were to go by Ravensnest, or by the new route that Onondago had mentioned. Path there was not, in either direction; but, we had land-marks, springs and other known signs on the former, while of the latter we literally knew nothing. Then Anneke and Mary Wallace, with their bright, blooming, sunny faces—bright and happy whenever we appeared most certainly, of late—were in the former direction, and even Dirck cried out 'for Ravensnest.' But, on that rout the Onondago refused to stir one foot. He stood, resembling a finger post, pointing northwesterly, with an immovable obstinacy, that threatened to bring the order of our march into some confusion.

"We know nothing of that rout, Trackless," Guert observed, or rather replied, for the Indian's manner was so expressive as to amount to a remark, "and we would rather travel a road with which we are a little acquainted. Besides, we wish to pay our parting compliments to the ladies."

"Squaw no good, now—war-path no go to squaw. Huron—French warrior, here."

"Ay, and they are there, too. We shall be on their heels soon enough, by going to Ravensnest."

"No soon 'nough—can't do him. Path long, time short. Pale-face warrior in great hurry."

"Pale-face warriors' friends are in a hurry, too—so you will do well to follow us, as we do not intend to follow you. Come, gentlemen, we will lead the Indian, as the Indian does not seem disposed to lead us. After a mile, or two, he will think it more honorable to go in advance; and for that distance, I believe I can show you the way."

"That road good for young men who don't want see enemy!" said Susquesus, with ironical point.

"By St. Nicholas! Indian, what do you mean?" cried Guert, turning short on his heels and moving swiftly towards the Onondago, who did not wait for the menacing blow, but wheeled in his tracks, and led off, at a quick pace, directly towards the northwest.

I do believe that Guert pursued, for the first minute, with no other intention than that of laying his powerful arm, on the offender's shoulder; but I dropped in on his footsteps, so soon,

Dirck following me and Jaap Dirck, that we were all moving off, Indian file, or in the fashion of the woods, at the rate of four miles in the hour, almost before we knew it. An impulse of that angry nature, is not over in a minute, and before either of us had sufficiently cooled to be entirely reasonable, the whole party was fairly out of sight of the hut. After that no one appeared to think of the necessity, or of the expediency of reverting to the original intention. It was certainly indiscreet thus to confide absolutely in the good faith of a savage, or a semi-savage at least, whom we scarcely knew, and whom we had actually distrusted; but we did it, and precisely in the manner, and under the feelings I have described. I know that we all thought of the indiscretion of which we had been guilty, after the first mile, but each was too proud to make the other acquainted with his misgivings. I say all, but Jaap ought to be excepted, for nothing in the shape of danger, ever gave that negro any concern, unless it was spooks. He *was* afraid of 'spooks' but he did not fear man.

Susquesus manifested the same confidence in his knowledge of the woods, while now leading the way, league after league, through the dark forest, as he had done when he took us to the oak with the broken top. On this occasion, he guided us more by the sun, and the course generally, than by any acquaintance with objects that we passed; though, three times that day, did he point out to us particular things that he had before seen, while traversing the woods in directions that crossed, at angles more or less oblique, the line of our present rout. As for us, it was like a sailor's pointing to a path on the trackless ocean. We had our pocket compasses, it is true, and understood well enough, that a north-west course would bring us out somewhere near the foot of Lake George, but, I much doubt if we could have made, by any means, as direct a line, by their aid as we did by that of the Indian.

On this subject we had a discussion among ourselves, I well remember, when we halted to eat and rest, a little after the turn of the day. For five hours had we walked with great rapidity, much as the bird flies so far as course was concerned, never turning aside, unless it might be to avoid some impassable obstacle, and our calculation was that we had made quite twenty, of the forty miles, we had to go over, according to the Onondago's account of the probable length of our journey. We had strung our sinews and hardened our muscles, in such a way as to place us above the influence of common fatigue, yet, it must be confessed, the Indian was much the freshest of the five when we reached the spring where we dined.

"An Indian does seem to have a nose, much like that of a hound," said Guert, as our appetites began to be appeased; "*that* must be admitted. Yet I think, Corny, a compass would carry a man through the woods with more certainty, than any signs on the bark of trees, or looks at the sun."

"A compass cannot err, of course, but it would be a troublesome thing to be stopping, every minute or two, to look at your compass, which must have time to become steady, you will remember, or it would become a guide that is worse than none."

"Every minute, or two! Say once in an hour, or once in half an hour, at most. I would engage to travel as straight as the best Indian of them all, by looking at my compass once in half an hour."

Susquesus was seated near enough to us three, to overhear our conversation, and he understood English perfectly, though he spoke it in the usual, clipped manner of an Indian. I thought I could detect a covert gleam of contempt in his dark countenance, at this boast of Guert's; but he made no remark. We finished our meal, rested our legs, and when our watches told us it was one o'clock, we rose in a body to resume our march. We were renewing the priming of our rifles, a precaution each man took twice every day to prevent the effects of the damps of the woods, when the Onondago, quietly fell in behind Guert, patiently waiting the leisure of the latter.

"We are all ready, Trackless," cried the Albanian; "give us the lead and the step, as before."

"No—" answered the Indian. "Compass lead, now. Susquesus no see any longer,—blind as young dog."

"Oh! that is your game is it! Well, let it be so. Now, Corny, you shall learn the virtue there is in a compass."

Hereupon Guert drew his compass from a pocket in his hunting-shirt, placed it on a log, in order to get a perfectly accurate start, and waited until the quivering needle had become perfectly stationary. Then he made his observation and took a large hemlock, which stood at the distance of some twenty rods, a great distance for a sight in the forest, as his land-mark, gave a shout, caught up his compass, and led off. We followed of course, and soon reached the tree. As Guert now fancied he was well entered on the right course, he disdained to turn to renew his observation, but called out for us to 'come on,' as he had a new tree for his guide, and that in the true direction. We may have proceeded in this manner for half a mile, and I began to think that Guert was about to triumph—for, to me, it did really seem that our course was as straight as it had been at any time that day. Guert now began to brag of his success, talking *to* me, and *at* the Indian, who was between us, over his shoulder.

"You see, Corny," he said, "I am used to the Bush, after all, and have often been up among the Mohawks, and on their hunts. The great point is to begin right; after which you can have no great trouble. Make certain of the first ten rods, and you can be at ease about the ten thousand that are to follow. So it is with life, Corny, boy; begin right, and a young man is pretty certain of coming out right. I made a mistake at the start, and you see the trouble it has given me. But, I was left an orphan, Littlepage, at ten years of age, and the boy that has neither father nor money, must be an uncommon boy not to kick himself out of the traces before he is twenty. Well, Onondago; what do you say to following the compass, now!"

"Best look at him—he tell," answered Susquesus, our whole line halting to let Guert comply.

"This d——d compass will never come round!" exclaimed Guert, shaking the little instrument in order to help the needle round to the point at which he wished to see it stand. "These little devils are very apt to get out of order, Corny, after all."

"Try more—got three—" said the Indian holding up the number of fingers he mentioned, as was his wont when mentioning numbers of any sort.

On this hint Dirck and I drew out our compasses, and the three were placed on a log, at the side of which we had come to our halt. The result showed that the three 'little devils' agreed most accurately, and that we were marching exactly south-east, instead of north-west! Guert looked on that occasion, very much as he did when he rose from the snow, after the hand-sled had upset with us. There was no resisting the truth; we had got turned completely round without knowing it. The fact that the sun was so near the zenith, probably contributed to our mistake, but, any one who has tried the experiment, will soon ascertain how easy it is for him to lose his direction, beneath the obscurity, and amid the inequalities of a virgin forest. Guert gave it up, like a man as he was, and the Indian again passed in front, without the slightest manifestation of triumph, or discontent. It required nothing less than a thunderbolt to disturb the composure of that Onondago!

From that moment, our progress was as swift as it had been previously to the halt; while our course was seemingly as unerring as the flight of the pigeon. Susquesus did not steer exactly north-west, as before, however, but he inclined more northerly. At length, it was just as the sun approached the summits of the western mountains, an opening appeared, in our front, beneath the arches of the woods, and we knew that a lake was near us, and that we were on the summit of high land, though at what precise elevation could not yet be told. Our rout had lain across hills and through valleys, and across small streams, though, as I afterwards ascertained the Hudson did not run far enough north to intercept our march; or, rather, by a sudden turn to the west, it left our course clear. Had we inclined westwardly ourselves, we might have almost done that which Col. Follock had once laughingly recommended to my mother, in order to avoid the dangers of the Powles Hook Ferry, gone round the river.

A clearing now showed itself a little on our right, and thither the Indian held his way. This clearing was not the result of the labours of man, but was the fruit of one of those forest accidents that sometimes let in the light of the sun upon the mysteries of the woods. This clearing was on the bald cap of a rocky mountain, where Indians had doubtless often encamped, the vestiges of their fires proving that the winds had been assisted by the sister element, in clearing away the few stunted trees that had once grown in the fissures of the rocks. As it was, there might have been an open space of some two or three acres, that was now as naked as if it had never known any vegetation, more ambitious than the bush of the whortleberry, or the honeysuckle. Delicious water was spouting from a higher ridge of the rocks, that led away, northerly, forming the summit of an extensive range in that direction. At this spring, Susquesus stooped to drink, then, he announced that our day's work was done.

Until this announcement, I do not believe that one of us all, had taken the time to look about him, so earnest and rapid had been our march. Now, however, each man threw aside his pack, laid down his rifle, and, thus disencumbered, we turned to gaze on one of the most surprisingly beautiful scenes, eye of mine had ever beheld.

From what I have read and heard, I am now fully aware that the grandest of our American scenery falls far behind that which is to be found among the lakes and precipices of the Alps, and along the almost miraculous coast of the Mediterranean, and I shall not pretend that the view I now beheld approached many, in magnificence, that are to be met with in those magic regions. Nevertheless, it was both grand, and soft, and it had one element of vastness, in the green mantle of its interminable woods, that is not often to be met with, in countries that have long submitted to the sway of man. Such as it was, I shall endeavour to describe it.

Beneath us, at the distance of near a thousand feet, lay a lake of the most limpid and placid water, that was beautifully diversified in shape, by means of bluffs, bays, and curvatures of the shores, and which had an extent of near forty miles. We were on its eastern margin, and about one-third of the distance from its southern to its northern end. Countless islands, lay almost under our feet, rendering the mixture of land and water, at that particular point, as various and fanciful as the human imagination could devise. To the north, the placid sheet extended a great distance, bounded by rocky precipices, passing by a narrow gorge into a wider and larger estuary beyond. To the south, the water lay expanded, to its oval termination, with here and there an island to relieve the surface. In that direction only, were any of the results of human industry to be traced. Everywhere else, the gorges, the receding valleys, the long ranges of hills, and the bald caps of granite, presented nothing to the eye, but the unwearying charms of nature. Far as the eye could reach, mountain behind mountain, the earth was covered with its green mantle of luxuriant leaves, such as vegetation bestows on a virgin soil beneath a beneficent sun. The rolling and variegated carpet of the earth resembled a firmament reversed, with clouds composed of foliage.

At the southern termination of the lake, however, there was an opening in the forest, of considerable extent; and one that had been so thoroughly made, as to leave few, or no trees. From this point, we were distant several miles, and that distance necessarily rendered objects indistinct, though we had little difficulty in perceiving the ruins of extensive fortifications. A thousand white specks, we now ascertained to be tents, for the works were all that remained of Fort William Henry, and there lay encamped the army of Abercrombie, much the largest force that had then ever collected in America, under the colours of England. History has since informed us that this army contained the formidable number of sixteen thousand men. Hundreds of boats, large batteaux, that were capable of carrying forty or fifty men, were moving about in front of the encampment, and, remote as we were, it was not impossible to discover the signs of preparation, and of an early movement. The Indian had not deceived us, thus far at least, but had shown himself an intelligent judge of what was going on, as well as a faithful guide.

We were to pass the night on the mountain. Our beds were none of the best, as the reader may suppose, and our cover slight; yet I do not remember to have opened my eyes from the moment they were closed, until I awoke in the morning. The fatigue of a forced march did that for us, which down cannot obtain for the voluptuary, and we all slept as profoundly as children. Consciousness returned to me, by means of a gentle shake of the shoulder, which proceeded from Susquesus. On arising, I found the Indian still near me, his countenance, for the first time since I had known him, expressing something like an animated pleasure. He had awoke none of the others, and he signed for me to follow him, without arousing either of my companions. Why I had been thus particularly selected for the scene that succeeded, I cannot say unless the Onondago's native sagacity had taught him to distinguish between the educations and feelings of us three young men. So it was, however, and I left the rude shelter we had prepared for the night, alone.

A glorious sight awaited me! The sun had just tipped the mountain-tops with gold, while the lake and the valleys, the hillsides even, and the entire world beneath, still reposed in shadow. It appeared to me like the awakening of created things, from the sleep of nature. For a moment or more, I could only gaze on the wonderful picture presented by the strong contrast between the golden hill-tops and their shadowed sides—the promises of day and the vestiges of night. But, the Onondago was too much engrossed with his own feelings to suffer me long to disregard what he conceived to be the principal point of interest. Directed by his

finger and eye, for he spoke not, I turned my look towards the
distant shore of William Henry, and at once perceived the cause
of his unusual excitement. As soon as the Indian was certain that
I saw the objects that attracted himself so strongly, he exclaimed
with a strong, guttural, emphatic cadence—

"Good!"

Abercrombie's army was actually in motion! Sixteen thousand
men, had embarked in boats, and were moving towards the
northern end of the lake, with imposing force, and a most beautiful accuracy. The unruffled surface of the lake was dotted with
the flotilla, boats in hundreds stretching across it in long dark
lines, moving on towards their point of destination, with the
method and concert of an army with its wings displayed. The last
brigade of boats had just left the shore when I first saw this striking spectacle, and the whole picture lay spread before me, at a
single glance. America had never before witnessed such a sight,
and it may be long before she will again witness such another. For
several minutes I stood entranced; nor did I speak until the rays
of the sun had penetrated the dusky light that lay on the inferior
world, as low as the bases of the western mountains.

"What are we to do, Susquesus?" I then asked, feeling how
much right the Indian now might justly claim, to govern our
movements.

"Eat breakfast, first—" the Onondago quietly replied; "then go
down mountain."

"Neither of which will place us in the midst of that gallant
army, as it is our wish to be."

"See, bye'm by. Injin know—no hurry, now. Hurry come, when
Frenchman shoot."

I did not like this speech, nor the manner in which it was uttered; but there were too many things to think of, just then, to be
long occupied by vague conjectures touching the Onondago's
evasive allusions. Guert and Dirck were called, and made to share
in the pleasure that such a sight could not fail to communicate.
Then it was I got the first notion of what I should call the truly
martial character of Ten Eyck. His fine, manly figure appeared to
me to enlarge, his countenance actually became illuminated, and
the expression of his eye, usually so full of good nature and fun,
seemed to change its character entirely, to one of sternness and
severity.

"This is a noble sight, Mr. Littlepage," Guert remarked, after gazing at the measured but quick movement of the flotilla, for some time, in silence— "a truly noble sight, and it is a reproach to us three, for having lost so much time in the woods, when we ought to have been *there*, ready to aid in driving the French from the Province."

"We are not too late, my good friend, as the first blow yet remains to be struck."

"You say true, and I shall join that army, if I have to swim to reach the boats. It will be no difficult thing for us to swim from one of these islands to another, and the troops must pass through the midst of them, in order to get into the Lower Lake. Any reasonable man would stop to pick us up."

"No need," said the Onondago, in his quiet way. "Eat breakfast; then go. Got canoe—that 'nough."

"A canoe! By St. Nicholas! Mr. Susquesus, I'll tell you what it is—you shall never want a friend as long as Guert Ten Eyck is living and able to assist you. That idea of the canoe is a most thoughtful one, and shows that a reasoning man has had the care of us. We can now join the troops, with the rifles in our hands, as becomes gentlemen and volunteers."

By this time Jaap was up, and looking at the scene, with all his eyes. It is scarcely necessary to describe the effect on a negro. He laughed in fits, shook his head like the Chinese figure of a Mandarin, rolled over on the rocks, arose, shook himself like a dog that quits the water, laughed again, and finally shouted. As we were all accustomed to these displays of negro sensibility, they only excited a smile among us, and not even that from Dirck. As for the Indian, he took no more notice of these natural, but undignified signs of pleasure, in Jaap, than if the latter had been a dog, or any other unintellectual animal. Perhaps no weakness would be so likely to excite his contempt, as to be a witness of so complete an absence of self-command, as the untutored negro manifested on this occasion.

As soon as our first curiosity and interest were a little abated, we applied ourselves to the necessary duty of breaking our fasts. The meal was soon dispatched, and, to say the truth, it was not of a quality to detain one long from any thing of interest. The moment we had finished, the whole party left the cap of the mountain, following our guide as usual.

The Onondago had purposely brought us to that lookout, a spot known to him, in order that we might get the view of its panorama. It was impossible to descend to the lake-shore, at that spot however, and we were obliged to make a detour of three or four miles, in order to reach a ravine, by means of which, and not without difficulty either, that important object was obtained. Here we found a bark canoe, of a size sufficient to hold all five of us, and we embarked without a moment's delay.

The wind had sprung up from the south, as the day advanced, and the flotilla of boats was coming on, at a greatly increased rate, as to speed. By the time we had threaded our way through the islands, and reached the main channel, if indeed any one passage could be so termed among such a variety, the leading boat of the army was within hail. The Indian paddled, and waving his hand in sign of amity, he soon brought us alongside of the batteau. As we approached it, however, I observed the fine, large form of the Viscount Howe, standing erect in its bows, dressed in his Light Infantry forest uniform, as if eager to be literally the foremost man, of a movement, in the success of which, the honour of the British empire, itself, was felt to be concerned.

Chapter XXIII

"My sons? It may
Unman my heart, and the poor boys will weep;
And what can I reply, to comfort them,
Save with some hollow hopes, and ill-worn smiles?"

Byron, *Sardanapalus*, IV. i. 210–214.

MY Lord Howe did not at first recognize us, in our hunting-shirts. With Guert Ten Eyck, however, he had formed such an acquaintance, while at Albany, as caused him to remember his voice, and our welcome was both frank and cordial. We enquired for the ————th, declaring our intention to join that corps, from the commander of which all three of us had reiterated and pressing invitations to join his mess. The intention of seeking our friend immediately nevertheless, was changed by a remark of our present host, if one may use such a term as applied to the commander of a brigade of boats.

"Bulstrode's regiment is in the center, and will be early in the field," he said, "but not as early as the advanced guard. If you desire good living, gentlemen, I am far from wishing to dissuade you from seeking the flesh-pots of the ————th; there being a certain Mr. Billings in that corps, who has an extraordinary faculty, they tell me, in getting up a good dinner out of nothing; but, if you want service, we shall certainly be the first brigade in action, and to such fare as I can command, you will be most acceptable guests. As for any thing else, time must show."

After this, no more was said about looking for Bulstrode, though we let our noble commander understand that we should tax his hospitality no longer, than to see him fairly in the field, after driving away the party that it was expected the enemy would send to oppose our landing.

Susquesus no sooner learned our decision, than he took his departure, quietly paddling away towards the eastern shore, no one attempting to intercept a canoe that was seen to quit the batteau that was known to carry the commander of the advanced brigade.

The wind freshened as the day advanced, and most of the boats having something or other, in the shape of a sail, our progress now became quite rapid. By nine o'clock we were fairly in the Lower Lake, and there was every prospect of our reaching our point of destination by mid-day. I confess the business we were on, the novelty of my situation, and the certainty that we should meet in Montcalm, an experienced as well as a most gallant foe, conspired to render me thoughtful, though I trust not timid, during the few hours we were in the batteau. Perfectly inactive, it is not surprising that so young a soldier should feel sobered by the solemn reflections that are apt to get possession of the mind, at the probable approach of death—if not to myself, at least to many of those who were around me. Nor was there any thing boastful, or inflated in the manner, or conversation, of our distinguished leader, who had seen much warm service in Germany, in the wars of his reputed grandfather and uncle, young as he was. On the contrary, My Lord Howe, that day, was grave and thoughtful, as became a man who held the lives of others in his keeping, though he was neither depressed nor doubting. There were moments, indeed, when he spoke cheerfully to those who were near him, though, as a whole, his deportment was, as I have just said, grave and thoughtful. Once, I caught his eye fastened on me, with a saddened expression, and I suppose that a question he soon after put me, was connected with the subject of his thoughts.

"How would our excellent and respectable friend, Madam Schuyler feel, did she know our precise position at this moment, Mr. Littlepage? I do believe that excellent woman feels more concern for those in whom she takes an interest, than they often feel for themselves."

"I think, my lord, that, in such a case, we should certainly receive the benefit of her prayers."

"You are an only child, I think she told me, Littlepage?"

"I am, my lord, and thankful am I that my mother cannot foresee this scene."

"I, too, have those that love me, though they are accustomed to think of me as a soldier, and liable to a soldier's risks. Happy is the military man who can possess his mind, in the moment of trial, free from the embarrassing, though pleasing and otherwise so grateful ties of affection. But, we are nearing the shore, and must attend to duty."

This is the last conversation I held with that brave soldier, and these were the last words of a private nature I ever heard him utter. From that moment, his whole soul seemed occupied with the discharge of his duty, the success of our arms, and the defeat of the enemy.

I am not soldier enough to describe what followed, in a very military or intelligible manner. As the brigade drew near the foot of the lake, where there was a wide extent of low land, principally in forest, however, some batteaux were brought to the front, on which were mounted a number of pieces of heavy artillery. The French had a party of considerable force to oppose our landing, but, as it appeared, they had not made a sufficient provision of guns, on their part, to contend with success, and our grape scouring the woods, we met with but little real resistance. Nor did we assail them precisely at the point where we were expected, but proceeded rather to the right of their position. At the signal, the advanced brigade pushed for the shore, led by our gallant commander, and we were all soon on *terra firma*, without sustaining any loss worth naming. We four, that is, Guert, Dirck, myself, and Jaap, kept as near as was proper to the noble brigadier, who instantly ordered an advance, to press the retreating foe. The skirmishing was not sharp, however, and we gained ground fast, the enemy retiring in the direction of Ticonderoga, and we pressing on their rear, quite as fast as prudence and our preparations would allow. I could see that a cloud of Indians was in our front, and will own that I felt afraid of an ambush; for the artful warfare practised by those beings of the wood, could not but be familiar, by tradition at least, to one born and educated in the colonies. We had landed in a cove, not literally at the foot of the lake, but rather on its western side, and room was no sooner obtained than Gen. Abercrombie, got most of his force on shore, and formed it as speedily as possible in columns. Of these columns we had four, the two in the centre being composed entirely of King's troops, six regiments in all, numbering more than as many thousand men, while five thousand provincials were on the flanks, leaving quite four thousand of the latter with the boats, of which this vast flotilla, actually contained the large number of one thousand and twenty-five! All our boats, however, had not yet reached the point of debarkation, those with the stores, artillery, &c., &c., being still some distance in the rear.

Our party was now placed with the right centre column, at the head of which marched our noble acquaintance. The enemy had posted a single battalion in a log encampment, near the ordinary landing, but finding the character of the force with which he was about to be assailed, its commandant set fire to his huts, and retreated. The skirmishing was now even of less moment, than it had been on landing, and we all moved forward, in high spirits, though the want of guides, the density of the woods, and the difficulties of the ground soon produced a certain degree of confusion in our march. The columns got entangled with each other, and no one seemed to possess the means of promptly extricating them from this awkward embarrassment. Want of guides was the great evil under which we laboured, but it was an evil that it was now too late to remedy.

Our column, notwithstanding, or its head rather, continued to advance, with its gallant leader keeping even pace with its foremost platoon. We four volunteers, acted as look-outs a little on its flank, and I trust there will be no boasting if I say, we kept rather in advance of the leading files, than otherwise. In this state of things, French uniforms were seen in front, and a pretty strong party of the enemy was encountered, wandering like ourselves, a little uncertain of the rout they ought to take, in order to reach their entrenchments in the shortest time. As a matter of course, this party could not pass the head of our column, without bringing on a collision, though it were one that was only momentary. Which party gave the first fire, I cannot say, though I thought it was the French. The discharge was not heavy, however, and was almost immediately mutual. I know that all four of us, let off our rifles, and that we halted, under a cover, to reload. I had just driven the ball down, when my eye caught the signs of some confusion in the head of the column, and I saw the body of an officer borne to the rear. It was that of Lord Howe! He had fallen at the first serious discharge made by the enemy in that campaign! The fall of its leader, so immediately in its presence, seemed to rouse the column, into a sense of the necessity of doing something effective, and it assaulted the party in its front, with the rage of so many tigers, dispersing the enemy like chaff, making a considerable number of prisoners, besides killing and wounding not a few.

I never saw a man more thoroughly aroused than was Guert
Ten Eyck, in this little affair. He had been much noticed by Lord
Howe, during the residence of that unfortunate nobleman at Albany, and the loss of the last, appeared to awaken all that there
was of the ferocious in the nature of my usually kind-hearted Albany friend. He acted as our immediate commander, and he led
us forward on the heels of the retreating French, until we actually
came in sight of their entrenchments. Then, indeed, we all saw it
was necessary to retreat in our turn, and Guert consented to fall
back, though it was done surlily, and like a lion at bay. A party of
Indians pressed us hard, in this retreat, and we ran an imminent
risk of our scalps, all of which I have ever believed would have
been lost, were it not for the resolution and Herculean strength
of Jaap. It happened, as we were dodging from tree to tree, that
all four of our rifles were discharged at the same time; a circumstance of which our assailants availed themselves to make
a rush at us. Luckily the weight of the onset fell on Jaap, who
clubbed his rifle, and literally knocked down in succession the
three Indians that first reached him. This intrepidity and success
gave us time to reload, and Dirck, ever a cool and capital shot,
laid the fourth Huron on his face, with a ball through his heart.
Guert then held his fire, and called on Jaap to retreat. He was
obeyed, and under cover of our two rifles, the whole party got
off, the red-skins being too thoroughly rebuked to press us very
closely, after the specimen they had just received of the stuff we
were made of.

We owed our escape, however, as much to another circumstance, as to this resolution of Jaap and the expedient of Guert.
Among the provincials was a partisan of great repute, of the
name of Rogers. This officer led a party of riflemen on our left
flank, and he drove in the enemy's skirmishers, along his own
front, with rapidity, causing them to suffer a considerable loss.
By this means, the Indians before us, were held in check, as there
was the danger that Major Rogers's party might fall in upon their
rear, should they attempt to pursue us, and thus cut them off
from their allies. It was well it was so; inasmuch as we had to fall
back more than a mile, ere we reached the spot, where Abercrombie brought his columns to a halt, and encamped for the night.
This position was distant about two miles from the works before
Ticonderoga, and consequently at no great distance from the

outlet of Lake George. Here the army was brought into good order, and took up a station for some little time.

It was necessary to await the arrival of the stores, ammunition and artillery. As the bringing up these materials, through a country that was little else than a virgin forest, was no easy task, it occupied us quite two days. Melancholy days they were, too, the death of Lord Howe acting on the whole army much as if it had been a defeat. He was the idol of the King's troops, and he had rendered himself as popular with us Americans, as with his own countrymen. A sort of ominous sadness prevailed among us, each common man appearing to feel his loss, as he might have felt that of a brother.

We looked up the ———th, and joined Bulstrode, as soon as we reached the ground chosen for the new encampment. Our reception was friendly, and even kind, and it became warmer still, as soon as it was understood that we composed the little party that had skirmished so freely on the flank of the right centre column, and which was known to have gone farther in advance than any one else, in that part of the field. Thus, we joined our corps, with some *éclat* at the very outset, every body welcoming us cordially, and with seeming sincerity.

Nevertheless, the general sadness existed in the ———th, as well as in all the other corps. Lord Howe was as much beloved in that regiment, as in any other, and our meeting and subsequent intercourse, could not be called joyful. Bulstrode had an extensive and important command for his rank and years, and he certainly was proud of his position, but I could see that even his elastic and usually gay temperament was much affected by what had occurred. That night we walked together, apart from our companions, when he spoke on the subject of our loss.

"It may appear strange to you, Corny," he said, "to find so much depression in camp, after a debarkation that has certainly been successful, and a little affair that has given us, as they assure me, a couple of hundred prisoners. I tell you, however, my friend, it were better for this army to have seen its best corps annihilated, than to have lost the man it has. Howe was literally the soul of this entire force. He was a soldier by nature, and made all around him soldiers. As for the Commander in Chief, he does not understand you Americans, and will not use you as he ought; then he does not understand the nature of the warfare of this

continent, and will be very likely to make a blunder. I'll tell you
how it is, Corny; Howe had as much influence with Abercrombie,
as he had with every one else, and an attempt will be made to introduce his mode of fighting, but such a man as Lord Howe requires another Lord Howe to carry out his own conceptions.
That is the point, on which I fear we shall fail."

All this sounded very sensible to me, though it sounded dis-
couragingly. I found, however, that Bulstrode did not entertain
these feelings, alone, but, that most around me were of the same
way of thinking. In the mean time, the preparations proceeded,
and it was understood that the 8th was to be the day that was to
decide the fate of Ticonderoga. The fort, proper, at this celebrated station, stands on a peninsula, and can only be assailed on
one side. The outworks were very extensive on that side, and the
garrison was known to be formidable. As these outworks, however, consisted principally of a log breastwork, and it could be approached through open woods, which of itself afforded some
cover, it was determined to carry it by storm, and, if possible,
enter the main work with the retreating enemy. Had we waited
for our artillery, and established batteries, our success would
have been certain; but the engineer reported favourably of the
other project, and perhaps it better suited the temper and impatience of the whole army to push on, rather than proceed by
the slow movements of a regular siege.

On the morning of the 8th, therefore, the troops were paraded
for the assault, our party falling in on the flank of the ———th,
as volunteers. The ground did not admit of the use of many
horses, and Bulstrode marched with us on foot. I can relate but
little of the general movements of that memorable day, the woods
concealing so much of what was done, on both sides. I know this,
however; that the flower of our army were brought into the line,
and were foremost in the assault; including both regulars and
provincials. The 42d, a Highland corps, that had awakened
much interest in America, both by the appearance and character
of its men, was placed at a point where it was thought the heaviest
service was to be performed. The 55th, another corps on which
much reliance was placed, was also put at the head of another column. A swamp extending for some distance along the only exposed front of the peninsula, these two corps were designated to
carry the log breast-work, that commenced at the point where

the swamp ceased; much the most arduous portion of the expected service, since this was the only accessible approach to the fortress itself. To render their position more secure, the French had placed several pieces of artillery in battery, along the line of this breast-work, while we had not yet a gun in front to cover our advance.

It was said that Abercrombie did not take counsel of any of the American officers with him, before he decided on the attack of the 8th of July. He had directed his principal engineer to reconnoitre, and that gentleman having reported that the defences offered no serious scientific obstacles, the assault was decided on. This report was accurate, doubtless, agreeably to the principles and facts of European warfare, but it was not suited to those of the conflicts of this continent. It was to be regretted, however, that the experience of 1755, and the fate of Braddock had not inculcated a more extensive lesson of discretion, among the Royal Commanders, than was manifested by the incidents of this day.

The ———th was placed in column, directly in the rear of the Highlanders, who were led on this occasion by Col. Gordon Graham, a veteran officer of great experience, and of an undaunted courage.* Of course, I saw this officer, and this regiment, being as they were directly in my front, but I saw little else; more especially after the smoke of the first discharge, was added to the other obstacles to vision.

A considerable time was consumed in making the preparations, but, when every thing was supposed to be ready, the columns were set in motion. It was generally understood that the troops were to receive the enemy's fire, then rush forward to the breast-work, cross the latter at the bayonet's point—if it should be necessary, and deliver their own fire at close quarters; or on their retreating foes. Permission was given to us volunteers, and to divers light parties of irregulars, to open on any of the French of whom we might get glimpses, as little was expected from us in the charge.

Nearly an hour was consumed in approaching the point of

---

*Holmes's Annals say that Lord John Murray commanded the 42d, on this occasion. I presume, as Mr. Littlepage was there, and was posted so near the corps in question, he cannot well be mistaken. Mrs. Grant, of Laggan, who was at Albany at the time, and whose father was in the battle, agrees with Mr. Littlepage, in saying that Gordon Graham led the 42d.—EDITOR.

attack, owing to the difficulties of the ground, and the necessity of making frequent halts, in order to dress. At length the important moment arrived when the head of the column was ready to unmask itself and consequently to come under fire. A short halt sufficed for the arrangements here, when the bagpipes commenced their exciting music, and we broke out of cover, shouting and cheering each other on. We must have been within two hundred yards of the breast-work at the time, and the first gun discharged was Jaap's, who, by working his way into the cover of the swamp, had got some distance ahead of us, and who actually shot down a French officer who had got upon the logs of his defences, in order to reconnoitre. That assault, however, was fearfully avenged! The Highlanders were moving on like a whirlwind, grave, silent and steady, cheered only by their music, when a sheet of flame glanced along the enemy's line, and the iron and leaden messengers of death came whistling in among us like a hurricane. The Scotsmen were staggered by that shock, but they recovered instantly and pressed forward. The ———th did not escape harmless, by any means, while the din told us that the conflict extended along the whole of the breast-work, towards the lake shore. How many were shot down in our column, by that first discharge, I never knew; but the slaughter was dreadful, and among those who fell was the veteran Graham, himself. I can safely say, however, that the plan of attack was completely deranged from this first onset, the columns displaying, and commencing their fire, as soon as possible. No men could have behaved better than all those I could see, the whole of us pushing on for the breast-work, until we encountered fallen trees, which were made to serve the purpose of chevaux de frise. These trees had been felled along the front of the breast-work, while their branches were cut, and pointed like stakes. It was impossible to pass in any order, and the troops halted when they reached them, and continued to fire by platoons, with as much regularity as on parade. A few minutes of this work, however, compelled different corps to fall back, and the vain conflict was continued for four hours, on our part almost entirely by a smart but ineffective fire of musketry, while the French sent their grape into our ranks, almost with as much impunity as if they had been on parade. It had been far better for our men had they been less disciplined, and less under the control of their officers; for the sole effect of steadiness, under such circumstances, is to leave the gallant and devoted troops, who refuse to fall back while they are unable to advance, only so much the longer in jeopardy.

Guert had shouted with the rest, and I soon found that, by following him for a leader, we should quickly be in the midst of the fray. He actually led us up to the fallen trees, and finding something like a cover there, we three established ourselves among them, as riflemen, doing fully our share of service. When the troops fell back, however, we were left in a manner alone, and it was rather dangerous work to retire; and finding ourselves out of the line of fire from our own men, no immaterial point in such a fray, we maintained our post to the last. Admonished, after a long time, of the necessity of retreating, by the manner in which the fire of our own line lessened, we got off with sound skins, though Guert retired the whole distance, with his face to the enemy, firing as he withdrew. We all did the last, indeed, using the trees for covers. Towards the close, we attracted especial attention, and there were two or three minutes, during which the flight of bullets around us, might truly, without much exaggeration, be likened to a storm of hail!

Jaap was not with us in this sally, and I went into the swamp to look for him. The search was not long, for I found my fellow, retreating also, and bringing in with him a stout Canadian Indian, as a prisoner. He was making his captive carry three discharged rifles, and blankets, one of which had been his own property once, and the others that of two of his tribe whom the negro had left lying in the swamp, as bloody trophies of his exploits. I cannot explain the philosophy of the thing, but that negro ever appeared to me to fight, as if he enjoyed the occupation as an amusement.

These facts were scarcely ascertained, when we learned the important intelligence that a general retreat was ordered. Our proud and powerful army was beaten, and that too by a force two-thirds less than its own! It is not easy to describe the miserable scene that followed. The transporting of the wounded to the rear, had been going on the whole time, and, as usually happens, when it is permitted, it had contributed largely to thin the ranks. These unfortunate men were put into the batteaux in hundreds, while most of the dead were left where they lay. So completely were our hopes frustrated, and our spirits lowered, that most of the boats pulled off that night, and all the remainder, quitted the foot of the lake early next day.

Thus terminated the dire expedition of 1758, against Ticonderoga, and with it our expectations of seeing Montreal, or Quebec, that season. I dare say we had fully ten thousand bayonets in the field that bloody day, and quite five thousand men closely engaged. The mistake was in attempting to carry a post that was so nearly impregnable, by assault, and this too without the cover of artillery. The enemy was said to have four or five thousand men present, and this may be true, as applied to all within the defences, though I question if more than half that number pulled triggers on us, in the miserable affair. There is always much of exaggeration in both the boasting and the apologies of war.

Our own loss on this sad occasion, was reported at 548 slain, and 1356 wounded. This was probably within the truth, though the missing were said to be surprisingly few, some thirty or forty in all, the men having no place to repair to, but the boats. Of the Highlanders, it was said that nearly half the common men, and twenty-five, or nearly *all* the officers, were either killed or wounded! One account, indeed, said that *every* officer of that corps, who was on the ground, suffered. The 55th, also, was dreadfully cut up. Ten of its officers were slain outright, and many were wounded. As for the ———th, it fared a little better, not heading a column, but its loss was fearful. Bulstrode was seriously wounded early in the attack, though his hurt was never supposed to be dangerous. Billings was left dead on the field, and Harris got a scratch that served him to talk of, in after life.

The confusion was tremendous after such a conflict, and such a defeat. The troops re-embarked without much regard to corps, or regularity of movement, and the boats moved away as fast as they received their melancholy cargoes. An immense amount of property was lost, though I believe all the customary military trophies were preserved. As the provincials had been the least engaged, and had suffered much the least in proportion to numbers, a large body of them was kept as a rear-guard, while the regular corps removed their wounded and *matèriel*.

As for us three, or four including Jaap, who stuck by his prisoner, we scarcely knew what to do with ourselves. Every body who felt any interest in us, was either killed or wounded. Bulstrode we could not see, nor could we even find the regiment. Should we succeed in the attempt at the last, very few now remained in it, who would have taken much, or indeed any concern in us. Under the circumstances, therefore, we held a consultation on the lake shore, uncertain whether to ask admission into one of the departing boats, or to remain until morning, that our retreat might have a more manly aspect.

"I'll tell you what it is, Corny," said Guert Ten Eyck, in a somewhat positive manner, "the less *we* say about this campaign, and of our share in it, the petter. We are not soldiers, in the regular way, and if we keep quiet, nobody will know what a t'rashing we t'ree, in particular, haf receivet. My advice is, t'at we get out of this army, as we got into it;—t'at is py a one-sided movement, and forever after holt our tongues, about our having had anyt'ing to do with it. I never knew a worsted man any the more respected for his mishap, and I will own that I set down flogging as a very material part of a fight."

"I am quite sure, Guert, I am as little disposed to brag of my share in this affair, as you, or any one can possibly be; but it is much easier to talk about getting away from this confused crowd, than really to do the thing. I doubt if any of these boats will take us in, for an Englishman flogged, is not apt to be very good-natured, and all our friends seem to be killed or wounded."

"You want go?" asked a low Indian voice, at my elbow. "Got 'nough, eh?"

Turning, I saw Susquesus, standing within two feet of me. Our consultation was necesarily in the midst of a moving throng, and the Onondago must have approached us, unnoticed, at the commencement of our conference. There he was, however, though whence he came, or how he got there I could not imagine at the time, and have never been able to learn since.

"Can you help us to get away, Susquesus?" was my answer. "Do you know of any means of crossing the lake?"

"Got canoe. That good. Canoe go though Yengeese run."

"That in which we came off to the army, do you mean?"

The Indian nodded his head, and made a sign for us to follow. Little persuasion was necessary, and we proceeded at his heels, in a body, in the direction he led. I will confess that when I saw our guide proceeding eastward, along the lake shore, I had some misgivings on the subject of his good faith. That was the direction which took us towards, instead of *from* the enemy, and there was something so mysterious in the conduct of this man, that it gave me uneasiness. Here he was in the midst of the English army, in the height of its confusion, though he had declined joining it previously to the battle. Nothing was easier, than to enter the throng, in its present confused state, and move about undetected for hours, if one had the nerve necessary for the service; and, in that property, I felt certain the Onondago was not deficient. There was a coolness in the manner of the man, a quiet observation, both blended with the seeming apathy of a red-skin, that gave every assurance of his fitness for the duty.

Nevertheless, there was no remedy but to follow, or to break with our guide on the spot. We did not like to do the last, although we conferred together on the subject, but followed, keeping our hands on the locks of our rifles, in readiness for a brush, should we be led into danger. Susquesus had no such treacherous intentions, however, while he had disposed of his canoe, in a place that denoted his judgment. We had to walk quite a mile ere we reached the little bush-fringed creek in which he had concealed it. I have always thought we ran a grave risk, in advancing so far in that direction, since the enemy's Indians would certainly be hanging around the skirts of our army, in quest of scalps; but I afterwards learned the secret of the Onondago's confidence, who first spoke on the subject, after we had left the shore, and then only, in an answer to a remark of Guert's.

"No danger," he said; "red-man gettin' Yengeese scalps, on the war path. Too much kill now, to want more."

As both governments pursued the culpable policy of paying for human scalps, this suggestion probably contained the whole truth.

Previously to quitting the creek, however, there was a difficulty to dispose of. Jaap had brought his Huron prisoner with him, and the Onondago declared that the canoe could not carry six. This we knew from experience, indeed, though five went in it, very comfortably.

"No room—" said Susquesus, "for red-man. Five good—six bad."

"What shall we do with the fellow, Corny?" asked Guert, with a little interest. "Jaap says he is a proper devil, by day-light, and that he had a world of trouble in taking him, and in bringing him in. For five minutes, it was heads or tails, which was to give in, and the nigger only got the best of it, by his own account of the battle, because the red-skin had the unaccountable folly to try to beat in Jaap's brains. He might as well have battered the Rock of Gibraltar, you know, as to attempt to break a nigger's skull, and so your fellow got the best of it. What shall we do with the rascal?"

"Take scalp—" said the Onondago, sententiously. "Got good scalp—war-lock ready—paint, war-paint—capital scalp."

"Ay, that may do better for you, Master Succetush—" so Guert always called our guide— "than it will do for us Christians. I'm afraid we shall have to let the ravenous devil go, after disarming him."

"Disarmed, he is already, but he cannot be long without a musket, on this battle ground. I am of your opinion, Guert;—so, Jaap, release your prisoner, at once, that we may return to Ravensnest, as fast as possible."

"Dat berry hard, Masser Corny, sah!" exclaimed Jaap, who did not half like the orders he received.

"No words about it, sir, but cut his fastenings—" Jaap had tied the Indian's arms behind him, with a rope, as an easy mode of leading him along. "Do you know the man's name?"

"Yes, sah—he say he name be Muss—" probably Jaap's defective manner of repeating some Indian sound, "and a proper muss he get in, Masser Corny, when he try to cotch Jaap by he wool!"

Here, I was obliged to clap my hand suddenly on the black's mouth, for the fellow was so delighted with the recollection of the manner in which he had got the better of his red adversary, that he broke out into one of the uncontrollable fits of noisy laughter, that are so common to his race. I repeated the order, somewhat sternly, for Jaap to cut the cords, and then to follow us to the canoe, in which the Onondago and my two friends had already taken their places. My own foot was raised to enter the canoe, when I heard heavy stripes inflicted on the back of some one. Rushing back to the spot where I had left Jaap and his captive, Muss, I found the former inflicting a severe punishment on the naked back of the other, with the end of the cord that still bound his arms. Muss, as Jaap called him, neither flinched nor cried.

The pine stands not more erect, or unyielding, in a summer's noontide, than he bore up under the pain. Indignantly, I thrust the negro away, cut the fellow's bonds with my own hands, and drove my slave before me to the canoe.

Chapter XXIV

"Pale set the sun—the shades of evening fell,
The mournful night-wind sung their funeral knell;
And the same day beheld their warriors dead,
Their sovereign captive, and their glory fled!"
                Felicia Hemans, "England and Spain," ll. 453–456.

I shall never forget the journey of that fearful night. Susquesus paddled the canoe, unaided by us, who were too much fatigued with the toil of the day, to labor much as soon as we found ourselves in a place of safety. Even Jaap lay down and slept for several hours, the sleep of the weary. I do not think any of us three, however, actually slept for the first hour or two, the scenes through which we had just passed, and that indeed through which we were then passing, acting as preventives to such an indulgence.

It must have been about nine in the evening, when our canoe quitted the ill-fated shore, at the southern end of Lake George, moving steadily and silently along the eastern margin of the sheet. By that time, fully five hundred boats had departed for the head of the lake, the retreat having commenced long before sunset. No order was observed in this melancholy procession, each batteau moving off, as her load was completed. All the wounded were on the placid bosom of the 'Holy Lake,' as some writers have termed this sheet of limpid water, by the time we ourselves got in motion, and the sounds of parting boats told us that the unhurt were following as fast as circumstances would allow.

What a night it was! There was no moon, and a veil of dark vapor was drawn across the vault of the heavens, concealing most of the mild summer stars, that ought to have been seen, twinkling in their creator's praise. Down, between the boundaries of hills, there was not a breath of air, though we occasionally heard the sighings of light currents among the tree-tops, above us. The eastern shore having fewer sinuosities than the western, most of the boats followed its dark, frowning mass, as the nearest route, and we soon found ourselves near the line of the retiring batteaux. I call it the line, for, though there was no order observed, each party making the best of its way to the common point of destination, there were so many boats in motion at the same time, that, far as the eye could penetrate by that gloomy light, an unbroken succession of them was visible. Our motion was faster than that of these heavily laden and feebly rowed batteaux, the soldiers being too much fatigued to toil at the oars, after the day they had just gone through. We consequently passed nearly every thing, and soon got on a parallel course with that of the boats, moving along at a few rods inshore of them. Dirck remarked however, that two or three small craft, even passed us. They went so near the mountain, quite within its shadows in fact, as to render it difficult to say what they were, though it was supposed they might be whale-boats, of which there were more than a hundred in the flotilla, carrying officers of rank.

No one spoke. It appeared to me that not a human voice was raised among those humiliated and defeated thousands. The plash of oars, so long as we were at a distance from the line, alone broke the silence of night, but that was incessant. As our canoe drew ahead, however, an hour or two after we had left the shore, and we overtook the boats that had first started, the moaning and groans of the wounded, became blended with the monotonous sounds of the oars. In two respects, these unfortunate men had reason to felicitate themselves, notwithstanding their sufferings. No army could have transported its wounded with less pain to the hurt, and the feverish thirst that loss of blood always induces, might be assuaged by the limpid element on which we all floated.

After paddling for hours, Susquesus was relieved by Jaap, Dirck, Guert and myself occasionally lending our aid. Each had a paddle, and each used it as he saw fit, while the Onondago slept. Occasionally I caught a nap, myself, as did my companions, and we all felt refreshed by the rest and sleep. At length we reached the narrow pass, that separated the Upper from the Lower Lake, and we entered the former. This is near the place where the islands are so numerous, and we were unavoidably made to pass quite close to some of the batteaux. I say to some, for the line became broken at this point, each boat going through the openings it found the most convenient.

"Come nearer with that bark canoe," called out an officer, from a batteau—"I wish to learn who is in it."

"We are volunteers, that joined the ————th, the day the army moved up, and were guests of Major Bulstrode. Pray sir, can you tell us where that officer can be found?"

"Poor Bulstrode! He got a very awkward hit, early in the day and was taken past me to the rear. He will be able neither to walk, nor to ride, for some months, if they save his leg. I heard the Commander in Chief order him to be sent across the lake, in the first boat with wounded, and some one told me, Bulstrode, himself, expressed an intention to be carried some distance, to a friend's house, to escape from the abominations of an army hospital. The fellow has horses enough to transport him, on a horse-litter, to Cape Horn, if he wishes it. I'll warrant you, Bulstrode works his way into good quarters, if they are to be had in America. I suppose this arm of mine will have to come off, as soon as we reach Fort William Henry, and that job done, I confess I should like amazingly to keep him company. Proceed gentlemen; I hope I have not detained you, but observing a bark canoe, I thought it my duty to ascertain we were not followed by spies."

This, then, was another victim of war! He spoke of the loss of his arm, notwithstanding, with as much coolness as if it were the loss of a tooth, yet, I question not, that in secret, he mourned over the calamity, in bitterness of heart. Men never wear the mask more completely than when excited and stimulated by the rivalry of arms. Bulstrode, too, at Ravensnest! He could be carried nowhere else, so easily, and, should his wound be of a nature that did not require constant medical treatment, where could he be so happily bestowed, as under the roof of Herman Mordaunt? Shall I confess that the idea gave me great pain, and that I was fool enough to wish I, too, could return to Anneke, and appeal to her sympathies, by dragging with me a wounded limb!

Our canoe now passed quite near another batteau, the officer in command of which, was standing erect, seemingly watching our movements. He appeared to be unhurt, but was probably entrusted with some special duty. As we paddled by, the following curious conversation occurred.

"You move rapidly to the rear, my friends," observed the stranger; "pray moderate your zeal; others are in advance of you with the evil tidings!"

"You must think ill of our patriotism and loyalty, sir, to imagine we are hastening on with the intelligence of a check to the British arms," I answered as drily, and almost as equivocally in manner, as the other had spoken.

"The check!—I beg a thousand pardons—I see you *are* patriots and of the purest water! Check is just the word, though check-*mate* would be more descriptive and significant! A charming time we've had of it, gentlemen! What say you; it is your move now."

"There has been much firmness and gallantry manifested by the troops," I answered, "as we, who have been merely volunteers, will always be ready to testify."

"I beg your pardons, again and again," returned the officer, raising his hat and bowing profoundly—"I did not know I had the honour to address volunteers. You are entitled to superlative respect, gentlemen, having come voluntarily into such a field. For my part, I find the honour oppressive, having no such supererogatory virtue to boast of. Volunteers! On my word, gentlemen, you will have many wonders to relate, when you get back into the family circle."

"We shall have to speak of the gallantry of the Highlanders, for we saw all they did, and all they suffered."

"Ah! Were you then near that brave corps!" exclaimed the other, with something like honest, natural feeling, for the first time exhibited in his voice and manner; "I honour men who were only *spectators* of so much courage, especially if they took a tolerably *near* view of it. May I venture to ask your names, gentlemen."

I answered, giving him our names, and mentioning the fact that we had been the guests of Bulstrode, and how much we were disappointed in having missed not only our friend, but his corps.

"Gentlemen, I honour courage, let it come whence it may," said the stranger, with strong feeling and no acting: "and most admire it when I see it exhibited by natives of these colonies in a quarrel of their own. I have heard of you, as being with poor Howe, when he fell, and hope to know more of you. As for Mr. Bulstrode, he has passed southward now, some hours, and intends to make his cure among some connections that he has in this province. Do not let this be the last of our intercourse, I beg of you, but look up Capt. Charles Lee, of the ———th, who will be glad to take each and all of you by the hand, when we once more get into camp."

We expressed our thanks, but Susquesus, causing the canoe to make a sudden inclination towards the shore, the conversation was suddenly interrupted.

By this time the Indian was awake, and exercising his authority in the canoe, again. Gliding among the islands, he shortly landed us at the precise point where we had embarked only five days before. Securing his little bark, the Onondago led the way up the ravine, and brought us out on the naked cap of the mountain, where we had before slept, after an hour of extreme effort.

If the night had been so memorable, the picture presented at the dawn of day, was not less so! We reached that lofty look-out, about the same time in the morning, as the Indian had awakened me on the previous occasion, and had the same natural outlines to the view. In one sense, also, the artificial accessories were the same, though exhibited under a very different aspect. I presume the truth will not be much, if any exceeded, when I say that a thousand boats were in sight, on this, as on the former occasion! A few, a dozen or so at most, appeared to have reached the head of the lake, but all the rest of that vast flotilla was scattered along the placid surface of the lovely sheet, forming a long, straggling line of dark spots, that extended to the beach under Fort William Henry, in one direction, and far as eye could reach, in the other. How different did that melancholy, broken, procession of boats appear, from the gallant array, the martial bands, the cheerful troops, and the multitude of ardent young men who had pressed forward, in brigades, less than a week before, filled with hope, and exulting in their strength! As I gazed on the picture, I could not but fancy to myself the vast amount of physical pain, the keen mental suffering, and the deep mortification that might have been found, amid that horde of returning adventurers. We had just come up from the level of this scene of human agony, and our imaginations could portray details that were beyond the reach of the senses, at the elevation on which we stood.

A week before, and the name of Abercrombie filled every mouth in America. Expectation had almost placed his renown on that giddy height, where performance itself is so often insecure. In the brief interval, he was destroyed. Those who had been ready to bless him, would now heap curses on his devoted head, and none would be so bold as to urge aught in his favour. Men in masses, when goaded by disappointment, are never just. It is indeed, a hard lesson for the individual to acquire; but, released from his close personal responsibility, the single man follows the crowd, and soothes his own mortification and wounded pride, by joining in the cry that is to immolate a victim. Yet, Abercrombie was not the fool-hardy and besotted bully that Braddock had proved himself to be. His misfortune was to be ignorant of the warfare of the region in which he was required to serve, and possibly to over-estimate the imaginary invincible character of the veterans he led. In a very short time he was recalled, and America heard no more of him. As some relief to the disgrace that had anew alighted on the British arms, Bradstreet, a soldier who knew the country, and who placed much reliance on the young man of her name and family, whom I had met at Madam Schuyler's, marched against Frontenac, in Canada, at the head of a strong body of provincials; an enterprise that, as it was conducted with skill, resulted in a triumph.

But with all this, my narrative has no proper connection. No sooner did we reach the bald mountain-top, than the Onondago directed Jaap to light a fire, while he produced from a deposit left on the advance, certain of the materials that were necessary to a meal. As neither of us had tasted food since the morning of the previous day, this repast was welcome, and we all partook of it, like so many famished men. The negro got his share of course, and then we called a council, as to future proceedings.

"The question is whether we ought to make a straight path to Ravensnest," observed Guert, "or proceed first to the surveyors, and see how things are going on in that direction."

"As there can be no great danger of a pursuit on the part of the French, since all their boats are in the other lake," I remarked, "the state of the country is very much what it was, before the army moved."

"Ask that question of the Indian—" put in Dirck, a little significantly.

We looked at Susquesus inquiringly, for a look always sufficed to let him comprehend us, when a tolerably plain allusion had been previously made.

"Black-man do foolish t'ing," observed the Onondago.

"What I do, you red-skin devil?" demanded Jaap, who felt a sort of natural antipathy to all Indians, good, or bad; excellent or indifferent; a feeling that the Indians repaid to his race, by

contempt indifferently concealed. "What I do, red-devil ha?—
dat you dares tell Masser Corny *dat*?"

Susquesus manifested no resentment at this strong and somewhat rude appeal, but sat as motionless as if he had not heard it.
This vexed Jaap so much the more, and, my fellow being exceedingly pugnacious on all occasions that touched his pride, there
might have been immediate war between the two, had I not
raised a finger, at once effectually stilling the outbreak of Jacob
Satanstoe's wrath.

"You should not bring such a charge against my slave, Onondago," I said, "unless able to prove it."

"He beat red warrior like dog."

"What of dat!" growled Jaap, who was only half-quieted by my
sign. "Who ebber hear it hurt redskin to rope-end him?"

"Warrior back like squaw's. Blow hurt him. He never forget."

"Well, let him remember den," grinned the negro, showing his
ivory teeth from ear to ear. "Muss was *my* prisoner, and what *good*
he do me, if he let go widout punishment. I wish you tell Masser
Corny *dat*, instead of tellin' him nonsense. When he flog me, who
ebber hear me grumble?"

"You have not had half enough of it, Jaap, or your manners
would be better," I thought it necessary to put in, for the fellow
had never before manifested so quarrelsome a disposition in my
presence; most probably because I had never before seen him at
variance with an Indian. "Let me hear no more of this, or I shall
be obliged to pay off the arrears on the spot."

"A little hiding does a nigger good, sometimes," observed
Guert, significantly.

I observed that Dirck, who loved my very slave principally because he was mine, looked at the offender reprovingly, and by
these combined demonstrations, we succeeded in curbing the fellow's tongue.

"Well, Susquesus," I added—"we all listen, to hear what you
mean."

"Musquerusque chief—Huron chief—got very tender back;
never forget rope."

"You mean us to understand that my black's prisoner will be
apt to make some attempt to revenge himself for the flogging he
got from his captor?"

"Just so. Indian good memory—no forget friend—no forget enemy."

"But your Huron will be puzzled to find us, Onondago. He will suppose us with the army, and should he even venture to look for us there, you see he will be disappointed."

"Never know. Wood full of paths—Injin full of cunning. Why talk of Ravensnest?"

"Was the name of Ravensnest mentioned in the presence of that Huron?" I asked, more uneasy that such a trifle would probably have justified me in confessing.

"Ay, something was said about it, but not in a way the fellow could understand," answered Guert, carelessly. "Let him come on, if he has not had enough of us, yet."

This was not my manner of viewing the matter, however, for the mentioning of Ravensnest brought Anneke to my mind, surrounded by the horrors of an Indian's revenge.

"I will send you back to the Huron, Susquesus," I added, "if you can name to me the price that will purchase his forgiveness."

The Onondago looked at me meaningly, a moment, then bending forward, he passed the forefinger of his hand around the head of Jaap, along the line that is commonly made by the knife of the warrior, as he cuts away the trophy of success, from his victim. Jaap comprehended the meaning of this very significant gesture, as well as any of us, and the manner in which he clutched the wool, as if to keep the scalp in its place, set us all laughing. The negro did not partake of our mirth, but I saw that he regarded the Indian, much as the bull-dog shows his teeth, before he makes his spring. Another motion of my finger, however, quelled the rising. It was necessary to put an end to this, and Jaap was ordered to prepare our packs, in readiness for the expected march. Relieved from his presence, Susquesus was asked to be more explicit.

"You know Injin," the Onondago answered. "Now he t'ink red-coats driv' away and skeared, he go look for scalp. Love all sort scalp—old scalp, young scalp—man scalp, woman scalp—boy scalp, gal scalp—all get pay, all get honour. No difference to him."

"Ay!" exclaimed Guert, with a strong aspiration; such as escapes a man who feels strongly— "he is a devil incarnate when he once gets fairly on the scent of blood! So you expect these French

Injins will make an excursion in among the settlers, out here to the south-east of us?"

"Go to nearest—don't care where he be. Nearest your friend; won't like that, s'pose?"

"You are right enough, Onondago, in saying that. I shall not like it, nor will my companions here like it, and the first thing you will have to do, will be to guide us straight as the bird flies to the Ravensnest, the picketed house, you know, where we have left our sweethearts."

Susquesus understood all that was said, without any difficulty, in proof of which he smiled at this allusion to the precious character of the inmates of the house Guert told him to seek.

"Squaw pretty 'nough," he answered, complacently. "No wonder young man like him. But, can't go there, now. First find friends measure land. All Injin land, once!"

This last remark was made in a way I did not like, for the idea seemed to cross the Onondago's brain so suddenly, as to draw from him, this brief assertion in pure bitterness of spirit.

"I should be very sorry if it had not been, Susquesus," I observed myself, "since the title is all the better for its having been so, as our Indian deed will show. You know, of course, that my father, and his friend Col. Follock bought this land of the Mohawks, and paid them their own price for it."

"Red man nebber measure land so. He p'int with finger, break bush down, and say, 'there, take from that water to that water.'"

"All very true, my friend; but, as that sort of measurement will not answer to keep farms separate, we are obliged to survey the whole off into lots of smaller size. The Mohawks first gave my father and his friend, as much land as they could walk round in two suns, allowing them the night to rest in."

"*That* good deed!" exclaimed the Indian, with strong emphasis. "Leg can't cheat—pen great rogue."

"Well we have the benefit of both grants, for the proprietors actually walked around the estate, a party of Indians accompanying them, to see that all was fair. After that, the chiefs signed a deed in writing, that there might be no mistake, and then we got the King's grant."

"Who give King land, at all?—All land here red-man land; who give him to King?"

"Who made the Delawares women? The warriors of the Six Nations was it not, Susquesus?"

"Yes—my people help. Six Nation great warrior, and put petticoat on Delawares, so they can't go on war-path any more. What that to do with King's land?"

"Why, the King's warriors, you know, my friend, have taken possession of this country, just as the Six Nations took possession of the Delawares, before they made them women."

"What become of King's warrior, now?" demanded the Indian, quick as lightning. "Where he run away to? Where land Ticonderoga, now? Whose land t'other end lake, now?"

"Why, the King's troops have certainly met with a disaster, and, for the present, their rights are weakened, it must be admitted. But, another day may see all this changed, and the King will get his land, again. You will remember he has not sold Ticonderoga to the French, as the Mohawks sold Mooseridge to us, and that, you must admit, makes a great difference. A bargain is a bargain, Onondago."

"Yes, bargain, bargain—that good. Good for red-man, good for pale-face—no difference—what Mohawk sell, he no take back, but let pale face keep—but how come Mohawk and King sell, too? Bot' own land, eh?"

This was rather a puzzling question to answer to an Indian. We white people can very well understand that a humane government, which professes, on the principles recognised by civilized nations, to have jurisdiction over certain extensive territories that lie in the virgin forest, and which are used only, and that occasionally, by certain savage tribes as hunting grounds, should deem it right to satisfy those tribes, by purchase, before they parcelled out their lands for the purposes of civilized life; but, it would not be so easy to make an unsophisticated mind understand that there could be two owners to the same property. The transaction is simple enough to us, and it tells in favour of our habits, for we have the power to grant these lands without 'extinguishing the Indian title,' as it is termed, but it presents difficulties to the understandings of those who are not accustomed to see society surrounded by the multifarious interests of civilization. In point of fact, the Indian purchases give no other title under our laws, than the right to sue out, in council, a claim to acquire by the grant of the Crown, paying to the latter such a consideration, as, in its wisdom, it shall see fit to demand. Still, it was necessary to make some answer to the Onondago's question, lest he might carry away the mistaken notion that we did not justly own our possessions.

"Suppose you find a rifle to your fancy, Susquesus," I said, after reflecting a moment on the subject, "and you find two Indians who both claim to own it; now, if you pay each warrior his price, is your right to the title any the worse for having done so? Is it not rather better?"

The Indian was struck with this reply, which suited the character of his mind. Thrusting out his hand, he received mine and shook it cordially, as much as to say he was satisfied. Having disposed of this episode thus satisfactorily, we turned to the more interesting subject of our immediate movements.

"It would seem that the Onondago expects the French Indians will now strike at the settlements," I remarked to my companions, "and, that our friends at Ravensnest may need our aid; but, at the same time, he thinks we should first return to Mooseridge, and join the surveyors. Which mode of proceeding strikes you as the best, my friends?"

"Let us first hear the Injin's reasons for going after the surveyors," answered Guert. "If he has a sufficient reason for his plan, I am ready to follow it."

"Surveyor got scalp, as well as squaw;" said Susquesus, in his brief, meaning manner.

"That must settle the point!" exclaimed Guert. "I understand it all, now. The Onondago thinks the Mooseridge party may be cut off, as being alone and unsupported, and that we ought to apprise them of their danger."

"All perfectly just," I replied, "and it is what they, being our own people, have a right to expect from us. Still, Guert, I should think those surveyors might be safe where they are, in the bosom of the forest, for a year to come. Their business there cannot be known, and who is there to betray them?"

"See," said Susquesus, earnestly. "Kill deer, and leave him in the wood. Won't raven find carcass?"

"That may be true enough, but a raven has an instinct, given him by nature to furnish him with food. He flies high in the air, moreover, and can see farther than an Indian."

"Nuttin' see farther than Injin! Red man fly high, too. See from

salt lake to sweet water. Know ebbery t'ing in wood. Tell him nuttin' he don't know."

"You do not suppose, Susquesus, that the Huron warriors
could find our surveyors, at Mooseridge?"

"Why, no find him? Find Moose; why no find ridge, too? Find
Mooseridge, sartain find land-measurer."

"On the whole, Corny," Guert remarked, after musing a little,
"we may do well to follow the Injin's advice. I have heard of so
many misfortunes that have befallen people in the bush, from
having despised Indian counsels, that I own to a little superstition on the subject. Just look at what happened yesterday! Had
red-skin opinions been taken, Abercrombie might now have
been a conqueror, instead of a miserable, beaten man."

Susquesus raised a finger, and his dark countenance became
illumined by an expression that was more eloquent even than his
tongue.

"Why no open ear to red man!" he asked, with dignity. "Some
bird sing a song that good—some sing bad song, but all bird
know his own song. Mohawk warrior use to wood, and follow a
crooked war path, when he meet much enemy. Great Yengeese
chief think his warrior have two life, that he put him before can-
non and rifle, to stand up and be shot. No Injin do so foolish—
no—never!"

As this was too true to be controverted, the matter was not discussed, but having determined among ourselves to let the Onondago take us back on the path by which we had come, we announced our readiness to start as soon as it might suit his
convenience. Being sufficiently rested, Susquesus, who did every
thing on system, manifesting neither impatience nor laziness,
arose and quietly led the way. Our course was just the reverse of
that on which we had travelled when we left Mooseridge, and I
did not fail to observe that, so accurate was the knowledge of our
guide, we passed many of the same objects as we had previously
gone near. There was nothing like a track, with the exception of
occasional foot-prints left by ourselves, but it was evident the
Onondago paid not the least attention to these, possessing other
and more accessible clues to his course.

Guert marched next to the Indian, and I was third in the line.
How often, that busy day, did I gaze at my file-leader, in admiration of his figure and mien! Nature appeared to have intended

him for a soldier. Although so powerful, his frame was agile, a particular in which he differed from Dirck; who, although so young, already gave symptoms of heaviness at no distant day. Then Guert's carriage was as fine as his form. The head was held erect, the eye was intrepid in its glance, and the tread elastic though so firm. To the last hour, on that long and weary march, Guert leaped logs, sprang across hollows in the ground, and otherwise manifested that his iron sinews and hardened muscles still retained all their powers. As he moved in my front, I saw for the first time, that some of the fringe of his hunting-shirt had been cut away in the fight and that a musket ball had passed directly through his cap. I afterwards ascertained that Guert was aware of these escapes, but his nature was so manly, he did not think of mentioning them.

We made a single halt, as before, to dine, but little was said at this meal, and no change in our plan was proposed. This was the point where we ought to have diverged from the former course, did we intend to proceed first to Ravensnest; but, though all knew it, nothing was said on the subject.

"We shall carry unwelcome tidings to Mr. Traverse and his men," Guert observed, a minute or two before our halt was up, "for, I take it for granted, the news cannot have gone ahead of *us.*"

"We first," answered the Onondago. "Too soon for Huron, yet. T'ink so—nobody know."

"I wish, Corny," pursued the Albanian, "we had thought of saying a word to Doortje about this accursed expedition. There is no use in a man's being above his business, and he who puts himself in the way of fortune, might profit by, now and then, consulting a fortune-teller."

"Had we done so, and had all that has happened been foretold, do you suppose it would have made any change in the result?"

"Perhaps not, since we should have been the persons to relate what we had heard. But, Abercrombie, himself, need have had no scruples about visiting that remarkable old woman. She's a wonderful creature, Corny, as we must allow, and a prudent general would not fail to respect what she told him. It is a thousand pities that either the Commander in Chief, or the Adjutant General, had not paid Doortje a visit before they left Albany. My Lord Howe's valuable life might then have been saved."

"In what way, Guert? I am at a loss to see in what manner any good could come of it."

"In what manner?—Why in the plainest possible. Now, suppose Doortje had foretold this defeat; it is clear Abercrombie, if he put any faith in the old woman, would not have made the attack."

"And thus defeat the defeat. Do you not see, Guert, that the soothsayer can, at the best, but foretell what *is* to happen, and that which *must* come *will*. It would be an easy matter for any of us to get great reputations for fortune-telling, if, all we had to do was to predict misfortunes, in order that our friends might avoid them. As nothing would ever happen, in consequence of the precautions taken to avert the evils, a name would be easily and cheaply maintained."

"By St. Nicholas! Corny, I never thought of that! But, you have been college-taught, and a thousand things are picked up at colleges, that one never dreams of at an academy. I see reason, every day, to lament my idleness when a boy, and fortunate shall I be, if I do not lament it all my life."

Poor Guert! He was always so humble when the subject of education arose, however accidentally or unintentionally on my part, that it was never commented on, that it did not give me pain, exciting a wish to avoid it. As the time for the halt was now up, it was easy to terminate the present discussion by declaring as much, and proceeding on our way.

We had a hard afternoon's walk of it, though neither of the five manifested the least disposition to give in. As for Susquesus, to me he never seemed to know either fatigue or hunger. He was doubtless acquainted with both, but his habits of self-command were so severe, as to enable him completely to conceal his sufferings, in this, as well as in most other respects.

The sun was near setting when we entered within the limits of the Mooseridge estate. We ascertained this fact, by passing the line trees, some of which had figures cut into their barks, to denote the numbers of the great subdivisions of the property. Guert pointed out these marks, being far more accustomed to the woods than either Dirck, or myself. Aided by such guides, we had no difficulty in making a sufficiently straight course to the hut.

Susquesus thought a little caution necessary, as we drew near to the end of our journey. Causing us to remain behind, he advanced in front himself, to reconnoitre. A signal, however, soon took us to the place where he stood, when we discovered the hut just as we had left it, but no one near it. This might be the result of mere accident, the surveying party frequently 'camping out,' in preference to making a long march after a fatiguing day's work, and Pete would be very likely to prefer going to join these men to remaining alone in the hut. We advanced to the building, therefore, with confidence. On reaching it, we found the place empty, as had been anticipated, though with every sign about it, of its tenants having left it, but a short time previously; that morning at the furthest.

Jaap set about preparing a supper, out of the regular supplies of the party, all of which were found in their places and in abundance. On inquiry of the fellow, I ascertained it was his opinion Mr. Traverse had gone off that very day, most probably to some distant portion of the patent, taking Pete with him, as every thing was covered up, and put away with that sort of care that denotes an absence of some little time. The Indian heard the negro's remark, to this effect, and tossing his head significantly, he said—

"No need guess—go see—light enough—plenty time. Injin soon tell."

He quitted the hut, on the spot, and immediately set about this self-assigned duty.

Chapter XXV

"Thou tremblest; and the whiteness in thy cheek
Is apter than thy tongue to tell thy errand."
                                    2 Henry IV, I.i. 68–69.

Curiosity induced me to follow the Indian, in order to watch his movements. Susquesus proceeded a short distance from the hut, quitting the knoll entirely, until he reached lower land, where a foot-print would be most likely to be visible, when he commenced a slow circuit of the place, with eyes fastened on the earth, as the nose of the hound follows the scent. I was so much interested in the Onondago's manner as to join him, falling in, in his rear, in order not to interfere with his object.

Of foot-marks there were plenty, more particularly on the low moist ground, where we were, but they all appeared to me to have no interest with the Indian. Most of our party wore moccasins, and it was not easy to see how, under such circumstances and amid such a maze of impressions, it could be possible for any one to distinguish a hostile from a friendly trail. That Susquesus thought the thing might be done, however, was very evident by his perseverance, and his earnestness.

At first, my companion met with no success, or with nothing that he fancied success; but, after making half the circuit of the hut, keeping always a hundred yards distant from it, he suddenly stopped, stooped quite to the earth, then arose, and sticking a broken knot into the ground as a mark, he signed to me to keep a little on one side, while he turned at right angles to his former course, and moved inwards towards our dwelling. I followed slowly, watching his movements, step by step.

In this manner we reached the hut, deviating from a direct line, in order to do so. At the hut, itself, Susquesus made a long and minute examination, but even I could see that the marks here, were so numerous as to baffle even him. After finishing his search at this point, the Indian turned, and went back to the place where he had stuck the knot into the ground. In doing this, however, he followed his own trail, returning by precisely the same deviating course as that by which he had come. This, alone, would have satisfied me that he saw more than I did, for, to own the truth, I could not have done the same thing.

When we reached the knot, Susquesus followed that (to me invisible) trail outside of the circle, leading off into the forest, in a direct line from the hut and spring. I continued near him, although neither had spoken during the whole of this examination, which had now lasted quite half an hour. As it was getting dark, however, and Jaap showed the signal that our supper was ready, I thought it might be well at length to break the silence.

"What do you make of all this, Trackless?" I inquired. "Do you find any signs of a trail?"

"Good trail—" Susquesus answered; "new trail, too. Look like Huron!"

This was startling intelligence, certainly; yet, much as I was disposed to defer to my companion's intelligence in such matters, in general, I thought he must be mistaken in his fact. In the first place, though I had seen many foot-prints near the hut, and along the low land on which the Indian made his circuit, I could see none where we then were. I mentioned this to the Indian, and desired him to show me particularly, one of the signs which had led him to his conclusion.

"See," said Susquesus, stooping so low as to place a finger on the dead leaves that ever make a sort of carpet to the forest, "here been moccasin—that heel; this toe."

Aided in this manner, I could discover a faint foot-print which might, by aid of the imagination be thus read; though the very slight impression that was to be traced, might almost as well be supposed any thing else, as it seemed to me.

"I see what you mean, Susquesus, and I allow it *may* be a foot-print," I answered, "but, then, it may also have been left by any thing else, which has touched the ground just at that spot. It may have been made by a falling branch of a tree."

"Where branch?" asked the Indian, quick as lightning.

"Sure enough; that is more than I can tell you. But I cannot suppose *that* a Huron foot-print, without more evidence than you now give."

"What you call that?—this—that—t'other?" added the Indian stepping quickly back, and pointing to four other similar, but very faint impressions on the leaves. "No see him, eh?—Just leg apart, too!"

This was true enough, and, now my attention was thus directed and my senses were thus aided, I confess I did discover certain proofs of footsteps that would, otherwise, have baffled my most serious search.

"I can see what you mean, Susquesus," I said, "and will allow that this line of impressions, or marks, does make them look more like foot-steps. At any rate, most of our party wear moccasins, as well as the red-men, and how do you know that some of the surveyors have not passed this way?"

"Surveyor no make such mark. Toe turn in."

This was true, too. But it did not follow that a foot-print was a Huron's, merely because it was Indian. Then, where were the enemy's warriors to come from, in so short a time as had intervened between the late battle and the present moment? There was little question all the forces of the French, pale-face and red man, had been collected at Ticonderoga to meet the English, and the distance was so great as almost to render it impossible for a party to reach this spot so soon, coming from the vicinity of the fortress, after the occurrence of the late events. Did not the lake interpose an obstacle, I might have inferred that parties of skirmishers would be thrown on the flanks of the advancing army, thus bringing foes within a lessened distance of us; but, there was the lake, affording a safe approach for more than thirty miles, and rendering the employment of any such skirmishers useless. All this occurred to me at the moment, and I mentioned it to my companion, as an argument against his own supposition.

"No true," answered Susquesus, shaking his head. "That trail—he Huron trail, too. Don't know red man to say so."

"But red men are human, as well as pale-faces. It must be seventy miles from this spot to the foot of Lake George, and your conjecture would make it necessary that a party should have travelled that distance in less than twenty-four hours, and be here some time before us."

"We no travel him, eh?"

"I grant you that, Trackless, but we came a long bit of the road in a canoe, each and all of us sleeping, and resting ourselves, in turns. These Hurons must have come the whole distance by land."

"No so. Huron paddle canoe well as Onondago. Lake there— canoe plenty. Why not come?"

"Do you suppose, Trackless, that any of the French Indians would venture on the lake, while it was covered with our boats, as was the case last night?"

"What 'our boat' good for, eh? Carry wounded warrior—carry run-away warrior—what he care? T'ink Huron 'fraid of boat? Boat got eye, eh? Boat see; boat hear; boat shoot, eh?"

"Perhaps not; but those who were in the boats can do all this, and would be apt, at least, to speak to a strange canoe."

"Boat speak my canoe, eh? Onondago canoe, strange canoe, too."

All this was clear enough, when I began to reflect on it. It was certainly possible for a canoe, with two or three paddles, to go the whole length of the lake, in much less time than we had employed in going two-thirds of the distance, and a party, landing in the vicinity of William Henry, could certainly have reached the spot where we then were, several hours sooner than we had reached it, ourselves. Still, there existed all the other improbabilities on my side of the question. It was improbable that a party should have proceeded in precisely this manner; it was still more improbable that such a party, coming on a war-path, from a distant part of the country should know exactly where to find our hut. After a moment's pause, and while we both slowly proceeded to join our companions, I suggested these objections to the Onondago.

"Don't know Injin," answered the other, betraying more earnestness of manner, than was usual with him, when he condescended to discuss any of the usages of the tribes, with a paleface. "He fight, first; then he want scalp. Ever see dead horse in wood—well, no crow there, eh? Plenty crow, isn't he? Just so, Injin. Wounded soldier carry off, and Injin watch in wood, behind army, to get scalp. Scalp good, after battle. Want him, very much. Wood full of Huron, along path to Albany. Yengeese down in heart, Huron up. Scalp so good, t'ink of nuttin' else."

By this time we had reached the hut, where I found Guert and Dirck already at their suppers. I will own that my appetite was not as good as it might have been, but for the Onondago's conjectures and discoveries, though I took a seat, and began to eat with my friends. While at the meal I communicated to my companions all that had passed, particularly asking of Guert, who had a re-

spectable knowledge of the bush, what he thought of the probabilities of the case.

"If hostile red-skins have really been here, lately," the Albanian
answered, "they have been thoroughly cunning devils, for not an
article in, or about the hut, has been disturbed. I had an eye to
that myself, the moment we arrived; for I have thought it far
from unlikely that the Hurons would be out, on the road between
William Henry and the settlements, trying to get scalps from the
parties that would be likely to be sent to the rear with wounded
officers."

"In which case our friend Bulstrode might be in danger?"

"He must take his chance, like all of us. But, he will probably be
carried to Ravensnest, as the nearest nest for him to nestle in. I
don't half like this trail, however, Corny; it is seldom a red-skin of
the Onondago's character, makes a mistake in such a matter!"

"It is too late, now, to do any thing to-night," Dirck observed.
"Besides, I don't think any great calamity is likely to befall any of
us, or Doortje would have dropped some hint about it. These fortune-tellers seldom let any thing serious pass without a notice of
some sort or other. You see, Corny, we went through all this business at Ty, without a scratch, which is so much in favour of the old
woman's being right."

Poor Dirck! that prediction had made a deep impression on his
character, and on his future life. A man's faith must be strong, to
fancy that a negative of this nature, could carry with it any of the
force of a positive, affirmative prediction. Nevertheless, Dirck
had spoken the truth, in one respect. It was too late to do any
thing that night, and it only remained to prepare to take our rest
as securely as possible.

We consulted on the subject, calling on the Indian to aid us.
After talking the matter over it was determined to remain where
we were, securing the door, and bringing every body within the
building, for the negroes and the Indians had been much in the
habit of sleeping about, under brush covers that they had erected
for themselves. It was thought that, having once visited the hut,
and finding it empty, the enemy, if enemy there were, would not
be very likely to return to it immediately, and that we might consider ourselves as comparatively safe, from that circumstance
alone. Then, there were all the chances that the trail might have
been left by friendly, instead of hostile Indians, although Sus-

quesus shook his head in the negative, whenever this was mentioned. At all events, we had but a choice of three expedients—to abandon the Patent, and seek safety in flight; to 'camp out;' or to shut ourselves up in our fortress. Of the first, no one thought for a moment, and of the two others, we decided on the last, as far the most comfortable, and, on the whole, as the safest.

An hour after we had come to this determination, I question if either of the five knew any thing about it. I never slept more profoundly in my life, and my companions subsequently gave the same account of their several conditions. Fatigue, and youth, and health gave us all refreshing sleep, and, as we lay down at nine, two o'clock came after so much time totally lost in the way of consciousness. I say two o'clock, for my watch told me that was just the hour, when the Indian awoke me, by shaking my shoulder. One gets the habits of watchfulness in the woods, and I was on my feet in an instant.

Dark as it was, for it was deep night, I could distinguish that Susquesus was alone stirring, and that he had unbarred the door of our cabin. Indeed, he passed through that open space, into the air of the forest, the moment he perceived I was conscious of what I was about. Without pausing to reflect, I followed, and soon stood at his side, some fifteen or twenty feet from the hut.

"This good place to hear," said the Indian, in a low suppressed tone. "Now, open ear."

What a scene was that, which now presented itself to my senses! I can see it, at this distance of time, after years of peaceful happiness, and years of toil and adventure. The morning, or it might be better to say the night, was not very dark in itself, but the gloom of the woods being added to the obscurity of the hour, it lent an intensity of blackness to the trunks of the trees, that gave to each a funereal and solemn aspect. It was impossible to see for any distance, and the objects that were visible were only those that were nearest at hand. Notwithstanding, one might imagine the canopied space beneath the tops of the trees, and fancy it, in the majesty of its gloomy vastness. Of sounds there were literally none, when the Indian first bade me listen. The stillness was so profound, that I thought I heard the sighing of the night air among the upper branches of the loftier trees. This might have been mere imagination; nevertheless, all above the summits of the giant oaks, maples and pines, formed a sort of upper world as regarded us; a world with which we had little communication, during our sojourn in the woods below. The raven, and the eagle, and the hawk, sailed in that region, above the clouds of leaves beneath them, and occasionally stooped, perhaps, to strike their quarry; but to all else, it was inaccessible, and to a degree invisible.

But, my present concern is with the world I was in; and, what a world it was! Solemn, silent, dark, vast and mysterious. I listened in vain, to catch the footstep of some busy squirrel, for the forest was alive with the smaller animals, by night quite as much as by day, but every thing, at that moment, seemed stilled to the silence of death.

"I can hear nothing, Trackless," I whispered—"Why are you out here?"

"You hear, soon—wake me up, and I hear twice. Soon come ag'in."

It did soon come again. It was a human cry, escaping from human lips in their agony! I heard it once only, but, should I live to be a hundred, it would not be forgotten. I often hear it in my sleep, and twenty times have I awoke since, fancying that agonizing call was in my ears. It was long, loud, piercing, and the word 'help' was as distinct as tongue could make it.

"Great God!" I exclaimed—"Some one is set upon, and calls for aid in his extremity. Let us arouse our friends, and go to his assistance. I cannot remain here, Susquesus, with such a cry in my ears."

"Best go, t'ink too," answered the Onondago. "No need call, though; two better than four. Stop minute."

I did remain stationary that brief space, listening with agonized uncertainty, while the Indian entered the hut, and returned, bringing out his rifle and my own. Arming ourselves, and shutting the door of the cabin, to exclude the night air, at least, Susquesus led off, with his noiseless step, in a south-west direction, or that in which we had heard the sound.

Our march was too swift and earnest to admit of discourse. The Onondago had admonished me to make as little noise as possible, and between the anxiety I felt, and the care taken to comply, there was, indeed, but little opportunity for conversing. My feelings were wrought up to a high pitch, but my confidence in my companion being great, I followed in his footsteps, as diligently as my skill would allow. Susquesus rather trod on air than walked, yet I kept close at his heels, until we had gone, as I should think, fully half a mile in the direction from which that awful cry had come. Here Susquesus halted, saying to me, in a low voice—

"No far from here—best stop."

I submitted in all things to the directions of my Indian guide. The latter had selected the dark shadows of two or three young pines for our cover, where, by getting within their low branches, we were completely concealed from any eye that was distant from us eight or ten feet. No sooner were we thus posted, than the Onondago pointed to the trunk of a fallen tree, and we took our seats, silently, on it. I observed that my companion kept his thumb on the cock of his rifle, while his fore-finger was passed around the trigger. It is scarcely necessary to say that I observed the same precaution.

"This good—" said Susquesus, in a voice so low and soft that it could not attract more attention than a whisper—"This very good—hear him ag'in, soon; then know."

A stifled groan *was* heard, and that almost as soon as my companion ceased to speak. I felt my blood curdle at these frightful evidences of human suffering, and an impulse of humanity caused me to move, as if about to rise. The hand of Trackless checked the imprudence.

"No good," he said, sternly. "Sit still. Warrior know how to sit still."

"But, Heavenly Providence! There is some one in agony, quite near us, man. Did you not hear a groan, Trackless?"

"To be sure, hear him.—What of that? Pain make groan come, alway, from pale-face."

"You think, then, it is a white man who suffers; if so, it must be one of our own party, as there is no one else near us. If I hear it again, I must go to his relief, Onondago."

"Why you behave like squaw? What of little groan? Sartain he pale-face; Injin never groan on war-path. Why he groan, you t'ink? Cause Huron meet him. That reason he groan. You groan too, no sit still. Injin know time to shoot—know time not to shoot."

I had every disposition to call aloud, to enquire who needed succour, yet the admonitions of my companion, aided as they were by the gloomy mysteries of that vast forest, in the hour of deepest night, enabled me to command the impulse. Three times, notwithstanding, was that groan repeated, and, as it appeared to me, each time more and more faintly. I thought, too, when all was still in the forest—when we sat ourselves in breathless expectation of what might next reach our ears— attentive to each sighing of the night air, and distrustful even of the rustling leaf—that the last groan of all, though certainly the faintest of any we had heard, was much the nearest. Once, indeed, I heard, or fancied I heard, the word 'water,' murmured in a low, smothered tone almost in my ear. I thought, too, I knew the voice; that it was familiar to me, though I could not decide, in the state of my feelings, exactly to whom it belonged.

In this manner we passed what, to me, were two of the most painful hours of my life, waiting the slow return of light. My own impatience was nearly ungovernable, though the Indian sat the whole of that time seemingly as insensible as the log which formed his seat, and almost as motionless. At length this intensely anxious and even physically painful watch drew near its end. Signs of day gleamed through the canopy of leaves, and the rays of dull light appeared to struggle downward, rendering objects dimly discernible.

It was not long ere we could ascertain that we had so completely covered ourselves, as to be in a position where the branches of the pines completely shut out the view of objects beyond. This was favorable to reconnoitring, however, previously to quitting our concealment, and enabled us to have some care of ourselves, while attending to the duties of humanity.

Susquesus used the greatest caution in looking around before he left the cover. I was close at his side, peeping through such openings as offered, for my curiosity was so intense that I almost forgot the causes for apprehension. It was not long before I heard the familiar Indian interjection "hugh!" from my companion; a proof that something had caught his eye of a more than ordinarily exciting character. He pointed in the way I was to look, and there, indeed, I beheld one of those frightful instances of barbarous cruelty, that the usages of savage warfare have sanctioned, as far back as our histories extend, among the forest warriors of this continent. The tops of two saplings had been brought down near each other, by main force, the victim's hands attached firmly to upper branches of each, and the trees permitted to fly back to their natural positions; or as near them as the revolting means of junction would allow. I could scarce believe my senses, when my sight first revealed the truth. But, there hung the victim, suspended by his arms, at an elevation of at least ten or fifteen feet from the earth. I confess I sincerely hoped he was dead, and the motionless attitude of the body gave me reason to think it might be so. Still, the cries for "help," uttered wildly, hopelessly, in the midst of a vast and vacant forest, the groans extorted by suffering, must have been his. He had probably been thus suspended and abandoned, while alive!

Even the Onondago could not restrain me, after I fully saw and understood the nature of the cruelty which had been exercised on the miserable victim who was thus suspended directly before my eyes, and I broke out of the cover, ready, I am willing to confess, to pull trigger on the first hostile red-man I saw. Fortunately for myself, most probably, the place had long been deserted. As the back of the sufferer was towards me, I could not tell who he was, but his dress was coarse and of the description that belongs to the lowest class. Blood had flowed freely from his head, and I made no doubt he had been scalped, though the height at which he hung, and the manner in which his head had fallen forward upon his breast, prevented me from ascertaining the fact, at once, by the aid of sight. Thus much did I perceive, however, ere the Indian joined me.

"See!" said Susquesus, whose quick eye never let any thing escape it long. "Told you so. Huron been here."

As this was said, the Indian pointed significantly at the naked skin which was visible between the heavy coarse shoes of the victim and the trowsers he wore, when I discovered it was black. Moving quickly in front, so as to get a view of the face, I recognised the distorted features of Petrus, or Pete, Guert Ten Eyck's negro. This man had been left with the surveyors, it will be remembered, and he had either fallen into the hands of his captors, while at the hut engaged in his ordinary duties, or he had been met in the forest, while going to, or coming from those he served, and had thus been treated. We never ascertained the facts, which remain in doubt to this hour.

"Give me your tomahawk, Trackless," I cried, as soon as horror would permit me to speak, "that I may cut down this sapling, and liberate the unfortunate creature."

"No good—better so," answered the Indian. "Bear—wolf can't get him now. Let black-skin hang—good as bury—no safe stay here long. Look round and count Huron—then go."

"Look round and count the Hurons," I thought to myself, "and in what manner is this to be done?" By this time, however, it was sufficiently light to see foot-prints, if any there were, and the Onondago set about examining such traces of what had passed at that terrible spot, as might be intelligible to one of his experience.

At the foot of a huge oak, that grew a few yards from the fatal saplings, we found the two wooden, covered pails, in which we knew Pete had been accustomed to carry food to Mr. Traverse and the chain-bearers. They were empty, but whether the provisions they unquestionably had contained fell to the share of those for whom they were intended, or to that of the captors, we never learned. No traces of bones, potato skins, or other fragments were discovered, and if the Hurons had seized the provisions they doubtless transferred them to their own repositories, without stopping to eat. Susquesus detected proof that the victim had been seated, at the foot of the oak, and that he had been seized at that spot. There were the marks of many feet there, and some proofs of a slight scuffle. Blood, too, was to be traced on the leaves, from the foot of the oak, to the place where poor Pete was suspended, a proof that he had been hurt, previously to being abandoned to his cruel fate.

But the point of most interest with Trackless, was to ascertain the number of our foes. This might be done, in some measure, according to his view of the matter, by means of the foot-prints. There was no want of such signs, the leaves being much disturbed in places, though after a short but anxious search, my companion thought it wisest to repair to the hut, lest those it contained might be surprised in their sleep. He gave me to understand that the enemy did not appear to be numerous at that spot, three or four at most, though it was quite possible, nay highly probable, that they had separated, and that their whole force was not present at this miserable scene.

It was broad daylight when we came in sight of the hut again, and I perceived Jaap was up and busy with his pots and kettles near the spring. No one else was visible, and we inferred that Guert and Dirck were still on their pallets. We took a long and distrustful survey of the forest around the cabin, from the height where we stood, ere we ventured to approach it any nearer. Discovering no signs of danger, and the forest being quite clear of underbrush or cover of any sort, large trees excepted, for some distance from the hut, we then advanced without apprehension. This open character of the woods near our dwelling was felt to be a very favourable circumstance, rendering it impossible for an enemy to get very near us by day-light, without being seen. It was owing to the fact that we had used so much of the smaller timber, in our own operations, while the negroes had burned most of the underbrush for fuel.

Sure enough, I found my two friends fast asleep, and certainly much exposed. When aroused and told all that had occurred to me and the Indian, their surprise was great, nor was their horror less. Jaap, who, missing us on rising, supposed we had gone in pursuit of game, had followed us into the hut, and heard my communications. His indignation was great, at the idea of one of his own colour's being thus treated, and I heard him vowing vengeance between his set teeth, in terms that were by no means measured.

"By St. Nicholas!" exclaimed Guert, who had now finished dressing, and who accompanied me out into the open air, "my poor fellow shall be revenged, if the rifle will do it! Scalped, too, do you say, Corny?"

"As far as we could ascertain, suspended as he was from the tree. But, scalped he must be, as an Indian never permits a dead captive to escape this mutilation."

"And you have been out in the forest, three hours, you tell me, Corny?—You and Trackless?"

"About that time, I should judge. The heart must have been of stone, that could resist those cries!"

"I do not blame you, Littlepage, though it would have been kinder, and wiser, had you taken your friends with you. We must stick together, in future, let what may happen. Poor Petrus! I wonder Doortje should have hinted nothing of that nigger's fate!"

We then held a long consultation on the subject of our mode of proceeding, next. It is unnecessary to dwell on this conference, as its conclusions will be seen in the events of the narrative, but it was brought to a close by a very sudden interruption, and that was the sound of an axe in the forest. The blows came in the direction of the scene of Pete's murder, and we had collected our rifles, and were preparing to move towards the suspected point, when we saw Jaap staggering along, coming to the hut, beneath the load of his friend's body. The fellow had stolen away unseen, on this pious duty, and had executed it with success. In a minute or two he reached the spring, and began to wash away the revolting remains of the massacre from the head of the Huron's victim.

We now ascertained that poor Pete had been badly cut by knives, as well as scalped, and suspended in the manner related. Both arms appeared to be dislocated, and the only relief to our feelings, was in the hope that an attempt to inflict so much suffering must have soon defeated itself. Guert, in particular, expressed his hope that such was the case, though the awful sounds of the past night were still too fresh in my ears, to enable me to believe all I could wish on that subject. A grave was dug, and we buried the body at once, rolling a large log or two, on the spot, in order to prevent wild beasts from disinterring it. Jaap worked hard, in the performance of these rites, and Guert Ten Eyck actually repeated the Lord's Prayer and the Creed over the grave, when the body was placed in it, with a fervour and earnestness that a little surprised me.

"He was but a nigger, Corny, it is true," said the Albanian, a little apologetically perhaps, after all was over, "but he was a very goot nigger, in the first place; then, he had a soul, as well as a white man. Pete had his merits, as well as a Tominie, and I trust they will not be forgotten in the last great account. He was an excellent cook, as you must have seen, and I never knew a nigger that had more of the dog-like fidelity to his master. The fellow never got into a frolick without coming honestly to ask leave, though, to be sure, I was not a hart master, in these particulars, on reasonable occasions."

We next ate our breakfasts, with as much appetite as we could. Shouldering our packs, and placing all around, and in the hut, as much as possible, in the condition in which we had found the place, we then commenced our march, Susquesus leading, as usual.

We went in quest of the surveyors, who were supposed to be in the south-east corner of the patent, employed as usual, and ignorant of all that had passed. At first, we had thought of discharging our rifles, as signals to bring them in; but these signals might apprize our enemies, as well as our friends, of our presence, and the distance was too great, moreover, to render it probable the reports could be heard by those for whom alone they would be intended.

The route we took was determined by our general knowledge of the quarter of the patent in which the surveyors ought now to be, as well as by the direction in which the body of Pete had been found. The poor fellow was certainly either going to, or coming from the party, and being in constant communication with them, he doubtless knew where they were at work. Then the different trails of the surveyors, were easily enough found by Trackless, and he told us that the most recent led off in the direction I have named. Towards the south-east, therefore, we held our way, marching as before, in Indian file, the Onondago leading, and the negro bringing up the rear.

Chapter XXVI

" 'Tis too horrible!
The weariest and most loathed worldly life
That age, ache, penury, and imprisonment
Can lay on nature, is a paradise,
To what we fear of death."

Measure for Measure, III.i. 127–131.

WE were not long in reaching the point of the patent in which the surveyors had been at work; after which, we could have but little difficulty in finding their present actual position. The marked trees were guides that told the whole story of their labours. For an hour and a half, however, we moved rapidly forward, Susquesus on the lead, silent, earnest, watchful, and I fear I must add, revengeful. Not a syllable had been uttered during the whole of that time, though our senses were keenly on the alert, and we avoided every thing like a cover that might conceal an ambush. Suddenly the Indian halted; at the next instant, he was behind a tree. Each of us imitated him, quick as thought, for this was our previous training in the event of encountering an enemy, and we all well knew the importance of a cover, in forest warfare. Still, no foe could be seen. After examining around us, in every direction, for a minute or two, and finding the woods vacant and silent as ever, Guert and I quitted our own trees, and joined the Trackless, at the foot of his own huge pine.

"Why this, Susquesus?" demanded the Albanian, sharply; for he began to suspect a little acting, got up to magnify the Indian's usefulness; "here is neither pale-face, nor red-skin. Have done with this folly, and let us go forward."

"No good—warrior been here; p'rhaps gone, p'rhaps no. Soon see. Open eye, and look."

As a gesture accompanied this speech we did look, again, and this time in the right direction. At the distance of a hundred yards from us, was a chestnut that might be seen from its roots to its branches. On the ground, partly concealed by the tree and partly exposed, was the leg of a man, placed as the limb would be apt to lie, on the supposition that its owner lay on his back, asleep. It showed a moccasin, and the usual legging of an Indian, but the thigh and all the rest of the frame was concealed. The quick eye of the Onondago had caught this small object, even at that distance, comprehended it at a glance, when he instantly sought a cover, as described. Guert and I had some difficulty at first, even after it was pointed out to us, in recognizing this object; but it soon became distinct and intelligible.

"Is that a red-skin's leg?" asked Guert, dropping the muzzle of his rifle, as if about to try his skill on it.

"Don't know—" answered the Indian— "got leggin', got moccasin; can't see colour. Look pale face most. Leg big."

What there was to enable one, at that distance, to distinguish between the leg of a white man and the leg of an Indian, at first greatly exceeded our means of conjecturing, but the Onondago explained it, when asked, in his own, usual, sententious manner, by saying—

"Toe turn out—Injin, turn in—no like, at all. Pale face big; Injin no very big."

The first was true enough in walking, and it did seem probable that the difference might exist in sleep. Guert now declared there was no use in hesitating any longer; if asleep, he would approach the chestnut cautiously, and capture the stranger, if an Indian, before he could rise; and if a white man, it must be some one belonging to our own set, who was taking a nap, probably after a fatiguing march. Susquesus must have satisfied himself, by this time, that there was no immediate danger, for merely saying "all go together," he quitted the cover, and led down towards the chestnut with a rapid, but noiseless step. As we moved in a body, all five of us reached the tree at the same instant, where we found Sam, one of our own hunters, and whom we supposed to be with Mr. Traverse, stretched on his back, dead; with a wound in his breast that had been inflicted by a knife. He, too, had been scalped!

The looks we exchanged, said all that could be said on the subject of the gravity of this new discovery. Susquesus alone was undisturbed; I rather think he expected what he found. After examining the body, he seemed satisfied, simply saying "kill, last night."

That poor Sam had been dead several hours was pretty cer-

tain, and the circumstance removed all apprehension of any immediate danger from his destroyers. The ruthless warriors of the
woods seldom remained long near the spot they had desolated,
but passed on, like the tornado, or the tempest. Guert, who was
ever prompt when any thing was to be done, pointed to a natural
hollow in the earth, one of those cavities that are so common in
the forest, and which are usually attributed to the upturnings of
trees in remote ages, and suggested that we should use it as a
grave. The body was accordingly laid in the hole, and we covered
it, in the best manner we could; succeeding in placing over it
something like a foot deep of light loam, together with several
flat stones; rolling logs on all, as we had done at the grave of Pete.
By this time, Guert's feelings were so thoroughly aroused, that, in
addition to the prayer and the creed, which he again repeated in
a very decorous and devout manner, he concluded the whole
ceremony, by a brief address. Nor was Guert any thing but serious
in what he did, or said, on either of these solemn occasions; his
words, like his acts, being purely the impulses of a simple mind,
which possessed longings after devotion and scriptural truths,
without knowing exactly how to express them; and this, moreover, in spite of the mere animal propensities, and gay habits of
his physical conformation and constitutional tendencies.

"Deat', my frients," said Guert, most seriously, becoming
Dutch, as usual, as he became interested— "Deat' is a sutten visitor.
He comes like a t'ief in the night, as you must all have often he'rt
the Tominie say, and happy is he whose loins are girtet, and
whose lamp is trimmed. Such I trust, is the case with each of you,
for, it is not to be concealet, that we are likely to have serious work
before us. Here have been Injins, beyont a question; and they are
Injins, too, that are out on the war path, in search of English
scalps; or, what is of equal importance to Mr. Follock and myself,
Dutch scalps in the pargain; which makes it so much the more
necessary for every man to be on his guart, and to stant up to
his work, when it may come, as the pull tog stants up to the ox.
Got forpit, t'at I should preach revenge over t'e grave of a frient,
but t'e soltier fights none the worse for knowing t'at he has peen
injuret in his feelin's as has certainly peen the case with ourselves.
Perhaps, I ought to say a wort in behalf of the teat, as this is the last,
and only time, that a fellow creature will ever have occasion to
speak of him. Sam was an excellent hunter, as his worst enemy

must allow; and now he is gone, few petter remain pehint. He had one weakness, which, stanting over his grave, an honest man ought not to try to conceal; he dit love liquor; put, in this, he was not alone. Nevertheless, he was honest, and his wort might pass where many a man's pont would be wort'less, and I leave him in the merciful hants of his Creator. My frients, I haf but little more to say, and that is this—that life is uncertain, and deat' is sure. Samuel has gone before us, only a little while, and may we all be equally preparet to meet our great account. Amen."

Did any one smile, at this address? Far from it! Singular, disconnected, and unsophisticated as it may seem to certain persons, it had one great merit that is not always discernible in the speeches of those who officiate at the most elaborate funeral rites. Guert was sincere, though he might not be either logical or very clear. This was apparent in his countenance, his voice, his whole manner. For myself, I will allow I saw nothing particularly out of place, in this address, at the time, nor do I now regard it, as either irreverent or unseasonable.

We left the grave of the hunter, in the depths of that interminable forest, as the ship passes away from the spot on the ocean, where she has dropped her dead. At some future day, perhaps, the plough-share may turn up the bones, and the husbandman ruminate on the probable fate of the lonely man, whose remains will then again be brought to the light of day. As we left the spot, the Indian detained us a moment, to put us on our guard.

"Huron do that," he said, meaningly—"No see difference, eh? Saw no hang up like Pete."

"That is true enough, Susquesus," Guert answered; for Guert, by his age, his greater familiarity with the woods, his high courage and his personal prowess, had now assumed, unresistingly on our parts, a sort of chieftainship over us. "Can you tell us the reason, however?"

"Muss, you call him, back sore—t'at all. Know him well; don't love flog. No Injin love flog."

"And you think, then, Jaap's prisoner has had a hand in this, and that the war path is open to revenge, as well as public service—that we are hunted less for our scalps, than to put a plaster on the Huron's back?"

"Sartain. T'ree canoe go by on lake—t'at Muss, you call him—know him, well. He no want sleep till back get well. See how he use nigger! Hang him on tree—only kill pale-face and take away scalp."

"Do you suppose that he made this difference in the treatment of his two captives, on account of the colour? That he was so cruel to Petrus because Jaap, another nigger, had flogged him?"

"Sartain—just so. Back feel better after t'at. Good for back to hang nigger. Jaap see, some time."

I will do my fellow the justice to say, that in the way of courage, few men were his equals. As I have said before, he only feared spooks, or Dutch ghosts; for the awe he had of me, was so blended with love, as not to deserve the name of fear. In general, unless the weather happened to be cold, his face was of a deep, glistening black; coffin-colour, as the boys sometimes called it; but, I observed, notwithstanding his nerve and his keen desire to be revenged for the cruel treatment bestowed on his companion and brother, that his skin now assumed a greyish hue, such as is seen only in hard frosts, as a rule, in the people of his race. It was evident that the Trackless' manner of speaking had produced an effect, and I have always thought the impression then made on Jaap was of infinite service to us, by setting in motion, and keeping in lively activity, every faculty of his mind and body. I had a specimen of this, as we moved off, Jaap walking, for some distance close at my heels, in order to make me the repository of his griefs and solicitude.

"I hopes, Masser Corny, sah," commenced the negro, "you doesn't t'ink any t'ing of what dis here Injin say?"

"I think, Jaap, it will be necessary for you to keep your eyes open, and by no means to fall into the hands of your friend Muss, as you call him, or he may serve you even worse than he served poor Pete. I hope, too, this will be a warning to you, of the necessity of treating your prisoners kindly, should you ever make another."

"I don't t'ink, Masser Corny, you consider pretty much, sah. What good it do a nigger to captivate an Injin, if he let him go ag'in, and don't lick him little? Only little, Masser Corny. Ebbery t'ing so handy too, sah—rope all ready, back bare, and feelin' up, like, after such a time in takin' 'e varmint, sah!"

"Well, Jaap, what is done, is done, and there is no use in regretting it, in words. Of one thing, however, you may be certain; no mercy will be shown *you*, should this fellow, Muss, be actually out here, on our heels, and should you be so unfortunate as to fall into his hands."

The negro growled out his discontent, and I could see that his mind was made up to give stout battle, ere *his* wool should be disturbed by the knife of a savage. A moment later, he stepped aside, and respectfully permitted Dirck to take his proper place, next to me, in the line.

We may have proceeded two miles from the spot where we had buried Sam, the hunter, when on rising a little hillock, the Indian tossed his arm, the sign that a new discovery was made. This time, however, the gesture was rather made in exultation than in horror. As he came to a dead halt, at the same instant, we all closed eagerly up, and got an early view of the cause of this exhibition of feeling.

The ground fell away, in a sort of swell, for some distance in our front, and, the trees being all of the largest size, and totally without underbrush, the place had somewhat of the appearance of a vast, forest edifice, to which the canopy of leaves above, formed the roof, and the stems of oaks, lindens, beeches and maples might be supposed to be the columns that upheld it. Within this wide, gloomy, yet not unpleasant hall, a sombre light prevailed, like that which is cast through the casements of an edifice of the ancient style of architecture, rendering every thing mellow and grave. A spring of sweet water gushed from a rock, and near it were seated, in a circle, Mr. Traverse and his two chain-bearers, seemingly taking their morning's meal; or, rather, reclining after it, with the pail, platters and fragments before them, like men reposing after appeasing their hunger, and passing a few minutes in idle talk. Tom, the second hunter and axeman, lay asleep, a little apart.

"Here has been even no alarm, thank Got," said Guert, cheerfully, "and we are in time to let them know their danger. I will give the call; it will sound sweetly to their ears!"

"No call—" said Trackless, quickly. "Hollow no good, now. Soon get there, and tell him, in low voice."

As this was clearly prudent, we pushed forward in a body, taking no pains, however, to conceal our approach, but making somewhat of a measured tread, with our footsteps. A strange sensation came over me as we advanced, and I found that neither of the surveyors stirred! A suspicion of the dread truth forced itself on my mind; but I can hardly say that the shock was any the less, when, on getting near, we saw by the pallid countenances, fixed glassy eyes, and fallen jaws, that all our friends were dead. The savage ingenuity of Indians had propped the bodies in reclining positions, and thrown them into attitudes that had a horrible resemblance to the species of indulgence that I have just described.

"Holy Heaven!" exclaimed Guert, dropping the butt of his rifle on the ground; "we are too late!"

No one else spoke. On removing the caps, it was found that each man had been scalped, and that all of those, whom we had left a few days before, proud of their strength, and instinct with life, had departed in spirit, soon to be seen no more. Jumper, the other Indian, alone remained to be accounted for. Rifle balls had been at work here, each of the four having been shot, Mr. Traverse in no less than three places.

I will confess that a suspicion of the Oneida crossed my mind, now, for the first time, and I did not scruple to mention it to my companions, as soon as either of us had power to speak, or listen.

"No true—" said Trackless, positively. "Jumper poor Injin—that so—love rum—no rascal to kill friend. Musohoconah warrior to do so. Just like him. No; Jumper fool—love rum—no bad Injin."

Where, then, was Jumper? He alone, of all whom we had left behind us, remained to be found. We made a long search for his body, but without any success. Susquesus examined the trails, and the bodies, and gave it as his opinion that the surveyor and chain-bearers might have been killed about three or four hours, and that the murderers, for such in our eyes they who had done the foul deed were to be accounted, had not been away from the place more than twenty minutes, when we arrived. This might well have happened, and we not hear the rifles, as the distance from the hut was several miles, and two hours before, we must have been not far from the place where we had passed the night. That the attack occurred after day-light, was reasonably certain, and, as Pete was surely seized while alive, some intelligence might have been obtained from him, that directed the savages to the point where the outlying party would probably be expecting him. Nevertheless, this was pretty much conjecture, and we never knew which victim fell first, or whether the negro was taken at all, near the spot, where he was gibbeted. The infernal cruelty of his conquerors may have kept him as a prisoner, for some time before the final catastrophe, and caused them to carry him about with them as a captive, in order to subject the wretch to as much misery as possible, for, as Susquesus said, Muss' 'back very sore.'

We buried poor Traverse, and his chain-bearers, near the spring, using one of the same natural hollows in the earth, as that in which we had interred the hunter. On a search, it was ascertained that their arms and ammunition had been carried off, and that the pockets of the dead men had been rifled. The American Indian is seldom a thief, in the ordinary sense of the term; but, he treats the property of those whom he slays as his own. In this particular, he does not differ materially from the civilized soldier, I believe, plunder being usually considered as a legitimate benefit of war. The Hurons had laid their hands on the compass and chains, for we could discover neither, but they had left the field-book and notes of Traverse, as things that, to them, were useless. In other respects, the visit of the savages to this fatal spot, left the appearance of having been hurried.

On this occasion, Guert made no attempts at morals, or eloquence. The shock had disqualified us all for any thing of the sort, and we discharged our duties with the earnest diligence, and grave thoughtfulness of men, who did not know but the next moment might bring themselves into the midst of a scene of deadly strife. We worked hard, and a little hastily, and were soon ready to depart. It was determined, on a hurried consultation, to follow the trail of the Hurons, as the most certain method of surprising them, on the one hand, and of preventing them from surprising us, on the other. The Indian would have no difficulty in pursuing the very obvious trail that was left, and which bore all the proofs of having been left by a dozen men.

The reader, who is unacquainted with the usages of the American savage, is not to suppose that this party had moved through the forest, in a disorderly group, regardless of the nature of the vestiges of their passage, left behind them. The native warrior never does that. Usually he marches in a line of single files, which has obtained the name of Indian file, with us, and, whenever there are strong reasons for concealing his numbers, it is his practice for each succeeding man to follow, as nearly as possible, in the footsteps of the warrior who precedes him; thereby rendering a computation difficult, if not impossible. In this manner our foes had evidently marched, but Susquesus, who had been busy examining the marks around the spring, the whole time we were occupied in burying the dead, gave it as his opinion that our enemies could not number less than a dozen warriors. This was not very pleasing intelligence, since it would render success in a conflict, next to hopeless. So, at least, I viewed the matter, though Guert saw things differently. This highly intrepid man, could not find it in his heart, to abandon the idea of driving foes so ruthless out of the country, and, I do believe, he would have faced a hundred savages at once, when we quitted the spring.

The Onondago had no difficulty in following the trail, which led us, at first, for some distance in a line towards Ravensnest; then made a sudden inclination in the direction of the hut. It was probably owing to this circuit and want of settled purpose in the Hurons, that we did not encounter them on our advance towards the "bloody spring"; as the spot where Traverse was slain, has been subsequently called.

It was not long ere we found ourselves quite near our own trail, though, perhaps fortunately for us, we did not actually strike it. Had our movement been discovered, doubtless the enemy would have got into our rear, a position in which Indians are always most formidable. As it was, however, we possessed that great advantage ourselves, and pursued our way with so much the greater confidence; knowing full well that danger was only to be apprehended in our front, the quarter on which all our eyes were fixed.

Although our return march was swift, it was silent as that of a train of mourners. Mourners we were, indeed, for it was not possible for human hearts to be so obdurate, as to feel insensible to the amount of misery that our late companions must have suffered, and to the suddenness of their fates. No one spoke, and Susquesus had never found us so close on his heels, as we kept ourselves all that morning. The foot of the file leader was scarcely out of its place, ere that of his successor covered the same spot!

The trail let us quite close to the hut, which we reached as near as might be to noon. On approaching the cabin, we used the utmost caution lest our enemies might then be in it, in ambush. The trail did not extend quite to the building, however, but diverged in a westerly direction, from a point that may have been a hundred yards distant from our habitation, though in full view of it. Here we found the signs of a gathering of the party into a cluster, and we inferred that a counsel had been held on the subject of once more going to the hut, or of turning aside to pursue some other object. Susquesus made a close examination at this spot, and gave it as his opinion, again, that the hostiles must, at least, number the dozen he had already mentioned. Leaving us to watch the signs about our dwelling, from covers we took for that purpose, he followed the trail for half a mile, in order to make certain it did not approach the log-house, on its opposite side. So far from this proving to be the case, however, he ascertained that it led off, in a straight line towards Ravensnest. This was, if anything, more unpleasant news to Guert and myself, than if the Onondago had brought back a confirmation of his first suspicion that the Hurons might be waiting for us, in our own temporary house. Complaints were useless, however, and we smothered our apprehensions as well as we could.

Susquesus was not a warrior to confide entirely in the signs of an open march. Experienced woodsmen frequently left their trails visible expressly to deceive, and the Onondago, who personally knew Muss, as Jaap called his prisoner, was fully aware that he had to deal with a profoundly artful foe. Not satisfied with even what he had seen, he cautioned us about quitting the cover, except under his guidance, and then commenced a mode of approach that was purely Indian, and which, in its way, had much of the merit of the approaches of more civilized besiegers, by means of their entrenchments, and zig-zags. Our advance was regulated in this way. Each man was told to select the nearest tree, that led him towards the hut, and to pass from the old to the new cover, in as rapid and sudden a manner as his agility would allow. By observing this precaution, and by using great activity, we had got within twenty yards of the door of the cabin, in the course of ten minutes. Guert could not submit to this slow, and, as he called it, unmanly procedure any longer, but quitting his cover, he now walked straight and steadily to the door of the cabin, threw it open, and announced to us that the place was empty. Susquesus made another close examination around the building, and told us he felt quite certain that the spot had not been visited since we had left it, that morning. That was grateful intelligence to us all, since it was the only probable clue by which our enemies could have learned our return to the patent, at all.

The question now arose as to future proceedings. Nothing was to be gained by remaining on the property, while prudence and the danger of our friends, united to call us away. We felt it would be a most hazardous thing to attempt reaching Ravensnest, though we felt it was a hazard we were bound to incur. While the matter was talked over, those among us who had any appetite, profited by the halt to dine. An Indian, on a war path, is equally ready to eat, or to fast, his powers of endurance both ways, more especially when the food is game, amounting to something wonderful.

While Susquesus, and Jaap, in particular, were performing their parts in a very serious manner, in this way, and the rest of us were picking up a few morsels more like men whose moral feelings checked their physical propensities, I caught a distant glimpse of a man's form, as it glided among the trees, at some distance from us. Surprise and awe were so strong in me, that I did not speak, but pointed with a finger eagerly, in the necessary direction, in order to let the Onondago see the same object too. Susquesus was not slow in detecting the stranger, however, for I think he must have seen him, even before he was descried by myself. Instead of manifesting any emotion, however, the Onondago did not even cease to eat; but merely nodded his head, and muttered— "Good—now hear news—Jumper come."

Sure enough, it was Jumper; and his appearance in the flesh, not only alive but unharmed, produced a general shout among us, as he came in, on such a long, loping gait, as usually marked a runner's movement. In a moment, he was among us, calm, collected, and without motion. He gave no salutation, but seated himself quietly on a log, waiting to be questioned, before he spoke; impatience being a womanly weakness.

"Jumper, my honest fellow," cried Guert, not without emotion, for joy was struggling powerfully with his organs of speech, "you are heartily welcome! These devils incarnate, the Hurons, have not injured *you*, at least."

Liquor had rendered Jumper's faculties somewhat obtuse, in general, though he was now perfectly sober. He gave a sort of dull look of recognition at the speaker, and muttered his answer in a low, sluggish tone.

"Plenty Huron," he said. "Clearin' full—Pale-face in fort— send Jumper with message."

We should have overwhelmed the fellow with questions, had

he not unfolded a corner of his calico shirt, and exhibited several letters, each of which was soon in the hand of the individual to whom it was addressed. Guert, Dirck and myself, severally got his communication, while there was a fourth, in the hand writing of Herman Mordaunt that bore the superscription of poor Traverse's name. Subsequent events have placed it in my power, to give copies of all the letters, thus received. My own, was in the following words:—

"My dearest father is so much occupied, as to desire *me* to write you this note. Mr. Bulstrode sent an express yesterday, who was bearer of the sad tidings from Ticonderoga. He also announced his own approach, and we expect him, in a horse litter, this evening. Reports are flying about the settlement, that savages have been seen in our own woods. I endeavour to hope, that this is only one of those idle rumours, of which we have had so many, lately. My father, however, is taking all necessary precautions, and he desires *me* to urge on *you* the necessity of collecting all your party, should you be again at Mooseridge, and of joining us *without delay*. We have heard of your safety and gallant conduct, through the man sent forward by Mr. Bulstrode, his master having heard of you all, safe in a canoe on the lake, the night after the battle, through a Mr. Lee, a gentleman of great eccentricity of character, though it is said of much talent, with whom papa happens to be acquainted. I trust this note will find you, at your hut, and that we shall see you all, with the least possible delay.

Anneke."

This, certainly, was not a note to appease the longings of a lover, though I had infinite gratification in seeing the pretty characters that had been traced by Anne Mordaunt's hand, and of kissing the page over which that hand must have passed. But, there was a postscript, the part of a letter in which a woman is said always to give the clearest insight into her true thoughts. It was in these words, viz:—

"I see that I have underscored the 'me,' where I speak of papa's desire that *I* should write to you, in preference to another. We have gone through one dreadful scene in company, and, I confess, Corny, I should feel far happier, if another is to occur, that *you*, and *yours*, should be with us, here, behind the defences of this house, than exposed, as you otherwise might be, in the forest. Come to us then, I repeat, with the least possible delay."

This postscript afforded me far more satisfaction than the body of the note, and I was quite as ready to comply with Anneke's request, as the dear girl herself, could be to urge it. Guert's letter was as follows:—

"Mr. Mordaunt has commanded Anneke and myself to write to those of your party, with whom he fancies each has the most influence, to urge you to come to Ravensnest, as speedily as possible. We have received most melancholy news, and a panic prevails among the poor people of this settlement. We learn that Mr. Bulstrode, accompanied by Mr. Worden, is within a few hours' journey of us, and the families of the vicinity are coming to us, frightened and weeping. I do not know that I feel much alarmed, myself; my great dependence is on a merciful providence, but the dread being on whom I rely works through human agents, and I know of none in whom I can place more confidence than on Guert Ten Eyck.

Mary Wallace."

"By St. Nicholas! Corny, these are such summonses as a man never hesitates about obeying," cried Guert, rising, and beginning to replace his knapsack. "By using great diligence, we may reach the Nest, yet, before the family goes to bed, and make not only them, but ourselves so much the more comfortable and secure."

Guert had a willing auditor in me, nor was Dirck at all backward about complying. The letters certainly much quickened our impulses, though, in fact, there remained nothing else to do; unless, indeed, we intended to lie out, exposed to all the risks of a vindictive and savage warfare. Dirck's letter was from Herman Mordaunt, and it told the truth in plainer language than it had been related by either of the ladies. Here it is.

"Dear Dirck,—The savages are certainly approaching us, my young kinsman, and it is for the good of us all to unite our forces. Come in, for God's sake, with your whole party, as speedily as possible. I have had scouts out, and they have all come in with reports that the signs of trails in the forest, abound. I expect at least a hundred warriors will be upon us by to-morrow, and am making my preparations accordingly. In approaching the Nest, I would advise you to enter the ravine, north of the house, and to keep within its cover, until you get to its southern termination. This will bring you within a hundred rods of the gate, and greatly increase your chances of entering should we happen to be invested when you get here. God bless you, dear Dirck, and guide you all safely to your friends.

Herman Mordaunt.

Ravensnest, July 11th, 1758."

Guert and I read this letter, hastily, before we commenced our march. Then abandoning the hut, and all it contained, to the mercy of any who might pass that way, we set off for our point of destination, on a quick step, carrying little besides our arms, ammunition, and the food that was necessary to assure our strength.

As before, Trackless led, keeping the Jumper a little on his flank, the danger of encountering foes being now considered to be greatly increased. It was true, we were still in the rear of the party that had committed the deeds at Mooseridge, but the Onondago no longer followed its trail, pursuing a different course; or one that led directly to his object.

Chapter XXVII

"My father had a daughter lov'd a man,
As it might be perhaps, were I a woman,
I should your lordship."

Twelfth Night, II.iv. 107–109.

As the reader must, by this time, have a pretty accurate idea of our manner of marching in the wilderness, I shall not dwell on this part of our proceedings, any longer. On we went, and at a rapid rate, the guide having abandoned the common route, which had got to be a pretty visible trail, and taking another on which, as it appeared to me, he had no other clue than an instinct. Guert had told Susquesus of the ravine, and how desirable it was to reach it, getting for an answer a quiet nod of the head, and a low ejaculation. It was understood, however, that we were to approach Herman Mordaunt's fortress, by that avenue.

It was past the turn of the day when we quitted Mooseridge, and none of us hoped to reach Ravensnest before dark. It fell out, as we expected, night drawing its veil over the scene, about half an hour, before the Trackless plunged into the northern, or forest-end of the ravine. Thus far, we had got no evidence, whatever of the proximity of foes. Our march had been silent, rapid and watchful, but it proved to be perfectly undisturbed. We knew, however, that the critical portion of it was still before us, and just as the sun set, we had made a halt, in order to look to our arms. It may now be well to say a word or two on the subject of the position of Herman Mordaunt's 'garrison' as well as of the adjacent settlement. I call Ravensnest the 'garrison,' for that is the word which New York custom has long applied to the fortress itself, as well as to those who defend it. Some critics pretend there is authority to justify the practice, and I see by the dictionaries that they are not entirely in the wrong.

The Nest stood quite half a mile from the nearest point of the forest, a belt of trees that fringed the margin, and which filled the cavity of the ravine, excepted. Near it, and in plain sight, was the heart of the settlement itself, which extended, in an east and west direction, fully four miles. This area, however, was cleared only in a settlement fashion; having patches of virgin forest scattered pretty profusely over its surface. The Mill Lot, as Jason's purchase was termed, lay at the most distant extremity of the view, but, as yet, the axe had not been applied to it. I had remarked in my last visit to the place, that, standing before Herman Mordaunt's door, something like a dozen log cabins were to be seen at a time, in different parts of the settlement, and that this number might have been increased to twenty, by varying the observer's position.

Of course, the whole of the open space was, more or less, disfigured, by stumps, dead and girdled trees, charred stubs, log heaps, brush, and all the other unseemly accompaniments of the first eight or ten years of the existence of a new settlement. This period in the history of a country, may be likened to the hobbledehoy condition in ourselves, when we have lost the graces of childhood, without having attained the finished forms of men.

Herman Mordaunt's settlement would have been thought a strong country, in one sense, for a field fight, had there been men enough to contend with a hostile party of any force. But, I have heard him say, that he had but about seventeen rifles and muskets that could be in the least relied on, inasmuch as some of his people were Europeans and had no knowledge of fire-arms, while experience had shown, that others, on the occurrence of an alarm, invariably fled to the woods, with their families, instead of rallying around the settlement colours. Such delinquencies usually take place, I believe, on all emergencies; love of life being even a stronger instinct than love of property. Here and there a sturdy fellow, however, would bar himself in, with a determination to go for the whole, under his own bark roof, and, occasionally, defences were made that would do credit to a hero.

It should be apparent to those who have any accurate notion of savage warfare, that the ravine, being, as it was, the only wooded spot near Herman Mordaunt's fortress, would be the place of all others most likely to contain an enemy who made his approaches against a garrison, by means of natural facilities alone. We were aware of this, and, Guert, who took an active command among us, as we drew near to danger, issued his commands for every man to be on the alert, in order that there might be no confusion. We were instructed as to the manner of proceeding the moment an alarm was given, and Guert, who was a capital mimic, had previously taught us several calls, and rallying signals, all of which were good imitations of the cries of different tenants of the woods, principally birds. These signals had their origin with the red men, who often resorted to them, and were said to be more successfully practised by our own hunters and riflemen, than even by those with whom they originated.

On entering the ravine, the order of our march was changed. While Susquesus and Jumper were still kept in advance, Guert, Dirck, Jaap and myself moved abreast, and quite close together. The density of the foliage, and the deep obscurity that prevailed in the bottom of this dell-like hollow, rendered this precaution necessary. It soon became so dark, indeed, that our only guide was the brook that gurgled along the bottom of the ravine, and which we knew issued into the open ground at its termination, to join a small river that meandered through some natural meadows to the westward of the Nest, but which, in the language of the country, was called a 'creek.' This abuse of good old English words, I am sorry to say, is getting to be only too common among us; yet I have heard Americans boast that we speak the language better than the mother country! That we have no class among us that uses an unintelligible dialect, like that of Lancashire or Yorkshire is true enough; and, that we have fewer persons who use decided vulgarisms, in the way of false grammar, than is the case in England, may be also accurate; but, it might be well for us to correct a great many faults into which we have certainly fallen, before we declaim with so much confidence about the purity of our English.* To return to the ravine.

*It is *northern* American, to call a small 'lake' a 'pond,' a small 'river' a 'creek,' even though it should be an 'outlet,' instead of an 'inlet,' &c. &c. It is a more difficult thing than is commonly supposed, to make two great nations, each of which is disposed to innovate, speak the same language with precise uniformity. The Manhattanese, who have probably fewer of the peculiarities of the inhabitants of a capital than the population of any other town in the world of four hundred thousand souls, the consequences of a rapid growth, and of a people who have come principally from the country, are much addicted to introducing new significations for words, which arise from their own provincial habits. In Manhattanese parlance, for instance, a 'square' is a 'park,' or, even a 'garden' is a 'park.' A promenade on the water, is a 'battery!' It is a pity that, in this humour for change, they have not thought of altering the complex and imitative name of their town.—EDITOR.

We had gone so far in the hollow, dark dell, as to have reached a point where the faint light of the open ground and the stars in the firmament became visible to us, when we suddenly found ourselves along side of the Trackless and Jumper. These Indians had halted, for their quick, jealous, eagle-like glances had detected the signs of enemies. Nor was this discovery very difficult to make, though some pains had actually been taken to conceal what was going on in our front. A party of some forty savages, every man of whom was in his war paint, had lighted a fire beneath a shelving rock, and were gathered around it at supper. The fire had already done its duty, and was now merely smouldering, throwing a faint, flickering light on the dark, fierce features of the group that was clustered round. We might have approached the spot in any other direction, without seeing the danger, in time to avoid it, but a kind Providence had carried the two Indians directly to a point, where the dying embers immediately caught their attention, and where they halted as has been said. I do not think we were more than forty yards from this fearful band of savages, when they first met my eye, and, hardened as I had certainly somewhat become, by the service and scenes I had so lately gone through, I will confess that my blood was a little chilled at the sight.

Our conference was in whispers. There we stood, huddled together beneath a huge oak, the shadow of which rendered the darkness that formed our only safe-guard, so much the more intense. So close were we, in fact, that even Jaap's body was in absolute contact with my own. Susquesus proposed making a *détour*, by crossing the brook, which, fortunately, tumbled down some rocks at this point, making a very favourable noise, and, thus, pass our enemies, who would not probably end their meal until we had time to reach the 'garrison.' To this Guert applied his veto. He was of opinion, and I have always thought it was the decision of a man born to be a soldier, that we were exactly in the position we might desire to occupy, in order to be of great service to the family, and to strike the enemy with a panic. By attacking, we should certainly surprise the party in our front, and might make such an impression as would induce them to abandon the settlement. Both Dirck and myself coincided in this opinion, which even received the support of Jaap's voice.

"Yes, sah! yes, Masser Corny, now 'e time to wengeance poor

Pete!" he muttered, and that rather louder than was thought quite prudent.

As soon as the Trackless found how things were going, he and Jumper prepared for the conflict, as coolly as any of us. Our arrangements were very simple, and were soon made. We were to deliver a single fire from the spot where we stood, shout, and charge with the knife and tomahawk. No time was to be wasted, however, and instead of remaining near the light, small as it was, we were to push for the mouth of the ravine, and thence make the best of our way, singly or in company, as chance should offer, to the gate of Ravensnest. In a moment, we were in open files, and had our orders.

"Remember Traverse!" said Guert, sternly—"remember poor Sam, and all our murteret frients!"

The reader knows that Guert was apt to be very Dutch, when much excited. We *did* remember the dead, and I have often thought, but never knew precisely, that each of us sacrificed a victim to the manes of our lost companions, on that stern occasion. Our rifles rang, or cracked would be the better word, almost simultaneously; a yell arose from the savages around the fire; our own shouts mingled with that yell, and forward we went, endeavouring to make our numbers appear as if we were a hundred.

One retains but very indistinct notions of a charge like that, made as it was in the dark, beyond its general characteristics. We swept directly among the slain and wounded, and I heard Jaap dealing one or two awful blows on the bodies, but no one opposed us. A moment after we had passed the smouldering fire, three or four shot were discharged at us, but there was no sign of their telling on any of our party. The distance from the fire to the mouth of the ravine, might have been a hundred yards, and the external light, or lesser darkness may be a better expression, served us for a guide. Thither we pushed, fast as we could, though by no means in compact order.

For this part of the affair, I can only speak for myself. I saw men moving swiftly among the trees, and I supposed them to be my companions, but we had become separated, it being understood that each man was now to shift for himself. As our rifles were discharged, and there was no time to reload them, there was little use, indeed, in any halt. Perceiving this, I did not issue from the ravine at the brook, but clinging more to its side, left it at a little height above the level of the adjacent plain. Here I paused to load, the cover being good, and the position every way favourable. While thus employed, I found time to look around me, and to ascertain the situation of things in the settlement, so far as the hour and the obscurity would permit.

The plain was glimmering with the remains of a dozen large fires, the ruins of so many log houses and barns. Their light amounted to no more than to render the darkness of the night distinctly visible, and to afford some small clues to the extent of the ravages that had been already committed. The house of Ravensnest, however, was untouched. There it stood, looking dark and gloomy; for, having no external windows, no other light was to be seen than a single candle that was probably placed in a loop-hole as a signal. Profound stillness reigned in and around the building, producing a species of mystery, that was in itself, under such circumstances, an element of force. There was not light enough to distinguish objects at any distance, and, having reloaded my rifle, I thought it wisest to make the best of my way to the gate. At that moment, the stillness in my rear seemed to possess something affirmatively fearful about it.

It was certainly a somewhat hazardous thing to break cover, at such a moment, and under such circumstances, but it was absolutely necessary to incur its risks. My first leap carried me halfway down the declivity, and I was soon on the level land. In my front were two men, one of whom seemed to me to be in the grasp of the other. As they were moving, though slowly, in the direction of the house, I ventured to ask 'Who goes there?'

"Oh, Corny, my lad, is that you?" answered Guert. "Got be praised! you seem unhurt, and are just in time to help me along with this Huron, on whom I blundered in the dark, and have disarmed and captured. Give him a kick or a push, if you please; for the fellow holds back like a hog."

I had too much knowledge of Indian vindictiveness, however, to adopt the means recommended, but seizing the captive by one arm, while Guert held the other, we ran him up to the *abbatis* that covered the gate of the 'garrison,' with very little difficulty. Here we found Herman Mordaunt, and a dozen of his people, all armed, ready to receive us. They were in expectation of our appearance, both on account of the hour, and on account of the clamor in the ravine, which had been distinctly heard at the house. In less than a minute, every body was in, safe and unharmed. The fact was, that our attack had been so sudden as to sweep everything before it, and the enemy had not time to recover from his panic, before we were all snugly housed. Once within the gate of Ravensnest, we ran no risks, beyond those which were common to all such log fortresses, in the warfare of the wilderness.

It would not be easy for a pen as unskilful as mine to portray the change, from the gloom of the ravine, the short but bloody assault, the shouts, the rush and the retreat, of the outer world, to the scene of domestic security we found within the Nest, embellished as was the last by woman's loveliness and graces, and, in many respects, by woman's elegance. Anneke and her friend received us, in a bright, cheerful, comfortable apartment, that was rendered so much the more attractive by their tears and their smiles, neither of which were spared. I could see that both had been dreadfully agitated; but joy restored their colour, and brought back the smiles to their sweet faces. The situation of the place was such, perhaps, as to render cheerfulness neither very lasting nor very lively, but the tenderest female can find her heart suddenly so lightened from its burthen of apprehensions, as to be able to seem momentarily happy, even when environed by the horrors of war. Such, in a measure, was the character of the reception we now received, together with a thousand thanks for having so promptly answered their letters, in person. The dear creatures had the ingenuity not to seem to ascribe that prompt obedience to their own requests, which we had manifested, to any care for ourselves, but solely to a wish to oblige and protect them. The reader will understand that all explanations still remained to be made, on both sides. These soon came, however, facts pressing themselves on the attention, at such times, with a weight that is irresistible. The ice was broken by Herman Mordaunt's entering the room, and speaking to us like one who felt that a great omission had been made.

"We had closed the gate, and set the look-outs at the loops, again," he said, "before I ascertained that all your party is not here. I see nothing of Traverse and his chain-bearers; nor of Sam or Tom, your hunters! Surely they are not left behind, in the forest?"

Neither of us three spoke. Our looks must have told the sad story, for Herman Mordaunt seemed to understand us, on the instant.

"No!" he exclaimed—"Can it be possible?—Not *all*, surely!"

"*All*, Mr. Mordaunt, even to my poor slave Petrus," answered Guert, solemnly. "They were set upon, while dispersed, I suppose, and have been murdered, while we were still absent, on our expedition."

The dear girls clasped their hands, and I thought Anneke's pallid lips moved, as if in prayer. Her father shook his head, and for some time he paced the room in silence. Then rousing himself, like one conscious of the necessity of calmness and exertion, he resumed the discourse.

"Thank God, Mr. Bulstrode reached us safely, last evening, just after we despatched the runner, and *he* is beyond the reach of these demons for the present!"

After this we were enabled to converse more connectedly, exchanging such statements as enabled each party to understand the precise condition of the other. We were then carried to Bulstrode's room, for he had expressed a desire to see us, as soon as we could be spared. Our fellow-campaigner received us in good spirits, for one in his situation, speaking of the events in front of Ticonderoga sensibly, and without any attempt to conceal the mortification that he felt, in common with the whole British Empire. His hurt was by no means a bad one; likely to cripple him for a few weeks, but the leg was in no danger.

"I have had the resolution and address, Corny, to work my way into good quarters, this unexpected siege excepted," he observed to me, when the others had withdrawn, leaving us alone. "This rivalry of ours is a generous one, and may now have fair play. If we quit this Nest of Herman Mordaunt's without ascertaining the true state of Anneke's feelings, we shall deserve to be condemned to celibacy for the remainder of our days. There never were two such opportunities for wooing to advantage!"

"I confess our situation does not strike me as being quite so favorable, Mr. Bulstrode," I answered. "Anneke must have too many apprehensions on her own account, and on account of others, to be as sensible to the tender sentiments of love, as might be the case in the peace and security of Lilacsbush."

"Ah! It is very evident you know nothing of the female sex,

Corny, by that remark. I will grant you, that unwooed previously, and without any foundation laid, if I may express myself so irreverently, your theory might turn out to be true; but not so under actual circumstances. Here is a young lady in her nineteenth year, who knows she is not only sought, but has long been sought, ay warmly, ardently sought by two reasonably unobjectionable young men, placed in the very situation to have all her sensibilities excited, by one or the other, and, depend on it, the matter will be determined within this blessed week. If I should prove to be the fortunate man, I hope to be able to manifest a generous sympathy; and *vice versa* I shall expect the same. Though this sad, sad business before Ty has been a good preparative for humiliation."

I could not avoid smiling at Bulstrode's singular views of our suits, but, as Anneke was ever with me an engrossing theme, spite of our situation, which certainly was not particularly appropriate to love, I did not feel equal to quitting it abruptly. The matter was consequently pursued. As I asked Bulstrode to explain himself, I got from him the following account of his theory.

"Why, I reason in this wise, Corny. Anneke loves *one* of us two, beyond all question. That she *loves*, I will swear; her blushes, her beaming eyes, even her beauty is replete with the loveliness of the sentiment. Now, it is not possible that she should love any other person, than one of us two, for the simple reason that she has no other suitor. I shall be frank with you, and confess that I think I am the favoured fellow, while, I dare say, you are just as sanguine and think it is yourself."

"I give you my honour, Major Bulstrode, so presuming, so improper a thought has never——"

"Yes, yes—I understand all that. You are not worthy of Anne Mordaunt's love, and therefore have never presumed to imagine that she could bestow it, on such a poor, miserable, worthless, good-for-nothing a fellow as yourself. I have a great deal of the same very proper feeling, but, at the same time, each of us is quite confident of his own success, or he would have given up the pursuit long since."

"I do assure you, Bulstrode, any thing but confidence mingles with *my* feelings on this subject. *You* may have reasons for your own security, but I can boast of none."

"I have no other than self-love, of which every man has a just portion, for his own comfort and peace of mind. I say that hope is indispensable to love, and hope is allied to confidence. My reasoning on these points is very simple. And, now for the peculiar advantages we enjoy for bringing matters to a crisis. In the first place, I am hurt, you will understand: suffering under an honourable wound, received in open battle, fighting for king and country. Then I have been brought fresh from the field, on my litter, into the presence of my mistress, bearing on my person, the evidence of my risk, and I hope, of my good conduct. There is not one woman in a thousand, if she hesitated between us, that would not decide in my favour, on these grounds alone. You have no notion, Corny, how the hearts of these sweet, gentle, devoted, generous little American girls melt to sympathy and the sufferings of a poor wretch that they know adores them! Make a nurse of a female, and she is yours, nine times out of ten. This has been a master-stroke of mine, but I hope you will pardon it. Stratagems are excusable in love, as in war."

"I have no difficulty in understanding your policy, Bulstrode, though I confess to some in understanding your frankness. Such as it is, however, I trust you feel certain it will not be abused. Now, as to my situation—what peculiar countervailing advantages do I enjoy?"

"Those of a defender. Oh, *that* is a battering-ram of itself! This confounded assault on the settlement, which they tell me is rather serious, and may keep alive apprehensions for some days yet, is a most unlucky thing for me, while it is of great advantage to you. A wounded man can not excite one-half the interest he otherwise might, when there is a chance that others may be slain, every minute. Then the character of a defender, is a great deal, and, being a generous rival, as I have always told you, Corny, my advice is to make the most of it. I conceal nothing, and intend to do all I can with my wound."

It was scarcely possible not to laugh at this strangely frank, yet I fully believe strangely sincere communication, for Bulstrode was a humorist with all his conventionalism and London notions and was more addicted to saying precisely what he thought than is common with men of his class. After sitting, and chatting with him, half an hour longer, on the subject of the late military operations, of which he spoke with both feeling and good sense, I took my leave for the night.

"God bless you, Corny," he said squeezing my hand, as I left him. "Improve the opportunity, in your own way, for I assure you I shall do it in mine. It is present valour against past valour. If it were not my own case that is concerned, there is not a man living to whom I should more freely wish success."

And I do believe Bulstrode did not exceed the truth, in his declarations. That I should succeed with Anneke, he did not think, as was apparent to me by his general manner, and the consciousness he must have possessed of his own advantages in the way of rank and fortune, as well as in having Herman Mordaunt's good wishes. Oddly enough, in quitting my rival, and under circumstances so very peculiar, I was accidentally thrown into the presence of my mistress, and that, too, alone! Anneke was the sole occupant of the little room in which the girls habitually staid, when I returned to it, Guert having managed to induce Mary Wallace to walk with him in the court, the only place the ladies now possessed for exercise, while Herman Mordaunt, Mr. Worden and Dirck, were together in the public room, making some arrangement with the confused body of the settlers who had crowded into the Nest, for the night watch. I shall not stop to express the delight I felt at finding Anneke there, nor was it, in any degree diminished, as I met the soft expression of her sweet eyes, and saw the blushes that suffused her cheek. The conversation I had just held, doubtless, had its effect, for I determined at once, that so favourable an occasion for pressing my suit, should not be lost. I was goaded on, if the truth must be told, by apprehension of Bulstrode's wound.

What I said precisely, in the commencement of that interview, is more than I could record, did I think it would redound to my advantage, as I fear it would not; but I made myself understood, which is more I fancy than happens to all lovers in such scenes. At first, I was confused and a little incoherent, I suspect, but feeling so far got the better of these defects as to enable me to utter what I wished to express. Towards the end, if I spoke in the least as warmly and distinctly as I felt, there must have been some slight touch of eloquence about my manner and language. This being the first occasion, too, on which I had ever had an opportunity of urging my suit very directly, there was so much to be said, so many things to be explained, and so many seemingly slighted occasions to account for, that Anneke had little else to do, for the first ten minutes, but to listen. I have always ascribed the self-possession which my companion was enabled to command during the remainder of this interview, to the time that was thus accorded her to rally her thoughts.

Dear, precious Anneke! How admirably did she behave that memorable night! It was certainly an extraordinary situation in which to speak of love, yet, I much question if the feelings be not more likely to be true and natural at such times, than when circumstances admit of more of the expedients of every-day life. I could see that my sweet listener was touched, from the moment I commenced, and that her countenance betrayed a tender interest in what I said. Presuming on this, or encouraged by her blushes and her downcast eyes, I ventured to take a hand, and perceived I was not repulsed. Then it was that I found words, that actually brought tears to my companion's eyes, and Anneke was enabled to answer me.

"This is so unusual—so extraordinary a time to speak of such things, Corny," she said, "that I hardly know what ought to be my reply. Of one thing, however, I feel certain; persons surrounded as we are by dangers that may, at any instant, involve our destruction, have an unusual demand on them for sincerity. Affectation, I hope, I am never much addicted to, and prudery I know *you* would condemn. I have a feeling uppermost, at this instant, that I wish to express, yet scarce know how—"

"Do not suppress it, beloved Anneke; be as generous as I am certain you are sincere."

"Corny, it is this. I know we are in danger—very great danger of being overcome; captured, perhaps slain, by the ruthless beings, who are prowling around our dwelling, and that no one in this house can count on a single day of existence even with the ordinary vain security of man. Now, should any thing befall *you*, after this, and I survive you, I should survive for the remainder of my days to mourn your loss, and to feel the keenest regrets that I had hesitated to own how much interest I have long felt in you, and how happy I have been with the consciousness of the preference that you so frankly and honestly avowed in my favour, months ago."

As the tears, as well as blushes of Anneke, accompanied these admissions, it was not possible for me to doubt what I heard. From that moment, a world of confidence, and a flow of pure,

sweet, strong, natural feeling bound us more and more closely together. Guert was in a happy mood to detain Mary Wallace, and
business greatly befriended me, as respected the others. More
than an hour had I Anne Mordaunt all to myself, and when the
heart is open how much can be uttered and understood, on such
a subject as love, in an hour of unreserved confidence, and of
strong feeling! Anneke admitted to me, before we separated,
that she had often thought of the chivalrous boy, who had volunteered to do battle in her behalf, when she was little more than a
child herself, and thought of him as a generous-minded girl
would be apt to think of a lad, under the circumstances. This very
early preference had been much quickened and increased by the
affair of the lion, and our subsequent intercourse. Bulstrode,
that formidable, encouraged rival, encouraged by her father if
not by herself, had never interested her in the least, beyond the
feeling natural to the affinity of blood, and I might have spared
myself, many hours of anxious concern, on his account, could I
only have seen what was now so unreservedly told to me. Poor
Bulstrode! a feeling of commiseration came over me, as I listened
to my companion's assurances that he had never in the least
touched her heart, while, at the same time, blushing very red, she
confessed my own power over it. An expression to this effect even
escaped her aloud—

"Have no concern on Mr. Bulstrode's account, Corny," Anneke
answered, smiling archly, like one who had well weighed the pros
and cons of the whole subject, in her own mind; "he may be a little mortified, but his fancy will soon be forgotten in rejoicing that
he had not yielded to a passing inclination, and connected himself with a young, inexperienced American girl, who is hardly
suited to move in the circles in which his wife must live. I do believe Mr. Bulstrode prefers me, just now, to any other female he
may happen to know; but his attachment, if it deserve the name,
has not the heart in it, dear Corny, that I know is to be found in
yours. We women are said to be quick in discovering when we are
really loved, and I confess that my own little experience inclines
me to believe that the remark does us no more than justice."

I then spoke of Guert, and expressed a hope that his sincere,
obvious, manly devotion might finally touch her heart, and that
my new friend, towards whom, however, I began already to feel
as towards an old friend, might finally meet with a return for a

passion that I was persuaded was as deep and as sincere as my own; a comparison that I felt was as strong as any I could make in Guert's behalf.

"On this subject, you are not to expect me to say much, Corny," answered Anneke, smiling. "Every woman is the mistress of her own secrets on such a subject, and, did I know fully Mary Wallace's mind, or wishes, in reference to Mr. Ten Eyck, as I do not profess to know either, I should not feel at liberty to betray her, even to you. I have no longer any secret of my own, as respects Corny Littlepage, but must not be expected to be as weak in betraying my whole sex, as I have been in betraying myself!"

I was obliged to be satisfied with this sweet admission, and with the knowledge that I had been long loved. When Anneke left me, which, at the expiration of more than an hour, she insisted on doing, under the consciousness of all that had passed between us, I had a good deal of difficulty in believing that I was not dreaming. This *eclaircissement* was so sudden, so totally unexpected I fancy to us both, that well might it so seem to either; yet, I fancy we did not part without a deep conviction that both were happier than when we met. I solemnly declare, notwithstanding, that I felt sorrow, almost regret, on behalf of Bulstrode. The poor fellow had been so evidently confident of success, only an hour or two before, that I could not have acquainted him with my own success, had he been up, and able to prefer his own suit; in his actual situation, such a procedure would have appeared brutal.

As for Guert Ten Eyck, he rejoined me sadder and more despairing than ever.

"It struck me, Corny, that if Mary Wallace had the smallest inclination in my behalf, she would manifest it at a moment, when we may all be said to be hanging between life and deat'. I have often heard it said that the woman who would trifle with a young fellow at a ball, or on a sleigh ride, and use him like a dog, while every one was laughing and making merry, would come round like one of the weather-cocks on our Dutch barns, at a shift of the wind, the instant that distress, or unhappiness alighted on her suitor. In other worts, that the very girl who would be capricious and uncertain, in happiness and prosperity, would suddenly become tender and truthful, as soon as sorrow touched the man who wished to have her. On the strength of this, then, I thought I would urge Mary, to the best of my poor abilities, and you know they are no great matter, Corny, to give me only a glimmering of hope, but without success. Not a syllable more could I get out of her than that the time was unseasonable to talk of such things; and I do think I should be ready to go and meet these Huron devils, hand to hand, were it not for the fact that the very girl who thus remonstrated, staid with me quite two hours, listening to what I had to say, though I spoke of nothing else. There was a crumb of comfort in that, lad, or I do not understand human nature."

There was, truly. Still, I could not but compare Anne Mordaunt's generous confessions, under the influence of the same facts, and fancy that the prospects of the simple-minded, warm-hearted, manly young Albanian were far less flattering than my own.

Chapter XXVIII

"Between two worlds life hovers like a star,
'Twixt night and morn, upon the horizon's verge:
How little do we know that which we are!
How less what we may be! The eternal surge
Of time and tide rolls on, and bears afar
Our bubbles; as the old burst, new emerge,
Lashed from the foam of ages; while the graves
Of empires heave but like some passing waves."
Byron, *Don Juan*, XV.xcix. 785–792.

I T was now announced by Herman Mordaunt in person, that the watch was set for the night, and that each man might seek his rest. The crowded state of the Nest was such, as to render it no easy matter to find a place, in which to sleep, straw being our only beds. At length we found our pallets, such as they were, and, spite of all that had passed that evening, truth compels me to admit that I was soon in a profound sleep. There was no exception to this rule among the Mooseridge party, I believe; fatigue proving to be more powerful, than either successful love, unsuccessful love, or personal apprehension.

It was about three o'clock, when I felt a significant pressure of the arm; such as one gives when he especially wishes to attract attention. It was Jason Newcome, employed in awakening the men of the house, without giving such an alarm as might reach the ears without. In a few minutes, every body was up and armed.

As the morning, just before the appearance of light, when sleep is heaviest, is the hour when savages usually attack, no one was surprised at these preparations, which were understood to be ordered by Herman Mordaunt, who was afoot and on the look-out, himself, at a place favourable to observation. In the mean time, we men, three or four and twenty in all, assembled in the court, in waiting for a summons to the gate, or the loop. Jason had executed his trust so dexterously that neither female nor child knew any thing of our movement, all sleeping, or seeming to sleep in the security of a peaceful home. I took an occasion to compliment the ex-pedagogue and new miller, on the skill he had shown, and we fell into a low discourse, in consequence.

"I have been thinking that this warfare may put a new face on these settlements, Corny," continued Jason, after we had conversed some little time, "more especially as to the titles."

"I cannot see how they are to be affected, Mr. Newcome, unless the French should happen to conquer the colony, a thing not very likely to happen."

"That's just it; exactly what I mean, as to principle. Have not these Hurons conquered this particular settlement? I say they have. They are in possession of the whull of it, this house excepted, and it appears to me that if we ever get repossession, it will be by another conquest. Now, what I want to know is this— does not conquest give the conquerors a right to the conquered territory? I have no books here, yet, but I'm dreadful forgetful, or I *have* read that such is the law."

I may say that this was the first direct demonstration that Jason ever made on the property of Herman Mordaunt. Since that time, he has made many more, some of which I, or he who may be called on to continue this narrative, will probably relate; but I wish to record, here, this as the first in a long series of attempts which Jason Newcome has practised, in order to transfer the fee-simple of the Mill Lot, at Ravensnest, from the ownership of those in whom it is vested by law, to that of his own humble, but meritorious person.

I had little time to answer this very singular sort of reasoning, for, just then Herman Mordaunt appeared among us, and gave us serious duty to perform. The explanations with which his orders were preceded, were these. As had been anticipated, the Indians had adopted the only means that could prove effective against such a fortress as the Nest, without the aid of artillery. They were making their preparations to set the building on fire, and had been busy all night, in collecting a large amount of pine knots, roots, &c., which they had succeeded in piling against the outer logs, at the point where one wing touched the cliff, and where the formation of the ground enabled them to approach the buildings, without incurring much risk. Their mode of proceeding is worthy of being related. One of the boldest, and most skilful of their number had crept to the spot, and posted himself so close to the logs, as to be safe from observation, as well as reasonably safe from shot. His associates had then extended to him one end of a long pole, they standing below, some on a shelf of the cliff, and the rest on the ground, all being safe from harm, so long as they kept close to their respective covers. Thus disposed, these children of the forest passed hours in patient toil, in forwarding by means of a basket, the knots and other combustibles, up to the warrior who kept his position close under the building, and who piled them in the way most favourable to his object.

Susquesus had the merit of discovering the projected attempt, the arrangements for which had completely escaped the vigilance of the sentinels. It would seem that the Onondago, aware of the artifices of the red-man, and acquainted in particular with the personal character of Jaap's friend Muss, did not believe the night would go by without some serious attempt on the house. The side of the cliff was much the weakest point of the fortress, having no other protection than the natural obstacles of the rocks, which were not inaccessible, though somewhat difficult of ascent, and the low picketing already mentioned. Under such circumstances, the Indian felt certain the assault would be made on that side. Placing himself on watch, therefore, he discovered the first attempts of the Hurons, but did not let them be known to Herman Mordaunt, until they were nearly completed; his reason for the delay, being the impatience of the pale-faces, which would not have suffered the enemy to accomplish his object, so far as preparations were concerned, the thing of all others he himself thought to be the most desirable. By allowing the Hurons to waste their time and strength in making arrangements for an assault that was foreseen, and which might be met and defeated, a great advantage was obtained; whereas, by driving them prematurely from an artifice they were known to be engaged in, they would have recourse to another, and the difficulty of discovery would be added to our other disadvantages. So Susquesus reasoned, as was said at the time, and it is certain that so he acted.

But, the time had come to meet these covert preparations. Herman Mordaunt now held a consultation, on the subject of our proceedings. The question submitted was whether we ought to let the Hurons go any further; whether we should shoot the adventurous savage who was known still to be posted under the logs of the house, and scatter his pile of knots, by a sortie; or, whether it were wiser to let the enemy proceed to the extremity of actually lighting his fire, before we unmasked. Something was to be said in favour of each plan. By shooting the savage who had made a lodgment under our walls, and scattering his pile, we should unquestionably defeat the present attempt, but, in all probability, another would be made the succeeding night; whereas, by waiting to the last moment, such an effectual repulse might be given to our foes, as would at once terminate their expedition.

On consultation, and weighing all the points as they offered, it was decided to adopt the latter policy. But one spot commanded a view of the pile at all, and that was a loop, that had been cut only the day before, and which looked directly down on the place, from a projection that existed in the second story, and which ran around the whole building. These projections were common enough in the architecture of the provinces, at that day, being often adopted in exposed positions, purposely to afford the means of protecting the inferior and external portions of the dwellings. The Nest possessed this advantage, though the loops necessary to complete the arrangement, had only quite recently been cut. At this loop, then, I stationed myself, for a short time, watching what was going on below. The night was dark, but there was no difficulty in distinguishing the pile of knots, which to me seemed several feet high, besides being of some length, or in noting the movements of the Indian who had built it. At the moment I took my stand at the loop, this man was actually engaged in setting fire to his combustibles.

For several minutes, Guert and I watched our enemy while he was thus employed, for the Huron was obliged to proceed with the utmost caution, lest a light prematurely shed around should betray him. He cautiously lighted his knots quite within the pile, having left a place for that purpose, and his combustibles were well in flames before the latter began to throw their rays to any distance. We had a quantity of water provided in the room from which we beheld all these movements, and might at any time have extinguished the fire, by pouring a stream through our loop, provided we did not wait too long. But Guert objected to 'spoiling the sport,' as he called it, insisting that the logs of the house would be slow to ignite, and that we might at any moment scatter the knots, by a rapid sortie. His wish was to let the enemy proceed in his designs, as far as would be at all safe, in order to render his defeat more overwhelming.

Owing to our position, directly over his head, we had no chance to see the face of the incendiary, while he was thus engaged. At length he cast a glance upward, as if to note the effect of the flames, which were beginning to throw their forked tongues above the pile, when we both recognised Jaap's prisoner, Muss. The sight proved too much for Guert's philosophy, and thrusting the muzzle of his rifle through the loop, he blazed away at him, without much regard to aim. This report was a sort of signal, for action, the whole house, and all the outer world appearing to be in a clamour in an instant. I had no means of seeing Muss, but some of our look-outs, who had him in view most of the time, told me after all was over, that the fellow seemed much astonished at the suddenness of this assault; that he gazed up at the loop an instant, uttered a loud exclamation, then yelled the war-whoop, at the top of his voice, and went bounding off into the darkness, like a buck put up unexpectedly from his lair. The fields all around the Nest, seemed to be alive with whooping demons. Herman Mordaunt had done little towards embellishing the place, and stumps were standing in hundreds, all about it, many having been left within twenty yards of the buildings. It now seemed as if every one of these stumps had an Indian warrior lodged behind it, while bands of them appeared to be leaping about in the gloom, under the rocks. At one time, I fancied we must be surrounded by hundreds of these ruthless foes, though I now suppose that their numbers were magnified by their activity and their infernal yells. They manifested no intention to attack, nevertheless, but kept screaming around us, in all directions, occasionally discharging a rifle, but, as a whole, waiting the moment when the flames should have done their work.

Considering the fearful circumstances in which he was placed, Herman Mordaunt was wonderfully collected. For myself, I felt as if I had fifty lives to lose, Anneke being uppermost in my thoughts. The females, however, behaved uncommonly well, making no noise, and using all the self-command they could assume, in order not to distract the exertions of their husbands and friends. Some of the wives of the sturdy settlers, indeed, actually exhibited a species of stern courage that would have done credit

to soldiers, appearing in the court, armed, and otherwise rendering themselves useful. It often happened that women of this
class, by practising on deer, and wolves, and bears, got to be
reasonably expert with fire-arms, and did good service in at-
tacks on their dwellings. I remarked in all the commoner class of
females, that night, a sort of fierce hostility to their savage foes, in
whom they doubtless saw only the murderers of children, and
wretches who made no distinction of sex or age, in pursuing their
heartless warfare. Many of them appeared like the dams of the
inferior animals when their young were in danger.

An interval of ten or fifteen minutes must have occurred, between the moment when Guert discharged his rifle, and that in
which the battle really began. All this time, the fire was gathering
head, our tardy attempts to extinguish it, proving a complete fail-
ure. But little apprehension was felt on this account, however, the
flames proving an advantage, by casting their light far into the
fields, and even below the rocks, while they did not reach the
court at all; thus placing a portion of the enemy, should they venture to attack, under a bright light, while it left us in darkness.
The only point, however, at which we could fear a serious assault
was on the side of the rocks, where the court had no other protection than the low, but close and tolerably strong picket. Fortunately, the formation of the ground, on that side, prevented one,
who stood on the meadows below, from firing into the court,
from any point within the ordinary range of the rifle. It was this
circumstance that had determined the site of the "garrison."

Such was the state of things, when Anneke's own girl came to
ask me to go to her mistress, if it were possible for me to quit my
station, were it only for a minute. Having no particular duty to
perform, there was no impropriety in complying with a request
which, in itself, was every way so grateful to my feelings. Guert
was near me, at the time, and heard what the young negress said;
this induced him to inquire if there was no message for himself,
but, even at that serious moment, Mary Wallace did not relent.
She had been kinder than common in manner, the previous
night, as the Albanian had admitted, but, at the same time, she
had appeared to distrust her own resolution so much, as even to
give less direct encouragement, than had actually escaped her,
on previous occasions.

I found Anneke expecting me in that little parlour, where I

had so recently listened to her sweet confessions of tenderness the evening before. She was alone, the instinct of her sex teaching her the expediency of having no witness of the feelings and language that might escape two hearts that were united as were ours, under circumstances so trying. The dear girl was pale as death when I entered; she had doubtless been thinking of the approaching conflict, and of what might be its frightful consequences; but, my presence instantly caused her face to be suffused with blushes, it being impossible for her sensitive mind not to revert to what had so lately occurred. This truth to the instinctive principle of her nature, could hardly be extinguished in woman, even at the stake, itself. Notwithstanding the liveliness and varying character of her feelings, Anneke was the first to speak.

"I have sent for you, Corny," she said, laying a hand on her heart, as if to quiet its throbbings, "to say one word in the way of caution—I hope it is not wrong."

"You *can* do nothing wrong, beloved Anneke," I answered, "or, nothing that would seem so in my eyes. Be not thus agitated. Your fears have increased the danger, which we consider as trifling. The risks Guert, Dirck, and myself, have already run are tenfold those which now beset us."

The dear girl submitted to have an arm of mine passed around her waist, when her head dropped on my breast, and she burst into tears. Enabled by this relief to command her feelings a little, it was not long ere Anneke raised herself from the endearing embrace I felt impelled to give her, though still permitting me to hold both her hands, and she looked up into my face, with the full confidence of affection, renewing the discourse.

"I could not suffer you to engage in this terrible scene, Corny," she said, "without one word, one look, one sign of the interest I feel in you. My dear dear father has heard all; and, though disappointed, he does not disapprove. You know how warmly he has wished Mr. Bulstrode for a son, and can excuse that preference; but he desired me, not ten minutes since, as he left me, after giving me a kiss and his blessing, to send for you, and to say that he shall hereafter look upon you as my and his choice. Heaven alone knows whether we are to be permitted to meet again, dear Corny, but, should that never be granted us, I feel it will relieve your mind to know that we shall meet as the members of one family."

"We are the only children of our parents, Anneke, and our union will gladden their hearts almost as much as it can gladden our own."

"I have thought of this, already. I shall have a mother, now; a blessing I hardly ever knew!"

"And one that will dearly, dearly love you, as I know by her own opinions, again and again expressed in my presence."

"Thank you, Corny—and thanks to that respected parent, too. Now, go, Corny; I am fearful this selfish gratification only adds to the danger of the house—go; I will pray for your safety."

"One word, dearest;—poor Guert!—You cannot know how disappointed he is, that I alone should be summoned here, at such a moment."

Anneke seemed thoughtful, and it struck me she was a little distressed.

"What can I do to alter this?" she said, after a short pause. "A woman's judgment and her feelings may not impel her the same way; then Mary Wallace is a girl who appreciates propriety so highly!"

"I understand you, Anneke. But, Guert is of so noble a disposition, and acknowledges all his defects so meekly, and with so much candor! Man cannot love woman better, than he loves Mary Wallace. Her extreme prudence is a virtue in his eyes, even while he suffers by it."

"I cannot change Mary Wallace's nature, Corny," said Anneke, smiling sadly, and, as I fancied in a way that said 'were it I, the virtues of Guert should soon outweigh his defects,' "but Mary will be Mary, and we must submit. Perhaps to-morrow may bring her wavering mind to something like decision, for these late events have proved greatly Mr. Ten Eyck's friends. But Mary is an orphan, and prudence has been taught her, as her great protection. Now go, Corny, lest you be missed."

The dear girl parted from me hurriedly, but not without strong manifestation of feeling. I folded her to my heart, that being no moment for affectations, or conventional distance, and I know *I* was, while I trusted Anneke might be, none the less happy, for remembering we had exchanged these proofs of mutual attachments.

Just as I reached the court, I heard a yell without, which my experience before Ty had taught me was the whoop the Hurons give when they attack. A rattling fire succeeded, and we were instantly engaged in a hot conflict. Our people fought under one advantage, which more than counterbalanced the disadvantage of their inferiority in numbers. While two sides of the buildings, including that of the meadows, or the one on which an assault could alone be successful, were in bright light, the court still remained sufficiently dark to answer all the purposes of defence. We could see each other, but could not be distinguished at any distance. Our persons, when seen from without, must have been confounded, too, with the waving shadows of the pickets.

As I approached the pickets, through the openings of which our people were already keeping up a dropping fire on the dark-looking demons who were leaping about on the meadows below, I learned from Herman Mordaunt himself, who received me by an affectionate squeeze of the hand, that a large body of the enemy was collected directly under the rocks, and that Guert had assumed the duty of dislodging them. He had taken with him on this service, Dirck, Jaap and three or four more of the best men, including both of our Indians. The manner in which he proposed to effect this object was bold, and like the character of the leader of the party. As so much depended on it, and on its success, I will explain a few of its more essential details.

The front of the house ranged north and south, facing westward. The two wings consequently extended east and west. The fire had been built at the verge of the cliff, and at the north-east angle of the building. This placed the north and east sides of the square in light, while it left the west and south in deep darkness. The gate opening to the west, it was not a very hopeless thing to believe it practicable, to lead a small party round the south-west angle of the house, to the verge of the cliff, where the formation of the ground would allow of a volley's being given upon those savages who were believed to be making a lodgment directly beneath our pickets, with a view of seizing a favourable moment to scale them. On this errand, then, Herman Mordaunt now gave me to understand, my friends had gone.

"Who guards the gate, the while?" I asked, almost instinctively.

"Mr. Worden, and your old acquaintance and my new tenant, Newcome. They are both armed, for a parson will not only fight the battles of the spirit, but he will fight those of the field, when concerned. Mr. Worden has shown himself a man, in all this business."

Without replying, I left Herman Mordaunt, and proceeded to the gate myself, since there was little to be done in the court. *There* we were strong enough; stronger, perhaps, than was necessary; but I greatly distrusted Guert's scheme, the guard at the gate, and most of all the fire.

I was soon at Mr. Worden's side. There the reverend gentleman was, sure enough, with Jason Newcome at his elbow. Their duty was to keep the gate in that precise condition in which it could be barred, or unbarred, at the shortest notice, as friends, or foes might seek admission. The parties appeared to be fully aware of the importance of the trust they filled, and I asked permission to pass out. My first object was the fire, for it struck me Herman Mordaunt felt too much confidence in his means of extinguishing it, and that our security had been neglected in that quarter. I was no sooner outside the buildings, therefore, than I turned to steal along the wall, to the northwest corner, where alone I could get a view of the dangerous pile.

The brightness of the glare that was gleaming over the fields and stumps, that came within the compass of the light from the fire, added to my security by the contrast, though it did not tell well for that particular source of danger. The dark stumps, many of which were charred by the fires of the clearing, and were absolutely black, seemed to be dancing about in the fields, under the waving light, and twice I paused to meet imaginary savages ere I gained the corner of the house. Each alarm, however, was idle, and I succeeded in obtaining the desired view. Not only were the knots burning fiercely, but a large sheet of flame was clinging to the logs of the house, menacing us with a speedy conflagration. The danger would have been greater, but a thunder-shower had passed over the settlement, only an hour before we were alarmed, and coming from the north, all that side of the house had been well drenched with rain. This occurred after 'Muss' had commenced his pile, or he might have chosen another side of the building. The deep obscurity of that gust, however, was probably one of the means of his success. He must have been at work, during the whole continuance of the storm.

I was not absent from the gate two minutes. That brief space was sufficient for my first purpose. I now desired Jason to enter

the court, and to tell Herman Mordaunt not to delay a moment
in applying the means for extinguishing the flames. There was
greater danger from them, than there possibly could be from any
other attack upon the pickets, made in the darkness of the morning. Jason was cool by temperament, and he was a good agent to
be employed on such a duty. Promising to be quick, he left us, and
I turned my face towards Guert, and his party. As yet, nothing
had been heard of the last. This very silence was a source of
alarm, though it was difficult to imagine the adventurers had
met with an enemy, since such a collision must have been somewhat noisy. A few scattering shot, all of which came from the west
side of the buildings, and the flickering light of the fire, were the
only interruptions to the otherwise death-like calm of the hour.

The same success attended me in reaching the south-west as in
reaching the north-west angle of the house. To me, it seemed as
if the savages had entirely abandoned the fields in my vicinity.
When I took my stand at this corner of the building, I found all
its southern side in obscurity, though sufficient light was gleaming over the meadows, to render the ragged edges of the cliff visible, in that direction. I looked along the log walls, to this streak
of light, but could see no signs of my friends. I was certain they
were not under the house, and began to apprehend some serious
indiscretion on the part of the bold Albanian. While engaged in
endeavouring to get a clue to Guert's movements, by devouring
every dark object I could perceive with my eyes, I felt an elbow
touched lightly, and saw a savage in his half-naked, fighting attire, at my side. I could see enough to ascertain this, but could not
distinguish faces. I was feeling for my hunting-knife, when the
Trackless's voice stayed my hand.

"He wrong—" said the Onondago, with emphasis. "Head too
young—hand good—heart good—head very bad. Too much
fire—dark here—much better."

This characteristic criticism on poor Guert's conduct, served to
tell the whole story. Guert had put himself in a position in which
the Onondago had refused to remain; in other words, he had
gone to the verge of the cliff, where he was exposed to the light of
the fire, and where he was necessarily in danger of being seen.
Still, no signs of him were visible, and I was on the point of moving along the south side of the building, to the margin of the rocks,
when the Trackless again touched my arm, and said "There!"

There our party was, sure enough! It had managed to reach the verge of the rocks at a salient point, which placed them in an admirable position for raking the enemy, who were supposed to be climbing to the pickets, with a view to a sudden spring, but at a dangerous distance from the buildings. The darkness had been the means of their reaching that point, which was about a hundred yards from the spot where I had expected to find them, and admirably placed for the intended object. The whole procedure was so much like Guert's character, that I could not but admire its boldness, while I condemned its imprudence. There was, however, no time to join the party, or to warn its leader of the risks he ran. We, who stood so far in the rear, could see and fully appreciate all the danger, while he probably did not. There the whole party of them stood, plainly though darkly drawn in high relief, against the light beyond, each poising his rifle and making his dispositions for the volley. Guert was nearest to the verge of the rocks, actually bending over them; Dirck was close at his side; Jaap just behind Dirck, Jumper close at Jaap's elbow, and four of the settlers, bold and hardy men, behind the Oneida.

I could scarcely breathe, for painful expectation, when I saw Guert and his companions thus rising from the earth, bringing their entire figures in front of the back-ground of light. I could have called out to warn them of the danger they ran; but it would have done no good; nor was there time for remonstrances. Guert must have felt he occupied a dangerous position, and what he did, was done very promptly. Ten seconds after I saw the dark forms, all their rifles were discharged, as it might be at a single crack. One instant passed, in death-like stillness, through all the fields, and in the court; then came a volley from among the stumps at a little distance from our side of the building, and the adventurers on the rocks, or those that could, rushed towards the gate. Two of the settlers, however, and the Oneida, I saw fall, myself. The last actually leaped upward, into the air, and went down the cliff. But Guert, Dirk, Jaap, and the other two settlers, had moved away. It was at that moment, that my ears were filled with such yells as I had not supposed the human throat could raise, and all the fields, on our side of the house, seemed alive with savages. To render the scene more appalling, that was the precise instant when the water, previously provided by Herman Mordaunt, fell upon the flames, and the light vanished, almost as one extinguishes a candle. But for this providential coincidence, there was scarce a chance for the escape of one of the adventurers. As it was, rifle followed rifle, from among the stumps, though it was no longer with any certain aim.

The battle had now become a *mêlée*. The savages went leaping and whooping forward in the darkness, and heavy blows were given and taken. Guert's clear, manly voice was heard, rising above the clamour, encouraging his companions to press through the throng of their assailants, in tones full of confidence. Both the Trackless and myself discharged our rifles at the foremost of the Hurons, and each certainly brought down his man; but it was not easy to see what we could do next. To stand aloof, and see my friends borne down by numbers, was impossible, however, and Susquesus and myself fell upon the enemy's rear. This charge of ours, had the appearance of a sortie, and it produced a decided effect on the result, opening a passage by which Dirck and the two settlers issued from the throng, and joined us. This was no sooner done, than we all had to stand at bay, retreating little by little, as we could. The result would still have been doubtful, even after we had succeeded in reaching the south-western angle of the building, had it not been for a forward movement on the part of Herman Mordaunt, at the head of half a dozen of his settlers. This reinforcement came into the affair with loaded rifles, and a single discharge, given as soon as we were in a line with our friends, caused our assailants to vanish, as suddenly as they had appeared. On reflecting on the circumstances of that awful night, in after-life, I have thought that the force in the rear of the Hurons began to melt away even before Herman Mordaunt's support was received, leaving their front weak and unsustained. At any rate, the enemy fled to their covers, as has just been related, and we entered the gate in a body, closing and barring it, as soon as possible.

I can scarcely describe the change that had come over the appearance of things, in that eventful night. The fire was extinguished, even to the embers, and deep darkness had succeeded to the glimmering, waving, red light of the flames. The yells, and whoops, and screams, and shouts, for our men had frequently thrown back the defiance of their foes in cheers, were done; a stillness as profound as that of the grave reigning over the whole place. The wounded seemed ashamed even to groan, but our hurt, of whom there were four, went into the house to be cared for, stern and silent. No enemy was any longer to be apprehended beneath the pickets, for the streak of morning was just appearing above the forest, in the east, and Indians rarely attack under the light of day. In a word, *that* night at least, was passed, and we were yet protected by Providence.

Herman Mordaunt now bethought him of ascertaining his precise situation, the extent of his own loss, and, as far as possible, of that which we had inflicted on the enemy. Guert was called for, to aid in this inquiry, but no Guert was to be found! Jaap, too, was absent. A muster was had, and then it was found that Guert Ten Eyck, Jaap Satanstoe, Gilbert Davis and Moses Mudge were all wanting. The Jumper, too, did not appear, but I accounted for him and for the two settlers named, having actually seen them fall. Day returned to us slowly, while agitated by the effects of these discoveries, but it brought no relief. We soon ventured to re-open the gates, knowing no Indian would remain very near the buildings, while it was light, and, having examined all the dangerous covers, we passed outside the court with confidence, in quest of the bodies of our friends. Not an Indian was seen, Jumper excepted. The Oneida lay at the foot of the rocks, dead, and scalped; as did Davis and Mudge on the summit. Everything else human had disappeared. Dirck was confident that six or seven of the Hurons fell by the volley from the cliff, but the bodies had been carried off. As to Guert and Jaap, no traces of them remained, dead or alive.

Chapter XXIX

"She looked on many a face with vacant eye,
  On many a token without knowing what;
She saw them watch her without asking why,
  And reck'd not who around her pillow sat;
Not speechless, though she spoke not; not a sigh
  Relieved her thoughts; dull silence and quick chat
Were tried in vain by those who served; she gave
No sign, save breath, of having left the grave."
                    Byron, *Don Juan*, IV. lxiii.497–504.

IT was a most painful moment to me, when Herman Mordaunt, an hour after all these facts were established, came to summon me to the presence of Anneke and Mary Wallace. One gleam of joy, one ray of the sunshine of the heart, shone on Anneke's sweet countenance, as she saw me unharmed enter the room, but it quickly disappeared in the strong sympathy she felt for the sufferings of her friend. As for Mary Wallace, death itself could hardly have left her more colourless, or with features more firmly impressed with the expression of mental suffering. Anneke was the first to speak.

"God be praised that this dreadful night is passed, and you and my dearest father are spared!" the precious girl said, with fervour, pressing the hand that had taken one of hers, in both her own. "For this much, at least, we can be grateful; would I could add for the safety of us all!"

"Tell me the worst at once, Mr. Littlepage," added Mary Wallace; "I can bear any thing better than uncertainty. Mr. Mordaunt says that you know the facts better than any one else, and that you must relate them. Speak, then, though it break my heart to hear it;—is he killed?"

"I hope, through Heaven's mercy, not. Indeed, I think not, though I fear he must be a prisoner."

"Thank you for that, dear, dear Mr. Littlepage! Oh! Thank you for that, from the bottom of my heart. But, may they not torture him?—Do not these Hurons torture their prisoners? Conceal nothing from me, Corny; you cannot imagine how much self-command I have, and how well I can behave. Oh! conceal nothing."

Poor girl! At the very moment she was boasting of her fortitude and ability to endure, her whole frame was trembling from head to foot, her face was of the hue of death, and the smile with which she spoke was frightfully haggard. That pent-up passion, which had so long struggled with her prudence, could no longer be suppressed. That she really loved Guert, and that her love would prove stronger than her discretion, I had not doubted, now, for some months; but, never having before witnessed the strength of any feeling that had been so long and so painfully suppressed, I confess that this exhibition of a suffering so intense, in a being so delicate, so excellent, and so lovely, almost unmanned me. I took Mary Wallace's hand and led her to a chair, scarce knowing what to say to relieve her mind. All this time, her eye never turned from mine, as if she hoped to learn the truth by the aid of the sense of sight, alone. How anxious, jealous, distrustful, and yet beseeching was that gaze!

"Will he be tortured?" She rather whispered huskily, than asked aloud.

"I trust, by God's mercy, not. They have taken my slave, Jaap, also; and it is far more probable that *he* would be the victim, in such a case, than Mr. Ten Eyck—"

"Why do you call him Mr. Ten Eyck?—You have always called him Guert, of late—you are his friend—you think well of him—you cannot be less his friend, now that he is miserable, than when he was happy, and the pride of all human eyes, in his strength and manly beauty!"

"Dear Miss Wallace, compose yourself, I do entreat of you—no one will cling to Guert, longer than I."

"Yes; I have always thought this—always *felt* this. Guert cannot be low, or mean in his sentiments, while an educated gentleman, like Corny Littlepage, is his friend. I have written to my aunt, and we must not be too hasty in our judgments. The spirit and follies of youth will soon be over, and then we shall see a shining character in Guert Ten Eyck.—Is not this true, Anneke?"

Anneke knelt at the side of her friend, folded her in her arms, drew the quivering head down upon her own sympathizing bosom, and held it there a moment, in the very attitude of protecting, solacing love. After a brief pause, Mary Wallace burst into tears, and I have ever thought that that relief, under God's mercy, saved her reason. In a few minutes, the sufferer became more calm, when she retired into herself, as was her wont, leaving Anneke and me, to discuss the subject.

After turning all the chances and probabilities in our minds, I promised my companions, not to lose a moment, but to use immediate means of ascertaining all that could be ascertained in Guert's behalf, and of doing everything that could be done, to save him.

"You will not deceive me, Corny—" whispered Mary Wallace, pressing my hand at leave-taking, in both her own. "I know I can depend on *you*, for he *boasts* of being your friend."

Anneke's painful smile, added force to this request, and I tore myself away, unwilling to quit such a sufferer, yet unable to remain. Herman Mordaunt was seen conversing with Susquesus, in the court, and I joined him at once, determined to lose no time.

"I was speaking to the Trackless on this very subject," answered Herman Mordaunt, as soon as I had explained my purpose, "and am now waiting for his answer. Do you think it, then, safe to send a messenger out to the Hurons, in order to enquire after our friends, and to treat with them!"

"No send?—Why not?" returned the Indian. "Red man glad to see messenger. Go when he want; come back, when he want. How can make bargain, if scalp messenger?"

I had heard that the most savage tribes respected a messenger, and, indeed, the necessity of so doing was of itself a sort of security that such must be the case. It was true, that the bearer of a flag might be in more danger on such an errand, than would be the case in a camp of civilized men, but these Canada Indians had been long serving with the French, and their chiefs, beyond a question, had obtained some of the notions of pale-face warfare. Without much reflection, therefore, and under an impulse in behalf of my friend, and my slave—for Jaap's fate was of lively interest with me—I volunteered to bear a flag myself. Herman Mordaunt shook his head, and seemed reluctant to comply.

"Anneke would hardly pardon me for consenting to that," he answered. "You must remember, now, Corny, that a very tender and sensitive heart is bound up in you, and you must no longer act like a thoughtless, single man. It would be far better to send this Onondago, if he will agree to go. He understands the red man, and will be able to interpret the omens with more certainty, than any of us. What say you, Susquesus; will you be a messenger to the Hurons?"

"Sartain—why no go, if he want? Good to be messenger, some-time. Where wampum—what tell him?"

Thus encouraged, we deliberated together, and soon had Susquesus in readiness to depart. As for the Indian, he laid aside all his arms, washed the war-paint from his face, put a calico shirt over his shoulders, and assumed the guise of peace. We gave him a small white flag to carry, feeling certain that the Huron chiefs must understand its meaning, and thinking it might be better in bearing a message from pale-faces, that he who carried it, should have a pale-face symbol of his errand. Susquesus found some wampum, too, having as much faith in that, probably, as in any thing else. He then set forth, being charged to offer liberal ransom to the Hurons, for the living uninjured bodies of Guert Ten Eyck and Jaap Satanstoe.

We entertained no doubt that the enemy would be found in the ravine, for that was the point, in every respect, most favourable to the operations of the siege, being near the house, having a perfect cover, possessing water, wood, and other conveniences. From that point the Nest could be watched, and any favourable chance improved. Thither, then, Susquesus was told to proceed, though it was not thought advisable to fetter one so shrewd, with too many instructions. Several of us accompanied the Onondago to the gate, and saw him moving across the fields, towards the wood, in his usual loping trot. A bird could scarcely have flown more directly to its object.

The half-hour that succeeded the disappearance of Susquesus, in the mouth of the ravine, was one of intensely painful suspense. We all remained without the gate, waiting the result, in-cluding Dirck, Mr. Worden, Jason, and half a dozen of the settlers. At length, the Onondago re-appeared, and, to our great joy, a group followed him, in which were both the prisoners. The last were bound, but able to walk. This party might have con-tained a dozen of the enemy, all of whom were armed. It moved slowly out of the ravine, and ascended to the fields that were on a level with the house, halting when about four hundred yards from us. Seeing this movement, we counted out exactly the same number of men, and went forward, halting at a distance of two hundred yards from the Indians. Here we waited for our messenger, who continued on, after the Hurons had come to a stand. Thus far every thing looked propitious.

"Do you bring us good news?" Herman Mordaunt eagerly asked. "Are our friends unhurt?"

"Got scalp—no hurt—take prisoner—jump on 'em, ten, two, six—cotch 'em, then. Open eyes; you see."

"And the Hurons—do they seem inclined to accept the ransom? Rum, rifle, blanket and powder; you offered all, I hope, Susquesus?"

"Sartain. No forget; that bad. Say take all that; some more, too."

"And they have come to treat with us? What are we to do, now, Susquesus?"

"Put down rifle—go near and talk. You go—Priest go—young chief go—that t'ree. Then t'ree warrior lay down rifle, come talk, too. Prisoner wait. All good."

This was sufficiently intelligible, and believing that any thing like hesitation might make the condition of Guert desperate, we prepared to comply. I could see that the Rev. Mr. Worden had no great relish for the business, but was ashamed to hang back when he saw Herman Mordaunt cheerfully advancing to the interview. We three were met by as many Hurons, among whom was Jaap's friend 'Muss' who was evidently the leading person of the party. Guert and Jaap were held, bound, about a hundred yards in the rear, but near enough to be spoken to, by raising the voice. Guert was in his shirt and breeches, with his head uncovered, his fine curly hair blowing about in the wind, and I thought I saw some signs of blood on his linen. This might be his own, or it might have come from an enemy. I called to him, therefore, enquiring how he did, and whether he were hurt.

"Nothing to speak of, Corny, I thank you," was the cheerful answer; "these red gentlemen have had me tied to a tree, and have been seeing how near they could hurl their tomahawks without hitting. This is one of their customary amusements, and I have got a scratch, or two, in the sport. I hope the ladies are in good spirits, and do not let the business of last night distress them."

"There is blessed news for you, Guert—Susquesus, ask these

chiefs if I may go near my friend to give him one word of consolation—On my honour, no attempt to release him will be made by me, until I return here."

I spoke earnestly, and the Onondago interpreted what I had said into the language of Hurons. I had made this somewhat hardy request, under an impulse that I found ungovernable, and was surprised, as well as pleased, to find it granted. These savages confided in my word, and trusted to my honour with a stately delicacy that might have done credit to the manners of civilized kings, giving themselves no apparent concern about my movements, although they occurred in their own rear. It was too late to retreat, and, leaving Herman Mordaunt endeavouring to drive a bargain with Muss and his two companions, I proceeded, unconcerned myself, boldly towards the armed men who held Guert and Jaap prisoners. I thought my approach *did* cause a slight movement among these savages, and there was a question and answer passed between them and their leaders. The latter said but a word, or two, but these were uttered authoritatively, and with a commanding toss of a hand. Brief as they were, they answered the purpose, and I was neither molested, nor spoken to, during the short interview I had with my friend.

"God bless you, Corny, for this!" Guert cried, with feeling, as I warmly shook his hand. "It requires a warm heart, and a bold one, too, to lead a man into this 'lion's den.' Stay but a moment, lest some evil come of it, I beg of you. This squeeze of the hand, is worth an estate to a man in my situation, but remember Anneke. Ah! Corny, my dear friend, I could be happy even here, did I know that Mary Wallace grieved for me!"

"Then be happy, Guert. My sole object in venturing here, was to tell you to hope every thing, in that quarter. There will be no longer any coyness, any hesitation, any misgivings, when you shall be once restored to us."

"Mr. Littlepage, you would not trifle with the feelings of a miserable captive, hanging between torture and death, as is my present case! I can hardly credit my senses, yet you would not mock me!"

"Believe all I say—nay, all you *wish*, Guert. It is seldom that woman loves as *she* loves, and this I swear to you. I go now, only to aid Herman Mordaunt in bringing you where your own ears shall hear such proofs of what I say, as have been uttered in mine."

Guert made no answer, but I could see he was profoundly affected. I squeezed his hand, and we parted, in the full hope on my side at least, that the separation would be short. I have reason to think Guert shed tears, for, on looking back, I perceived his face turned away from those who were nearest to him. I had but a single glance at Jaap. My fellow stood a little in the rear, as became his colour, but he watched my countenance with the vigilance of a cat. I thought it best not to speak to him, though I gave him a secret sign of encouragement.

"These chiefs are not very amicably disposed, Corny," said Herman Mordaunt, the instant I rejoined him. "They have given me to understand that Jaap will be liberated on no terms whatever. They must have his scalp, as Susquesus tells me, on account of some severity he himself has shown to one of these chiefs. To use their own language, they want it for a plaster to this warrior's back. His fate, it would seem is sealed, and he has only been brought out, yonder, to raise hopes in him, that are to be disappointed. The wretches do not scruple to avow this, in their own sententious manner. As for Guert, they say he slew two of their warriors, and that their wives will miss their husbands, and will not be easily quieted unless they see his scalp, too. They offer to release him, however, on either of two sets of terms. They will give up Guert for two of what they call chiefs, or for four common men. If we do not like those conditions, they will exchange him, on condition we give two common men for him, and abandon the Nest to them by marching out, with all my people, before the sun is up above our heads."

"Conditions that you cannot accept, under any circumstances, I fear, sir?"

"Certainly not. The delivery of any two is out of the question—would be so, even to save my own life. As for the Nest, and its contents, I would very willingly abandon all, a few papers excepted, had I the smallest faith in the chiefs' being able to restrain their followers; but, the dreadful massacre of William Henry, is still too recent to confide in any thing of the sort. My answer is given already, and we are about to part. Possibly, when they see us determined they may lower their demands a little."

A grave parting wave of the hand was given by Muss, who had conducted himself with great dignity in the interview, and the three Hurons walked away, in a body.

"Best go," said Susquesus, significantly. "Maybe want rifle. Hurons in 'arnest."

On this hint, we returned to our friends and resumed our arms. What succeeded, I learned in part, by the relations of others, while a part was witnessed by my own eyes. It seems that Jaap, from the first, understood the desperate nature of his own position. The remembrance of his misdeeds in relation to Muss, whose prisoner he had now especially become, most probably increased his apprehensions, and his thoughts were constantly bent on obtaining his liberty, by means entirely independent of negotiation. From the instant he was brought out of the ravine, he kept all his eyes about him, watching for the smallest chance of effecting his purpose. It happened that one of the savages so placed himself before the negro, who was kept behind all near him, as to enable Jaap to draw the Huron's knife from its sheath without being detected. He did this while I was actually with the party, and all eyes were on me. Guert and himself were bound, by having their arms fastened above the elbows, behind the back, and when Guert turned aside to shed tears, as mentioned, Jaap succeeded in cutting his fastenings. This could be done, only while the savages were following my retreating form with their eyes. At the same time, Jaap gave the knife to Guert, who did him a similar service. As the Indians did not take the alarm, the prisoners paused a moment, holding their arms as if still bound, to look around them. The Indian nearest Guert had two rifles, his own and that of Muss, both leaning negligently against his shoulder, with their breeches on the ground. To these weapons Guert pointed, and, when the three chiefs were on the point of rejoining their friends, who were attentive to their movements in order to ascertain the result, Guert seized this savage by his arm, which he twisted until the Indian yelled with pain, then caught one rifle, while Jaap laid hold of the other. Each fired and brought down his man; then they made an onset with the butts of their pieces on the rest of the party. This bold assault, though so desperate in appearance, was the wisest thing they could do, as immediate flight would have left their enemies an opportunity of sending the swift runners of their pieces in pursuit.

The first intimation we had of any movement of this sort was in the reports of the rifles. Then, I not only saw, but I heard the tremendous blow Jaap gave to the head of Muss; a blow that demolished both the victim and the instrument of his destruction. Though the breech of the rifle was broken, the heavy barrel still remained, and the negro flourished it with a force that swept all before him. It is scarcely necessary to say Guert was not idle in such a fray. He fought for Mary Wallace, as well as for himself, and he overturned two more of the Indians, as it might be in the twinkling of an eye. Here Dirck did good service to our friends. His rifle was in his hands, and levelling it with coolness, he shot down a powerful savage who was on the point of seizing Guert, from behind. This was the commencement of a general war, volleys now coming from both parties; from ourselves, and from the enemy who were in the cover of the woods. Intimidated by the fury of the personal assault under which they were suffering, the remaining Indians near Guert and the negro leaped away towards their friends, yelling; leaving their late prisoners free, but more exposed to fire than they could have been when encircled even by enemies.

Every thing passed with fearful rapidity. Guert seized the rifle of a fallen Indian, and Jaap obtained another, when they fell back towards us, like two lions at bay, with rifle bullets whizzing around them at every step. Of course, we fired, and we also advanced to meet them, an imprudent step, since the main body of the Hurons were covered, rendering the contest unequal. But, there was no resisting the sympathetic impulses of such a moment, or the exultation we all felt at the exploits of Guert and Jaap, enacted as they were, before our eyes. As we drew together, the former shouted and cried——

"Hurrah! Corny, my noble fellow—let us charge the woot—there'll not be a ret-skin left in it, in five minutes. Forwart my friends—forwart, all!"

It certainly was an exciting moment. We all shouted in our turns, and all cried 'forward' in common. Even Mr. Worden joined in the shout, and pressed forward. Jason, too, fought bravely, and we went at the wood like so many bull-dogs. I fancy the pedagogue thought the fee-simple of his mills depended on the result. On we went, in open order, reserving our fire for the last moment, but receiving dropping shots that did us no harm, until we dashed into the thicket.

The Hurons were discomfited, and they fled. Though a panic is not usual among those wild warriors, they seldom rally on the field. If once driven, against their will, a close pursuit will usually disperse them for a time; and such was the case now. By the time I got fairly into the ravine, I could see or hear of no enemy. My friends were on my right and left, shouting and pressing on, but there was no foe visible. Guert and Jaap were in advance, for we could not overtake them, and they had fired, for they got the last glimpses of the enemy. But one more shot did come from the Hurons in that inroad. It was fired from some one of the retreating party, who must have been lingering in its rear. The report sounded far up the ravine, and it came like a farewell and final gun. Distant as it was, however, it proved the most fatal shot to us, that was fired in all that affair. I caught a glimpse of Guert, through the trees, and saw him fall. In an instant, I was at his side.

What a change is that from the triumph of victory to the sudden approach of death! I saw by the expression of Guert's countenance, as I raised him in my arms, that the blow was fatal. The ball, indeed, had passed directly through his body, missing the bones, but injuring the vitals. There is no mistaking the expression of a death-wound, on the human countenance, when the effect is direct and not remote. Nature appears to admonish the victim of his fate. So it was with Guert.

"This shot has done for me, Corny," he said, "and it seems to be the very last they intended to fire. I almost hope there can be no truth in what you told me of Mary Wallace!"

That was neither the time nor the place to speak on such a subject, and I made no answer. From the instant the fall of Guert became know, the pursuit ceased, and our whole party collected around the wounded man. The Indian alone, seemed to retain any consciousness of the importance of knowing what the enemy was doing, for his philosophy was not easily disturbed by the sudden appearance of death among us. Still he liked Guert, as did every one who could get beyond the weaknesses of his outer character, and fairly at the noble traits of his manly nature. Susquesus looked at the sufferer a moment, gravely and not without concern; then he turned to Herman Mordaunt, and said—

"This bad—save scalp, that good, though. Carry him in house. Susquesus follow trail and see what Injin mean."

As this was well, he was told to watch the enemy, while we bore our friend towards the Nest. Dirck consented to precede us, and let the melancholy truth be known, while I continued with Guert, who held my hand the whole distance. We were a most melancholy procession for victors. Not a serious hurt had any of our party received, in this last affair, the wound of Guert Ten Eyck, excepted; yet, I question if more real sorrow would have been felt over two or three other deaths. We had become accustomed to our situation; it is wonderful how soon the soldier does; rendering death familiar and disarming him of half his terrors, but calamities can, and do occur, to bring back an army to a sense of its true nature and its dependence on Providence. Such had been the effect of the loss of Lord Howe, on the troops before Ticonderoga, and such was the effect of the fall of Guert Ten Eyck, on the small band that was collected to defend the possessions and firesides of Ravensnest.

We entered the gate of the house, and found most of its tenants already in the court, collected like a congregation in a church that awaits the entrance of the dead. Herman Mordaunt had sent an order to have his own room prepared, for the sufferer, and thither we carried Guert. He was placed on the bed; then the crowd silently withdrew. I observed that Guert's eyes turned anxiously and inquiringly around, and I told him, in a low voice, I would go for the ladies myself. A smile, and a pressure of the hand showed how well I had interpreted his thoughts.

Somewhat to my surprise, I found Mary Wallace, pale it is true, but comparatively calm and mistress of herself. That instinct of propriety which seems to form a part of the nature of a well-educated woman, had taught her the necessity of self-command, that no out-break of her feelings should affect the sufferer. As for Anneke, she was like herself, gentle, mourning, and full of sympathy for her friend.

As soon as apprised of the object of my visit, the two girls expressed their readiness to go to Guert. As they knew the way, I did not attend them, purposely proceeding in another direction, in order not to be a witness of the interview. Anneke has since told me, however, that Mary's self-command did not altogether desert her, while Guert's cheerful gratitude probably so far deceived her as to create a short-lived hope that the wound was not mortal. For myself, I passed an hour in attending to the state of things, in and around the house, in order to make certain that no negligence occurred, still to endanger our security. At the end of that time, I returned to Guert, meeting Herman Mordaunt near the door of his room.

"The little hope we had is vanished," said the last, in a sorrowful tone. "Poor Ten Eyck has, beyond a question, received his death-wound, and has but a few hours to live. Were my people safe, I would rather that every thing at Ravensnest, house and estate, were destroyed, than had this happen!"

Prepared by this announcement, I was not as much surprised as I might otherwise have been, at the great change that had occurred in my friend, since the time I quitted his room. It was evident he anticipated the result. Nevertheless he was calm; nay, apparently, happy. Nor was he so much enfeebled as to prevent his speaking quite distinctly, and with sufficient ease. When the machine of life is stopped by the sudden disruption of a vital ligament, the approaches of death, though more rapid than with disease, are seldom so apparent. The first evidences of a fatal termination are discovered rather through the nature of the violence, than by means of apparent effects.

I have said that Guert seemed even happy, though death was so near. Anneke told me, subsequently, that Mary Wallace had owned her love, in answer to an earnest appeal on his part, and, from that moment, he had expressed himself as one who was about to die contented. Poor Guert! It was little he thought of the dread future, or of the church on earth, except as the last was entitled to, and did receive on all occasions, his outward respect. It seemed that Mary Wallace, habitually so reserved and silent among her friends, had been accustomed to converse freely with Guert, and that she had made a serious effort, during her residence in Albany, to enlighten his mind, or rather to arouse his feelings on this all-important subject, and that Guert, sensible of the pleasure of receiving instruction from such a source, always listened with attention. When I entered the room, some allusion had just been made to this theme.

"But for you, Mary, I should be little better than a heathen—"

said Guert, holding the hand of his beloved, and scarce averting his eyes from their idol, a single instant. "If God has mercy on me, it will be on your account."

"Oh! no—no—no—Guert, say not, think not *thus!*" exclaimed Mary Wallace, shocked at this excess of his attachment even for herself at such a moment. "We all receive our pardons through the death and mediation of his Blessed Son. Nothing else can save you, or any of us, my dear, dear Guert; and I implore you not to think otherwise."

Guert looked a little bewildered; still he looked pleased. The first expression was probably produced by his not exactly comprehending the nature of that mysterious expiation, which baffles the unaided powers of man, and which, indeed, is to be felt, rather than understood. The look of pleasure had its origin in the 'dear, dear Guert,' and, more than that, in the consciousness of possessing the affections of the woman he had so long loved, almost against hope. Guert Ten Eyck was a man of bold and reckless character, in all that pertained to risks, frolick and youthful adventure, but the meekest Christian could scarcely possess a more lowly opinion of his own frailties and sins, than this dashing young fellow possessed of his own claims to be valued by such a being as Mary Wallace. I often wondered how he ever presumed to love her, but suppose the apparent vanity must be ascribed to the resistless power of a passion that is known to be the strongest of our nature. It was also a sort of moral anomaly that two so opposed to each other in character; the one verging on extreme recklessness, the other pushing prudence almost to prudery; the one so gay as to seem to live for frolick, the other quiet and reserved, should conceive this strong predilection for each other, but so it was. I have heard persons say, however, that these varieties in temperament awaken interest, and that they who have commenced with such dissimilarities, but have assimilated by communion, attachment and habits, after all, make the happiest couples.

Mary Wallace lost all her reserve, in the gush of tenderness and sympathy, that now swept all before it. Throughout the whole of that morning, she hung about Guert, as the mother watches the ailing infant. If his thirst was to be assuaged, her hand held the cup; if his pillow was to be replaced, her care suggested the alteration; if his brow was to be wiped, she performed that office for him, suffering no other to come between her and the object of her solicitude.

There were moments when the manner in which Mary Wallace hung over Guert, was infinitely touching. Anneke and I knew that her very soul yearned to lead his thoughts to dwell on the subject of the great change that was so near. Nevertheless, the tenderness of the woman was so much stronger than even the anxiety of the Christian, that we perceived she feared the influence on his wound. At length, happily for an anxiety that was beginning to be too painful for endurance, Guert spoke on the subject himself. Whether his mind adverted naturally to such a topic, or he perceived the solicitude of his gentle nurse, I could not say.

"I cannot stay with you long, Mary," he said, "and I should like to have Mr. Worden's prayers, united to yours, offered up in my behalf. Corny will seek the Dominie, for an old friend?"

I vanished from the room, and was absent ten minutes. At the end of that time, Mr. Worden was ready in his surplice, and we went to the sick room. Certainly, our old pastor had not the way of manifesting the influence of religion, that is usual to the colonies, especially to those of the more northern and eastern portion of the country; yet, there was a heartiness in his manner of praying, at times, that almost persuaded me he was a good man. I will own, however, that Mr. Worden was one of those clergymen who could pray much more sincerely for certain persons, than for others. He was partial to poor Guert, and I really thought this was manifest in his accents, on this melancholy occasion.

The dying man was relieved by this attention to the rites of the church. Guert was not a metaphysician, and, at no period of his life, I believe, did he ever enter very closely into the consideration of those fearful questions which were connected with his existence, origin, destination, and position in the long scale of animated beings. He had those general notions on these subjects, that all civilized men imbibe by education and communion with their fellows, but nothing more. He understood it was a duty to pray, and I make no doubt he fancied there were times and seasons in which this duty was more imperative than at others, and times and seasons when it might be dispensed with.

How tenderly, and how anxiously did Mary Wallace watch over her patient, during the whole of that sad day! She seemed to know neither weariness nor fatigue. Towards evening, it was just as the sun was tinging the summits of the trees with its parting light, she came towards Anneke and myself, with a face that was slightly illuminated with something like a glow of pleasure, and whispered to us, that Guert was better. Within ten minutes of that moment, I approached the bed, and saw a slight movement of the patient's hand, as if he desired me to come nearer.

"Corny," said Guert, in a low, languid voice—"it is nearly all over. I wish I could see Mary Wallace once more, before I die!"

Mary was not, *could* not be distant. She fell upon her knees, and clasped the yielding form of her lover to her heart. Nothing was said on either side; or, if aught were said, it was whispered, and was of a nature too sacred to be communicated to others. In that attitude did this young woman, long so coy and so difficult to decide, remain for near an hour, and in that quiet, cherishing, womanly embrace did Guert Ten Eyck breathe his last.

I left the sufferer as much alone with the woman of his heart, as comported with prudence and a proper attention on my part, but it was my melancholy duty to close his eyes. Thus prematurely, terminated the earthly career of as manly a spirit as ever dwelt in human form. That it had imperfections my pen has not concealed, but the long years that have since passed away, have not served to obliterate the regard so noble a temperament could not fail to awaken.

Chapter XXX

"How slow the day slides on! When we desire
Time's haste, he seems to lose a match with lobsters;
And when we wish him stay, he imps his wings
With feathers plumed with thought."

Thomas Tomkis, *Albumazar*,
II.vi. 10–14.

IT is unnecessary to dwell on the grief that we all felt for our loss. That night was necessarily one of watchfulness, but few were inclined to sleep. The return of light found us unmolested, however, and an hour or two later, Susquesus came in, and reported that the enemy had retreated towards Ticonderoga. There was nothing more to fear from that quarter, and the settlers soon began to return to their dwellings, or to such as remained. In the course of a week the axe again rang in the forest, and rude habitations began to reappear, in the places of those that had been destroyed. As Bulstrode could not well be removed, Herman Mordaunt determined to pass the remainder of the season at Ravensnest, with the double view of accommodating his guest, and of encouraging his settlers. The danger was known to be over for that summer, at least, and, ere the approach of another, it was hoped that the humiliated feelings of Great Britain would so far be aroused, as to drive the enemy from the province; as indeed was effectually done.

On consultation, it was decided that the body of Guert ought to be sent, for interment among his friends, to Albany. Dirck and myself accompanied it, as the principal attendants, all that remained of our party going with us. Herman Mordaunt thought it necessary to remain at Ravensnest, and Anneke would not quit her father. The Rev. Mr. Worden's missionary zeal had, by this time, effectually evaporated, and he profited by so favourable an occasion, to withdraw into the safer and more peopled districts. I well remember as we marched after the horse-litter that carried the remains of poor Guert, the divine's making the following sensible remarks:—

"You see how it is, on this frontier, Corny," he said; "it is premature to think of introducing Christianity. Christianity is essentially a civilized religion, and can only be of use among civilized beings. It is true, my young friend, that many of the early apostles were not learned, after the fashion of this world, but they were all thoroughly civilized. Palestine was a civilized country, and the Hebrews were a great people; and I consider the precedent set by our blessed Lord is a command to be followed in all times, and that his appearance in Judea is tantamount to his saying to his apostles, 'go and preach me and my gospel to all *civilized* people.'"

I ventured to remark that there was something like a direct command to preach it to *all* nations, to be found in the bible.

"Ay, that is true enough," answered Mr. Worden, "but it clearly means all *civilized* nations. Then, this was before the discovery of America, and it is fair enough to presume that the command referred solely to *known* nations. The texts of scripture are not to be strained, but are to be construed naturally, Corny, and this seems to me to be the natural reading of that passage. No, I have been rash and imprudent in pushing duty to exaggeration, and shall confine my labours to their proper sphere, during the remainder of my days. Civilization is just as much a means of providence, as religion itself, and it is clearly intended that one should be built on the other. A clergyman goes quite far enough from the centre of refinement, when he quits home to come into these colonies, to preach the gospel; letting alone these scalping devils the Indians, who, I greatly fear, were never born to be saved. It may do well enough to have societies to keep them in view, but a meeting in London is quite near enough ever to approach them."

Such, ever after, appeared to be the sentiments of the Rev. Mr. Worden, and I took no pains to change them. I ought, however, to have alluded to the parting with Anneke, before I gave the foregoing extract from the parson's homily. Circumstances prevented my having much private communication with my betrothed before quitting the Nest, for Anneke's sympathy with Mary Wallace was too profound, to permit her to think much, just then, of aught but the latter's sorrows. As for Mary herself, the strength and depth of her attachment, and grief, were never fully appreciated, until time came to vindicate them. Her seeming calm was soon restored, for it was only under a tempest of feeling that Mary Wallace lost her self-command, and the affliction that was inevitable and irremediable, one of her regulated temperament and high principles, struggled to endure with Christian submission. It was only in after-life that I came to know how intense and absorbing had, in truth, been her passion for the gay, high-spirited, ill-educated, and impulsive young Albanian.

Anneke wept for a few minutes in my arms, a quarter of an hour before our melancholy procession quitted the Nest. The dear girl had no undue reserve with me, though I found her a little reluctant to converse on the subject of our own loves, so soon after the fearful scenes we had just gone through. Still she left me in no doubt on the all-important point of my carrying away with me, her whole and entirely undivided heart. Bulstrode she never had, never *could* love. This she assured me, over and over again. He amused her, and she felt for him, some of the affection and interest of kindred, but not the least of any other interest. Poor Bulstrode! now I was certain of success, I had very magnanimous sentiments in his behalf, and could give him credit for various good qualities that had been previously obscured in my eyes. Herman Mordaunt had requested nothing might be said to the Major of my engagement, though an early opportunity was to be taken by himself, to let the suitor understand that Anneke declined the honour of his hand. It was thought the information would best come from him.

"I shall be frank with you, Littlepage, and confess I have been very anxious for the union of my daughter and Mr. Bulstrode," added Herman Mordaunt, in the interview we had, before I left the Nest, "and I trust to your own good sense to account for it. I knew Bulstrode, before I had any knowledge of yourself, and there was already a connection between us, that was just of a nature to render one that was closer, desirable. I shall not deny that I fancied Anneke fitted to adorn the station and circles to which Bulstrode would have carried her, and perhaps it is a natural parental weakness to wish to see one's child promoted. We talk of humility and contentment, Corny, though there is much of the *nolo episcopari* about it, after all. But, you see that the preference of the child is so much stronger than that of the parent, that it must prevail. I dare say, after all, you would much rather be Anneke's choice than be mine?"

"I can have no difficulty in admitting that, sir," I answered, "and I feel very sensible of the liberal manner in which you yield your own preferences to our wishes. Certainly, in the way of rank and fortune, I have little to offer, Mr. Mordaunt, as an offset to Mr. Bulstrode's claims, but in love for your daughter, and in an ardent desire to make her happy, I shall not yield to him, or any other man, though he were a king."

"In the way of fortune, Littlepage, I have very few regrets. As you are to live in this country, the joint means of the two families, which some day, must centre in you and Anneke, will prove all-sufficient; and, as for posterity, Ravensnest and Mooseridge will supply ample provisions. As the colony grows, your descendants will increase, and your means will increase with both. No, no—I may have been a little disappointed—that much I will own, but I have not been, at any time, displeased. God bless you, then, my dear boy; write us from Albany, and come to us at Lilacsbush in September. Your reception will be that of a son."

It is needless to dwell on the melancholy procession we formed through the woods. Dirck and myself kept near the body on foot, until we reached the highway, when vehicles were provided for the common transportation. On reaching Albany, we delivered the remains of Guert to his relatives, and there was a suitable funeral given. The bricked closet behind the chimney, was opened as usual, and the six dozen of Madeira, that had been placed in it, twenty-four years before, or the day the poor fellow was christened, was found to be very excellent. I remember it was said generally, that better wine was drunk at the funeral of Guert Ten Eyck, than had been tasted at the obsequies of any individual, who was not a Van Rensselaer, a Schuyler, or a Ten Broeck, within the memory of man. I now speak of funerals in Albany, for I do suppose the remark would scarcely apply to many other funerals, lower down the river. As a rule, however, very good wine was given at all our funerals.

The Rev. Mr. Worden officiated, and was universally regarded with interest, as a pious minister of the gospel, who had barely escaped the fate of the person he was now committing 'dust to dust,' while devotedly and ardently employed in endeavouring to rescue the souls of the very savages who sought his life, from the fate of the heathen.

I remember there was a very well worded paragraph to this

effect in the New York Gazette, and I have heard it said, but do not remember to have ever seen it myself, that in one of the reports of the Society for the Promulgation of the Gospel in Foreign Parts, the circumstances were alluded to, in a very touching and edifying manner.

Poor Guert! I passed a few minutes at his grave before we went south. It was all that was left of his fine person, his high spirit, his lion-hearted courage, his buoyant spirits and his unextinguishable love of frolic. A finer physical man I never beheld, or one who better satisfied the eye, in all respects. That the noble tenement was not more intellectually occupied, was purely the consequence of a want of education. Notwithstanding, all the books in the world, could not have converted Guert Ten Eyck into a Jason Newcome, or Jason Newcome into a Guert Ten Eyck. Each owed many of his peculiarities, doubtless, to the province in which he was bred and born, and to the training consequent on these accidents, but nature had also drawn broad distinctions between them. All the wildness of Guert's impulses could not altogether destroy his feelings, tone and tact as a gentleman; while all the soaring, extravagant pretensions of Jason never could have ended in elevating him to that character. Alas! Poor Guert! I sincerely mourned his loss for years, nor has his memory yet ceased to have a deep interest with me.

Dirck Follock and I would have been a good deal caressed at Albany, on our return, both on account of what had happened, and on account of our Dutch connections, had we been in the mood to profit by the disposition of the people. But, we were not. The sad events with which we had been connected were still too recent to indulge in gaieties, or company, and, as soon as possible after the funeral, we seized the opportunity of embarking on board a sloop bound to New York. Our voyage was generally considered a prosperous one, lasting indeed, only six days. We took the ground three times, it is true, but nothing was thought of that, such accidents being of frequent occurrence. Among the events of this sort, one occurred in the Overslaugh, and I passed a few hours there very pleasantly, as it was so near the scene of our adventure on the river. Anneke always occupied much of my thoughts, but pleasing pictures of her gentle decision, her implicit reliance on myself, her resignation, her spirit, and her intelligence were now blended, without any alloy, in my recollections.

The dear girl had confessed to me, that she loved me even on that fearful night, for her tenderness in my behalf dated much farther back. This was a great addition to the satisfaction with which I went over every incident and speech, in recollection, endeavouring to recall the most minute tone or expression, to see if I could *now* connect it with any sign of that passion, which I was authorized in believing did even then exist. Thus aided, equally by Anneke's gentle, blushing admissions, and my own wishes, I had no difficulty in recalling pictures, that were infinitely agreeable to myself, though possibly not minutely accurate.

In the Tappaan Sea, Dirck left us, proceeding into Rockland to join his family. I continued on in the sloop, reaching port next day. My Uncle and Aunt Legge were delighted to see me, and I soon found I should be a lion, had I leisure to remain in town, in order to enjoy the notoriety my connection with the northern expedition had created. I found a deep mortification pervading the capital, in consequence of our defeat, mingled with a high determination to redeem our tarnished honour.

Satanstoe, with all its endearing ties, however, called me away, and I left town, on horseback, leaving my effects to follow by the first good opportunity, the morning of the day succeeding that on which I had arrived. I shall not attempt to conceal one weakness. As usual, I stopped at Kingsbridge to dine and bait, and while the notable landlady was preparing my dinner, I ascended the heights to catch a distant view of Lilacsbush. There lay the pretty cottage-like dwelling, placed beneath its hill, amid a wilderness of shrubbery, but its lovely young mistress was far away, and I found the pleasure with which I gazed at it, blended with regrets.

"You have been north, I hear, Mr. Littlepage," my landlady observed, while I was discussing her lamb, and peas, and asparagus; "pray, sir, did you hear or see any thing of our honoured neighbours, Herman Mordaunt and his charming daughter?"

"Much of both, Mrs. Light, and that under trying circumstances. Mooseridge, my father's property in that part of the province, is quite near to Ravensnest, Herman Mordaunt's estate, and I have passed some time at it. Have no tidings of the family reached you, lately?"

"None, unless it be the report that Miss Anneke will never return to us."

"Anneke not return! In the name of wonder, how do your hear this?"

"Not as *Miss* Anneke, but as Lady Anneke, or something of that sort. Isn't there a General Bulstrom, or some great officer, or other, who seeks her hand, and on whom she smiles, sir?"

"I presume I understand you, now. Well, what do you learn of him?"

"Only that they are to be married next month—some say they *are* married already, and that the old gentleman gives Lilacsbush, out and out, and four thousand pounds currency, down, in order to purchase so high an honour for his child. I tell the neighbours it is too much, Miss Anneke being worth any lord in England, on her own, sole, account."

This intelligence did not disturb me, of course, for it was tavern-tidings and neighbours' news. Neighbours! How much is that sacred word prostituted! You shall find people opening their ears with avidity to the gossip of a neighbourhood, when nineteen times in twenty it is less entitled to credit, than the intelligence which is obtained from a distance, provided the latter come from persons of the same class in life as the individuals in question, and are known to them. What means had this woman of knowing the secrets of Herman Mordaunt's family, that were one-half as good as those possessed by friends in Albany, for instance? This neighbourhood testimony, as it is called, does a vast deal of mischief in the province, and most especially in those parts of it, where our own people, are brought in contact with their fellow-subjects, from the more eastern colonies. In my eyes, Jason Newcome's opinions of Herman Mordaunt and his acts, would be nearly worthless, shrewd as I admit the man to be; for the two have not a distinctive opinion, custom, and I had almost said principle, in common. Just appreciation of motives and acts can only proceed from those who feel and think alike, and this is morally impossible where there exist broad distinctions in social classes. It is just for this reason, that we attach so little importance to the ordinary reports, and even to the sworn evidence, of servants.

Our reception at Satanstoe was just what might have been expected. My dear mother hugged me to her heart, again and again, and seemed never to be satisfied with feasting her eyes on me. My father was affected at seeing me, too, and I thought there was a very decided moisture in his eyes. As for old Capt. Hugh Roger, three-score-and-ten had exhausted his fluids, pretty much, but he shook me heartily by the hand, and listened to my account of the movements before Ty with all a soldier's interest, and with somewhat of the fire of one who had served himself in more fortunate times. I had to fight my battles o'er and o'er again, as a matter of course, and to recount the tale of Ravensnest in all its details. We were at supper, when I concluded my most laboured narrative, and when I began to hope my duties, in this respect, were finally terminated. But my dear mother had heavier matters still, on her mind, and it was necessary that I should give her a private conference, in her own little room.

"Corny, my beloved child," commenced this anxious and most tender parent, "you have said nothing *particular* to me of the Mordaunts. It is now time to speak of that family."

"Have I not told you, mother, how we met at Albany, and of what occurred on the river—" I had not spoken of that adventure in my letters, because I was uncertain of the true state of Anneke's feelings, and did not wish to raise expectations that might never be realized—"and of our going to Ravensnest in company, and of all that happened at Ravensnest, after our return from Ty?"

"What is all this to me, child! I wish to hear you speak of Anneke—is it true that she is going to be married?"

"It is true—I can affirm that much from her own mouth."

My dear mother's countenance fell, and I could hardly pursue my wicked *equivoque* any further.

"And she has even had the effrontery to own this to *you*, Corny?"

"She has, indeed; though truth compels me to add that she blushed a great deal while admitting it, and seemed only half disposed to be so frank; that is at first; for, in the end, she rather smiled than blushed."

"Well, this amazes me! It is only a proof that vanity and worldly rank, and worldly riches, stand higher in the estimation of Anneke Mordaunt, than excellence and modest merit."

"What riches and worldly rank have I, mother, to tempt any woman to forget the qualities you have mentioned?"

"I was not thinking of you, my son, in that sense at all. Of course, I mean Mr. Bulstrode."

"What has Mr. Bulstrode to do with my marriage with Anne Mordaunt, or any one else, but her own sweet self, who has consented to become my wife; her father, who accepts me for a son; my father, who is about to imitate his example, by taking Anneke to his heart as a daughter, and you, my dearest, dearest mother, who are the only person likely to raise obstacles, as you are now doing."

This was a boyish mode of producing a most delightful surprise, I am very ready to acknowledge, and, when I saw my mother burst into tears, I felt both regret and shame at having practised it. But youth is the season of folly, and happy is the man who can say he has never trifled more seriously with the feelings of a parent. I was soon pardoned—what offence would not that devoted mother have pardoned her only child!—when I was made to relate all that was proper to be told of what had passed between Anneke and myself. It is scarcely necessary to say, I was assured of the cheerful acquiescence in my wishes, of all my own family, from Capt. Hugh Roger, down to the dear person who was speaking. They had set their minds on my becoming the husband of this very young lady, and I could not possibly have made any communication that would be more agreeable, as I was given to understand from each and all, that very night.

My return to Satanstoe occurred in the last half of the month of July. The Mordaunts were not to be at Lilacsbush until the middle of September, and I had near two months to wait for that happy moment. This time was passed as well as it could be. I endeavoured to interest myself in the old Neck, and to plan schemes of future happiness there, that were to be realized in Anneke's society. It was and is a noble farm; rich, beautifully placed, having water on more than three of its sides, in capital order, and well stocked with such apples, peaches, apricots, plums and other fruits as the world can scarcely equal. It is true that the provinces a little further south, such as New Jersey, Pennsylvania, Maryland and Virginia, think they can beat us in peaches, but I have never tasted any fruit that I thought would compare with that of Satanstoe. I love every tree, wall, knoll, swale, meadow and hummock about the old place. One thing distresses me. I love old names, such as my father knew the same places by, and I like to mispronounce a word, when custom and association render the practice familiar. I would not call my friend Dirck Follock, any thing else but Follock, unless it might be in a formal way, or when asking him to drink a glass of wine with me, for a great deal. So it is with Satanstoe; the name is homely, I am willing to allow, but it is strong, and conveys an idea. It relates, also, to the usages and notions of the country, and names ought always to be preserved, except in those few instances in which there are good reasons for altering them. I regret to say, that ever since the appearance of Jason Newcome among us, there has been a disposition among the ignorant and vulgar, to call the Neck, Dibbleton; under the pretence I have already mentioned, that it once belonged to the family of Dibblees; or, as some think, as a pious diminutive of Devil's Town. I indignantly repel this supposition, though I do believe that Dibbleton is only a sneaking mode of pronouncing Devilton, as, I admit, I have heard the old people laughingly term the Neck. This belongs to the "Gaul darn ye" school, and it is not to my taste. I say the 'ignorant and vulgar' for this is just the class to be squeamish on such subjects. I have been told—though I cannot say that I have heard it myself—but I am told, there have been people from the eastward, among us, of late years, who affect to call "Hell-Gate," "Hurl-Gate," or "Whirl-Gate," or by some other such sentimental whirl-a-gig name, and these are the gentry who would wish to alter "Satanstoe" into "Dibbleton!" Since the eastern troops have begun to come among us, indeed, they have commenced a desperate inroad on many of our old venerated Dutch names; names that the English direct from home, have generally respected. Indeed, change—change in all things, seems to be the besetting passion of these people. We, of New York, are content to do as our ancestors have done before us, and this they ridicule, making it matter of accusation against us that we follow the notions of our fathers. I shall never complain that they are deserting so many of *their* customs, for I regard the changes as improvements, but I beg that they may leave us ours.

That there is such a thing as improvement, I am willing enough to admit, as well as that it not only compels, but excuses changes; but, I am yet to learn it is matter of just reproach, that a man follows in the footsteps of those who have gone before him. The apothegms of David, and the wisdom of Solomon, are just as much apothegms and wisdom, in our own time, as they were the day they were written, and for precisely the same reason—their truth. Where there is so much stability in morals, there must be permanent principles, and something surely is worthy to be saved from the wreck of the past. I doubt if all this craving for change has not more of selfishness in it, than either of expediency, or of philosophy; and I could wish, at least, that Satanstoe should never be frittered away into so sneaking a substitute as Dibbleton.

That was a joyful day, when a servant in Herman Mordaunt's livery rode in upon our lawn, and handed me a letter from his master, informing me of the safe arrival of the family, and inviting me to ride over next day, in time to take a late breakfast at Lilacsbush. Anneke had written to me twice previously to this; two beautifully expressed, feminine, yet spirited, affectionate letters, in which the tenderness and sensibility of her nature were barely restrained by the delicacy of her sex and situation. On the receipt of this welcome invitation, I was guilty of the only piece of romantic extravagance, that I can remember having committed in the course of my life. Herman Mordaunt's black was well treated, and dismissed with a letter of acceptance. One hour after he left Satanstoe—I *do* love that venerable name, and hope all the Yankees in Christendom, will not be able to alter it to Dibbleton—but, one hour after the negro was off, I followed him myself, intending to sleep at the well-known inn, at Kingsbridge, and not present myself at the Bush, until the proper hour next morning.

I had got to the house of the talkative landlady, two hours before sunset, put up my horse, secured my lodgings and was eating a bite myself, when the good housewife entered the room.

"Your servant, Mr. Littlepage," commenced this loquacious person; "how are the venerable Captain Hugh Roger, and the Major, your honoured father? Well, I see by your smile. Well, it is a comfortable thing to have our friends enjoy good health—my own poor man enjoyed most wretched health all last winter, and is likely to enjoy very much the same, that which is coming. I should think you had come to the wedding at Lilacsbush, Mr. Corny, had you not stopped at my door, instead of going on direct to that of Herman Mordaunt."

I started, but supposed that the news of what was to happen, had leaked out, and that this good woman, whose ears were always open, had got hold of a neighbourhood-*truth*, for once in her life.

"I am on no such errand, Mrs. Light, but hope to be married one of these days, to some one or other."

"I was not thinking of your marriage, sir, but that of Miss Anneke, over at the 'Bush, to this Lord Bulstrom. It's a great connection for the Mordaunts, after all, though Herman Mordaunt is of good blood, himself, they tell me. The knight's man often comes here, to taste our cider, which he admits is as good as English cider, and I believe it is the only thing which he has found in the colonies that he thinks is one half as good; but Thomas tells me all is settled, and that the wedding must take place right soon. It has only been put off on account of Miss Wallace, who is in deep mourning for her own husband, having lost him within the honey-moon, which is the reason she still bears her own name. They tell me a widow who loses her husband in the honey-moon is obliged to bear her maiden name; otherwise Miss Mary would be Mrs. Van Goort, or something like that."

As it was very clear the neighbourhood knew little about the true state of things in Herman Mordaunt's family, I took my hat and proceeded to execute the intention with which I had left home. I was sorry to hear that Bulstrode was at Lilacsbush, but had no apprehensions of his ever marrying Anneke. I took the way to the heights, and soon reached the field where I had once met the ladies, on horseback. There, seated under a tree, I saw Bulstrode alone, and apparently in deep contemplation. It was no part of my plan to be seen, or to have my presence known, and I was retiring, when I heard my name, discovered that I was recognised, and joined him.

The first glance at Bulstrode showed me that he knew the truth. He coloured, bit his lip, forced a smile, and came forward to meet me, limping just enough to add interest to his gait, and offered his hand with a frank, manliness that gave him great merit in my eyes. It was no trifle to lose Anne Mordaunt, and I am afraid I could not have manifested half so much magnanimity. But, Bulstrode was a man of the world, and he knew how to command the exhibition of his feelings, if not to command the feelings themselves.

"I told you, once, Corny," he said, offering his hand, "that we must remain friends, *coute qui coute*—you have been successful, and I have failed. Herman Mordaunt told me the melancholy fact before we left Albany, and I can tell you, *his* regrets were not so very flattering to you. Nevertheless, he admits you are a capital fellow, and that if it were not for Alexander, he could wish to be Diogenes. So you have only to provide yourself with a lantern and a tub, marry Anneke and set up housekeeping. As for the honest man, I propose saving you some trouble, by offering myself in that character, even before you light your wick. Come, take a seat on this bench, and let us chat."

There was something a little forced in all this, it is true, but it was manly. I took the seat, and Bulstrode went on.

"It was the river that made your fortune, Corny, and undid me."

I smiled, but said nothing; though I knew better.

"There is a fate in love, as in war. Well, I am as well off as Abercrombie; we both expected to be victorious, while each is conquered. I am more fortunate, indeed; for he can never expect to get another army while I may get another wife. I wish you would be frank with me, and confess to what you particularly ascribe your own success."

"It is natural, Mr. Bulstrode, that a young woman should prefer to live in her own country, to living in a strange land, and among strangers."

"Ay, Corny, that is both patriotic and modest, but it is not the real reason. No, sir; it was Scrub, and the theatricals, by which I have been undone. With most provincials, Mr. Littlepage, it is a sufficient apology for any thing, that the metropolis approves. So it is with you colonists, in general; let England say yes, and you dare not say, no. There is one thing that persons who live so far from home, seldom learn, and it is this:—there are two sorts of great worlds; the great vulgar world, which includes, all but the very best in taste, principles, and manners, whether it be in a capital, or a country; and the great *respectable* world, which, infinitely less numerous, contains the judicious, the instructed, the intelligent, and on some questions, the good. Now, the first form fashion; whereas the last produce something far better and more enduring than fashion. Fashion often stands rebuked in the presence of the last class, small as it ever is, numerically. Very high rank, very finished tastes, very strong judgments, and very correct principles, all unite, more or less, to make up this class. One, or more of these qualities may be wanting, perhaps, but the union of the whole forms the perfection of the character. We have daily examples of this at home, as well as elsewhere, though, in our artificial state of society it requires more decided qualities to resist the influence of fashion, when there is not positive social rank to sustain it, perhaps, than it would in one more natural. That which first struck me, in Anneke, as is the case with most young men, was her delicacy of appearance, and her beauty. This I will not deny. In this respect, your American women have quite taken me by surprise. In England, we are so accustomed to associate a certain delicacy of person and air, with high rank, that I will confess I landed in New York with no expectation of meeting a single female, in the whole country, that was not comparatively coarse, and what we are accustomed to consider common, in physique; yet, I must now say that, apart from mere conventional finish, I find quite as large a proportion of aristocratical-looking females among you, as if you had a full share of Dutchesses. The last thing I should think of calling an American woman, would be coarse. She may want manner, in one sense; she may want finish, in a dozen things; she may, and often does want utterance, as utterance is understood among the accomplished, but she is seldom indeed, coarse, or vulgar, according to our European understanding of the terms."

"And of what is all this *ápropos*, Bulstrode?"

"Oh! of your success and my defeat, of course, Corny," answered the Major, smiling. "What I mean is this—that Anneke is one of your second class, or is better than what fashion can make her, and Scrub has been the means of my undoing. She does not care for fashion in a play, or a novel, or a dress even, but looks for the proprieties. Yes, Scrub has proved my undoing!"

I did not exactly believe the last, but, finding Bulstrode so well disposed to give his rejection this turn, it was not my part to contradict him. We talked together, half an hour longer, in the most amicable manner, when we parted; Bulstrode promising not to betray the secret of my presence.

I lingered in sight of the house, until evening, when I ventured nearer, hoping to get a glimpse of Anneke, as she passed some window, or appeared, by the soft light of the moon, under the piazza that skirted the south front of the building. Lilacsbush deserved its name, being a perfect wilderness of shrubbery, and favoured by the last, I had got quite near the house, when I heard light footsteps, on the gravel of an adjacent walk. At the next instant, soft, low voices met my ears, and I was a sort of compelled auditor of what followed.

"No, Anne, my fate is sealed for this world," said Mary Wallace, "and I shall live Guert's widow, as faithfully and devotedly, as if the marriage vow had been pronounced. This much is due to his memory, on account of the heartless doubts I permitted to influence me, and which drove him into those terrible scenes, that destroyed him. When a woman really loves, Anneke, it is vain to struggle against any thing but positive unworthiness, I fear. Poor Guert was not unworthy in any sense; he was erring and impulsive, but not unworthy. No—no—not unworthy! I ought to have given him my hand, and he would have been spared to us. As it is, I can only live his widow in secret, and in love. You have done well, dearest Anneke, in being so frank with Corny Littlepage, and in avowing that preference which you have felt almost from the first day of your acquaintance—"

Although this was music to my ears, honour would not suffer me to hear more, and I moved swiftly away, stirring the bushes in a way to apprise the speaker of the proximity of a stranger. It was necessary to appear, and I endeavoured so to do, without creating any alarm.

"It must be Mr. Bulstrode," said the gentle voice of Anneke, "who is probably looking for us—see, there he comes, and we will meet—"

The dear speaker became tongue-tied; for, by this time, I was near enough to be recognised. At the next instant, I held her in my arms. Mary Wallace disappeared, how or when, I cannot say. I place a veil over the happy hour that succeeded, leaving the old to draw on their experience for its pictures, and the young to live in hope. At the end of that time, by Anneke's persuasion I entered the house, and had to brave Herman Mordaunt's disposition to rally me. I was not only mercifully, but hospitably treated, however, Anneke's father merely laughing at my little adventure, saying that he looked upon it favourably, and as a sign that I was a youth of spirit.

Early in October we were married, the Rev. Mr. Worden performing the ceremony. Our home was to be Lilacsbush, which Herman Mordaunt conveyed to me the same day, leaving it, as it was furnished, entirely in my hands. He also gave me my wife's mother's fortune, a respectable independence, and the death of

Capt. Hugh Roger, soon after, added considerably to my means. We made but one family, between town, Lilacsbush, and Satanstoe, Anneke and my mother, in particular, conceiving a strong affection for each other.

As for Bulstrode, he went home before the marriage, but keeps up a correspondence with us, to this hour. He is still single, and is a declared old bachelor. His letters, however, are too light-hearted to leave us any concern on the subject; though these are matters that may fall to the share of my son Mordaunt, should he ever have the grace to continue this family narrative.

Explanatory Notes

4.17 tree "known by its fruit": Matthew 12.33.

4.28 "every body's business": Izaak Walton, *The Compleat Angler*, part 1, ch. 2.

8.28 West-Chester: Westchester county included all the territory east of Manhattan to Connecticut and north along the Hudson River to the Highlands.

10.9-10 as long . . . grass shall grow: a variant of an anonymous North American expression for the terms of a treaty.

11.20-21 Felipses, or Philipses . . . Hudson: The manor of Philipsborough in Westchester county was a small part of the holdings of Frederick Philipse, who had inherited both this property and the large grant in Putnam county known as Philipse's Highland patent from Adolphe Philipse, who acquired it in 1697.

11.22 de Lanceys: The de Lanceys were connected with many of the important Colonial families mentioned in *Satanstoe*. Cooper married Susan Augusta de Lancey (1792-1852), daughter of John Peter de Lancey (1753-1828) and granddaughter of James de Lancey (1703-1760) who served as Chief Justice of the Supreme Court and as Lieutenant Governor of New York from 1753-1755 and from 1757 until his death. His wife Anne was the daughter of Col. Caleb Heathcote (see pages 19-20). Susan's great-grandfather, Étienne or Stephen de Lancey (1663-1741) had married Ann Van Cortlandt, daughter of Gertrude Schuyler and Stephanus Van Cortlandt, the first mayor of New York City to have been born in America.

11.24 Kingsbridge: township in the Bronx containing the King's Bridge, named for William III who provided this link between Manhattan and the mainland. The approach to the bridge was at the present intersection of West 230th Street and Kingsbridge Avenue. The present bridge, located elsewhere, dates only from 1900.

13.33 Sir Charles Hardy: Governor of New York from 1755 to 1757, Hardy participated in the unsuccessful campaign

of the Earl of Loudoun to capture Louisbourg in the
summer of 1757.

13.34 Sir Danvers Osborne: Governor of New York who hanged
himself two days after taking office in 1753.

14.16 Byram River: The westernmost river in Connecticut.

17.20 His Excellency: William Shirley (1694-1771), colonial
Governor of Massachusetts (1741-1756) and
Commander-in-Chief of the British forces in America
(1755-1756).

17.28-29 Barnwell . . . Tuscarora expedition: Between January
and April of 1712, Col. John Barnwell led an expedition
of some 50 whites and 350 Indian allies into North
Carolina to help settlers fight off Tuscarora Indians who
were retaliating against kidnappings and encroachments
on their hunting grounds.

19.18 Col. Heathcote: Col. Caleb Heathcote, a vestryman of
Trinity Church instrumental in establishing Church of
England congregations in New York, was the
father-in-law of Lt. Gov. James de Lancey.

20.17-18 the Rt. Rev. Wm. *Heathcote* de Lancey, the Bishop of
Western New-York: Cooper's brother-in-law who lived
from 1797 to 1865.

22.23 Nassau Hall: later Princeton University.

26.40 Powles Hook: Jersey City, New Jersey.

27.3   Tobb's Ferry: Dialect for Dobbs' ferry, the first ferry
service on the Hudson River, initiated by Jeremiah
Dobbs in 1698.

31.37 architect: The architect of the third Trinity Church, built
in 1841-48, was Richard Upjohn of Boston, an
Englishman who had come to America in 1828.

32.10-12 residence of Stephen de Lancey . . . tavern: Built
about 1730 by Stephen de Lancey, this house became the
residence of James de Lancey and then, in 1754, was
converted into an inn called the Province Arms or the
City Arms. Still later, as the City Hotel, it was the site of
the farewell banquet given Cooper by the Bread and
Cheese Club in May 1826 before he went to Europe. He
regularly stayed there until it was changed into stores in
1849.

52.30 Hampshire Grants: During a dispute over the boundary
between New Hampshire and New York in the 1750's
and 60's, the government of New Hampshire granted
patents to land claimed by New York. After 1764, when
the Crown found in favor of the New York claim, settlers
who had purchased these disputed grants would not
accept the decision and riots ensued. The issue was

finally resolved when Vermont was admitted to the
Union in 1791.

54.19-21 Mr. Washington . . . Braddock's defeat: Col. George
Washington was an aide to General Braddock at the
Battle of the Monongahela, July 9, 1755.

61.28 Communipaw: a village in Bergen County, New Jersey,
named for the original grantee, Michael Pauw, a director
of the Dutch West India Company.

78.33 Mr. Speaker Nicoll: William Nicoll began service as
Speaker of the Provincial Assembly in 1702 and was
re-elected to that office for sixteen consecutive years.

79.23 Col. Nicoll: Col. Richard Nicolls (1624-1672) presided
over the bloodless surrender of New Netherland by the
Dutch, took possession of New Amsterdam on September
8, 1664, and changed both its name and that of the
entire province to New York.

85.29 Smybert: John Smibert (1688-1751), a Scottish portrait-
and landscape-painter, came to America in 1729 and
designed Boston's Faneuil Hall in 1742.

85.29 Watson: John Watson (1685-1768), a Scottish portrait
painter who arrived in Perth Amboy, New Jersey, in
1714, may have had the earliest art collection in
America, paintings he imported from Scotland in 1730
and displayed in his home.

85.29 Blackburn: Joseph Blackburn, an English portrait painter
who lived and worked in New England between 1754
and 1763 when he returned to London.

86.1-25 The Thespian Muse . . . result: Lewis Hallam, his wife,
three of his children, and ten members of his troupe
arrived in Williamsburg in September 1752 from
England. They performed there, and in Charleston,
Philadelphia, and New York until 1755. Hallam built a
theater in New York on the east side of Nassau Street
between Maiden Lane and John Street in 1753. Hallam
died in Jamaica in 1756, and his widow married David
Douglass, a theater operator in Jamaica, who formed the
American Company out of Hallam's old troupe with the
former Mrs. Hallam as leading actress. Douglass brought
the company back to New York where he built a
temporary theater on Cruger's Wharf; performances
were held there until February 1759. (See 136.11-12.)

86.13 second regular theatre: The first theater in America was
probably the Play House in Williamsburg mentioned by
Hugh Jones in *The Present State of Virginia*, 1724.

92.14-16 the Crown and Bible . . . Hugh Gaine: Hugh Gaine
printed "The New York Gazette and The Weekly

Mercury" at the sign of the Bible and Crown in Hanover Square.

109.9 Lord Loudon: John Campbell, 4th Earl of Loudoun (1705-1782) was Commander-in-Chief of British forces in North America from January 1756 to December 1757 when he was recalled.

136.7 Abercrombie: James Abercromby (1706-1781) replaced Lord Loudoun and was Commander-in-Chief of British forces in North America in 1758.

148.24 The spires of two churches: In the 1750's the two principal churches in Albany were the Dutch Reformed church and St. Peter's (Anglican). The Dutch Reformed church, which had been in Albany since 1642, built its third structure, the Stone Church, in 1715 and demolished it about a century later. The first church of St. Peter's was built in 1715-16, a steeple added in 1751, and it was demolished in 1802.

181.25 Peter Cuyler: Three Cuylers have been Mayors of Albany: Johannes in 1725-26, Cornelius in 1742-46, and Abraham in 1770-78. No Cuyler was Mayor in 1758, however, the Mayor of Albany at that time being Sybrant G. Van Schaick.

183.39-40 Philip Van Rensselaer: Mayor of Albany, 1799-1815 and 1819-1821.

199.27 *in petto*: literally "in breast," Italian expression for something preserved as a secret.

276.31 Lord Howe: George Augustus, third Viscount Howe, born in England c. 1724, died at the foot of Lake George after being shot 6 July 1758.

282.24-25 *coute qui coute*: cost what it may (French).

[283].35-36 clever colonels at need: Cooper deleted the rest of this note, which is given in the "Note on the Manuscript" in the present volume.

288.30 poor Munro: Lieutenant-Colonel George Monro (which Cooper spelled Munro in *The Last of the Mohicans*) was in charge of Fort William Henry in the summer of 1757 and was forced to surrender to the superior forces of Montcalm when he and Montcalm both learned that Monro's superiors were not going to send reinforcements. The famous massacre, which Cooper described in *The Last of the Mohicans*, followed.

289.3 Gen. Bradstreet: John Bradstreet served with the British and Colonial forces from 1735-74 and distinguished himself in the capture of Fort Frontenac in 1758.

291.36 'is the tribute . . . virtue.': Maxim #218 of La Rouchefoucauld is "Hypocrisy is the homage that vice

offers to virtue." *The Maxims of La Rouchefoucauld,*
translated with an Introduction by Louis Kronenberger
(New York: Random House, 1959), p. 73.

305.15-16 *pari passu*: at an equal pace (Latin).

309.25 "Count leaves: Here, as he had done in *The Last of the
Mohicans,* Cooper paraphrases from an Indian runner's
report to Montcalm about how many British were
approaching. "'If you can count the leaves on the trees,
you can count them.'" David Humphreys, *An Essay on the
Life of the Honourable Major-General Israel Putnam*
(Hartford, 1788), p. 41.

331.19-20 Col. Gordon Graham: As Cooper's note says, Mrs.
Grant's *Memoirs* reports that the forty-second regiment
was commanded by this veteran "who had the first point
of attack assigned to him; he was wounded at the first
onset." *Memoirs of an American Lady* (Boston, W. Wells et
al, 1809), II.37.

334.22-23 The 55th . . . cut up: Mrs. Grant wrote, "Of the fifty
fifth regiment, to which my father had newly been
attached, ten officers were killed, including all the field
officers." Ibid.

[339].23 the "Holy Lake": Discovered by Isaac Jogues, S.J., in
1646 and christened Lac du Saint Sacrament by him,
Lake George was re-named by Sir William Johnson in
1755 to assert British dominance over the area.

342.37 Capt. Charles Lee: Captain Lee is also mentioned in
Mrs. Grant's *Memoirs* (II.33) in terms that may have
suggested his rather high-handed manner to Cooper.

435.15 "Gaul darn ye": Buckingham, writing in the *New
England Magazine* in 1832 said, "We have . . . 'Gaul darn
you' for G-- d--- you . . . and other like creations of the
union of wrath and principle." (III.380)

Textual Apparatus

Textual Commentary

Cooper turned over his holograph preface and 241 pages of manuscript of *Satanstoe* to John Fagan, his trusted stereotyper, between 4 March and 15 May 1845. He wrote Fagan 4 March,

> *By express* to-day, I send you a few chapters of new book. Begin *at once*, as I am in a great hurry, and wish to save time. I shall be at Heads on Tuesday or Wednesday night, probably the last, and I hope to find a great bundle of proofs ready.
> The running title must be, "Satanstoe."[1]

The proof sheets Cooper read are not extant, but his trips to Philadelphia to read proof suggest strongly that he followed his usual practice of going over the proofs carefully and revising them in ways that are consistent with the patterns of revision we see in the holograph manuscript itself.[2] While the present edition accepts such revisions, it rejects compositors' misreadings that Cooper missed and restores Cooper's idiosyncratic puctuation that always seems to have been governed more by his ear than by any mechanical rules for punctuation.

Published in New York on 18 June 1845 by Burgess, Stringer & Co.[3] and in London on 9 June 1845 by Richard Bentley, *Satanstoe* had an extraordinarily uncomplicated publishing history for a Cooper novel. While the Bentley edition did make some typographical errors and changes in accidentals that are useful in tracing the transmission of the text,[4] only two substantive changes appear in the texts of *Satanstoe* after the first American edition. These changes, which originated in the Bentley edition, are: "in America" for Cooper's "among us" at the first edition's I.vi.22 (Bentley I.v.15-16) and "America" for "this country" in the first line of the text. Bentley also added "June, 1845" to the end of the preface. This stemma gives the line of descent of the text through the Townsend-Darley edition that was published in 1859, after Cooper's death.

Satanstoe (1845-1859)

AMS
↓
Burgess, Stringer & Co., New York, 1845
↓
Richard Bentley, London, 1845
reimpression, 1847
↓
A. & W. Galignani, Paris, 1845
Baudry (Galignani), Paris, 1845

Reimpressions by Stringer & Townsend
(New edition) 1852, 1855, 1856;
reimpressions by W. A. Townsend &
Company 1859
↓
Piracy: G. Routledge & Co., London, 1856

The manuscript for *Satanstoe* is complete and serves as copy-text for this edition. The revisions Cooper made in this manuscript are, in turn, clearly related to the further revisions he made when he read the proof of *Satanstoe* in Philadelphia. Since Cooper apparently did not read proof against the manuscript, however, some two hundred substantive errors went undetected in the text of the first edition and have been perpetuated in all subsequent editions.

These errors result in passages that would not necessarily bother a reader who already knew the story, as Cooper obviously did, but might perplex the attentive first-time reader. For instance, Corny Littlepage, our narrator, and his party, entering the forest, have "three white labourers to clear the woods." Of what? Corny also says that the people of Fishkill "made little of the war, and asked us many questions concerning the army, its commanders, its force, and its objects." If they made little of the war, why were they so curious about it? Major Bulstrode is said at one point to be "almost entranced." How much more of the heroine's singing does he need or how much better singer must she be to finish the job? The manuscript answers all these questions by showing that the labourers were to clear the *roads*, that the people of Fishkill *knew* little of the war, and that the major was *actually* entranced. The following list locates in the present edition some other interesting or important errors in the first edition.

Page & Line	First Edition	Manuscript
99.22	departed	separated
118.35	wound	wormed
127.17	lands	laws
135.7	manners	manner
137.14	procured	produced
145.21	sup	sleep
147.31	traveller's dresses	travellers' dress
153.1	in turn	in time
171.23	calf	oaf
193.14	And she	Anneke
219.33	themselves	ourselves
224.4	intensely	intently
273.4	where	when
426.31	trial	time
434.36	swell	swale

Other errors might not mislead the reader, but do delete nuances Cooper wanted. For example, the compositor's misreading of Cooper's *now* for *soon* destroys the humor of Corny's discovery about the heroine when she disapproves of a cynical remark made by his rival.

> I thought something like displeasure settled on the fair, polished, brow of Miss Mordaunt, who I could now see, possessed much character and high principles for one of her tender years. (90.7-10)

The eleven compositors who were setting the text of *Satanstoe* were working from a manuscript written in Cooper's small handwriting. He usually managed to put more than forty lines of script on a sheet that had thirty-five lines marked on it. He often jammed words against the right margin, crammed revisions and insertions between lines, and put lengthy additions to existing paragraphs in whatever space he could find. As a result, marks of punctuation and even terminal letters are sometimes missing. Knowing that Cooper did not intend such incomplete punctuation or spelling, the editors have made the necessary corrections after consulting the first edition, the proofs of which Cooper did correct and revise. All such corrections of the copy-text are, of course, listed as Emendations.

The manuscript shows three different stages of composition. Some additions, deletions, or corrections of the original draft were clearly made at the time of the original writing or so close to that time that the ink and pen are the same as those used for the first draft. A second stage of revision was made at a different time and in much darker ink, and Cooper was at this time revising the text and also clarifying letters that a compositor might misread. A third set of revisions was undertaken by John Fagan on Cooper's orders. For example, he wrote Fagan on 4 March 1845:

> You will find the name of the heroine printed "Aneke"—It must be altered wherever it occurs to "Anneke," or with two n's—I add, when it is used the first or second time, "Anne"—This must be altered in this way. "Anneke (Anna Cornelia, abbreviated)."[5]

Accordingly, a second *n* is written above the first almost every time Anneke's name appears in the manuscript through Chapter XX (manuscript leaf 160, line 41). Beginning with Chapter XXI, Cooper himself wrote the double *n*. This correct spelling is treated as Cooper's throughout and not as an emendation. Similarly, Cooper occasionally left blanks in the manuscript when he temporarily forgot a proper name. Dorrichay (at 260.29) and Doorichaise (261.40) are written in by a hand other than Cooper's, and the name Doortje is written, in the black ink of Cooper's second revisions, several times by Cooper but also by someone else, probably Fagan. Cooper also left a blank at 431.34 after "Mrs" and in the manuscript (between lines 15 and 16 on leaf 236) he wrote "(look for the name in about Capt. [sic] 4. or 5)"; someone duly retrieved the name of Mrs. Light. Since Cooper corrected proof in addition to giving specific instructions, such insertions, even though not in his handwriting, are considered his.

While reading proof, Cooper apparently continued to make the kinds of revisions that he had begun earlier in altering the manuscript. Typical of his efforts to make his writing more concise are these changes, chosen at random:

217.40	at seven, or even eight	*becomes*	at eight
234.23	have ever seen	*becomes*	ever saw
407.10-11	at least somewhat	*becomes*	somewhat

Other changes made the meaning more specific, as when "some contractor" becomes "an army contractor" at 159.33. Also typical of Cooper's revisions are the increases in dialect for those characters who speak a dialect. We find three such corrections in one typical passage when he substitutes

172.4	trove	*for*	drove
181.18-19	ter gentleman	*for*	the gentleman
182.36	t'an	*for*	than

The most frequent kind of revisions, also continuing a process begun in the manuscript alterations, is made to avoid repeating a word or a sound. He changed "followed" to "succeeded" in this sentence (84.39): "There was a good deal of general and disjointed conversation that followed; which I shall not pretend to follow . . . ." He changed the first "only" to "merely" in this passage (104.2): ". . . with only a second class dog, and only one." "Appeared" becomes "entered" at 109.10: "As the company appeared, these domestics disappeared . . . ." At 259.36-37 a paragraph ends: "When all was ready, we went finally forth, on our business." "Business" was later changed to "errand," and the reason is found in the next paragraph when the Rev. Mr. Worden says, "I go with you Corny, on this foolish business. . . ."

In the manuscript, Corny several times refers to Anneke as "Annie," but Cooper checked Corny's familiarity while reading proof and she is always Anneke or Anne to him in the printed version. Restoring the formalities proper to their relationship not only makes Anneke and Corny look better, but it also makes Jason Newcome's brashness look worse.

The text of this edition is the copy-text as emended by changes the editors believe Cooper made while correcting and revising proof for the first edition. The only substantive changes initiated by the Cooper Edition without being discussed in a textual note are those which supplement Cooper's identification of the source of his epigraphs. These emendations are, however, listed as such.

Punctuation is a problem since the first edition reflects housestyling rather than Cooper's manuscript. As we have noted, Cooper himself tended to punctuate as though he were marking the manuscript to be read aloud. For example, leaf 42 of the manuscript reads, at lines 17-19:

My aunt was descending from the drawing-room, in dinner dress, for that no lady ever neglects, even though she dines on a cold dumpling, as I opened the street door. Mrs. Legge was not coming down alone to take her seat at table, but having some extra duty . . . .

Trying to simplify the syntax of the first sentence, the compositor made a hash of the second, so that I.86.34-37 in the first edition (81.3-7 in the present edition) read:

> My aunt was descending from the drawing-room, in
> dinner dress—for that no lady ever neglects, even
> though she dines on a cold dumpling. As I opened the
> street-door, Mrs. Legge was not coming down alone to
> take her seat at table, but, having some extra duty . . . .

The present edition follows Cooper's punctuation except
when emendation seems absolutely necessary; consequently,
there is a lack of consistency in punctuation except for three instances in which consistency has been imposed. In the first of
these, the editors routinely place commas and periods within closing quotation marks even though Cooper was inconsistent about
such spacing. Secondly, he frequently placed an apostrophe
directly over the *s* of a possessive, so that words like *wolves'* and
Guert's are assumed to be what Cooper wanted rather than *wolve's*
and *Guerts'* (Guert being the name of a character). Finally,
Cooper's known preference for quotation marks before and after
each epigraph (or "motto" as he called it) is followed by the
Cooper Edition and duly listed as an emendation wherever
Cooper neglected to furnish the necessary punctuation.

The manuscript of *Satanstoe* is like other Cooper manuscripts
in containing what we might consider capitalization by contagion.
He frequently precedes or follows one capitalized word with
another, so that we find, in mid-sentence, such pairs as God Bless,
By George, Blessed Lord, Dutch Edifice, Spanish Gold, English
Crown, and even Beneficent and Gracious Lord. Slips of the pen
and inadvertent capitalization are emended and recorded. At the
beginning of a word, Cooper's *s*, *t*, and *g* could either be capitals
or lower case; consequently, the transcription is governed by in-
terpretation of his intentions. Capitals are obviously called for at
the beginning of a sentence and on proper nouns, while lower-
case is needed on words like "some," "the," and "good" occurring
within a sentence.

Cooper often used a short line, placed low at the level of the
lines on the paper, as a period. These are fairly easy to distinguish from his dashes, which he also used frequently, but sometimes the compositors erred, particularly if the dash-period was
followed by one of the ambiguous capitals just mentioned. For
example, at 277.22 a sentence ends with "term" and a long, syn-
tactically complicated sentence begins with "They." The printer,
however, mistook the short dash for a full dash at AMS 149.39
and printed it as such.

Writing with pens that needed mending, Cooper often left con-
fusing spaces in the middle of compound words. Confronted with
"in deed," the compositors had to compare that space with the equally large spaces, on the same line, in "h and" and "Mor d aunt" and

print "indeed" as one word. As a rule, however, he seemed to prefer "anywhere" and "everywhere" as one word, while "any thing" and "every thing" are generally written as two words.

Where Cooper deleted a word or phrase, but neglected to delete (by a stroke of the pen) the accompanying punctuation, this edition assumes that he meant to cancel the punctuation as well. For instance, at 13.2 Cooper ended the sentence with "disturb" followed by a period, then canceled "disturb" and wrote "create" above it, also followed by a period. The Cooper Edition does not consider this as a case of doubled punctuation and reports no emendation.

Double punctuation is reported, however, when it occurs as a result of an addition or revision that leaves the original punctuation undisturbed. One such example occurs at 231.21 where the sentence ends with the word "island" before Cooper adds the qualifying "at present." He inserted a comma next to the old period after "island" and this double punctuation is duly recorded in the Emendations list and preceded by a degree sign (°).

Cooper's spelling of words has been retained when such spelling is sanctioned as early-nineteenth-century usage by the *Oxford English Dictionary* or by the 1828 edition of Noah Webster's *Dictionary*. Words that he habitually misspelled, such as "particularly" ("particularily"), "athwart" ("atwart"), "receive" ("recieve"), "coolly" ("cooly"), and "fortnight" ("forthnight") have been emended, as have other words ("route" and "rout") where an acceptable spelling ("rout") could be misleading in the context in which it appears.

The text of *Satanstoe*, then, is a transcription of Cooper's manuscript as emended by Cooper for the first American edition in 1845 and with additional corrections of errors of spelling and punctuation that he would not have sanctioned had they come to his attention. All changes, whether accidental or substantive, have been recorded in the list of Emendations.

Notes:

1. *The Letters and Journals of James Fenimore Cooper*, ed. James Franklin Beard. 6 Vols. (Cambridge: Harvard University Press, Belknap Press, 1960-1968), V.12 (hereafter cited as *Letters and Journals*). Cooper's letters show that he was in Philadelphia between 30 April and 15 May, 1845, and he wrote Bentley that the "remainder" of *Satanstoe* would leave by the steamer "of the 16th May" (*Letters and Journals*, V. 19, 22, 24, 26, 27.)

2. See "Note on the Manuscript."

3. For Hinman collation of first editions, J. F. Beard 1 was used as the standard of collation. Collation of J. F. Beard 2, Yale Iw/C786/845s, and Dartmouth PZ/3/.C786/.S revealed no substantive differences. A typographical error, "yonr" for "your" at II.30.34, is present in all four books. The standard of collation has a different type face at I.106.19-34 while the Dartmouth copy has a different type face at I.108.13-32.

4. The accidentals mentioned include Bentley's printing Dei for Deir (I.37.24) and capitalizing Cooper's fort proper (II.113.6 in the American first edition) to become Fort Proper (III.71.7 in the first English edition) followed by Galignani at 261.24. The Bentley edition of the University of Illinois (813/C78s/1845a) was sight-collated against the first American edition, and the Galignani edition (James F. Beard #1) was sight-collated against the Bentley edition.

The same printers, Fain and Runot, printed both the Galignani edition and the Baudry's European Library edition, which is a reimpression of the Galignani on cheap paper and bound in an inexpensive binding. The Baudry and Galignani *Satanstoe* of 1845 are both in the American Antiquarian Society collection and were spot-collated there.

5. *Letters and Journals*, V. 12.

Note on the Manuscript

The Preface and pages 121-241 (corresponding to Volume II of the first edition) of the manuscript of *Satanstoe* belonged to the late Paul Fenimore Cooper, Jr. and are currently housed at the American Antiquarian Society. Manuscript pages 1 through 120 (the text for Volume I of the first edition) are in the Pierpont Morgan library in New York. No title page seems to exist, but otherwise the manuscript is complete. The Preface is written on both sides of an unnumbered sheet; the rest of the pages are numbered consecutively. The epigraphs, which Cooper called "mottos," to each chapter are written on the back of the leaf that begins the chapter except for leaf 9, the beginning of the second chapter, where Cooper's customary instruction to the printer "(Motto—turn over)" has been crossed out and the quotation from *The Winter's Tale* inserted above the text. The other authorial and "editorial" notes printed in the text are usually written on the verso of the manuscript leaf. Some penciled mathematical calculations, probably made in the printing shop, occur on the verso of pages 18, 72, and 119. A large doodled "Satanstoe" and an equally large "by J Fenimore Cooper" are both scratched out on the verso of leaf 147.

The Preface is written in black ink on faintly lined white paper 8" by 12 5/8". The manuscript is on foolscap originally measuring 16" by 12 5/8" then torn or cut to produce leaves of 8" by 12 5/8". There are 35 faint lines to a page, and a margin at the top that varies from 3/4" to 1". Leaves 1 through 158 are on bluish-gray paper, but leaf 1 has faded to greenish gray and leaf 120 (the last of Volume I) has faded to brownish gray (recto) and greenish gray (verso). Leaves 159 through 182 are on brighter blue paper, and leaves 183 through 240 are on white paper. The last leaf, 241, appears to have been white paper but is now discolored to a grayish beige. The pages contain few visible markings. On leaf 203 an impression in the upper left corner reads OHEN & HURBUT/ SO LEE/ MASS in a frame, and small impressions of P&S appear in the upper left corner of odd-numbered leaves on the darker blue paper.

The manuscript of Volume I has been neatly patched, probably by the binder, beginning with page 12, where the two parts of the sheet have been taped on the verso with a 1/4"-wide strip of paper of a quality that matches the surrounding matting. Additional reinforcement occurs on pages 15, 16, 21, 22, 54, 64, 78, 85, 93, 111, and 118. The manuscript of Volume II is loose in a folder, and leaf 128 has had 3 5/8" removed from the bottom; the missing part, however, is now held to the page by two pieces of paper cut from a printed page and pasted onto the verso. One piece mentions eight pounds while the other says "complete ptysalism has set in." Page 142 was cut apart in the middle of line 16 so that Barton could start a stint, but the two parts are now together, though unattached, in the folder. Besides printers' names and inked page numbers corresponding to page numbers in the first edition, smears, ink blots, and stains are found throughout the manuscript. Small tears, particularly at the corners, occasionally involve parts of words.

Cooper routinely began to write in the margin at the top of the page, and usually put over forty lines to a page—sometimes going as high as fifty. He wrote, and made his first revisions, in a black ink now faded to dark gray. Later revisions were made in an ink that is still very black and easy to distinguish from the earlier writing.

Cooper's initial changes in the manuscript generally involve nuances of meaning ("seemed" for "appeared" or "acceptable" for "desirable") or smooth out the syntax. The most frequent revisions are those that provide a synonym for a word already used, or which avoid repetition of similar sounds. Longer additions to the original text were sometimes made to render the circumstances more specific. For instance, as Herman Mordaunt's harnessed horses are swept downstream past Corny and Anneke, Cooper inserts a sentence that describes the shriek that comes "from one of the fettered beasts" thus greatly increasing the verisimilitude Cooper always sought. Other substantial additions occur frequently at the end of paragraphs when Cooper, revising, decided that some topic needed more explanation. He often made such additions when describing Jason Newcome or commenting on the New England character.

Deletions in the manuscript are usually done to tighten the prose and make it more precise. Several long deletions are, however, worth noting. On leaf 31 Cooper canceled "(turn over)" written above "White Wine" and canceled the accompanying note on the verso which reads: "(Note. "White Wine" agreeable to the parlance of the New York Cries meant "Butter≠milk," even as recently as five and twenty years since. Editor.)" He obviously decided at this time not to define the term but to dramatize it in the scene that ends this chapter (IV). On the verso of leaf 142, the current footnote ending with "in our own times." at 264.40

of the present volume was followed by thirty-nine lines in which Cooper described the behavior of one Richard Jackson, "a coloured man of very good character" who had been hypnotized and had given testimony about a robbery. In some five hundred words of this canceled note Cooper went on to say that he had "magnetized" Richard Jackson himself "more than once, and certainly have heard strange things from him, while in that state." One time he took Richard, in a trance, to his home and Richard described a yellowish-green bird from Florida that had just died that morning and was still lying in the cage.

Clearly relevant to his personal problems in 1845 and to the concerns of *Satanstoe* is the other long passage that Cooper canceled, this one on the verso of leaf 153, after the footnote at 283.35-36 ending "at need."

> This should be the use of the rank of Commodore, while Admirals formed the gradation in the line of regular promotions. There being no admirals in the militia, however, it is next to hopeless to expect that they will be given to the navy.
>
> In this country, Commodores in the navy, strictly fill the same place. We should have had Admirals, long since, but for that peculiarily [sic] American vice, envy: which renders the very ordinary minds, of which Congress is so largely composed, indisposed to grant a title, as military appellations, that is not known to the militia! <Editor.> ↑That this reluctance to do justice to a body of men of whom the nation is free enough to boast, does not proceed from a jealous, though mistaken love of liberty is evident from the fact that it so quietly and so generally submits to the odious and vulgar tyranny of its press. <and> A↑n active↓ love of true liberty would have driven the American press, as it now exists, out of being, a quarter of a century since. Editor.↓

Textual Notes

The following comments refer to specific decisions to emend or not to emend requiring fuller explanation than could be provided in the Textual Commentary.

[3].20   The capitalization of the first American edition indicates Cooper's wish to emphasize a main concern of the trilogy of which *Satanstoe* is the first volume.

[21].29   Cooper originally wrote "such a thing as training in false notions, as well as a training in such that are true." He then inserted "a lad" after "as training" and "him" after "a training" and changed "in such" to "in those" but did not cancel the article before the second "training."

34.13   The name Cooper originally chose for his heroine was "Sally," which was crossed out here. For his instructions about the name of Anneke, see the Textual Commentary.

46.1   The last syllable on leaf 11 was "no-" and Cooper failed to complete the word "notions" on his next page.

54.3   Cooper changed "to do this" to "to find their land" by crossing out "do this" and writing the revisions below; however, "this" remains easy to read.

85.29   In the manuscript, Cooper left a long space between "Smybert" and "the people" and put two commas in the space to remind himself to fill in the names. When he added "Watson" and "Blackburn" he gave them their own commas and failed to cancel the other two.

[92].2   The quotation marks breaking up Thurio's speech in the manuscript are almost certainly not Cooper's.

95.1   When he added "Many of" Cooper did not change the *T* to a lower case.

102.25   The manuscript is torn on the lower left corner where "of" would be.

[137].2   Again, the quotation marks at the ends of the lines of the epigraph are probably not Cooper's.

148.20   Cooper crossed out "the" and probably meant to write "one," but left off the *e*, so the printer restored "the."

175.24   In the confusion of this passage, the printer probably failed to notice Cooper's addition of "old <Doriche> Doortje" above the line.

176.16   Cooper had substituted "every one" for "all" in the manuscript, but failed to add "of" at the time.

184.37   Cooper wrote "episcop-" at the margin of the page and began the next line with "alian," which he later canceled.

[196].3   The quotation marks here and before the next line may have been added by a printer.

218.11   This is a clear reference to Mrs. Van der Heyden. At 217.17 and 217.33 Cooper canceled "Bogart" and inserted "Van der Heyden" but failed to change this.

[226].1   Cooper numbered his chapters consecutively, but the first American edition was printed in two volumes.

229.30   Cooper had canceled "so"; yet it is still legible.

238.38   This reading, taken with the one that follows, forms a good example of eye-skip error.

243.17   Going over the manuscript, Cooper enlarged the *e* in "gravest" to the size of a capital *E*, which the printer misread as a *t*.

248.4   The word "on" is written in above the line.

249.16   Cooper wrote "were brought," then canceled "brought" and substituted "came" but failed to cancel "were."

255.16   Cooper moved beer in the list to get it next to cider and away from lemons and sugar.

261.12   Cooper left a blank space where a name could be inserted after "Mother," but the printer just ended the sentence. The first set of punctuation marks are probably the compositor's.

262.33   The lower left corner of manuscript page 141 has been torn off, leaving only the *n* of "on."

264.34   Cooper wrote "already busy" first; then he wrote "engaged" above "busy" without canceling it.

271.12   The last sentence of the paragraph, which makes this change of names imperative, was added after the original paragraph was written.

274.33   Cooper deleted "on"; it is, however, clearly legible.

280.21   In revising, Cooper canceled "Nay" and wrote a capital *M* over the lower-case *m*. The change was obviously made because the following paragraph also starts with "Nay."

281.29   Cooper deleted everything but "that" from "that he might not live to return."

290.39   This word is at the end of a line and almost illegible.

291.12   This word is also at the end of a line and the compositor had to guess what it was.

291.36   Trying to quote from memory, Cooper was apparently not sure whether the quotation included "which" or should begin "is." La Rouchefoucauld's maxim #218 actually reads: "Hypocrisy is the homage that vice offers to virtue."

301.22   Cooper meant to say "so soft and mild were its tones," but he did not have space at the right margin for a clear *s*. Confronting "were . . . tone" in proof, he changed "were" to "in."

306.9   The "us" is another example of a printer's ignoring a cancellation.

306.34   Cooper had tried to delete the last two letters from "their" to make "the," but the *h* and the telltale dot of the *i* led the printer to print "his."

309.12   The double commas are left over from the original "us, Trackless, from the red coats."

[310].4   The Riverside edition of Shakespeare gives "Birnan" for the name of the wood instead of "Birnam."

329.2   Cooper wrote "a" over "its," but "its" got printed.

334.7   This truncated word is the last word on the manuscript leaf, and Cooper normally would put "ing" at the top of the next page. Some interruption is suggested by the fact that the color of the paper changes with the following page.

[339].11-12   The last word in the line is "us," and Cooper crowded "three" in above it at the right margin, but the compositor apparently did not see it.

342.23   Cooper's *r* here looks very much like a *g*, and anyone
              guessing at a word beginning with *m* and ending with *g*
              would, given the context, guess "meaning."

345.19   The "I" is left over from "do I," which Cooper meant to
              replace with "who ebber hear me."

[368].3   Someone, probably not Cooper, put double quotation
              marks at both end of lines three through six and deleted
              a comma after "imprisonment."

369.12   The word "most" is directly above "pale face" in the
              manuscript, but it is followed by a clear period and a
              double quotation mark. Cooper later deleted the quotation
              mark and added "Leg big."

398.37   The constant problem of deciding whether Cooper ended
              a word with *s* or not becomes particularly vexing in his
              description of Ravensnest. The terminal *s* is, however,
              clearly present enough times to show that Cooper
              sometimes thought of Ravensnest as one building, and at
              other times considered the wings as separate buildings.

407.9   Cooper wrote "adventures," leaving out the final *r*, which
              led the compositor to read his *s* as an *r* and print
              "adventurer."

[411].2   Someone other than Cooper put double quotation marks
              at the end of this and the next six lines of poetry, and the
              beginning of lines 2 through 8 on the manuscript. These
              marks were rightly ignored by the compositor who set the
              first American edition.

416.28   The top right corner of leaf 228 has been lost.

[426].31   Cooper's terminal *e* here resembles a capital letter and is
              as high as an *l* would be.

431.34   Between lines 15 and 16 on leaf 236 of the manuscript,
              Cooper wrote, above the blank he left, "(look for the name
              in about Capt. [sic] 4 or 5)" and Fagan or someone else
              retrieved Mrs. Light's name.

Emendations

This list records all readings of the Cooper Edition which differ from those of the copy-text. Readings to the left of the brackets are those adopted by this edition; readings immediately to the right of the brackets are from the copy-text. Readings from the first American edition are also given when they differ substantively from both the adopted readings and those of the copy-text. Sources of the readings are identified by abbreviations: AMS is the author's manuscript, A is the first American edition, and CE is the Cooper Edition. In emendations of punctuation, a curved dash (~) to the right of the bracket represents the same word as the one to the left of the bracket, and a caret (ᴧ) indicates the absence of punctuation in the copy-text. A dagger (†) calls attention to entries in which the copy-text form occurs at the end of a line of script, usually at the crowded right margin of the leaf. A degree sign (°) marks entries in which the copy-text form is influenced by interlinear insertion in the manuscript. An asterisk indicates that the reading is discussed in the textual notes. When identical emendations occur three or more times, they are listed in a single entry at the initial occurrence.

The following texts are referred to:

AMS   Author's Manuscript

A   New York: Burgess, Stringer and CO., 1845

Tp.10-11 "The . . . truth."]A; [AMS titlepage lacking]
Tp.12 William Cowper, "The Task," III.268-269]CE; Spenser A
[3].3 development]A; developement AMS
[3].19 "Satanstoe"]A; " ~ ' AMS
[3].19 "Chainbearer,"]A; ' ~ ' AMS
*[3].20 ANTI-RENTISM]A; anti-rentism AMS
[3].26 &c.]A; ~ ᴧ AMS *Also* emended at 32.28, 33.9, 33.30 (*twice*), 46.39, 126.15, 139.1, 154.4, 159.39 (*twice*), 160.18, 161.7, 162.28, 179.3, 186.8, 311.24, 327.1 (*twice*), 384.30 (*twice*) and 398.34.
[3].26 Mr.]A; Mʳ ᴧ AMS *Also* emended at [3].27, 17.38, 20.14, 22.15, 22.26, 23.4, 24.8, 24.18, 25.1, 25.10, 25.14, 26.29, 26.35, 26.38, 28.9, 28.18, 29.14, 31.27, 34.35, 37.6, 38.7, 38.21, 38.28, 38.37, 39.29, 40.4, 41.7, 41.17, 41.21, 43.33, 44.27, 44.30, 44.34, 45.11, 45.35, 46.6, 46.22, 46.23, 46.29, 52.25, 54.19, 56.7, 58.34, 58.37, 62.20, 67.40, 68.4, 68.18, 68.25, 68.39, 69.13, 73.3 (*twice*), 73.19,

73.34, 73.35, 75.11, 75.25,
77.8, 77.13, [78].33, 79.22,
79.23, 79.27, 79.35, 82.3,
83.14, 83.15, 84.14, 84.28,
84.30, 86.25, 86.38, 87.8,
87.25, 87.38, 88.13, 88.22,
88.36, 89.1, 89.3, 89.6, 89.8,
89.15, 89.20, 89.30, 89.37,
90.1, 90.4, 90.14, 90.30, 91.8,
91.13, [92].9, [92].17 (*twice*),
[92].28, 93.21, 94.36, 95.10,
95.36, 97.21, 97.23, 97.24,
97.27, 97.36, 97.38, 98.21,
98.29, 99.38, 101.7, 101.13,
101.20, 102.5, 102.13, 102.16,
102.28, 103.5, 103.9, 105.17,
[107].16, 111.4, 111.28,
111.33, 112.1, 112.15, 112.27,
114.35, 114.39, 115.14, 115.18,
116.14, 116.36, 118.40, 119.36,
119.38, 120.18, 123.15, 123.26,
123.30, 123.34, 123.37, 124.7,
124.32, 125.6, 125.34, 126.1,
126.23, 127.6, 127.14, 127.33,
127.40, 128.5, 128.18, 128.23,
130.25, 130.36, 132.25, 133.16,
133.33, 142.21, 142.33, 142.34
(*twice*), 142.40, 143.8, 143.19,
144.7, 144.38, 147.22, 148.6,
149.9, 149.12, 149.19, 149.27,
150.15, 150.24, [151].7,
[151].20, [151].27, 152.31,
153.1, 153.38, 154.35 (*twice*),
155.23, 155.35, 155.40, 156.7,
156.21 (*twice*), 156.28, 157.19,
157.25, 158.17, 158.34, 158.37
(*twice*), 159.1, 159.12, 159.20,
159.40, 160.20, 161.18, 161.37,
161.40, 162.1, 162.4, 162.5,
162.17, 163.7, 163.16, 163.28,
163.37, 164.1, 164.23, 164.30,
164.34, 165.1, 165.5, 167.9,
167.15, 167.20, 167.23, 167.28,
169.14, 169.16, 169.33, 170.40,
171.2, 172.12, 172.16, 172.36,
173.14, 173.21, 173.22, 173.25,
173.29, 174.20, 174.36, 175.18,
175.34 (*twice*), 175.35 (*twice*),
176.8, 176.32, 176.33, 177.4
(*twice*), 177.9, 177.13, 177.25,
177.36, 178.19, 178.25, 178.29,

179.11, 179.25, 179.33, 180.7,
180.14, [181].8, [181].16,
[181].17, [181].19, [181].20,
[181].33 (*twice*), 182.3, 182.5,
182.12, 182.14, 182.21, 182.22,
182.25, 182.26, 182.36, 182.37,
183.12, 183.17, 183.19, 183.28,
184.5, 184.6, 184.17 (*twice*),
184.21, 184.26, 184.28, 184.33,
185.4, 185.10, 185.17, 185.33,
186.1 (*twice*), 186.13, 186.15,
186.25, 186.31, 187.3, 187.18,
187.19, 187.22, 187.27, 187.32,
188.2, 188.5, 188.9, 188.11,
188.25, 188.39, 189.3, 189.16,
189.20, 189.31, 189.37, 190.22,
190.30, 192.16, 193.8, 193.37,
194.26, [196].35, 197.3, 197.6,
197.25, 197.33, 197.36, 198.5,
199.12, 199.22, 202.29, 206.29,
208.6, 209.10, 210.2, [211].20,
216.3 (*twice*), 216.9, 216.13,
216.32, 221.29, 223.28, 224.37,
[226].36, 248.3, 248.6, 250.17,
250.34, 251.3, 251.40, 252.31,
255.10, 255.22, 255.25, 255.29,
255.35, 258.4, 258.37, 259.21,
259.29, 259.39, 260.4, 263.20,
263.35, 264.3, 264.7, 264.17,
264.32, [269].15, 270.13,
270.33, 270.37, 271.17, 271.26,
272.8, 274.2, 275.6, 275.14,
275.23, 275.32, 276.40, 279.25,
285.2, 286.10, 286.16, 286.26,
286.27, 287.14, 287.15, 287.22,
287.25, 288.15, 288.16, 289.9,
290.28, 291.25, 291.37, 292.4,
292.19, 292.21, 292.28, 292.36,
293.4, 295.31, [297].11,
[297].20, 298.4, 298.19,
299.18, 300.9, 301.32, 305.26,
305.37, 306.15, 307.37, 309.2,
[310].24, 322.1, 322.16,
[324].21, 325.28, 331.37,
331.39, 342.33, 351.20, 353.16,
364.12, 369.32, 370.31, 373.25,
374.14, 379.10, 379.20, 379.22,
380.7, 380.11, 380.12, 389.5,
389.14, 389.36, 392.17, 394.24,
394.31, 395.7, 398.6, 403.34,
404.30, 405.38, 406.1, 406.8,

[411].26, [411].27, [411].33, 412.24, 412.25, 414.33, 415.21, 416.33, 419.37, 424.14, 424.17, 424.23, [426].30, 427.14, 427.30, 428.27, 429.4, 429.5, 429.34, 431.30, 433.40, 434.1, 436.28, 436.34, 438.19, 438.24, 440.22 *and* 440.36.

°[3].28-29 "Chain⫫bearer,"]A; 'Chainbearer.' AMS

°4.2 by its]A; by the its AMS

4.3 conceive]A; concieve AMS *Also corrected at* 4.19, 251.3 *and* 423.29.

4.11 the Union]A; this Union AMS

4.16 individuals,]A; ~ ∧ AMS

4.17-18 actions, and the "tree is known by its fruit," God help us]A; acts, God Help Us AMS

4.28-29 nobody's]A; nobody AMS

[7].4 *As You Like It*, II.iv.19-21]CE; As You Like It AMS

[7].34 committed mine]A; committed my mine AMS

8.16 enrol]A; enrole AMS

8.28 Satanstoe]A; Satan's Toe AMS *Also emended at* 9.2, 9.19, 10.3, 10.5, 10.18, 10.29 *and* 11.18.

8.32 bless]A; Bless AMS *Also emended at* 132.18, 225.2 *(twice)*, 248.8, 280.29, 282.23, 381.7, 392.1, 416.22 *and* 429.15.

8.36 "neck"]A; '~' AMS

8.37 "head and shoulders,"]A; '~ ~ ~', AMS

9.3 sixty-three]A; ~ ∧ ~ AMS *Numbers are also hyphenated at* 10.40, 11.1, 11.2, 21.1, [50].9, 53.20, 65.13, 85.12, 122.17, [137].10, 152.4, 162.21, 162.35, 170.15, 170.17, 174.15, 183.34, 203.17, 205.20, 252.34, 252.35, 252.37, 255.28, [269].26, 287.15, 304.11, 308.5, 309.5, 311.10, 311.11, 319.18, 326.40, 333.34, 334.20, 356.34, 357.16, 391.27, 429.25, 432.22 *and* 433.2.

°9.5 soil on earth]A; ~.~ ~ AMS

9.9 neck proper]A; Neck Proper AMS

9.10 was to inherit]A; had inherited AMS

9.14 colony to the]A; Colony of the AMS

°9.15 born, in]A; ~; ~ AMS

°9.16-17 ancestors; here]A; ~. ~ AMS

9.21 well-known]A; ~ ∧ ~ AMS

9.28 well-known]A; ~ ∧ ~ AMS

10.9-10 grass shall grow]A; grass grow AMS

10.14 *"standing* order"]A; '~ ~' AMS

10.19 Devil's]A; Deevil's AMS

10.20-21 father-in-law purchased]A; ~ ∧ ~ ∧ ~, ~ AMS

10.22 half-a-dozen]A; ~ ∧ ~ ∧ ~ AMS *Also hyphenated at* 18.14 *and* [181].32-33.

10.30 particularly]A; particularily AMS *Also emended at* 15.2, 16.4, 59.31, 60.13, 63.20, [64].14, 80.11, 81.16, 88.34, 110.36, 116.1, 123.11, 132.40, 143.34-35, 143.38, 158.22, 174.10, 198.3-4, 203.38, 208.28, 219.40, 227.4, 232.14, 262.9, 276.10, 284.18, 289.25, 311.5-6, 320.26, [354].13, 355.22, 357.40, 371.16, 390.16 *and* 438.17.

10.35 story and a half]A; story, and half AMS

11.9 ceilings]A; cielings AMS

11.13 King's]CE; Kings AMS; king's A *Apostrophe also added to show possession at* 23.23, 25.38, 28.23, 31.23-24, 31.24, 40.1, 46.5, 54.21, 58.26-27, [78].6, 79.41, 116.19, 116.29, 133.23, 148.38, 171.20, 176.32, 198.33, 206.14, 208.6, 214.25, 217.33, 219.15, 219.31, 229.3, 229.27, [240].21, 251.5, 274.14, 345.15, 355.17 *and* 417.35.

11.15 portion]A; portions AMS

11.26 vie.]A; ~.. AMS

12.20 fifty]A; forty AMS
12.29 Corny]A; Corney AMS *Also emended at 12.32, 25.24, 27.19, and 28.39.*
12.32 Corny Littlepage]A; Corney Littlefield AMS
12.34 feeling that]A; feeling AMS
13.25-26 afforded]A; offered AMS
13.33 Monckton]A; Moncton AMS
14.3 Louisbourg]A; Louisburg AMS
14.17 states]A; States AMS
14.20 received]A; recieved AMS *Also corrected at* 41.21, 55.14, 60.25, 67.37, 67.38, 72.27, 73.10, 81.13, 81.39, 82.9, 84.4, 89.18-19, 93.19, 101.39, 110.32, 123.9, 123.10-11, 135.5, 135.24, 139.31, 173.31, [196].11, 207.35, 209.33, 244.15, 257.3, 289.38, 302.39, 307.2, 307.16-17, 312.35, 328.25, 334.32, 337.19, 349.11, 379.7, 380.10, 385.39, 388.14-15, 388.25, 389.21, 391.6, 405.15, 409.29, 421.10 *and* 422.10.
15.22 led]A; lead AMS
15.27 former]A; old AMS
15.33 benefited]A; benefitted AMS
15.36 moving about]A; travelling AMS
15.40 venerable progenitor,]A; grandfather AMS
16.11 difference;]A; ~, AMS
16.14 heathens]A; heathen AMS
16.18 would be better]A; would better AMS
16.19 more righteousness]A; more of righteousness AMS
16.37 discoursing]A; discussing AMS
16.40 "Major"]A; '~' AMS
16.40 "Captain"]A; '~' AMS
17.1 fonder]A; founder AMS
17.6 familiarly]A; familiarily AMS
17.6 Hodge]A; Hugh AMS
17.8 Hugh]A; Hodge AMS
17.23 out of his]A; out his AMS
17.35 is now very particular]A; is very particular now AMS

17.37 Hodge]A; Ro AMS
17.38 *It]A; (Note, It AMS
17.40 also.]A; ~.) AMS
18.5 '10,]A; '~; AMS
18.8 some time]A; some little time AMS
18.13 "vantage ground"]A; '~ ~' AMS
18.27 by George]A; By ~ AMS
18.27 he]A; she AMS
18.28 his son]A; her son AMS
18.29 the girls]A; she AMS
19.2 and with]A; with AMS
19.4 how]A; How AMS
19.5 "the Yankee expedition,"]A; '~ ~ ~,' AMS
19.12 language—which]A; ~, ~ AMS
19.13 end—treat]A; ~, ~AMS
19.23 our]A; our own AMS
19.28 heathenish]A; Heathenish AMS
19.34 "I]A; '~ AMS
19.35 heathenish]A; Heathenish AMS
19.36 here,"]A; ~,' AMS
20.3 drill."*]A; ~.'ˣ (Note AMS
20.10 *On]A; Note (On AMS
20.11 died more than]A; died about AMS
20.11 at Mamaroneck]A; in Mamaroneck AMS
†20.12 Co.,]A; ~ ∧ ∧ AMS
20.17 belong]A; belongs AMS
20.17 Wm.]A; Wᵐ∧ AMS
20.20 Louisbourg]A; Louisburg AMS
20.24 *plunder.*—Editor.]A; ~.∧~∧) AMS
[21].3 rest."]A; ~:— AMS
[21].4 *The Winter's Tale,* III.iii.59-61]CE; Winter's Tale AMS
†[21].25 doctrine that the]A; doctrine that that the AMS
*[21].29 as training]A; as a training AMS
22.2 Latin]A; latin AMS *Also emended at* 41.19, 86.11, 89.37 *and* 90.3.
22.2 Greek]A; greek AMS

22.11 gauge]A; guage AMS
22.13 invariably]A; always AMS
22.16 Æneids]A; Eneades AMS
°22.29 prodigy in]A; ~.~ AMS
23.2 Christmas]A; christmas AMS
23.5 Valkenburgh]A; Valkenberg
AMS *Also emended at* 23.9,
26.32 *and* 38.17.
23.6 'Brom]A; ∧ ~ AMS *Also
emended at* 24.23 *and* 26.21.
23.20 vogue then, as well as]A;
vogue, then as AMS
23.21 he pe]A; he be AMS
23.24 "college-l'arnt"]A; '~-~'
AMS
°23.27 sent, even]A; ~. ~ AMS
23.27 admitting that he]A;
admitting he AMS
23.31 colleges, dat]A; ~ ∧ 'dat
AMS
23.36 ist]A; is AMS
23.39 college]A; College AMS
24.1 Don't]A; Dont AMS
24.6 pack]A; back AMS
24.21 coolly]A; cooly AMS *Also
corrected at* 76.33, 223.14,
251.10 *and* 386.4.
24.22 trade.]A; ~." AMS
24.25 breaches]A; preaches AMS
24.37 ter Neck]A; The Neck AMS
24.37-38 Presitent]A; President
AMS
24.38 r o o f, ruff]A; ~. ~ AMS
25.11 ascetic]A; ascetick AMS
25.13 blessed]A; Blessed AMS
25.27 ter sight]A; de sight AMS
25.32 dull-seeming]A;
dull-looking AMS
26.12 Colonel]A; colonel's AMS
°26.29 religion,]A; ~. AMS
27.9 propositions]A; truths AMS
27.11 they]A; the AMS
27.16 Ter journey]A; The
journey AMS
27.17 ter exercise]A; the exercise
AMS
27.17 Ter Major]A; The Major
AMS
27.25 whenever that event
might]A; when ever that
might AMS

°27.26 father]A; grand-father
AMS
27.30 identical]A; much alike
AMS
27.32 tifferent]A; different AMS
27.39 Major Evans]A; Capt.
Hugh AMS
28.2 peen]A; been AMS
28.3 vast]A; wast AMS
28.4 yonter]A; yonder AMS
28.12-13 "terriple ferry"]A;
'~ ~', AMS
28.13 itself, had]A; ~ ∧ ~ AMS
28.23 representatif]A;
Representatif AMS
28.29 Jaap]A; Jake AMS
28.30 Yaap]A; Yop AMS
29.14 Mrs.]A; Mʳˢ∧ AMS *Also
emended at* 58.30, 59.10, 81.5,
[92].17, 95.10, 180.11, 186.31,
186.34, 214.18, 214.22, 216.39,
217.17, 217.32, 218.11, 220.17,
220.28, 220.32, 221.31, 221.33,
223.9, 224.28, 246.3, 246.6,
248.5, 248.16, 331.38, 431.34,
437.1 *and* 437.16.
29.20 question]A; subject AMS
29.27 supper]A; table AMS
29.28 table]A; supper AMS
30.3 tried]A; contrived AMS
30.6 of gala-day]A; of a gala-day
AMS
30.20 blacks, you]A; ~ ∧ ~ AMS
°30.22 asking it.]A; ~."~. AMS
°30.33 party.]A; ~." AMS
30.40-31.1 to-day]A; ~ ∧ ~ AMS
31.16-17 colony.*]A; ~.ˣˣ AMS
31.26 *The]A; Note (The AMS
†31.42 —Editor.]A; ∧ ~ ∧ AMS
32.4 walking]A; moving AMS
32.11 Trinity,*]A; ~,ˣ AMS
32.18 went]A; passed AMS
32.22 gone by]A; passed AMS
32.24-25 Lanceys]A; Lancey's AMS
32.28 house†]CE; ~ ˣˣ AMS
32.38 *The site]A; ˣ(Note—The
site AMS
32.38 Hotel.—ED.]A; ~ ∧ ∧ ~.)
AMS
32.39 †Now]CE; ˣˣ(Note—Now
AMS

32.39 —ED.]A; ∧ ~.) AMS
33.13 wearing]A; in AMS
33.13 hat; and]A; hat, as usual, and AMS
33.16 army.*]CE; ~.ˣˣ AMS
33.24 *This]CE; ˣˣ(Note. (This AMS
33.24 Rensselaer]A; Renselear AMS *Also corrected at* 33.30, 33.36, 140.12, 140.15-16, 157.9-10, 183.39-40 *and* 429.29.
33.28 county]A; Co. AMS
33.29 Colonel]A; Col. AMS
33.41-42 man.—Editor.]A; ~.~.) AMS
°34.2 come out]A; ~, ~ AMS
34.5 groups]A; groupes AMS
*34.13 Anneke (Anna Cornelia, abbreviated)]A; Aneke AMS
34.20 Whether 'a]A; ~ ∧ ~ AMS
34.22 coach,']A; ~,∧ AMS
35.1 Anneke*]A; Aneke∧ AMS
35.4 *Pronounced On-na-*kay*, I believe.—Editor.]A; [lacking] AMS
[36].4 singing."]A; ~.∧ AMS *Terminal quotation marks also provided at* 52.31, 54.2, 78.4, 142.5, 179.20, [226].5, [240].10, 251.10, 262.7, [269].8, 282.25, [297].5, [324].5, [339].5, 345.34, [354].3, [426].5, 427.29 *and* 437.2.
[36].5 *The Winter's Tale,* IV.iv.202-3, 211-12]CE; *Winter's Tale* AMS
[36].7 term]A; time AMS
[36].11 books]A; Books AMS
[36].13 philosophy]A; Philosophy AMS
[36].15 moons.]A; ~ ∧ AMS *Period also added to sentence at* 54.9, †54.31, 55.40, †59.17, †63.39, 65.32, 80.23, 91.2, †145.31, †163.26, †172.6, 179.20, [196].33, 198.39, 201.37, †206.9, 231.24, 231.32, 238.29, 241.20, †263.34, °265.10, †267.6, 276.11, 277.11, 277.27, 292.8, †315.6,

350.34, 389.39, °405.11, †410.13, 414.29 *and* 435.30.
[36].35 our class]A; the class AMS
37.14 ideas]A; thoughts AMS
37.20 praised]A; Praised AMS
37.21 ferry]A; ferry again AMS
38.10 Dirck's]A; Dirckie's AMS
38.27 £50 per annum]A; £50, per. ann. AMS
38.31 Christian]A; christian AMS *Also capitalized at* 56.7, 62.17, 423.19 *and* 428.4.
39.8 Philipses]CE; Felipse's AMS
39.13 Lanceys]A; Lancey's AMS
°39.13 &c.]A; ~., AMS
39.21 or, as]A; ~ ∧ ~ AMS
39.22 appellation himself]A; ~, ~ AMS
†39.27 jet-black]A; ~ ∧ ~ AMS
39.27 greasy-looking]A; ~ ∧ ~ AMS
39.28 procuring for him]A; procuring him AMS
39.39 Newark,—]A; ~,∧ AMS
40.1 book]A; bible AMS
40.10 supper,—]A; ~,∧ AMS
40.17 "neighbours"]A; '~' AMS
40.19 supervisors!]A; ~, AMS
40.23 lying!]A; ~. AMS
40.39 taught no]A; taught an AMS
40.40 that is]A; that was AMS
†41.1 innocent,]A; ~ ∧ AMS
41.5 dependent]A; dependant AMS
41.7 looked, the]A; ~ ∧ ~ AMS
41.8 time we]A; ~, ~ AMS
41.9-10 a much]A; much a AMS
°41.20 hunter,]A; ~., AMS
41.27 say, "hat]A; ~, '~ AMS
41.35 latter]A; later AMS
41.40 "election-day"]A; 'Election Day' AMS
42.17 a-n]A; a n AMS
42.19 "English,"]A; '~ ∧' AMS
42.19 "*Ing*lish"]A; '~' AMS
42.20 "*Eng*lish"]A; '~' AMS
42.20 "nothing"]A; '~' AMS
42.21 *noth*-ing]A; *Noth*ing AMS
42.21 *naw*thin]A; *Naw*thin AMS
42.25 "none," (nun,)]A; '~ ∧ ∧(~ ∧)" AMS

42.26 "stone," "stun,"]A; "~ ∧"
　"~.∧ AMS
42.26 "home,"]A; "~ ∧" AMS
42.28 "hearth," "h'arth;"]A;
　"~ ∧" "harth," AMS
42.28 though]A; but AMS
42.29 "Been,"]A; '~ ∧' AMS
42.30 "roof,"]A; '~ ∧' AMS
42.30 "ruff"]A; '~" AMS
43.8 conceit]A; conciet AMS *Also
　corrected at* 43.22-23, 61.35 *and*
　96.5.
43.26 which]A; that AMS
43.30 disposition]A; character AMS
43.30 manner]A; manners AMS
43.35 fortnight]A; forth night
　AMS *Also emended at* 46.18,
　[50].14, 89.7, 132.6, 132.13,
　138.32, 249.34, 255.40, 306.6,
　[310].13 *and* 312.17.
44.7 have]A; feel AMS
44.23 "your folks,"]A; '~ ~ ∧'
　AMS
45.15 you?]A; ~! AMS
°45.30 certificate."]A; ~ ∧ ∧ AMS
45.31 "recommend"]A; '~' AMS
45.31-32 "recommendation"]A;
　'~' AMS
*†46.1 notions]A; no- AMS
46.21 'huffs,']A; '~ ∧" AMS
46.33 prove to]A; show AMS
46.36 language, viz:—]A;
　~—~— AMS
46.39 &c."*]A; ~."ˣˣ AMS
46.40 *This]A; Noteˣ (This AMS
47.1 said]A; cried AMS
47.14 her a]A; her AMS
47.27 hemisphere?]A; ~. AMS
47.35 Italy itself]A; ~; ~ AMS
47.42 excellence.—Editor.]A;
　~.∧ ~ ∧) AMS
48.16 regularly]A; regularily AMS
48.40 was]A; is AMS
49.5 and, I]A; ~ ∧ ~ AMS
49.6 think, reasonably]A; ~ ∧ ~
　AMS
49.14 "extraordinary"]A; '~' AMS
°49.15 unconsciously,]A; ~. AMS
[50].6 Longfellow, "A Psalm of
　Life," 11.33-36]CE;
　Longfellow AMS

52.9 father has]A; ~, ~ AMS
52.14-15 recommendation?]A;
　~. AMS
52.20 Dirck]A; Corny AMS
52.25 A.B.,]A; A.B ∧ ∧ AMS
52.26 institution.]A; ~." AMS
52.36 as the]A; as they AMS
52.40 breast]A; pocket AMS
53.14 English-made]A; ~ ∧ ~
　AMS
53.18 first quality]A; ~-~ AMS
53.19 English-made]A; ~ ∧ ~
　AMS
53.20 ninety-six]A; ninty ∧ ~
　AMS
53.25 suppose]A; hope AMS
53.31 it?]A; ~. AMS
54.5 fast!]A; ~. AMS
54.19 Virginia—]A; ~, AMS
54.21 south—]A; ~, AMS
54.24-25 Mississippi]A; Mississipi
　AMS
54.26 fact]A; facts AMS
54.36 under discussion]A; in
　doubt AMS
†54.38 cooking,]A; ~ ∧ AMS
54.39 this]A; that AMS
55.4 below, gave me some useful
　information]A; below AMS
55.17 stone—]A; ~, AMS
55.17 common]A; usual AMS
55.18 country—]A; ~, AMS
55.18 long,]A; ~ ∧ AMS
55.40 cousin,]A; ~ ∧ AMS
56.1 or,]A; ~ ∧ AMS
56.1 pronounced,]A; ~ ∧ AMS
56.1 Harman]A; ~, AMS
†56.21 relations?]A; ~. AMS
57.5 Anneke]A; Annie AMS *Also
　emended at* 67.35, 76.5, 83.36,
　84.14, 84.34, 87.21, 91.4,
　96.22, 97.12, 97.37, 98.39,
　101.12 *and* 108.32.
57.15 with it]A; with AMS
57.16 (On-na-*kay*)]A; (An-e-ke)
　AMS
57.30 not]A; never AMS
†57.34 and]A; an AMS
58.15 relished]A; enjoyed AMS
58.19 the same]A; less AMS
°59.6 already.]A; ~." AMS

59.22 young friend]A; friend
 AMS
59.32 Lane]A; Road AMS
59.34 should]A; would AMS
59.37 Queen]A; Queen's AMS
60.15 irresistible]A; irresistable
 AMS
60.26 half-past]A; ～ ∧ ～ AMS
 Also hyphenated at 60.36, 80.31,
 82.24 *and* 155.25.
60.28 genteel.*]A; ～.ˣˣ AMS
60.31 *The]A; ₍(Note—The AMS
60.36 half]A; ½ AMS
°61.11-12 arrangement]A; ～.
 AMS
61.19-20 opinion. ¶ Just]A; ～. ～
 AMS
61.25 wine!]A; ～, AMS
61.26 White wine]A; 'White
 Wine' AMS
61.37 north-west]A; ～ ∧ ～ AMS
 Directions also hyphenated at
 314.36-37, 315.28, 347.2,
 360.33, 366.38, 367.13, 405.26,
 405.30, 407.14 *and* 407.15.
61.40-41 experience!—Editor.]A;
 ～.——～ ∧) AMS
62.6 holiday]A; Holiday AMS
62.13 "reasonable."]A; '～.'. AMS
°62.17 hence,]A; ～,. AMS
°62.26-29 beauty. There are air
 . . . man. A square . . .
 pleases."]A; beauty. A square
 may be a parallelogram, or a
 triangle, or any other shape
 one pleases. There are air and
 beauty enough, to satisfy any
 reasonable man. ∧ AMS
62.38 sixty]A; six AMS
63.22 'white wine']A; "White
 Wine," AMS
63.29 white wine]A; "White
 Wine" AMS
63.37 St. Jingo]A; ～ ～, AMS
63.37 "darnation"]A; '～' AMS
63.37 "darn you"]A; '～ ～' AMS
[64].2 "Here's]A; '～ AMS
[64].5 *New York Cries.*]A; New
 York cries ∧ AMS
[64].10 white wine]A; White
 Wine AMS

[64].13 unless he]A; unless it
 might be that he AMS
[64].16 white wine]A; White
 Wine AMS
[64].22 "shining"]A; '～' AMS
°65.16-17 laughing,]A; ～. AMS
65.22 features]A; feature AMS
65.22-23 distinguish]A;
 distinguishes AMS
65.39 receiving]A; recieving
 AMS *Also corrected at* 93.21,
 162.22, 200.12-13, 201.23,
 227.6, 256.33, 257.30, 278.21,
 294.17, 420.3 *and* 422.37.
66.7 when, unconsciously, I got
 separated]A; when I got
 unconsciously separated AMS
°66.28 before.]A; ～,. AMS
66.35 curtsey; upon]A; ～. After
 AMS
67.10 genttleum]A; genttlem AMS
67.11 *"Anneke,"*]A; '～,' AMS
67.11 "gentleman]A; '～ AMS
67.12 appearance."]A; ～,' AMS
67.12 "Can]A; 'can AMS
67.12 Dirck?"]A; ～,' AMS
67.16 "cousin Anneke."]A; '～ ～.'
 AMS
°67.18 Mordaunt,]A; ～. AMS
67.31 unintelligible]A;
 unintellable AMS
67.36 face—]A; ～, AMS
68.22 when]A; Yesterday, when
 AMS
68.32 regularly]A; regularily AMS
69.2 Littlepage?]A; ～. AMS
69.17-18 perceive]A; percieve
 AMS *Also corrected at* 264.19,
 363.23 *and* 407.25.
69.24 some]A; many AMS
69.29 habitation]A; structure AMS
70.6 semi-savage]A; ～ ∧ ～ AMS
70.10 peculiarly]A; peculiarily
 AMS
70.11 endeavoured]A; attempted
 AMS
70.37 Yaap]A; Yap AMS
70.40 Pinkster field, a]A;
 Pinkster a AMS
71.29 mistress]A; Mistress AMS
72.1 animal's]A; animal AMS

72.16 however]A; hower AMS
73.8 sisters]A; sister AMS
°73.20 tickets.]CE; ~." AMS
73.33 treat?]A; ~. AMS
74.5 saved me]A; saved AMS
74.15 been]A; felt AMS
74.18 Corny]A; Coorney AMS
74.27 conceiving]A; concieving AMS
75.21 genteelly]A; genteely AMS
75.22 ungenteelly]A; ungenteenly AMS
75.24 'Seminarian]A; "~ AMS
75.26 Boys']A; Boy's AMS
75.27 visitors]A; visiters AMS
76.17 keeper]A; Keeper AMS
77.1 for]A; by AMS
77.5-6 particularly]A; particulearily AMS
77.7 happened]A; passed AMS
77.18 Anneke]A; Anne AMS *Also emended at* 85.14, 86.33, 89.35, 91.23, 98.39, 101.14, 108.21 *and* 126.29.
[78].5 *Cymbeline*, III.iv.165-167]CE; Cymbeline AMS
[78].7 Street,*]A; ˣˣ(Note— AMS
[78].13 much of his]A; most of my AMS
[78].25 so]A; as AMS *Also emended at* 182.27, 199.2 *and* 201.19.
[78].26 "Park"]A; 'park' AMS
[78].28 valleys]A; vallies AMS *Also emended at* [137].21, 227.16, 318.15 *and* 319.28.
[78].30 one]A; once AMS
[78].33 Nicoll*]A; ~ˣˣ AMS
[78].34 *Now, Liberty Street.]A; ^~, ~ ~.) AMS
[78].35 †The]CE; Note ˣ (The AMS
79.4 birth]A; death AMS
79.27 relic]A; relick AMS
79.29 Old]A; old AMS
79.42 government.—Editor.]A; ~.^~.) AMS
80.37 ¶ Marriages]A; [no ¶] AMS
81.13 any.]A; ~? AMS
81.18 receive]A; recieve AMS *Also emended at* 81.21, 81.32, 82.3, 93.19, 93.20, 110.29,

113.33, 129.25, 133.23, 135.1, 160.23, 185.2, 207.22, 213.22, 217.1, 217.8, 217.23, 242.16, 249.32, 251.36-37, 306.31, 325.31-32, 331.28, 387.39, 422.31 *and* 423.6.
81.26-27 Herma*a*nus]A; Herma*w*nus AMS
81.30 speak]A; speake AMS
82.6 highest-bred]A; ~ ^ ~ AMS
82.17 she in]A; she even in AMS
82.20 weakness]A; weaknesses AMS
82.21 recollect that]A; recollect AMS
82.29 sat]A; even sat AMS
82.30 even later]A; later AMS
82.39 Colony,]CE; ~., AMS
83.4 most intimate]A; intimate AMS
83.19 *"cousin*]A; '~ AMS
83.19 and I]A; and that I AMS
83.20 interpret this as]A; interpret into AMS
83.23 cause]A; cause me AMS
83.36 half-hour]A; ~ ^ ~ AMS *Also hyphenated at* 184.39, 207.2, 247.3 *and* 414.30.
84.21 fields]A; Feilds AMS
84.21 frolicks]CE; Frolicks AMS
84.39 succeeded]A; followed AMS
85.4 titles]A; tittles AMS
*85.29 Watson,]A; ~,, AMS
85.29 Blackburn,]A; ~,, AMS
85.32 day—]A; ~, AMS
85.33 generations—]A; ~, AMS
86.5 Hallam]A; Hellam AMS
86.11 Greek]A; greek AMS
86.13 ever]A; every AMS
86.15 place.*]A; ~.ˣˣ Note AMS
86.24 felt]A; took AMS
86.34 *tête-à-tête*]A; ~ ^ ~ ^ ~ AMS
86.40 *The]A; (~ AMS
86.40 church]A; church itself AMS
86.40 Post Office.—Editor.]CE; ~ ~ ^——~.) AMS
87.23 so far to]A; to so far AMS
87.29 it is his]A; it his AMS
87.40 it is his]A; it his AMS
°88.11 weight.]A; ~." AMS

88.39 representations?]A; ∼.
AMS
90.5 'that]A; "∼ AMS
90.6 starves.'"]A; ∼" AMS
90.13 starves!"]A; ∼."! AMS
°91.1 ignorance,]A; ∼. AMS
91.14 "This]A; ∧ ∼ AMS *Initial*
quotation marks also added at
111.38, 157.3, [166].2, 213.11,
[226].2, [240].2, [254].2,
[269].2, [297].2, 322.3, [324].2,
364.4, [368].2, 380.20, [382].2,
[397].2, 404.27 *and* [426].2.
*[92].2 I;]CE; ∼;" AMS
[92].3 I]CE; "∼ AMS
[92].3 endanger]A; ∼" AMS
[92].4 His]A; "∼ AMS
[92].4 not:]CE; ∼:" AMS
[92].5 I]CE; "∼ AMS
[92].6 *Two Gentlemen of Verona*,
V.iv.132-135]CE; Two
Gentlemen of Verona AMS
[92].19 patronymics]A;
patronymicks AMS
†°[92].23 relatives]A; rela⧸tives
AMS
[92].28 Bulstrode. They]A;
∼;—they AMS
94.10 Green.*]A; ∼.ˣˣ AMS
94.13 front,]A; ∼; AMS
94.19 brick]A; bricks AMS
94.36 *Mr.]A; Note. Mʳ ∧ AMS
94.38 causes]A; cause AMS
94.39 third-class street]A; third
class of street AMS
94.40-41 apology.—Editor]A;
∼.∧ ∼ AMS
*°95.1 the hills]A; The hills AMS
95.8 Lieutenant]A; ruling Lt.
AMS
95.17 back-ground]A; ∼ ∧ ∼ AMS
95.24 moral.*]A; ∼.ˣˣ AMS
95.27 follows that]A; follows AMS
95.29 Blossoms]A; Bloemiches
AMS
95.36 *The]A; Note (The AMS
95.38 church]A; Church AMS
95.40 superior.—Editor.]A;
∼.∧ ∼ ∧) AMS
96.5-6 intimates that "Corny]A;
∼ '∼ ∧ ∼ AMS

96.7 Colony."]CE; ∼.' AMS
96.8 mothers]A; Mothers AMS
°96.30 cousins,]A; ∼. AMS
96.36 feared]A; pined AMS
96.37 and angel-like]A; angel
like AMS
96.38 feared]A; pined AMS
97.9 parted?]A; ∼. AMS
97.11 bow to]A; help entertain
AMS
†97.33 enemies,]A; ∼ ∧ AMS
98.5 "as]A; '∼ AMS
98.5 me,"]CE; ∼,' AMS
98.10 Annie]A; Anne AMS
°98.14 dread.]A; ∼, AMS
98.23 adding 'and very]CE;
∼ ∧ ∼ '∼ AMS
98.24 unsought,']A; ∼,∧ AMS
98.28 To-night]A; ∼ ∧ ∼ AMS
98.37 Henry]A; Harry AMS
99.1 permitted]A; permitted of
AMS
99.21 my]A; My AMS
°99.25 training. And]CE; ∼." ∼
AMS
99.27 fashion."]A; ∼.' AMS
100.2 obtain]A; attain AMS
†100.5 should]A; shoul AMS
100.10 Duke]A; Duke's AMS
100.11 lodgings]A; lodging's AMS
100.17 a man]A; men AMS
100.20 answered.]A; ∼; AMS
101.5 patrician]A; Patrician AMS
101.25-26 birthright]A; birth
right AMS
101.27 Harris's]A; Harris' AMS
101.29-30 the young man in
question]A; him AMS
102.20 'that]A; "∼ AMS
*102.25 alongside of]A; along
side AMS
102.25 daughters.']A; ∼.∧ AMS
103.4 waive]A; wave AMS
103.5 to-day. This]A; ∼; this AMS
103.17 next to that of]A; next AMS
103.29 reason]A; occasion AMS
104.2 merely]A; only AMS
104.14 Wallace]A; Wallace
merely AMS
104.38 however;]A; ∼, AMS
104.39 gave]A; give AMS

105.16 threatening]A; '~' AMS
[107].2 God's]CE; Odd's AMS
[107].2 bodkin]CE; bodikins AMS
[107].7 *Hamlet*, II.ii.529-532]CE;
Hamlet AMS
[107].12 'the virtuous]A; "~ ~
AMS
[107].32 may have]A; may AMS
108.24 concealed]A; covered AMS
108.26 shade]A; cover AMS
109.10 entered]A; appeared AMS
109.20 thing]CE; things AMS
109.29 perceived]A; percieved
AMS *Also emended at* 321.2,
364.38, 417.6, 424.8 *and*
424.12.
109.36 had]A; was AMS
110.4 Syphax]A; Sypax AMS
110.12 offence.*]A; ~.^{xx} AMS
110.13 Harris's]A; Harris' AMS
110.15 "virtuous Marcia"]A;
'~ ~' AMS
110.15 came]A; come AMS
110.36 "virtuous Marcia"]A;
'~ ~' AMS
110.37 *In]A; (Note. In AMS
110.40 herring.—Editor.]A;
~.∧~∧) AMS
111.6-7 itself. ¶ The]A; ~. ~
AMS
111.11 courted]A; sued AMS
111.33 Hon.]A; ~∧ AMS
111.38 Jane"—]A; ~—" AMS
112.4 Henry]A; Harry AMS
112.24-25 Marcia.'"]CE; ~." AMS
112.29 better]A; best AMS
114.13 regret that]A; regret AMS
114.18 prodigious]A; particular
AMS
114.21 arrives]A; arrive AMS
114.27-28 Miss Markham]A; Miss
[space] AMS
114.30 Miss Markham]A; Miss
[space] AMS
†114.39 Mordaunt.]A; ~, AMS
°116.10 question.]A; ~ ∧ AMS
°116.11 particularly]A;
particularil AMS
116.16 allowed]A; allow AMS
116.21 a dozen]A; dozen AMS
116.34 that person]A; them AMS

117.13 acquirements]A;
aquirements AMS
117.39 getting]A; by getting AMS
118.12 commodious]A; very
commodious AMS
118.18 Lane]A; Road AMS
118.29 appeared that]A;
appeared AMS
119.3 notion that]A; notion AMS
119.4 natural that]A; natural AMS
119.4 that right]A; that a right
AMS
119.7 New York]A; York AMS
119.20-21 sometimes]A; often AMS
120.29 would]A; could AMS
[122].6 Reginald Heber,
"Happiness," ll. 17-20]CE;
Heber AMS
[122].11 heights]A; hieghts AMS
[122].15 wall-like]A; long
wall-like AMS
124.11 a greater]A; as great a
AMS
124.11 than a]A; as a AMS
124.16 heights]A; hieghts AMS
124.26 seats as]A; seats of AMS
124.29 foretell]A; foretel AMS
°125.32 Anneke said]CE; Aneke
said AMS; said Anneke A
126.4 Everywhere]A; Every
where AMS
126.18 highly-finished]A; highly
wrought AMS
126.22 that impressed]A; as to
impress AMS
127.4 learning useful things]A;
learning AMS
127.6 Newcome]A; Newcombe
AMS
127.9 enemies]A; enimies AMS
127.17 "poority,"]CE; '~,' AMS
127.40 entreat]A; intreat AMS
128.12 so."]A; ~?' AMS
128.23 labours]A; labous AMS
128.29 ribands]A; ribbands AMS
128.31 be owing]A; be AMS
128.32 being 'treated']A; 'seeing
sights' AMS
130.8 and I]A; but I AMS
°130.11 Anneke]A; Aneke' AMS
130.19 Jason; that]A; Jason, since

most of that AMS
131.5 awful]A; desperate AMS
131.10 agin']A; ag'in AMS
131.10 real title]A; title AMS
°131.16 induce]A; induces AMS
131.22-23 "Esquire."]CE; '~.'
AMS
131.35 head.*]A; ~.ʌ AMS
131.36 *As]A; (Note. As AMS
131.38 that which]A; for what AMS
132.4 one which]A; one that AMS
132.20 I waited]A; waited AMS
132.27-28 "his grace,"]A; '~ ~,'
AMS
132.32 sufficiently far]A; far
enough AMS
132.41 York.—Editor.]A;
~.ʌ~.) AMS
133.28 'her]A; ʌ ~ AMS
133.29 understand]A;
understood AMS
133.39 Corny,"]A; ~!' AMS
134.1 also an only]A; also only
AMS
°134.13 great-great-
grandmother]A; ~ ʌ ~ ʌ ~
AMS
134.37 by mail]A; by my mail
AMS
135.26 kindred]A; Kindred AMS
135.31 sunset]A; the sun set AMS
135.40 adequately]A; strongly
AMS
136.7 in the command]A; in
command AMS
*[137].2 joy]A; ~" AMS
[137].3 Expands]A; "~ AMS
[137].3 Savoy!]A; ~!" AMS
[137].4 Doom'd]A; "~ AMS
[137].4 roam,]A; ~ ʌ" AMS
[137].5 Each]A; "~ AMS
[137].5 home,]A; ~," AMS
[137].6 My]A; "~ AMS
[137].6 sooth'd]A; soothe'd AMS
[137].6 end:]A; ~;" AMS
[137].7 I]A; "~ AMS
[137].8-9 Joel Barlow, "The
Hasty Pudding," Canto I.
57-62]CE; Barlow AMS
[137].25 promising.*]A; ~.ˣˣ
AMS

[137].30 *Forty]A; (Note. Forty
AMS
[137].36 answer.—Editor.]A;
~.ʌ ~ ʌ) AMS
138.18 Corny,"]A; "~, AMS
138.23-24 possible to do]A;
possible AMS
139.9 Yaap]CE; Yop AMS; Jaap A
Also emended at 145.36, 146.1,
146.16 *and* 146.24.
139.17 Yaap's]A; Yap's AMS
139.32 "office;"]A; '~'; AMS
139.32 "study,"]A; '~ ʌ' AMS
140.7 too;]A; ~, AMS
140.11 colonies; full]A; ~. Full
AMS
140.12 Rensselaers]A;
Rensselears AMS
140.15-16 Rensselaers]A;
Rensselears AMS
141.14 deceive]A; decieve AMS
Also emended at 259.23, 377.18
and 413.11.
141.23 conveniences; that
looks]A; conveniences that
look AMS
141.27 may]A; can AMS
142.35 conceives]A; concieves AMS
143.36 (*twice*) buffalo]A; buffaloe
AMS *Also emended at* 144.4.
144.22-23 near the sea]A; nearer
the streams, AMS
144.24 grandfather's]A;
grand-father's AMS
144.26 party]A; journey AMS
144.34 hasty-pudding]A; '~-~'
AMS
144.35 "suppaan."]A; '~." AMS
145.4 "south wind"]A; '~ ~' AMS
145.5 "softly,"]A; '~,' AMS
°145.6 running]A; runing AMS
145.13 air]A; airs AMS
145.40 us:]A; ~. AMS
146.15 "yah-yah-yahs"]CE;
"~-~-yah'sʌ AMS
146.17 time.]A; ~." AMS
146.20 de barns]A; the barns AMS
146.23 "cold negro"]A; '~ ~'
AMS
146.31-32 Livingstons]A;
Livingstones AMS

147.4 Albany,]A; ~ ∧ AMS
147.33 idea]A; ideas AMS
147.36 woollen]A; woolen AMS
*148.20 up the]A; up on AMS
†148.24 visible,]A; ~ ∧ AMS
148.31 east.*]A; ~.ˣˣ AMS
148.32 *In]A; Note—(In AMS
149.11 terms—]A; ~ ∧ AMS
149.31 athwart]CE; atwhart AMS
149.34 moment]A; motion AMS
149.36 Jersey or]A; Jersey and AMS
149.40 least.—Editor.]A;
     ~.∧ ~ ∧) AMS
150.9 Half-dozen]A; ~ ∧ ~ AMS
150.17 who was known]A; whom
     it knew AMS
[151].2 "But bid]CE; ∧Bid AMS
[151].2 veins]A; viens AMS
[151].3 new-set]A; ~ ∧ ~ AMS
[151].4 love."]CE; ~.∧ AMS
[151].5 Edward Young, *The
     Revenge,* I.i.186-188]CE;
     Young AMS
[151].8 pursuers]A; persuers AMS
152.13 it were]A; it might AMS
152.17 singularly]A; singularily
     AMS *Also emended at* 153.11
     and 176.38.
152.31 their]A; thier AMS
152.40 embellishments]A;
     emblishments AMS
153.22 street.*]A; ~.ˣˣ AMS
153.33 *The]A; (Note—The AMS
153.41 capitals.—Editor.]A;
     ~.∧ ~ ∧) AMS
154.2 turkeys]A; turkies AMS
154.11 turkeys]A; turkies AMS
154.22 pea-green]A; ~ ∧ ~ AMS
154.22-23 woollen]A; woolen
     AMS
154.32 appearances.*]A; ~.ˣˣ
     AMS
154.36 *There]A; (Note. There
     AMS
154.39-40 since.—Editor.]A;
     ~.∧ ~ ∧) AMS
155.21 "macaronis"]A; 'bucks'
     AMS
155.22 "buck"]A; '~" AMS
155.38 on.]A; ~? AMS

156.4 dere]A; der AMS
156.7 Got pless]A; God bless AMS
156.36 "York Colony."]A; '~ ~.'
     AMS
156.40 eye-brows]A; eye's brows
     AMS
157.1 sort of]A; sort AMS
157.2 there]A; '~ AMS
157.3 "and]A; ∧ ~ AMS
157.4 deceptions,"]A; ~,' AMS
157.11 those]A; these AMS
157.13 God.*]A; ~.ˣˣ AMS
157.23 Corny?]A; ~, AMS
157.27 owners']A; owner's AMS
157.28 *I]A; (Note. I AMS
157.36-37 altar. ¶ It]A; ~. ~ AMS
157.41 "that]A; '~ AMS
†157.41 before,"]A; ~,∧ AMS
157.42 past.—Editor]A; ~.∧ ~
     AMS
158.2 Corny?]A; ~, AMS
158.7 Bishop,]A; Bishops∧ AMS
158.31 known to]A; know AMS
159.2 Worden.]A; ~? AMS
159.3-4 "assistance!"]CE; '~'!
     AMS
159.15 had]A; had yet AMS
159.22-23 accommodation]A;
     accomodation AMS
159.33 an army]A; some AMS
159.33 contractor]A; contracter
     AMS *Also emended at* 160.16,
     160.20, 160.25, 160.30,
     161.20-21, 161.34, 161.37,
     162.4, 162.20, 162.36-37,
     174.38 *and* 202.38.
160.1 shake]A; squeeze AMS
160.23 half-joes]A; ~ ∧ ~ AMS
     Also emended at 161.36 *and*
     162.21.
160.29 it!]A; ~. AMS
161.10 head]A; heads AMS
161.26 "and]A; '~ AMS
161.32 beast.]A; ~? AMS
161.40 assents]A; assent AMS
°162.8-9 acquaintance.]A; ~, AMS
162.17 scarcely]A; scarely AMS
162.35 March—]A; ~, AMS
162.36 season—]A; ~, AMS
162.39 that he]A; that that he
     AMS

163.4 operations]A; operantions AMS
163.12 rount]A; arount AMS
163.27 subject.]A; ~.' AMS
163.31 but no]A; by no AMS
164.5 quite as much]A; quite much AMS
164.12 development]A; developement AMS
164.13 than that]A; but that AMS
164.17-18 resemble]A; resemblance AMS
164.24 wonder]A; surprise AMS
164.25 surprised]A; surprise AMS
164.30-31 for what I]A; for I what AMS
[166].5 are now]A; now are AMS
[166].5 botheration."]A; ~;∧ AMS
[166].6 *The Punning Society*]A; The Punning Society AMS
[166].14-15 "coasting,"]A; '~,' AMS
[166].18 Church—]A; ~; AMS
167.1 went, like the]A; went like AMS
167.28 Littlepage!]A; ~; AMS
167.28 Capt.]A; ~ ∧ AMS
167.33 Hon.]A; ~ ∧ AMS
167.36-37 *"lady-fashion"*]A; '~-~', AMS
168.2 "destined element,"]A; '~ ~,' AMS
168.8 almost]A; scarcely AMS
°168.9 through]A; though AMS
168.19 Guert!"]A; ~!," AMS
169.2 hand-sled]A; ~ ∧ ~ AMS
169.15 misunderstood]A; misinterpreted AMS
169.18 Guert]A; Dirck AMS
169.22 awkwardness]A; awackwardness AMS
169.23 entreat]A; intreat AMS
169.33 Eyck,"]A; ~,' AMS
170.14 hand-sled]A; ~ ∧ ~ AMS
171.20 friend's]A; friends AMS
172.1 Littlepage?]A; ~. AMS
172.3 t'ough]A; dough AMS
172.4 trove]A; drove AMS
172.6 t'ings]A; things AMS
172.13 met;]A; ~, AMS

172.14 days.']A; ~.∧ AMS
172.14 t'at]A; that AMS *Also emended at* 176.26, 177.8, 335.12 *and* 335.13.
172.17 Dirck?]A; ~. AMS
173.39 phlegmatic]A; plegmatick AMS
174.3 set-to]A; ~ ∧ ~ AMS
174.12 "Dominie"]A; '~' AMS
175.16 moment]A; minute AMS
175.17 of]A; of a AMS
175.23 "old]A; '~ AMS
175.23 ducks"—]A; ~—" AMS
175.24 all"—]A; ~—" AMS
°175.25 strangers"—]A; ~"∧ AMS
°175.33 words:]A; ~. AMS
°176.3-4 game-like way]A; ~ ∧ ~-~ AMS
°176.4 market-hall]A; ~.~ AMS
176.8 Eyck!"]A; ~,' AMS
176.9 say?]A; ~. AMS
*°176.16 one of]A; one AMS
°176.18 theft!]A; ~!" AMS
176.23 expense]A; expence AMS
176.33 time,]A; ~. AMS
177.9 it!]A; ~— AMS
177.17 intelligibly]A; intelligably AMS
177.18-19 clothes-baskets]A; clothes' baskets AMS
°178.1 gate]A; ~. AMS
178.15 servant whom]A; servant AMS
178.28 manage]A; mange AMS
178.34 articles]A; dishes AMS
178.40 been very]A; been AMS
178.40 detect]A; have detected AMS
179.23 Church."']A; ~.∧" AMS
179.28 Gentlemen,]A; ~ ∧ AMS
179.34 being very]A; being AMS
180.9 night?"*]CE; ~ ?"ˣ AMS
180.10 *In]A; Note.ˣ In AMS
180.14 Littlepage.—Editor.]A; ~.∧ ~ ∧ AMS
[181].2 Masters,]A; ~ ∧ AMS
[181].5 *Much Ado About Nothing*, IV.ii.20-22]CE; Dogberry AMS
[181].17 "here]A; '~ AMS
[181].18-19 ter gentleman]A; the gentleman AMS

182.20 perceive]A; perciev AMS
182.22 affair?]A; ~, AMS
182.34 looking]A; looking back
   AMS
182.35 shoulder]A; should AMS
182.36 t'an]A; than AMS
182.36 potty]A; poty AMS
183.4 jokes]A; scrapes AMS
183.7 it has]A; it is has AMS
183.10 Alderman.*]A; ~.ˣˣ AMS
183.11 put to]A; put AMS
183.25 moost]A; must AMS
183.27 olt—]A; ~, AMS
183.33 *The]A; ˣNote. The AMS
183.41 Mayor."—Editor.]A;
   ~."ʌ ~ ʌ) AMS
184.27 Eyck?]A; ~. AMS
184.28-29 Tominie,']A; ~,ʌ AMS
184.29 'rapscallion]A; ʌ ~ AMS
184.29 frient]A; friendt AMS
184.35 shirt."*]A; ~."ˣˣ AMS
184.36 *This]A; ˣ(Note)—This
   AMS
*184.37 non-Episcopal]A;
   non-episcop AMS
184.40 edifice]A; Edifice AMS
185.3 authoritatively]A;
   authoratatvily AMS
185.21 angelic]A; angelick AMS
185.21-22 *forgiving*]A; *forgivnging*
   AMS
185.40 *twice.*—Editor.]A;
   ~.ʌ ~ ʌ) AMS
186.5 incursion]A; invasion AMS
186.9 afterwards]A; afterward,
   AMS
186.21 veins]A; viens AMS
186.26 manner]A; feelings AMS
186.27 services]A; service AMS
186.31 table?]A; ~. AMS
186.37 who]A; whom AMS
187.4 around]A; round AMS
187.12 at the]A; at AMS
187.23 Madeira]A; madeira AMS
187.35 Guert;]A; ~, AMS
187.37 imagine]A; fancy AMS
188.12 deceived]A; decieved AMS
188.37 mother.]A; ~! AMS
189.14 than an]A; than AMS
190.12 'Loping Dominie,']CE;
   "~ ~," AMS

190.23 receives]A; recieves AMS
190.24 great]A; good AMS
191.17 wear]A; enter AMS
191.21 attention]A; eye AMS
191.29 and which I]A; and I
   which I AMS
191.39 sally]A; remark AMS
192.29 plainly]A; plain AMS
193.33 chooses]A; choose AMS
†193.34 nay?]A; ~ ʌ AMS
194.15 suitor?]A; ~. AMS
194.37-38 impressed upon]A;
   impressed on AMS
*[196].3 With]A; "~ AMS
[196].4 Thus]A; "~ AMS
[196].6 Away!]A; ~, AMS
[196].6 pains."]A; ~.ʌ AMS
[196].7-8 Caroline Norton, "The
   Arab to His Favorite Steed,"
   ll.1-2, 47-48]CE; The Arab to
   his Steed AMS
198.15 judgments]A; judgment
   AMS
200.15 him to]A; him AMS
200.18 up]A; out AMS
200.22 'a]A; "~ AMS
200.22-23 asunder.'"]A; ~.'" AMS
201.7 proved]A; prov'd AMS
201.14 asthmatic]A; astmhatick
   AMS
201.34 him]A; whom AMS
202.6-7 come from]A; come of
   AMS
202.13 look on]A; look upon AMS
202.16 colony?]A; ~. AMS
202.29 attend]A; see AMS
202.32 provinces]A; Provinces
   AMS
202.40 gold]A; Gold AMS
203.4 eight]A; Eight AMS
203.4 dollars]A; Dollars AMS
203.6 notes]A; Notes AMS
203.7 colony bills]A; Colony Bills
   AMS
203.9 gold]A; Gold AMS
203.10 silver]A; Silver AMS
203.11 main]A; Main AMS
204.2 neatness; for]A; ~. For AMS
204.10 glancing]A; glanced AMS
204.27 Mary Wallace]A; Mary
   AMS

205.23 do?]A; ~; AMS
†206.6 blue,]CE; ~ ∧ AMS
†206.16 quantity.*]A; ~ ∧ˣ AMS
206.22 *As]A; Note ˣ (As AMS
†206.24 round]A; roun AMS
206.25 fastened]A; attached AMS
206.36 "Sleigh,"]A; '~ ∧' AMS
206.38 "sled,"]A; '~ ∧' AMS
206.38 "sledge."]A; '~.' AMS
206.40 "sled,"]A; '~ ∧' AMS
206.41 saying]A; say AMS
206.41 "coach"]A; '~' AMS
206.41 "wagon"]A; ∧waggon∧
  AMS
206.41 "Sleigh"]A; '~' AMS
†206.41 English]A; Englis AMS
206.43 needed.—Editor.]A;
  ~.∧~∧) AMS
207.4 men in]A; men of AMS
208.1 perceiving]A; percieving
  AMS *Also emended at* 264.35,
  [310].14, 319.40, 320.1 *and*
  386.40.
208.7 Schuyler,]A; ~; AMS
208.9 all-important]A; ~ ∧ ~
  AMS
209.2 "aunt"—]A; "~ ∧— AMS
209.6 "blood"]A; '~' AMS
209.9 Littlepages]A; Littlepage's
  AMS
209.16 sleigh]A; sliegh AMS
[211].5 walls!"]A; ~!∧ AMS
[211].6 Robert Southey, "Lord
  William," ll.73-76]CE; Lord
  William AMS
[211].19 short, steep]A; ~ ∧ ~,
  AMS
†[211].20-21 notwithstanding]A;
  notwith/standing AMS
212.8 atmosphere]A; weather AMS
212.11 vehicles]A; vehicle's AMS
212.18-19 magical. ¶ "Here]A;
  ~. '~ AMS
212.35 window]A; windows AMS
213.34 this]A; that AMS
213.39 or no]A; or AMS
214.4 inquiringly]A; anxiously
  AMS
214.18 connection]A; connexion
  AMS *Also emended at* 214.20,
  217.21 *and* 224.28.

214.24 church]A; Church AMS
214.30 turned to speak]A; spoke
  AMS
214.31 propriety]A; subject of
  the propriety AMS
215.2 to town]A; to the town AMS
215.6-7 exertions]A; intentions
  AMS
215.23 northern]A; Northern
  AMS
216.11 James]A; James' AMS
216.12 say that]A; say AMS
216.14 that]A; but that AMS
216.16 foreign-dislike]A;
  forign-dislike AMS
216.20 entreat—]A; ~. AMS
216.21 church]A; Church AMS
216.25 peculiarly]A; peculiarily
  AMS
216.30 too]A; to AMS
216.39 at]A; on AMS
216.39 got]A; get AMS
°216.40 will]A; ~. AMS
217.2-3 competitor]A; competiter
  AMS
217.7-8 always be]A; be always
  AMS
217.13 dwellers]A; people AMS
217.17 short]A; little AMS
217.40 at eight]A; at seven, or
  even eight AMS
218.6 stories and]A; stories of
  AMS
*218.11 Van der Heyden]CE;
  Bogart AMS
†218.28 occur]A; occu AMS
218.34 suitor]A; suiter AMS
219.9 went,]A; ~; AMS
219.12 their journey]A; thei
  exertion AMS
219.22 mentioned]A; named AMS
220.18 'Albany,']A; "~ ∧" AMS
220.18 river."]A; ~.∧" AMS
°220.24 he had]A; he he had AMS
220.39 the consequences
  proved]A; that the accidents
  turned out to be AMS
°221.18 hamlet]A; ~. AMS
221.24 speak to us]A; speak us
  once more AMS
221.25 men?]A; ~, AMS

221.30 any]A; any one AMS
°222.13 caused by]A; caused by of AMS
222.23 'Albany']A; "~" AMS
222.23 'river.']A; '~." AMS
222.23 this]A; this last AMS
°222.27 utter,]A; ~. AMS
222.33 spook]A; sprite AMS
223.4 exhilaration]A; exhiliaration AMS
223.5-6 that which]A; that AMS
223.7 rifles would produce, was]A; rifles, was AMS
223.14 wrong,"]A; ~,' AMS
223.27 not be]A; not to be AMS
224.6 involuntary]A; involuntarily AMS
224.21 over]A; across AMS
[226].6 Robert Southey, "Lord William," ll.69-72]CE; Lord William AMS
[226].8 a place]A; places AMS
[226].15 flood—when]A; ~, ~ AMS
[226].18-19 anywhere]A; any where AMS *Also emended at* 235.4 *and* 237.5.
[226].24 banks]A; Banks AMS
227.11 west—]A; ~, AMS
227.12 colony—]A; ~, AMS
227.30 recall]A; recal AMS
227.41 —Editor.]A; ∧ ~ ∧) AMS
228.15 efforts—]A; ~, AMS
228.16 race-course—]A; ~-~, AMS
228.37-38 galloped]A; galopped AMS
229.5 "Moses"]A; '~' AMS
°229.8 beyond]A; ~, AMS
229.9 ridge,]A; ~ ∧ AMS
229.30 any]A; the least AMS
230.2 us,—]A; ~,∧ AMS
230.5 impassable]A; impassible AMS
230.39 another]A; that AMS
231.4 were no grounds]A; was no ground AMS
231.5 anxiously]A; solemnly AMS
°231.11 desperate]A; ~. AMS
231.13 be,]A; ~ ∧ AMS
°231.21 island, at]A; ~., ~ AMS

232.6-7 remonstrances]A; remonstrance AMS
232.24 affright—]A; ~, AMS
232.40 than]A; than thus AMS
233.3 stronger—]A; ~. AMS
233.29 islands]A; ~, AMS
233.29 Hudson]A; ~, AMS
234.11-12 feasible]A; feasable AMS
234.13 and,]A; ~ ∧ AMS
234.23 ever saw]A; have ever seen AMS
235.1 straitening]A; straitning AMS
235.24 first,]A; ~ ∧ AMS
235.32 grandly,]A; ~ ∧ AMS
236.4 doubtless]A; doubtess AMS
236.5 minutes that]A; minutes AMS
236.14 entreated]A; intreated AMS
236.23 knees: the]A; ~. The AMS
°236.27 desolation,]A; ~. AMS
°236.27 Anneke]A; ~. AMS
°236.31 instant,]A; ~. AMS
236.37 you!]A; ~— AMS
236.37-38 torpor]A; torpour, AMS
237.2 *you*]A; you AMS
237.3 father?—]A; ~;∧ AMS
237.4 No, no, no!]A; ~——~—~, AMS
237.19 dependence]A; dependance AMS
237.20 effect]A; affect AMS
237.24 believe]A; beleive AMS
237.27 learning]A; knowing AMS
†237.30 walked,]A; ~ ∧ AMS
238.8 bank—]A; ~, AMS
†238.15 of our]A; of ou AMS
°238.17 winds,]A; ~. AMS
238.27 head]A; forehead AMS
238.29 hoofs]A; hoof AMS
°238.30 exclaimed]A; ~, AMS
238.35 it at]A; it AMS
238.36 horses,]A; ~ ∧ AMS
239.3 was,]A; ~ ∧ AMS
[240].15 Eyck's]A; Eick's AMS
†[240].16 minute]A; minut AMS
[240].22-23 heart-piercing]A; heart-pearcing AMS
[240].26 excite]A; arouse AMS
[240].26 now]A; still AMS

°241.28 less]A; ~. AMS
241.38 maintaining]A;
　maintainting AMS
242.14 close to]A; near AMS
243.11 under the weight]A; in
　consequence AMS
243.16 slightest]A; slighest AMS
243.34 shooting]A; drifting AMS
244.28 the banks]A; two banks
　AMS
244.29 houses—]A; ~, AMS
244.32 before,]A; ~; AMS
244.39 late;]A; ~, AMS
°244.39 for; it]A; ~. It AMS
244.40 shelter]A; house AMS
245.21 hither]A; in this AMS
245.39 assistance—]A; ~, AMS
246.4 dwelling—]A; ~ ∧ AMS
246.17 believe that]A; believe
　AMS
246.30 Heaven!]A; ~ ∧ AMS
246.31 offer.]A; ~— AMS
247.1 what]A; all AMS
247.4 wagon]A; waggon AMS
247.5 women—]A; ~, AMS
247.6 course—]A; ~, AMS
247.24 current,]A; ~; AMS
248.10 you; but]A; ~. But AMS
248.12 ill-omened]A; ~ ∧ ~ AMS
248.12-13 messenger." ¶
　Guert]A; ~." ~ AMS
248.14 house—in]A; ~, ~ AMS
*° 249.16 came]A; were came AMS
249.17 swum]A; swam AMS
249.40 carrying]A; carrying
　down AMS
250.2 surface—]A; ~, AMS
250.2 bodies—]A; ~, AMS
†250.4 sleigh,]A; ~ ∧ AMS
250.10 of my]A; of our AMS
250.27 army!]A; ~. AMS
250.28 As soon as]A; The instant
　AMS
°250.31 instant]A; instant that
　AMS
250.35 Sir]A; ~. AMS
251.24 hands!]A; ~. AMS
†251.31 manner;]A; ~ ∧ AMS
°251.38 indecorum]A;
　indecorums AMS
252.5 innocently]A; miss AMS

252.13 for a]A; for AMS
253.13 settlement]A; settlements
　AMS
[254].6 *Macbeth,* I.iii.51-54]CE;
　Banquo AMS
[254].18 Albany,]A; ~ ∧ AMS
[254].23 viz.]A; ~ ∧ AMS
[254].29 shades]A; points AMS
[254].31-32 characteristic]A;
　characteristick AMS
255.11 viz.]A; ~ ∧ AMS
255.14 him at]A; him over at AMS
*255.16 beer, cider]A; tobacco,
　cider AMS
255.17 lemons, sugar]A; lemons,
　beer, sugar AMS
†255.32 omitted]A; omitte AMS
255.33 everybody's]A; every
　bodys AMS
256.3 Satanstoe—]A; ~, AMS
256.4 language—]A; ~, AMS
256.5 *"grands couchers"*]A; '~ ~'
　AMS
256.5 *"petits couchers"*]A; '~ ~'
　AMS
256.8 "grands couchers"]A;
　'~ ~' AMS
256.15 *"grands couchers"*]A;
　'~ ~' AMS
256.15 rarely—]A; ~, AMS
256.19 *"grand coucher"*]A; '~ ~'
　AMS
256.19 Albany—]A; ~; AMS
256.20 forbade—]A; ~; AMS
256.29 "great]A; '~ AMS
256.29 bed"]A; ~' AMS
256.29 "little]A; '~ AMS
256.29 bed"]A; ~' AMS
256.31 "lever]A; '~ AMS
256.32 "to]A; '~ AMS
256.32 rise"]A; ~' AMS
256.32 get up]A; ~-~ AMS
256.35 classes,]A; ~ ∧ AMS
256.35-36 *petit lever*]A; petit lever
　AMS
256.36 getting-up]A; ~ ∧ ~ AMS
256.37 X.]A; Xth AMS
256.39 marriage—]A; ~, AMS
256.40 personage—]A; ~, AMS
256.40 "petit lever"]A; '~ ~'
　AMS

256.41 two.—Editor.]A; ~ . ∧ ~ ∧
AMS
257.4 fancied that]A; fancied AMS
257.16 foolishly]A; had AMS
257.30 "no"]A; '~' AMS
257.35 "no"]A; '~' AMS
258.10 fortune-teller]A; ~ ∧ ~
AMS
258.28 accompany]A; go with AMS
258.40 —Editor.]A; ∧ ~ ∧) AMS
259.37 errand]A; business AMS
260.13 ultra-tidy]A; ultra-neat
AMS
260.22-23 fortune-teller's]A;
~ ∧ ~ AMS
260.30 want]A; wan't AMS
261.4 manner,]A; ~ ," AMS
*261.12 Mother."]A; ~ ∧" # ."
AMS
261.14 Ah! there's]A; ah. There's
AMS
261.17 this]A; that AMS
261.19 is—and]A; ~ ; ~ AMS
262.26 after-life]A; ~ ∧ ~ AMS
*262.33 influence on]A;
influence n AMS
263.30 many]A; some AMS
263.37 celebrated]A; regular AMS
263.38 regularly]A; regularily
AMS
264.7 Mother]A; mother AMS
Also emended at 265.7, 265.22,
266.6, 266.12, 266.39 *and*
267.17.
264.25 Come,]A; ~ ∧ AMS
°264.28 closely?]A; ~ . AMS
264.29 loping]A; Loping AMS
264.29 loping]A; Loping AMS
264.31 him!]A; ~ . AMS
*264.34 busily engaged]A; busy
engaged AMS
264.38 Mademoiselle]A;
Madamoisell AMS
264.40 taking the]A; taking AMS
264.40 times.—]A; ~ . ∧ AMS
265.1-2 the table]A; her table AMS
°265.10 it.]A; ~ , AMS
†265.17 geese,]A; ~ ∧ AMS
265.17 game-cocks,]A; ~ ∧ ~ ∧
AMS
265.17-18 one who]A; ~ , ~ AMS

265.40 1845.—Editor.]A;
~ . ∧ ~ ∧) AMS
266.10 good; three]A; ~ . Three
AMS
266.17 mind?]A; ~ ; AMS
266.17 For]A; for AMS
266.18 sake,]A; ~ ∧ AMS
266.24 seems]A; does seem AMS
266.36 aspen-leaf]A; pople leaf
AMS
266.38 lost]A; loss'd AMS
267.5 their]A; thier AMS
†267.6 America.]A; ~ ∧ AMS
267.7 I have]A; have I AMS
267.12 head!]A; ~ . AMS
267.12 *you*]A; you AMS
267.13 *you*]A; you AMS
267.15 truly. Know]A;
truly—know AMS
267.19 Good! go]A; ~ ; ~ AMS
267.19 him—absence]A; him.
Absence AMS
267.21 fired,]A; ~ ∧ AMS
267.37 life-time]A; ~ ∧ ~ AMS
267.38 Kt.]A; ~ ∧ AMS
267.39 of]A; of the AMS
267.40 .—Editor.]A; ∧ ∧ ~ ∧ AMS
[269].9 Shelley, "Mutability,"
ll.8-14]CE; Shelley AMS
[269].18 sort—]A; ~ , AMS
[269].19 Albany—]A; ~ , AMS
[269].25 Ten]A; ten AMS
°[269].29 character;]A; ~ . AMS
[269].31 him—]A; ~ , AMS
270.4 Moses!]A; ~ . AMS
270.31-32 intercourse.]A; ~ ."
AMS
†°271.7 pretence.]A; ~ ∧" AMS
*271.12 Major Bulstrode]A;
Herman Mordaunt, AMS
271.17 Bulstrode]A; Mordaunt
AMS
271.32 fidgeting]A; fidgetting
AMS
272.26 Messrs.]A; ~ ∧ AMS
272.26 and Van]A; & Van AMS
272.36 Mordaunt]CE; Mordaunts
AMS; Mordaunt's A
273.35 got]A; go AMS
274.21 head-quarters]A; ~ ∧ ~
AMS

274.25 north,]A; ∼ ∧ AMS
274.29 Bulstrode]A; ∼, AMS
274.29 was to]A; was AMS
274.40 young]A; two AMS
275.6 Littlepage,]A; ∼! AMS
275.16-17 may appear]A; now
  appears AMS
°275.20 work;]A; ∼, AMS
275.34 history?]A; ∼. AMS
276.4 is as]A; is AMS
276.7 conceal]A; con conceal AMS
276.23 Knights-Barrow*nights*]A;
  ∼ ∧ ∼ AMS
276.23 believed]A; believe AMS
277.17 Mooseridge,]A; ∼ ∧ AMS
277.25 twenty-fold]A; ∼ ∧ ∼ AMS
277.32-33 "told . . . church"]A;
  '∼ . . . ∼' AMS
277.39 "well acquainted,"]A; '∼
  ∼ ∧' AMS
278.13 strong,]A; ∼ ∧ AMS
278.13 spacious,]A; ∼ ∧ AMS
278.33 at any]A; ∼, ∼ AMS
278.33 thousands of]A; half a
  dozen AMS
278.37 two]A; ∼, AMS
279.8 but]A; by AMS
279.14 me—you]A; ∼; ∼ AMS
279.14 *dear*]A; *dear* to me AMS
280.15 give you]A; give AMS
*°281.29 might]A; that might
  AMS
281.33 well as]A; well AMS
[283].2 "Come]A; '∼ AMS
[283].5 nigger.]A; *nigger*— AMS
[283].6 Burns, "The Ordination,"
  IV.28-31]CE; Burns AMS
[283].12 thirty or]A; thirty and
  AMS
284.14-15 were particularly]A;
  happened to be AMS
284.24 indeed,]A; ∼ ∧ AMS
285.10 males,]A; ∼ ∧ AMS
285.17-18 so; a precaution that is
  sometimes useful in the
  woods]A; so. I owe my life to
  this circumstance AMS
285.23 removed,]A; ∼ ∧ AMS
285.32 natural]A; native AMS
†286.2 admirably]A; admiraly
  AMS

°286.19 gown,]A; ∼. AMS
286.40 quarter]A; part AMS
†287.39 placed in]A; placed in in
  AMS
288.25 expedition]A; exhibition
  AMS
289.32 on]A; in AMS
290.9 route]A; rout AMS
290.10 head-waters]A; ∼ ∧ ∼
  AMS
290.31 fall in with]A; overtake
  AMS
290.36 we were]A; we AMS
290.39 of the]A; of AMS
291.16 Jack!]A; ∼. AMS
*291.35 which]A; '∼ AMS
292.25 without]A; with out AMS
292.27 Whist]A; whist AMS *Also
  capitalized at* 292.32, 292.35
  and 293.4.
292.27-28 Picquet]A; of picquett
  AMS
293.3-4 Picquet]A; picquet AMS
294.15-16 accommodation]A;
  accomodation AMS
°294.27 choice]A; ∼, AMS
294.32 a property]A; an estate
  AMS
294.34 tracts]A; estates AMS
294.42 abandoned.—]A; ∼. ∧
  AMS
295.14 quit-rents]A; ∼ ∧ ∼ AMS
295.39 get—]A; ∼, AMS
296.5 King]A; king AMS
296.6-7 Yankee]A; yankee AMS
296.22 in case]A; in the case AMS
296.23 parallelogram]A;
  parelelogram AMS
296.24 strong picket]A; stone
  wall AMS
296.28 picketed]A; picketted AMS
296.32 straitened]A; straitined
  AMS
[297].6 Freneau, "The Indian
  Burying-Ground,"
  ll.37-40]CE; Freneau AMS
°[297].20 Guert,]A; ∼ ∧ AMS
[297].20 Traverse]A; Taverse AMS
†[297].22 well-armed]A; ∼ ∧ ∼
  AMS
[297].25 called]A; ∼, AMS

°[297].33 hard;]A; ~. AMS
[297].35 borne]A; born AMS
298.10 but without]A; without
    AMS
298.12 the journey]A; the rest of
    his journey, AMS
298.34 the year]A; a year AMS
298.35 had]A; all AMS
298.36 fiftieth]A; fiftyeth AMS
298.39 Nations.—]A; ~.ʌ) AMS
299.5 led]A; took AMS
299.11 exists,]A; ~ ʌ AMS
299.36 brought me]A; brought
    AMS
300.1 they've]A; thev'e AMS
300.12 Jumper,]A; ~ ʌ AMS
300.13 described?]A; ~. AMS
300.17 tree?"]A; ~.ʌ AMS
*†301.22 tones]CE; tone AMS
°301.24 Traverse,]A; ~. AMS
301.31 stands?]A; ~. AMS
301.37 yonder]CE; younder AMS
302.17 keen-scented]A; ~ ʌ ~
    AMS
302.24 with]A; with a AMS
303.18 inner]A; outer AMS
303.20 outward]A; inward AMS
303.20 from]A; toward AMS
†303.22 chain-bearers]A; ~ ʌ ~
    AMS
303.28 moose]A; Moose AMS
304.1 everybody]A; every body
    AMS
304.31 surprise,]A; ~ ʌ AMS
304.33 cross-pieces]A; ~ ʌ ~ AMS
305.8 great lots]A; Great Lots
    AMS
305.17 lot]A; Lot AMS
305.19 of the trees]A; of trees
    AMS
306.29 athwart]A; atwart AMS
306.32 beneficence]A;
    benificence AMS
306.40 Mooseridge']A; ~" AMS
307.8 matters]A; things AMS
307.27 plentiful]A; plenty AMS
307.33 beneficent]A; Beneficent
    AMS
307.33-34 gracious]A; Gracious
    AMS
308.24 T'e]A; The AMS

308.26 chaps]A; men AMS
309.3 A Huron]A; The Hurons
    AMS
*309.12 us,]CE; ~,, AMS
309.12 Trackless?]A; ~, AMS
309.25 'em]A; them AMS
309.18-19 Ticonderoga]A;
    Tyconderoga AMS *Also
    emended at* 421.17-18 *and*
    [426].12.
[310].2 "Fear not,]A; ʌ ~ ~ ʌ
    AMS
[310].3 Dunsinane.]A; ~ ʌ AMS
*[310].4 *Macbeth,* V.v.43-44]CE;
    Macbeth AMS
[310].11 returning,]A; ~ ʌ AMS
[310].19 health,]A; ~ ʌ AMS
[310].34-35 sealed. ¶ Herman]A;
    ~. ~ AMS
311.21 'made by men']A; by the
    landlord AMS
°311.25 Mooseridge]A; ~. AMS
311.37 land-holder]A; ~ ʌ ~ AMS
311.39 *It]A; ˣNote (It AMS
311.40 years.—Editor.]A;
    ~.ʌ)~ ʌ AMS
°312.28 proceed,]A; ~. AMS
313.1 ready—]A; ~, AMS
313.26 ready, though]A; ~ ʌ ~
    AMS
313.31 bestirred himself]A;
    shouldered his rifle AMS
313.37-38 patronymic]A;
    patronymick AMS
314.9 Ravensnest']A; ~" AMS
°314.19 Huron—]A; ~,— AMS
°314.23 do]A; ~. AMS
†316.22 o'clock,]A; ~ ʌ AMS
°316.30 longer,—blind]A; longer.
    "Blind AMS
316.34 hunting-shirt]A; ~ ʌ ~
    AMS *Also hyphenated at* [324].8
    and 351.10.
317.3 true]A; right AMS
317.5 triumph—]A; ~, AMS
†317.8 us,]A; ~ ʌ AMS
317.21 tell,]A; ~. AMS
317.32 that the]A; that the the
    AMS
317.33 south-east]A; South East
    AMS

317.34 north-west]A; North West
AMS
318.4 thunderbolt]A; thunder
bolt AMS
318.9 north-west]A; North West
AMS
318.23 his]A; its AMS
318.34 spouting]A; spirting AMS
318.38 believe that]A; believe
AMS
319.15 diversified]A; diversed
AMS
319.26 relieve]A; releive AMS
319.27 Everywhere]A; Every
where AMS
320.32-33 hill-sides]A; ~ ʌ ~ AMS
320.35 moment]A; minute AMS
320.37 sides—]A; ~ ʌ AMS
321.17 again]A; ever AMS
322.3 "a truly]A; ʌ ~ ~ AMS
322.32 as to]A; than to AMS
323.12 any one]A; any AMS
323.18 forest uniform]CE; Forest
Uniform AMS
[324].5 ill-worn]A; ~ ʌ ~ AMS
[324].6 Byron, *Sardanapalus*,
IV.i.210-214]CE;
Sardanapalus AMS
[324].18 field."]A; ~,' AMS
[324].18 "but]A; '~ AMS
[324].28 hospitality]A; hispitality
AMS
°325.13 around]A; ~. AMS
325.16 grandfather]A;
grand-father AMS
325.28 excellent]A; admirable
AMS
325.37 risks]A; risk AMS
326.20 sustaining]A; meeting
with AMS
°326.21 four,]A; ~,, AMS
°327.38 it assaulted]A; assaulted
AMS
328.5 kind-hearted]A; ~ ʌ ~
AMS
°328.22 retreat,]A; ~., AMS
°328.25 closely,]A; ~,, AMS
328.27 We]A; "~ AMS
328.29 partisan]A; partizan AMS
328.34 Rogers's]A; Roger's AMS
328.36 inasmuch as]A; ~, ~ AMS

329.5 else]A; other AMS
329.20 *éclat*]A; éclat AMS
329.25-26 extensive and
important]A; important and
extensive AMS
329.34 me,]A; ~ ʌ AMS
°329.36 has.]A; ~." AMS
330.14 outworks]A; out-works
AMS
330.15 outworks]A; out works
AMS
331.9 8th of]A; 8th AMS
331.11 scientific]A; scientifick AMS
331.29 breast-work]CE; ~ ʌ ~
AMS
331.36 Holmes's]A; Holme's AMS
331.36 42d]A; 42th AMS
331.40 42d.—Editor.]A; 42d. AMS
332.13 avenged]A; revenged AMS
332.20 breast-work]CE; ~ ʌ ~
AMS
332.23 Graham]A; ~. AMS
333.14 sound]A; whole AMS
333.17 close]A; last AMS
333.23 Canadian]A; Canada AMS
333.25 rifles,]A; ~ ʌ AMS
333.29 to me]A; me to me AMS
†333.34 own!]A; ~ ʌ AMS
333.40 most]A; many AMS
*†334.7 attempting]A; attempt-
AMS
334.17 thirty or forty]A; 30 or 40
AMS
334.39 scarcely]A; scare AMS
335.1 see]A; find AMS
335.12 t'ree]A; three AMS
335.12 haf]A; have AMS
335.12 receivet]A; recieved AMS
335.14 holt]A; hold AMS
335.14 anyt'ing]A; any thing AMS
335.19 be; but]A; be. But AMS
335.22-23 good-natured]A; ~ ʌ ~
AMS
335.35 which we]A; which AMS
336.26 said; "red-man]A; said.
"Red man AMS
336.26 gettin']A; getting AMS
[339].6 Felicia Hemans,
"England and Spain,"
ll.453-456.]CE; Mrs Hemans
AMS

[339].23 the 'Holy Lake,']A; The Holy Lake AMS
340.9 parallel]A; paralell AMS
340.35 we were]A; we AMS
340.40 it."]A; ~.' AMS
341.1 army]A; armed AMS
341.12 wishes]A; wish AMS
341.18 spies."]A; ~.' AMS
341.20 were]A; were merely AMS
341.34 paddled]A; paddle AMS
342.1 equivocally]A; cynically AMS
342.5 check-*mate*]A; chek-*mate* AMS
342.7 now."]A; now." ¶ We could not help laughing. AMS
°342.28 friend]A; friends AMS
343.10 look-out]A; ~ ʌ ~ AMS
343.11 awakened]A; awoke AMS
°345.4 heard it]A; ~. ~ AMS
*°345.19 me]A; me I AMS
345.21 not]A; never AMS
345.33 Susquesus,]A; ~; AMS
°346.11 about]A; ~, AMS
346.21 by the]A; by AMS
†346.23-24 significant]A; signifcant AMS
346.24 which he]A; which AMS
347.8 picketed]A; picketted AMS
347.18 spirit.]A; ~." AMS
347.25 'there]A; "~ AMS
347.26 water.'"]A; ~." AMS
347.29 into]A; in AMS
347.40 King?]CE; King. AMS
348.3 warrior]A; warriors AMS
348.3-4 petticoat]A; petticoats AMS
348.9 warrior]A; warriors AMS
348.10 lightning]A; lightening AMS
348.38 title]A; tittle AMS
349.11 his hand]A; a hand AMS
349.21-22 surveyors,]A; ~? AMS
349.36 won't]A; wont AMS
350.8 advice]A; advise AMS
350.10 Indian counsels]A; Injin Councils AMS
350.16 tongue.]A; ~." AMS
350.40 mien!]A; ~. AMS
351.2 he]A; it AMS
351.2 Dirck]A; Dirck's AMS
351.35 that remarkable]A; the AMS

351.35 woman]A; woman, himself AMS
352.1 Guert?]A; ~; AMS
352.8 foretell]A; foretel AMS
352.15 St.]A; ~ ʌ AMS
353.7-8 to remaining]A; than to remain AMS
°353.13 supplies]A; ~, AMS
353.24 self-assigned]A; ~ ʌ ~ AMS
[354].2 "Thou]A; '~ AMS
[354].4 *2 Henry IV*, I.i.68-69]CE; Shakspeare AMS
355.27 foot-print]A; impression AMS
355.35 lightning]A; lightening AMS
355.40 to]A; out AMS
°356.13 was a]A; was AMS
356.16 moment?]A; ~. AMS
356.27 me at]A; me on AMS
356.28 his own]A; his AMS
†357.7 care?]A; ~— AMS
357.21 proceeded in precisely]A; preceded us, precisely in AMS
357.34 t'ink]A; think AMS
357.34 nuttin']A; nothin' AMS
358.19 notice]A; ~. AMS
358.23 Dirck!]A; ~, AMS
358.36 empty,]A; ~ ʌ AMS
359.2 expedients—]A; ~; AMS
359.36 bade]A; bad AMS
360.7 in; and]A; in. And AMS
360.8 was!]A; ~. AMS
360.26 ears]A; ear AMS
360.27 t'ink]A; think AMS
360.28 minute."]A; ~.' AMS
360.31 his]A; his own AMS
361.18 then]A; then we AMS
362.4 forest—]A; ~, AMS
362.5 ears—]A; ~, AMS
362.7 leaf—]A; ~, AMS
362.21 discernible]A; discernable AMS
362.32 "hugh]A; 'Hugh AMS
362.35 indeed,]A; ~ ʌ AMS
363.1 near them]A; near it AMS
363.1 as the]A; as these AMS
363.7 "help"]A; '~,' AMS
363.36 facts]A; fact AMS
363.37 remain]A; remains AMS

363.40 liberate the]A; liberate this AMS

364.4 Hurons,"]A; ~,' AMS

364.5 "and]A; '~ AMS

364.5 done?]A; ~.' AMS

364.11 saplings,]A; ~ ∧ AMS

364.15 they were]A; it was AMS

364.16 potato]A; potatoe AMS

364.37 broad daylight]A; broad-day light AMS

366.40 but]A; ~; AMS

367.1 friends,]A; ~ ∧ AMS

367.10 at work]A; to be found AMS

*[368].3 The]A; "~ AMS

[368].3 life]A; ~" AMS

[368].4 That]A; "~ AMS

[368].4 imprisonment]A; ~" AMS

[368].5 Can]A; "~ AMS

[368].5 paradise,]A; ~ ∧" AMS

[368].6 To]A; "~ AMS

[368].7 *Measure for Measure*, III.i.127-131]CE; Measure for Measure AMS

[368].24 foot]A; root AMS

°369.23 stranger,]A; ~ ∧ AMS

°369.37 undisturbed;]A; ~, AMS

370.25 he'rt]A; heart AMS

370.26 girtet]A; girted AMS

370.36 knowing]A; feelin' AMS

370.36 peen]A; been AMS

371.3 dit]A; did AMS

371.6 his]A; His AMS

371.6 haf]A; have AMS

371.9 preparet]A; prepared AMS

371.12 discernible]A; discernable AMS

†371.22 plough-share]A; share AMS

371.29 age]A; greater age AMS

372.35 little?]A; ~. AMS

373.12 instant]A; time AMS

373.19 lindens,]A; ~ ∧ AMS

374.8 "we]A; '~ AMS

374.18 listen.]A; ~." AMS

374.39 gibbeted]A; gibbetted AMS

°375.2 with them as a captive]A; with his captors AMS

°375.3 possible, for, as]A; possible. As AMS

°375.3 'back very sore.']A; back was very sore." AMS

°375.27 us,]A; ~. AMS

377.4 opinion,]A; ~,, AMS

377.19 personally knew Muss]A; knew Muss, personally AMS

377.26 way. Each]A; way. ¶ Each AMS

377.31 could not]A; could AMS

378.12 picking up]A; picking AMS

378.16 speak, but]A; speak; but I AMS

378.18 slow in]A; slow at AMS

378.19 descried]A; seen AMS

378.21 but]A; he AMS

378.25 gait]A; movement AMS

378.38 Pale-face]A; Pale faces AMS

379.9 *me*]A; me AMS

379.30 that hand]A; the last AMS

380.6 follows:]A; ~ ∧ AMS

380.20 summonses]A; summons AMS

380.33 Dirck,—]A; ~,∧ AMS

381.7 dear]A; Dear AMS

[382].5 *Twelfth Night*, II.iv.107-109]CE; Viola AMS

[382].26 word or two]A; word AMS

°383.17 forms of men]A; form of manhood AMS

383.31 hero]A; heroe AMS

383.36 alone]A; only AMS

383.38 commands]A; orders AMS

384.29 It]A; (~ AMS

384.29 pond,' a]A; ~." A AMS

384.30 of an]A; an an AMS

384.31 great]A; populous AMS

384.41 town.—Editor.]A; ~.∧ ~.) AMS

†385.5 eagle-like]A; eagle AMS

°385.8 on]A; ~. AMS

385.31 garrison.']A; ~." AMS

†385.36 surprise]A; meet AMS

†387.24-25 half-way]A; ~ ∧ ~ AMS

387.28 there?']A; ~." AMS

387.29 you?]A; ~! AMS

387.29 Got]A; God AMS

387.35 seizing]A; siezing AMS

387.36 other,]A; ~ ∧ AMS

388.4 everything]A; all AMS

°388.17 smiles,]A; ~. AMS

388.39 your hunters]A; the hunters AMS

389.33 days]A; day AMS
390.11-12 same. Though]A; ~;
though AMS
391.15 out of]A; in AMS
391.23 itself!]A; ~. AMS
392.33 utter]A; say AMS
†392.37 occasion,]A; ~ ∧ AMS
393.9 every-day]A; ~ ∧ ~ AMS
393.14 perceived]A; found
AMS
393.22 prudery I]A; prudery I I
AMS
394.23 her]A; me AMS
394.24 Have]A; Feel AMS
394.34 we]A; they AMS
395.20 than when]A; than AMS
°395.20 notwithstanding,]A;
notwithstand AMS
395.21 regret,]A; ~ ∧ AMS
395.25 procedure]A; proceedure
AMS
395.30 deat']A; death AMS
395.36 worts]A; words AMS
396.7 had to]A; had AMS
396.10 was,]A; ~ ∧ AMS
396.10 Anne]A; Annie AMS
[397].9 waves."]CE; wave. AMS
[397].10 Byron, *Don Juan*,
XV.xcix.785-792]CE; Byron
AMS
[397].33 neither female]A; not a
female, AMS
[397].33-34 nor child]A; or child,
AMS
398.20 will]A; shall AMS
399.19 picketing]A; picketting
AMS
399.24 pale-faces]A; Pale-faces
AMS
399.28 time]A; ~, AMS
399.30 by driving]A; in driving
AMS
399.36 our]A; the AMS
400.4 lodgment]A; lodgement
AMS
400.12 place]A; spot AMS
400.23 seemed]A; seemed to be
AMS
400.30 He cautiously]A; He AMS
400.33 distance]A; distance
around them AMS

°401.16-17 war-whoop]A;
war-hoop AMS
†402.25 rifle.]A; ~.. AMS
°402.29 were it]A; were AMS
402.34 even at]A; at AMS
402.34 moment]A; moment, even
AMS
403.4 as were]A; as AMS
403.6 entered; she]A; entered,
for she AMS
403.21 run]A; ran AMS
403.25 her feelings]A; herself
AMS
403.31 "without]CE; ∧ ~ AMS
404.16 this?]A; ~, AMS
404.18 way; then]A; way, and
AMS
404.22 candor!]A; ~. AMS
404.27 defects,']A; ~, ∧ AMS
404.28 and we]A; "~ ~ AMS
405.22 and on its]A; and its AMS
°405.24 south,]A; ~. AMS
405.27 building]A; buildings AMS
406.18 northwest]A; north west
AMS
407.2 the means]A; his means AMS
407.3-4 any other]A; any AMS
*407.9 adventurers]CE;
adventures AMS; adventurer A
407.10-11 somewhat]A; at least
somewhat AMS
407.24 endeavouring]A;
endevoring AMS
407.26 half-naked]A; naked AMS
407.28 hunting-knife]A; ~ ∧ ~
AMS
407.29 stayed]A; staid AMS
407.33 served]A; answered AMS
407.40 "There!]A; '~. AMS
408.27 at a single]A; in a single
AMS
409.27 after-life]A; ~ ∧ ~ AMS
409.33 had come]A; had now
come AMS
409.35 darkness]A; ~, AMS
409.38 done]A; mute AMS
410.22 Everything]A; But every
thing AMS
*[411].2 eye,]A; ~," AMS
[411].8 served]A; served her
AMS

[411].10 Byron, *Don Juan,*
    IV.lxiii.497-504]CE; Byron
    AMS
[411].27 bear]A; bare AMS
412.7 pent-up]A; ~ ∧ ~ AMS
412.19 beseeching]A; beseecting
    AMS
412.22 mercy]A; Mercy AMS
413.9 everything]A; all AMS
413.23 send?]A; ~. AMS
413.29 would]A; might AMS
413.34 slave—]A; ~, AMS
413.35 me—]A; ~, AMS
†413.35 volunteered]A;
    volunteer AMS
413.39 you must]A; must AMS
†414.8 Indian,]A; ~ ∧ AMS
414.9 calico]A; calicoe AMS
414.26 Several]A; Many AMS
415.6 unhurt?]A; ~. AMS
415.7 scalp]A; scalps AMS
415.7 prisoner—jump]A; ~.
    Jump AMS
415.15 Susquesus?]A; ~. AMS
415.26 bound,]A; ~ ∧ AMS
416.24 lion's den]A; Lion's Den
    AMS
*†416.28 grieved]A; grie AMS
417.32 any two]A; any hero,
    AMS
417.34 willingly]A; willing AMS
417.39 their]A; thier AMS
418.5 'arnest]A; earnest AMS
418.37 then they]A; then AMS
419.15-16 volleys]A; vollies AMS
°419.31 Jaap,]A; ~ ∧ AMS
419.39 bull-dogs]A; ~ ∧ ~ AMS
420.1 fee-simple]A; ~ ∧ ~ AMS
420.23 arms,]A; ~ ∧ AMS
420.26 death-wound]A; ~ ∧ ~
    AMS
420.30 intended]A; intend AMS
420.37 disturbed]A; disturb AMS
°421.25 then]A; ~, AMS
421.26 eyes]A; eye AMS
421.37 apprised]A; apprized AMS
422.11 death-wound]A; ~ ∧ ~
    AMS
422.38 allusion]A; allusions AMS
†423.7 Blessed]A; Blesse AMS
423.14 had its]A; had it is AMS

423.25-26 opposed]A; opposite
    AMS
423.33 habits]A; habit AMS
423.38 assuaged]A; assauged AMS
424.6 near.]A; ~: AMS
424.14 prayers,]A; prayer's AMS
425.7 Corny,"]A; ~,' AMS
425.18 but it]A; and it AMS
[426].6-7 Thomas Tomkis,
    Albumazar, II.vi.10-14]CE;
    Albamazar AMS
427.2 Christianity]A; christianity
    AMS
427.8 blessed]A; Blessed AMS
427.11 people.'"]A; ~.' AMS
427.14 enough,"]A; ~,' AMS
428.4 after-life]A; ~ ∧ ~ AMS
428.6 ill-educated]A; ~ ∧ ~ AMS
428.13 all-important]A; ~ ∧ ~
    AMS
428.40 mine?"]A; ~?' AMS
429.23 closet]A; ~, AMS
429.38 life,]A; ~ ∧ AMS
430.8-9 unextinguishable]A;
    unestinguisable AMS
430.18 wildness]A; rowdyism AMS
430.25 what had]A; all that AMS
431.5 recall]A; recal AMS
*431.34 Light]A; [lacking] AMS
432.4 Isn't]A; Is'n't AMS
432.4 Bulstrom]A; Bultrone AMS
432.10 down]A; [ms torn] own
    AMS
432.19 from]A; [ms torn] m AMS
432.21 means]A; [ms torn] eans
    AMS
432.37 Our]A; My AMS
432.38 her heart]A; my heart AMS
434.3 father,]A; ~ ∧ AMS
434.9 am]A; am now AMS
435.15 ye"]A; ~' AMS
435.17 told—]A; ~, AMS
435.18 myself—]A; ~ ∧ AMS
435.20 "Hell-Gate"]A; '~ ∧ ~'
    AMS
435.20 "Hurl-Gate"]A; 'Hurll ∧ ~'
    AMS
435.20 "Whirl-Gate"]A; '~ ∧ ~'
    AMS
435.22 "Satanstoe"]A; '~' AMS
435.22 "Dibbleton"]A; '~' AMS

†435.35 that]A; tha AMS
436.5 a substitute]A; an
   alternative AMS
†436.12 spirited]A; spirite AMS
†436.14 delicacy]A; delicac AMS
436.15 welcome]A; wellcome
   AMS
436.22 well-known]A; ~ ∧ ~ AMS
436.27 housewife]A; housewife,
   herself AMS
436.36 Mordaunt]A; Mordaunt's
   AMS
436.37 was to]A; was AMS
437.1 Light]A; [lacking] AMS
437.4 Bulstrom]A; Bulstrone AMS

437.13 honey-moon]A; ~ ∧ ~
   AMS
437.14 honey-moon]A; ~ ∧ ~
   AMS
438.18 success.]A; ~ ? AMS
438.22 patriotic]A; patriotick AMS
†439.27 even,]A; ~ ∧ AMS
439.28 Yes,]A; ~ ∧ AMS
440.3 Anne]A; Annie AMS
440.28 place]A; draw AMS
441.1 means]A; fortune AMS
441.3 conceiving]A; concieving
   AMS
441.7-8 light-hearted]A; ~ ∧ ~
   AMS

Rejected Readings

This list records all readings from the first American edition that differ substantively from those of the copy-text but have not been accepted as authorial. In addition to variants in words or word-order, the list includes variants in the spelling of dialect words. Words to the left of the brackets are from the manuscript (AMS) and are accepted by this edition; readings to the right of the brackets are from the first American edition (A) and are rejected. An asterisk to the left of the entry indicates that a textual note comments on the decision to retain the copy-text reading.

The following texts are referred to:

AMS   Author's Manuscript

A   New York: Burgess, Stringer and Co., 1845

11.18 for a property]AMS; for
    property A
13.32 II^d]AMS; II. A
14.25 while]AMS; whilst A
14.31-32 Dutch, and]AMS;
    Dutch, who A
14.37 island]AMS; land A
16.28 had come]AMS; who had
    come A
19.23 Manors]AMS; Manor A
23.7 happened]AMS; happen A
25.27 poy]AMS; boy A
26.7 My]AMS; The A
26.22 dissenting]AMS; distressing A
28.30 he too had]AMS; he had A
33.24 lived]AMS; live A
[36].23 a Euripides]AMS; an
    Euripides A
38.15 drank to]AMS; drank A
38.36-37 resignation]AMS;
    emigration A
39.12 Mamaroneck]AMS;
    Mamanneck A
43.14 unaccustomed]AMS;
    accustomed A

46.25 pronounc'ation]AMS;
    pronunciation A
47.29 expressions]AMS;
    expression A
47.29 escape]AMS; escapes A
47.37 West-Indian]AMS;
    West-India A
51.5 autumns]AMS; autumn A
51.25 truth]AMS; trutth A
53.20 t'irteen]AMS; thirteen A
*54.3 their]AMS; this A
56.30 in the winter]AMS; in
    winter A
58.11-12 accessories]AMS;
    accessions A
62.23 it is]AMS; is is A
63.31 hands]AMS; hand A
63.37 as]AMS; and a A
65.1 common there was]AMS;
    common, then, was A
65.16 most]AMS; worst A
65.21 soul]AMS; man A
66.2 fields]AMS; field A
67.15 hand]AMS; hands A
68.39 Nor]AMS; How A

69.6 uttered]AMS; called A
69.31 negro men]AMS; negroes never A
69.32 fields]AMS; field A
70.36 remains]AMS; remained A
73.18 she]AMS; and A
74.27 farther]AMS; further A
76.7 interposed]AMS; interfered A
76.12 run]AMS; ran A
84.22 year]AMS; season A
86.40 —Editor.]AMS; [missing] A
90.8 now]AMS; soon A
97.36 accepts]AMS; accept A
99.22 separated]AMS; departed A
101.21 of Bulstrode's]AMS; of Mr. Bulstrode's A
105.30 actually]AMS; almost A
111.40 Mordaunt's]AMS; Mordaunt A
112.32 served]AMS; seemed A
117.21 recover]AMS; renew A
118.17 lilacs]AMS; lilac A
118.35 wormed]AMS; wound A
127.12 Now, York]AMS; New York A
127.17 laws]AMS; lands A
131.17 titles]AMS; title A
135.4 county]AMS; country A
135.7 manner]AMS; manners A
136.10 new comers]AMS; new forces A
[137].14 produced]AMS; procured A
139.15 careers]AMS; career A
143.4 trust]AMS; trusts A
145.21 sleep]AMS; sup A
145.23 knew]AMS; made A
147.14 marten's skin]AMS; martens' skins A
147.29 companions]AMS; companion A
147.31 travellers' dress]AMS; traveller's dresses A
149.4 usually]AMS; exactly A
[151].4 into]AMS; unto A
152.7 honour]AMS; honours A
152.9 honours]AMS; honour A
153.1 time]AMS; turn A
153.22 street]AMS; streets A
154.37 *around*]AMS; *round* A
155.8 prutent]AMS; prudent A

156.29 service]AMS; services A
158.1 set]AMS; sit A
165.13 eyes]AMS; eye A
171.11 as]AMS; so A
171.13 youths]AMS; youth A
171.23 oaf]AMS; calf A
171.27 cried]AMS; said A
175.10 careers]AMS; career A
*175.24 quails"—"old Doortje"—"knows]AMS; quails"—"knows A
177.26 this wild]AMS; the wild A
178.39 change]AMS; changes A
182.19 relatives]AMS; relations A
183.27 pe]AMS; be A
183.31 Guert up]AMS; up Guert A
184.7 Doortje's]AMS; Dootje's A
184.28 Doortje's]AMS; Dootje's A
185.1 know]AMS; have A
193.14 Anneke]AMS; And she A
198.37 matters]AMS; matter A
199.38 answers]AMS; answer A
201.21 *raisins*]AMS; *raisons* A
201.21 *Fontainebleau*]AMS; *Fontainbleau* A
202.2-3 yourself]AMS; yoursel A
206.39 thing]AMS; things A
207.40 towards her]AMS; towards the A
209.39 think]AMS; that A
210.4 were]AMS; was A
214.9 never]AMS; had never A
214.33 rains]AMS; wind A
214.39 produced]AMS; produces A
215.36 Anneke]AMS; Anneke's A
216.24 saw]AMS; see A
217.18 some]AMS; some little A
219.24 curtain]AMS; ocean A
219.33 ourselves]AMS; themselves A
223.39 break *has*]AMS; *break has* A
224.4 intently]AMS; intensely A
*[226].1 XVI]AMS; I A
*229.30 had]AMS; had so A
232.26 their]AMS; heir A
233.33 giant]AMS; great A
235.9 those]AMS; these A
236.20 downward]AMS; downwards A
237.16 in behalf]AMS; on behalf A

238.19 barrier]AMS; barriers A
*238.38 was]AMS; was once
more A
238.39 runners, once more]AMS;
runners A
[240].1 XVII]AMS; II A
243.9 knew]AMS; know A
*243.17 gravest
circumstance]AMS; greatest
circumstances A
246.8 wardrobes]AMS; wardrobe A
246.38 bitter]AMS; better A
247.25 forests]AMS; forest A
247.30 in one]AMS; on one A
*248.4 as on]AMS; as A
248.31 were]AMS; even A
249.31 one]AMS; our A
252.6 your]AMS; yonr A
[254].1 XVIII]AMS; III A
255.12 the immoderate]AMS;
immoderate A
255.39 example]AMS; examples A
257.3 more]AMS; much A
257.6 advance]AMS; advances A
257.17 service]AMS; services A
259.14 streets]AMS; street A
260.37 tell]AMS; tells A
262.3 rose]AMS; arose A
262.35 temperaments]AMS;
temperament A
266.34 doesn't]AMS; does not A
267.10 Jack and]AMS; Jack and
and A
267.30 is queen]AMS; is a queen A
267.39
Knights-Barrow*night*]AMS;
Knight or Barrow*night* A
[269].1 XIX]AMS; IV A
271.13 Doortje]AMS; Doortje's A
271.28 these]AMS; that A
273.4 when]AMS; where A
*274.32-33 determined]AMS;
determined on A
276.13 Doortje's]AMS; Doortje A
278.30 long trains]AMS; a long
train A
*280.21 My]AMS; Nay, my A
[283].1 XX]AMS; V A
284.40 roads]AMS; woods A
286.12 great]AMS; good A
*290.39 hour]AMS; time A

*291.12 look]AMS; stand A
294.16 settlers]AMS; settler A
[297].1 XXI]AMS; VI A
*301.22 were its]AMS; in its A
301.38 quiet dignity]AMS; great
dignity A
302.32 near]AMS; near to A
*306.9 bring]AMS; bring us A
*306.34 from the]AMS; from his A
308.31 manner]AMS; manners A
[310].1 XXII]AMS; VII A
313.32 pouch]AMS; pack A
318.15 across]AMS; along A
319.22 devise]AMS; desire A
322.20 hands]AMS; hand A
[324].1 XXIII]AMS; VIII A
328.25-26 we were made of]AMS;
of which we were made A
*329.2 a station]AMS; its station A
331.1 ceased]AMS; ceases A
332.27 those]AMS; that A
[339].1 XXIV]AMS; IX A
*[339].11-12 us three]AMS; us A
[339].17 southern]AMS; south A
*342.23 manner]AMS; meaning A
342.27 guests]AMS; guest A
348.24 humane]AMS; human A
349.29 their]AMS; this A
349.34 there]AMS; then A
[354].1 XXV]AMS; X A
[354].34 into]AMS; in A
357.25 companions]AMS;
companion A
357.36 suppers]AMS; supper A
361.31 our own]AMS; our A
362.31 apprehension]AMS;
apprhension A
366.31 hart]AMS; hard A
[368].1 XXVI]AMS; XI A
*369.12 pale face most.
Leg]AMS; most pale-face; leg A
370.7 upturnings]AMS;
upturning A
370.19 possessed]AMS; possesses A
370.36 t'e soltier]AMS; the
soltier A
371.31 parts]AMS; part A
371.33 t'at]AMS that A
[382].1 XXVII]AMS; XII A
[382].30 as to those]AMS; as
those A

384.5 red men]AMS; red-man A
385.24 shadow]AMS; shade A
388.36 look-outs]AMS; look-out A
389.35-36 so favorable]AMS; as
favourable A
390.15 suits]AMS; suit A
392.6 I do]AMS; I A
[397].1 XXVIII]AMS; XIII A
*398.37 buildings]AMS;
building A
406.26-27 I gained]AMS; I had
gained A
410.15 effects]AMS; effect A
410.18 buildings]AMS; building A

[411].1 XXIX]AMS; XIV A
414.2 man]AMS; men A
416.12 retreat]AMS; retract A
418.11 now]AMS; more A
419.34 ret-skin]AMS; reat-skin A
[426].1 XXX]AMS; XV A
*[426].31 time]AMS; trial A
427.9 times]AMS; time A
430.1 I have]AMS; I had A
434.36 swale]AMS; swell A
437.7 our cider]AMS; new cider A
437.21 apprehensions]AMS;
apprehension A
437.29 lip]AMS; lips A

Word-Division

List A records compounds hyphenated at the end of the line in the copy-text and resolved as hyphenated or one word as listed below. If the compound occurs elsewhere in the copy-text or if Cooper's manuscripts of this period fairly consistently followed one practice respecting it, the resolution was made on that basis. Otherwise first editions of works of this period were used as guides. List B is a guide to transcription of compounds hyphenated at the end of the line in the Cooper Edition; compounds recorded here should be transcribed as given; words divided at the end of the line and not listed should be transcribed as one word.

LIST A

9.8	salt-meadow	147.5	inland
10.16	himself	174.4	Dutchman
15.37	grandfather	184.6	myself
18.20	demijohn	194.27	understand
19.24	grandfather	213.26	self-humiliation
26.5	cock-fighting	227.4	northward
39.34	dunghill	228.15	supernatural
40.35	warm-hearted	246.5	farm-house
48.38	moreover	247.12	highway
68.28	school-master	282.15-16	warmy-cold
85.31	grandchildren	332.28	breast-work
97.15	understand	340.14	whale-boats
104.28	background	344.17	mountain-top
109.40	gentlemen	364.28	footprints
142.14	grandmother	377.17	woodsmen
144.30	hypercriticism	437.23	horseback

LIST B

30.40-31.1	to-day	[211].22-23	half-hour
93.37-38	scarlet-coats	216.15-16	home-love
116.38-39	self-love	227.39-40	self-admiration
117.33-34	to-morrow	[240].22-23	heart-piercing
125.23-24	out-buildings	248.34-35	re-crossed
134.11-12	great-great-grandmother	[254].20-21	town-morality
143.29-30	sky-blue	257.15-16	tongue-tied
167.30-31	lady-fashion	267.23-24	half-joes
167.36-37	*lady-fashion*	276.10-11	Knights-Barrow*nights*
177.18-19	clothes-baskets	303.23-24	quick-sighted
193.12-13	hen-coops	304.22-23	log-houses

311.18-19	six-pence	387.24-25	half-way
314.23-24	Pale-face	396.12-13	warm-hearted
320.32-33	hill-sides	398.22-23	fee-simple
335.22-23	good-natured	401.16-17	war-whoop
341.11-12	horse-litter	405.13-14	dark-looking
346.33-34	red-coats	429.10-11	all-sufficient
355.31-32	foot-print	432.26-27	fellow-subjects
357.28-29	pale-face	441.7-8	light-hearted